MW01248865

THE DESOLATION CHRONICLES

By

Theodore J. Nottingham

Published by Theosis Books

© 2012 by Theodore J. Nottingham

ISBN 978-0-9827609-4-9

Printed in the United States of America.

BOOK 1

THE FINAL PROPHET

CHAPTER 1

New York City—June 2032

The television studio, a vast jungle of electronic equipment, was teaming with frantic workers preparing for the most ambitious event of their careers. This day was the climactic moment awaited round the world. A daily avalanche of media coverage had prepared billions of viewers for this phenomenon. A live satellite uplink, carried from one orbiting dish to another over every corner of the planet, was to transmit the telecast of the century. One man would sit before the eye of humanity and speak to every living human being in the same instant. Nothing would ever be the same afterward.

The prophecies of spiritual masters and illumined visionaries heralded this event as the turning point in the evolution of human consciousness, the moment of mass awakening to a level of awareness and insight that would break through the opaque clouds of separate consciousness into the vistas of union with universal life.

All work was at a standstill. Offices were dead silent as employees stood motionless before television sets. Millions upon millions were frozen into one common beam of attention.

Instant translation of each word pronounced by the speaker into every known language would insure a synchronization of hearing and understanding, thanks to the colossal powers of techno-genius that circled the globe like one great nervous system, connecting every nerve to the central vortex of activity. Satellite dishes looked toward the heavens in front of countless churches, temples, ashrams, mosques, universities, and hotels—all packed with silent, expectant faces.

Red lights flashed on and off with urgent words. Ten minutes and counting before the worldwide telecast. Cameramen adjusted their headphones, nerves on edge with the magnitude of the moment. Producers hurried back and forth, called out orders to assistants, checked their watches obsessively. Sweat gleamed on brows that had seen it all, veterans of the great feats of global broadcasting. But this one was different. This was an encounter between humanity and its destiny. This was the final revelation to a race come of age.

Technology and science had established this possibility now facing the world. History's painful road had reached its *kairos* time, its transitional point.

"Where is he?"

Jeanne Fleming, network producer extraordinaire, shot out her question to no one in particular. The floor director looked anxiously into the control room, hoping somebody had an answer. He motioned like a panicked mime at the shadows commandeering the booth.

"You tell me!" yelled back an outraged director. His face ravaged by thirty years of tantrums over tight deadlines and prima donnas, the man hadn't a drop of patience left in his system. Especially this evening.

Frank Ross rushed out of the control room, into the studio, and sought out the producer like a loose bull in a Spanish fiesta.

"This is your fault, Jeanne!"

She turned around and faced her assailant.

"How dare you! I had the agenda worked out to the minute."

Ross knew that, having done over twenty shows with her. But he needed to vent his frustration on someone.

"What the hell are we going to do now?"

Jeanne removed a lock of red-dyed hair from between her eyes and took a deep breath.

"I was told by his people that they would have him here twenty minutes before air time."

"Twenty minutes? You know that's unheard of for a live telecast! Why'd you agree to that? There's half a dozen guys with heart conditions in this studio!"

"We're not dealing with someone whose schedule can be controlled!" Jeanne fired back angrily. "I did the best I could."

Ross turned in circles several times, taking in the hectic scene around them.

"I better not lose my job over this," he muttered.

"Take it easy, Frank. The world will wait for him."

The aging, worn out director stopped his anxious pacing. He looked into the eyes of his colleague. For an instant, he lost track of the noise whirling around them. Jeanne Fleming, aggressive go-getter and unflinching personality, felt herself soften as a smile crossed her lips. The reality of the moment came back to her and lifted her above the whirl of emotions that was such a part of her daily activity.

"They'll wait for him . . . " she repeated gently with a strange, distant voice. Ross felt a chill rise up his spine and goose bumps spread across his entire body. He was far from being religious, but there was something special—sacred—about this event. Even a jaded TV director recognized the exceptional quality of the moment.

"It's bigger than the Oscars, isn't it?" he said, paradoxically feeling the weight of worry evaporate from his chest and shoulders.

"You bet," Jeanne retorted. "You go on back to your chair and do your job."

"Right," he agreed with a new determination.

Ross watched her walk off into the crowd of technicians. He shook his head in amazement and returned to the control room.

"So what's the deal?" asked one of the assistants at the switch.

"You tell me," Ross grunted as he grabbed his headphones.

The audio man looked up from his vast board of knobs and buttons and nearly jumped out of his seat. Rex Conway, senior vice-president of programming, was standing over him peering through the wall-length window.

"Mister Ross, sir, I think there's someone here to see you."

Ross had just seated himself comfortably in his cushy swivel chair.

"Are you joking? We're going live in minutes."

"Not if the set is empty, we're not!"

The VP was now in the control room, his cultivated baritone voice booming over the dozen people in the booth.

Ross swallowed hard. Top brass only showed up in his work area when things were going very wrong.

"What's the backup plan?" the director asked as calmly as he could.

"There is no backup plan, Ross!" Conway cried out. The ugly tone of his voice clashed with his shiny, perfectly tailored Italian suit. Everyone seemed to shrivel at his rage. Conway looked at them with that arrogant air made possible by too much power and a huge bank account.

"We've got over five hundred million dollars of corporate sponsorship hanging on this thing. It's your job to make us look good."

"So do we run the logo and put up a 'please stand by' slate?" Ross dared to ask. The VP flashed him a disdainful look.

"Put a gazillion people on hold? It could start a war!"

Conway nervously ran his manicured fingers through the scented grease holding his hair back.

"I knew we shouldn't have agreed to this. It's too weird . . . and too dangerous."

He noticed that the pretty engineer by the vectorscope overheard him.

"What can you do when the President gives you a call and the World Federation Secretary himself walks into your office?"

He held in check a sheepish look which might have betrayed the limitations of the power that gave him his bombastic confidence. The young woman was not impressed. The eagerly anticipated presence of today's visitor to the studio obliterated all pretense to self-importance. A mind-bending breakdown of imaginary hierarchies and power bases had invaded the building since early morning. Nothing was the same, and the man had not even made his appearance.

* * *

A door opened, and the prophet appeared, surrounded by a nervous entourage. A great hush came over the studio as he slowly walked toward the lighted stage where the cameras awaited him. Tall, intense, ruggedly handsome, he looked more like a film star than a wonder worker. But there was something about his presence that was unlike anyone else. An aura of all-seeing awareness accompanied him like a luminous cloud. Those who came under his gaze, however briefly, were seen through and through.

His disciples flanked his side more like bodyguards than devotees. Several hurried ahead and confirmed where he was to sit. A make-up artist was angrily told to forget about powdering their leader's forehead. It just wasn't done.

Producers, directors, and technicians watched with stunned silence as the man walked onto the set and took his seat. Presidents and other world leaders had come before them in the past, and these professionals had long ago lost any trace of fascination with celebrities. But this man was different. He was more than a famous person. In his wake, he seemed to carry some mysterious power from the heart of the universe. He had performed miracles before the eyes of a cynical, suspicious world. No one doubted anymore.

"Roll camera!" Ross shouted with a blend of relief and enthusiasm.

The prophet sat stoically before the eyes of the world.

"Many have come before to warn you of what lay ahead. But I have come to tell you that the warnings are over. The Tribulation, the age of transition, is here!

"Each of you who listen to me must awaken now to your true nature so that you may not only survive the cataclysms and tragedies that are about to devastate the world, but most especially—so that you may participate in the rebuilding of the aftermath.

"A new beginning will rise out of the destruction and purification of the old. Prepare yourselves now to become instruments of the higher realm that seeks to bring light to this forsaken place. Otherwise you will be mere fodder for the terrible calamities that are already on their way.

"What is the nature of this change you must undergo? First, centuries-old misconceptions must be uprooted. Among them are the idolatry of the self and the legions of evil that come with it: separation, violence, greed, reckless abuse of the earth.

"Turn your attention from yourselves to the Source of your existence. This is what you were created to do and be: co-workers in the completion of creation, not its vultures and destroyers. You cannot participate in the building of a new age without serving a higher world by letting it work through you.

"How is this done?"

He paused for a moment.

"We must get beyond religion."

The words were stated slowly and emphatically. A worldwide audience watched in stunned silence. The man on the television screen stared unblinking at the camera that was sending his message around the planet, live and instantly translated.

"The forms must die so that their true content can be released."

The serene speaker knew that every sentence he pronounced could be a death warrant. But this moment was the climax of his strange and wondrous journey on this plane of existence. It was for this that he was born.

Hardly middle aged, the prophet of the new millennium was a man of mystery. His life was virtually anonymous until the previous year when his fame exploded across the globe. Now he spoke from the depths of his mysterious soul to a critical mass of humanity. The outcome could change entire societies and lead to an enlightened epoch for all peoples.

"We are one family. All of our intuitions of the Sacred are partial truths. The time has come to tear down the barriers between us. Religious institutions have failed humanity and the teachers they claim to represent. A new day has arrived. Today, we can each recognize the oneness within all authentic religious teaching. We must now turn beliefs into experience. The only genuine sanctuary is within each one of you, not in buildings. Rituals are only useful if they lead us into the depths of our own heart."

A hushed crew watched intently in the darkness of the vast studio. The solitary man sat peacefully on a stool beneath a dozen lights. Alone and uncompromising, he addressed the world.

In the bowels of the cavernous studio, hurried footsteps echoed toward the control room. An anxious Rex Conway burst into the room.

"We've got to cut him off! The phones are ringing off the hook! We'll lose every one of our sponsors!"

Frank Ross rose from his chair and cried out impatiently.

"The World Federation has approved the appearance of this man on the International Link! What he says is their concern, not ours."

The vice-president, more nervous than ever, was losing his mask of suave confidence and turning into a bundle of twitches.

"This heresy is not Federation-approved! It can't be! In less than a minute, the man's made himself the number one enemy of every religion on the planet!"

"So?"

Conway stopped short and looked into the eyes of the director. Their cold, disinterested gaze said it all.

"One more dead lunatic won't bring the world government to an end," he added with a certain pleasure. "He's making his bed. Let him lie in it."

The executive turned to the large window opening onto the studio. The solitary man was still talking in a slow and steady voice to a shocked world audience.

CHAPTER 2

Enid, Oklahoma—October 2031

It had all started on a quiet night in the middle of nowhere, less than a year before.

A light was on in the library of the old Gothic seminary building. It was nearly two o'clock in the morning. Hardly another light could be seen for a hundred miles in the barren plains of Oklahoma. The library was on the top floor of the cathedral-like building and overlooked the small city of Enid like a misplaced monument from another age.

Perched above the roof, surrounded by gargoyles and statues of forgotten saints, was a narrow tower. It was from here that the solitary light shimmered in the darkness. Inside the tower were kept old books that no one had studied for half a century or more. Decaying covers lined the walls like abandoned sarcophagi guarding unimaginable treasures. The wisdom of mystics and scholars across two millennia was gathered there, mute legacies crying out from their hopeless confinement.

Neither professors nor students came to visit these orphans of the most illumined minds of the past. Dismissed as irrelevant and even ignorant, these books from the loftiest souls of the race were rejected in favor of the latest academic best-seller gracing the book review pages of important journals, assuring tenure and pay raises for their authors.

One man still visited the tower and its disdained treasures. An old professor, soon to reach his eightieth birthday and kept on the faculty out of charity, spent his evenings here. Dr. Anton Hogrogian, an Eastern European scholar once beloved by generations of students, was now long past his prime. Though he had published several books in his day, he had committed more time to teaching than to advancing his fame among his peers.

During his forty years at the seminary, he had outlived the entire faculty several times, had watched his wife slowly die of cancer, and was now utterly alone in the world. No one took him seriously anymore, not even freshman students who considered the slow talking, slumped over old man little more than an easy course to get through. The latest president had tried several times to force him into retirement, but always found himself unable to pronounce the words when gazing into those large, dark and melancholic eyes that saw through to the core of his soul.

Dr. Hogrogian was considered an eccentric and patronizingly called a "mystic," without any understanding of what the word meant. But the few who came to know him were clear that he was indeed a mystic whose powers of mind blended with keen intuition and certain innate psychic capabilities. The aged professor was also a striking example of humility, the kind that could only be forged in a lifetime of inner spiritual effort. He never put forth his unusual talents and brilliant learning unless they could benefit another person, and even then it was with an unassuming aura that often veiled his profound contributions.

Despite a serious heart condition and a laundry list of physical ailments, the professor was in the tower again on this night. Sitting at the small wooden table in the corner of a room jammed with books, he was leaning over yellow, water-stained pages attempting to decipher the fading print.

Something was different on this silent night. Never before had the professor remained in the tower at such a late hour. Never before had his shriveled skeleton of a body been wracked with an intensity that bordered on frenzy.

Before him lay writings dating back to the first century AD. The words were in Hebrew. Dr. Hogrogian slowly, relentlessly moved his finger across the page from right to left. In an excited whisper, he translated the ancient words to himself.

"And there shall be two . . . "

The trembling finger stopped and remained on the end of the sentence, shaking like a reed in a howling wind. The aged professor turned to his battered briefcase that sat open on the desk next to him. With his other hand, he rummaged through the mess of papers and books and pulled out a shiny new paperback that seemed oddly out of place in this mortuary of withered works. He fumbled through it, searching for a passage he had marked in ink the day before.

The top of his balding head turned a scarlet red. His worn and wrinkled face suddenly began to beam with a youthful energy, a momentary Indian summer peering through the late autumn of his life. The book was the latest publication on the findings of the Dead Sea Scrolls. Lost for centuries and accidentally found in caves near the sight of the mysterious Essene sect, these treasures were still being deciphered for the general public. He read from a chapter on one of the most intriguing scrolls to be pieced together, the "Manual of Discipline." It contained both the way of life and the teachings of the esoteric community at Qumran in the heart of the Judean desert, not far from the wilderness where John the Baptist had called his people to spiritual renewal.

"Another Messiah . . . " the old man murmured in awe. "There is to be another Messiah for our time . . . "

He threw the book down and pulled from his pocket the morning edition of the local paper. Spreading the newspaper out before him, he turned to the back page of the second section. His finger once again undertook its scanning efforts, this time rushing down through the columns of print.

He came across a small, insignificant article hidden away in the lower third of the page. The headline read: *The Tale of the McCormick boy: Some say it's a miracle*. The professor came to sentences he had underlined with a shaky pen: "The part-time pastor, a student at the local seminary, was unavailable for comment."

Dr. Anton Hogrogian, Ph.D. from Oxford, professor Emeritus and lifelong student of things sacred, sat back in his little wooden chair. He closed his tired eyes and breathed deeply. A tear appeared in the thick crow's feet at the corner of his eye and slowly wound its way down his cheek.

"Could it be?" he sighed. "Holy God, could it be?"

After a moment, he opened his eyes and looked toward the window. Pale moonlight streamed into the room, peaceful and serene.

"Am I just an old fool?" he wondered out loud. The stars shimmered in the night. They seemed to answer the old philosopher with their mysterious light journeying down to him from unimaginable distances. Their stability comforted him. They mirrored the changelessness of some eternal truth shining down on a world gone mad.

After all his years of study, Dr. Hogrogian was certain of one thing: History had reached an impasse, religion was nearly dead, and civilization was wandering aimlessly without direction. It was time for a new revelation!

CHAPTER 3

The formation of the World Federation, which replaced the anemic and impotent United Nations, had given hope to nations wracked with instability. The centralizing of power and economic trade barely managed to slow the disintegration of societies and the imbalance of the haves and the have-nots. Born from twenty years of negotiations and cantankerous debates, the design of this amalgamation of governing powers included all sorts of clauses to safeguard the population from total oppression.

Certain birthrights were no longer so, but this was justified for the sake of the larger picture. In the last years of the twentieth century, it had become clear to everyone that the world family would either sink together or find new ways of living together. A quarter of a century later, the World Federation still seemed like a good idea. Oversight of national crises was carefully monitored. Crop failures were anticipated well in advance and preparations made on another side of the globe to ease the oncoming famine. Renegade leaders were dealt with swiftly and efficiently: War planes from a dozen nations flew in, locked onto their target, and didn't leave until the remains of the culprit were identified in the debris. Laser powered X ray detectors were all the rage in these search and destroy missions. No one could hide anywhere. No matter how far underground the bunker was buried, regardless of the layers of steel and rock, the enemies of the Federation would be discovered with the ease of a hunting dog sniffing the trail.

The peoples of Earth were willing to pay the price for relative safety. And pay they did. Everything was now within reach of the all-powerful world government, from stock markets to individual credit and medical histories. Monster computers stored information bytes on every living person and, at the tap of a button, revealed intimate details that had once been off-limits. Genetic and DNA structures had long replaced fingerprints as marks of identification. Personality profiles dissected every potential job candidate and filed them under categories that determined their future.

Freedom and privacy had sold out to efficiency and security, even though the Federation could only oversee the growing chaos.

Within five years of this new configuration of power, the signs of breakdown were evident everywhere. National pride and prejudice still grumbled beneath the veneer of international unity and was kept in its cage only through the threat of severe reprisal. Crime was still vying for ultimate control of the streets, despite sophisticated methods of spying and infiltration. The board rooms of great industrial conglomerates were glowing with a new level of greed and success, and the very rich were getting ever richer. But for the average person just trying to get by, the unification of policies and trade meant very little. Worst of all, the human soul had been left to continue its downward fall into despair and meaninglessness.

With the linking of cultures and nations into one giant Pangea-like government came an ever greater mechanization of society. People were now cogs in a more complex and immense wheel that generated the survival of all inhabitants of Earth. The pooling of resources meant an increase in commitment to the big picture and a disinterest in individual need. All religions were held in check for the sake of order and reduced to their most superficial, external manifestations. The World Federation approved what was made available to the believer. That was the answer to religious fanaticism: Water it down and make it essentially meaningless. Religion was one more controlled substance for the consumer, one more stimulant in the escapist fare provided for the anthill of the working masses. Efficiency had no room for spiritual awakening and devotion to a Being who did not seem to contribute to the economic health of the Federation. Besides, history proved that religion was a failure, a major contributor to violence and instability. However, the Federation honored each religion as a pillar of social stability as long as it remained within the boundaries of its particular guidelines. The purpose of religious institutions was no longer the pursuit and veneration of Truth, but the support of the status quo.

In order to keep this new multi-ethnic, multi-cultural hodgepodge of civilization from shattering into fragmented subcultures, it was necessary to relativize all morality and values. Anything too hard-edged was suspect and entered into the central computer system of the Federation's Security Department. To achieve balance and harmony among the yoked nations, the power-possessors had chosen as their creed the only option before them: Nothing is sacred, everything serves the global effort of maintaining order.

But the architects of this new unified world and its fragile balancing act had grossly miscalculated. Though the surface of society seemed to run relatively smoothly under the subtle tyranny of the Federation, the intense dissatisfaction with such a "generic existence" was creating secret pockets of rebellion whose leaders were more zealous than ever. Social upheaval could be held in check and trade deficits balanced out at the end of the year, but the human soul could not be reduced to a well-functioning automaton in the service of planetary stability.

Most people were quite content with their little share of goods and services. Though taxes had gone through the roof in the last two decades in order to underwrite a central controlling agency, the shopping malls and groceries stores were well-packed with the necessities of life. The World Federation even approved the latest international film stars, making sure they did not violate some group's sensitivities so that they could be idolized throughout all cultures. This supervision not only guaranteed gargantuan profits from all parts of the world, but also insured that most everyone was kept satisfied with the distractions made available to them. And distractions were very big business.

One hundred years of motion pictures had evolved from mere entertainment to vital fixes for addicts of escapism. Keeping the world population in hypnotic contentment was a key strategy of the Federation. Revolutionaries rarely arose out of the ranks of the numb and apathetic. It was even rumored among the more courageous journalists that the Federation quietly accepted the international drug cartel's business dealings. Not only was it one of the most efficient and successful trading partners in the worldwide market, but the goods it circulated assisted in the overall goal of the government: Keep the masses content and in a daze. No expert on human psychology had come up with a better plan to stop humanity from destroying itself.

New generations born into this anesthetized and carefully monitored society were trained to think of themselves as world citizens rather than children of specific nationalities. The philosophy behind this effort sounded good on paper and from the lips of three decades of politicians, but the end result was becoming demonic. With this new identity also came an arch-patriotism: Loyalty was now demanded by the Federation in the name of humanity rather than in the name of some particular flag. To be human meant to be in line with the accepted norms provided by the World Government. To think for oneself was as dangerous as ever. There were means of identifying and isolating those individuals who persistently refused to participate in the grand parade of sustaining the planetary economy.

Behind the power of the World Federation stood the genius of high-tech wizardry. From miniature cameras to integrated computer systems analyzing probabilities of human behavior, the very soul of the government lay in the electronic chips that gave it access to every conceivable bit of information. Liberated from absolute values, the authorities were free to pursue all avenues of science, including DNA manipulation and subliminal education.

The freedom of the press was as relative as religious doctrine, and only naive reporters imagined that they were allowed to provide information unsanctioned by the powers that be. Getting on the air meant facing several billion people across the continents, and the Federation was not foolish enough to leave that kind of access to just anyone. The information superhighway of the late twentieth century had created a network so potent in its outreach that the privilege of communication was now restricted to government-approved organizations. Though individual modems could talk to the other side of the globe, so could the international police scanners and anyone caught generating inflammatory information was sure to be found out. Particular words transmitted via fiber optics would set off search and scanning devices so intricate that before the sender finished his sentence, his address would be flashing in fluorescent red on a central office computer. There was little room for stepping out of line. That was the price for world peace, a peace that existed only on the surface.

At the turn of the century, a conflict in the Middle East broke out that started with terrorists and evolved into an all-out war involving a dozen countries. The devastation of chemical warheads shocked the world so greatly that a new demand for international control brought about the first stirrings of what would later become the World Federation.

Technology had broken new barriers, many of which only further destabilized humanity's precarious situation. Organ harvests and other horror stories concerning the misuse of science were pervasive and virtually impossible to control. The knowledge was out, and like Pandora's box, there was no putting the furies back.

Spiritual teachings of the past that had generated a fever-pitch of interest in the last decades of the previous century were now nearly forgotten by the majority of people who were too busy trying to survive from day to day as cogs in a giant machine. To be rejected from that system meant that there was no way to make a living or feed oneself. Survival meant control, and control meant loss of freedom. Loss of freedom meant loss of self-respect. Many people were beaten down and turned into Medieval serfs who were slaves to the technology that had originally been invented to serve them.

A backlash had taken place among the descendants of the spiritual seekers of a previous age, and religion was dried up and fossilized all the more. Yet many had returned to religion, primarily for the sake of the communal network that served their basic social needs and gave them a superficial sense of meaning in their dreary lives. The clergy had become powerful once again after enduring ridicule from society for more than half a century. They were a small elite that the Federation used in its subtle efforts to establish a social hierarchy. People knew their place in this kind of a world, and the clergy saw themselves as power brokers in the structure.

Yet most churches, temples and synagogues continued their hundred-year fall into decay as the majority of society lost all sense of a reality beyond the one dimensional version that gave them so much stress. The Federation had developed extraordinary expertise in the art of distraction to keep great masses of people passive and seemingly content. Entertainment so dominated the world that it was a virtual mind-control system. What was heard and seen from the first days of life carefully upheld the belief systems and world views that the Federation wanted to maintain, not because they had any meaning, but because they contributed to the stability of the economic structure.

Television was the great umbilical cord that fed its illegitimate children. People lived from it thoughtlessly, and had long forgotten that only critical discernment could save them from its subliminal ability to shape their perceptions. If this mother force decided there was no God, then one way or the other the world would become molded to this perspective through the relentless manipulation that overwhelmed it every minute of every day.

Human beings were shaped for whole lifetimes without suspecting anything—passive clay in the hands of an invisible potter whose purposes were not benevolent. Those who remained independent thinkers were enemies of the state and chastised mercilessly from grade school onward.

In this rigidly structured world society, people were kept in separate compartments. The haves did not see the have-nots, and the have-nots did not see the haves, many of whom hired their own private security forces to protect their goods against the desperate hordes.

The poor of the world groveled in greater numbers than ever before in world history. Famine was a constant nightmare for a third of the globe. The yearly eruptions of deadly contagious diseases were unstoppable. Those in power concluded that the upside of this catastrophe was the weeding out of a population that the earth could not sustain. This grotesque view was characteristic of a system that had lost its soul long ago.

The Federation provided a pittance to most of the penniless citizens that could be accounted for. Not enough to keep them alive, but enough to keep them in need. Beneath the surface broiled a blind insanity that threatened to explode onto the surface at any moment. World armies were permanently on a state of alert.

The unfulfilled prophecies of the previous centuries, which many unconsciously hoped would end their misery, left a spiritual void that nothing could fill. The whole idea of the end of the world was thrown aside with disdain once again. If it hadn't happened in the year 2000, it wasn't going to happen, at least according to the Federation's spin masters.

CHAPTER 4

Located at the end of a red dirt road, the McCormick farm was surrounded by an ocean of fields. The empty wasteland of tilled soil gave the place a feeling of desolation that bordered on gloom. No sign of life anywhere. Miles and miles of bleak space without a tree or hill to break the monotony. If there was such a place as nowhere, this was it.

An old Buick appeared on the horizon, bouncing over every rock and pothole like a ship in peril. A giant cloud of dust pursued it across the narrow road bordered by barbed wire fences.

Hunched over the wheel was the little silhouette of Dr. Hogrogian, nervously making his way through the endless obstacle course.

The professor had never learned the skill of driving, having let his wife take the wheel during their five decades together. Now that he was on his own, he had no choice but to develop skills which simply were not part of his makeup. He held onto the steering wheel for dear life and peered through the dirty window with desperate determination.

When the farm finally came into view, he let out a great sigh of relief, knowing that this trip was potentially fatal for him.

The rusted old car shook and rattled its way off the road into the front yard of the farm. A large, black and brown spotted dog barked ferociously, yanking on its chain. The professor remained in his vehicle, frightened by the beast's unfriendly welcome. He waited for someone to appear from the farmhouse.

"Hey there!"

Dr. Hogrogian turned himself with difficulty, grimacing at his arthritic pain. He could see no one.

"Over here!" a strong female voice called out.

"Where over here?" the professor muttered impatiently, turning to and fro in his seat. He finally caught sight of a figure waving at him from the barn. A portly lady, twice his size, with a scarlet jovial face, headed toward him. The professor fumbled with the door and managed with difficulty to extract himself from his car.

"What can I do for you?" the lady shouted with a beaming smile.

"The dog . . . " Dr. Hogrogian stuttered, still uncertain as to the length of the chain holding it back from tearing at his flesh.

"Oh, don't worry about Dixie! She won't bite."

"Does she know that?" the old man asked, starring in horror at the irrational creature barking its head off.

The woman whistled a powerful, shrill note that nearly burst the professor's eardrum. The dog immediately halted the display of savagery and returned to its shady spot near the porch. Dr. Hogrogian turned in amazement toward the woman who wielded such power.

"Are you lost, Mister?"

"Not if this is the McCormick farm."

The lady stopped a few feet away from him and studied him suspiciously.

"You're not one of them newspaper people, are ya?"

"No, Madam, that I most surely am not," the professor said with a chuckle. "Are you Mrs. McCormick?"

"Who wants to know?"

The generous, hospitable look on the woman's face gave way to a dangerous glare that seemed ready to defend its territory. The professor removed his hat with long lost European manners and presented himself with a dignity that hardly matched his worn clothing.

"Dr. Anton Hogrogian, professor of Early Church History, at your service."

A warm glow returned to the farmlady's features.

"Well, hello, Mister professor. Your kind ain't never set foot on our place before."

"Is that so? With the seminary just down the road, you would think . . ."

"We're a million miles from nowhere out here, even if the distance ain't that far. So what brings you to our home?"

The professor placed his hat back on his head to shut out the cold breeze coming in off the barren plains. He reached into his pocket and pulled out the newspaper article.

"This . . . this is what brings me here."

Mrs. McCormick took the clipping from his hand and peered at it carefully.

"This don't tell the half of it."

"There is more?"

"Mister, my son wasn't just healed of his illness."

"What do you mean?"

Mrs. McCormick handed back the clipping as tears welled up in her bright blue eyes.

"Do you know what was wrong with my son?"

"Well, he had . . . he is a hemophiliac," the professor stammered searching through the newspaper article.

"That's right. But that's not what his problem was. My son had been given some bad blood."

"Bad blood?" Dr. Hogrogian still did not understand.

"My son had AIDS; that man of God cured my son of AIDS! That means that he brought him back from the dead."

The old professor turned ghostly pale. Tears streamed down the farm lady's rugged cheeks. She clasped her hands together in prayer.

"God is good," she whispered as a radiant joy shone through her tears.

Dr. Hogrogian was speechless. Unconsciously, he crossed himself in the ancient orthodox manner as the faithful had done over the centuries when encountering the holy.

The two strangers stood together in a timeless moment of silent thanksgiving. A veil seemed to lift, revealing the invisible dimension of reality. The peace of the surrounding countryside echoed the reverence of their experience. No temple or cathedral could offer a better sanctuary for their gratefulness to the beneficent Creator.

"Why did you not tell the press?" Dr. Hogrogian finally managed to ask.

"He would not have wanted me to."

"Did he ask that of you?"

"No. I just knew."

Dr. Hogrogian could hardly contain himself. He felt his heart pound against his chest and took in a deep breath to ease his excited state.

"Why are you telling me?"

The woman smiled a giant grin and replied with earthy honesty.

"You don't look like you would do anybody any harm."

"Thank you. Would you let me see your son?"

She hesitated a moment. A shadow swept across her features.

"Why?"

"I would like to know what he experienced."

"And why are you so interested?"

"I know this man . . . "

"How do you know him?"

"He was my student."

"Are you his friend?"

"Yes. And more . . . I am his student now."

Mrs. McCormick was struck by the old man's humility and the gentleness emanating from his person.

"I'll let you see my son. But just for a minute. And you have to promise that you'll never write about what you see."

"You have my word."

She led him toward the house.

A twelve year old boy, skeleton thin and white as snow, lay in a large unkempt bed in a corner of a room. Premature dark circles gave the child's eyes the eerie look of an old soul trapped in a young body. He was reading a book when the door opened and his mother entered.

"Tommy, you've got a visitor."

The boy's face suddenly became flushed with enthusiasm.

"He's here? He came back?"

"No child, not him. A professor friend of his."

The boy's excitement immediately vanished and he fell back into his morose state. Dr. Hogrogian timidly peered into the room.

"May I come in?"

"Please do and watch your step. It's always messy in here," Mrs. McCormick said with no apologies. "Tommy, this gentleman wants to ask you a couple questions."

"What for?" the boy mumbled defiantly, crossing his arms around his chest as though prepared to keep a secret to himself.

"What for? Because I said so, that's what for," his mother responded with a temper that would have sent a wild dog running for cover.

Hat in had, the professor approached the bedside with a look of awe.

"I am sorry to bother you, young man. I just need to know . . . how did it happen?"

The boy looked up at his mother, scowling.

"Do I have to?"

"It's okay, son, he use to be his teacher."

Tommy's eyes lit up.

"You were?"

Dr. Hogrogian nodded his head with a certain pride.

"That's great! Did you teach him how to . . . "

The professor held up his hand and abruptly interrupted him.

"I only taught him what is to be found in books. The rest is beyond my powers."

Mrs. McCormick pulled a chair toward the bed and motioned for the old man to sit.

"Thank you. Tell me, young man, what exactly took place here?"

The boy closed his book and leaned back against the pillows.

A mysterious smile crossed his lips.

"He came to see me the last time I was in the hospital. I was in awful pain. The doctors didn't look real happy either. They said they were doing everything they could. I remember when he first came in, I couldn't see very well. Everything was fuzzy. He took my hand. There was this heat. I felt it in my fingers at first. Then it went all the way up my arm, and the next thing I knew, I could see better."

The boy's face took on a glowing expression. Dr. Hogrogian could hardly control his emotions as he listened breathlessly.

"He spoke to me . . . and he said that I would be going home soon and that everything would be all right. I knew he was telling me the truth. Not like the doctors or Reverend Morgan. It wasn't just my mind. My body knew."

Tommy was silent, experiencing the moment again. His mother wiped away her tears with a soaked handkerchief.

"So you were brought back home?" Dr. Hogrogian finally asked.

Tommy nodded.

"And he came to see you again?"

"The doctors thought we were crazy," Mrs. McCormick interjected.

"They told me he wouldn't make it through the night. He'd already lived six weeks longer than expected. But when I saw that look on his face and the color change in his skin, I knew something had happened."

"He sat right where you're sitting, in that same chair."

The professor felt his body shiver and hid his fingers in the folds of his hat.

"He sat there and held my hand," the boy went on. "I don't know how long it was. It felt like all day."

"It was just an hour, Tommy," his mother said gently.

"And he spoke to me . . . "

"What did he say?"

"That I had a long life ahead of me. That I would have a family to care for. That I had good things to do before leaving this world."

Mrs. McCormick leaned over and whispered in the professor's ear.

"He told him he would be a scientist who'd invent things to help others. That was at the end, when Tommy fell asleep."

"I could feel my sickness leave me and I asked him where it was going."

"What did he answer?"

"He just smiled. But I could tell that he was in pain."

"You mean . . . " Dr. Hogrogian couldn't finish his question.

"He took it into himself. That's what I think. Besides, his hand got all puffy and red."

"So then he got up and left?"

"I fell asleep, and when I woke up, he was gone. And so was my sickness."

The old man turned to the mother for confirmation.

"Not only was his fever and pain gone, but he ate like a horse for the first time in over a year. And it wasn't thirty-six hours before his lesions healed."

"How do you mean, healed?"

"They were gone."

"You mean they stopped bleeding?"

"I mean they were gone, scabs and all. Nothin' but a little scar left where they'd been. Look for yourself."

She took her son's arm and stretched it out before the professor. Moving her finger along the forearm, she pointed out tiny white marks spotting the skin.

"It was all open wounds before."

The professor stood up, uncertain that his legs would hold him.

"How do you feel now?" he asked Tommy.

"I wanna play baseball, but Mom won't let me."

"Not just yet," Mrs. McCormick said with a glorious smile.

Dr. Hogrogian took the boy's hand and shook it gently.

"Thank you so much for what you've shared with me. It has healed me too, in a way. I hope you get to hit a home run very soon."

He winked at Tommy and patted him on the head. Mrs. McCormick escorted him out of the room.

Tommy called out as they vanished from view.

"If you ever see him, you tell him I'm going to grow up to be just like he said. You tell him that's a promise from my heart."

CHAPTER 5

The setting sun stretched out across the vast skies of the Southwestern plains, spreading rich hues of orange, red, and pink in all directions. The sharp line of the horizon, unencumbered by trees or buildings, awaited the golden disk's descent with awed stillness.

Dr. Hogrogian stirred the pea soup coming to a boil on his old-fashioned gas stove. The kitchen was a disaster area of forgotten dishes and pots and pans stored carelessly wherever room could be found. Tidiness had vanished from the professor's home on the day of his wife's funeral. Very few things mattered to him anymore, the least of which was housekeeping. Besides, he had not learned the skills of working a kitchen until after his seventy-fifth birthday. There weren't many new tricks this old dog cared to know about.

A slice of rye bread jumped out of the toaster with such loud noise that the professor nearly dove for cover. He never could get used to the unexpected timing of the toaster, especially after a day that had so rattled his nerves. Spreading big chunks of butter on his bread, he did his best not to burn his fingers. But the pain hardly reached his awareness anyway. Little Tommy still haunted his mind's eye.

"I must be crazy," he muttered to himself as he scooped the last remains of raspberry jam out of a sticky jar. He slapped the contents of the spoon on his toast with vehemence, frustrated with the machinations of his mind.

"Why now?" he wondered out loud as he absentmindedly turned on a little TV set placed precariously over the sink to keep him distracted whenever he did the dishes. A news report was in process.

"The spokesman stated that the resources of the World Federation are stretched to the breaking point. There seems to be little interest in this tragedy among the Western nations. In another development, inspectors announced that plutonium has indeed been stolen from the nuclear reactor . . . "

Dr. Hogrogian turned the volume down. He couldn't take the flood of horror coming from the nightly news anymore. Everything was getting worse everywhere. "Why not now?" he suddenly blurted out.

"Why not at such a time of decay and barbarism and despair?"

He felt dizzy as his mind went into overdrive with a million and one thoughts pouring in at the same time. Raspberry jam landed on his pant leg and pulled him out of the dangerous vortex. He growled at himself and grabbed a towel to remove the mess from his favorite clothing, the only pair of pants that didn't look like they came out of long abandonment in a thrift shop.

He mechanically turned the TV back up as he washed his hands.

"On the local scene, a three alarm fire broke out early this morning at the Pleasant Valley Community Church near County Line Road. Firemen were on the scene early enough to save the main church building, but the parsonage was completely destroyed. A gasoline can was found at the scene. Arson is suspected. The pastor was not at home and cannot be reached for comment."

The old man choked on his last bite of toast. He rushed to the phone and dialed frantically. "Mrs. Violet Simmons? This is Dr. Hogrogian. Do you know which one of our student pastors is currently at Pleasant Valley?"

"I don't have my files at home, Dr. Hogrogian," answered a wavering voice. "But I do believe that one of our recent graduates is still there."

"And who would that be?" the professor asked impatiently as beads of perspiration gathered on his forehead.

"Oh, the quiet one, what's his name . . . you know, with the strange eyes."

"I need his name, Mrs. Simmons," the professor barked.

A heavy silence came across the phone line.

"Forgive me, Mrs. Simmons, but this is an emergency. Can you recall his name?"

"You must be thinking of Adam Hawthorn."

This time, it was the professor who was silent.

"Hello?"

"He is the pastor at Pleasant Valley? Are you sure?"

"Yes, I'm quite sure of it. In fact, I remember receiving some complaints about him from members of the congregation. And others for that matter."

Dr. Hogrogian looked over at the television set still broadcasting pictures of the smoldering parsonage.

"What sort of complaints? And what other people?"

"I'm in the middle of dinner, Dr. Hogrogian. Can we talk about it tomorrow?"

"What did you mean by other people?" the professor insisted, suddenly acting on an intuitive feeling rising from deep within.

"Well, some students were quite upset at Reverend Hawthorn's theological perspectives. I have to go now. Goodnight, Dr. Hogrogian."

The phone abruptly clicked in his ear. Hogrogian felt numb all over. Something undefinable was troubling him. He felt himself on the verge of a disorienting fear. Instinctively, he turned up the TV to pull himself out of the state into which he was slipping.

A gigantic farmer in overalls was answering a reporter's questions.

"Can't imagine who would do a thing like that. My pa helped build the house. It meant a lot to folks round here. But I knew something bad was gonna happen."

"Why is that?" the reporter asked, smelling a story.

"Them newfangled ministers comin' out of that school. They don't preach the Book no more. And this here Reverend Hawthorn, he got folks real upset."

"Are you saying that someone wanted to harm the pastor of this church?"

"I'm sayin' that you can't be tellin' folks things about religion that get them all in a rage. This ain't some big city where anything goes, no sir. We're plain folks and we like our religion the ol' fashion way."

"What did your pastor say that would cause such anger?"

"It ain't stuff for the TV. He was just . . . different."

With that, the farmer lowered his cap over his eyes and walked away from the camera.

"Well, there you have it, Dave and Tina," the reporter said, turning to the camera, "a mystery fire with overtones of religious dissension. Back to you."

Hogrogian smacked the off button and the picture vanished into a dot of electronic light. He hurried over to a tall, green filing cabinet and threw open the top draw. Folders crammed with papers of all sorts were squeezed together so tightly that, once removed, there was little chance of replacing them. The old man fumbled through the scribbled class names that identified the mass of paper. He came across a folder titled "The Mystics of the Church, Summer course."

"That's it!" he cried out as he tore at it seeking to displace it. Opening it on the table, papers sprang out like furies contained in some Pandora's box. Within moments, the table was covered with term papers, lists, notes, and lectures.

"Where is it? Where is it?"

He came across a syllabus to which was attached students' names.

"Here we go. Harris, Hartman, Hatcher, Hawkins, Hawthorn."

The professor located a phone number by the name and hurried to the phone. An obnoxious sound pierced his ear, followed by a computerized voice stating that the number was disconnected. The old man was approaching a state of panic.

"Who can help me? Who knew him? Which classmate might have befriended him?"

His frenzied momentum suddenly froze as he visualized the classroom where he had last seen Adam Hawthorn. The tall, silent figure always sat in the back and rarely spoke. Hogrogian recalled how he was always aware of his presence, even with his back to the man. The professor was struck, in their brief interaction, by the serenity of his personality. In his late thirties, he was classified as a second career student, although no one knew what he had done in the previous years. His manner was unpresumptuous and soft-spoken, a sharp contrast to his intense, dark eyes and aquiline profile. A Semitic ancestry commingled with Northern European blood to create an unusual combination: straight black hair, blue eyes, light brown skin, Romanesque features.

The professor remembered him as not especially handsome, but with a captivating quality that came from a powerful alertness, like the buzzing of a high-powered electric fence. All this energy was focused in a way that was aimed both inward and outward.

This was only the first characteristic that had impressed Hogrogian.

The man exhibited the signs of one who practiced what the ancient books of the early spiritual teachers of the Faith counseled: watchfulness, detachment, humility, and especially unseen warfare. It was clear to the professor who had read so many documents on the matter during his career that this man knew something about the control of will and attention.

Hogrogian didn't remember him ever chatting with other students, although his demeanor was not unfriendly. He was serious, but not rigid—aloof but not conceited.

"Jeremy!" the old man called out. "Jeremy Wilkes was a friend to him."

He searched through the names again and located a phone number. This time his call was answered by a real voice.

"Jeremy Wilkes? This is Dr. Hogrogian. Yes, from last year's Church History class . . . I am well. Sorry to call at this hour, but I am trying to locate a fellow classmate of yours. I believe the two of you worked on a project for me: Adam Hawthorn."

"Has something happened to him?" The voice on the other end asked.

"I'm not sure. Why do you ask?"

"I knew there would be trouble sooner or later," the concerned young man answered.

"What makes you say that?"

"It's a long story."

"I must meet with you."

"Well, my schedule . . . "

"This is all-important."

"It is?"

"Do you know where Adam Hawthorn is right now?"

"I have no idea."

"Have you seen the news?"

"No."

"His parsonage was burned to the ground."

A heavy silence came over the phone wire before Jeremy spoke. "How about eight o'clock tomorrow morning at the diner?"

"I'll be there."

Hogrogian put the phone down and dropped into a chair. He felt too old for this. But something very big was taking place and he was compelled to pursue it, even if it killed him.

CHAPTER 6

"What'll it be?"

"Coffee, black, and your number three special."

The waitress jotted down the order and poured a stream of steaming caffeine into the waiting cup. Hogrogian sipped it immediately. He hadn't slept an hour the night before and he dearly needed the jump start from the coffee.

Something had to keep him going.

He opened the tattered briefcase at his side and pulled out a folder jammed with handwritten notes. Instinctively, he looked around to insure that no one could peer over his shoulder. He was still haunted by an unnamable fear that gnawed at his stomach and disturbed his dreams with dark phantasms. From the day—even the moment—that he had been struck with the thought of Adam Hawthorn's identity, a dark cloud had come over his psyche.

Hogrogian placed his cup on its plate with a loud clink that shook his system more intensely than the Colombian coffee bean extract. He looked into the black liquid in the saucer. That was the very expression of the feeling running through the corridors of his soul: black, steaming, potent. Involuntarily, he crossed himself. The old habit, inherited from a thousand year legacy of faithful believers, carried power for him. The invocation of spiritual forces eased his anxiety and settled his stomach.

His lifelong association with ancient Christian rites informed his deeper mind of the true sources of action on this plane. Good and evil were not merely personality traits or genetic accidents. Greater forces were at work.

"You're early!"

The old man looked up from his gloomy thoughts to find the enthusiastic presence of Jeremy Wilkes standing before him. Radiant with youthful energy, he was the very antithesis of the professor's dimming life-force.

"Thank you for coming," Hogrogian stated as he put out his hand to greet him. "Forgive me if I don't stand. This weather is not friendly to my knees."

Jeremy took a seat across from him and studied him closely.

"You look very tired, Dr. Hogrogian."

"I'm no longer the dashing youth I once was."

"Have you been unwell?"

"Old age is a synonym for unwell. I've had trouble sleeping. But we're not here to talk about me."

"No, of course not. What exactly are we here to talk about? My curiosity is driving me crazy."

"Did you see the news this morning?"

"I did."

"Well?"

Jeremy leaned forward and gazed at the aged but glimmering eyes of his former teacher.

"You didn't invite me for breakfast to discuss a matter for the fire department?"

"Why did you tell me that you expected trouble for Adam Hawthorn?"

The change of subject caught him off guard and Jeremy found himself speechless. The waitress appeared in time to give him a chance to recover. He glanced at the menu and asked for whatever came first into his vision.

"You knew him better than any of his classmates, is that correct?"

Jeremy nodded with a certain hesitation.

"As well as he would let himself be known. He was not very approachable."

"How do you mean?"

"He never engaged in small talk, or in virtually any other kind of talk for that matter. It's not that he was an introvert as much as the fact that he always seemed involved with something else."

"Something else?"

"I've never met anyone more centered and focused and yet so completely immersed in some other . . . dimension. Does that make any sense?"

"I understand. And that other dimension, as you call it, wasn't mere daydreaming or the activity of his own preoccupation's?"

"No, and don't ask me how I know. I just do. He was plugged into some stronger current. A higher frequency."

"That is what I observed as well." Jeremy's eyes opened wide. He never guessed that the old professor was such a sharp student of human nature. The astute observer lay camouflaged behind drooping eyebrows and an intellectual's "lost in space" characteristics. Jeremy suddenly experienced a new level of respect for the unassuming gentleman.

"So how does all this tie together?"

"Jeremy, I need to be able to trust you."

The young man's statement of assurance was immediately interrupted by Hogrogian's eagle-eyed glare.

"I am taking a risk with you beyond all reason. We have only known each other from behind desks. But I need someone to help me and you are the only one I can turn to."

Jeremy straightened himself in his chair and focused all his attention on the old professor. The waitress approached with their meals and the two men remained frozen in a state of urgent expectation until she left them.

"I have come to the conclusion that Adam Hawthorn is here among us on a mission that does not originate in this world. I believe that his role is crucial to our times and to the future of humanity. I further believe that his work will not easily come to fruition, and that opposing forces will interfere at every opportunity."

Jeremy's entire body reacted to the words. He felt dehydrated all of a sudden and instantly covered with perspiration. A wave of nausea followed as he lost his inner balance and felt somehow caught between reality and the dream world. Some sort of metaphysical vertigo took hold of him. He managed to speak after a moment.

"You think he is a kind of prophet?"

"Not just a prophet. The ultimate prophet. The Messiah. The Holy One of God!"

"You mean, like the Second Coming?"

"In a way."

"The return of Christ?"

"I believe he is another Messiah, the one foretold by the Essenes over two thousand years ago."

"Another one? That goes against all creeds!"

"We speak of things that no human can fully comprehend."

Jeremy strained to function from his reasoning powers which threatened to wash away beneath the flood of emotions swirling within.

"You think that Adam Hawthorn, the man who sat across from me in Church History class, is both human and divine; begotten, not made; one with the Father?"

The words burned his mouth like hot coals as they were voiced.

"I believe he is the final incarnation of the Word of God before the Great Tribulation. The one who will bring us together or let us fall into annihilation."

The food was getting cold, but neither man had any appetite. Cigarette smoke drifted by from other tables along with the clang of silverware. Their surroundings were as far from them as the next galaxy.

"Do you still want to help me?"

"I don't know, to be quite honest."

"That's understandable. Let me ask you this: If you were to confirm the veracity of what I have told you, would you reconsider?"

"Of course!"

"Then let us agree to go that far."

"What do you propose?"

"We have to find him."

Jeremy tried a bite of his breakfast and put it aside. It was only an excuse to buy some time anyway.

"How do we do that?"

"That's where you come in. I don't have the stamina to go on a wild goose chase. You would have to do the detective work. I believe he is still in the state."

"What makes you say that?"

"Because I sense his presence nearby."

That was too much for the young man. After all, he had graduated *magna cum laude* from an academic institution. This whole affair was just too out of step with the standard norms that everybody else held to be true.

"Jeremy, this is too important for you to dismiss on the grounds that your little mind cannot grasp it. This is no time for arrogant dismissal of things that we are in no position to judge."

Jeremy bit his lip trying to contain his indignation. "I didn't come here to get insulted!"

"So why did you come here?"

"I came here because of my admiration for you, Dr. Hogrogian. Because of my desire to be helpful to you. I could tell over the phone that you were really troubled and, quite frankly, I was concerned about your health."

"At my age, humans become rather fragile. Is that all?"

"No. I have always known that there was something very special about Adam Hawthorn."

"What makes you say that?"

Jeremy paused to consider the few experiences he had shared with the unusual man. How could he describe the first time he saw him standing outside the seminary in the shade of a giant willow tree? He knew then that this was the man who would teach him what he had yearned to discover from the depths of his soul.

How could he explain the feeling that went through him when the man looked at him and saw to the very core of his being? He had felt himself stripped naked of his vain personality and imaginary ideas of himself. He was left to stand in all his helplessness before that knowing gaze.

How could he explain the awe that came over him whenever he crossed the man's path?

His respect for his fellow student was the same as that which was felt toward a grandmaster in the Himalayas. There was something ageless about his fellow student who was so unlike all the other students. It seemed ridiculous for Adam Hawthorn to be sitting at a desk receiving so-called learning from people far below his level of insight. There was a resonance to his voice, a quiet certitude in his manners, and an obvious inner strength that could overcome anything.

Jeremy had asked him once where he was from, hoping to engage him in conversation. The man responded with a melancholic half-smile. He said, "I come from far away." Jeremy remembered making some awkward response that left him feeling very stupid.

But he knew at that moment that there was a deeper mystery about this person which he felt driven to uncover. That was why he was sitting in the cafe with the old professor.

"All right!" he announced with determination, "I'll go that far with you. I'll find Adam Hawthorn."

Tears of gratitude welled up in the professor's tired eyes.

He reached over and took hold of his hand. Both men knew that they had just vowed themselves to an awesome covenant, one that could only be signed in blood.

CHAPTER 7

Cleejay Hobbs pulled out a spark plug and cleaned it with a greasy rag. With the expert knowledge of a do-it-yourself mechanic, the giant farmer looked over the engine of his battered pickup truck and quickly assessed its condition.

Like other farmers in this lonely wasteland, he had to solve all his problems by himself, whether in the field or in the workings of a Caterpillar.

The son of survivors of the second dust bowl plague early in the third millennium, he was the very incarnation of the anachronistic pioneer spirit: fiercely independent, self-sufficient, hard working. The man was a living relic of another age, the last of his kind and soon to be extinct, just like the family farm.

Times were hard for such people. The clock of so-called progress was ticking away and a new day had arrived for the agricultural needs of the world. Most of Hobbs' fellow farmers were already bankrupt, and heart-rending tales of tragedy were virtually the only talk left in the community.

A certain bitterness and gloomy sense of unalterable destiny was etched on the face of every farmer in the area.

The natural virtues of their way of life—hospitality, neighborliness—now suffered the strain of a life gone off track. It was only a matter of time before they were all displaced persons, and the fact that the World Federation promised to take care of them was no consolation.

Hobbs turned his weather-beaten face in the direction of the dirt road running past his property. A cloud of dust announced the approach of a vehicle. As the road led nowhere but into his fields, he knew that a visitor was headed his way. A grimace cramped his features. He didn't like unannounced visits. Not anymore. Not since the trouble had started.

The car pulled into his front yard. Three mud-caked dogs dashed out of the barn, barking savagely. They surrounded the car. Hobbs squinted to see the face of the driver before calling off his animals.

"What do you want?" he called out suspiciously.

Jeremy rolled down his window part way, a worried eye on the dogs.

"Are you Mr. Hobbs?"

"Who wants to know?"

"Jeremy Wilkes."

"Never heard of you."

"I'm a friend of Reverend Hawthorn. I understand that you're a member of his congregation." Hobbs chose not to call off his dogs.

"State your business, mister."

"Can I get out of my car?" Jeremy called out with irritation.

Hobbs whistled and the dogs stopped their barking, moving away from the vehicle. Jeremy stepped out cautiously.

He walked over to the huge man and put out his hand. Hobbs stared at him with disdain. Jeremy was taken aback by his unfriendliness.

"I'm looking for Reverend Hawthorn. No one seems to know where he's been staying since the fire."

"So why do you come to me?"

"One of the members of the church informed me that you were the last to see him."

"Who told you that?" Hobbs asked angrily.

"That's not important. Do you know where he is?"

"No idea. I got no time to shoot the breeze. I'm busy."

He turned back to his truck. Jeremy sensed that something was very wrong.

"Look, Mr. Hobbs, I need to locate your pastor. Do you know . . . "

"He ain't my pastor!" the farmer spat out with disgust.

"What do you mean? You're a member of Pleasant Valley, right?"

The farmer put down his wrench and faced Jeremy.

"Yeah, I'm a member. My pa built the place. I grew up there. Never missed a Sunday. But that Reverend Hawthorn ain't my pastor."

"I take it you didn't care for his theology?"

"His what?"

"His ideas about God."

"I don't know nothin' about God. I know about plantin' an harvestin'. And I do know when a man ain't preachin' the Bible like he's s'ppose to."

"Didn't Reverend Hawthorn assist your wife in her illness?"

The rugged farmer's features took on a frightening look of rage. "How do you know that?"

Jeremy instinctively took a step back. He could feel the man's capacity for violence just below the surface mounting quickly.

"I would think you'd be grateful for the help he was to your family."

"He filled her head with all kinds of ideas. That wasn't no help!"

"Did you share your concern with Reverend Hawthorn on his last visit?"

"I sure did. He meddled with my family in a way that ain't right. Even my kids fell for his bull crap."

"I understand you wanted him removed from the pulpit."

"You bet I did. I'm president of the congregation. That's what I'm s'ppose to do when the preacher's no good."

"But the other members wouldn't go along with you?"

Hobbs took a threatening step forward.

"What the hell are you asking me all this for?"

Jeremy stood his ground. "Tell me where the Reverend is."

"How should I know? I just told him never to come back. So I guess he left."

"What do you know about the fire?" Jeremy asked boldly.

Hobbs grabbed his wrench, eyes glazed with rage.

"Get outta here before I crack your skull!"

"I'm leaving, but I'm going to find the Reverend and he better be in good health."

"You threat'nin' me, mister?" Hobbs cried out, following him to the car. Jeremy opened the door, but the farmer slammed it shut.

The two men faced each other.

"No, I'm not threatening you, Mr. Hobbs," Jeremy stated as calmly as he could. "It looks like that's what you're doing to me, however."

"You don't come to a man's home and throw accusations at him!"

"I'm not accusing you of anything. I just thought you could help me find the Reverend."

"Check out the jailhouse. He spent more time there than with the people who paid his salary."

"Thank you, that's all I needed to know," Jeremy said as he opened the car door again.

"Don't ever let me find you on my property again! Any friend of that man is not welcomed here!"

"I can see that."

Jeremy turned the ignition key and threw the stick shift in reverse.

"I mean it, mister. Don't come here again!"

The car pulled away rapidly. Cleejay Hobbs watched it disappear down the road, clenching the wrench like a weapon. Violent hate burned through his features, dissipating whatever humanity was left in him. As he turned back toward the farmhouse, his dogs hurried off, sensing the danger in their master's rage.

CHAPTER 8

Jeremy drove directly to the county jail, a place he had visited several times before as part of his field education. It was a gruesome hovel built in the early part of the previous century when there was no concern for humane conditions for the prisoners. The sheriff and his men took pleasure in tearing out the last shreds of human dignity from the inmates. The jailhouse was more like a Medieval dungeon than like the lockups found in modern cities with their two-way television systems and laser-activated security systems. It smelled of urine, had little light, was stifling hot in the summer and freezing cold in the winter.

Jeremy had never been exposed to such human misery before, and avoided the place like the plague. It had defined for him the direction of his ministry, away from such dreadful conditions and toward the middle class congregational maintenance that now seemed so perverse to him. For Adam Hawthorn, however, this horrid place was the beginning of his ministry.

He entered the building, taking one last breath of fresh air before plunging into the stench and dinginess awaiting him inside. He was hoping to avoid seeing any of the prisoners, for their faces stayed with him long afterward. On he's last visit, he had encountered a criminal incarcerated for multiple murders, and he still shuddered at the remembrance of the dead eyes and lack of conscience in that wretched human soul. The man was a deserter from the World Federation security forces and was therefore a highly trained extermination machine. On the loose and out of control, he had left a trail of gore across the North American continent until his arrest in these barren plains.

"State your business," the officer said in a mechanical voice.

Jeremy approached the caged-in office.

"Is the chaplain in?"

"What do you want with him?"

"I'm from the seminary. I need to speak with him."

"Are you clergy?"

"I am."

"Down the hall, second door to the left."

Jeremy braced himself and headed deeper into the building. Further down the corridor he could hear the echo of raucous laughter and cursing coming from the cells like fumes from the lower depths. He found the chaplain's office and stood before the door for a moment. How long was it since he had last seen Adam Hawthorn? Perhaps a year or more. He felt his heart beating faster. Why did this happen to him every time he came into his presence? He still didn't know. But he did remember that each time their eyes met, a feeling was conveyed deep within his soul in a way that happened with no other person. There was something more than human about it, something profoundly mysterious and overpowering.

He knocked at the door.

"Come in."

With great anticipation, he entered the room. Shock struck him like a baseball bat. Sitting at the desk was not Adam Hawthorn, but Raymond Sutherland, a former student and the exact opposite of the man he expected to see. Sutherland was a staunch fundamentalist with fascist-like views concerning dogma and the letter of the law. Rotund and shifty-eyed, prematurely balding and with a heavy Southern drawl, Sutherland was the incarnation of everything Jeremy hated about formal Federation-approved religion. The man was a loyal sergeant-at-arms of the institution. They had been in numerous classes together, all of which Sutherland had interrupted with self-indulgent, obnoxious soliloquies that frustrated professors and classmates to no end. A real shock came from expecting the peaceful and serene sight of Adam Hawthorn and finding instead that of Raymond Sutherland.

It was light and dark, black and white, perhaps even good and evil.

"What are you doing here?" Jeremy asked angrily.

"I work here, Wilkes. What do you want?"

"I came here to see someone else."

A sly smile crossed Sutherland's jovial, sweaty face. "You mean Hawthorn, don't you? You came to see Adam Hawthorn."

"That's right."

Raymond's face tightened like a fist.

"Well, he's not here anymore."

"When did this happen?"

"Just a couple of weeks ago."

"Where might I find him?"

"I don't have the slightest idea."

Jeremy sensed that Raymond was holding something back.

"Why did he leave this position?"

"Oh, he didn't leave it voluntarily. He was told to leave."

"By whom?"

"By the people in charge, who do you think?"

"Why? What happened?"

"The very same thing that happened at his church."

"And what would that be?"

"Look, Wilkes, you know that I don't like the guy, never have. I've known for years that he was nothing but some way out heretic. And I'm not the only one who feels that way. He came here and started doing weird things, just like I predicted."

"What kind of weird things?"

"For one, he affected the inmates."

"What do you mean, he affected the inmates?"

"The sheriff told me about this prisoner held for attempted murder and armed robbery. Every time he saw the Reverend Hawthorn come by, he started crying like a baby and wouldn't stop for hours."

"Is that a fact?"

"It turns out Hawthorn never cracked open a Bible with them, never gave them any lessons in Scripture or led any worship services. He just sat with them and listened to them. One time he did some kind of magic on this inmate who was real sick."

"Magic? What are you talking about?"

"Ask the sheriff. This Joe Kramer, he'd been sick for a week. Couldn't keep anything down. Hawthorn went into his cell and put his hands over his stomach, and next thing you know the guy was in perfect health. It freaked out his cell mates, I'll tell you that. Just not the kind of thing a chaplain's suppose to do."

"So they fired him?"

"Oh, yeah."

"And hired you in his place?"

"That's right. Bible-based sermon, a couple hymns, and no mumbo-jumbo. And especially no making grown men cry for no good reason. What an embarrassment that guy is!"

Jeremy didn't know what to say. For years he had fought his feelings of repulsion toward this man, attempting to forgive him and accept him for what he was. But there was something mean, cruel even, in his rigid so-called religion. Jeremy turned toward the door.

"If you find him, tell him to get outta this state. We don't want him around here."

Jeremy suddenly had an intuition.

"Raymond, you don't know anything about the fire that took place at Pleasant Valley Church, do you?"

The man's face froze and Jeremy watched it turn red from the neck up to the ears and across the forehead. After an awkward moment, he said, "What fire?"

The two men stared each other down with the intensity of gunfighters. Jeremy slammed the door behind him.

CHAPTER 9

The professor pulled his dusty car into the church parking lot. He had awakened that morning with a cold shiver rising up his spine. He knew there was a terrible urgency in finding Adam Hawthorn. But he had so little strength left for this effort. He had to speak with Jeremy.

Hogrogian sat in his car for a moment, debating whether he really should disturb his former student during his work hours. He was beginning to question whether his mind was altogether stable. Was old age finally catching up with him? Maybe some kind of senility was interfering with his rational mind. Why couldn't he just retire quietly and be done with it? Why did his life have to end with struggle just as it had begun? Had he not seen enough adventures in his time?

Then he saw the senior minister come out of the church. Robert Morgan was as arrogant a man as he had ever known, the very opposite of a pious human being. The professor had known him years ago when he had been a student at the seminary. Even back then he knew that the man would rise up through the ranks quickly due to his aggressive personality and his slippery skills at satisfying the Federation guidelines. He was now pastor of the largest church in town, a member of numerous national committees, and president of the International Association of Registered Clergy. Such an obscene idea filled the professor with righteous indignation. Here was the reason to continue struggling. This Pharisee of Pharisees was a master hypocrite parading in clergy robes while inwardly living the life of the worst of the godless. This man was on the verge of national prominence and would undoubtedly catch the eye of some well-placed Federation deputy. That was the beginning point for all serious upward mobility.

Hogrogian watched the man get into his car, the latest electrical, computer-driven model. He studied him intently. With his keen insight into human nature, he could see the darkness of the man's soul engraved in his cold, haughty features. He could also see that there was some inner brewing rising to the surface through the intensity of his glare. The man was up to something.

Suddenly, as Morgan started his engine, he turned and noticed the professor. The minister reacted with a jolt, realizing that the old man had been secretly observing him. For a split second, his face turned sour with the bile of anger. He caught himself and spread a big smile across his face in a grimace that was meant to hide what was really there. The professor barely nodded in response and watched the grimace fade away instantly as the minister drove off.

This was no mere pathetic egotist. This was a dangerous man.

Hogrogian entered the church and found Jeremy in his study in the company of his wife, Lynn. He knocked on the open door to make his presence known. He could tell that he was interrupting some private and painful scene.

Jeremy looked up. On his face were the marks of anxiety and distress.

"Hello, Professor."

Lynn turned around. The professor had always admired Jeremy's wife. She was a rare kind of person, radiant with intelligence and compassionate sensitivity. Her good heart was supported by a powerful personality. She too was a seer into the human soul. Hogrogian thought of her as a sister, despite their distance in age and background.

"Well, hello Dr. Hogrogian," she said as she gave him a warm hug.

"How nice to see you again, Lynn. I hope I am not interrupting."

Neither Lynn nor Jeremy responded, knowing that the professor was aware that he was indeed interrupting them. But somehow they also knew that his unexpected visit was linked to their concerns.

"Has something happened?" Hogrogian asked.

"No, it's nothing," Jeremy responded.

The professor glanced at Lynn and saw that her expression did not support that answer.

"Is it about Adam Hawthorn?"

"Nothing significant, professor," Jeremy insisted.

The old man knew better.

"This is not the time to keep things from me, Jeremy. We are all in this together now. Tell me what I need to know."

Jeremy had no intention of rattling his old teacher's nerves.

"If you don't tell him, I will," Lynn stated in her usual straightforward manner. "Jeremy went to the county jail and discovered that Adam Hawthorn is no longer employed there, and that Raymond Sutherland has taken his position."

"What does that mean?" Hogrogian asked.

"Don't go on with this, Lynn," Jeremy requested.

"It wouldn't mean much, professor," she continued, "except that when Jeremy came to work today, Reverend Morgan put him on notice. He told him that any further effort to contact Adam Hawthorn would result in his reporting him to the Suspect Persons Network."

"How is that possible?" the professor exclaimed.

"Apparently," Lynn went on with the insight of a detective's mind, "Sutherland placed a call right after Jeremy's visit and this is where he called."

She turned to her husband, seeking his approval for her next statement. He nodded reluctantly.

"Jeremy thinks Sutherland may be connected to the fire."

"Is that why he called Reverend Morgan?" the professor asked.

"Why would Morgan be concerned that Jeremy not speak with Adam?" Lynn followed up. "I think it's because the good Reverend Morgan has something to do with this as well."

Hogrogian dropped into a chair and removed his hat.

"That is quite a claim. The man is the president of the IARC."

"That's right," Jeremy muttered.

"Why on earth would Reverend Morgan be concerned with Adam Hawthorn?" Hogrogian insisted.

"Because he is a threat to his kind and to all that makes him seem important," Lynn stated boldly. "He is a devoted pawn of the Federation. He'd love the opportunity to get their attention."

"Do you also believe that this man is seeking to destroy Adam Hawthorn?"

The professor felt a knot of tension tighten his stomach. He sensed a giant web of evil gathering around them.

"One thing is certain," Lynn observed intently, "Morgan is going to get Surveillance after us if Jeremy isn't more careful. We can't afford to become branded as anarchists."

The professor stood up and approached the couple. He reached out for their hands.

"That mustn't happen. I couldn't live with myself. All this could be just the mad ravings of an old man. It is not worth putting yourselves at risk. So this is what we shall do. I will take up the search on my own and . . . "

"But your health, professor!" Jeremy interrupted.

"My health will be much worse if you are in the unemployment line on my account. I will continue to share with you what I come upon, but you mustn't be directly involved."

"We had an agreement," Jeremy insisted.

"Please hear me. You and Lynn must not be victimized. I want your promise that you will do what you must in order to keep your job."

"But . . . "

"Listen to the man," Lynn stated firmly. "He doesn't want you to take these chances. And he'll keep us informed. We've got other responsibilities."

The three friends held hands tightly. They each sensed that this was only the beginning of their troubles.

CHAPTER 10

The full moon stared down from the sky, glowing mysteriously. The little western city was quiet, as usual. Only the locust kept up their nocturnal racket, a strange contrast to the stillness of the desert plains.

Dr. Hogrogian's hunched silhouette slowly wandered about the neighborhood, cane in hand. The old professor was in the habit of taking evening walks for almost half a century now. It relaxed him after a hard day's mental strain dealing with scholarly reflection and teaching. But this evening was different. The professor was weighed down by a terrible sense of responsibility that was all-encompassing for the human race. Why him? he wondered. Why should the last chapter of his life be thrown into such dramatic upheaval? But he couldn't escape it. He knew that something extraordinary was about to take place and, for whatever reason, no one in the world but him had any sense of its approach.

The intuition that ate at his innards and forced him onward on this bizarre journey was so powerful that it squelched the doubts of his rational mind and the fear that he was going senile. He really had no choice. The urge within would give him no rest. He had to go in search of this man. He didn't know what the outcome would be, but he simply knew that he had to find him.

Hogrogian sensed that awesome forces were involved, forces that might destroy him. Adam Hawthorn had a great mission to accomplish in this age and somehow the little old scholar was charged with being useful to him. Perhaps it was a reward for a life of faithful commitment and study. Or perhaps it was the absurd luck of circumstance. Hogrogian no longer had the energy to philosophize on such matters. The facts were before him and he had to deal with them.

So where to begin? Where would this prophet, this Messiah-like figure wander off to at the beginning of his ministry to the world? Hogrogian looked up at the black skies and the glowing orb watching him relentlessly. He followed its pale shaft of light down across the horizon, beyond the town's buildings and outlining the desert expanse for miles around. The desert! Of course! Where else but the desert? Had not the Christ chosen that place as his retreat for regeneration and guidance? The same could be said of Moses and Mohammed and so many other holy men who had walked the face of the earth. The desert and its awesome solitude was their true home, the location of their most intense alignment with the transcendent mysteries that spoke to them. The desert was also one of the last places on earth where the Federation had not established a surveillance system.

The professor scanned the plains, seeking an answer to how he might find the solitary man. Who would know the desert? The dim outline of a rugged face began to take shape before his inner vision. He closed his eyes, attempting to make it out. What was this apparition? A man with long gray hair and high cheek bones. A Native American. Who else knew the desert, and who else would a man like Adam Hawthorn be willing to trust? In his many years at the seminary, Hogrogian had come to know a number of the elders of the Cherokee nation who lived nearby. He was, in fact the only professor to have reached out to them as a brother. He appreciated their wisdom and keen sense of the sacredness of life.

On several occasions, Hogrogian was reprimanded for inviting guest speakers of that community who offered to the students a spritual view that made their brand of religion seem artificial. There was one medicine man in particular, Stargazer, who outraged the seminary leadership with his sharp critique of the white man's lack of holistic insight. During a worship service at the seminary chapel, the man had burnt sage and passed it around to everyone present, asking that they breathe it deeply as part of the ceremony.

Then it hit him. This was the man whose face was manifested before him, and this was the man whom Adam Hawthorn had befriended on his visits to the seminary. He remembered now seeing the two of them in whispered conversation, oblivious of the world around them, communing in a striking commonality of understanding.

Hogrogian knew the reservation well and was even familiar with the old Indian's dwelling. The tribal elder had extended his hospitality to him in gratitude for his appreciation of their culture. Tomorrow, the professor would undertake the trip to the secluded village and see what he could find out.

Just as those thoughts concluded, another picture shaped itself in his mind. This one had an aura of doom about it; it was not a face, but a shadowy landscape seen from the ground: a strangely formed barren cliff, and the silhouette of an eagle drifting by high in the cloudless sky. An ominous feeling filled his soul. The old man shook his head, looked up at the sky, and breathed in deeply. He would not allow fear to deter him from what he knew he had to do.

He turned and resolutely headed for his home. Shortly after he had disappeared behind a building, the darkness was broken by a pair of headlights flashing on. A car moved out of the shadows and headed off into the night.

* * *

The light of dawn was just stretching upward from the horizon, casting colored streaks across the cloak of night. The Southwestern plains were silent and immobile, except for an old Buick rattling along a two lane road.

Hogrogian had hardly slept. He knew that with the sunrise would come a day of great significance. Before starting up his engine, he had called Jeremy and told him of his brainstorm. Surely he would find the prophet on the reservation.

The professor was so intent on his quest and so concerned with the struggle of keeping his car on the road that he failed to notice a moving light detaching itself from among the stars. A stealth helicopter was following him.

The car bounced and shook its way past the reservation entrance and headed for a shack isolated from the other homes. Every time he came to this place, Hogrogian couldn't help but shake his head at the lack of development made available to these people. Deep into the twenty-first century, in a unified world booming with technological improvements, nothing seemed to have changed on these reservations. How could the World Federation disregard their plight while solving so many other global problems? Somehow, the disinterest in this one segment of humanity was proof that the great ideals of the Federation were faulty and doomed to failure. Either they led all of humanity into a better future, or everyone would eventually flounder on the rocks of misery.

The dignified tribal elder was sitting on his dilapidated porch as though anticipating his early morning visitor. Hogrogian pulled up alongside a pile of rusted farm equipment from the last millennium and eagerly stepped out of his car.

"Stargazer! My good friend, how are you?" he called out as he hurried over to him.

The somber Indian rose from his chair and watched him approach without expression.

"Professor Hogrogian . . . I've been expecting you."

The two men shook hands. Hogrogian immediately perceived that his intuition had been right.

"You know why I am here?"

"Certainly," the powerful man mumbled as he gazed across the horizon. "You haven't been followed, have you?"

"Not that I know of," Hogrogian answered, looking over his shoulder nervously. "I can't imagine who . . . "

"Come now, you're not that lost in your books are you, old friend?"

"What do you mean?"

The dignified medicine man gestured to a rickety chair. Hogrogian sat himself carefully.

"The dominators want to find him also."

Dominators. That was the name the mysterious elder gave to the powerful world government officials. Hogrogian found it to be a most appropriate expression.

"Why would they be interested in Adam?"

Stargazer raised his hand. "Don't use that name. We don't call him that here."

"Oh?"

"He is known to us as "the Visitor.""

The professor was familiar with the colorful ways in which Native Americans identified each other, and he understood that a name captured an essential quality of someone's being.

"Why that name?"

"That is his secret. We can only recognize that he has such a secret and honor him."

"Very well. So you know that I am looking for him."

"Of course."

"Can you take me to him?"

Stargazer shook his head negatively.

"Why not?" Hogrogian cried out, virtually pleading.

"He will have to come to you."

"But you do know where he is, don't you?"

"So do they."

The words caught Hogrogian off guard. For a moment, he stared at him in confusion.

"I don't understand."

"Dark deeds are surrounding us."

A chill shot through the professor's aged body.

"Are you afraid, Professor Hogrogian?"

"Should I be?"

"Yes."

Hogrogian found himself wishing he had never taken off on this crazy search.

"Why would I be in danger?"

"You don't understand what is at stake."

"Do you?"

The Indian shrugged his shoulders enigmatically. "The Visitor is here to change everything. The Dominators don't want change. They are pleased with the way things are."

"Have you seen these changes in a dream?" Hogrogian dared to ask on a hunch.

"I've seen the Visitor."

"How is it that you can know such things?"

"I look at what is not visible."

Hogrogian smiled. Here was a true mystic, one of the last in a world chained to a wretched materialism.

"I want to help him if I can," the professor stated softly after a moment of silence.

"No one can help him. But maybe he can help you."

"Why can I not help him?"

"Because his destiny is already clearly traced and he is here for a purpose that cannot be altered."

Hogrogian asked him if he knew what that was.

A twinkle lit up the eyes of the stoic tribal elder. "That depends on where you think he is from."

"What do you mean?" Hogrogian asked breathlessly. Suddenly, he had an intuition. "How is it that you came to call him *the Visitor*?"

The man sat silently for a moment and drank in the horizon with his piercing gaze. "We call him the Visitor because he is not from around here. There's an ancient legend among my people. It's also found in other tribes, especially among the Mayans and the Hopis. A legend of a prophet who is to come from far away . . . "

"Could that be a metaphor for a spiritually enlightened being?"

"It could be."

"But you don't think so?"

A trace of irritation fluttered across the elder's face. He did not like answering so many questions.

"I don't mean to pry, friend, but if I am placing myself in danger, I ought to know something about all this, shouldn't I?"

"Isn't your concern pure enough? Does it require further justification in following your sense of what is right?"

"No, I suppose not."

"Then let it be, professor."

"Why shouldn't I know what you seem to know?"

"Because you wouldn't know what to do with the information."

Hogrogian couldn't help but feel insulted. As a scholar of mystics, no one knew better than he about the ineffable mysteries of the spirit. Stargazer turned to him as though having read his thoughts.

"We live in an age when everything is out of balance. And only a balanced one can solve our situation. Such persons once lived among us."

"You mean the wise ones of old?"

"I mean . . . before the ice ages . . . "

Hogrogian heard a buzz ring through his brain. The old Cherokee was right. This was information he didn't know what to do with.

"Are you referring to a civilization that existed prior to recorded history?"

Stargazer did not answer. He was intently staring at the morning sky which had turned blood red. Hogrogian persisted, even though he knew that the man had retreated into the abyss of his soul.

"What are you telling me, Stargazer? Do you believe he is from another time?"

Slowly, the old Indian raised his hand and pointed his finger to the sky.

"Another world . . . " he mumbled.

Hogrogian would have questioned him further had he not noticed a shadow darkening his friend's features.

He turned and looked in the direction in which he was pointing. The silhouette of a small helicopter hovered in the distance. Hogrogian knew immediately that they were being watched and probably heard by the sophisticated equipment on board.

As panic took hold of him, Stargazer motioned for him to be silent and pointed in the direction of the cliffs behind his home.

"You must go," he whispered.

"Where to?"

"Just go . . . you'll find what you came for."

"But I don't want to lead anyone to him!"

"It's too late for that."

"Oh, my God, what have I done?"

"It was written, friend. You had no choice."

Professor Hogrogian understood then that he had never realized what true mysticism might entail. He arose and placed his hand on Stargazer's shoulder.

"What will happen to you?" he asked.

"It doesn't matter. I am at peace. The question is: Are you?"

Hogrogian was suddenly aware for the first time that his life was in danger. He took a deep breath and found himself more intensely present to this moment of his life. The deep peacefulness of his

Indian companion led him into his own center.

"I am proud to count you as my friend," Hogrogian said in a quivering voice. The tribal elder looked at him unblinking and nodded slightly, which spoke reams of his appreciation for the old professor. Hogrogian hurried off the porch and stumbled toward the cliffs. By then the helicopter had reached the entrance of the reservation. Dust clouds along the road announced the approach of fast moving vehicles.

Sweating and quickly out of breath, the old man hurried up the slopes. With every step he knew that his time had come. It was clear to him that he was part of something infinitely greater than the sum total of his life. He fell on his face in the desert sand and coughed. How ridiculous it was for him to be running from some unknown enemy. He was too old for this. Perhaps in some paradoxical way, he was playing a useful part in this mysterious drama. He had learned long ago that events are seldom what they seem on the surface. Perhaps his presence here would in some way spark the work that the prophet had to undertake.

He stood and wiped the sand from his mouth. He took a deep breath and moved deeper into the ravine that lay open before him. He let himself roll down a sharp incline toward the bottom of a dry river bed. He knew he was lost, and yet he felt closer to his destination than ever before. The very silence of the desert, piercing in its oppressive tranquillity, spoke to him of the goal of his life: union with the One.

In spite of himself, he cried out, "Where are you, Adam? Let me speak with you, please!"

He moved forward without any idea of where he was headed. A person could hide in countless crags along the cliffs. He came to another incline and proceeded to climb it with his last bit of strength. Suddenly he felt an evil presence behind him. Almost unconsciously, he turned around. And there across the river bed, on the top of the hill, appeared uniformed silhouettes hurrying after him. Instinctively, the professor turned away and rushed for cover. A terrible cramp suddenly paralyzed his heart.

Hogrogian fell hard on his back behind a boulder. He knew he was going into shock. He knew he was going to die. He felt himself drift into a valley of peace.

The old professor opened his eyes one last time. The scene came into focus: the cloudless sky, the barren cliff, and then the slow flight of an eagle crossed the frame of his vision. The shock of knowing that he had seen this very image in his mind's eye the night before brought a surge of adrenaline back into his dying body. For a moment, he saw with intense clarity.

Suddenly, a shadow slipped between the bright sky and his vision. The shadow of a man. Hogrogian felt a shiver run through his entire body. The silhouette standing over him raised his right hand—slowly, deliberately—the open palm held above him and aimed at his forehead. Instantly, Hogrogian was reminded of the countless icons of Christ and of the saints that had been such a part of his life, their hands of blessing held up from the eternal realm to humanity. He knew that this was what he was now seeing. A profound, measureless peace flooded him, extinguishing all pain and anxiety. He knew that the silhouette before him was Adam Hawthorn.

The tall man, in dusty clothing, stood like a rock before the dying professor. His face was unshaven, his hair matted and unkempt. But it was his eyes, gleaming with unearthly brilliance and staring unblinking into Hogrogian's eyes, that brought an aura of holiness to the moment.

With his last breath, he whispered: "Who are you?"

The prophet replied, but without words. Hogrogian heard his voice in his own mind, telepathically. *I am who you think I am.*

Save yourself, he thought, too weak to pronounce the words. He heard an answer.

I am not here to save myself.

In an instant, the dying man sensed the tragic mission laying ahead for his former student, with its inevitable persecution and hardship that were sure to come.

Why must it be this way? he wondered. The prophet leaned toward him and placed a finger on the old man's forehead. A flood of magnificent light filled his vision and thrilled his soul. He had no more questions, only a strange joy, despite this desolate ending in the wilderness.

A serene smile softened the professor's features. He raised his weak hand as though receiving the invisible power communicated from the man standing over him.

He closed his eyes and, with utter acceptance and peace, slipped into another world.

* * *

The prophet was thrown in jail without due process. Sheriff Bancroft and his men had judged and condemned him and were already celebrating the victory which was sure to make them look good in the next day's front page.

Jeremy paced back and forth, outrage boiling through his veins. He had to release it or explode. Upon hearing of the events in the desert, he had insisted that the sheriff let him into the cell with Adam Hawthorn. In the shadows, Adam sat silently on the edge of a bench, as peaceful as someone gazing at the ocean on a gentle summer day.

Jeremy abruptly stopped his frantic pacing. He felt ashamed of his lack of control and approached the man in the shadows with remorse.

"Hello, Jeremy. It's been a long time . . . "

His voice carried a soothing quality that immediately eased Jeremy's anxiety.

"Yes it has, Adam. Two years or so. Dr. Hogrogian and I have been looking for you." He felt his throat tighten at the mention of his old mentor's name.

"You have?" Adam responded with a knowing half-smile.

"We heard about the fire, and we were worried about your safety."

"That was thoughtful of you."

Jeremy sat by his side, feeling strangely timid over such proximity to a man who had once been merely a fellow student.

"Are there people seeking to do you harm?"

"There must be . . . " he answered mysteriously.

"It was the professor who wanted so desperately to find you."

They sat in silence. Jeremy shook his head. "I can't believe Dr. Hogrogian is gone."

"It was his time," Adam stated softly.

"He had me convinced of the craziest thing . . . "

"What would that be?"

"He said . . . I can't even bring myself to repeat it . . . " Jeremy muttered. Then he looked at his listener. A shudder went up his spine and shot throughout his body. The man's eyes radiated an intense gaze that penetrated the deepest recesses of Jeremy's soul. A quality of utter calm kept the hypnotic beams of fire from completely overwhelming the young man. He felt exposed, known to the core of his being.

"He said that you were some kind of second Messiah."

The two men stared at each other in the dim light of the jail cell. An unearthly silence fell over them and time seemed to stand still. Jeremy lost all awareness of his surroundings as though he had suddenly fallen into another dimension and lost his bearings. He could see nothing but those eyes—dark, intense, probing—and tranquil, like galaxies slowly moving through infinite space.

To break the spell, Jeremy grabbed onto a question.

"The McCormick boy . . . you made him better."

Adam maintained his gaze without response.

"What was the matter with him? The papers said it was like some kind of miraculous healing."

Adam made no comment.

"What was his illness?" Jeremy inquired, still trying to make conversation and break the odd sensation of being in the glare of the blazing eyes.

"Don't you know?" Adam finally said in a slow, distant voice.

"No. The article referred to a blood disease. The professor told me it was a mutation of the AIDS virus."

"He was right."

Jeremy leapt from the bench, tearing himself away from the overpowering presence of the man. He was filled with high-powered energy as a result of the bizarre experience. But he didn't know what to do with it.

"You're not telling me you cured the boy of AIDS, are you? That's impossible."

"The impossible is at the heart of your religion, Jeremy."

Still under the sway of electrifying energy, the young man couldn't help but turn it into inappropriate anger and frustration.

"Sure, but we don't take it that literally now. It's all been rationalized. There are no more miracles!"

"Really?"

Adam's simple question struck him like a thunderbolt. He felt dizzy. His world had suddenly been turned upside down right in this dreary cell that smelled like a toilet. How could he believe that reality was different than it seemed in a place like this?

Exhausted, Jeremy sat down and dropped his head into his hands. Memories flooded his mind as he drifted far from the dingy prison cell.

CHAPTER 11

A soft light fell through the stained glass windows, sending a colored ray into the empty sanctuary. It spot lit a golden cross on the altar at the center of the chancel. A dazzling reflection sparkled from the crucifix, offering the momentary illusion that some mysterious cosmic life-force was emanating from the instrument of torture.

In the deep silence, the sanctuary took on a quality of the sacred. Absolute stillness and peace filled the consecrated space. An ancient abandoned temple would not have radiated a more numinous feeling. Perhaps the Divine was in this place after all.

Suddenly the door swung open and a hurried man shattered the reverent atmosphere. He called out in a loud crass voice a superficial greeting to someone in the narthex, and raced through the sanctuary like some pagan intruder pillaging the Holy of Holies. This man, full of disregard for the space he was disturbing with his irreverent attitude, was the senior minister of the church.

Robert Morgan, pastor Bob as his congregation called him, was a big man in his early fifties. He wore his white minister's robe like a Roman centurion's tunic, back erect, chest puffed out. He had been in the ministry some eighteen years and had pastored this particular church nearly ten. As he placed his sermon note cards on the pulpit and tested the microphone, he looked out at the empty pews which would soon be filled with nearly five hundred people.

Though he had preached thousands of times, it still gave him a thrill to stand before a captive audience and put on a show—his show, his one-man show, jokes and all. This Sunday morning was especially exciting as he anticipated the joining of a new member, a young woman with tantalizing eyes. How many times these past few Sundays had he felt those familiar delicious goose bumps rise as he projected in his rich baritone voice some monologue about himself passed off as a sermon and sensed those eyes gazing at him with warm admiration.

Pastor Bob had been particularly careful to select one of his past sermons which offered him an opportunity to be dramatic. He had a natural skill for improvisation, and whether or not the content had any value, he could fool his listeners into imagining that he had proclaimed something of importance. His sermons were little more than a chaotic medley of ingredients with no complete meal as the outcome: a sad story here, a couple of jokes there, a dash of quotes from often quoted books, the usual self-aggrandizing illustrations pulled from various experiences of the past week. All this was mixed with a mild reference to Holy Scripture, and presto—another Sunday sermon to make his people feel good about having performed their weekly duty of listening to the "Word of God."

Pastor Bob walked over to the altar and dusted bits of lint from the communion cloth. He again tested the microphone which stood on a stand behind the altar. A smirk of disdain twisted his features as he set the mic stand. With his singer's background and extroverted theatrics, he had no problem in sending his voice booming across the sanctuary. His young associate, however, was another matter altogether.

Soft-spoken and introverted, Jeremy was unable to project with the gusto of his colleague and boss. For Pastor Bob, a man bred on the antiquated values of machismo, this was a sign of weakness and, as he suspected, would prove to be a bad omen for their relationship. Back-slapping and loud laughter was, as far as he was concerned, at least as important to a minister's make-up as theological depth and Biblical study.

The narthex doors opened again and Jeremy stepped into the sanctuary. Pastor Bob immediately looked away and began straightening the candles so as to hide the venomous energy which glazed in his eyes every time he encountered his associate.

Jeremy laid a stack of bulletins on a table by the doors. He knew only too well the icy tension that existed between them. Within two weeks of having been hired by the board of the congregation, their relationship had slipped into a degeneration from which it was not to recover. Jeremy and Lynn had been part of the community of Hillcrest Christian Church for eight months now. And in that time the young man's life had become a relentless, raging nightmare.

Many members of the congregation had come to love him dearly for his insight into the meaning of the Scriptures and the practical elements of the spiritual life. These were not skills automatically handed the typical seminary graduate.

Most of them had never been exposed to the ideas which Jeremy shared with them from the pulpit and in their living rooms. They were gems born in the fire of experience, suffering, and intensive searching. Jeremy and Lynn were seekers of truth who had traveled the back roads of self-discovery and enlightenment long before the call to ministry had come into their lives.

"Everything all set?"

Jeremy looked up at Pastor Bob whose back was still turned to him.

"Yes," he responded in a sad tone. No matter how hard he tried, he could not accustom himself to the alienation and warlike atmosphere which had shattered their working relationship.

"Then go out there and greet the people!" Pastor Bob called out in a harsh voice. Wearing a big smile, however artificial, was the only sacred requirement on Sunday mornings for the senior minister, and he knew how difficult that was for his associate.

Jeremy shook his head as he found himself once again forced to accept the unacceptable—the performance of the worship of God, the Divine Love empowering all things in the midst of hatred, hypocrisy, and ignorance.

He hesitated a moment, trying to think of some conciliatory statement which would dissolve the agonizing blood clot between them, some word which might bring them together onto common ground.

"Well?"

Pastor Bob turned around, glaring coldly at Jeremy. He was a man who believed in authority and its swift obedience. Moreover, he found great satisfaction in forcing his associate to bend his will and ideas in submission to his own. The two ministers' eyes locked on each other.

Here was the ageless battleground of the old and the new. Here was the recurring struggle of every generation, every century, and the dark side of religion: blind leaders and crucified mavericks. In this Southwestern church, where mainstream Protestantism was maintained like a stagnant swamp, the forces of darkness and light confronted each other.

Jeremy felt nauseous. He thought of Lynn, his spouse and soul mate, who alone shared his vision. Strong and fearless, she would have told him to fight back, to tell the man exactly what he knew him to be. But that was not Jeremy's way. Even after all the horrors he had witnessed in his brief encounter with so-called Christianity, even after all the abuse he had taken, Jeremy could not bring himself to initiate all-out war with Pastor Bob. Nor did he wish to divide the congregation into party lines as happened too often in the denomination. So he accepted this umpteenth humiliation and bowed to the orders of his superior, impostor though he was.

Jeremy opened the doors and a flood of noise entered the sanctuary. The narthex was packed with people in their Sunday best. An intense smell of perfumes invaded Jeremy's nostrils and intensified the sickness in the pit of his stomach. He glanced at the faces in the crowd: Everyone was showing teeth and shaking hands as they did each Sunday morning. It was as though some unofficial requirement stipulated that, upon entering through the church doors, every person was to act happy and eager to greet everyone else. Never mind the agony that might be torturing their souls, or the brokenness of their lives that needed mending so desperately. That stipulation was especially true for the ministers who were the very conductors of this masquerade of artificial behavior.

Jeremy suddenly felt dizzy. Out of his subconscious came waves of memories, repressed memories of his earliest efforts to awaken to a greater reality. Confronted with the circus of polyester religion in which he was now enmeshed, each memory was like a red-hot sword striking his heart. Nevertheless, he forced himself to step into the crowd and began shaking hands. As coincidence would have it, Jeremy first encountered Mr. and Mrs. Reynolds. They were all smiles and fit in just right with the rest of the faces. But Jeremy had learned from a friend that Mrs. Reynolds had been brutalized daily by her husband for twenty-five years, all the while faithfully attending this church, smiling alongside her torturer. Neither the sermons, nor the Bible studies, nor the fellowship meals had affected their lives in the least. And the few visits from Pastor Bob and his predecessors had only amounted to small talk and more smiles over tea.

"How are you, Mrs. Reynolds?" Jeremy asked in earnestness, looking deep into her anguished soul. Mrs. Reynolds struggled to keep her happy mask on, but her eyes moistened as she intuitively felt that the young man sensed her pain. Mr. Reynolds, a founding member of the church and large contributor to its upkeep and development, was a past-master at the Sunday morning "look how warm a Christian I am" game. His jolly air was all the more emphasized by the constant hugging and squeezing and kissing to which he subjected every woman he could find before and after the service. In fact, Mr. Reynolds' bear hugs were a popular legend in the church which everyone smiled at in order to overlook the lecherous enjoyment he got from them.

The young women tried especially hard to find it cute and a natural part of "Christian fellowship," while their bodies were telling them in silent screams that they were being molested right in the House of the Lord. Only one woman refused to be subjected to Mr. Reynolds' sweaty hugs. The first time Lynn laid eyes on the man, she knew what he was. As they were introduced, and as he approached to wrap his arms around her, she gave him a look that literally froze him in his tracks. It was the kind of look that no one dared to manifest for fear of shattering with honesty the artifice of this "Christian behavior."

Unfortunately, Lynn had paid a great price for that look: Pastor Bob's undying hatred, for Mr. Reynolds was a favorite of the pastor's, due to his financial contributions and the Christmas bonuses which he semi-anonymously sent him every year.

From that first encounter, Mr. Reynolds eyed the young associate with suspicion and distrust. On weekdays when he came by the church to chat with the senior minister, Mr. Reynolds would give Jeremy the cold shoulder. But on Sunday mornings he was all smiles. And this Sunday would have been no exception, but for the fact that Jeremy's face reflected such a serious concern for his wife's welfare.

"We're just fine," Mr. Reynolds insisted loud and clear as he pulled his wife away from Jeremy. Mrs. Reynolds looked back at him as they quickly disappeared into the crowd of merry greeters.

He recognized a desperate cry welling up from her soul, and shuttered as he witnessed her being sucked into the whirlpool of hypocrisy and pretense.

How many lives were truly in pain and turmoil right here in this room, he thought to himself. Behind all those masks was such need for healing, for peace, for illumination, for forgiveness. And Jeremy felt all the more overwhelmed by the utter emptiness of the so-called worship service which they were about to attend. In this opportunity to be exposed to the Presence of the Divine, to hear of God's nearness and to learn ways of receiving that transforming power, these people were to be given a bombastic soliloquy signifying nothing, dragged through a set of silly rituals, standing and sitting in a ridiculous game of "Simon says," and finally left with that numb feeling of emptiness which prayer and worship were meant to fill in the first place. The blasphemy of it all sickened him to the very core of his spirit and he rushed into his office adjacent to the narthex.

Jeremy collapsed into his chair. He closed his eyes and breathed deeply. A strange silence filled his office. The intensity of the quiet came not only because of its contrast with the noise of the narthex but from a mysterious quality—as though the silence was filled to the brim with "presence." A bird whistled outside his window.

Bird songs had always been for Jeremy messages from a higher world, reminders of Divine Love in the midst of a harsh, unfriendly environment. Often in his life those sweet, ethereal sounds had healed his pain and given him hope. But on this day, the mother bird's spring harmony struck another chord within him.

It shook loose a forgotten memory from the abyss of his despair. And with that sliver of recollection came a tidal wave from his turbulent past.

Beyond his office door and the small hallway which separated it from the crowded narthex, Jeremy knew that madness awaited him. He had journeyed so long and suffered so much to uncover truth and meaning above the chaos of the modern world with its competing religions, dull materialism, and heart-wrenching injustices. In that process he had given up many of his cherished dreams of youth. And having come through the wild storms of such a lonely search, full of deadly pitfalls and hypnotizing illusions, he now found himself grinding to a halt in the mud of suburban, whitewashed religion into which the unpredictable winds of destiny had hurled him.

He looked up at his large bookshelf which spanned the width of his office wall and rose nearly to the ceiling. It was jam-packed with books, many of them torn from years of study and continuous traveling. They traced his journey: existential European philosophers, the writings of Hindu gurus, esoteric teachers the world had never heard of, the great mystics of the Church who embodied the teachings of the living Christ. Here were the relics of an unrelenting search that had spanned three continents and had brought Jeremy in touch with extraordinary individuals, little known to History and never seen on television but who held the keys to the transformation of human consciousness and the uncovering of its great potential. They had been his mentors, his dearest friends, his harshest challengers. Some had died centuries ago and yet were more alive through their writings than those faces in the crowd who led a purposeless existence and, though alive in the flesh, had long ago died in the spirit. Others were psychics, eccentrics, teachers, artists, loners, charlatans, wisemen . . . whatever weaknesses they may have had, not one of them was guilty of sleepwalking through a religion made of petrified dogma and lifeless repetition. They would all have wondered what their friend Jeremy, outsider and truth seeker, was doing at the heart of social convention and artificial respectability, not merely participating in it but legitimizing it by his very presence in their midst.

As the seconds slowed and the surroundings faded away, Jeremy's agony dissolved with the reality of the moment, giving way to another reality, an invisible one populated with all that had gone before. For Jeremy, its sudden intrusion into the moment swept him up into another dimension that brought him face to face with the ghosts of the past who so haunted his present.

* * *

"Wait for me here. I'll be back in a moment."

Little Jeremy, age ten, stood in the ancient cathedral and watched his daddy step into a nearby office with the parish priest. The boy was alone in the dark, cold sanctuary. Alone except for an old woman on her knees deep in prayer near the altar. Her silhouette was as frozen as the medieval statues of apostles and saints which lined the walls.

The little boy shivered. Outside, the summer sun drenched the fields with heat. But in the cathedral, the Gothic pillars and stone floors held an icy cold that had been kept captive there for some seven hundred years. In his shorts and summer shirt, the boy felt the ancient dampness chill him to the bone.

The darkness terrified him. It seemed to contain the bloody history of the place. The same stones, the same dampness, the same old women at prayer had been here in the days of Joan of Arc. Heavy swords had echoed against these walls as men of armor invaded the stillness, bringing into these hallowed corridors the fury of battle and the stench of death. To little Jeremy's imagination, steeped in the blood bath of European history, the silence was filled with screams of anguished humanity in strange harmony with the chants of the monks.

"Daddy!"

The cry came from a place beyond his control. It echoed through the cathedral in an ominous, urgent chorus. The old woman looked up. Little Jeremy caught sight of her disapproving look amidst a mass of scowling wrinkles. Her peasant features, a sight rarely seen in the city where he lived, caused the hair on his neck to stand on end. In the dark shadows, lit only by flickering candles, the woman seemed the very incarnation of evil.

Jeremy hurried away, running into the wooden chairs which served as pews. The high-pitched screech of the legs on the stones polished by countless feet sent an echo like that of laughing furies tearing through the solemn silence. Jeremy frantically looked for his father. But the door at the far end of the sanctuary was closed, just like the door to his father's heart, the father who so many times before had left his son alone and frightened to wait endlessly for his return from some meeting or other.

His fear rising out of control, the little boy felt himself locked and forgotten in a tomb whose occupants he had rudely disturbed. Never before had he felt so strongly the presence of an invisible universe populated with beings who transcended space and time. They were more real to him than the artifacts that loomed in the shadows. Somehow his frenzied emotional state had placed him on a wavelength through which he sensed the energies that had once circulated in this monument and that seemed to have been hanging from the rafters like bats waiting for the disappearance of the light of day to hurl themselves down upon their prey.

The boy had been told that kings and bishops were buried in the crypt beneath his feet. Now the feeling of death rose into his awareness like the shadows of the candle flames dancing along the walls. Never before had the boy tasted such oppressive, omnipotent power. He felt suffocated by his own terror. In desperation, he ran back into the center of the sanctuary where dim sun rays broke through the eerie darkness.

He looked up at the stained glass windows, instinctively seeking comfort from the high places through which streamed the sun. The impassive faces of the saints stared back at him. And beyond them, the giant image of the Christ, holding up his right hand in a sign of blessing to the world.

The boy suddenly felt a strange, wondrous relief fill his soul as he looked into the gentle eyes of the great icon. The face of the Son of God drew him in with a magnetic power utterly unknown to his experience.

A profound measureless peace broke through his fear. The tension in his body melted under the mystic warmth of the Divine Presence, easing his aloneness. He stared unblinking at the image of the Christ which was inexplicably healing him like the warm embrace of his mother. He basked in a glow of unconditional love raining down upon him from the very heart of the cosmos. The blessing of the Logos painted on the ancient wall vibrated through

Jeremy's being with greater power than any feeling he had ever encountered.

He intuitively knew that from this day on he would never again feel completely abandoned or lost in hopelessness. The mysterious presence of this life-giving Love would always be there, even without his awareness of it.

After awhile, the boy began to become aware of himself. He was surprised to feel a wide smile stretching across his features. And he had the queer impression that his feet were not touching solid ground. Then Jeremy realized that he had temporarily lost all sense of his physical body, as though his soul had been drawn out of him and plunged into an ocean of light.

"Jeremy! Jeremy!"

It took him a moment to recognize his father's voice.

"What on earth are you doing?"

He turned around and found his father standing behind him, an irritated look etched on his features.

"I've called you five times now!"

Jeremy felt as though he were struggling to wake from a dream, but he wasn't sure which was the dream and which the reality. His father seemed so small and even silly with his habitual irritation, like a circus clown upset over a fly on his nose. For the first time, the boy saw his father stripped of the imaginary power and importance that children see in their parents.

"I . . . I was looking at . . ."

He pointed at the great painting near the dome of the cathedral. He found himself without words to name the image. There was something too sacred about it that couldn't be expressed through concepts and familiar names. Unable to articulate even the name, Jeremy was struck with the shocking realization that he could never verbalize his awesome experience, that he could never share it with anyone else unless they too had tasted its numinous impact at the core of their being.

"Nice painting. Early fourteenth century, I'd guess."

Jeremy had always admired his father's vast knowledge of history, art, and culture. But in that moment, witnessing his father's split-second glance and labeling of the object of his encounter with the Sacred, Jeremy perceived the blindness of intellectual knowledge devoid of spiritual experience. He knew as he had never known anything before that the image overlooking them had brought him in touch with some greater dimension, some eternal reality which was closed off to those who would merely classify it in the context of its time and place. The artwork's potential for opening the temple veils separating human consciousness from the Divine Presence was utterly lost when seen with eyes that could not transcend its temporal creation in favor of its eternal meaning. The little boy followed his father out of the cathedral.

Unbeknownst to his parents, he was no longer the same person who twenty minutes before had entered the church. Jeremy's first glimpse of these deeper feelings had awakened his spirit, generating hunger pangs for more contact with the world of spirit.

It would be a long time before Jeremy encountered the mysterious and overwhelming power that had reached out to him in the ancient cathedral and forever influenced the course of his destiny.

Jeremy's father was a good man who tried to inculcate in his son a strange form of religion: plenty of concern for the poor and oppressed of the world, but no focus on the mysterious Presence of the Divine, though it was both the origin and purveyor of love for others. So while Jeremy went to church every Sunday year after year throughout his childhood, he met with no experience of that unconditional Love which had touched his soul. The teachings of the man from Nazareth were offered as a guide to moral behavior, but not as a radical challenge to live exclusively for the transcendent, invisible Force he called "Abba."

It was only on his walks in the countryside that the boy encountered fragments of that experience that had overwhelmed him in the old cathedral. The fragrance of rain, the gentle dance of trees in the wind, a whispering river—these were the ministers of the Divine Power which had reached out to him and blessed him with the consciousness of Its presence. The men and women in the pulpit on Sunday morning were purveyors of boredom and repetition, leaders of empty rituals that only the children seemed to realize held no real purpose. Unlike the boy who pointed out the emperor's nakedness in the tale of the "Emperor's New Clothes,"

Jeremy felt that honesty and the obvious could not be discussed in church. There were hymns to be sung—again and again—long sermons to sleep through, and stories from the Bible to be learned like those bland history lessons in mindless secular classrooms.

On the day of his baptism, at the age of twelve, Jeremy had stopped looking for anything meaningful in the institution that had spoon-fed him platitudes from his earliest memories. There were seven children to be immersed that day. They were members of a Protestant denomination born out of the Reformation, and which believed firmly that baptism made sense only when adults, in full possession of their will and faculties, made a conscious decision. Oddly enough, by the twenty-first century, this truth which many had died martyrs' deaths for, had been reduced to an absurd caricature. When children of church members turned twelve, they spent a few weeks in a pastor's class and poof—they were considered mature and capable enough to make a fundamental choice in matters of the spirit, which most of the adults themselves did not understand. However, it made all the parents smile and feel proud and have another occasion to sit down for big dinners.

So Jeremy put on the white robe, and rehearsed the walk down into the baptismal pool, and learned when to hold his nose and when to lean back as the minister dipped him under water. He got his picture taken with the rest of the group and his mother cried, but he never felt the presence of the Holy Spirit or heard the voice of God, nor even had the thought of changing his behavior on the following day. It would be years before he even understood what the purpose of this ritual was originally meant to convey, and years beyond that to learn that the silly business he had undergone on that day had been a sacred act of the secret Essene brotherhood in the deserts of Judea among people who had committed their lives to one purpose—the constant worship of the living God.

With that stamp of approval from the organization to which his family belonged, Jeremy could then participate in communion, yet another ritual no less raped of its meaning. When the plates with the little tasteless tablets of who-knows-what came across the pew, he would pop one into his mouth along with everyone else, take a shot glass of Welch's grape juice, and listen to a mumbled prayer from the elders who generally seemed to be in dire pain as they performed their public duty for the week. He would watch everyone's arm go up as they threw back the grape juice down their gullets in unison. Somehow, this was suppose to have something to do with sacrifice and forgiveness and the partaking of Christ's blood.

Jeremy spent a lot of mental energy trying to understand what it was meant to do or represent. As with so many in this world, he had long ago sensed the unique quality of the kind young rabbi from long ago who had brought a new teaching and reached out to all with compassion. The tragedy and gory details of his death had cut Jeremy to the core and taught him early on that the world of human beings was full of evil, ignorance, and danger.

But what that soul-stirring story had to do with the weekly ingestion of crumbs and juice, he could not for the life of him figure out. The best part of that ritual was the peaceful music the organist played while the elements were being passed around—the only time in the service when the organ was not pounding the ear drums with obnoxious chords whose only virtue was to cover up the outrageously off-key voices shrieking around him. How far removed this all was from the gentle, life-giving words that had echoed down through history, shedding hope and light on millions groveling in the darkness of human error and stupidity. When would he ever find someone to give him real answers?

* * *

A guard entered the corridor and brought Jeremy back into the narrow confines of the jail cell. Jeremy hurled himself at the bars and released his fear and confusion in a burst of rage.

"What is he being charged with?"

The guard stepped back instinctively, then gave him a mocking smirk, knowing that all the power was on his side.

"We can hold him for twenty-four hours without charges."

"This man is not a wanted criminal!" Jeremy cried out as he pointed at the silhouette in the shadows.

"We don't know that yet, do we, son?"

"What kind of law is this? I want to make a phone call!"

"Sure, we'll let you make a call."

As the guard searched for his keys, several men appeared in the hallway. Jeremy let out an involuntary gasp. One of the visitors was Reverend Morgan, closely flanked by the sheriff. Jeremy retreated to the back of the cell as the men entered. Morgan gave him a mocking glance.

"The two of you know each other, I'm sure," the rotund sheriff said to Adam. Morgan squinted beneath the greenish lights and peered at the silent, seated man. The minister's eyes brimmed with disdain and arrogance.

Guards brought in two chairs and the men sat squarely in front of Adam.

"We want to talk to you about the fire at the church. What can you tell us about it?" the sheriff asked.

The prophet gazed upon his two judges, seeing them in the all-revealing light of powerful intuitive perception. Both men felt ill at ease and hid all the more behind their self-important personas.

"I was at my desk at the time of the fire," Adam said simply.

"You mean you left the scene?" the sheriff responded eagerly, sensing a way to pin something on him. "That's a misdemeanor right there."

"It was a matter of self-preservation."

"What do you mean?" the minister asked with a twinge of nervousness.

"I saw someone set the fire," Adam stated calmly.

"You what?"

The sheriff nearly jumped out of his chair.

"He moved right passed my window with a can of gasoline in his hand."

"Who was it then?" the policeman cried out.

"I did not actually see his face. Just a silhouette."

"Why should we believe you?" Morgan questioned with vehemence.

"You don't need to believe me. Ask that man." Adam pointed over their heads. They turned around to find Cleejay Hobbs standing in the jail's corridor. A haunted, grief-stricken look held his features captive. He was in a state of great agitation.

"Cleejay! What brings you here?" the sheriff asked his old acquaintance.

"Heard you arrested the pastor."

"We sure did."

"I gotta see him."

"What for?"

The gigantic farmer disregarded the question and approached the cell bars.

"My wife is dying, pastor . . . she told me to come and find you. I'll do anything to make her better."

Adam studied him silently.

"Then you know what you must do," he finally stated.

"But who will care for her then?" he responded as though he had heard the prophet telepathically.

"She'll be caring for you."

Hobbs turned to the sheriff, his eyes filling with tears.

"I done it, sheriff. I set the fire."

The policeman jumped out of his chair.

"Why would you do a damn fool thing like that, Cleejay?"

"I heard this man at a town meeting," he answered pointing to Reverend Morgan. "He was calling the pastor a dangerous heretic."

Morgan's face turned bright red and he tried to mumble some sort of justification. The sheriff interrupted him.

"You know what this means, don't you, Cleejay?"

The man nodded and turned to Adam in desperation.

"Call her," the prophet stated gently.

Hobbs hurried to the nearby pay phone and within moments was weeping with gratitude. Everyone in the cell held their breath in amazement as they witnessed the strange incident. Hobbs hung up the phone and hurried back into the cell. He fell to his knees before Adam.

"How can I ever thank you. I beg your forgiveness. What can I do to . . . "

Adam touched the man's head and silenced him. The rugged old farmer looked up, his face glistening with tears.

"Be a good man. That's what you're here for."

The tough, weather-beaten farmer glowed with joy. There was nothing left of the violent, rude individual who had inhabited his psyche all these years. His personality had undergone a veritable meltdown.

CHAPTER 12

The prophet was released the next morning before dawn. As they walked along the quiet road, Jeremy was flooded with the sensation that he was at a crossroads, and that if he did not act now, he would miss an opportunity that would never return to him.

"What are your plans, Adam?"

"To move on."

"Where to?"

"Wherever I am led."

Jeremy couldn't control a negative reaction. His rational mind would not accept such faith in an invisible power so deeply involved in the affairs of human beings. Even as a minister, such a concept was too great a clash with his twenty-first century version of reality.

"You're quite a skeptic, Jeremy."

Adam had somehow read his mind.

"All this talk of providence and guidance is just too spiritual even for a minister, is it?"

"It seems to me that we must obey the laws of this world."

"What laws?"

"Oh, like making money to pay the rent, having to pay your taxes, and making decisions that are economically sane . . . "

"Ah, money concerns."

"Well, that for one. I guess you're not tied down by anyone else."

"Your relationships should liberate you, not tie you down, Jeremy. They're an antidote to our natural selfishness, so you're the lucky one, not me."

"I'm not free to take off into the wild blue yonder."

"How do you know? Maybe she would go with you."

"Do you remember Lynn?" Jeremy asked, surprised at Adam's memory.

"I do. She was the best candidate for ministry in the entire seminary, even though she wasn't a student."

"Are you suggesting that we pack up and go with you, wherever you're going?"

"I'm not suggesting anything. I merely told you that I was moving on. You do what you need to do."

"What are you going to buy yourself a cup of coffee with along the way?"

"I'm more interested in the big picture. What's ultimately ahead rather than what I'll be doing this afternoon. The coffee will take care of itself."

"What about the things that you leave behind?"

"Such as?"

"Dr. Hogrogian."

"His work is finished here."

"I mean the funeral. Don't you want to stay for the funeral?"

Adam stopped walking and looked up at the sky. The colored light of dawn was just beginning to seep through the night.

"You're quite right, Jeremy. I want to be here for that event."

"Would you be willing to say a word at the grave site?"

Adam looked at him for a moment, pondering the question.

"You do realize that what I would have to say would not be appreciated by some."

"I think you should say whatever is in your heart. He was special to both of us."

"It might cause trouble for you, Jeremy."

"I'm only interested in an authentic farewell to our dear professor."

"Then I'll take you up on it, friend. We'll let the chips fall where they may."

* * *

A large crowd gathered at the cemetery where the remains of Dr.

Hogrogian were to be interred. Students, colleagues of the academic world, neighbors, ordinary folk who had been touched by the man's rare sensitivity and compassion stood silently in the sunshine. The leadership of the denomination was also there, headed by Reverend Morgan, who was always one for proper protocol, even though he had despised the eccentric gentleman.

In the back of the crowd, statuesque and motionless, stood Stargazer, the Cherokee wise man. He was strangely out of place in his faded jeans and windbreaker among all the suits and ties. A podium and microphone had been erected by the grave. Jeremy gave a subdued and thoughtful eulogy. Lynn sat under a small canopy filled with flowers and wept quietly as she remembered the gentleman from the old world whose mystical wisdom had given her hope for human beings.

Adam Hawthorn stood to one side of the coffin, staring intently into the hole that would be the final resting place of his beloved mentor. The sun was bright and he wore thick sunglasses to protect his eyes. But they couldn't conceal the intensity of his gaze and the single-mindedness of his purpose on this day. He knew that in the crowd stood dozens of Dr. Hogrogian's enemies, men in positions of power and authority, well known for making and breaking careers. Adam knew that to honor his old friend he would have to end his career in this organization right here in this peaceful cemetery where the dead watched with sadness the strange affairs of the living.

Adam stepped up to the podium.

"The man we are to remember," he began, "had many friends and many enemies. His students loved him and recognized in him a man with a great heart and a mysterious capacity to understand them and connect with their innermost soul. This man also had many people who fiercely disliked him and sought to destroy his career. One might wonder why this compassionate, sensitive man would generate such anger among his colleagues. For his enemies were all among the academic authorities, many of whom are sitting here today."

He looked across the faces of the stern professors standing about, looking more and more uncomfortable.

"What was it about this gentle man that made him such a threat to the powers that be, to the institution that he served so loyally? I believe the very beauty of his soul, so well known to his students, revealed the sterility of the academic world around him which sought not to enlighten the soul, but to train the mind according to its version of reality."

Reverend Morgan looked over at the president of the seminary and shook his head angrily.

"Why would men and women who claim to teach younger generations the wisdom of their religion seek to destroy a man who incarnated that very thing? Perhaps it is because they are frauds and have no such wisdom!"

A loud gasp came from the audience and the professors began to move about nervously, unable to contain their rage. Morgan smiled cynically and whispered to a colleague.

"He's just buried himself with Hogrogian. His career is over."

Lynn looked up at Adam, worried that he was going too far. Jeremy took her hand and tried to comfort her.

"I say to you today that in remembering the life of Dr. Hogrogian, we must not overlook the last two decades of his life in which he was hounded by so-called Christians. And he was hounded because he was a truly spiritual man and did not fit in their little mental box where they put everyone and everything, including their god. They stand guard around this little box which their mind has created and protect it with great zeal, because from these boxes they receive awards and titles and pensions and all the attention that satisfies their egos."

Angry words were now rising from the crowd. People were no longer able to put up with what was being said from the podium.

"Dr. Hogrogian's simplicity, humility and deep devotion was alien to their arrogance and hunger for power. Such a man put them all to shame. And in response, they sought to crucify him and chase him from their world."

"That's enough!" someone cried out.

"Silence!" Adam responded with thundering authority. The man turned pale before the prophet's glare.

"You disrupted this man's life; you will not disrupt his funeral! You tried to bury him before his physical death, to erase his name from memory. You tried to keep him out of print and forgotten so that his witness to the Truth would be remembered no more, and your version that pays you well and fattens you up and makes you feel important will go on unchallenged. But Dr. Hogrogian will not be forgotten despite all your efforts, for he was the real thing, and those with eyes to see and ears to hear will always remember his unique gifts and his compassionate heart. You, on the other hand, will vanish like the grass you stand on and fall into the outer darkness which is already in your empty souls."

"That's it!" Reverend Morgan shouted as he walked away. Most of the professors followed him out of the cemetery.

"Please leave! You do not deserve the right to be here on this special occasion as we honor Dr. Hogrogian," Adam said into the microphone for all to hear.

"We'll deal with you later!" Morgan cried out.

"Beware!" Adam responded. "I'm not an old man you can kick around at will!"

The other mourners stood around the grave frozen in shock, and red with discomfort.

"Friends," Adam continued, " this is as it should be. These men and women did not have the right to be here. Their hypocrisy was a blasphemy before God. So now we are left with his true friends, and we can begin the authentic rite of passage and bid farewell to this noble soul who gave us all so much. I want to tell you a story about Dr. Hogrogian, one that is not on his resume, but that he shared with me some years ago."

Adam stepped away from the podium and approached the open grave. He crossed himself in the manner of Dr. Hogrogian's tradition and began to speak.

* * *

Even as a child, Hogrogian had sensed the presence and action of spiritual reality. He was a descendant of an ancient Slavonic family whose religious conversion predated the beginnings of holy Russia. For over twelve hundred years, the atmosphere of the Hogrogian home was permeated with an intuitive consciousness of the invisible depths of existence.

The Turkish invasion in the Middle Ages brought Islam to the Balkans, but the proud people of Montenegro took to the mountains and remained true to their beliefs. This defiant, stubborn and courageous stand against overwhelming forces entered the soul of each new generation. Struggle was as natural as breathing, and the birth of every first male child was greeted with the saying "may he be the first of nine!" Nine that would carry on the fight for independence.

Anton Hogrogian was born into that turbulent milieu and incarnated its features to an extreme degree. His personality was both fiercely courageous and profoundly pious. No one followed the rituals of the Church with more devotion. Even the village priest would lose his patience with the boy, and later the young man, who insisted on performing every prostration, every signing, every prayer in conformity with the ancient liturgy of Saint John Chrysostom.

He would have become a priest had not ethnic cleansing pulverized all his hopes and dreams. Hardly into his twenties, Hogrogian was under attack from both the Muslims and the Nationalists who hated his piety. The young man was given the rare "privilege" of looking into the face of demonic evil on a scale unparalleled in human history. His only option was to head for the border.

"What is your name?"

The soldier held his rifle aimed at the young Serb's chest.

"Hogrogian, Anton."

"Show me your papers."

Hogrogian reached into his jacket pocket. He knew they were in order. He had made sure of that before planning his escape.

Nevertheless, all men were suspected fighters, regardless of their profession.

The officer studied the documents carefully. Hogrogian looked at the scenic view of his homeland: round hills rich with woods and meadows, old church towers and castle ramparts rising above the trees, winding rivers in every valley.

This was all a part of him, as essential as his hands and legs.

But there was no turning back now. He would have to walk away from it all like Abraham heading for the desert. Except that Abraham didn't have to make it past hordes of fanatic separatists, all of whom were bent on destroying the likes of him.

"Where are you headed?"

"Home." The ironic answer stuck in his throat. Home would now be everything that was not home. Home would have to be made of something other than physical reality if he were ever to have one again.

The soldier handed his papers to him and motioned for him to move on. Hogrogian took his first step toward freedom. Or so he thought. The border was still five miles away.

His powerful legs carried him swiftly through forests and groves. Despite the beauty and peace of his surroundings, Hogrogian could not benefit from the nature world he had communed with so often as a child. He could not rid himself of the face of his mother and sisters as he had seen them on his last glance over his shoulder. The little woman in a black gown, old before her time, with the timeless look of a mother's grief etched upon her classic Slavonic features. Three young girls, once full of giggles and playfulness, now weighed down to the end of their days with the tragedy of war.

He knew he would never see them again. All he had left of them were memories that some day were sure to fail and leave him with only dim images. But he also carried them in his blood, that strong Montenegran blood that had the power to endure.

He would remember the lessons of life passed on to him by his culture and his church through the innate wisdom of his mother and father. He was taking with him the last of an ancient legacy that made freedom and reverent humility one and the same. And it was this God, whose presence was kept alive by the flame of faith passed on from heart to heart, who would truly keep him going.

Hogrogian paused in the midst of a small clearing and listened to the birds. A deep tranquillity came over him as he noticed the sun rays breaking through foliage and creatures of the wild scurrying about their business, oblivious of the human madness. With peace appeared a new awareness of the axis of his life—the divine presence. Everything was shattered expect that. Every hope of his life was broken, and yet something held him up over the abyss of despair. He looked at the moss-covered trees and the graceful ivy climbing toward the sky. In that brief instant, something of eternity revealed itself to him.

Though lost, he knew there was a way out. Though alone, he knew he couldn't be. As solid as the ground he stood on and as palpable as the warmth of the summer sun shimmering down through the trees, so was his awareness of an unseen power sustaining him in the midst of chaos. All was lost, and yet everything was his, as long as he remained true to the force that held him up.

A dead body lay spread-eagle on the edge of the woods. Hogrogian almost fell over it as he came out from the brush. This was not the first corpse he had seen, yet he was unable to restrain a shout of horror. The dead man was his age, shot full of holes from his head to his feet. Hogrogian felt as though he were looking at his own fate if his escape was unsuccessful.

The open eyes stared into nothingness, proclaiming the preciousness of life against the backdrop of nonlife. A sparkle on his bloody hand revealed a wedding ring and the certainty that a good number of people would soon feel the agonizing pangs of his loss, and a part of them would also die from the murderer's bullets.

"Hey you! Don't move!"

Hogrogian came out of his reflection and with lightning speed found himself in the throes of terror. Several hundred yards below him, at the bottom of the hill, soldiers were steadying their weapons in his direction. Without thinking, he dashed off toward the woods like a hunted rabbit. The crackle of gunfire exploded around him, knocking down tree limbs and bits of bark.

He raced at full speed through the forest, dodging trees and bushes, not feeling any of the thorns that tore at him as he ran by. The two years of war had yet to instill the kind of fear that now burned through his nerves. This was the first time that death was out for him specifically.

Over the sound of his desperate panting, he could hear the stomping of army boots crashing through the underbrush. An extra jolt of adrenaline increased his speed as he reached the outer edge of the woods. Now the chemicals of fear were spiced with those of anger. What indignity to be chased in his own backyard like a beast of prey! He swore to himself that he would never run again.

He burst out of the woods and found himself in a lovely meadow. In the midst of it, surrounded by flowers of all colors, stood an old chapel. Out of breath, Hogrogian made a supreme effort to race toward the chapel. Sweat poured from him like a river and his heart no longer beat in rhythmic fashion. Halfway to the chapel, his legs collapsed beneath him and he fell into the tall grass. Any moment now, the soldiers would appear in the clearing and he too would be staring blindly at the summer clouds above.

Every inch of his body was on fire with pain. Never had he forced it to run so intensely for so long. No doubt his speed had neared Olympic standards, and now he was paying the price. He considered not getting up again. Rolling over, he caught sight of the light blue sky smiling above him. The vision was suddenly marred by the thunder of boots nearing the meadow.

"Damn it!" he cried out. "I won't let you take it from me!"

Without knowing how, he made it to his feet and ran to the chapel. His legs were powered by outrage. They had destroyed his country, made his family homeless, and ruined his dreams. He was not going to let them tear out the gift of life and blind him to its glory. Not without the kind of fight that was the special talent of the mountain men of Montenegro.

As he came around to the front of the little chapel, he stumbled over another dead body. The corpse was dressed in a soldier's uniform even though he was an aged man. His gun still protruded from its holster. Without thinking, Hogrogian pulled out the pistol and approached the chapel entrance.

He recognized the little building as the hermitage of a revered monk who had died not long ago. The man was widely regarded as a holy man, and the place was considered sacred.

He opened the door and entered a dark world. As his eyes adjusted to the lack of sunshine, he noticed large silhouettes peering at him. At the end of the room, a small window let in a stream of summer light. Faces slowly appeared on the walls. Bearded and serene, they were the icons of ancient saints.

Guttural orders were barked outside. The soldiers hurried toward the chapel.

Hogrogian checked the pistol for bullets as he had learned to do in the obligatory military training of his youth. He cocked the weapon. He knew there were three soldiers after him and he was prepared to drill them with holes. Not only was he on fire with the effort to stay alive, but a powerful rage roared within him against these men who were so recklessly destroying civilization.

The soldiers entered. He placed his hand on one of the old chairs to steady it and aimed his gun at the door.

Outlined by the light of the open door, the soldiers huddled together. It would be a simple affair for him to shoot all three before any of them could react.

Hogrogian closed one eye and placed the first soldier in the pistol's cross hairs. All the horrors that he had witnessed and wept over these last two years were about to be revenged in one swift and terrible moment. But just as his finger began to squeeze the trigger, he heard an inner voice speak to him.

"Be not afraid of them that kill the body, and after that have no more that they can do. But fear Him who has the power to cast into hell."

The voice was so clear that he looked up as though it had come from someone next to him. His eyes fell upon the icons of the prophets, martyrs and apostles all gathered together to celebrate the mystic feast with the Holy One of God whose giant icon filled the back of the chapel. But now the icon of Christ that had first conveyed compassion, radiated an expression of anger.

Hogrogian was suddenly flooded with the strange sensation that the transcendent world was more real than the danger in which he found himself.

The inner voice spoke to him again. "He who takes up the sword, dies by the sword."

The chapel suddenly filled with an atmosphere of terrible awe. He looked back at the door. The soldiers had turned on their flashlights and moved into the room. They were easy targets for him. Then in the doorway he saw the glowing outline of another figure. He blinked, thinking that his imagination had gone wild because of the trauma of the moment. It seemed to him that the saintly old hermit was standing there, holding a chalice in his hand and looking directly at him as though inviting him to participate in the symbolic union in which the spiritual beings on the wall were engaged.

He looked back at the icons. The Last Supper was painted over the altar and fell on Hogrogian like a tidal wave. It seemed to him that a celestial assembly was gathered together, one in which the Anointed One was the host and the saints and angels His guests. The overwhelming power of another spiritual reality was vividly present, a thousand times more real than the soldiers and his fear. He felt like an intruder in this sacred space.

Ancient words of scripture came to him. "Surely the Lord is in this place. This is none other than the house of God and the gate of heaven."

He realized at that moment that the only difference between himself and the violent men searching for him was the fact that he believed in a spiritual reality. His fear of the soldiers felt puny compared to the sensation of sacredness weighing down upon him. His thoughts of killing made him feel ashamed in this holy place. The palpable presence of the spiritual beings represented on the walls so overwhelmed his concern for his existence that he lost all desire to kill for it. He laid the gun on the floor. It no longer mattered if the soldiers caught him and shot him on the spot.

His devotion to the higher world was more important than his own life. He saw another icon in the back of the room, picturing Christ silencing the storm. It spoke to him directly and intimately. It was his storm and his need that the Son of God was stilling in that moment. The synchronicit of his circumstances and the meaning of the image gave the icon intense significance. The presence of the Eternal made itself intimately known to him. He knew that he would never again doubt the reality of the spiritual world and those who had come from it to save humanity. He would trust them more than his loaded gun.

"There he is!" one of the soldiers cried out.

The flashlights fell on him. He held up his hands. The soldiers surrounded him immediately, leveling their weapons at his head. They too were agitated by being in this mysterious and ghostly place. In spite of their brutality, something about the chapel made them strangely uncomfortable.

Hogrogian closed his eyes, expecting to be shot right there beneath the icons.

"Look! There's a gun on the floor!" one of the soldiers called out.

Another soldier picked it up. "It's cocked and loaded!"

"Why didn't you shoot us?" the third one asked.

Hogrogian opened his eyes.

"He who lives by the sword, dies by the sword."

The men were stunned by his response.

"You had that gun aimed at us and you chose not to fire? Even though you knew we were going to kill you?"

"That's right. He reminded me."

The men turned in the direction where he was pointing. Their flashlights illuminated the serene features of the Christ whose gaze seemed alive and staring straight at them. They were shaken by the stern impression of the sacred face. One of them lowered his gun.

"Let him go," he said.

"Are you crazy?" another one whispered.

"I can't shoot this man either," the third soldier said.

"But he's an enemy!"

"He chose not to be our enemy. I choose not to be his."

The first soldier looked at his companions and realized that he felt the same way as well.

"Don't come around here again!" he said to Hogrogian as they turned away.

When they had gone, Hogrogian found a candle and lit it before the icons. He offered up prayers of gratitude. From that day on, he lived and breathed for the sake of that higher world that had reached through space and time and taken hold of his heart.

* * *

"Anton Hogrogian has now joined that gathering of saints whom he encountered all those years ago. He is one of them in the realm of light," Adam concluded.

The shadows were growing long across the cemetery lawn. No one had moved in the time that Adam was talking, mesmerized by the tale of the old man's life. They were finally realizing how fine a soul had lived among them. The service ended as the prophet, now a public enemy of the institution that had prepared him for his ministry, sent a shovel-full of earth upon the coffin of his beloved teacher.

CHAPTER 13

Jimmy Maloney sat in his tiny office at the North American Branch of the World Federation Headquarters. It was three in the morning and no breaking news had come into the main computer storage center for nearly an hour.

Jimmy lit his tenth cigarette since the beginning of the night shift. He was bored out of his mind. This was the easiest job he had ever held, but sometimes it tested even his capacity for total isolation.

He had risen high enough in the bureaucracy to hold a security-clearance position. In this international operation, it took years of drone desk work to prove one's loyalty and dependability. Jimmy had a penchant for solitary, meticulous activity. He didn't particularly like people. Compiling bits of data into a myriad of files that no one would ever be interested in suited him just fine. His job was to catalog all information that came in over the Southwestern sector of the United States. From car thefts to corporate takeovers, he was the cog in the engine that took in the facts and dispersed them into giant data banks.

He put out his cigarette and placed another one between his lips, mechanically searching for a lighter in his shirt pocket. Then he caught himself, remembering that he was trying to quit. Ever since the fear campaign of the nineties concerning nicotine, it was politically incorrect to enjoy the act of swallowing smoke. But Jimmy enjoyed being different and had started the habit just to spite society's disdainful attitude. Besides, the tobacco kept him awake during the long nights in his cubicle all alone with the flashing lights of his computers. The cigarettes kept him company. They were all the emotional assistance he needed to make it through his work hours.

In his apartment on forty-fifth street, he had an old ferret that gave him some sense of relationship with living creatures. Yet even though the animal had been with him for some five years, his favorite companions were his computers. He collected old laptops from the end of the last century and hooked them together to terminals of earlier models. Every chance he got, he performed wizardries that only his mind understood.

He navigated the WorldNet with the ease and precision of an experienced captain on the high seas. The automated minds of his machines were more real to him than his neighbors and passersby in the street. He enjoyed working when everyone slept and reveled in the solitude that made possible his life at the keyboards. His acquaintances considered him odd and antisocial. But he had come to grips with his nature and was contented with being who he was.

As he swirled in his worn chair and lit the cigarette, his eyes turned upon one of the six computer screens that surrounded him. On the largest terminal, the twenty-seven incher, a continuous stream of information scrolled by, coming through on-line from across his sector. The little white lines of type came and went almost as fast as he could blink. From long practice, he had learned the skill of catching the location and first words of each news item to grasp the gist of the information. His job was merely to catalog events for some other bureaucrat in some other cubicle on the floor above him to pass on to someone on the floor above him. This was the way of the World Federation, and it paid his rent and his groceries, so he had no complaints.

He yawned and looked at his watch. At this hour, not much was going on and even the large screen was beginning to show blank spaces between bits of information. He took a drag from his cigarette, feeling the acrid smoke sting his throat and lungs. He blew perfect circles as he released it back into the air. Then out of the corner of his eye, he saw a new bite of news appear on the screen. He caught the words Enid, Oklahoma.

He was one of the very few workers in the building to recognize the name.

"So what's going on in Enid?" he said out loud.

Speaking to himself was a habit he had picked up in his solitary living.

He leaned forward, squinted, and read the screen.

"Enid, Oklahoma: three-thirty A.M. A local minister was assaulted at a friend's home by masked assailants. They broke into the house and beat him severely. One of the intruders was shot by the homeowner. The minister crawled over to the wounded man and placed his hands on the wound.

"The intruder watched with understandable astonishment as the man he had come to kill healed his serious wound within moments. He was so grateful that he begged forgiveness from the minister and revealed his identity as an off-duty policeman. He claimed that he was ordered to commit this crime by his superiors. At Bass Memorial Hospital, doctors confirmed the apparently miraculous healing."

Jimmy was a skeptic from birth and had no patience for the mysteries of the supernatural. His fingers flew across the keyboards. A melodious sound of chimes came out of the computer's speaker as it saved the information to a file and then shot it over to the printer. In an instant, the story appeared in hard copy form. Jimmy grabbed the paper, blew out a puff of smoke, and studied the message again.

There was something familiar about this story. His mind went to work, seeking to retrieve data just like his computers. Perhaps that was why he loved them so much. There were word and idea links in his memory that gave him access to a vast array of information at even greater speed than his beloved machinery. What was there about a strange tale coming out of a little town in the Southwest? He closed his eyes and focused his mind. Somewhere in his mental files, there was another bit of information captured from the information highway.

Something important was underlying these brief paragraphs that the national news had not found worthy to pick up. Enid . . . a strange figure with unusual powers . . . The silence of the night floated through the room with a weight that had not been there before, as though his environment was hushed by his need to remember.

He suddenly leaped out of his chair. "That's it! I knew I'd seen it before!" He threw his cigarette into an overburdened ashtray. His fingertips fell on the keyboards like a concert pianist's and began to speak to the computer. Directories, sub-directories and file searches flew across the screen as he went after one sentence in an ocean of countless words.

"There it is!" he cried out. If anyone had been in the room, they would have thought that he had found a treasure map. On the screen, little words blinked in their ghostly light against a blue neon background. Another story from Enid about a minister healing a little boy from a hopeless condition.

"It's got to be the same man!" Jimmy said. His heart kicked into high gear. He had one other hobby besides computer wizardry, and that was mystery stories. Arthur Conan Doyle and Alfred Hitchcock were his heroes. He loved to hunt for clues and connections. What else was there to do at three a.m. all alone in a tiny, dark space?

* * *

The World Federation's U.S. offices were headquartered in a heavily fortified forty story building in upper Manhattan. The dreary concrete monument housed a variety of departments. The executives occupied the top five floors overlooking the city on one side and a park on the other. The hourly wage earners like Jimmy Maloney were huddled in the basement and lower floors without windows or proper air circulation.

In the middle section of the building, hidden from the eyes of the world, was the top secret command post for the military side of the World Federation. No elevators opened onto these floors. Hidden moving stairways that connected to underground bombproof chambers transported people with special security clearances.

In his eight years on the job, Jimmy had only caught sight of one individual working in that section. He recognized him by his obvious military bearing and personality, and by the bulge of a huge gun in his jacket.

Even the knowledge of what was on those middle floors was top secret. Peons and bean counters like Jimmy knew only rumors that they kept to themselves with priestly confidentiality.

This was not an age in which to be caught sharing secrets. The world government was merciless with leaks of any kind. They dealt with them in the manner of gangsters and dictators. There was no due process for traitors and loose tongues, only death in a back alley.

An atmosphere of paranoia and constant stress permeated the entire complex. The world was less safe than it had ever been, even though power was centralized and carefully organized through high-tech surveillance of the population.

It was mid-morning, several hours past the end of his work day, when Jimmy stepped into the elevator and pushed the button for the third floor. He had been waiting impatiently for time to pass and to build up the courage to do what he felt he had to do. The third floor was lodged just below the secret military headquarters and the last place before the no man's land of concrete walls and infrared devices that guarded the temple of power hidden in the building.

Jimmy wiped beads of sweat from his prematurely balding brow and straightened his jacket. He tightened his grip on the folder that contained the output of the messages that concerned him. He hated traveling away from his quiet, dark cubicle and entering the bright, neon-lit offices of his supervisor. He avoided it like the plague and hadn't made the trip in six months. But he had a hunch about this one, and though he was more inclined to live by his intellect rather than by his intuitions, this feeling was too strong to overlook.

He had been told a hundred times in his first years on the job that anything which struck him as peculiar or potentially destabilizing had to be brought to the attention of his superior. That was his purpose buried in the basement night after night. He was the eyes of the World Federation and was often told to be proud of that. Though he was only two small pupils in an immense ocean of eyes watching everything closely, his optical nerves were tied to the very survival of world civilization. There was no room for risking the oversight of small disturbances—not in a world that was constantly on the brink of nuclear destruction, nationalistic revolution and religious uprisings. If a Mid Eastern Iman with terrorist inclinations blinked, the World Federation wanted to know about it.

As the elevator stopped at the second floor, opened and closed its doors on an empty hallway, Jimmy studied the contents of his folder and reflected on his decision to take this matter upstairs. Would he be laughed at, yelled at, fired even? His boss was one of those men who had no tolerance for incompetence and thoroughly enjoyed lording it over his underlings. Jimmy was one of dozens of such servants to Hank Bracken, middle management tyrant.

"Why this story and not another?" he wondered to himself. What was it about this news that stirred such an inexplicable response in him? Then he remembered his boss's often quoted rhyme: "Yours is not to wonder why, just be a spy." Being a spy for the safety of the world gave him a sense of importance that his paycheck and working environment could not offer him. So he was dutifully carrying his catch off the radar screen of his computerized ocean of information. If he was mocked, so be it. It wouldn't be the first time, nor the last. He had adapted to the humiliation of being weak of body and oddly lackluster in personality. Those were the cards he had been dealt. But some day he hoped to break a big story, one that would send shock waves all the way to the top floor.

The elevator came to a stop at the third floor. Jimmy nervously patted down what hair he had on his head and prepared himself to walk among fellow humans, one of the more distasteful obligations of life, as far as he was concerned. The doors opened onto a vast room broken up into dozens of cubicles. He made his way past what seemed like zombies at their computer terminals, each one storing facts and figures for the giant global operation. He realized that no one noticed him, another humiliation he was used to, although it always stung him somewhere in the recesses of his heart.

At the far end of the room were enclosed offices where the higher-ups hid behind doors and darkened glass, where they could watch their workers unobserved. He knocked at door number five.

"Come in!" a gruff voice responded.

Jimmy took a deep breath, braced himself, and entered. Hank Bracken was a large, rotund man in his fifties with a bulldog face and a mane of wild gray hair that was incapable of being tamed.

He had once been an athlete, and though his muscles had turned to fat, his character still emanated a powerful and competitive disposition.

"Maloney! What brings you out of your hole?" the man said without looking up from his paperwork.

"I . . . I . . . " Jimmy couldn't find the words to present his concern.

"Spit it out!" his superior ordered, still focused on other matters.

"There's something I thought I should bring to your attention," Jimmy said as he held his file folder in two slightly trembling hands.

"What is it?"

"Some news out of Oklahoma, sir."

"What news?"

"Well, it's rather strange . . . "

This time Bracken looked up.

"What the hell are you talking about?"

Jimmy handed the folder to him as though feeding a tiger through the bars of its cage. Bracken snatched it out of his hands.

"You gotta be more articulate, Maloney. I don't have time to beat around the bush."

He opened the file and looked at the two sheets on which a few lines were printed.

"What am I looking at, Maloney?"

"There's something going on here, sir."

Bracken dropped the papers on his overcrowded desk and scratched his head with impatience.

"I don't have time for this nonsense! What is it that concerns you about this?"

Jimmy swallowed hard, took a deep breath and did his best to step out of the cave of his introversion.

"There seems to be a man out there with unusual powers that could be a threat to the peace of the region."

His boss sat back in his large, comfortable chair and looked at him with mounting anger.

"Are you telling me that some backwards religious foolishness should worry security agents of the World Federation?"

Jimmy tried to respond but Bracken interrupted.

"Don't you remember our policy regarding these matters? If folks want to live in the Dark Ages, let them—as long as they keep it to themselves. It's as effective as any other form of distraction to keep them in line."

"But sir, this man seems to be actually manifesting supernatural abilities. It could scare people."

"Well it sure scares me, Jimmy my boy," Bracken retorted in mockery. "I can tell you that. Yeah, I'm just shiverin' all over. What the hell did you expect out of the Southwest? By the time we colonize another planet, they'll still be harking back to the frontier days."

"Sir, what if this is for real? What if this man can actually cure rare diseases?"

"How would that be a problem for us besides costing doctors some profit?"

"Well, sir, imagine . . . "

Bracken slammed his large fist on the desk.

"I'm not in the business of imagining, Maloney! We deal with concrete information here. No room for fantasy. This is the real world."

Jimmy felt compelled to make his point.

"Sir, if this man is some kind of mystic healer, it could create chaos. People from all over the world might come to him for cures."

His boss let out a loud laugh. "You spend too much time alone in the dark, son. You gotta step out and smell the fumes of our world. There are no mystics today! There are terrorists and thieves and revolutionaries. A whole bunch of lunatics. But I haven't seen a mystic yet in my thirty years on the job. And even if there were such persons, there's no room for them in this day and age. That all died out with the twentieth century."

Jimmy was out of words. He couldn't think of what else to say.

"Go on, get outta here!" Bracken barked as he returned to his stacks of papers. "Don't bother me until you come across something really important to our global security."

Jimmy stood silently before him for a moment. He was in a strange state of shock and his gut-feeling shouted loud and clear through the synapses of his brain. Something serious was about to happen out of these obscure events. But he couldn't put his finger on it.

Bracken peered up from his work and glared at him, virtually pushing him out the door with the irritation in his eyes. Jimmy picked up the folder on the desk, turned around and walked out.

He moved into the busy labyrinth, shoulders slumped over, his head looking down in embarrassment and confusion. He crashed into someone hurrying by. Papers flew in the air. A young woman stood before him, trying to catch the materials that were falling out of her arms.

"Jimmy!" she cried out in frustration. "Watch where you're going!"

"Hi, Michelle," he said, suddenly mesmerized. The young woman had lovely features, and was radiant with intelligence and a dynamic personality. Michelle Blair was a level three security agent who had already made a reputation for herself in a short period of time. He had seen her on and off over the past several years. She was a distant goddess in his sad and lonely life, one that he could never come near. Yet his flesh had just touched hers. He could feel his face turn scarlet red. It was such a soft and wonderful sensation, even though she had bruised his arm in the encounter.

"Don't look at me like that! Help me get my papers together," she said impatiently.

To Jimmy, those were the most beautiful words he'd ever heard. He quickly kneeled down beside her and gathered the mess. He handed her the papers and she looked up at him. A blond curl of displaced hair fell over her green eyes. It added a sensuous quality to her otherwise businesslike demeanor. He stared at her in awe. He could feel her breath on his face. Her nearness utterly enthralled him. This was the most exciting moment of his life.

She smiled sweetly. He had never seen such white, lovely teeth.

"Thanks, Jimmy."

"You're . . . you're welcome," he answered as they both stood up.

He caught sight of the soft pale skin of her breast and the lace of her bra as she rose. He felt his legs go weak.

"Are you okay?" she asked naively, completely unaware of what was going on in his head. "What's the matter?"

He was paralyzed, unable to speak or think. She found a way to break the awkward moment.

"What brings you up here?"

"A strange . . . a strange story out of the Southwest."

"Oh? I love strange stories."

"Well, Mr. Bracken doesn't."

"Is this it?" she asked with a coquettish glance at the folder he was holding.

"That's it."

"May I see it?"

"Well, I don't know . . . "

"Now Jimmy, my security clearance is as good as yours. You don't need to hide anything from me."

"I'm not! Really!" he said defensively.

She opened the folder and was surprised to find only a few lines of type on the sheets.

"Not much here for a story that deserves to be brought up to this office."

His face turned red again and the old familiar feeling of failure made his heart sink. This was the one person whose opinion really mattered to him. He had admired her beauty and bright intelligence since the day she had come on board.

She read the first page to herself and then quickly looked at the second sheet. He stood before her, ready to take the folder back and to apologize for wasting her time with his silly and illogical reaction. But when she looked up at him, he knew instantly that she too had been struck to the core with the tale of the mysterious healer.

"This is incredible!" she whispered. "I've never read anything like this."

"Me neither," he added, thrilled to find a sympathetic response.

"It's a wonderful story! But what made you bring it here? It seems so irrelevant to security operations."

Jimmy found himself suddenly filled with extroverted energy with which he was unfamiliar. He heard himself babbling at full speed.

"Can you imagine what would happen if somebody really had

powers like that, somebody who could heal people of the mutated viruses of AIDS? There would be a colossal panic across this country, the world even. Who wouldn't want to go find him?"

She reflected on the matter. Then she looked at him with great seriousness.

"Jimmy, how 'bout if you and I go out to lunch and talk this over?"

Those were the most wonderful words he had ever heard in his entire life. He felt his heart beating in his eardrums.

"I'd love to!" he said somehow.

She looked at the gold watch on her thin, graceful wrist. "I guess it's still early for that."

"No, it isn't," he said quickly. "I haven't had breakfast."

"I haven't either. I got an early start today. So what are you doing just now?"

"Absolutely nothing."

"Are you ready to go?"

"I'm ready," he answered, unable to keep his voice from shaking.

* * *

The restaurant was almost empty at this off-hour. Though it was just across the street from the building, Jimmy had never been there because it was generally packed shoulder to shoulder with employees of the Federation and other clerical types in the area. He had seen the crowd once from the sidewalk and immediately - became claustrophobic without even entering the place.

He sat across from Michelle in a booth, still in shock from this turn of events. Not in his wildest dreams had he imagined this scene ever taking place. He hadn't shared a meal with another human being in years. And suddenly out of the blue, there he was—with the one woman who had looked upon him with kindness and care.

She sipped on a straw dipped in her soda. He downed a cup of coffee that he no longer needed, though he hadn't slept in nearly twenty-four hours. His nervousness kept growing in intensity as they dealt with the simple but intimate activities of ordering food and preparing to eat face to face. She recognized his state but did him the favor of not seeming to notice it. This kind of a meeting was a regular habit for her. She held them several times a week with colleagues and visitors. But she realized that this night owl was a creature of a different sort. She watched patiently as he knocked over a cup of water and grabbed napkins to clean up the mess, his ears scarlet red.

"I think I'd like to look into this story, Jimmy," Michelle said quietly as she spread a napkin on her lap.

"What do you mean?"

"It's my job to look into such things."

"But don't you need special authority to go to that expense?"

"Maybe you don't know that I've recently been promoted. I'm a senior investigator and I decide what I need to do with my travel account according to my best judgment. That's why they pay me so well."

She wished she hadn't said that, realizing that she was in the presence of someone who made far less than she did, probably barely surviving from check to check.

"What if it's a dead end?" he asked, worried that his bringing this to her attention would cause trouble for her.

"Well, that's a chance I'll have to take."

"How would you go about dealing with this?"

"It's pretty straightforward, Jimmy," she said as a waitress placed their sandwiches in front of them. "I'll fly out to Enid on our chartered jet, locate this man and try to talk to him."

"I don't know if you can do that," he blurted out nervously.

"I can talk to anyone I want! That's why they hired me."

"But this involves other things."

"Like what?"

"I don't know . . . mystical, occult stuff . . . he could be dangerous."

"According to the stories that you showed me, he seems to be the opposite of a dangerous man."

"Except that he obviously has enemies."

"Well, that's part of the story too. It's almost as interesting as his mysterious powers. Why would officials disguise themselves and do this to him? Why is he a threat?"

"Maybe it's just a small town thing. Everybody knows -

everybody. Somebody's cousin wanted him hurt . . . "

"Could be."

They ate in silence. He did his best not to spill his food on himself in front of this beautiful woman.

"What's the worst thing that could happen?" she said as she swallowed a bite of sandwich. "I go there, nobody wants to talk to me, or it's a one dimensional story, and I get on the plane and come home. Right?"

"Doesn't Mr. Bracken have anything to do with your activities?"

"He does, but he doesn't scare me like he does you."

He looked at her sheepishly and she smiled with a certain pleasure at displaying the strength of her character and the freedom she had from the grip of men like Bracken.

"I couldn't live with myself if there was any danger involved, and if you got . . . hurt."

"Why would I get hurt? Nobody's going to hurt me. Besides, you know that I can communicate with the agencies that will bring me backup. I'm also a black belt in the martial arts. Did you know that?"

Jimmy shook his head in amazement.

"That's one reason I got the job. I can take care of myself."

"But I feel so responsible."

"I'll tell you what." She put down her sandwich and looked at him straight in the eyes. "How about if I stay in touch with you through your e-mail while I'm in the field and keep you informed of my activities. Will that keep your fears at bay?"

"You would do that?" he asked, overwhelmed with her consideration of his feelings.

"Sure, Jimmy, that's the least I can do for bringing this story to my attention. Who knows, this could be a big break for me. You know what happens to those investigators who uncover really significant events."

"No, what?"

"We get a major bonus and an opportunity for a next level position. That's when the fun really begins. I'd be making the big decisions. I'd get to fly to Europe once a week and talk to colleagues over there. That'd be nice, wouldn't it?"

"I suppose," he said unenthusiastically. He was not a ladder climber by any means, and he recognized that he couldn't hope to have her around very long. She was definitely a rising star and would no doubt marry some hot-shot top management character with a shiny suit and a huge bank account. Jimmy consoled himself with the fact that she was here with him alone. That was enough for now.

"You can help me with this investigation, you know. I think you've got a good feel for potentially destabilizing events," she said sweetly.

The compliment brought new life into his limbs. He felt a smile brightening his features.

"Most people would have overlooked this, but you caught it. I've been to many seminars concerning the Federation's views on the dangers of religion, and the most volatile situations arise around individuals with Messiah-like ideals. They usually drag a lot of people down with them and stir up deadly social disturbance."

"People like this man?"

"Exactly. Somebody with charisma, eloquence, an ax to grind, or even unusual powers. Just one of that kind can throw a whole society into upheaval. And you know that's the number one concern of the Federation—keeping such things from happening so that the whole world doesn't go down in flames."

"Do you think a little story like this from the Southwestern desert can have an impact on another continent?"

"Why certainly. That's the wonder and horror of our times. Everything is connected and influences everything else. All it takes is one spark and pow! One lunatic can cause worldwide devastation. There are maniacs by the thousands out there waiting for any excuse to bomb something. We've been on the brink for so long now that a light breeze could send us tumbling over the edge."

"You're too pretty to be in the middle of all these terrible things."

Jimmy couldn't help himself. It just came out and there was nothing he could do about it. She did her best not to take it as an insult and accepted it as an awkward compliment from an awkward young man.

"I was made for this, Jimmy. I've got adventure in my blood. I'm as curious as a cat. My daddy taught me to be street wise and fancy free."

Jimmy studied her with unbridled admiration. What a stunning human being she was: strong, bright, beautiful, and most of all, kindhearted. For the lonely young man who lived in a basement with blinking computer screens as friends, this woman represented an oasis in a desert of contempt.

CHAPTER 14

Lynn sat in the public laundromat reading a newspaper while waiting for a bundle of clothing to dry. Dressed in jeans and a sweatshirt, she fit right in with the crowd of small-town folks and drifters who were passing through this land of dust and wheat fields. She felt like one of them now, on the road with the prophet and her husband, not knowing where they were headed or even why she had agreed to uproot their lives and take off in the middle of the night.

The terrible incident that had thrown them out of their former lives still felt as though it had happened moments ago, although two days had gone by.

She found it difficult to concentrate. She would lose track of what she was reading every few lines of newsprint and find herself caught in the trauma of that awful night when four men broke into her home and attacked Adam Hawthorn.

She had been awakened by the sound of breaking glass and sensed immediately that intruders were in the house. Jeremy slept soundly next to her and had not budged. She shook him violently, swept up in a whirlwind of sudden terror.

It took a moment for Jeremy to come to his senses, and by that time the men had already discovered the person they were after. He had been sleeping on the couch in the living room and was sitting up waiting for them before they even entered the house.

Lynn insisted that Jeremy get his father's old pistol that had been laying for years in the back of a drawer, loaded but untouched. The thought was despicable to the young minister but he trusted his wife's common sense and acquiesced to her insistence. He wanted her to remain in the bedroom while he went downstairs. By this time the thud of blows could already be heard. They both realized what was going on. There was no way he could keep her from coming with him. She grabbed a baseball bat that they kept behind the bedroom door along with a flashlight and raced down to the living room.

Sitting in the laundromat staring at the rhythmic pattern of the drying clothes, she remembered vividly that by the time they reached the living room, she was no longer scared but full of anger. She had always had a temper that she tried hard to control, but this was more than anger—it was rage, raw and out of control. How dare these men attack her saintly friend! She guessed already that they were hired hands, paid for by the likes of Reverend Morgan. She aimed the flashlight on the scene.

She knew now that she would never be able to rid herself of the image. It was scorched in her mind forever.

Adam was standing, surrounded by four brutes, receiving their blows to his head, back and stomach without any response. His only effort seemed to be to remain on his feet out of sheer dignity. Her flashlight illuminated the horrible sight just as one of the assailants raised a tire iron, intending to bury it in the prophet's skull. If she had held the gun, she would have fired it.

Jeremy had not shot a pistol in years, but his aim was sure. He hit the man near his neck. Lynn remembered her feelings at that moment—she would have aimed for the head. The man fell back with a loud yell and the other three looked up in fear. They ran like rats for the open window. They hadn't planned on coming across a clergyman with a weapon. But their cowardly work was done. Adam was covered in blood.

Lynn and Jeremy hurried to him. Jeremy wanted to pursue the men and shoot them as they ran across his yard, but Adam grabbed his arm and looked at him through the blood dripping down his face and running down the side of his eyebrows. He nodded negatively, making a stunning impression on them with his utter calm and acceptance of this vicious attack on his person. Jeremy turned his anger upon the man laying on the floor. Again Adam held him back.

Tears welled up in Lynn's eyes as she sat in the laundromat. She hid her face behind the newspaper so that the others around her wouldn't see her emotions. It came back to her in slow motion as she watched the prophet kneel beside his enemy and gently, lovingly almost, place his hand on the bullet hole in his flesh. The man was bleeding profusely. The bullet had pierced through his body and nicked an artery. Blood gushed like a fountain onto the carpet. He moaned like a helpless child.

Within moments of Adam's palm coming over the wound, the blood stopped flowing. Lynn and Jeremy watched in wonder as the man quieted down and his body stopped shaking. Soon there was no more pain. He looked at Adam through his ski mask and began to weep. Lynn had never seen such wrenching crying before. The tears gushed out of his eyes just as the blood had from the wound moments ago. It was as though his very soul was wracked with the consciousness of his evil deed. He raised his hand and touched Adam's bloody cheek.

Tears slid down Lynn's cheeks as she remembered the words he spoke with pure sincerity: "I'm so sorry . . . I'm so sorry." Adam had done more than heal his wound. He had given the man a taste of unconditional love and it worked its miracle on his soul. He seemed transformed in that moment. He pulled off his mask still weeping uncontrollably. They helped him sit up. It was then that she heard his confession and the terrible revelation that confirmed her intuition. Sure enough, he had been ordered to commit this malefic crime by the sheriff and therefore by the church leaders of the community.

She tried to read the paper for distraction. The idea that powerful religious leaders like Morgan had the capacity for such evil was unbearable to her. She didn't want to think about it because it completely destroyed the integrity of the institution for which she and her husband had offered their lives. For most of her existence, she had felt that the church was the last place in society where one could find authentic humanity rather than greed and deceit. She knew, of course, of all the deviant behaviors that were part of the history of religion, but in this age there was no other institution that stood for good and that alone.

She was prepared to live in poverty. She was willing to raise a family and care for her husband under conditions that were below her gifts. Ironically, she had now committed herself to even greater destitution and uncertainty in choosing to leave with their friend and spiritual teacher. She was still in shock over the impulsive decision to drop everything and join him on his unknown destiny. But she was certain of one thing: Adam Hawthorn was an incarnation of that unconditional goodness that rains down on all alike from the heart of the universe.

She had no idea if he was on a mission or had a plan to help a desperate world. She wanted to be part of it because she could trust his complete integrity, and even more, his extraordinary awareness of the spiritual world.

The powerful moment returned to her, as vibrant and alive as it was forty-eight hours ago. She and Jeremy had made the decision simultaneously. What else could two people committed to the Good do when Goodness itself was standing before them? All the religious, mystical and esoteric books they had read could not match the presence of the man who was now their guide. His simple serenity and uncompromising authenticity was the very summit of what they sought through their long, arduous years in search of meaning and truth.

Mixed with her fear and uncertainty was also an exhilarating feeling of utter freedom and liberation born from the all-or-nothing commitment she had just made to the principles which were most important to her. She knew that she would have the inner strength to endure everything for the sake of serving and receiving from the depths of Being evidently present in the man they called Adam.

The cycle ended and she retrieved the clothing. A sweet joy dawned within her as she folded the clothes of her beloved husband and of the man she admired with all her soul. The humble work of folding his socks thrilled her with a sense of participating in something so much greater than she was. Certainly, he was a man of flesh and blood like others, but there was clearly a quality within him that opened onto another dimension in a way more tangible than in any other human being she had come across. She recognized that he had chosen to die as an ordinary individual and give himself to a holy cause.

She realized that she now had to live only on her intuition and float in the winds like a glider, dependent on currents far beyond her own capacities. She smiled to herself as she finished folding the clothes and placed them in the basket, realizing that she had prepared for these circumstances her entire life. She had sharpened her skills of listening to her heart which knew things that the mind did not. That special kind of knowledge had been hers since childhood.

Born into a military family, she grew up under a reign of terror that crushed the sweet innocence of childhood and matured her far beyond her years. Her father was a drunkard who savagely abused his power over his family. Her only comfort throughout her early years was to escape into a little oasis of nature where she could find some moments of peace. The relentless suffering taught her to rely on her instincts long before her peers had awakened from the fantasies of a child's world.

In her moments of aloneness and quiet, she had learned to pray, though she knew not to whom she was praying. The anguish of fear and despair had ripped open her heart and revealed a world that only those who suffer deep pain are privileged to encounter—a transcendent emotional sensitivity for other beings. She consciously chose to live in that atmosphere rather than become hardened and embittered by the darkness into which she was born.

Out of this empathy for others had also arisen a strong psychic awareness. Perhaps it had come out of a survival instinct intensified by the daily dangers of her father's violent instability. At a glance she could tell whether the beast within him was about to arise and assault them with his belt for no particular reason, except perhaps to release the poisons that made his soul toxic.

It had taken her years to overcome the terrible results of her father's abuse, years of seeking a wholeness that would heal those awful wounds to her essence. She knew that it would take something spiritual to permanently free her from the effects of those psychological bruises, but she had yet to find that balm in her experience of religion.

She stepped outside with her basket of laundry. A hot, bright Southwestern sun instantly warmed her from head to foot and invaded her like oil penetrating paper. It was the physical equivalent of that spiritual healing that would take away the shadows of her past. She knew already that being in the presence of the prophet would bring her that kind of regeneration. The uncertainties of their future and financial condition paled before the potential of such profound rebirth.

She drove along the dusty road leading to the motel where they were staying. It was a decrepit, rundown building constructed at the turn of the century. Leaning against its side was a desolate greasy-spoon restaurant ironically named the Oasis Cafe. Through the window, she saw Adam and Jeremy sitting at a booth and waved at them as she went into the motel with her basket. She felt butterflies in her stomach looking at the silhouette of the man sitting as straight as a Buddha statue and radiating a palpable peacefulness that affected—even unconsciously—everything around him. She couldn't wait to join her husband and share the privilege of conversation with this extraordinary individual.

Jeremy sipped his coffee, deep in thought. Lines of worry and fatigue already aged his face. Adam's clear, glimmering eyes turned upon him and he smiled gently. The bruises and cuts on his face had healed and left only a slight trace of the brutality inflicted on him the other night.

"Why worry, Jeremy? It's a beautiful day."

Jeremy came out of his thoughts with a jolt.

"Huh? Beautiful day?"

He glanced out the window. "Yes, it's beautiful. Doesn't solve our problems, though."

"What problems would those be?"

"You're kidding!" Jeremy stumbled over his words, feeling irritation rising within, but quickly evaporating in the presence of the man's great serenity. "Well, for one, we've got enough money on us to keep a roof over our heads for about a week. And then what?"

"Are you having second thoughts about leaving Enid?"

"No, not at all," Jeremy insisted, trying to convince himself. "We couldn't stay there. Besides, we want to be with you."

"Why?"

"Why? Well, I'm not sure why, to tell you the truth. I don't even know what your plans are. It just seemed like the right thing to do at the time."

Adam looked out the window at the wheat fields across the road. They undulated in the wind like ocean waves as far as the eye could see.

"Jeremy, you have to come to grips with the fact that if you are going to join me, it must be a definitive, irrevocable decision."

"I know that."

"No, you don't. You have no idea what you are involved with, and that's how it has to be. But if you make a choice to be part of it, you cannot look back."

Jeremy felt humiliated by the mirror the prophet was putting up before him. He sensed that this would be the first of many times when such revelation of himself would come about in this man's presence.

"I am committed to doing what is right. If that means following you to the ends of the earth at all cost, then that's what I will do."

"It will mean overcoming your pride, Jeremy."

"Gee, I thought I was doing pretty good at that so far."

"You haven't even started, my friend."

The observation stung him like a whip across his back. He reacted with anger, but held it in check. Adam's intense eyes fell on him like laser beams, pulverizing the facade he held before him to hide his real feelings.

"Jeremy, you became a disciple and the mark of a disciple is to be like his master. You know the words that master has spoken. He has revealed to us long ago that our false sense of self-importance is our great enemy. Morgan and the others are mere pawns in a play. The real enemy is within."

"This is true," Jeremy admitted, remembering that he had heard that idea echoed in every mystical treatise he had ever picked up.

"It's a hard road, least of all because of financial uncertainty. If we have to bag groceries from town to town to make our pennies, that's what we will do."

"Bag groceries?" Jeremy said in horror.

"Whatever it takes."

"I've got a master's degree!" he cried out in outrage. Remorse immediately overwhelmed him as Adam studied him with the unblinking awareness of his own conscience.

He tried to change the subject. "So what do you propose we do at this point?"

"Have our breakfast."

"I mean where do we go from here?"

"We'll follow the signs."

"To highway 31?"

"No, the signs that are given to us."

"Oh . . ."

For the first time, Jeremy felt his confidence in the prophet's mysterious ways shaken.

"They come to us at every moment. We're just not awake enough to see them."

"You mean, there's a sign coming at us right now, here in this cafe?"

"Certainly."

Jeremy looked around somewhat sarcastically. All he could see were a few old men, a bored waitress, and flies buzzing along the window sills.

"Sometimes the signs are so obvious that we look right past them."

Jeremy looked again. This time he noticed a poster on the wall right behind the prophet. It was the picture of a hungry child along with words asking for assistance. Jeremy almost dropped his cup.

"That's right," Adam said softly. "That's what we're going to do."

"Help needy children?" Jeremy asked, still confused.

"Just be of help, period. That's what we're here for, as I'm sure you'll agree. And need is everywhere."

"But shouldn't we head for a larger city? You don't want to hang around these desolate parts of the country, do you?"

"I prefer these out of the way places, myself. They're more peaceful."

"Don't you think we should publicly denounce the hypocrites

who pass themselves off for spiritual leaders?"

"All in good time, Jeremy, all in good time. For now, we'll trust in what Providence will send our way."

"Adam, I don't want to be disrespectful, but I get the feeling that you know more than you're willing to tell me. Am I right?"

"If you were right, you'd know not to ask me the question."

"But look at the sacrifice I'm making! Don't I deserve some idea of where we're headed?"

"Sacrifice? You don't know the meaning of the word, Jeremy."

This time, the young man couldn't contain his anger despite his deep admiration for the prophet.

"Damn it! I've given everything up! What else is there?"

"You'll see," Adam said quietly.

"Tell me you're on a great mission for this wretched world. Tell me that there's something big about to happen."

The prophet looked at him sadly. "Isn't it enough to know that you're committing your life to what your heart believes in most?"

He took pity on Jeremy's confused and hesitant expression.

"Don't worry. You'll have a important role to play in your time. The world is going to need all the decent people it can get."

"How do you mean?"

"There's only so far the caretakers of this planet can degenerate before something must be done. The Tribulation is upon us. The prophecies have foretold this cataclysm for centuries."

"Is there any way we can avoid it?"

"There was hope that the momentum could be turned around. But it wasn't. People have become so completely unconscious that they have let themselves become tools to dark influences that are bent on nothing but destruction of the ordained order of the universe."

"What do you mean by people becoming unconscious?"

"The great masses of humanity are lost in distraction, most often by distractions that manipulate them. They passively fall in line with the agenda set by those in control. Their lack of attention to the real things of life has dehumanized their priorities. From birth to death, life for such people is superficial, utterly pointless, and serves the wrong masters. Human beings have been turned into both slaves and consumers of the very product that they are enslaved to create! It works out very nicely for international corporations, but not for the spiritual welfare of this planet and the life forms that inhabit it.

"People have lost all sense of their birthright—to exist as conscious members of the wondrous phenomenon of life in the cosmos."

"How did we manage to fall so low?"

"Look at the utter contempt in which spiritual reality is held in this day. We have lost sight of the most significant aspect of our being that gives meaning and purpose to existence itself. Without it, people are reduced to living according to the grotesque laws of eat or be eaten. They wallow in instant gratification for a short while and die a miserable, tragic death where everything seems to be taken away."

"Is it too late for humanity?"

"It is too late for the world, both for nature and for the so-called civilized societies that modern humans have created. But it is not too late for individuals. One at a time, each person must seek and find that part of themselves that opens onto the deeper reality. With new understanding of the purpose of life, a new way of being will be born. Then humanity will start again, in another direction. A more evolved direction."

"Is this your purpose here?" Jeremy asked timidly.

"I have something specific to accomplish, yes. It's not time yet to speak of it."

"Is it related to the coming of . . . the Tribulation?"

"Yes."

Jeremy waited to hear more. But Adam kept a cloak of secrecy over his mission.

"Can you tell me this," Jeremy asked after an awkward moment, "can the catastrophes be avoided?"

"No. Many prophets have warned humanity for centuries. From the Sibylline oracles to the Hebrew prophets, to Sun Bear of the Chippewa tribe to Nostradamus and Edgar Cayce. Not to mention the Mayans and the visionaries of all faiths. But the message did not get through. Generation after generation chose the easy way of blindly following the mass mind and its self-indulgences which have led to this inevitable conclusion."

Jeremy was at a loss for words. He realized there was no way he could get anymore information if Adam was not prepared to give it to him. Lynn entered the cafe and came to sit at her husband's side.

"You're glowing today, Lynn," Adam said sweetly.

She smiled back, unable to define the wonderful ecstasy that had taken hold of her unexpectedly.

"May you return to this state continually all the days of your life. It's not easy to sustain," Adam stated as a subtle blessing.

"I can't imagine anything changing my state today," she said breathlessly. "I feel so light and free."

Jeremy looked at her, surprised. He wished he could feel that way also, rather than dragged down by the mundane concerns of daily survival.

"Don't be fooled into believing that such a state of consciousness is dependent on external circumstances. We must learn to live in that rarefied air even during the hard times."

"Well, these are them," Jeremy said.

"No," Adam responded. "These are actually the good times. Enjoy them while you can or there'll be nothing to enjoy."

Jeremy was depressed all the more by his words. Lynn ran her fingers through the hair on the back of his head, an expression of affection that always soothed his pessimistic spirit. He smiled and relaxed.

"If we're to be traveling companions, let's at least enjoy each other's company," Lynn suggested.

"He won't tell me where we're going!" Jeremy said to Lynn in one last attempt to grasp at any information.

"I'll tell you where we're not going," Adam said in a soft but commanding voice. "We'll stay away from any kind of media, any kind of limelight, and remain as unseen and unheard as possible."

"Well, this is the place to achieve that goal," Jeremy retorted.

"Is it possible to avoid the Federation's surveillance?" Lynn asked.

"If one doesn't make any waves," Adam responded.

"We blew that one in Enid, didn't we!" Jeremy said with a chuckle.

"We must avoid publicity at all cost," Adam stated again. "That is rule number one."

Jeremy felt himself react negatively to the suggestion of rules, a knee-jerk reaction he had suffered from since childhood. But he realized that the decision to join the prophet placed them under his direction. There was no avoiding the authority that he emanated.

"You don't like the idea of rules very much, do you Jeremy?" Adam said with empathy.

Jeremy looked down, embarrassed at being seen so clearly.

"Please understand that this is not in any way a desire on my part to have power over you and your choices, simply the critical fact of our situation."

Jeremy and Lynn looked at each other. They both knew that they had just received a tiny piece of the puzzle that formed the destiny into which they had been swept up. Obviously, Adam knew more than he was willing to say.

"It would seem to me that a public forum would allow you to express your views and help people find their way in this madness."

"I'm not here to express my views."

"Isn't that a form of assisting the world?"

"It can be done without trumpeting one's opinions, otherwise one merely adds to the noise that interferes with the experience of Truth. So until that can be presented without degeneration into petty arguments over subjective perspectives, it's best to simply . . . be."

"Simply be?" Jeremy asked.

"That's why Lynn is experiencing such joy just now. She is just being in the moment, without the baggage of worries and fears that you carry. It is that quality of awareness that can be useful to others. Otherwise we are as sick and miserable as they are."

Jeremy felt a certain jealousy for his wife's superior state of mind in that moment. But he repressed the childish notion and accepted with humility that he had much to learn, not only from the prophet, but from everyone and everything.

"You've taken your first step on the path," Adam said, letting him know that he was aware of what was going on in his mind and heart.

The young man felt goose bumps throughout his body. He realized the extent of the man's unusual powers. He understood finally that he was on an incredible adventure where everything he had yearned to know and become would be made available to him.

"The first and most fundamental effort is the objective awareness of yourself," Adam said all of a sudden. The tone of his voice had changed. He had shifted gears on his friends once again. Before them, there appeared now a teacher of the highest order, offering them nuggets of wisdom that they had searched after for years. There was an infinite light in his eyes.

With those very first words of disseminating his understanding, Adam became a master-teacher to his friends, revealing yet another aspect of his mission.

"Why?" Jeremy asked, falling into the student/teacher relationship as though this had been their roles forever.

"Because nothing real can take place until we know what we're dealing with. We can't take for granted that we know how or why we function the way we do.

"So try observing yourself from a completely neutral standpoint. Don't judge what you see. Just see it. Observe your reactions, your attitudes, your moods and the many aspects of yourself that take charge from moment to moment. If you do this with sincerity and courage, not justifying every action and passing thought, a deeper dimension of yourself will begin to be nourished."

Jeremy and Lynn looked at each other, marveling at the morsels of practical spiritual information being offered to them in this dingy cafe out in the middle of nowhere.

Adam continued in a strong, determined voice that magnetized their attention.

"This simple effort begins the process of creating a space within you that is not completely hypnotized by external events. Though you still react to outer circumstances through ingrained habit, there is now this sliver of your deeper Self that is not pulled out of you. A new space of inner freedom is being created along with a new sense of what constitutes your true nature.

"Another critical aspect of this observation is the study of your negative states. You'll be amazed at how much of your time is spent under the dominance of these dark moods and thoughts.

"Nothing healthy can grow under the constant downpour of this acid rain within you. Eventually, you'll discover that you can free yourself from such unpleasant behavior and states of mind. Step one is to turn off the leaking faucet—Stop expressing negative and violent emotions!"

The couple looked at each other, feeling as though the words just spoken had cut them to the quick and revealed their secret weaknesses and personal troubles.

"This effort of not manifesting such feelings is the beginning of separating yourselves from them. You don't have to accept living in those dark states. You are not them. They are bad habits acquired over a lifetime and the result of unconscious influences. If you want healing and joy in your life, you must stop the momentum of negativity. If you want to grow, you can't feed on such rotten states of mind."

Jeremy and Lynn drank in his words with their coffee and orange juice. They realized that he was preparing them, molding them for their tasks in the future.

"One of the other important things to notice about negative states is how much energy they drain out of you. If you're aware of yourself before and after a moment of rage, you'll see very clearly how much energy has been lost in that brief moment. We only have so much of that precious life force available to us each day, and we can use it to be healed and renewed—which then makes us useful to the purposes of creation—or we can squander it thoughtlessly.

"This is the beginning of clearing the path for new states and qualities of consciousness, where the spirit is regenerated and strengthened with the nourishment of another way of being in the world.

"So notice your thoughts before they plant themselves in your feelings and eventually manifest in your actions. Stop being asleep at the switch! Or you may end up becoming the unwitting tool of forces that are not interested in your welfare. They can only reach you through your mind and your imagination. They will take control of you if you're not paying attention."

Lynn's face turned pale. She had a strange intuition that Adam was warning them of the onrush of dramatic events from which they could only protect themselves through such inner discipline.

"After self-observation and separation from negative states

comes the next all-important practice: becoming present to the moment. Experience the moment as it is, for what it is. Becoming present grounds you in reality here and now and takes you out of the tempests of imagination and inner talking that fill the mind with so much noise. Become present not only to your surroundings, but to your body. Relax the tensions that you haven't even noticed before: in the shoulders, in the jaws, in the stomach. Begin to experience the revitalizing peace of being alive in this moment."

He paused, letting the insights sink in.

"Are you familiar with meditation?" he asked softly.

They both nodded, having experimented with a variety of teachings.

"Then you know how helpful it is to regulate your breathing in order to center yourself. Just breathing in and out slowly to ease the inner tensions is a powerful tool for nourishing your spirit in the moment. Learn to sit quietly for awhile. This is no luxury or idle behavior. Most people are so wracked with stress and worry that they can't even get back in touch with themselves until they've managed to release themselves from the grip of their anxieties.

"We rob ourselves of the very joy of living when we let ourselves fall into endless worry and nervous tension. Take time to let go of all that."

He paused again. They sat in silence, experiencing the sweet simplicity of this moment of their lives, free from the shadows of the past and the dangers of the future.

Adam took a sip of water and continued in the same steady rhythm that carried his words deep into their minds and hearts.

"This daily effort will teach you to stop, or at least to step back from, the constant flow of thoughts that create reality for you. This means that most of your worrying and anxious considerations fall by the wayside and you're able to rise above the clouds of your immediate concerns to the larger picture of your existence as a whole.

"Sometimes, however, the flood of thoughts refuses to slow, no matter what you do. Nerves are so frayed that you can't achieve the simple peace of looking out the window and enjoying the view without anything coming to mind. That's when you might employ the stop exercise. In the midst of a thought or daydream, tell yourself to stop and abruptly cut short what is going on in your mind. Then relax your body and look around you, just seeing what is there."

Jeremy broke into the flow of his teacher's gift of wisdom.

"So the daily practice for the inner nourishment of the spirit includes objective observation of our selves, separation from negative states, quieting the mind, and becoming present to the moment? Is that correct?"

Adam nodded with a compassionate smile. His friend was assuming that such a task was a straightforward, simple matter. The day would come when the pain and wonder released from these efforts would utterly transform him.

"You'll notice how these practices begin to take you out of your usual nervous tension. They'll keep you from mindlessly responding to everything around you by turning a portion of your attention inward, and by expanding your perspective in the moment so that you begin to be more than just your self-centered, habitual mass of reactions.

"If you apply these techniques regularly—and that's the key, consistency—you'll soon find yourself living more frequently in that space of centeredness, of liberation from being victims of your automatic reactions.

"Then you'll find that you become capable of a serenity, of an acceptance of what is, and of a surrender of selfishness that empowers you to help others as well as yourself. That's when you begin to tap into the power within where true nourishment—the daily bread that seekers of spiritual awakening long for—becomes available."

"What is this daily bread?" Lynn asked, realizing she had never really understood this metaphor that she had lived with her entire life.

"It's the spiritual empowerment that enables us to accept life as it comes, even with all its tragedies, and gives us the capacity to act for the higher good in any given situation. An old tradition calls it the indwelling of the uncreated. This inner power is also a link with spiritual reality which creates a free human being who is no longer entangled in his or her selfishness and constant stream of fears and desires. Such a person can journey through life with wisdom and compassion. Such a person can, and in this age of transition must, participate in the renewal of the world . . . someday."

Jeremy and Lynn both understood that he was hinting at something as yet unimaginable. They were both stunned by the revelation of his potent insights and by the realization that they were being made ready for a mighty work.

Jeremy had to look away from his friend and teacher to hide the tears in his eyes as he experienced a profound gratitude for having been given this strange privilege. He looked over toward the counter. A large television screen was flashing a local news bulletin with the Federation's familiar symbol for getting attention from its passive viewers—a blinking multicolored light in the midst of a three-dimensional computerized effect which gathered to itself the programmed minds of the populace.

As his eyes stopped upon the screen, he remembered Adam's words about a sign in every moment. A commentator came on the screen, well known in the Southwest, reading his story from a news bulletin handed to him in the studio. The sound was too low for Jeremy to hear, but he instinctively tuned his ear to the broadcast. Suddenly, his jaw dropped and he heard a sound of shocked surprise come out of his mouth. Adam and Lynn turned toward what he was looking at.

On the TV screen, behind the commentator, was a black and white photograph of Adam taken five years ago at the seminary.

"What is that?" Jeremy cried out. He nearly pushed Lynn out of the booth and hurried over to the screen so that he could hear what was being said.

The waitress was already turning it up by the time he got to the counter. Everyone paid attention when these news flashes came on. The anchorman spoke in the neutral tone that was a mark of his profession.

"The minister, considered a heretic by the Ministerial - Association of the Greater Southwest, abruptly left town after being released from prison. His former colleagues had this to say about the matter."

Video footage of Reverend Morgan appeared full screen.

Jeremy's hands went to his head in anger and horror.

"He was always a strange one. I had my eye on him years ago when he was in seminary and I knew that he would eventually be trouble. He's now on the loose, and I just want everyone to know that we at the Ministerial Association no longer support his ministry and are revoking his credentials. I consider him a dangerous man who should be avoided at all cost."

"You bastard!" Jeremy yelled, singed to the core of his being. The folks at the counter turned to him, stunned by his outburst. The commentator came back on the air.

"If you see this man—who goes by the name of Adam Hawthorn—you are asked to contact your local police department. Though no warrants for his arrest have been issued, authorities do want to question him regarding a shooting that occurred two nights ago, and the Ministerial Association wishes to formally revoke his license in a public hearing. The number on this screen is open twenty four hours."

Jeremy returned to the booth watched by everyone in the cafe. Someone recognized Adam's distinctive features.

"Hey, that's him, ain't it? That's the guy wanted on the TV!"

"It sure looks like him!" the waitress said as she scribbled down the phone number.

"Call somebody, Louise!"

Jeremy stood by the booth, trembling with outrage. He couldn't believe what he had just seen.

"We've got to get out of here!" Lynn whispered.

"Everything's all right. Don't worry," Adam responded. "It's not such a big surprise."

"How can you say that! These people are after you and you haven't done anything!"

"Are you that naive, Jeremy? Men like Morgan understand power only in terms of domination. They need to have control, and people whom they cannot get under their control they must crush. It's an old, old tale that apparently won't go away."

Lynn turned away from the people at the counter who were staring at them wide-eyed, and covered her mouth as she whispered.

"The waitress is calling right now! We need to go."

"That's fine," Adam said, sending his peacefulness into his friends to ease their fear. "Let's pay the bill and calmly walk to the car. We'll get our things and be on our way."

They stood up. Jeremy went through his wallet looking for some money. A big man at the counter, younger than the others, rose from his seat.

"Hey you! You better stay right there till the cops show up!"

Lynn headed toward the door, car keys in hand. Adam paid no attention to the gruff man who stepped forward to block his way.

"I think you better wait, mister! The sheriff wants to talk to you."

"We've already spoken, friend. There's nothing more to be said. There's no warrant served. I'm not under any legal obligation. Thank you for your concern."

The man came closer. Jeremy stepped between Adam and the big farmer.

"This is none of your business! Back off!" Jeremy grumbled angrily.

"Who do you think you're talking to? You tryin' to scare me, city boy?"

"Come along, Jeremy. It's time for us to go. No need for trouble," Adam whispered to his friend.

"Yeah, there is. You ain't leavin'!" the man shouted.

"Oh yes he is!" Jeremy said, ready to fight. His hands formed fists by his side.

"You don't really think you can take me, do you, buddy?" the man said with a grin that revealed his rotting teeth and lust for violence. "I can eat your kind for lunch."

Jeremy was losing control. All the rage of the last few weeks—the death of Dr. Hogrogian, the assault on Adam, and now the horrible injustice of being turned into fugitives—all came to a boiling point. He hadn't swung his fists since his high school days, but he felt the irresistible momentum shoot through his veins like a forest fire.

Then he felt Adam's touch on his shoulder. His adrenaline rush instantly vanished and his hands relaxed. He felt ashamed of his bestial reaction.

"We're leaving now," Adam said in a voice that would not accept any resistance. He gently moved Jeremy away from the man.

Now Adam stood face to face with the large brute.

"Why must you keep seeking violence all your life, Johnny?"

The man's features nearly exploded in shock.

"Why don't you stop this cycle of destruction that your father started so long ago? Find some peace for yourself and for those around you."

The man's lips trembled uncontrollably, as though he were faced with the ghosts of his past and the picture of the wretched life he had lived because of them.

"It's never too late to start over. Be at peace."

"How do you know my name?" he managed to mutter as his knees weakened and he was overcome with sorrow.

Adam placed his palm over the man's heart.

"Be at peace, Johnny. Be a good man."

He fell backwards, crashing down onto a table, then to the floor. He lay there, weeping like an infant. The people at the counter jumped up, terrified.

"He'll be all right," Adam said. "He'll be all right. Except that he's got a serious heart condition. Tell him to have it checked when he's able to."

With that, he turned and walked out of the cafe.

CHAPTER 15

The small jet landed at the Enid airport. Michelle Blair hurried out of the plane. A Federation car awaited her and she was soon on the road. She turned on a sophisticated computer inlaid in the dashboard and picked up a microphone.

"This is Michelle Blair. Security number 4432 dash one. Come in."

A voice crackled from a speaker imbedded in the computer.

"This is Jimmy Maloney, receiving you loud and clear."

"Jimmy, what are you doing on the job at this hour?"

"I'm on double shift. I want to keep track of how things are going for you."

"I just got here! It's really hot, that's all I can say for now."

"Have you seen the local news reports?" Jimmy's voice continued, sounding as though he were speaking in a tin can.

"Nothing came across the plane's computer."

"I picked up a local bulletin just about an hour ago. I'm sending you the information right now."

The mini computer screen blinked and the transcript of the television broadcast appeared in compact paragraphs.

"Good job, Jimmy. Give me a chance to listen to it."

"You go right ahead. I'll be right here."

She pushed the audio button and a nearly human computer voice read the material to her as she sped along the desolate roads of the Southwest.

When the voice finished, she pressed the return button that

brought the Federation acronym and symbol—an eagle with its claws buried in the blue planet—back onto the screen.

"That's really interesting, Jimmy. Our man's wanted but not wanted. I never heard of that one before."

"I've picked up another message on the local police line. I thought you might be interested in this as well."

"Wow, you can get into everything, can't you?"

"That's my job."

Another message appeared on the screen. She pressed the audio button again.

A deep voice, damaged by multiple recordings and transfers, crackled over her speaker.

"This is Sheriff Bancroft calling for Reverend Morgan."

"Reverend Morgan here."

"Reverend, we've got a report of a strange incident ten miles east of Ponca City. Thought you might want to hear about it."

"Go ahead, please."

"A waitress at the Oasis Cafe called in and said the man we're looking for was sitting right there in front of her."

"We got him!"

"Well, he left before the deputies showed up. But he did something to one of the people in the diner."

"What do you mean, he did something?"

"It's hard to explain. A man by the name of John Lang . . . he touched him and people at the cafe say that when he got up off the floor, he was nothing like the man they'd known all their lives. He changed instantly from a tough character with multiple arrests to some kinda quiet, introspective, docile guy that scared the hell outta them. He's remained in that state ever since."

"Well, I'll be . . . I told you he was dangerous, sheriff!"

"We've got the highway patrol after him. He can't be too hard to find now. Over and out."

"Thank you, sheriff."

Michelle turned off the audio button.

"Unbelievable," she murmured.

"What did you say?" Jimmy's voice came through the electronic equipment on a wave of static.

"I said it's unbelievable. Something about this story really bothers me."

"Gives me the creeps. Like he's some kind of magician or something."

"I can't tell if we're going after a good guy or a bad guy."

"Remember, Miss Blair, if it upsets the locals, he's bad, regardless of any other standards. That's what the regulation book says."

"I know the book, Jimmy. Listen, I need to concentrate on where I'm headed now. We'll keep in touch."

"Be careful."

She turned off the equipment and focused her gaze on the vast emptiness in front of her. Confused emotions stirred within her. What was she getting herself into? She had a disturbing sensation that this was a case that placed her at odds with the basic principles from which she had always operated. She shook her head to free herself from the mental gremlins and turned on the radio for distraction.

Country music came on, loud and full of twang. She smiled at the culture shock. Then she tried to lose herself in the ballad which erased the discomfort in her solar plexus. It wasn't working, not because of the song's limitations. Michelle couldn't keep her inner anguish from surfacing.

A memory had been triggered by these events. It seemed like another lifetime, though it was only fifteen years ago. She was just on the threshold of adulthood, full of idealism and yearning for something she couldn't define. Her father, an important operative in the Federation's Security Division, got her in the door at the ground level of his department. She was on her first infiltration mission. These were routine undercover jobs that often led nowhere but were the mainstay of the Federation's efforts to keep ahead of all suspicious activities.

A strange character had been spotted in some small city in the hinterlands of the Midwest. He had no money or power, but he was too free with his opinions. Especially about the last war. The alliances at the Federation were still burning from the catastrophe of the Syrian conflict. More than two million dead and nothing accomplished, expect for the toppling of a dictator who was quickly succeeded by another made of the same cloth. For many around the world, this nasty skirmish was the war to end all wars. Not because an ironclad worldwide peace treaty would be signed, but because there would be too little left of the human species or of the planet for anything approaching civilization to continue.

The war was short—eight months—but included chemical warheads and savage assaults on civilians with smart bombs that weren't so smart. The only victor was disillusionment. And George Bowers was the very incarnation of that awful discontent born from witnessing too much senseless horror.

She was introduced to him at a party which agents artfully arranged as an entry point for the infiltration. Though she had done more traveling than most people her age, Michelle had never met anyone like Bowers. From the first moment she laid eyes on him, she knew there was something to be learned from this man.

"Hi, I'm Michelle Blair."

She extended her hand to the large silhouette in the shadows and found no response. As she began to feel embarrassment creep through her with her hand extended into space for no apparent purpose, she sensed someone studying her intently.

"George Bowers."

A hand came through the shadows and grasped hers with unusual strength.

"Have a seat."

Michelle sat in a large cushioned chair next to the throne-like seat that George occupied. They sat in silence for a moment, which created a restless awkwardness in the young woman.

"What are you filling your mind with these days?"

"Sorry?" Michelle asked, thinking she must have misunderstood.

The question was not in keeping with the loud rock beat and the flowing alcohol. All around them people were socializing, eagerly seeking to land a willing sex partner before the evening was over.

"What are you reading these days?"

"Carlos Castanedas," Michelle answered without hesitation. For the past six months, thanks to this forgotten and dismissed writer of the last century, she had been living through her imagination in the Mexican desert, following Don Juan, spiritual "warrior" and teacher extraordinaire, through his peyote lessons and amazing insights.

"What are they looking for?"

Michelle turned to her questioner, wanting to see the features of one who could get so directly to the point of everything the young woman cared about. A rim of bluish moonlight outlined George Bowers' massive head. Though the rest of his body vanished into the darkness of the room, Michelle could tell that he was a bear-like man, prematurely aged, who radiated an unusual magnetism. Even in silhouette, a perceptive observer could tell that this man was not a part of his surroundings. He had a sullen and distant quality in his bearing and seemed to exist separately from others, as though he were an outside observer objectively viewing the life of humanity.

"Truth."

The words came out in a whisper. Michelle hoped no one had heard them, including George.

"Why?"

The question was harsh, merciless, admitting of no platitudes.

"Because life is unlivable without it."

The man in the shadows took a drink from his brandy glass. Michelle awaited a response, but none came. Yet in George's very silence, she sensed a reaction that affirmed her answer in emotions too deep for words.

A fog of unspeakable sadness enveloped the two of them.

Michelle turned her attention to the young men and women dancing and flirting a few feet away. Someone past her a joint. Michelle hesitated. She had smoked marijuana in college and found liberation in its release from the inhibitions of her military-style upbringing, but it had only taught her to act silly without remorse. In the heavy atmosphere that emanated from George Bowers, creating an oasis of serenity in the midst of the foolishness of the party, it seemed inappropriate to lose control.

She turned to Bowers. A massive hand was protruding from the shadows waiting to receive the hand-rolled cigarette. Michelle had the instant impression that this hand was reaching for relief from pain. She felt the need to follow him into whatever world he wandered through so she inhaled the acrid smoke as deeply as her lungs would take it.

"The first one's free," George said stoically as he took the cigarette.

"What do you mean?"

"You gotta pay the piper once you start dancin' to his music."

Bowers leaned forward as he inhaled. For the first time, Michelle caught sight of his features. The heavy, jovial face was lined with a ragged beard. Several small scars on the stubby nose betrayed a violent past. The head was balding, and the eyes were small but beaming with intensity.

"The truth will set you free. This won't," George stated as he sat back in his chair. Somehow Michelle knew that he was already taking her under his wing and hoping to protect her from the mistakes that had damaged his life.

Before long, Michelle's head was spinning. The raucous beat of the music, the thick smoke, and the flashing lights all conspired to draw her into a bizarre, noisy dreamlike state. The drums pounded in her bloodstream side by side with her heartbeat; the dark colors and wild laughter disoriented her; and in the midst of it all, those fiery eyes set in a face impassive as granite watched the scene, watched her.

Michelle tried to engage Bowers in conversation, but the drug had disconnected her control over her mouth. It sounded to her as though her words came out in slow motion.

"You were in the Middle-East conflict?"

Bowers inhaled another drag of the marijuana cigarette. He seemed entirely unaffected by it.

"Got there the day before the Syrian offensive."

"You're kidding," Michelle responded with a silly grin.

Bowers looked at her intensely. Michelle felt as though a stake were being driven into her heart, and a wave of remorse came over her. She regretted having smoked.

"I went from computer programming to picking up body parts in the desert."

Michelle stared at him wide-eyed. His grim, shadowed features looked like the very face of tortured humanity. She knew that this man had seen more of life's horrors than she ever would. And that very fact caused Michelle to feel drawn to him in hopes of learning from his experiences. Her purpose there as a Federation agent was nearly forgotten.

"I was a medic . . . I had crispy critter duty."

"What's that?" asked Michelle, not certain she wanted to know.

"After a skirmish, we'd go out with these big green trashbags and pick up all the pieces of torn flesh so when the platoon went through, it wouldn't drive the grunts insane."

Michelle was thunderstruck. With the noise of the party all around her and the disconnected feeling instilled by the herb, the impact of this horrific revelation tore through her soul. The laughter from the drunken crowd resonated like the mockery of Lucifer surveying the results of his influence on humanity.

Bowers watched the young woman's face turn pale. For the first time, a snicker broke his poker-face mask. He was getting some perverse pleasure from jolting his young admirer out of her comfortable, squeaky-clean existence.

"I had to choose who got morphine and who didn't. Those who couldn't be saved, I'd shoot 'em up with an overdose. And then I'd shoot myself up right there in the middle of the battlefield, in the blood-soaked sand with shrapnel flying all around."

Michelle had never been so close to the ugly side of reality. She was both fascinated and repulsed.

"You had to decide who was going to live and die?"

"Yeah . . . the ones who died were the lucky ones."

Bowers' eyes dimmed as the faces of friends killed in combat came back to him. A black cloud seemed to envelop him as he struggled to repress unspeakable agony.

"The good ones didn't make it back."

Michelle wanted to reach out to him and heal the pain, but she sensed that nothing she could do or say would ease those terrible wounds. Besides, she could see that already Bowers' iron mask was clamping shut over the momentary vulnerability. It was as though a "No Trespassing" sign was posted over his bloody inner world. Michelle realized that only a skilled surgeon of the soul could put this man back together again.

"What did you do after the war?" she asked, trying to change the subject.

"Lived in Turkey a couple years."

"Doing what?"

"Nothin' legal . . . tryin' to put things together again. Finding alternatives."

"Alternatives?"

"Yeah . . . other possibilities."

Bowers seemed to retreat into an inner world shrouded in mystery. Michelle felt she had no right to intrude. They sat in silence. The young woman had the odd feeling that somehow she was sharing in the private agony of her new acquaintance simply by partaking in his painful silence.

A drunken young man suddenly burst into their makeshift sanctuary and sat next to Michelle.

"Let's dance!" he said loudly, blasting her in the face with a strong smell of whiskey.

"No thanks," Michelle responded gently. She hated dancing, for no other reason than her body had never figured out how to tune into the rhythm of the music and gyrate in sync with it. Besides, her mind was still in the desert of the Middle-East.

"Oh, come on. Don't be a party-pooper."

He jumped up and grabbed her arm, trying to yank her out of her chair. The unexpected physical assault sent a surge of adrenaline into her bloodstream like a spark thrown into a truckload of gasoline.

"What the hell do you think you're doing?" she cried out as she shook the man off her arm. Her rage shocked the young man out of his drunken haze, replacing it with anger. For an instant, she thought a fist was going to indent the side of her face.

Michelle stood rigidly before him, her features twisted in outrage. Then a strange thing happened. In the midst of the noise and flashing lights and violent anger charging through her nervous system, Michelle was suddenly lifted out of herself and dropped into some kind of vacuum, some eye of her inner hurricane, in which she saw herself impartially, like a disinterested observer. It was a seeing from within. She saw the anger not with her eyes, but with her heart's sight. She saw the tension in her muscles, the warrior stance of her body, the aggressive reaction of the man standing before her, the dancers in the background, the mocking look from George Bowers, and above all, the utter stupidity of her sudden reaction.

"Forget it," she mumbled as she sat down. The man hurried off cursing at her.

Michelle felt as though she was a hot air balloon that had sprung a leak. The tension and emotion dissipated. Her repulsion at her overreaction was as powerful as her amazement at the neutral ground she had just discovered within herself. Or was it above herself? The sensation was more intense than the impact of the drug she had inhaled. With this sudden breakthrough into another dimension of her consciousness, she had uncovered an extraordinary treasure. Like an archeologist stumbling onto the wealth of a pharaoh's tomb, Michelle had stepped into a place of inner peace completely fortified from the events of the outside world, a place sealed even from her own follies. It was like a secret garden described by those Arabian poet-mystics, a garden filled with intoxicating fragrances.

"Got too stoned?" Bowers asked as he watched the young woman vanish into a black hole of introspection.

"I've never seen clearer . . . "

"Not a pretty sight."

"What's that?"

"Seeing yourself as you really are."

Michelle looked at him, surprised that this cynical war veteran was so perceptive.

"Quite a mess in there. A whole army of crazy people. With no general to keep control."

George Bowers stared intently at Michelle to see if his words were generating any recognition. He watched her turn red with shame and he passed her the joint to ease the pain. Michelle took it and inhaled gratefully, hoping to bury the stinging insight that had so disrupted her comfort. She smiled to herself as she realized that Bowers was still the medic in the desert, out to heal the agony of his comrades. But this time he was dealing with psychological wounds.

He seemed to read her thoughts.

"This kind of pain doesn't go away like it does for a battle wound. The body eventually heals itself or adapts. The kind of wound you got doesn't go away till you transmutate."

Michelle laughed, partly to hide her unease with this man who seemed to see her through and through.

"Till I transmutate?"

Bowers leaned toward her. His demeanor abruptly changed from disinterested onlooker to intense conveyor of knowledge.

"You heard about the Alchemists of the Middle Ages?"

"Sure. They tried to change stone into gold."

"Well, you gotta do the same with yourself if you wanna escape the pain of bein' crazy."

Michelle looked deep into his eyes. She could barely withstand the energy pouring like waterfalls from within Bowers' soul. In that moment, Michelle knew that she was being given a secret, a cosmic secret concerning the potential of human nature. From this odd bearer of spiritual insights, Michelle was receiving the first clues concerning that goal which she dimly sensed she must journey toward.

From that first evening, Michelle began to spend more and more time with Bowers. She was, of course, paid to do so, and she dutifully filed her report to the appropriate supervisor. But, in her youthful naiveté, she was making the fatal error of confusing her mission with her humanity. There was something about him that stirred a deep yearning within her.

It certainly wasn't pleasure which she found in the man's company, for she was often humiliated by the razor-sharp insights that cut through her image of herself and revealed both the artifice and the true person whom she had lost along the way. Nor did she spend most of her evenings in George's dark, sparsely decorated apartment for the sake of friendship. Bowers was a tormented man who, despite his exposure to spiritual teaching, was not capable of genuine compassion and warmth.

The war had killed him even though he had not returned in a body bag. Like so many young men of his generation and of generations before them, George had been pulled from his middle class surroundings, his baseball team and computer games, to be hurled into a world of horror and atrocities. He had once attempted to describe a small detail of the monstrous insanity of war by telling Michelle about the day when he was on his stomach crawling under the spray of mortar. A black soldier was laying ahead of him, his insides spilling out onto the sand. As George prepared to administer a lethal dose of morphine to put him out of his misery, he heard someone come up behind him. The sight astonished him: an army clerk, briefcase in hand, was crawling over to them, waving a pen.

"I need that soldier's absentee vote!"

"You gotta be kiddin'."

"It's for the presidential elections back home."

The clerk reached the dying soldier and insisted that he cast his ballot right there in the middle of the fire fight as he held his intestines in his hand. Bowers would have struck the clerk with his rifle, but the soldier agreed to comply. In a supreme final act of contempt for a world which had destroyed his future and made him die far from home, the young black man voted for the leading neo-nazi and hate monger of the day. He expired damning the evils of life.

On his wall, Bowers had a dim photograph of his platoon buddies. Not one of them had made it home. Michelle often studied the picture because it held an eerie fascination for her. The faces of the young soldiers all had an expression of grim condemnation which the camera had captured as a legacy for the living. These were faces that had seen too much to have hope for any goodness, for any God. And their violent deaths only seemed to confirm their opinion.

Bowers had that same look. He was like a ghostly representative of all those who had gone to their death cursing the universe that had given them such purposeless and tragic lives. He was a messenger of the unjustly killed walking among the living, and though alive himself, he was more at home in the land of the departed. Yet he had to live. For a number of years after his discharge from the army, he had kept himself going with opium and other heavy drugs.

Because he existed on the fringes of society, rejecting - everything considered acceptable by that world that had massacred his friends and the children of three Arab countries, he had stumbled across the strange and mysterious writings of other outsiders. These writers also rejected all the ordinary beliefs of the dormant masses of humanity who were both the cause and the victims of wars. Yet they had not been brutalized to the point of rejecting the possibility of something higher, something better than the life which produced such senseless horror and misery.

Wandering through the Middle East and the subcultures of the West, Bowers had compiled a large collection of materials unknown to mainstream society. Like the peasant who had uncovered long lost early Christian gospels in the Libyan desert and used them to feed the fire of his oven, Bowers carried these writings with him without realizing that they were the very medicine that could heal his alienation, his agony and cynicism.

Bowers was laying on his couch looking out the window at the summer weather on this lazy Sunday afternoon. Michelle sat in an antique chair her friend had purchased at an auction. The shape of the chair kept her back erect like a Brahman's meditative posture. She had been studying the writings of Indian yogis for several months and was beginning to put some of their exercises into practice. She would sit for hours in lotus position listening to Bowers' colorful monologues. It wasn't long before she had discovered that a straight backbone and intentional slow breathing were having an effect on her state of awareness.

She was able to bring her body into a relaxed condition that made it possible for her to divide her attention between listening to Bowers and awareness of herself. This split attention meant that she could see her reactions to ideas and events without being instantly victimized by her response to the stimulus.

This in turn allowed her to remain in a state of serenity that gave her both a feeling of healing and liberation. Sometimes, it was more the quiet sitting than the avalanche of offbeat ideas which fed Michelle's hungry soul on her visits to Bowers' home.

Most important of all was the experience she was having in her hands. One day, while sitting in the chair with her palms up, resting atop each other against her stomach, she sensed an incredible wave of heat flow through them. At the same time she realized that they were both swollen, as though they were absorbing the warm energy circulating through them and, in so doing, retaining that energy in her fingers and palms.

With this sensation of warmth came an increase in the inner peace that swept through her like a gentle mountain breeze. It reminded her of a moment she had tasted on a summer vacation with her father, sitting next to a waterfall in the sanctuary of undisturbed nature. A feeling of profound peace brought in its wake an inexpressible joy—a joy as vast as the ocean, a joy illuminating the limitlessness of her soul.

"Every so often, spiritual masters appear at special times in history to shed new light on the old subject of spiritual transformation."

Bowers rubbed his eyes to push away the fatigue overtaking him. The peacefulness of the day was making him drowsy.

"Why is it that no one believes this anymore?" Michelle wondered.

"Such a one will come again in our time. No doubt about it. And he will enlighten some and cause others to hate him. As always."

Something stirred in Michelle's heart. It seemed that she knew that man, as though his presence was somehow familiar to her. The mysterious sensation ran through her like wildfire. Was this the man she had been unknowingly waiting for? Was this the teaching that would provide her with a key to a new dimension of reality?

"I've got some books on these matters," Bowers stated as he took notice of Michelle's excited state. "But I'm warning you now, if you step into this world, you won't come out the same."

"That's exactly what I'm looking for! Transformation!"

"It's no intellectual exercise. The messengers will crack your foundations and walk away when you call for help. The ideas themselves have incredible power. Terrible power."

Michelle looked at her strange friend and suddenly realized that he had stopped short of entering the realm of these messengers. Even after his experiences in the Syrian conflict, this minefield of exposure of self to Self was too intense and dangerous for him.

That's when it hit her. George had a role to play in her life and this was his purpose: to introduce her to material that he himself had left untouched. The man was a dead-end street, used up before his time. He had cursed the social norms that had spawned the horrors of the war, but had not found the ladder which would bring him out of his own pit of damnation. He rejected everything but had nothing to replace it with. He could mock the life of ordinary people, yet remained one himself, unwilling to step onto the narrow way which led to awakening to a new meaning.

George was satisfied with lounging on his couch and watching the sports channels, all the while recognizing life's absurdity. Michelle, on the other hand, was looking for an open door to find the deeper meaning of things. In that moment, looking at her odd friend laying on his couch with a big glass of brandy in his hand, she knew that she would have to journey alone on unmarked paths with no help in sight.

Then her world came crashing down upon her. A phone call in the middle of the night informed her that security agents had raided Bowers' home. The decision had been made by her superior based on her reports. The man's maverick viewpoints were considered a security risk. But Bowers was still a soldier and he resisted. It cost him his life.

Michelle insisted on seeing the body, and when she saw the bullet hole in his head, all of her youthful zest for things spiritual vanished into some black hole in her heart. From that moment on, she was a professional, highly acclaimed and on the fast track to success. She threw herself into her work and left behind the young woman who hungered for something the Federation knew nothing about.

Now, for the first time in over a decade, she was suddenly haunted by that painful past. It wasn't even the guilt of causing Bowers' death that soured her stomach and cramped her heart, but a fear, a dreadful fear that this strange man she was chasing down would reawaken that part of her she thought she had buried in Bowers' coffin.

CHAPTER 16

Andrew Bradshaw was the thirty year old son of one of the wealthiest men in the Southwest. For over two hundred years, his family had made money in cattle. Then as beef became unpopular and diseases made it dangerous, they turned to real estate and made a new fortune with hundreds of prefabricated instant communities. His relatives were also oilmen from the earliest days, and when that market dried up and the world switched to new forms of energy, they transferred their investments to genetic engineering in the field of world agriculture. Their inherited luck and savvy continued down through the generations and they became responsible for the creation of a laboratory-produced fast growing plant that could feed the millions of hungry mouths around the world.

It just happened that their lavish wealth was also a positive contribution to the human race. The Bradshaws had no interest in philanthropy or any other kind of sharing with the world. But Andrew was different. Born with that silver spoon squarely planted between his teeth, he had learned long ago the emptiness of material possessions. A feeling of utter alienation began to invade him at a young age.

Matters only got worse as Andrew grew up under the shadow of the local church and its "supervision" of his religious education. Andrew couldn't understand why his parents continued to show up every Sunday to listen to inane sermons whose utter pointlessness infuriated them to such an extent that it ruined the big family lunch which followed like an extended ritual.

"Why do you keep going?" he would ask.

"Because it's important to go to church."

"Why don't we try finding a better minister?"

"This is the best one in the city."

So Andrew had to obey the family marching orders: go to church and shut up about it. The love of God and the transformation of the human spirit had nothing to do with it. Moreover, the adolescent selfishness and mistakes that he was beginning to fall into went unchecked by any example of a better way to live. The only thing people expected out of church on Sunday morning was that the coffee be good and ready as soon as they got out of the sanctuary.

Without even noticing it, Andrew found himself slipping away from any interest in "religion" as he was experiencing it. Mediocrity, platitudes, and insipidness were all he could find in this rusted remnant of a once vital faith. At the same time, something was stirring within him, something mysterious and radically foreign to the influences that played upon the lives of teenagers. It made itself known like some long forgotten dream floating by his inner sight and vanishing almost as soon as it was detected.

Those brief moments of sudden nostalgia were enough to send waves of dissatisfaction throughout his being. He knew that behind the multitude of teenage activities, behind the fantasies of a glorious future, something fundamental was missing, something which was his key to happiness and fulfillment.

He had no way of defining what this powerful, shattering yearning was. The church had no answers for him. It didn't even know what the questions were anymore. The hunger of the soul for all that was labeled "God" was as passé as monasteries and praying on one's knees.

Though the foolishness of the world, with all its dull materialism and cheap entertainment, threatened to drown him in a sea of wastefulness, a tiny corner of his soul remained as impregnable as a medieval castle on a mountain summit.

One of the primary reasons for the strength of his inner world was the searing suffering which he lived in daily. Andrew was a victim of the violence of the crowd.

He had first seen this monster's face in first grade, at recess. A group of farm boys circled him and kicked at him, mocking him for being from a wealthy family and not one of their kind. In that instant of desperate aloneness, hopelessly overwhelmed with the mindlessness of a group formed by cruelty and ignorance, Andrew tasted the universal tragedy of prejudice and rejection. In the midst of a country school yard, he came face to face with the demons of hate and brutality, roaring through children's voices and smoldering in innocent eyes. In his pain and fear, he became a brother to the disdained of all times and places, and an outsider to the secure world of sameness and corporate identity.

Looking at those screaming, angry boys, young Andrew discovered his separate individuality like never before, and witnessed the awesome deceit of education with its effort to mold everyone into a common way of thinking. Over the years, such scenes repeated themselves all too often, and Andrew learned to see that those mocking faces were cowardly; they turned on him only when strengthened by the crowd. One on one, the attackers rarely assaulted him.

How many times had he suffered insult and even physical injury from the absurd dislike of being a Bradshaw! How much worse it was for those whose skin pigmentation was different, or whose thyroid glands made them larger than others, or whose sensitive souls would create future artists rather than praised athletes.

Andrew soon learned that there simply was no reason behind that kind of prejudice. Only gross stupidity, below even the consciousness of beasts. Out of that abyss of blackness came all the horrors of human history.

His father insisted that he be educated among the people of their environment rather than in a private school. He wanted his son to come up the hard way and to learn what life was really like for those who did not go home to a giant mansion. He forced him to participate in all the social activities of his peers, from sports to local clubs.

His teen years were spent in a blur of twisted values, reinforced by wrestling coaches who attempted to create an emotional cripple out of him in four short years of sweat and competition. The gym room became a more powerful chamber of transformation than the sanctuary. The worship of winning and of the mighty idol known as "team spirit" completely obliterated the deeper sensitivities that had taken root in Andrew's heart.

It seemed as though high school coaches were devoted to the utter annihilation of any real feeling in the teenage boys under their control. They molded their minds with humiliation and tyranny, forcing them to become members of that male fellowship bent on power and dominance which caused and fought the wars of past and future. Innocence and emotion were crushed under the rules of brute force and hatred of the adversary. The wrestling mat became a terrible rite of passage as effective as any tribal ritual for integration into the ways of the jungle.

Andrew suffered his share of spiritual emasculation for the sake of "being part of the team." Wrestling was a sport especially prone to generate intense psychological agony. It was only him and the other guy out there in the middle of the gym as hundreds of fans screamed for blood. The cheerleaders sat in circles around the mat and got a front row seat at the humiliation of a young man doing his best not to get his neck broken. The last few moments were the worst. With every tendon stretched beyond its limit, the struggle would wind down to slow motion as it approached that instant when both shoulders touched the mat at the same time and the referee, his face inches away from the agonizing wrestlers, slapped the rubber floor with a sharp, quick, decisive sound. The crowd would jump to its feet along with the victorious wrestler while the loser laid prostrate on the mat, his disgrace complete and inescapable. There could be no more vivid failure in front of girlfriends, parents, teammates, teachers, and the entire cast of one's high school life. Only the coach's—and his father's—look of disappointment could make it worse.

How many times had he gone off into the night after a lost match, his pride shredded and hung up like a criminal in the town square for all to mock. He would fall into a bottomless pit of anger and bitterness, and there he would come face to face with the demon of self-hatred. Those were the first occasions of pouring alcohol over his open psychic wounds.

The child within was buried alive, and each coffin nail pierced his heart and spirit. The pain was so fierce that he could not see what had happened. In spite of himself, in spite of his outsider's view of the culture surrounding him, he had sold out to its values and made himself a slave to its illusions. Like so many other teenage boys, he built up his muscles and tore down his spirit. It wasn't long before a veritable coat of armor surrounded his soul, reducing him to a kind of teenage barbarian, on the same self-destructive spectrum as those predators who roamed the streets of big cities. He was doomed to travel far from his inner homeland until the spell was broken.

But it would be a long and arduous return to the self that was lost on those bloodstained mats and in those crowded school hallways where the integrity of the individual was devoured by the all-powerful spirit of the mass mind.

It was called "peer pressure" but this was surely a weak name for that vampire spirit that sucked the joy out of young lives and turned them into arrogant fools or mindless imitators of whatever models society flashed before them.

Like the wolf packs of the wilds, it was a matter of raw survival. The loner got eaten, the crippled were abandoned, and the one with the biggest teeth won all the wolverines. Andrew Bradshaw was nearly driven insane by the fact that everything and everyone conspired to sustain the power of the pack. Movies depicted what a man or a woman was supposed to be; teachers spoon-fed the culture's priorities and punished deviance; parents supported the engines that vomited out the propaganda through television, radio and the WorldNet; sports directed the flow of young souls straight into the prefabricated molds approved by society; and burgeoning sexuality provided the electricity that kept everyone moving through the assembly line.

Andrew's independent mind was not strong enough to battle the lure of mythic stories and sensual pictures which, like parasites, ate their way into his soul. By the time he graduated from high school, there was hardly anything left of him. The "team spirit" had beaten his individuality into submission, the cheerleaders had enticed him into a false idea of manhood, the coaches had reduced the spiritual side of his being to ashes, and his parents and the church had blessed the whole massacre as the proper way to grow up.

* * *

One quiet summer day, in his eighteenth year, Andrew Bradshaw found himself sitting by a small river winding its way through the quiet countryside. He escaped to this natural sanctuary at every opportunity so that he might find some peace and attempt to cure the deep melancholia that was settling into his soul. Life had gone from bad to worse for him as he approached adulthood in a culture completely disinterested in the stirrings of his soul.

The agony of this alienation was rarely alleviated. It didn't take long for a raging fire of anger to burn inside him. The fierceness of the fireball was all the greater because it was completely repressed. No one knew of his secret pain. As the years passed, it began to rise to the surface in violent outbursts which only increased his misery.

Sitting by the water, a deep peace came over him. A peace he hadn't tasted in years. The gentle, monotonous song of the flowing water spoke to him of lost innocence and forgotten dreams. A rare sense of certainty came over him. He had decided to do it.

The sharp kitchen knife sliced across his wrist. The blade reached his vein and a thin stream of blood shot up from his arm. Andrew looked at the jet pouring out of his limb as from a broken pipeline. There was no pain. There was no emotion. A strange calm overtook him as though he were viewing the scene from far away. Andrew was surprised at his objectivity and at the profound peace which was now welling up from deep within.

Still in his teens, he was ending his life and had no regrets. He would now be set free from the agony and frustrations of his youth that were haunting his young adult life as well. He lay on the river bank and stretched out his bleeding arm, letting the blood pour into the slow-moving waters. There was nothing to do now but wait. Wait for that eternal peace that would carry him away from the alienation and rejection he had known in the world of human beings.

Never had he experienced such peace, such detachment. Then, in the midst of this still vacuum within, there suddenly appeared a thought. The source of this intruder would always remain unknown to him. Was it an accidental association, was it the grace of God or the work of Providence? This thought, disturbing the great calm which anticipated oblivion, said to him: "You are needed for a mighty work."

Without hesitation, Andrew was on his feet heading for his home. Though his life meant nothing to him and his future seemed utterly hopeless and empty, he could not resist the certainty and power of the inner voice. He entered the kitchen, covering the red jetstream with his hand. He found a cloth and placed it over the wound. In an instant, it was soaked with blood. Dazed, Andrew picked up the telephone receiver and dialed the number of his only friend.

"Come over . . . something's happened."

Andrew would find out later that his friend was on the way out the door when the phone rang. A few seconds more and there would have been no one to help him. Again the question came that would gnaw at him relentlessly from then on: was it accident or fate?

His friend, Paul, entered the house and immediately had to suppress his reaction. Blood covered the kitchen walls and floor. But what shocked Paul more than the gore he had stepped into was the utter disinterest on Andrew's face.

The incident was forgotten, except for a scar that would always remind him of that moment, that strange peace, and the events that had saved his life. He now had to face the problem of what to live for. Why had he been kept alive? Was there purpose uncovered at rock bottom, at the heart of that darkness that had almost engulfed his young life?

Andrew was certain of one thing: life could never be the same. He could not come so close to death, reach out to it and accept it, and then return to sleepwalk through a dreary existence. If something had indeed lifted him out of his descent toward annihilation at the last moment, "it" must have had a purpose, a plan for the use of his life.

At first, he spent his days sitting in total silence, staring off into space. Or he would gaze at a rose in the garden for hours at a time. He found himself entering into a simple, uncluttered consciousness of the present moment. Since there was nothing to attract his mind, nothing to tempt his desires, nothing to cause him anxiety, he was free—for the first time since early childhood—free to just be. In this quiet encounter with the little things around him, without reference to himself or his ambitions, his likes or dislikes, Andrew began to uncover a new sense of reality, an undiscovered or long forgotten dimension in which wonder and connectedness with surrounding life became the true source of meaning.

Then, one day, while sitting in his chair in the garden looking at butterflies with no thought in his mind, Andrew was suddenly filled with a tidal wave of joy. The inflow of delight seemed to heal his inner wounds and melancholia all at once. He began to laugh in an uncontrollable reaction to the foreign infusion of pure happiness shining through his soul for no apparent reason. He felt himself radiating with light and warmth, in love with all that surrounded him.

When the extraordinary feeling left him, Andrew knew that everything had changed. From that moment on, he entered upon a great search, seeking to identify the source of this regenerating and transforming life, seeking to find ways of recovering this wonderful consciousness that he intuitively knew to be the greatest treasure anyone could wish for.

Andrew took on a variety of odd jobs. He had dropped out of college, driven by an unquenchable thirst for something more, eager to search the world for his undefinable Holy Grail. His father, an international entrepreneur, took him to every continent, thinking that he was creating the perfect businessman of the future. Multilingual, world traveled, aware of the flux of markets, and with a global vision—such a son was to take his place some day in the long line of money-making barons that had made the family proud and excessively rich.

But Andrew rebelled against his father like everyone else, and focused on areas that were anathema to his old man's view of life. It so happened that at the top of the list were things spiritual. Religion was something that the Bradshaws used only as a prop for respectability. Privately, they found it all utterly absurd.

Still unmarried, Andrew had become an embarrassment, and all sorts of rumors circulated among his wealthy peers. It was known that he experimented with the subculture of the supernatural, only to tire of that and come back home to his books. Some thought he was washed up at thirty and would live out his life in a room ordering rare books on the WorldNet. A waste of a man, a waste of a fortune, a waste of a life. His father had come to hate his son because all his dreams for Andrew's important role in the world were shattered. He had made sure that the boy had grown up strong, physically and mentally, and somehow his plans still hadn't worked out. Something in Andrew kept him from fitting the mold that his father had so carefully created for him.

In the midst of his uncertainty and lack of direction, Andrew had retained one thing from his bohemian travels, and that was his sense of the tapestry of destiny. He felt certain that he had a purpose, just as the saving voice had told him in his days of wanderlust. He was clairvoyant enough to know that somehow his purpose would reveal itself in his home, in the very place where his hopes and dreams were despised. He had seen enough to be disappointed by the degeneration of the human experiment. Modern civilization had failed to give the individual freedom and happiness. Instead, it had surrounded him with a world of technical wizardry that turned against him.

His father was by now retired and his overbearing character was fading, but he still had plenty of energy to condemn his son's behavior and try to push him out of the dead end he had fallen into.

Andrew had a need to do something for his fellow humans in a hands-on way. To his father's great humiliation, he went weekly to the local mission house and worked in the kitchen to feed the homeless and the vagrants passing through. He didn't know what his life's work would turn out to be, but he knew that he had to offer himself in service in any way that he could.

Andrew also cultivated flowers in his impressive garden. He learned from the earth to be patient and bide his time. Spring would come eventually. Little did he know that spring would come in the form of an old rickety car bouncing along the back roads of his properties, seeking refuge from the searching eye of Federation agents.

* * *

The mission house was unmistakable to those who came through the area. It stood right on Main Street and any vehicles passing through had to drive by its dilapidated front doors. Very little traffic came through this out of the way place. The only visitors were desperate illegal immigrants and lost souls. It was in front of this mission house that the prophet requested that the car come to a stop. Jeremy looked out the front window at the rundown building and sighed.

"Pretty grim."

"Looks like the last outpost for the hopeless," Lynn said sadly as she studied a few wretched people sitting on the front steps.

"That's what it is," Adam stated. "An outpost in the wilderness. Just what we're looking for."

"Oh great," Jeremy mumbled.

"Why don't you go in and locate the person in charge and tell them we're here to offer our services."

"What do you mean, offer our services?" Jeremy asked with alarm.

"We're going to make ourselves available for anything that might need to be done here, in return for lodging."

Jeremy looked around nervously. "I don't see any motels around here."

"Maybe we can stay at the mission house," Adam suggested.

"I don't want my wife living in a place like that!"

"We should ask how she feels about it."

"I'm ready for anything," Lynn said from the back seat.

Jeremy reached over and took hold of her hand. He squeezed it lovingly. He was so proud of her courage and self-sacrificial dedication. She would never cease to amaze him.

He stepped out of the car and headed toward the building. The people on the stairs, unclean and in distress, looked at him with haunted eyes. He braced himself for the strength to endure what was ahead.

The inside was as shabby as the exterior; hot and stuffy, dimly lit, overcrowded. The place was a pit of human unhappiness. He had worked in soup kitchens before. His church participated in a mission house in his former parish, but this one was different. It reflected the desolation of the locale in which it was situated—a forgotten, abandoned place where the twenty-first century had not yet landed. If one wanted to hide away from the world, this was certainly the place.

Jeremy wandered past several families of people from distant lands. He thought he recognized the characteristics of Peruvian descent, the noble races of the Incas and Mayans, and perhaps some Eastern European features as well. These were the backwaters of the American dream where the poor and the tired had washed up onto a shore that was nothing like what they had imagined. There were no more opportunities for such as these, just the daily effort to stay alive.

He heard some pots and pans clanging in the kitchen and headed toward the sound. He opened the door and found himself confronted with a chaos of dirty dishes piled on top of each other. A lone individual was beginning the dreary task of cleaning the mess that had taken a week to accumulate.

He approached the person and was surprised to find a tall, lanky, clean-cut man. He looked more like a concert pianist than a volunteer for a soup kitchen.

"Hello," Jeremy said.

The man turned around. His sad eyes, drooping with dark circles, studied Jeremy with curiosity.

"May I help you?"

"Actually, that's my question."

"I beg your pardon?"

"My friends and I are here to help you."

Andrew Bradshaw became suspicious. "What are you talking about?"

"Forgive me, let me introduce myself properly. I'm Jeremy Wilkes. I'm here with my wife and a friend, and we are offering our services to your mission."

Andrew looked at him in stunned silence. He didn't know how to respond. Jeremy stood there awkwardly as the man looked him over, trying to detect where he was from and what he was up to. Finally, Jeremy had to break the silence.

"I don't suppose you get too many strangers showing up to volunteer, do you?"

"None," Andrew said grimly. "Nobody comes here except people in great need."

"Who else works here?"

"Besides me, there's the owner who comes in once in awhile, Mrs. Logan. She's getting up there in years and can't really work much any more. We use to have a few people from local churches, but they seem to have lost interest. It's not much fun."

"I'm sure it isn't. What's your name?"

"My name? It's Andrew."

"How do you do, Andrew?" Jeremy said as he extended his hand.

Andrew wiped his soapy fingers on his pant leg and reluctantly shook Jeremy's hand. Jeremy was surprised at the softness of his skin. He deduced that he was dealing with a man who lived more in his intellect than in manual labor, and who obviously had some kind of privileged life.

"My friends are waiting in the car. May I bring them in to see the place?"

"I don't know . . . "

"We'll help you with these dishes here."

"What?"

"I said we'll wash the dishes with you. Looks like that other room needs a good sweeping."

"Who are you people?" Andrew asked, this time with irritation in his voice.

"Me, I'm a minister, currently without a congregation. My wife is my companion in ministry, and my friend is also in that same vocation, sort of."

"You're just wandering the countryside looking for a place to work?"

"Something like that."

"We can't pay you anything."

"That's not a problem. However, we'll need some help finding lodgings. Let me introduce you to them."

Jeremy turned around and headed for the front door. Andrew hesitated, then timidly followed him, a look of concern on his face. Adam and Lynn were already standing in the doorway.

"Lynn, I want you to meet . . . Andrew is it?"

"Yes," Andrew said as he relaxed upon seeing Lynn's friendly, honest face.

Jeremy turned to Adam. "And this is . . . " He hesitated using

Adam's real name. They hadn't talked about camouflaging his identity.

"Adam's the name," the prophet said as he extended his hand. Andrew was struck by the man's clear, intense eyes. When he took his hand, he was shocked by the heat coming from his palm.

"I'm Andrew Bradshaw."

"Yes," the prophet responded, as though he already knew. "How good to meet you."

Andrew almost expected him to say "at last." The thought was so strange to him that he had to just let it go by.

"Let's get to work," Adam stated.

They headed for the kitchen. It was the beginning.

CHAPTER 17

Within three hours of the prophet and his friends settling in the upstairs rooms of the mission house, the first miracle occurred.

Andrew was sweeping the front steps when an old rusty pickup truck pulled up in front of the building. A farmer jumped out, panicked.

"Help me!" he shouted to Andrew. "Help me!"

Andrew dropped his broom and hurried down the stairs. The farmer leaned into the back of the truck. In between hay bails and farm equipment lay a young girl about to give birth.

"What's the matter?" Andrew asked nervously.

"My daughter . . . she's gonna have a baby!"

"What did you bring her here for? Take her to the hospital!"

"It's too far away. Her water's already broke. There's something wrong. She'll never make it!"

Andrew looked at the young woman. She was moaning in terrible agony, both hands on her protruding stomach. Blood ran in rivulets to the edge of the truck and down over the license plate.

"My God!" Andrew cried out in horror. "We've got to get her to a doctor!"

"Please!" the girl cried out. "Help me! Make the pain go away!"

She was already delirious with pain and fever. Andrew was swept up in the panic and could not think straight. He knew there was no doctor within ten miles. Bouncing along the dirt roads might be fatal to her. His mouth turned dry as he desperately tried to figure out what to do.

"Don't let her die!" the man yelled, tears running down his cheeks. "She's only twelve years old. Have mercy on us!"

He crossed himself even though he hadn't been to church in the last half century of his existence. But in his despair there was no one else to turn to. He knew they were beyond human help. The young girl went into convulsions.

"Jesus, save us!" the man cried out.

Andrew's sides cramped in utter terror. He knew he was completely helpless. Then he sensed a soothing presence nearby. In the midst of his fear and anguish, a calming energy—like a gentle sun ray warming his neck—penetrated into his soul and inexplicably gave him hope. He turned around to see Adam coming down the steps.

He stepped out of the way as the prophet leaned into the pickup truck and placed his hand on the girl's forehead. Her eyes rolled back into her head. Within moments, the convulsions stopped. Her breathing stabilized and she turned large brown eyes toward Adam. They were no longer filled with terror. Though she was shivering and bleeding, a smile brightened her face. She felt herself safe in his magnetic and healing presence.

"Let's take her into the house," Adam said quietly. "Andrew, do you have a stretcher in there?"

"Yes, we do."

"Get it for us, please."

Andrew ran like a madman into the building. His panic was now mixed with a dizzying sense of wonder at what he had witnessed. He came back out with an old, stained stretcher and they placed her on it with great care. Blood poured freely from her body. She was becoming very weak, but her fear was gone. Her father wept helplessly as the two men carried her into the building.

"God forgive me! Forgive me!" he mumbled to himself.

He was walking behind Adam as they entered through the doorway. The prophet turned around and gave him a cold, distant look.

"Stay out here!" he said to him in a commanding voice that made it clear he knew the dreadful, incestuous story. The man shrunk back and fell to his knees on the steps, shivering in remorse and fear.

Lynn and Jeremy hurried down the stairway to join them and immediately set to work finding water and towels. Andrew stood against the wall, trembling like an autumn leaf. Adam leaned over the girl laying on the couch in the main room. He took her hand as Lynn felt her pulse and tried to slow the bleeding.

"Jeremy, call somebody. She's dying," she whispered.

No longer afraid, the young girl stared unblinking at the face of the prophet, glued to his eyes which filled her with profound peace. Her skin turned pallid and her breathing slowed as the blood continued to drip to the floor. Andrew wept, seeing her life-force evaporate. A heavy silence fell over the room. Only her labored breathing could be heard. Then it stopped.

Everyone froze as they watched a sacred and terrible event—life vanishing and death settling in.

"No!" Andrew moaned. "No!"

Lynn and Jeremy stared in shock at the sweet, angelic face of the dead girl. Only the blood drops falling to the floor interrupted the eerie silence. Adam leaned toward her and breathed out onto her face as he caressed her forehead. The three others thought it was his way of saying good-bye to the gentle soul that had left so soon.

Suddenly, the little girl's body heaved. All three let out a cry of fear. Her torso lifted from the couch in a violent convulsion. Adam stood up over her, raising his hand in the ancient sign of blessing. The intensity on his face was almost unbearable. Sweat poured from his features like a dam breaking loose.

"God in heaven!" Andrew cried out as he realized that her body was responding to some emanation of energy that Adam was sending into her. The young girl breathed in loudly and exhaled. Her eyes opened. She was alive again.

Jeremy and Lynn cried out in joy and wonderment, tears bursting from their eyes. Andrew fell to his knees, overwhelmed. The prophet lowered his hand and smiled gently at the little girl who stared at him wide-eyed and confused. She recognized him.

"I saw you there," she whispered. "In the light."

"Give her some water," Adam said.

Lynn was so shaken with emotion, she couldn't move. Jeremy

hurried into the kitchen and came back with a glass of water. He
handed it to the prophet who put it to the girl's lips. She sipped it,
looking at him with astonishing affection. A new maturity was in
her face, far beyond her years, as though her spirit had aged a
decade in an instant.

"It was beautiful," she said to him.

"Yes," he responded softly.

"Look!" Lynn cried out in awe.

There was a movement between the girl's legs as a baby's head
appeared.

"Push!" Lynn cried out, laughing and crying at the same time.
"Push, darling!"

The girl closed her eyes and strained with all her might as the
prophet held her hand. A tiny baby came out into Lynn's hands.
She cleared its mouth and it announced its presence to the world
with a great cry.

Andrew wiped his face so he could see through his tears. He
couldn't tell if he was hallucinating.

"Give the child to its mother," Adam said to Lynn.

She placed the newborn in the girl's arms. She held it lovingly
as though she had long experience as a mother. It was a bizarre
sight to see a little girl radiating with such a mature character. She
would clearly be able to care for this infant.

"Behold your children, Lynn," Adam said.

Lynn looked at him in shock. She turned back and studied the
little girl and her child. Her heart filled to the brim with the desire
to care for them as her own. She brought her hands to her face and
wept with joy.

Adam turned away from the girl and headed toward the door.
She called out to him.

"Don't leave me!"

He turned back. "I'll always be near you, Juanita. Always."

His words comforted her and she smiled. He motioned for
Jeremy to hold her hand, then he stepped outside. Andrew
struggled to rise to his feet, shivering and weeping. He was
completely obliterated by what he had witnessed. He looked out
the window to gaze, mesmerized, upon the man whose miraculous
deed he had seen with his own eyes.

Adam approached the father, a stocky, dull-featured individual with a sailor's tattoos on his arms. The man looked like he had lived an ugly, violent life. He stood up and faced Adam.

"How's my daughter?"

"She's no longer your daughter," Adam said sternly.

"What the hell are you talking about?"

"From this moment on, you have forfeited your right to be her father and caretaker. We will be her family."

"Are you crazy? You can't do that!"

Adam pierced him with his eagle-eyed glare and said very slowly.

"I know what you did."

The man was speechless, unable to hide from the gaze that penetrated deep into his buried conscience.

"You are not to see her again or to come near this place!"

The man managed to snap out of his state of shock.

"You have no right to do this!"

"If you come near her, I will deal with you myself."

"Who do you think you are? You can't threaten me!" the man growled as he rolled up his sleeves.

Andrew ran to the door, realizing that the man was turning violent. He approached Adam just as the prophet said to the man in a loud, imperative voice:

"Be gone!"

The wretched man backed away, thunderstruck by the power of the prophet's order. Andrew realized that he would not need to defend him. The man seemed to shrink under the prophet's glare and hurried away without a word. He jumped into his truck and tore off down the road without looking back.

Andrew stood behind Adam who was frozen in place for a moment. Though he couldn't see his face, Andrew sensed that he was recomposing himself after that release of intense energy. He turned around and Andrew caught a glimpse of his expression. He was surprised that it wasn't anger but sorrow. The shadow vanished from his face as soon as he saw Andrew standing before him. They studied each other.

"Who are you?" Andrew whispered in amazement. Adam said nothing, and in his silence and limpid eyes, Andrew understood without need for words that this was the man he had been waiting for all these years. He had finally found his purpose in life.

* * *

Twenty-four hours had gone by since Jimmy had received a report from Michelle. He was getting worried. In his little cubicle, he talked to the computer through his fingers, trying to locate any bulletins he could find from the Northeast sector of the Southwest. But all was quiet.

It seemed that his friend and the man she was seeking had dropped off the radar screen, something that just didn't happen at the World Federation headquarters.

Suddenly the door at the end of the dark room opened and the stocky silhouette of Hank Bracken appeared before him. Jimmy nearly jumped out of his seat. His boss never, absolutely never came down into the sub-basement. He watched the bullish man swagger over to him at a quick pace. This could only mean that he was very upset. Sure enough, Bracken headed directly for him, his face a scarlet red.

"What the hell's going on, Jimmy?"

"What do you mean, sir?"

"You know what I mean! Blair, what is she up to?"

"Michelle Blair?"

"Of course! She's in the field, and apparently she's only in contact with you. Talk to me!"

"Well, she's on an investigation."

"Really?" the man said fuming. "And why do I not know about it?"

"I . . . I don't know, sir. She made the decision and I thought she had the authority to do so."

"Only technically. She knows damn well that I need to be made aware of what the agents in my sector are doing. Spill the beans, son. What's going on?"

"You remember the news items I brought to you the other day?"

"No."

"Regarding the man with the strange powers."

"Oh yeah, right. What about him?"

"Well, she's gone to find him."

"She what?"

"She decided that the story was worth investigating."

"Without a second opinion?"

"She's a level three agent and is not required to do that."

"Doesn't my opinion count for anything around here anymore? I don't like this going behind my back business!"

"I wouldn't call it that, sir."

"I don't care what you'd call it, boy! She needs to be more of a team player and communicate with her peers. Especially Miss Blair."

"Why her in particular, sir?"

"Because I worked with her father for twenty-five years and I owe him a few favors. One of them is to make sure his daughter doesn't get herself hurt. At least not too badly."

"This investigation doesn't seem to be a dangerous mission, Mr. Bracken."

"What the hell would you know about it, buried here in your cubicle?"

"You're right. I don't know anything about it. Except that my knowledge of the circumstances suggests that there's no danger of bodily harm involved. We're not dealing with terrorists here."

"And how do you know that?"

"He's a religious man who's healing people. Why would that be harmful to agents of the Federation?"

"That's why I work upstairs and you work down here, son. He's probably a major fanatic, and if he attracts a bunch of other fanatics, there's bound to be nasty consequences. Surely you've heard of the stories in the last century of such cult leaders: Jim Jones, the Waco disaster, the Cult of the Sun, the blind Japanese guru and his chemical weapons . . . hell, it's only gotten worse since then! Religion is the most dangerous of all our watch zones. It's as dangerous as the political one. In some ways, it's even more volatile."

Jimmy looked away, ashamed and confused that he might have contributed to placing Michelle in danger.

"So where is she now?"

"I don't exactly know, sir."

"Say again?"

"She hasn't checked in since yesterday."

"That's against regulations! Field agents must check in every twelve hours at the minimum. Is she breaking the rules now?"

"I don't know, sir . . . "

"I'm taking over, Jimmy. First thing to happen is that she's to communicate directly with me, not with you. I don't know how this got set up, but it's ridiculous. I never heard of an agent communicating with a level one employee. That ends right now."

Jimmy grit his teeth at the insult and at the intrusion into his relationship with Michelle Blair.

"As soon as you hear from her, you let me know. Is that understood?"

"Yes, sir."

"I'm gonna send another agent out there to back her up as soon as you know her location. This little private affair of yours is gonna end up costing us a fortune."

"With all due respect, sir, I don't think it's going to be for nothing."

"Really? Why's that?" Bracken asked as he leaned toward him with a threatening glare.

"I'm getting regular reports from the area regarding this case that suggest we're dealing with a phenomenon that isn't going to go away."

"A phenomenon, eh? That's not in the agency's vocabulary. A madman, a trouble maker, a disturber of the peace, a lawbreaker . . . you gotta come up with something a little more specific than 'a phenomenon.' I wanna see everything you've got on the case in my office in fifteen minutes!"

He turned his back on Jimmy and stomped out of the room.

"Damn!" Jimmy whispered to himself. The last thing he wanted was to cause trouble for Michelle. He had a feeling all along that she was headed for trouble by going out on a limb without due consideration for the standard procedures of the agency.

He tapped on his keyboard to scan the breaking news coming in from the Northeast quadrant where Adam Hawthorn was last spotted. He generated a word search, seeking to narrow down the material that was coming across the screen.

A bulletin board came up letting him know that nothing was

found in the parameters of his search. He went back to the general news items coming in from reporters, police departments, and WorldNet hackers. He scanned the headlines, about to give up on his effort. A word caught his interest, though it seemed to have nothing to do with what he was looking for.

"Bradshaw heir donates a million dollars to cause of healer."

Jimmy was always fascinated by the life and neuroses of the wealthy, partly out of jealousy and partly because it helped him appreciate his life more when they were in trouble. Their troubles made him feel a little less depressed about his situation. He looked across the first few lines of the news bulletin, hoping to find something to feed his desire for gossip. Sure enough, he found character-defaming words about Andrew Bradshaw and his eccentric ways. A family friend was quoted as saying that something like this had always been expected from the heir to the fortune, and that he would waste large sums in some foolish fantasy. He might even deplete the family's wealth for generations to come. This latest venture was well-intentioned enough in that it was aimed at the homeless and the poorest of the poor, but instead of investing in a reputable charity as other philanthropists did, Bradshaw was giving it all to a community that was being formed in the middle of nowhere.

It seemed as though the eccentric Bradshaw had gotten himself involved in some sort of cult, or at least with a charismatic figure whose intentions were unclear.

That's when it hit him. Jimmy's intuitions kicked into high gear. Somehow he knew who that figure had to be. Despite his boss's angry repudiation, he knew that he was right all along. Something big was coming in the wake of this mysterious healer. He printed out the story and was about to take it upstairs when he checked himself.

"Wait a minute!" he said out loud. "He'll never go for this." There was no clear-cut connection between the stories, no guarantee that Jimmy was right about what lay between the lines.

He played in his mind the kind of humiliation and rage he might encounter, and decided against presenting the material. He would stick to his secret communication with Michelle Blair and take his chances. Besides, it was a cheap thrill to resist his superior's orders.

His screen filled with blue and red, the signal of a field agent's incoming message. He jumped to the keyboards as the first words appeared in the haze of colored light.

"Hello, Jimmy. How are you today?"

"Michelle, where are you? I've been worried," he typed in response.

"Settled in Enid. Been doing background research."

"Why didn't you check in?"

The words came back quickly. "Too busy."

He scratched his head nervously, then typed away at lightning speed.

"Bracken's been here. He knows what you're doing and he's really upset."

Words came back in caps. "Too bad."

"He insists that I link you with him and that he take over the communication with you."

The screen was blank for a moment.

"I don't think so." The words came slowly but with obvious determination.

"Why not?"

"Because the story's too good to let it fall into his hands. He'll drop the ball."

Jimmy shook his head, knowing this could only mean trouble. He typed away.

"I think I know where our man is."

The words came back instantly. "Where?"

"I'll send you the story. It just came in."

He located the file and pressed the enter key. It downloaded immediately. He waited for a moment, knowing that she was reading the material with avid interest. He reveled in the feeling that her excited attention was directed toward him.

* * *

Michelle was led into the large, luxurious office of Reverend Morgan by a dutiful secretary. The powerful minister looked her over with a barely concealed lustful glance, then slipped into his plastic self-righteous persona.

"Hi there, it's good to see you."

He came around his marble desk and shook her hand.

"Thank you for taking time to grant me an interview," Michelle said graciously.

"My pleasure. I enjoy speaking with representatives of the Federation. Especially such lovely ones, if you don't mind my saying so. I've met your father before."

"Have you?"

"Yes, years ago at an Association meeting. He gave the keynote address on the need for religious leaders to work hand in hand with the Federation's security agents. Strangely enough, it was precisely to avoid incidences like this one."

"How do you mean?" she asked as he pointed her to a seat.

"Come now, young lady, do I look like a fool to you? I know why you're here."

"You do?"

"Why certainly. You know, as president of the Ministerial Association, I do have friends in high places."

"Really?"

"Indeed. As I said, your father and I came to know each other. I've visited the headquarters several times. I've even been to the top floor."

"Is that a fact?" she said, rather disgusted by his boasting.

"That's right. I've played golf with General MacDaniel and his colleagues."

"Who won?" she asked sarcastically.

"I did, if you want to know the truth."

"Interesting."

"I've built my own golf course behind my house. I practice as often as I can."

"I guess there are some privileges that come with your profession."

"And why not?" he asked with an edge of irritation. "I've worked for it. I've done more funerals and weddings in my time than you could ever imagine. So, how may I help you?"

"As you pointed out, I'm interested in the case of this Adam . . . "

"Hawthorn."

"That's right. I understand you've been directly involved with this matter."

"And I'll continue to be until we bring him before the Commission on Ministry and strip him of his ordination."

"Do you feel it's necessary to do that?"

"Of course! The man is a dangerous heretic."

"In what way?"

Morgan sat back in his chair. "These theological matters are too complicated for you."

She resented his patronizing tone. "Try me."

"I'll make it plain and simple. The man thinks he's a messenger from God. That kind of Messiah Complex is the last thing we need right now in these uncertain times."

"What makes you say that?"

"Well, he goes around trying to heal people without the help of doctors. This is the twenty-first century! We don't need to be sold snake oil."

"Hasn't he been successful?"

"I'm sure he's failed a lot more than he's succeeded. I'd say its either coincidence or dumb luck."

"You don't believe in those kinds of healing powers?"

"I'm a modern man, young lady. I've seen my share of the sick and the dying. You bet I believe in high-tech medicine."

"But you worship such a healer, don't you?"

"Like I said, I'm a twenty-first century man. I don't expect to find what may have happened in a distant time."

"May have happened?" Michelle asked with surprise.

"You know that our scholars have demythologized the scriptures and put them in perspective. If we are ever going to have any hope of getting people to act right, we'd better bring things up to date. Otherwise we alienate the best and the brightest."

"So you don't particularly believe in the revelation you preach about every Sunday?"

"Now, Miss Blair, you're overstepping your boundaries. You didn't come here to interrogate me, did you? I'm not your story."

"No, I didn't. My apologies. I was just curious. How long have you known this man?"

"Oh, I first became aware of him about four years ago when he appeared out of nowhere at our local seminary. I'm on the Board of Trustees. I participate in the preparation of our students and certify them. I knew right away that we had a bad apple in the barrel."

"You did?"

"He was different all right. He never socialized, never showed up at fellowship events. He didn't seem to pay much attention to professors. Just an all around strange guy."

"Why is the police involved in looking for him? This doesn't seem to be a matter for them."

Morgan looked at her coldly, and tried to hide his discomfort at her question.

"He's a threat to all good people, not just church goers. He seems to damage the minds of people who come too close to him. I'd say he's a time bomb ready to go off. Such people are a serious concern to our authorities, as you well know."

"Isn't it true that the people who have been affected by him turned out for the better?"

Morgan jumped out of his chair, outraged.

"Young lady, you have much to learn! The issue is not how they've turned out, but the fact that they've been dramatically altered. Anyone who's got that kind of power over others is a danger to all of us. Anyone can see that! Why can't you?"

"But it's part of your religion that people go through transformation, isn't it?"

"I don't know what religion you're talking about. In my religion, people go to church, honor their God and their leaders, volunteer for good causes, contribute financially to the organization, and live clean lives. They don't go through major psychological breakdowns. I've seen his wizardry happen with my own eyes. Believe me, it's a frightening sight."

"Are you telling me, Reverend Morgan, that people who are changed by intense experience and become kinder, nonviolent individuals are a menace to society?"

Morgan's face was turning red and his well-trained mannerisms began to fall apart. He stumbled over himself trying to respond.

"What I'm saying is that no one has a right to mess with people's psyche like that, regardless of the outcome. That isn't religion! It's black magic!"

"But the results are positive."

"It's not what we train people to do in seminary, I'll tell you that much!" he yelled, smacking his hand on the desk. In that moment, Michelle saw the face of a mean-spirited individual who had nothing in common with the kind of man one would expect a minister to be.

She stared at him silently, watching him twitch with anger. He managed to control himself, straightened his tie, and sat back down.

"What exactly are you here for, Miss Blair?"

"I'm investigating the information we've received concerning this Adam Hawthorn."

"It sure seems to me like you've got a prejudiced viewpoint from the get-go. That's a breach of policy in your department."

"No sir, I don't believe I'm prejudiced in this case. I'm simply trying to get a good grasp of the facts. That's my job."

"If you're going to err, do so on the side of safety to society, not on the side of a loose canon with no accountability to anyone. I've got work to do now."

"One last question, Reverend Morgan," she said as she rose.

"What is it?"

"What would you like to see happen to this man?"

Morgan put down his pen, crossed his hands over his papers and studied Michelle.

"It is my opinion that he should be put away in a cell for the criminally insane for the rest of his life and never be allowed to speak to another human being until he drops dead."

Her blood ran cold at his words. She couldn't believe this "man of God" was so merciless. Her mind flashed onto the ancient images of the Inquisition and gruesome scenes of religious intolerance that had darkened human history for thousands of years. She turned away.

"Say hello to your father for me."

She did not respond and closed the door behind her.

CHAPTER 18

Word of the prophet's appearance spread quickly across the international vistas of the WorldNet. Andrew Bradshaw was a lifelong aficionado of cyberspace communication and had visited most of the links to the subcultures of spiritual seekers across the world.

His years of solitude were only physical, for he chatted nightly with his bodiless friends across the world who shared his passion for something more than the dull version of reality undergirded by the Federation and its armies of like-minded bureaucrats.

Andrew could not keep what he had witnessed at the mission house to himself. After having searched the continents for such a one as this, the fact that he had appeared at his doorstep made it all the more dramatic. All his intuitions were confirmed at once and energized him with a tidal wave of enthusiasm. He was a new man, clear about his purpose and his single-minded commitment. His time had finally arrived to be useful to the universe.

Within twenty-four hours, thousands of e-mail addresses and a dozen Web sights had received a simple and stunning message: "He has arrived." The readers and lurkers on the Net understood what these coded words meant. It was the fulfillment of a common longing that had reached a critical mass among the discontent in societies without direction.

From the dusty, barren plains of the Southwest came an underground news bulletin that would stir the hearts and minds of outsiders and mavericks from every country. Links, newsgroups, and chat worlds buzzed with Andrew Bradshaw's announcement.

The soil was fertile for such a claim.

The night after he input the passionate testimonial of his experience, he received some one hundred and fifty messages: "Tell us more . . . Can we come to see him? . . . What are his plans? . . . Can we send money? . . . How do we get there? . . . I'm on my way!"

Andrew himself was stunned by the response and tormented by the fear that he had made a mistake. Perhaps he should have asked permission to share his witness with the world. He was so used to solitude and intimate one-on-one encounters with fellow seekers by the light of a computer screen that he had no idea of the volume of persons eagerly anticipating such news.

His fear increased as he realized that he had further jeopardized the man he so admired by making himself vulnerable to Federation surveillance in cyberspace. Such a massive flow of e-mail in his direction might cause those hidden eyes to turn unwanted attention upon him. But he couldn't help himself. The joy and wonder of what had been brought into his life was too powerful to keep silent. He wanted everyone to know that such a man existed, that there was hope for finding authentic spiritual teachers in a world built solely on military and economic power. He felt that he owed it to the friends he had made on the Net, fellow solitaries who were adrift on an ocean of confusion and despair. Such people were intensely aware of the darkness of the age and the gruesome reduction of human nature to functional units in a highly efficient production line. Andrew couldn't imagine that it wasn't a good thing to announce the appearance of such a man as Adam Hawthorn. What more appropriate reaction than to trumpet a new day for those seeking meaning and purpose?

They began to arrive one at a time. Soon it was a continuous stream of individuals making their way to the place with no name where Adam Hawthorn had gone to hide and to serve those he came across.

It was Lynn who realized what Andrew must have done after the tenth person had appeared on the steps of the mission, seeking to be useful to the prophet. She confronted him in the kitchen where they were preparing a meal for both the vagrants and the visitors.

Andrew was working at her side. He had already begun to pour his wealth into their activities. There were supplies piled up everywhere.

"What have you done, Andrew?" she asked him as they peeled carrots side by side.

"I've got some funds and I wanted to make good use of them."

"I don't mean the money, Andrew. How is it that people know about Adam?"

He didn't want to have to tell her. He was beginning to suspect that he had made a mistake. But Lynn was the kind of person that he couldn't lie to. Her goodness of heart had made itself so transparent to him in their short time together that he recognized her as a noble soul. Besides, she seemed to be capable of reading people as though the prophet's abilities were contagious for those nearest to him.

"I told some friends on the WorldNet about him," he confessed.

She did not respond for a moment. Already she had learned to accept events as part of a great play designed for an important purpose. She no longer reacted in her old ways to such things. She accepted what was meant to happen.

"Are you aware that he is wanted by persons who wish him evil?" she asked quietly.

"I did not!" he replied in shock. "Why would anyone want to harm him?"

"The powers that be consider him a threat."

"That's ridiculous!"

"Surely it sounds familiar to you, doesn't it?"

"What do you mean?"

"Don't you know that everyone like him who has come among us has been assaulted by the authorities?"

"That's true, but we live in different times now. He's needed more than ever."

"All the more reason why he's dangerous to those who are supported by the status quo."

"Haven't we learned those lessons from history yet?"

"We never do. That's the main lesson."

"Well, it's going to be different this time!" Andrew said as he threw down the carrots. Lynn looked over, surprised at his reaction.

"Why do you think so?"

"For one thing, if a man like this doesn't influence our world, we're doomed to ultimate destruction! Secondly, this time around, such a man will not be without the power of this world."

"I don't understand."

"I mean to say that he'll have the necessary funds to fulfill whatever mission it is that he must accomplish."

"He's not looking for donations."

"It doesn't matter if he's looking for cash or not. I'm going to give it to him."

"You've got money, do you?"

He looked at her and smiled. "Yes, I do. And I'm going to put it to good use finally."

"Okay. But don't you think you should ask him first?"

"I'm sure he wants whatever will help his cause."

"I don't know if he has a cause, Andrew."

"He serves the cause of good in this world!"

"He's told us a number of times that all he wants to do is be helpful to whomever crosses his path."

"In this age, he can't retire to these backwaters. The world needs him as much as Juanita did the other day. He can't be wasted. We've been waiting too long for someone like him."

"You're not proposing to dictate his agenda, are you?"

"Not at all. But I will provide whatever I can to enable his work in the world."

He took her arm and looked at her earnestly. "Will you help me figure out how to best use the funds that I'm going to make available to him?"

"I don't know anything about that sort of thing."

"Surely you have ideas of how it could best be used right now."

"I don't know ... besides providing needed things for the mission house."

"That's loose change."

"Build him a house if you want."

"I'll do that. I'll build him a whole town."

"Really? You've got that much cash?"

"I'm filthy rich, Lynn. It's made me sick all my life until now. As of today, it will fuel something worthwhile."

"Talk to him about it."

"I did. I offered him a million dollars yesterday. He said he wasn't interested."

"I'm not surprised," Lynn said with a knowing smile.

"I asked him if he couldn't make good use of that, and he said no and walked away. So if I have to do it indirectly, I will."

Lynn thought for a moment. "It could be that certain practical matters escape him. Maybe we can quietly make available what is needed without him particularly noticing. We might give him a decent place for his own private time."

"That's what I'm asking you to do—handle his affairs so he doesn't have to worry about it."

"I'll talk to Jeremy about it and get back to you."

They returned to their meal preparation, both deeply concentrating on how they might best assist the extraordinary man who had come among them.

* * *

By the time Michelle Blair drove into the ghost town where the mission stood, massive construction was already taking place. Not only was the mission house being reconstructed, but a number of buildings were going up nearby which would serve both as homes and meeting places for the people arriving from all corners of the earth.

A dozen tents were erected in the empty fields surrounding the desolate area. Among the people milling about, Michelle noticed Lynn and little Juanita pushing the baby in a stroller along the side of the dusty road. There was something so beautiful about the love that exuded from Lynn and the helpers busily caring for the mission house that Michelle felt she was witnessing the birth of a new human community. There was a quality in these faces entirely different from the society she came from.

Up ahead, the road was being paved to enable trucks to get in and out of the area with their heavy equipment and construction materials. She felt caught up in an energy vortex that seemed to be hovering over this otherwise dreary environment. It made her heart beat faster.

Michelle parked, jumped out of her car, and approached Lynn.

"Hello there!" she called out.

Lynn looked over and was immediately suspicious, noticing her fine clothing. Most of the people showing up to be near the prophet were dressed in clothes very different from those worn by the successful of the world.

"May I help you?" Lynn asked.

"Yes, I'm Michelle Blair. I'd like to talk with Mister Hawthorn."

"Why do you want to talk to him?"

"I'm a news reporter and I'm interested in what is going on here."

"He's not available right now."

"But is he here?"

"Yes, he's meeting with some of the people who've come to see him from far away."

Michelle looked around. "I can't believe how many people are here! Who are they?"

"I don't know myself. They seem to appear from out of nowhere."

"What is their purpose here, if I may ask?"

"The same as yours."

"I see . . . I noticed a few people in wheelchairs on the way in. Are they here to find healing?"

"Some are. Most are here to learn from him and make themselves useful in one way or another."

"You mean they just dropped everything and traveled to this place?"

"That's right."

Michelle gazed at the motley groups of people participating in construction work and running errands to and fro. She recognized clothing characteristic of several foreign countries.

"I see you've got some international visitors here as well."

"We do," Lynn said, growing more suspicious of Michelle's careful study of the surroundings.

"Did they also drop everything to fly over here?"

"Yes they did. Most of them have taken one way tickets."

"Is that a fact? This Adam Hawthorn must be quite an individual."

"He is."

"What must I do to get an audience with him?"

"Nothing special. When you see him, just go up to him. There is no protocol here. He has no secretaries or schedules."

"How will I recognize him?"

"You'll recognize him," Lynn said with a smile. "But he's hard to pin down. He's very busy."

"Busy doing what exactly?"

"Helping people," Juanita said with a big smile. "Making them better."

Michelle suddenly guessed the identity of the young girl. Jimmy had faxed her the story.

"Is this your child?" she asked Juanita, approaching to look at the infant.

"Her name is Angel."

"And you're the one he . . . " she could hardly bring herself to say it, "he brought back."

Lynn gave her a scolding look. "We don't talk about that."

"Yes I am. I died and he brought me back."

"How do you know that you were gone?" Michelle dared to ask.

"I wasn't in my body anymore. I was flying through a tunnel of light. Then I felt a pull. I knew it was him, bringing me back."

Michelle couldn't argue with Juanita's straightforward statement. She felt her heart tighten in her chest and did her best to repress the feeling that she was dealing with something authentic.

"You said he's in the mission house over there?"

"Yes, in the main room," Lynn answered.

Michelle hurried away as Lynn watched her closely. She knew that eventually the growing crowds would bring people with harmful intentions. But there was nothing she could do to stop the flow of humanity toward the prophet.

Inside the mission house, Michelle walked through the dust and noise of construction. The entire building was being remodeled. She came into a large room where two dozen people sat on furniture and on the floor. They surrounded a man who sat peacefully on a wooden chair, patiently answering questions. She knew immediately that he had to be Adam Hawthorn.

Michelle quietly slipped behind the back row. No one noticed her as they listened intently to the prophet.

Adam was answering someone's question.

"Humanity has run out of time. This is our last chance to change our course."

"How do you mean, sir?" someone asked.

"Most people live now only to serve the needs of the state without any awareness of why they exist in the universe. It has taken hundreds of years to reach this level of spiritual annihilation. There are consequences to such depths of darkness. Consequences that affect the health of the species and of the planet itself. Degeneration cannot go on forever. There comes a point when it bottoms out."

"And we are at this point?" a person with a thick accent asked.

"I think you know the answer to that question."

"Then what must we do?"

"Things must change in this generation or there will be no recovery after the time of disasters."

"I'm prepared to give my life to that effort," another person said. "What would you have us do?"

"There must be enough people willing to commit themselves to a radical rediscovery of their spiritual selves so that they may be of service to the forces of light seeking to renew this world."

Michelle had heard this kind of talk before. She'd read some old books that had once been popular in the New Age fad at the turn of the century, but were now forgotten on dusty library shelves. She knew that her grandparents' generation had been utterly disillusioned during that surge of hunger for meaning, and like countless others had given up their forays into the deeper mysteries of life in order to survive in a world seeping into global ruin. She had long ago lost patience with the subject, and yet this man's flaming eyes and simple expression carried a dynamism that touched something deep within her.

"Teachers and avatars have said this before," someone said. "Do you bring anything new?"

Adam looked intently at his questioner. "Friend, I bring the final call before the night settles in forever."

A chill came over the crowd. Everyone fell silent.

"What I say is not new. But the circumstances in which I say them creates a new urgency."

"What makes you say this is the final call? Humanity has been in a wretched state before," a person with a European accent called out.

"Indeed it has. But the clock has run out. Our technological progress has so outstripped our spiritual evolution that for the last hundred years we've had the capability of destroying all life on earth. Now, with all the immense poverty, famine and hopelessness of so much of humankind, we've reached the threshold. Our worst nightmares are coming true."

"Are you saying that you're the last one to call us to this awakening?" someone with a Hindu accent asked.

Adam looked at the crowd. Jeremy was among them, eagerly listening to every word, eyes wide open, waiting for Adam's answer. Outside, all the construction sounds suddenly stopped at once. A frightening silence fell over them. Adam spoke in a slow, deliberate tone.

"I am the final prophet . . . "

No one spoke. Michelle could hear the thumping of hearts. She couldn't resist the sensation that filled the room and now penetrated her soul as well. She forced herself out of her mesmerized state, remembering that she was an agent of the World Federation Security forces. She told herself that this man was either crazy or extremely dangerous. What he couldn't be was right.

Jeremy was as stunned as any of the people in the room. He had never heard Adam speak like this before. He didn't know what to make of this turn of events. Even the miraculous healings he had witnessed could not prepare him for this revelation.

Adam sat quietly, completely unaffected by the shocked faces staring at him.

"The world needs to know this!" Andrew finally said, coming out of his own trance. "If you're the final call to spiritual awakening, it must be heard loud and clear around the world!"

"Otherwise, how will people know?" someone said.

"The time must be right for that moment," Adam stated. "It cannot be forced or hurried. But you're right, Andrew. I am here to let the world know. And when I am heard, everyone will have an ultimate choice to make."

"What about us who hear you now? What must we do?" someone else asked.

"Change yourselves. There is no more time for procrastination."

"How do we do that?" a voice cried out.

"Put your hand to the plow and do not turn back. Know that you will be plowing your own field, pulling up the weeds of ignorance and selfishness within you in order to receive the seeds of knowledge that will awaken your spiritual selves and link you with the powers of light. In all centuries, this has been the work of those who sought enlightenment and freedom from inner chaos. Now this chaos has been thoroughly externalized and it rules the world. If you do not get to work, you will be useless in the struggle for the future of this planet and its inhabitants.

"This knowledge is not intellectual. It is the art of being your true selves, free from the accumulated baggage of wrong thinking. The darkness has actually created a special opportunity for those who seek the light. There is a shortcut now to a way of being that can allow you to encounter what you seek. This shortcut is generated by the very darkness that keeps everyone from knowing who they truly are."

"Are you saying that it is in living differently that we find the key?"

"That is correct. Virtually everything that is acclaimed and taught by our societies is the opposite of what it takes to find true wisdom. In order to become what your heart calls you to be, you must relinquish the direction that the forces of this world point toward, whether they be political or religious."

"Are you saying that our religions can no longer teach us the way?"

"That is what you are hearing me say. This age has fallen into such complete ignorance of humanity's destiny and purpose that everything serves the powers of this world. We have lost the most basic, instinctive sense of right living that might have been taken for granted in the distant past. When was the last time any of you chose to sacrifice your self-interest and desires for the sake of right action in the world? When was the last time you made an effort to go out of yourself for the sake of a higher purpose without any strings attached? It is a return to authentic living, free from the weight of the artificial ego that is the only path left now.

"Religious rituals have become meaningless and religious leaders corrupt. Even the highest teachings are no longer understood and are learned by rote and therefore made vacant of all meaning. You must rediscover meaning by encountering it directly. That begins with transcendence of your artificially constructed selves."

"Suffering and sacrifice, is that the only road to spiritual evolution?" someone cried out.

"No, however liberation from mass hypnosis is the path. The culturally-formed ego creates a virtual reality for us that is disconnected from the vast world from which we all come."

"If you say you're the final prophet," Jeremy said in a trembling voice, no longer speaking to his friend but to an awesome stranger, "does that mean that you have some knowledge of a future catastrophe?"

"The catastrophe is already here, Jeremy. Humanity has failed so many times in the opportunities given to it for rising to its higher potential that it is pointless to send any more messengers."

"Messengers?" someone asked in a heavy Australian accent. "Who is sending the messengers?"

"Friends, be sure that your curiosity is founded on the need for your own evolution and your service to a greater cause, not in mere intellectual interests. Hear what I say and either accept it or reject it. And I will say again: this is the age in which a hand is being extended from above for the last time. Reach for it."

Several people in the room began to weep. One of them cried out.

"Humanity will be left to itself? How can a loving Creator do this?"

"How many saints, teachers, apostles, and prophets have been sent in the last three thousand years? They are almost countless, from world-renowned saviors to unheralded and forgotten people with radiant hearts. They have come among us again and again. Most of them have been mistreated, rejected, or murdered. Don't you think that divine justice requires a completion of this seemingly futile effort? Is it not right to have a limit to this relentless sacrifice?"

"How can we accept your word on this, that you are the last one? What can you show us to prove such a statement?" someone with a German accent questioned.

Adam smiled. "Friend, look around you. The world is in a throttle hold. All of our technology has been turned against us. The information age has become the surveillance age. Our science has created unspeakable evils, most of which you don't even know about—such as the harvest of human organs, the manipulation of genetic material to create beings according to human blueprints. We have trespassed for several hundred years now, way beyond where a civilized people should have gone. All it will take is a spark to ignite this planet, whether it comes from the impoverished countries, or some wretched megalomaniac, or brutal terrorists.

"We've fed ourselves poison by satisfying our most depraved indulgences through our entertainment. We've brought up generations of men and women whose minds are completely molded and brainwashed by the twisted values of a greed-driven, self-gratifying social order. There are consequences to such disintegration and we are living them out now. You know this as well as I do. It's headline news on a daily basis. The multiplication of horrors cannot go on indefinitely.

"So the time is here to give oneself to the higher aspirations of our humanity and serve the needs of spirit, or to wallow in the wretchedness that is all around us. Hear me well, the messengers of light are numbered and it has been ordained that I am to be the last of them before the Tribulation. After me will come desolation and destruction. And human beings will become sub-animal."

Michelle was thunderstruck by his words. Her mind rebelled against them, but her heart believed him in spite of herself. The prophet spoke again.

"You've asked me what you can do, those of you who are ready to make this ultimate dedication of your lives. You can join me in following through with the mission that must be accomplished regardless, of the cost. Or you can go back to the world you came from. There is no room here for halfhearted people."

He looked at the crowd. His eyes landed on Michelle. She had to keep herself from falling back against the wall in reaction to the power of his gaze. It took all the strength of character she could muster to withstand his stare and not reveal her intentions to him. Somehow she realized that he knew anyway, reading her life story faster than any computer yet invented. She also sensed that he did not hold it against her.

But in that split second of their encounter, the memory of George Bowers appeared in her mind. A chill went through her whole body as she sensed that he had dragged it up out of her past and placed it before her inner sight. With that image came the memory of her long repressed desire for deeper meaning. But her intellect refused to accept what her heart perceived. It couldn't be. No one could stir such private memories.

"Will you come to our country?" an Asian person asked, "and speak what you know?"

"A sign of the age is that it is possible to speak to everyone everywhere without wandering the world. This is the setting for the last call. How could it be otherwise? Do you see the divine justice of it? Everyone will have a chance to hear before night falls forever on the human spirit. But do not be fooled. There are tremendous forces against even the effort to call people to their higher selves. It is a threat not only to the powers of the world, but to the powers of darkness that seek your absolute captivity. And they will send their minions against this final call and against you. So if you decide to stay with me, know that it is nothing less than surrendering your lives to a greater cause."

"I'm prepared to do so!" someone said.

"I am as well!"

"And so am I!"

Most of the group responded likewise.

"That is the price for finding what you seek, my friends. A messenger of the past century said it well: 'Truth that costs nothing is a lie.' Your hearts know already that what you will find will be worth the cost."

"Are you proposing the overthrow of the established order?"

Michelle couldn't believe that the question had come out of her mouth. He looked at her, not surprised that it would be she who asked that question.

"If you mean, do I seek to rule over others, the answer is no. But if your real question is, am I a danger to the established order, the answer is most assuredly yes. I am here to reveal the inhumanity of this order and the falsity that it stands for. The only hope for our species is, in fact, to break out of the mindset and way of life that is provided by the powers of this world and to seek a radically different relationship with life. There is no compromise possible anymore. We cannot serve both the forces of darkness and the forces of light."

It was clear to Michelle that he was telling her precisely what she was hoping not to hear, that he was an enemy of the World Federation, possibly their number one enemy. For he was not interested in starting a revolution and changing a country's flag, but in bringing about the utter annihilation of all that shaped and guided the human mind, sustaining the socioeconomic system that kept everything afloat.

The deadening silence was suddenly shattered by Michelle's beeper going off. She fumbled to shut it down, but the damage was done. Everyone turned to look at her. She felt shades of red rise up her cheeks while she quieted her beeper as though she were strangling it. She looked up to see all eyes upon her, including the luminous beams from Adam. No one there was the type of person to carry such signs of servitude to the electronic web tightly wrapped around most of society. It seemed particularly out of place here in the presence of the man who had come to condemn the triumph of technology over the human spirit.

She mumbled "sorry," but it was too late. Jeremy and Andrew both rose to their feet, intending to find out who she was and what her purpose was among them. But Adam raised his hand as though to say "let her be." They sat back down.

"Please feel free to answer your call," he said in a kind voice. The emphasis he placed on "your" suggested that her kind of call was quite different from his kind. Even then, he did not wish to diminish her in the eyes of the others. In fact, it was clear to him that there was a seeker of light buried within her as well. She gave the prophet an appreciative glance for freeing her from the terrible awkwardness in which she was suddenly caught, and abruptly left the room.

She hurried to her car, wishing she had never come to this place.

Not only had she failed to turn off her beeper—the most obvious of requirements under such circumstances—but she was also in turmoil over what she had seen in the eyes of Adam Hawthorn. She knew that she was not on an ordinary case.

She opened the car door and saw a light flashing on her computer, letting her know that headquarters was trying to get hold of her. She sat in the car and pushed a few buttons as she breathed deeply to regain her composure.

"Are you there?"

The voice of Hank Bracken came out loud and clear.

"Yes, I'm here."

"Didn't you receive my message to contact me several hours ago?"

"I did, sir, but I've been caught up in circumstances beyond my control."

"Sure you have. Can you hear me clearly right now?"

"I can."

"As of this moment, you're off the case."

"I beg your pardon?"

"You heard me."

"That makes no sense, Mr. Bracken. I've just come from meeting the prophet . . . the subject . . . for the first time. I'm about to get the information I came to find."

"I don't care if you've got a gygabite of information to send me. I want you back here pronto!"

Michelle grit her teeth. She couldn't accept that kind of tyrannical authority, not from her boss or her father or anybody else. She had grown up under it and she was downright allergic to it.

"I will not leave this case without an explanation!"

"You want an explanation? I'll give you one. If you don't do what I tell you, I'll have you demoted. I'll put you behind a desk for the next five years. Need more?"

"I've never been asked to leave a case without an explanation, sir. This makes no sense."

"What makes no sense is what you're doing, Miss Blair! It's flagrantly against company policy. You've got no backup, your supervisor's not aware of your activities. I thought you were better trained than that."

Michelle was angry now. "Hank Bracken, don't you patronize me like this! You had no interest in this case and I've got the authority to look into it!"

"Not anymore you don't!"

"Oh really?"

"The order doesn't come from me, my dear," Bracken said in a softer voice. "It comes from upstairs."

"Upstairs?"

"Top floor."

"You're kidding? Why in the world would they be interested in this kind of investigation?"

"You got me. It comes directly from General MacDaniel's office."

"General MacDaniel?" she said in shock. "Wait a minute. I'll bet I know why this is happening. Reverend Morgan made a phone call."

"Who?"

"Reverend Morgan is a friend of General MacDaniel."

"Why in hell would a minister in some backwater corner of the world have influence over a four star general in the top leadership of the Federation?"

"You tell me, Hank. Morgan sure wasn't happy with our conversation."

"He wasn't?"

"No. He definitely wants this man put away, guilty or innocent."

"Is that a fact?"

She had hit the right button. Bracken could be bullheaded and overbearing, but one thing he wasn't was unfair. He lived and died by his sense of justice.

"You think the minister caused this order to come down the pike?"

"No doubt in my mind, Hank. He went ballistic over this Adam Hawthorn. I'm beginning to see why."

"I'll tell you what, Michelle . . . we didn't have this conversation."

"Say again?"

"I haven't been able to reach you yet. And you haven't gotten this order from me."

"I can't thank you enough, Mister Bracken," she said with a grateful smile.

"Don't be thanking me. Nothing's happened yet. I can't guarantee you I won't be calling you back in five minutes. But I sure as hell am not gonna let our tail be wagged by a clergyman who's in tight with the top brass. That's just not the way we do things around here."

"Good for you, Hank!"

"I want your reports filed directly to me, not passed on to Jimmy."

"'I'll do that. By the way, it's going to be worth your attention. This is no backwoods event. I'll give you a full report in the next few hours. This man's out to change the tides of history."

"Is he now?"

"He's got a charisma that won't stop. Apparently with the supernatural power to back it up."

"I don't want that word in your report. Supernatural is not in our vocabulary."

"I don't know what else to call it."

"Find another word, you hear? No mumbo jumbo. Let's keep this clean."

"Yes sir."

"Over and out."

A button clicked and Michelle was alone again. She smiled to herself. He was hard to deal with, but inside there lay hidden a good man. No wonder he got along so well with her father. He had heart as well as brawn.

She was about to turn off her on-board computer when another light flashed. She knew it had to be Jimmy.

"Hey, Jimmy!"

"Michelle! What's going on?"

"I've had my first look at our man."

"Tell me about him."

"Can't do that right now. I've got a delicate situation here. And I'm obligated to file my reports directly to Bracken."

"You can't cut me out of the loop completely! I'm the only one who's feeding you news bulletins."

"I won't cut you out, Jimmy, but we're going to have to play by the rules now. There are too many people watching."

"I saw a code blue flash next to the bulletins. You know what that means, don't you?"

"Of course."

"The higher ups earmarked this case for special attention."

"When did this start happening?"

"Late this morning."

"That would be about right."

"What do you mean?"

"There are folks here on the ground who are calling the shots with the big boys."

"Sounds pretty upside down."

"The world seems to be that way. It's hard to say who the power brokers are. I thought they were all in our building, but it seems there are some of them out here too."

"So you've seen him?"

"I have."

"What's he like?"

"Very intriguing individual. He's got this awful way of seeing right through you. Listen Jimmy, let me know if and when Bracken sends backup. I want to know who all is involved, who's watching who. I don't want to end up being bait for someone else."

"Will do. I've already got the in-house scanning on."

She leaned over to turn off the computer.

"Michelle?"

"Yes?"

"Be careful. Please."

"Don't worry about me, Jimmy. I'll be fine."

She tapped the off button, disturbed by the tone in his voice. She wondered whether he knew more than he was letting on.

Michelle got out of the car and locked it. She leaned back against it, trying to figure out what to do next. Suddenly, Jeremy and Andrew were standing beside her.

"What may I do for you, gentlemen?" she said as calmly as she could.

"You can go back to where you came from, that's what you can do for us," Andrew responded sternly.

"That's not very hospitable."

"We know you're not here for charitable reasons," Jeremy said angrily. "We're not going to stand for infiltrators."

"I'm no infiltrator!" she replied, irritated by the insult.

"Then what exactly are you here for?" Andrew fired back.

"I'm a news reporter."

"Sure you are. That's quite a gizmo you've got in your car for a news reporter," he said, pointing at her sophisticated computer built into the dashboard.

"It's just a standard communication system. Nothing special. Many reporters have them."

"Lady, we're going to protect Adam with everything we've got," Jeremy stated with determination. "And we expected people like you to show up. Not quite this soon, but here you are. So we want you to leave now. You're not welcomed here."

She wanted to argue with Jeremy but knew from the look in his eyes that it was pointless.

"Listen fellas," she said finally. "What if I told you I was really interested on a personal level in what this man has to say, regardless of my occupation."

"That would be a first. An undercover agent interested in things spiritual," Andrew reacted sarcastically.

She didn't respond, refusing to confirm their suspicions.

"If I told you from my heart that I have no intention to damage what you folks are doing here, that in fact I'm interested in making sure that Adam Hawthorn doesn't get in harm's way, would you let me stay for awhile?"

"We're not taking any chances," Jeremy responded. "There's too much at stake."

"Let me put it to you this way," Michelle stated impatiently. "I spoke with Reverend Morgan this morning . . . "

She watched Jeremy's face knot into a grimace.

"I thought you'd recognize the name," she continued. "I know he doesn't wish Mr. Hawthorn good health. I wasn't pleased at all with what I saw in that individual. If I'm able to get an objective picture of what is going on here, of who he is and what he's after, I may be very helpful to your cause at a time when no one else will be."

The two men turned to each other, uncertain as to what they should do. Lynn came up behind them.

"Let her stay," she said.

They all looked at her in surprise.

"You know I can tell about these things, Jeremy. I think we should give her a chance. One thing's for sure, we're going to need all the help we can get when all this goes public. A well-meaning person in her position may be very important to us."

"Don't you think we should find out exactly who she works for?" Andrew asked, eyeing Michelle suspiciously.

"It doesn't matter," Lynn replied. "If her heart's in the right place, she'll do the right thing."

Michelle felt as though she'd been knifed in the chest. It was more painful to be thought of as a potentially good person than as a security agent and spy. She'd spent so long behind the mask of a strong investigator that she'd forgotten how to be vulnerable. She sensed that Lynn's words were calling to a part of herself that had been dormant for a long time. She wasn't sure she wanted to be such a person, but it was already too late. The dam had broken and feelings deep within were bubbling up and leaking into her consciousness.

"Thank you," Michelle said to Lynn. "I appreciate your willingness to trust me, and I'll do my best to live up to your assumptions about me. Would you be kind enough to tell me where I might stay for the evening?"

"There are no rooms around here," Andrew said. "You have to camp out in your car. . .unless you want to risk staying at a fleabag motel up the road."

Michelle decided she would choose her car, even though it had been a long time since she'd had to live in it. This case was getting stranger by the minute. But her ace investigator's instinct told her loud and clear that this was a big one. How big, she couldn't possibly have imagined.

CHAPTER 19

Morgan threw down the newspaper, steaming with fury. He paced back and forth in his office, releasing the toxic energy that filled his being and cursing under his breath. He returned to his desk and picked up the front section of the paper. The bold headlines read: "A prophet in the American desert!" A large photograph of the rising community took up nearly a third of the page. All other news was pushed aside for this story.

Morgan reread the words out loud. "Man heals dozens of AIDS patients. Doctors and scientists astonished. Local authorities estimate over one hundred people a day are appearing in the little community that has been named Renouveau, the French word for renewal."

"I can't believe it!" he cried out to himself. "How did this get so out of hand?"

He pushed a button on his phone. It immediately dialed a memorized number. A secretary's face appeared on a small phone monitor.

"Good morning, Reverend Morgan. How may we help you today?" the carefully groomed secretary said in a professionally friendly voice.

"I need to talk to the general!"

"General MacDaniel is preparing for a major conference, sir. He gave specific orders not to be disturbed."

"I don't give a damn what he said! You tell him that it's the President of the Ministerial Association and that we have a serious emergency on our hands."

"But sir, the general was adamant about . . . "

"You wanna keep your job or not?"

The digital image on the screen was clear enough to reflect the woman's efforts to hide her outrage at his comments.

"I'll do what I can, Reverend Morgan."

She put him on hold and the symbol of the World Federation came on the screen.

"Don't make me wait!" he said as he looked at his watch.

After a moment, the face of a stern, bald-headed man appeared on the screen. Thick black eyebrows shaded his small grey eyes that had seen and inflicted plenty of gore in their day. His beak-like nose made him look like a stalking animal. The frame included his four star epaulettes.

"What is it Morgan? I'm busy!"

"General, you know I wouldn't bother you if it wasn't really serious."

"That's what you said last time."

"It's gotten totally out of control. Can you see this?" He held up the newspaper over the tiny lens at the top of the monitor.

The general rubbed his glistening dome, trying to remain patient. "No, I can't."

"It says that one hundred people a day are showing up at Hawthorn's hideout. I'm told the WorldNet is buzzing with the news. People are flying in from around the world."

"What kind of people?"

"All kinds, not just the loonies looking for a guru. Sick people with incurable diseases are showing up and apparently going home cured."

"Don't be ridiculous!"

"That's what it says here, general. Whether it's true or not, it's causing a sensation. I hear the traffic is backed up so bad in that area, the locals can't go about their business anymore. I told you we had an explosive situation on our hands, and by God it's exploded!"

"So what do you want me to do about it, Morgan?"

"We've got to get rid of him before he gets too big! This is all happening at lightning speed. Before you know it, he'll be on national television. There's no way the media's not going to pick up on this."

"Is he breaking any laws?"

"He's breaking laws of nature. But that's not the point. I'm telling you, he's going to destabilize the population."

"I can't send troops in."

"No, but you can send some undercover agents. Get the real story of what's going on. If we can get some dirt on him, we can put him away. If we can't find dirt, let's make some up."

The general snickered, revealing big yellow teeth that had smoked many a cigar. "You never cease to amaze me, Reverend."

"Just trying to do my duty, general."

"Listen, I gotta go. I'll talk to head of security and we'll send people out there."

"Please keep me informed of their reports, general. If I can get enough information, I can have him defrocked at a distance."

"Will do."

The image disappeared and the Federation symbol returned on the screen. Morgan turned off his phone. He looked at the newspaper and thought for a moment. He studied the new buildings in the picture.

"Somebody's funding this," he said to himself. "If we can cut off the source, we might send him back into obscurity."

The secretary knocked on the door and entered.

"Reverend, there's someone here to see you."

"I don't want to see anyone. Who is it?"

"One of your pastors, sir. From the Northeast sector."

"Really? Show him in."

Harry Novack entered the room. He was a thin, wiry man with shifting eyes that couldn't look at people directly. He sported a little mustache and a shiny suit. No corporation would have hired him in a leadership position, but he had managed to land a respectable job as a minister by catering to the people in power and by giving his congregants whatever they wanted to hear.

"Mornin' Bob."

"Good morning, Harry. What brings you this way?"

"I see you've read the news already."

"Sure have."

"It's nuts up there! My people can't even make it to church. All the roads are blocked. It's bumper to bumper all the way from the airport. He's turned the place into some kind of mini Lourdes up there! You've got to put a stop to it."

"You drove all the way here to tell me this, did you?"

"No, I came here to ask for your help."

"What can I do?"

"You need to show up there, Bob, and straighten things out."

"Me? I can't go there."

"If someone in authority denounces him, maybe people will turn away."

"How did he build a town overnight? Do you know who's paying for all this?"

"Yes I do."

"Tell me!"

"It's Bradshaw money, Bob."

"The Bradshaws, as in Bradshaw International and Bradshaw industries?"

"The very ones."

"How is that possible? They wouldn't have anything to do with this!"

"The old man wouldn't. It's his crazy son. He's got plenty of his own cash. I understand he's worth a hundred mill all by himself."

"The Bradshaw son is footing the bill?"

"Yep."

"That's valuable news there, Harry. If we can turn the tap off, we'll slow things down. What can we dig up on that guy?"

"He's got enough skeletons in the closet to provide us with just about any story we want."

"Wonderful! If we can't get to Hawthorn, we'll get to his people."

"Do you know that Jeremy Wilkes is his lieutenant or something?"

"I'm not surprised. He was my assistant for a time. I knew he'd end up going off the deep end."

"I'm told that his wife is kinda like a business manager for the operation."

"Lynn? How do you know this?"

"The bankers in town told me. I do have some connections, you know."

"Well, I knew they'd end up doing something crazy."

"I think we should take the whole Ministerial Commission up there and excommunicate him right there on sight."

"Any chance that could be dangerous?"

Harry scratched his ear nervously. "Well, his followers are multiplying every day, no question. Typical lost souls who think he's the Second Coming. Makes me sick. It's like some kind of international fair out there. Never seen so many foreigners. I don't know how the hell they found out about it, but they're pouring in."

"So what do the locals think about all this?"

"They're very upset. However it's been a real boon for the business folk, I gotta admit. People who come to find some kind of miracle cure have to stay someplace and eat somewhere. I've seen more fast food places open up in the last week than in the last fifteen years. Some of our farmers have become restaurateurs all of a sudden. But I would guess most of them want him out."

"Well, I'm working on it as we speak. What we need to do is soil his name somehow. We have to keep this from going beyond a regional thing."

Harry rubbed his hands together with glee. "You mean, cut his legs out from under him. Destroy his reputation. That shouldn't be too hard. It's been done before."

Morgan gave him a look that shut him up.

"We do what we have to do. And as far as I'm concerned, this is the most dangerous case we've dealt with in my entire career."

"He's definitely not one of us," Harry said. "That's for sure. We gotta get rid of him. All this healing stuff makes me look pretty bad to my people. They start expecting me to have some kind of ability instead of just doing my job."

He realized what he had said and tried to rectify his statement.

"I know what you mean," Morgan interrupted. "So here's what has to happen. We have to create a sex scandal. Set him up with somebody."

"Can we use the same people we used last time?"

"I don't see why not. It worked like a charm. You'll make the contact?"

"I certainly will," Harry stated with lust seeping out of every pore in his body. He couldn't wait for an excuse to return to the world of prostitution, especially when it was for a "good cause" and he could hide his pathetic weaknesses under some self-righteous cloak.

"Make it quick and give top dollar for it. Be sure to contact me only on my private phone and keep anybody else involved to a strict minimum."

"You can count on that, Bob."

"Don't mess this one up. There's a whole lot at stake."

"I understand."

Harry stood up, and his colleague waved him away, not wanting to shake his clammy, slippery hand again.

* * *

Reverend Harry Novak made his way directly to the home of Peggy Bonnot. He didn't trust any other form of communication, since anything that went out over fiber optics was traceable. He found the woman lounging about in her nightgown, reading magazines. Peggy was considered beautiful according to the social mores, with her bleach blonde hair and heavy makeup, but it barely concealed a pitiful lost soul who had sold out every shred of her dignity for the mighty dollar.

She was unmarried and had no children. Even at this relatively young age, she knew that decades from now she would still be in the same lonely situation, if she wasn't dead from some social disease. But she accepted her condition, knowing that such was the price to pay for her lucrative business. It gave her plenty of toys and nice clothes which, in her twisted mind, she counted as more valuable than a close relationship with another human being.

She opened the door in her bathrobe and looked down on the little nervous man ogling her with unabashed desire. Peggy didn't recognize him at first. Her list of clients was rather significant and she never paid much attention to the individuals she had to deal with.

"Don't you remember me?" Harry asked in a trembling voice as he stared at the décolletage. She looked back at him with a blank expression.

"I'm Harry Novak, remember?"

She shook her head, not willing to unchain the door in case she was facing another lunatic. They appeared in her life by the handful. Such was the nature of her business. Her loveless use of sex beckoned forth the lowest vermin of society, with the consequences that she often had to deal with psychopaths. But she was generally tougher than they were.

"I'm the minister," he whispered guiltily. He hated to admit his profession under such circumstances. The paradox was too gruesome, even for his spineless character.

"Oh yeah, right. The set-up guy."

"Shhh!" he whispered, even though there was no one in sight of her large home and vast expanse of lawn.

"Is it time to take down somebody else?"

He nodded.

"My price has gone up for that sort of thing, you know. It left a bad taste in my mouth. The poor jerk lost his job and his family. If I'm not mistaken, he finally committed suicide, didn't he?"

Harry didn't want to talk about it. "May I come in?"

She unlatched the door and he entered like a rat scurrying into the sewers. The woman's home was a gaudy museum of trinkets piled up to the ceiling. Paintings, games, pottery—she was obsessed with accumulating possessions as a way of hiding from the tragedy of her life. There were several lush sofas decorated with bright-colored flowers, matching a wallpaper that was so busy it made one dizzy with visual saturation. Three full-size plastic statues of naked Greek goddesses adorned the room, surrounded by large potted plants. They represented her fantasy of herself—a goddess to the lowliest of men.

Harry looked around, thrilled by the phantasmagoria of the place. He was excited just being in her living room. Peggy was not a very bright individual, but she had turned her capacity to have power over men into an art form. She could sense instantly when she had magnetized a man's attention and could tell in an almost psychic way the level of her control over him. Reverend Novak was too easy, as were most of the men she dealt with.

"Can I get you something, Harry?"

"No thank you."

She leaned over to water an ivy plant that crawled up the side of a white column in the middle of her living room. It wasn't that the plant needed water. She knew that the mere act of bending over would cause the man to go into near convulsions. It was all she had, besides her things, this power over wretched males who lived according to their loins. She hadn't graduated from high school, yet in one week she could make a school teacher's yearly salary. Society had set the stage for such degenerate human relationships and all she had to do was harvest the results by making herself available.

Peggy was not yet thirty, but less than a decade into this profession the challenge had dried up. The whole thing was getting rather boring. All that was left to her was the cheap thrill of watching men fall under her spell. Though she couldn't bite their heads off like a praying mantis, she knew that she could destroy their will power and turn them into bumbling fools. That was her ultimate revenge.

"So what is it you want this time?"

"We need you to work your magic on a particular individual and make arrangements to get photographs of the event."

"Photos this time is it? That's really gonna cost you. I don't do photos very often."

"You name your price, we'll pay it."

"Sounds good to me."

"I'm going to give you two names in case the first one cannot be seduced."

"I haven't met the man I can't seduce."

"This might be him."

"That makes it intriguing. What about the other guy?"

"He won't be as difficult. We want one or the other."

"Same price?"

"Yes."

"Give me the details and I'll take it from there."

"The man we're after is named Adam Hawthorn. You may have read about him in the papers or on television."

"Nope. Is he another minister?"

"Yes."

"What makes you think he'd be hard to get?"

"He's different than the usual."

"You mean different than yourself?"

Harry turned red, but he couldn't deny it.

"He has a way with people. You'll want to be careful."

"What kind of a way?"

"He sort of changes them."

"Ain't nobody gonna change me, honey!" she said with a lustful grin. "I'm set in my ways for life and that's the way I like it."

"That's why we know you can do the job for us."

"When do you want this to happen?"

"As soon as possible."

Harry stood up and pulled out a wad of cash from his pocket.

"You don't carry the amount of cash I'm going to need for this."

"This is not for that job," he said as he separated a handful of bills.

* * *

The area surrounding the mission house was unrecognizable. A compound of buildings had been erected virtually overnight. Traffic streamed from all directions. Word was getting out on a daily basis concerning the astonishing healings that were taking place. People with desperate and incurable diseases were going home completely healed. Volunteers appeared from everywhere, creating a work force totally dedicated to the prophet.

Adam was now teaching as well as healing, and those who came to listen to him knew they had found what they were looking for: a source of authentic life-transforming wisdom. They were also mesmerized by his certainty about dramatic events in the near future and their long-term aftermath. The network of spiritual seekers, underground for half a century and no longer approved by society, was on fire with reports, anecdotes, and phrases remembered by his avid listeners.

Lynn, Jeremy, and Andrew were laboring eighteen hour days, barely able to keep up with the intensification of the work in which they were caught up. With extraordinary ease, the prophet had moved into his new role and accepted the quickly changing circumstances as though he had anticipated them. No one quite knew where all this was headed, but the momentum was mounting relentlessly.

The Bradshaw wealth undergirded the creation of this new community which was becoming populated with persons of every walk of life. Old, young, religious, occult—all starving seekers who had been left without a shepherd for decades. Jeremy attended every teaching session he could, in between washing dishes and helping Lynn with the administration of the community. He felt carried along on a tidal wave of events that astonished him daily. But the greatest surprise of all was to witness Adam blossom into a world class spiritual teacher, radiant with inspiration and simplicity.

Only Lynn perceived that there was a sadness deep within his inscrutable soul. This adulation and attention was not his wish but his sacrifice. She knew that he would have preferred never to have come out of the desert. She often resented Andrew's role in creating this flood of epic proportions, but then she would remember Adam's own words about the acceptance of providential activity in whatever form it came. People were often merely pawns in a game devised and played from a higher realm.

Adam's only advice to her regarding the construction of this community of renewed humanity was not to build too solidly. It had taken her weeks to grasp his meaning, but she was now beginning to understand. The buildings and the community itself were not the ultimate purpose of his work and would eventually be placed aside for something else. She was overseeing the construction of a set for a specific event that would come and go on the world scene. While others became part of this new society with the intention of settling in for a lifetime, free from the perversion of the larger culture, Lynn recognized that it was all temporary. The prophet had not come to build in the physical realm but in the spiritual realm.

Andrew was one of those who thought he was financing a new civilization. He funneled his money by the millions into a dream he hoped would last a thousand years. Soon they were purchasing, with the help of their new friends, rare books and works of art from around the world, gathering the finest achievements of the human spirit to save them from vanishing in the quicksands of degenerating societies that were drowning in violence and chaos.

Michelle was now participating fully in the birthing of this new world, amazed by the lightning speed with which things were happening. She attended the meetings, which were at first informal and then became more structured, and did the manual labor that was part of the teaching's method. She immersed herself in the lifestyle that was being created before her eyes. She also filed her reports dutifully, but her heart was not in that work.

Like everyone else, Michelle marveled at what was taking place. This was the very event that the World Federation did not want to see come into being: an independent community unattached to any of the Federation's requirements and without any of the economic and electronic ties to the larger world which swept everyone else into its orbit. She knew that in the long run this phenomenon would become intolerable to those with the power to destroy it, but for now she enjoyed the ecstatic feeling of new possibilities that shined on every face. Something beautiful was taking place in a world that had given up hope in such developments. She planted trees, made meals for the community, and stayed up late into the night conversing with people from all walks of life.

At first, she was reluctant to become part of the community. What kind of people would she come across? What would they require of her? But her initial encounter with this new world soon silenced her concerns.

A man was pacing the pathway in front of a large building where Michelle was assigned to live. He was compulsively smoking a cigarette. When he saw Michelle approach, a friendly smile broke the intense concentration etched on his rather oddly shaped face. He had been waiting for her.

"You must be Michelle. I'm Eric. We've been expecting you."

The young woman was immediately put at ease by the genuine welcoming energy. She entered the house and found herself in another world. Though sparsely decorated, the front rooms vibrated with a deep peace and "cleanliness," an emotional cleanliness as though the world of violence and anger had been left outside like an old pair of muddy boots. Paintings by De Vinci, Raphael, and Rembrandt hung on the walls. They were not museum pieces, but purposeful "energies," filling the rooms with a special quality. Classical music came from a sound system, -

underscoring the atmosphere with the gentle sophistication of a higher civilization far removed from the chaos beyond its doors.

"So long as man is not horrified at himself, he knows nothing about himself." So read a quotation signed by a spiritual master of the past century and written in careful calligraphy on a card laying on a nearby table.

There were chairs forming a circle in the middle of the living room. Several people were milling about. They were mostly in their thirties and forties, each radiating a similar quality of warmth, openness, and peace. Even though Michelle had a natural aversion to groups, she was put at ease by these people of a different sort. A pleasant young woman invited her to sit as the others joined the circle.

For several hours, she listened to a summary exposition of insights from Adam Hawthorn that were meant to be applied to one's daily life. It was evident to her that the behavior of these students already bore witness to the fruit of such work. They were free of artifice, defense mechanisms, quick tempers and touchy egos. Most of them were veterans of long and solitary journeys through the dark forests of esotericism, Eastern religions, and other teachings on the evolution of the human soul. Some had traveled far and wide, from the jungles of South America where ancient Mayan temples still attracted seekers of ultimate meaning to the slopes of the Himalayas where Tibetan monasteries still guarded spiritual treasures unsoiled by twenty-first century technolust.

Above all, these strangers were companions on an invisible way, each one possessed by a force that transcended their petty selves and searched for something higher and still unknown.

There was much that was left unsaid about the prophet's vision of the future. Michelle was offered basic information as to the purpose of the teachings and the reasons why the students had joined together. The intricate knowledge made available to them by the prophet—a knowledge that seemed to be the very essence of all religious, psychological, and philosophical truth—was without question information of great power that even a secular woman like Michelle could recognize as a rare treasure for those who knew how to use it.

One of the first requirements placed on her by the new world she had entered was to live at the "Teaching House." Though she had mixed feelings about this experimental community with its mysterious prophet and the communal living so foreign to her lifestyle dictated by the larger society, she was utterly fascinated by the psychological insights offered to her. It was clear that this was information which was not available at the local bookstore or on computer and television screens.

William was the "House Director." He was a good natured, rolly-polly character who had dabbled in Zen Buddhism and Medieval mysticism before landing upon the news of Adam's appearance. Like many of the other members of the group, he bore the marks of a generation whose childhood had been marred by the violence of the Middle Eastern wars and whose young adulthood had sought new directions through the widespread use of drugs. He had survived all of that and was now entering middle age with a stability unimaginable just a few years before.

But it wasn't merely the maturing into responsibility that had brought him the sanity and self-confidence which he now manifested with such ease. There was something within him, something other than his personality and ego that guided his behavior with a sure and impartial hand. William had been in the community from the very first month of its formation. He knew the prophet well and had clearly absorbed a good deal of practical wisdom.

"So who is this "prophet" anyway?"

Michelle stared intently at William, searching out any clues that might not be made known through words. She sat in a circle of chairs among the other students, all of whom had been in the community for some time and looked upon her as a kind of newborn chick.

Michelle noticed that the gentle, heavy-set leader was uncomfortable with her question. It was clear that there was a wall of mystery in this organization which could only be scaled by those who had paid their dues through commitment and hard work. Michelle couldn't help resenting the inner sanctum atmosphere which outlined in broad strokes her "unworthiness." Yet it made sense to her that there had to be steps to climb for anyone to have access to greater insight. Lynn had warned her that she had to not only be able to understand the truth of Adam's teaching, but also be capable of withstanding it.

Reading the accounts left behind in the wake of great spiritual teachers made it evident that there were unusual and extraordinary individuals hidden in the mass of humanity who had rare gifts and astonishing insight into the meaning and purpose of life. Adam himself had let it be known that there were communities like Renouveau hidden away in remote regions where men and women came in touch with a degree of consciousness unlike anything which their fellow human beings ordinarily experienced.

"He is a conscious being," William said in answer to her question.

"A conscious being?"

Michelle was still struggling with this peculiar terminology that created a whole new worldview and couldn't be found in dictionaries.

"A man who is in touch with his higher mind. In other words, a man who is spiritually awake."

Michelle felt a surge of adrenaline heat her veins. For years now, she had hoped to come across a person who was not like other people, a wise man, a master who could point her in the right direction and forever change her life. She was convinced that such teachers were not the product of imaginative writers, but flesh and blood who breathed the same air she did, even though they were infinitely above the limitations of her own understanding.

"Is he a good man, a kind man?" Michelle asked.

"Of course he is!" Marilyn cried out in her Southern drawl. She was a Louisiana girl full of exuberance and seemingly unlimited joy. It was, in fact, her smile and the smiles of the seven other students that had first set Michelle's mind at ease. They all seemed cleansed from the poisons of harshness and alienation that so typified most of the people she knew.

Even among the artists she had come across, who were a few notches freer and more broad-minded than the average individual, she had found that everything led back to selfishness. But these students were apparently transcending their likes and dislikes, coming in touch with a vast consciousness, a more compassionate Self in touch with a higher world. And they were doing it without drugs or shaving their heads.

"When can I talk to him?"

"Soon," William stated gently.

The students guarded the prophet with a strange jealousy.

"It's an honor you have to earn," another student said.

Michelle turned to the man who had spoken. Alan was a tall, rugged character who had gone through the meat grinder of life more than once. His scraggly beard and hawklike features were unsettling in this atmosphere of gentility. But Michelle was instantly attracted to him, sensing that here was a seeker who had traveled the world to find meaning. He didn't fit anyone's picture of a person thirsting for spiritual transformation, and that was perhaps the greatest reason why Michelle was fascinated by him.

It wouldn't be long before she learned of Alan's past. As she had imagined, it was full of dramatic experiences that might have destroyed a less persistent man. Alan had wandered through the jungles of Central and South America, studying the ancient temples of long gone peoples. He had been a Theosophist and a Rosacrucian, filling his mind with encyclopedic knowledge of esoteric lore. From Hermes through Plato to peyote, he had lived the spectrum of the inner search without ever landing on the living bread that could satisfy him at long last.

There was a darkness to this man, for though his spirit had not yet been disillusioned or broken, it had fallen into the pits of self-indulgence and corruption more often than not. Alan was a living monument to the strange fact that seekers of truth were not necessarily bastions of virtue. There was a hunger in his eyes, a lust even, not for higher consciousness but for personal powers, psychic powers with which he could manipulate others. In her naiveté, Michelle found his tragic life all the more interesting because of the anguish that had tortured it for so long. This maverick student of the esoteric, this plunderer of mystic mysteries, could perhaps become her mentor, offering her a harvest of exotic ideas stolen from the secret halls of arcane temples.

"Does he have absolute power?" Michelle asked with some concern.

"We don't work that way here," William was quick to interject.

That made Michelle feel better. At least this community wasn't turning into a cult centered around the worship of a man raised to godlike stature. The horror of Jonestown was in every history book with its graphic images of piles of bodies three layers thick. The days of the adored guru were over. Too many frauds had given the teacher-student relationship a bad name. The great ones— Yogananda, Meher Baba, Gurdjieff—had died long ago, and those who had come along to replace them in the last half-century, such as Rajneesh and his Rolls Royce fetish and Reverend Moon and his bizarre mind control skills, were clearly of a different caliber.

The idealism of the last decades of the twentieth century had decomposed and left in its wake the gruesome remains of unfulfilled longings. The spirituality that had once broken through conformity and obedience to temporal authorities had turned into a marketplace, the very den of thieves that had caused such outrage in the prophet from Nazareth. It could only disintegrate from there and some day start afresh.

Michelle was no longer concerned that she was getting into something oppressive and dangerous. Certainly, this community was a subculture, a world apart, but it was founded on timeless ideas, the kind that had fed the minds of humanity's finest. Here was culture and nonviolence, cleanliness and peace, order and harmony.

William took some papers out of a folder and cleared his throat. "We'll read the latest words from Adam that he shared with us last week at our general meeting. This will serve as a kind of introduction for Michelle."

She nodded appreciatively, relaxed in her chair and listened closely.

William read slowly and deliberately:

"'Our world today is not conducive to a healthy inner life. In fact, it knows virtually nothing of that dimension of our being. What is meant by the inner self? Quite simply, it is the essence of who we are, that consciousness of ourselves that has been with us since our earliest memories. This inner self is located deep down in the most intimate psychological and spiritual places where we live and move and have our being.

"'Our society lives and worships only the surface of things, including the surface of human beings. How we look and what we can accomplish are more important issues than the maturity of character that can find peace in the midst of hardship and mastery over our emotional turmoil. There was a time in civilization when wisdom was praised as the highest virtue.

"'Today we have sunk to the crudest materialistic, external levels of consciousness: aggressive ambition or muscle tone seem to be all-important. The greatest loss in this sad state of affairs is the spiritual nature of the individual. Whatever religious belief or non-belief you may hold to, there is no denying the invisible dimension of each human being.

"'Though we are present to this inner self like the fish are to the ocean, we are generally unaware of its needs. Our focus is outward, hypnotized by the noise and colors of our surroundings.

"'Our very life-force is pulled out of us all day long, whether by the TV set, the concerns of business, or the demands of others. We are seldom at home within ourselves. Yet it is only in that proper alignment with our deeper consciousness that we can be truly useful to ourselves and to others.'"

Michelle moved in her seat, uncomfortable with the words that seemed to be directed right at her. She hoped others felt the same.

William continued the reading:

"'So the first step in healing the inner self is to become aware of it, then the healing process proceeds of its own accord. All spiritual traditions teach methods on how to accomplish this critical awakening. But keep in mind that spiritual awakening is not dependent on any method or external activity.

"'Quiet the mind. Anyone who has attempted this knows that it is no easy task. In fact, we seldom reach a stage where there is absolute silence. We must learn to reach the deeper silence behind the noise of our thoughts, like stepping into a cave on the other side of a waterfall.

"'Slow your breathing. Most methods of spiritual development emphasize this simple but transformative effort. Become aware of inhaling and exhaling. Breathe slowly and deeply. You can actually lower your blood pressure and reduce your heart rate. Eventually, you may realize that the act of inhalation is a reception of the cosmic life-force within all existence, and exhaling is the release of tensions and self-centered attitudes.

"'Relax your body. Sitting with your backbone straight but not rigid allows the energy to flow with less obstruction. Proof of this can be easily demonstrated; In a moment of fatigue, when you are bent over your desk, straighten up your back and you will immediately feel an increase of energy.

"'Concentrate on the areas of tension in your body—your shoulders, face, arms, stomach, legs. Merely becoming aware of each knot will release the tension which is both a physical and psychological blockage.

"'Bring your hands together. One hand placed over the other, palms up, allows the energy to circulate in the same way as connecting a circuit. With a little patience, you might notice your hands warm up with a gentle, healing energy.'"

Michelle was struck by these words which described the very experience she had felt over a decade ago in the company of George Bowers. Her body reacted oddly to the reawakening of these repressed memories. She began to perspire profusely and felt a shortness of breath as though someone were strangling her. But she knew that someone was herself, the part of her that wanted to keep her away from this knowledge that threatened to change her life completely.

William glanced at her, knowing that she was going through a strong reaction. He continued:

"'Sit in silence. Just twenty minutes a day will recharge your energies more powerfully than several hours of sleep. It won't be long before you will want to increase that private time because it is not just refreshing, but life giving.

"'Most of us experience such frantic, nerve-jangling daily lives that the simple effort of sitting still is an alien, uncomfortable operation. Even in many churches, silent moments last no more than a few seconds because it is all the worshipers can put up with. We are strangers to ourselves and spend most of our lives trying to live outside of ourselves.

"'In former centuries, this kind of healing, regenerating way of life was more natural. Think of the hours spent by the fireplace or on a river bank. These gentler rhythms are lost to us, replaced with the rush of the twenty-first century and all its requirements. We must take responsibility for the welfare of our inner selves, because no one else will do it for us. What is the use of caring for the outer self, if the inside is dark, mildewed and full of cobwebs? This is where we find our true humanity through which we can be of service to the world around us. But we can bring no peace and no love to anyone unless we have found these states within ourselves.

"'Seeking the inner stillness can do more for you than any doctor or any pay increase. All the mysteries of life are there in that "no-place" where everything began.'"

Tears rolled down Michelle's cheeks even though she fought them with all her might. She knew she had encountered the truth that her heart had hungered for since childhood. Her mother's early death had left a void that nothing could fill. Out of that youthful agony had arisen the sense of something to be found in life that could not be taken away. And she had just found it in this room, among these quiet and devoted people.

* * *

An unofficial structure was falling into place as this eclectic community gathered around the prophet. Though a certain democracy reigned among the seekers and volunteers, it didn't take long for some to be more authoritative than others. The younger members were at the bottom of the rung, and the more mature and those who had been there from the beginning were the decision-makers. None of this was supervised by Adam, whose time was no longer his own. Every waking hour he was advising, healing, teaching, and comforting. He provided the vision of where they were headed on a day to day basis.

People gravitated to various roles according to their skills. Those who spoke several languages became instant translators, others with construction skills participated in the relentless building, creating homes for this extended family. A number of those who had been cured had also experienced a spiritual renewal so intense that they remained with the group and gave themselves to whatever work needed to be done. Though everything was fluid and uncertain, each person there knew that they had come in contact with a unique source of transcendent power and wisdom.

Lynn and Jeremy were overwhelmed with work from the

moment they got up to the moment they went to bed, but the excitement around them was so strong that they were continually energized. Before their very eyes, this organism of human souls committed to the prophet's mission was taking shape out of nothing, like Creation itself.

Among the throngs that were appearing on the dusty roads leading to Renouveau were persons with serious mental troubles who were not prepared to be healed psychologically and to find the wholeness that was being made available to everyone. Within the first month, a number of people were forced to leave because their intentions were clearly at variance with those of the community.

That problem required some kind of structure, however loose and non-coercive. Andrew took the brunt of that job, so concerned was he with infiltrations and scandals. He knew that the ground beneath them was not really solid and that the great balloon that they were becoming could pop in an instant. He was also more realistic than Jeremy and Lynn in recognizing the degree of brokenness among the people who came to join them. There were entire generations that had grown up without a shred of insight regarding their spiritual nature. Like the Russians after their revolution in the early twentieth century, they had lived in the long, dark night of a one dimensional experience of reality. The results were devastating, as many people lacked the fundamentals of conscience and any sense of propriety. But the momentum was unstoppable. Too many amazing events were taking place every day. The testimonials of those healed was heard around the world.

Often Lynn wasn't sure whether she was running a hospital or a mental ward. Adam was as occupied with spiritual damage as he was with the physical kind. But most of all, there was joy. The joy of creating a new community unfettered by the rigid oppression of a high-tech world that had turned its skills against its creators. No one here was merely a cog in the crushing wheel called "economic progress." Greed and violence were left at the doorstep when people came to Renouveau.

The only dogma in Adam's teaching was the necessity of recovering childhood's state of wonder, and drinking in deeply each moment of life without the burden of the ego's imagined requirements. Perhaps one of the greatest miracles of all was seeing people so quickly shed their unnecessary suffering and dive deeply into the long-lost innocence of their original being.

There were many tears and exhilarating experiences every day. People walked about with a new song in their hearts, a sense of fulfillment which nothing could compare with in the sophisticated, regimented world.

Love affairs were rampant, despite the overall focus of attention on reaching for a higher level of oneself. Lynn often heard rumors about illicit behavior and personality struggles. She had thought rather naively that everyone would share a common aim, make similar efforts and seek the same results. But everyone came with their own agendas and their own psychological baggage.

Nevertheless, most members of this motley remnant of humanity, who had escaped from the imprisonment of the degenerate world culture were deeply affected by the prophet's presence and words. Overall, there was a unity of purpose and devotion that made them a harmonious body.

One day, Adam was walking through the newly planted gardens, enjoying the peaceful beauty that was being created in the barren landscape. Lynn was patiently working with tomato plants that had grown five feet tall.

"Have you noticed, Lynn, that some of our friends are having trouble aligning themselves with their deeper selves?"

"I have," she said as she wiped the sweat from her brow, and she stood up. "I've noticed a lot of things that concern me."

"You haven't mentioned this to me before."

"I thought they were petty issues that would go away by themselves. They shouldn't take up your time."

Adam shaded his eyes from the sun and looked at his beloved friend. "That's thoughtful of you, Lynn, but the health of our little community is an issue that must be attended to or a cancer will grow that could be fatal to it. What do you think we should do about this problem?"

"Well, Adam," she said as she took off her muddy gloves, "I think we should be more organized so that people can be instructed more intentionally and not left to themselves to develop their own understanding."

"Organized in what way?"

"I've thought about this for some time. It seems to me that people need particular times of study, practice, and even worship. It might keep them focused."

Adam closed his eyes and reflected on the matter, turning his face to the sun. She studied him in his contemplation, noticing once again the extraordinary peace radiating through the very marrow of his bones. She knew by now that such a state was not a natural phenomenon, but the result of great and sustained effort. And she loved him even more for his sacrifice.

"There's always a danger in this, you know," he said. "Structures can so easily petrify into cages rather than springboards for new discoveries. They crystallize in very little time."

"But how do we deal with those who need guidance and some form of discipline? Maybe we need to limit our numbers."

"I wouldn't want to do that, Lynn. Everything that has happened here has been a spontaneous development that should not be inhibited."

"What happens to these people if this community does not continue some day?"

"They'll have to rely on their own understanding. That's the only aim here. They cannot become dependent on others whose lives are as transient as theirs. Each must find his or her own stable foundation. Otherwise we create followers, not whole people. We musn't let that happen."

He looked away with a certain sadness coloring his features.

"You know, Lynn, every time this has been done, even with the greatest of messengers, the followers have always betrayed and distorted the message. That's why—this time—it's not anything visible that matters. People must find their own link with the Source. There will be so few other options soon. Other help will not be available. Everyone must become auto-determined, rather than a puppet whose strings are pulled by the outside world. This is urgent business. First, because everything outside of us will soon be undependable, if not entirely destroyed. Second, because mastery of ourselves is the only way to block the influence of dark forces seeking to infiltrate this realm through us."

He walked away, heading for an orchard that bordered a small creek. Lynn watched him vanish in the sunlight, pondering his words. She couldn't avoid hearing what was left unsaid. She kneeled and continued her work with new attention to this moment and the simple pleasure of caring for a tomato plant. Never again would she take for granted the sweetness of life's ordinary tasks. Nothing lasted for long.

CHAPTER 20

Michelle wandered through the compound, familiarizing herself with the area. There were a number of prefabricated cottages at the far end of the property. All were empty as everyone was working in the main buildings at this hour.

She was about to turn back when she saw a flash of light reflected in the window of the cottage furthest removed from the road. She couldn't imagine what would create such a phenomenon unless something had blown up or caught fire. She hurried to the little house. As she approached, another flash lit up the window, but this time it stayed like a glow from some source within the house.

Michelle fell to the ground, half-expecting the place to explode. But the peaceful countryside remained undisturbed. She rose and ran to the door. It was unlocked. She entered and was unable to restrain a gasp. In the far end of the room, beneath the window, the prophet sat on a small rug. He was motionless, staring at an ancient icon depicting a vision of the celestial realm. His entire body was glowing with an intense white light. It was so bright that she couldn't make out parts of his shape behind the glare of the unnatural radiation.

He turned and looked upon her. The light was pouring out of his eyes, out of his whole face. The intensity of the brightness suddenly diminished. She turned to leave, frightened by the sight and ashamed of her intrusion, when he held up his hand.

"Come closer, Michelle Blair."

She hesitated. Her curiosity overcame her fear and she stepped forward.

"I would rather you not speak of what you have just witnessed," he said gently.

Michelle moved further into the room, her courage enticed by the wonder she was seeing.

"You're not here just to heal sick people, are you?"

He didn't answer, and that was answer enough.

She stopped a few feet away from him. She could feel the heat of the light emanating from him. It was like the warmth of a midday sun.

"Who are you?" she whispered in awe.

"I am a messenger," he responded simply.

A flash of intuition shot through her being. She hadn't experienced that sensation since the age of twelve when she somehow knew that her best friend had been involved in a serious accident.

"With a message concerning the future?"

He nodded lightly.

"You're truly a prophet then! Your special gifts, your clairvoyance, your mission . . . yes, you're an authentic prophet. It makes sense now."

"Why must it make sense? Reality doesn't add up like a child's math problems."

She kneeled beside him, some five feet away. She had never been so close to him. Though he was a handsome man with incredible magnetism, there was something so other-worldly about him that she banished from her mind and body any sexual attraction.

"What do you mean?"

"It could be different than you imagine. Maybe I'm not bringing anything good for the world."

"That's not possible!" she protested. "You're a great teacher. You could single-handedly renew the quest for spiritual awakening in our time."

A look of deep melancholy darkened his inscrutable features.

"What if I were a bearer of terrible things?"

"Don't say that!" she said, confused and strangely disturbed by his words.

Adam looked back at the icon that stood before him on the small table.

"After me comes desolation."

She felt as though a powerful hand had reached into her stomach and clenched it with all its might. The atmosphere of the room became heavy and the colors seemed to transform into darker shades.

"In every culture, on every continent, there have been messengers of light whom people have called prophets. A prophet is not merely someone who foretells the future. If it were that alone, his or her work would only be a parlor trick. The genuine work of the prophet is to bring to humanity a new awareness of its true identity and of the reality of the spiritual world. Each time a so-called prophet sacrifices himself for this cause, it is because the unfathomable realm of spirit from which we all come is reaching out once again to its lost children. You might say that prophets are like kamikaze pilots of the last century. They are sent in on a suicidal mission in the heat of the battle."

"Is this true for you as well?"

He looked out the window. A soft rain was falling from grey clouds passing overhead.

"I will only say this. Don't concern yourself with me. Concern yourself with the state of humanity. The mass mind thought that entering the new millennium without an apocalyptic ending meant that they could be freed from those fears. But the prophecies of the ages cannot be put aside so lightly. This world has failed to take the warnings seriously. This is the last warning. After me, there will be no more time."

"Why don't you tell this to the world now? There are a hundred reporters on the edge of the property wanting to ask you questions."

"I will only speak when I can speak to everyone at once, and I will only speak one time. That is how it must be."

"How could that be accomplished?"

He looked at her with an ironic glint in his eyes.

"You'll see. It will happen as it is meant to happen."

She knew it was time for her to go. She stood and thanked him for his words and these private moments. She left quietly. The prophet remained motionless in the shadows, a glow still surrounding his body. He closed his eyes and re-entered the realm of peace from which he had been disturbed. He needed to commune with it more than his lungs needed oxygen.

* * *

Jimmy stood before his boss and watched the bullish man read Michelle's report. He knew that Bracken would detect the source of his own concern. Despite her concise, professional presentation of the facts, there were unmistakable clues that she was being drawn into the community on a personal level. That, of course, was the ultimate sin a Federation agent could commit in an investigation.

Bracken read the hardcopy out loud, glancing up at Jimmy every so often with a worried look.

"The students come from all walks of life, all socioeconomic levels and educational backgrounds. They have one thing in common: a burning desire for spiritual awakening. Most of them have been seeking knowledge of this kind for years. Some have traveled as far as Tibet and India. I was told of two students who became disciples of a Tibetan holy man who, after some time, told them to go back to America to find a teaching that would prepare them for the future and the coming catastrophes. He then gave them a latitude and longitude that turned out to be this very spot in the Southwest. I have seen the prayer blanket given to these students high up in the Himalayas by this anonymous enlightened teacher.

"Adam Hawthorn is said to be a prophet of the highest order, someone whose inner vision and spiritual powers are undeniable. He is certainly unlike most anyone you are likely to meet, particularly at Federation headquarters. His gaze pierces right to the marrow of one's being and leaves us helplessly exposed in all our imperfections. He is a man who has overcome violence in himself and radiates a strange blend of gentleness and inner strength.

"His wisdom seems to be culled from ancient teachings and religions presented in incredibly pragmatic ways that make possible genuine personal change. There is no question here of some vague faith in a spiritual promised land or future state of bliss. He requires his students to make great personal efforts and provides the psychological tools for individual application.

"Members of this community make tremendous sacrifices. We live in "teaching houses," where part of the instruction is to learn to put up with each other. There are weekly meetings and daily chores that force the body to submit itself to one's higher aims.

"This subculture gives us rare opportunities to rediscover our essential nature beneath the facades of personality. We learn to free ourselves from the unnecessary anger and irritation that poison our lives. We marvel at the depth of the human potential as revealed by the best minds of civilized humanity: Pythagoras, Plato, Epictetus, Goethe, Blake, and many more who have been forgotten by our society.

"For some of the people here, this experience seems to be a matter of life and death. The prophet often quotes an old saying which states that it is only when we discover that life is leading us nowhere that it begins to have meaning. People here are prepared to sacrifice everything—ambition, family, comfort—in order to find regenerating meaning and purpose.

"Adam Hawthorn tells his followers that they must recover the wonder toward life so important in the teachings of the mystics, the willpower so fundamental to all esoteric methods, and the unconditional goodness revealed at the heart of all religions.

"This is a community of people in the process of being purified of their petty selfishness. They are manifesting a new dignity and control over their irrational impulses and unpleasant manifestations.

"And yet, there are signs of conflicts surfacing among us. Who is closest to the teacher? Who has been around the longest? Who is qualified to give orders? Even the power of the man who has altered the course of our lives seems insufficient to overcome that all too familiar human pettiness.

"In analyzing this discrepancy between the potential of human transformation available to us and the increasingly absurd conflicts arising among the people of the community, I noticed the following factors:

—The organization is becoming more important than the ideas that founded it.

—The life-style of effort and sacrifice that we willingly entered into is becoming a dogmatic requirement rather than a personal commitment.

—Students who once searched for higher consciousness with pure motives are now satisfied with positions of authority within the little society they have helped to created.

—The teacher who was once at the center of activities is now becoming more inaccessible and surrounded by a protective entourage.

—The teachings of the prophet are often reduced to learning by rote rather than used in dynamic application. A robot-like atmosphere is being created as people share memorized platitudes rather than insights born from the furnace of intimate experience.

"My observations lead me to conclude that this community has a specific life-span. Adam Hawthorn continually states that individuals must understand his teachings in their own way and eventually re-create the forms in which they are lived out."

Hank Bracken dropped the papers on his desk and shook his head.

"She can't handle this by herself! I'm gonna send backup."

"What if you just pull her out of there?" Jimmy asked in a shaky voice, daring to advise his moody supervisor.

"That's a stupid idea, Maloney! She's taken root, like we say, and it would look all the more suspicious if we yank her outta there now. But I'll tell you what. If she gets into trouble, I'm gonna hold you responsible!"

"Me?"

"Yeah, you! You got her into this."

"I just showed . . . "

"Don't justify yourself! Take some responsibility. In fact, I'll give it to you. If things get outta control, your head rolls!"

Jimmy felt his body turn clammy. He could never have imagined that his discovery of this story would lead to this. Why didn't he just keep his mouth shut and live out his career quietly in his dark cubicle? Why did he try to go beyond the call of duty?

Then a strange thought appeared in his turbulent mind: maybe he never had a choice in the matter!

* * *

Every evening, people gathered in small groups and spoke eagerly late into the night. Jeremy and Lynn, Andrew and Michelle often missed a whole night's rest. The topic invariably came back to the identity of the prophet.

"Jeremy, you knew him years ago in seminary, is that right?" Michelle asked.

"I knew him as much as anybody could know him. He was not very communicative."

"Does anybody know where he comes from?"

"No. I believe it was Dr. Hogrogian who told me that he had been orphaned at a young age and grew up rather wild. I guess his grandfather took care of him for a short time. He was apparently a saintly man. Then Adam entered a spiritual journey that took him all over the world. There's evidence that he was in a monastery for some time, in ashrams, and some esoteric circles."

"The strangest tale of all was from old Stargazer, the Indian mystic," Lynn said with a flutter of emotion. "The moment he met Adam he called him the Visitor, as though he wasn't even from this planet."

"Some of us would have agreed with that conclusion," Jeremy said jokingly.

"Stargazer wasn't kidding. He seemed to recognize in him something different and other-worldly that came from some other dimension. There's no telling how he acquired that capacity."

"Would it be wrong to ask him about his background?" Michelle asked, prying as subtly as possible.

"I think so," Lynn answered. "I believe there's a lot of personal tragedy there, and to the best of my knowledge, he refers to his past as simply fodder for who he is now. In a sense, it's irrelevant."

"But it isn't!" Michelle insisted. "People have to have some sort of credentials for what they do."

"Do they?" Jeremy responded. "I'm afraid they don't offer degrees for prophets and healers. Not in this society. In fact, if someone does have a degree, you can be pretty sure that he doesn't qualify for those kinds of roles."

"You want to know the strangest story I ever heard about him?" Lynn asked. "It was told to me by an old woman who apparently had known him sometime in his past. She'd given him shelter when he had no home at all and first appeared in this part of the country. She told me that he never had any parents. According to her, he was actually found in a garbage dump where he'd been abandoned. The person who found him kept him as her own for a time. She was a homeless woman. One day he was taken away from her and put into foster homes."

"Are you telling me there are no birth certificates on him, no hospital records, nothing?" Michelle wondered with a slight tremor.

"Nope."

"Someone got hold of his background papers," Jeremy remembered, "from the admissions office. We were curious back then also. If I'm not mistaken, my friend who went through his files reported that they were completely blank from age eighteen back. No reference to high schools, elementary schools, no legal guardians."

"What do you make of that?" Michelle asked, trying to figure out the puzzle.

"He's a mysterious man indeed," Lynn stated.

"But he is a human being, right?" Andrew asked in an uncertain voice. "What else could he be?"

"He's a human being all right," Jeremy replied. "But only on the outside. On the inside, he lives in another world. No doubt about that."

"Do you think it's possible for ordinary humans to achieve what he has?" Andrew asked again.

"Only with the greatest of efforts and self-sacrifice," Jeremy said. "That's the real difference between us and him. He went all the way."

They sat in silence for a time, sipping tea and pondering the strange mystery of the man they all loved.

"Do you think he is the one that was announced by the great religions and the visionaries down through the ages?" Andrew whispered in wonderment.

"What do you mean?" Michelle asked, embarrassed to reveal her ignorance.

Lynn turned to her. "Before his death, the Buddha spoke of one who was to come at the end of time whom he named Maitreya. In Hinduism, there is the prophecy of the appearance of the avatar Kalki, and Saoshyant of the Zoastrian Vedas. Nostradamus foretold of 'the Awaited One' and the seer de Sabato spoke of 'a mysterious man.' In his trances, Edgar Cayce perceived a 'World Unifier' and Indonesian prophets talk of the 'Spiritual King to come.'

"The Moslems believe that Muntazar is coming at the end of time. Other texts talk of a 'Man of Power,' Jeremy added.

"In the Bhagavad Gita, Lord Krishna says 'I will come to this world, as in ages past,'" Andrew contributed excitedly. "Central Asia has the tale of 'White Burkhan' who will bring spiritual rebirth. Mahayana Buddhism teaches of the appearance of enlightened beings."

Lynn leaned forward and looked at her friends intently. "But there's something different in what Adam is saying. All of these prophets were said to appear after the devastation has taken place. Adam says that he comes as a messenger just prior to the destruction."

"So there is one to come after him?" Andrew wondered.

"He told me something very strange," Michelle ventured timidly, knowing she was among people who were far more knowledgeable on this subject. "He told me that there would be help from many sources some day."

"What are you suggesting?" Andrew asked.

"Maybe all of those teachers will come back. Rather than being references to one single individual, they might be visions of separate enlightened ones. Maybe a number of them will return!"

The companions spoke late into the night, tossing about theories and intuitions regarding the mysterious whirlwind in which their lives were caught up. Michelle was no longer there as a Federation agent, but as a human being vitally concerned about meaning and purpose in the light of the prophet's appearance. She sensed that not even the Federation would be able to hold the world together when the time finally came for the final collapse of civilization.

* * *

Jeremy had purchased a small television set, although he knew Adam would frown on any intrusion of the manufactured culture into their community. But he felt it necessary to keep an eye on world news.

One evening, after a particularly hard day's work, he and Lynn rested in their little cottage. Too tired to read, he turned on the box that would connect them to the world. A miniature satellite dish linked them with hundreds of channels.

Jeremy switched channels mechanically, his arm around Lynn. Both of them were half-asleep. It was the usual lineup of merchants selling their wares and silly entertainment that had numbed the minds of humanity for close to a century. They were pleased that they had long ago dropped the habit of wasting their lives away staring passively at the screen.

Lynn's eyes widened and she was suddenly wide awake.

"Go back to that channel!"

Jeremy pressed the buttons on the remote control. Two men were sitting in a studio set surrounded by potted plants, talking to each other. The host was some well-known personality whose name they had now forgotten.

"So you're saying, Reverend Morgan, that this man's messiah-like claims are to be completely disregarded."

A close-up of Bob Morgan filled the screen. He was perfectly coiffed and with his carefully oiled personality, he was well-suited for the role of playing to an audience that could be easily manipulated.

"Well, Dan, I don't know what exactly he claims to be. He's one of those sly ones who makes sure he doesn't say the wrong thing so that he won't be caught. But we've gotten word that he's gone from this healing business to forecasting, would you believe, the end of the world."

"Again?" the host said mockingly. "Haven't we gotten past that one?"

"You would think that humanity would have matured beyond that old myth," Morgan said with a sarcastic grin. "But apparently not. Here we are, the most highly advanced civilization ever on this planet, and we still have to deal with eccentric solitaries full of gloom and doom. I'll tell you what I hate about it most, Dan," Morgan said as he leaned forward, playing to the camera. "Men like Adam Hawthorn take hope away from people. They tell them there's nothing to look forward to, that they have to become what they're not or else, and people just can't do that. It disturbs the little lives they've managed to carve out for themselves. Now where's the good in that, I ask you?"

A two-shot of the men came on the screen.

"So you don't feel there is any need to be concerned about this kind of continued insistence on some global catastrophe?"

"Of course not!" Morgan said adamantly. "Our scholars have proven that biblical prophecy is symbolic, related to other times and places. It's a mistake to take them literally. Besides, every time they are taken that way, the foretellers of the apocalypse are proven wrong. As you know, we reached a climax at the turn of the century with people coming out of the woodwork talking about the end times. And here we are today, doing just fine. I'd say better than ever, thanks to the World Federation and continued technological improvements. We're going up, not down."

"Have you heard any particular prophesies from this man? I don't think I've read anything about that."

"My sources tell me that he not only claims to be a prophet, but actually the final prophet. The last one before some mammoth catastrophe that will end history as we know it. How about that for an ego trip, eh? The man's dangerous, as I've stated repeatedly."

"Does he offer any evidence for his claim?"

"Just the usual things, with his so-called powers of healing and the influence he has on people. But I knew him when he was just an ordinary man and I had no reason to believe that he was anybody special. Unusual perhaps, but no different than you and I. How he went from a seminary student to the final prophet of the age, I'll never know."

"He didn't speak of anything like that in the days when you knew him?"

"He didn't speak, period. He was the quietest minister I've ever seen. As you know, in our profession that's the wrong personality attribute to have."

"So what do you think ought to be done with him?"

"If you want to know the truth, I think the Federation should arrest him for disturbing the peace and the sanity of gullible people. That community of his has all the signs of a cult in the making. I understand that reporters can't even get on the property. I know that some of our local pastors have tried and they've been barred. That tells you right there that we're dealing with another fringe group like the ones that were around fifty years ago. I thought people were better educated now, but apparently not. That kind of thing's always under the surface."

"Well, we're out of time. Thank you for sharing your thoughts, Reverend Robert Morgan. Next week, our program will . . . "

Jeremy pressed the off button and the screen went dark. They sat in silence for a moment.

"Are we gullible, Lynn?" Jeremy asked, half-seriously.

"There's nothing fake about Adam Hawthorn."

"That's true, but where's all this headed? This is no way to create a future for the baby we want to have some day."

"No it isn't," she said as she took his hand. "But I don't think we have any choice. Something of great importance is taking place and we can't just walk away from it to seek security in the world out there. We'd end up being worse off than living with the shifting sands of this situation."

He kissed her gently on the forehead. Their love surfaced, chasing away all fears and uncertainties. He hugged her and they slipped under the covers.

* * *

Andrew had recruited a small army of vigorous men and women whose devotion to the prophet was unquestioned and who were also capable of defending themselves. He posted them in guard houses around the property where they kept a twenty-four hour watch. Though Adam had not given his approval for this decision, and would probably have rejected the idea, Andrew and Jeremy felt strongly that there had to be some protection from the invasion of the outside world.

Not only were they concerned about the world media creating disruption in their little world, but they also wanted to gain some control over the flood of people entering the compound. This was a virtually impossible task, but they had to attempt it. The least they could do was to identify the new visitors in order to know who was among them. They had no doubts that undercover agents and other individuals with harmful intentions were infiltrating their community. Without turning Renouveau into a military camp, they did their best to keep watch over the crowds seeking access to the prophet.

On a peaceful Wednesday morning in spring, along with a large crowd of the sick, the curious and the seeking, Peggy Bonnot appeared in the community. She had left behind her fake hair color and facial makeup. Like a method actress of the past, she had managed to transform herself into the appearance of another bewildered and simple soul searching for meaning. Acting was a youthful fantasy of hers that she had been forced to leave behind early on. The opportunity to employ that skill again was a great fringe benefit in this business transaction.

She had been informed of the identity of another undercover agent already present on sight and knew who to contact for any assistance. She saw Adam on the very first morning as he addressed the new batch of people that she had come in with. Some fifty people stood or sat in a large, newly constructed room whose walls had not yet gone up.

Adam stood on a platform, speaking into a microphone. His soft voice reverberated through large speakers mounted in half a dozen places twenty-five feet over the listeners.

"Those of you who have come here to find healing, either physical or spiritual, must begin by opening your minds to the possibility of new life. Wherever you come from, whatever your experience has been, you are offered the chance for renewal by the very fact that you are here now.

"These words are not platitudes. You might remember the ancient saying: "Come to me, all who are weary . . . " This call is issued once again. The heart of the cosmos is reaching out to you, its children. You can find cleansing, new life, true joy and peace. The cost is not small, however. It is not a monetary cost. That would be too easy. It is a decisive dedication to a new relationship to reality.

"You are not merely your bodies, you are spiritual beings embedded in matter for a special cosmic purpose. You are not functionaries of the state or consumers in the marketplace. You are children of the universe and you have an important role to play on a scale that your mind cannot comprehend. Each of you has the birthright to live in peace, contentment and fulfillment through the right use of the gifts which have been provided to you by the sacred forces that created you.

"Nothing was given to you to be used for petty, selfish purposes. You are not your own. And it is only through transcendence of your self-centered mindset that you will enter into the freedom and wholeness that are the treasures you were meant to find in this life."

While others listened in awe, Peggy did her best to conceal her disdain and mockery of such words. She had so abandoned her authentic self that there was hardly anything left of it. And the constant desecration of her body buried her soul deeper in some void within her. Barren emptiness took the place of her spirit now. However, she found herself uncomfortable trying to look at this intense, mystical man as a potential client. There seemed to be an invisible shield around him that kept him immune to the sexual energy of others. He lived in another dimension where bodily lust was utterly unknown. When he looked at people, he saw the essence of their being, not the contours of their flesh. Despite her darkened mind, she recognized that rare element of his nature on an instinctive level. The awareness that told her of men's attraction to her picked up on this unusual characteristic and knew that it would find no response, even if she were to stand before him naked in all her voluptuousness.

At that very moment, his eyes fell upon her. Though they soon moved on to someone else, she felt an electric charge shoot through her heart. The way he looked at her brought forth a remembrance of herself as a little girl, as though he had torn through the wretchedness and perversity of her adulthood and gone directly to the lost child whom she still was in her essential being. The child whose father had abandoned her and left her with a hatred and need for men that had led her on this path of self-destruction.

The sensation was fleeting but overwhelming. Her mouth went dry, and for a brief moment, her arrogant attitude fell from her and shattered like a plate-glass window. The vulnerability that was left exposed sent shivers of terror through her, and she quickly attempted to recompose herself and hide behind the persona she had worked so hard to create. No question about it, she would not even attempt to approach this man. She left the room ahead of the others, unable to bear the experience that had so shaken her. She feared that he would look at her again and cause it to return. Peggy felt sick to her stomach, as though her own being rebelled against the betrayal of the child she had once been. She walked along the path in a daze, doing her best to get hold of the self with which she was familiar and comfortable.

A middle-aged man suddenly came up to her.

"What the hell are you doing?"

She looked at him, surprised.

"What?"

"I know who you are and you should know who I am. Why aren't you in there?"

"You're an agent."

"That's right. Try not to be too obvious about it."

She looked him over. He was stocky and athletic like most security agents, and his ragged clothing couldn't hide from her the military training that he had undergone.

"Your job is to help me, mister, not to boss me around," she said angrily. "I don't work for you."

The agent repressed a violent reaction to her disrespectful words. He realized that she spoke the truth. He wasn't used to dealing with her kind and resented being soiled by having to support her. Oddly enough, it was only on a case dealing with religious people that he had to work with a prostitute. It was by no means part of the Federation's methods.

"I need you to point out to me who Andrew Bradshaw is. He's the guy I'm gonna deal with," she demanded in her regal way.

"Bradshaw's in the kitchen at the mission house, right down the road on your left. He's tall and bony with short dark hair."

She walked off without thanking him. He watched her move down the path. Even in jeans and a sweatshirt she exuded sensuality. He shook his head at the tactics being employed on this case. But he was a man whose religion was following orders, and he thought no more about it.

Peggy walked up the steps of the mission house, making her way through crowds of people gathered to eat their meal—a strange blend of the desperately poor and people from all parts of the world looking for God. She elbowed people to get through and finally made her way to the kitchen. She came upon another dense crowd of people preparing food and working on huge stacks of dishes. Some sang in foreign languages, others chatted softly. At the far end, she easily caught sight of Andrew who stood head and shoulders over most of the people there. He was silently spraying hot water on used plates, strangely concentrating on inner thoughts undoubtedly stimulated by the prophet's teachings.

She made her way to his side.

"Hi! Are you Andrew?"

He turned to her in surprise, as most people had no idea of his name.

"I am. Who are you?"

She did her best not to act too coy in this first encounter, even though that was her standard procedure.

"I'm Marsha. I just got here and I'm ready to go to work."

"There are some potatoes to be pealed over there."

"I've got all kinds of food allergies. I'd rather do the dishes."

"Okay. Grab that sponge and join me. What brings you here?"

"Same as everybody else, I guess."

"Everyone's got their own purpose."

"I'm looking for . . . " she hesitated, trying to come up with something, "myself."

"Aren't we all," he answered pensively.

"How long have you been here?" she asked, subtly pressing her body against his as they worked side by side.

"From the beginning . . . six months. Feels more like six years."

"You're one of the originals?"

"So to speak. I was here when there was nobody but me in the kitchen."

"Is that right?" she said, putting on her most admiring face. He looked at her and received her wide-eyed "you're so wonderful" look square between the eyes. He turned away, unsettled by her feminine wiles. She knew she had her man.

* * *

Within forty-eight hours, Peggy's professional skills had succeeded. It was midnight and she was lying in bed next to Andrew. His lack of experience with women made him an easy prey and she had quickly found the way to excite his passions to the point of thoroughly confusing his mind. But when the moment came and she was in his room naked, something changed. Her lovemaking had no love in it. By the time he turned away from her, he felt more empty and alone than ever. Her flirting skills and his - attraction to her had cheated him. When all was said and done and there was no more mystery, the dehumanizing element of loveless sex revealed the meaningless illusion of the game. It wasn't anything like what he had hoped it would be. It was a mechanical act that led nowhere, except to the desecration of their bodies and the reduction of a sacred act to animal behavior.

Even Peggy had not enjoyed herself. It was all rather routine to her. The exciting part was the twenty thousand dollars she had just made. It was like taking candy from a baby. The hidden mini camera was set in her purse on a table near the bed and had captured the brief but fatal mistake.

Andrew felt terribly ashamed at having let himself fall victim to his lust so soon after finding the spiritual reality he had been seeking for so long. In fact, that had been a part of what had fooled him. His guard was down. The heightened energy of the monumental event in which he was centrally involved had led him to believe that he was on the right track and that nothing could go wrong now. But all it took was the age-old trick to pull the rug out from under him. Now that he had satisfied his baser nature, he felt that he had betrayed not only the prophet and the spiritual forces involved in this historic event, but most of all, himself.

One moment of inattention and all that he most cherished was forgotten for a pleasure that could not compare to the self-respect that he had just lost. Peggy felt sorry for the poor fool who had fallen into her trap without any hesitation. When she discovered how wealthy he was, she thought perhaps there was more money to be made in this brief encounter. He might be naive enough to fall madly in love with her and become her sugar daddy. But when she saw the utter simplicity of the life-style he lived in and the virtually barren place he called home, she realized that she was dealing with someone who didn't know how to make good use of his financial luck.

In many ways, he was her opposite—quiet and retiring while she was a lavish exhibitionist. It was that very difference that made him attractive to her in some small way. She had trained herself not to have any interest in her clients, but this one was different in that he neither paid for it nor sought it out. Like a schoolboy, he had been caught up in her charm and helplessly manipulated. All she had to do now was turn in the film which would generate the still pictures to be published in newspapers across the world. Her mission was accomplished. She was already spending the money in her head while lying next to her victim.

Andrew got up and began to dress. She turned to him, surprised that he was already leaving her side.

"Don't you want to linger a bit?"

"What for?"

"We can talk. Get to know each other."

She was still making use of her acting abilities.

"I don't see the point."

"Who knows, maybe you'll fall in love with me."

He stopped and looked over at her. "You don't mean that, do you? This is just a cheap thrill for you."

"What makes you say that?" she asked, concerned that he had

picked up on something.

"I could tell that there was no affection when I held you in my arms."

"You could? Then why did you go through with it?"

"I don't know," he answered, looking away in shame.

Something deep within her sank into the morass of unhappiness which was secretly suffocating her spirit. A part of her wanted to hear him say that he cared about her in some way other than the usual animal attraction. But it was not meant to happen, and she was doomed to a life without such an encounter. She had to accept it once again.

"You'll have to get home. I'll be working in a couple hours. There might be some people coming by. I don't want them to see you leaving."

"You're ashamed of me, are you?"

He didn't answer as he finished dressing.

"If you have to work in a little while, why don't you come back to bed?"

"I don't think I can sleep."

She threw off the covers and started dressing angrily. She didn't like it when people were ashamed of being with her. The least they could do was to wait until they were out of her presence to express it. Her mind returned to the twenty thousand dollars that awaited her. They made her feel better.

"Where are you staying?"

"They gave me a place in building number four."

"Listen," Andrew said gently. "I don't mean to insult you. It's just that this hasn't happened to me in years. I didn't want it to be this way. I didn't mean to hurt you."

"I'm not hurt, you can be sure of that."

"One night stands are not unusual for you?"

She turned to him with glaring eyes. "Like you said, it was a cheap thrill."

"I apologize if I hurt your feelings . . . "

"Shut up already," she shouted.

Peggy finished dressing, grabbed her purse and left the room. Andrew stood in the shadows, a inexplicable sense of impending doom hanging over him.

CHAPTER 21

The prophet spent many hours with the people who came to him. They were like starving waifs, many of whom had been longing for such knowledge for a lifetime. Those who had managed to find out-of-print books on the deep matters of the human spirit were not satisfied with mere head knowledge. They thirsted for direct communication with someone who lived and breathed regenerating wisdom.

Wisdom fell from the prophet's soul as life-giving rain on parched earth. When he spoke, even the birds seemed to quiet down in the trees. The people listened with intense concentration, breathlessly absorbing the meaning of his words. His words were simple, genuine, personal, and most of all—transforming.

It was a cool day in March, and the people who had come to find new life in this community sat outside in the grass under the trees listening to the last prophet to come in this age.

"Modern society has virtually eradicated sacred spaces that humans of all times and places needed for their reintegration, for their evolution, for their sanity.

"The age of materialism and rigid rationalism has rejected humanity's natural inclinations toward things spiritual and crushed its desire for those experiences. Instead, we are served up fantasies from the world of electronic communication that masquerade as reflections of reality.

"Even our places of worship have been reduced to social gatherings whose superficial activities complete the process of alienating the soul from its true home.

"In previous ages, there were esoteric schools where the architects of cathedrals learned of the relationship between space and human experience of the sacred. Sanctuaries were designed to create the maximum impact on every individual, regardless of education or religious knowledge. Even brutish warriors were humbled upon entering these buildings that grabbed hold of the deeper layers of human consciousness and eloquently spoke of the vast dimensions of reality. From the deep silence, high vaulted ceilings, and effects of color and light came a harmony that was - unmistakable. Human arrogance had to bow down before this vivid witness to something greater than itself.

"These same effects are found in Asian temples, in Hindu ashrams, in mosques and synagogues. They are also found in the heart of undisturbed Nature. Human beings learned to capture and focus aspects of these numinous qualities almost from the beginning of our species—the great pyramids, Stonehenge, the dolmens of ancient Gaul. Native Americans knew all about sacred space and communed with the invisible powers of the Great Spirit from the Black Hills to the deserts of Arizona.

"Energy fields within the earth identify specific locations of special power. We are such minuscule creatures on such a colossal backdrop of greater forces that we will find no end to the mysteries around us.

"But the most important location of sacred space is not found in the plains of Salsbury or in the decaying monuments of the past. The most powerful sacred space of all is the human soul. It is there that we can become aware of and align with the very Source of life in the universe."

Adam stopped for a moment and looked at the hundreds of people staring back at him. He wanted them to understand what lay beyond the words coming from his mouth.

"We are seeking to create a sacred space here at Renouveau that can assist in each one's awakening.

"When several people gather together to access these intimate yet universal depths within them, then real power is encountered. The joining together of human consciousness in an effort to encounter the sacred is one of the fundamental purposes of human existence in the cosmos. We have forgotten this utterly and completely.

"Because we are so dependent on our senses, we need all the help we can get from our surroundings. Even though your kitchen could become sacred space in a moment of higher consciousness or of profound communing with another person, it is important to have and go to places that are especially set aside for these efforts. That, of course, is what a church or temple is meant to be. But the tragic superficiality of modern consciousness has turned most places of worship into empty spaces rather than sacred spaces."

Adam raised his hand and pointed at the decorations scattered about, brought from dozens of different cultures and religions.

"If institutional religion has lost the ability to provide it for us, then we must use our creativity and yearning to reconstruct such spaces. They are the cornerstone to finding our true selves along with the purpose and meaning of our existence."

Adam was asked to say a word on a subject that was especially obscure and confusing to the children of the twenty-first century.

"The act of prayer has often been misunderstood and distorted into what it is not. It is generally reduced to a grocery list of needs and wants presented in times of trouble to some higher power that may or may not respond.

"Notice that in this kind of behavior, there is no concept of change of self or of deeper insight into reality.

"We are left with the impotence of an individual calling out to a distant, unknown entity. All religions have been carriers of this kind of prayer, from the primitive tribal rite to the kneeling believer in a Gothic cathedral.

"The great mystics, saints, and teachers of all traditions reveal in their own lives that prayer is ultimately a uniting of human consciousness with a vaster life that they called divine, the Source of our existence.

"For the greatest spiritual visionaries, prayer merges with the very act of breathing. It becomes moment to moment awareness. Consciousness of being alive becomes intense receptivity to a higher reality.

"Each of you can experience moments of illumination where a mysterious joy or gratitude floods your heart. We are then lifted out of the mundane day-to-day consciousness which we mistakenly take for reality and experience a freedom, peace, and a capacity to love that transcends our ordinary inclinations."

He stopped to let his companions absorb this revelation. If any one of them could make those words live in his or her full being— body, soul, and spirit—they would find the key to all the mysteries contained within them.

"The transforming power of prayer deals with a more attuned awareness, an exalted consciousness of the present moment, and a liberation from the psychological baggage that blocks out our true identity. Consciousness is energy, and with a little observation of ourselves, we can easily notice the difference in quality in our various states.

"Notice what happens to you in the presence of beauty and deep stillness: you're standing in a wooded area blanketed with freshly fallen snow, staring at an ice-covered creek, listening to the deep silence.

"Notice the lightness in your heart and mind, and the feeling of well-being that takes over from the usual traffic jam of your thoughts and worries.

"We are generally entirely unconscious of our inner state, of the energy circulating within us and the quality of our awareness of the outside world. These energies are like vibrations or colors that are constantly shifting and filtering our experience of reality.

"Prayer stabilizes and focuses these energies, thereby changing their quality. Once we get past the natural urge to ask for help, we can become receptive to and even mirror a higher state of existence. This effort is marked by a warming of the heart, a refreshing stillness of mind, and a refinement of our energies to the point where our bodies no longer weigh us down.

"Energy and higher vibration metamorphosize into relationship and union. This quality of receptivity and attention takes us to the threshold of the true purpose of prayer—the experience of that mystery humanity has called the Sacred. We are then in touch with an expanded consciousness that transcends time and space. It is then that "miracles" can happen: a loving thought directed toward a sick friend that generates healing, an adjustment of one's fundamental attitude to life, an awakening to new understanding."

Adam paused again and looked at the tree branches swaying gently in the breeze.

"We learn in such moments that we must become good stewards of our energies for they are not isolated from the ocean of Spirit that fills the universe. It is possible to find peace in the midst of the storms of confusion and torment!

"We can and must—because it is our birthright—discover the higher altitudes that fill us with strength and hope and wisdom. There is a magnetic power to these states. They call to us. Our true nature is found in these higher levels of consciousness where light replaces darkness and union melts down separation.

"Then our prayer becomes life-giving, not just for ourselves but for all things because they are influenced in one way or another by the energies that each one emits. We can generate higher or lower frequencies and affect someone unaware far away. Each of you affects the world far more than you realize. That, in fact, is why we have come to this time of transition.

"The world is not merely the three dimensional experience entering our five senses. On the subatomic level of reality, we are all connected and the mysteries of telepathy and intuitive perception are just the tip of the iceberg.

"Quantum physics tells us that the center of the expansion of the universe is everywhere. We are infinitely more than we can conceptualize ourselves to be, and our capacity for good is virtually unlimited. Prayer is the means of insuring that we become positive forces grounded in the goodness of the transcendent spheres from which we come."

"Talk to us of love," someone asked breathlessly.

Adam took in a deep breath and sat silently for a moment. He looked upon the motley group with great compassion. They were so lost and helpless, broken pieces of a society that had failed them in every way.

"Most often, the use of that word is made in a very self-centered context. Love is generally mixed up with what I need, what I want, what makes me feel good. This is not the kind of love that will fulfill a human life. In fact, this is not love at all. It may be desire, attraction, or a passing feeling, but it is not love. It is only gratified self-love.

"The love that transforms human life is seen most dramatically in an ancient image: the crucifixion. Here we are faced with the radical giving of self for the sake of others. Here we see a picture of such transcendence of the human ego that its power is said to overcome death itself. And what is the central characteristic of this image that has shaken humanity to its core? Not good feeling or sweet intentions, but all-consuming sacrifice of self-interest.

"This image of love which has changed the course of world history is not one of gruesome masochistic martyrdom. For the people who first responded to this event, it was a sign of victory— the overcoming of darkness, particularly the darkness within. Two thousand years later, this mighty paradox of victory in sacrifice is still one of the great mysteries of the cosmos.

"It's the kind of mystery that will transform the life of the one who is informed by its wisdom. This expression of love tells us that a certain kind of death to self gives rise to a vast life. Such an idea will always be socially unacceptable, but is so now more than ever, when self-gratification is sanctified as self-esteem, freedom and even spiritual activity.

"This other view tells us that the way of self-transcendence is the breakthrough to enlightenment and true fulfillment. Yet by its very nature, it defies all self-centered motivation. Only those who consciously choose to die to their self-interest will enter into this mystery and discover a depth of meaning, purpose and connectedness entirely unknown to others.

"Clearly, such a manifestation of love reveals a whole new dimension to the word. Imagine the power of will that must be harnessed in order to overcome all the pettiness that makes up our nature. That kind of selfless love anchors us irretrievably in a way of life that is completely at odds with everything our society bows before.

"But our disintegrating civilization is neurotically focused on personal satisfaction at all cost. Even the concept of love has been perverted into a narcissistic pleasure which can be switched on and off according to whatever whim takes over. Divorce rates top seventy percent of all marriages, children by the millions are growing up without guidance, the elderly are warehoused like discarded furniture, and sex is a primary marketing tool in the international corporate world. So much for the idea of love in our time.

"Who has the strength of character to love another for richer or poorer, in sickness and health—or in other words—come hell or high water? Where are the heroic spirits of mercy and goodness giving themselves for the sake of others?

"Not in our national magazines or on world television. But they are out there, unheralded, disdained, forgotten. Such rejection doesn't matter to them because they walk the narrow and difficult path of love which is an all or nothing proposition. They have left comfort, vanity, and need for approval far behind.

"You won't hear many songs describing that kind of love. But it is the hope of humanity nonetheless. Without such strong and sacrificial love we are doomed to shallow, restless lives, forever seeking something we cannot define. The human spirit is designed with the capacity of the total gift of self in the name of an unconditional Love. That is our true nobility and purpose."

The people sat around Adam, intensely attentive, aware that what they were hearing was a matter of life and death, not only for themselves, but for the future of the race.

* * *

It was a broiling day across the Southwestern desert, even though spring had yet to give way to summer. The change in weather patterns over the last fifty years had thrown everything off kilter. Another dust bowl had arisen across the Southern states as a result of relentless droughts, while in other parts of the country, floods had devastated vast areas of farmlands. The West was torn apart by violent earthquakes and the East was plagued with polluted tides and hurricanes. The whole world was threatened by damaged ozone. Chaos was everywhere and had risen to a great crescendo across the world. It was rumored in the scientific community that the earth was about to shift its axis and that even greater natural calamities were at hand.

Here in the desert sands, the vistas of emptiness and their silence remained the same. For thousands of years this wilderness was held sacred by Native Americans. They recognized the presence of a special power in its very unfriendliness toward human life. The desert witnessed to a stability that could not be found anywhere else. There was something primeval about this wasteland that gave it the capacity to survive the vortex of madness into which the world was collapsing.

Stargazer climbed to the top of a cliff overlooking the ocean of sun, cactus and tumbleweed. He had come here since his youth when he was taught how to absorb the unique energies of this sacred space. This day, however, was different. He'd had a premonition in a dream several nights before that he was to receive a message from this mysterious spot.

He came to the top of the cliff. A strong wind was howling through the crags like an angry, restless wanderer. The old elder looked out at the limitless horizon surrounding him on all sides. He contemplated the great expanse and the powerful peace that hovered over it. It had been too long since he had last come to this place.

He emptied his mind of all thoughts and tuned himself to the secrets of the world around him. His long locks of grey hair shivered in the whistling breeze. His rugged features seemed to unite with the rocks that rose up about him in a similar stillness and meditative pose.

An eagle cried overhead. The old Indian's eyes opened wide. He came out of the abyss of his reflection. The great bird's echoing scream was a sound held in great reverence by his people. This day it spoke to him of becoming prepared and braced for an intrusion from the spirit world. He looked about, expecting to see an omen manifest before him.

Out of nowhere, a large feather danced gracefully down to his feet. With eyes that few others possessed, he perceived the riddle. The feather was that of a hawk, which his tribe wore in battle in ancient times. He knew what this meant—be ready for combat. He quieted himself again to make room for the spirit to speak to him.

An animal suddenly slithered out of a cave and hurried down the path. It was a wildcat carrying stolen food, escaping before the deadly owner's return. Stargazer understood that something underhanded was afoot. In the distant haze of heat layering the air with odd undulating waves, he thought he saw the silhouette of a man walking toward him. His feet were not touching the ground. He wasn't sure whether this was a vision or an actual event.

He focused his gaze, but the image vanished, leaving the desert to its hollow void.

A word escaped his lips. "The Visitor!"

It all came together. He realized that what he'd been given to see were signs that the prophet was in trouble. He looked across the horizon to the North. A black mountain of angry clouds was moving toward him, bringing deadly lightning and tornados in its wake. The menacing image of devastation spoke to him of the legends of his people concerning the future.

A voice, with the resonance and insistence of a war drum, beat in his head as though the coming thunder had penetrated his soul.

"The Fourth World shall end soon, and the Fifth World will begin. This the elders everywhere know. The Signs over many years have been fulfilled, and few are left.

"This is the First Sign: white-skinned men will come to our lands and take them from us, striking their enemies with thunder. The Second Sign: spinning wheels of wood filled with voices will overrun our lands. Third Sign: a strange beast, like the buffalo, with great horns will cover the land in great numbers. The Fourth Sign: snakes of iron will cross the land. The Fifth Sign: a giant spider's web will hang over the prairies. The Six Sign: rivers of stone that make pictures in the sun will cover the land. The Seventh Sign: the sea will turn black and much death will come from it. The Eighth Sign: many youths with long hair like our people of old will come to the tribes and learn their ways.

"The Ninth and Last Sign: a dwelling place in heaven, above the earth, will appear as a blue star and fall with a great roar. Then the ceremonies of our people will end. Then the world will shake, and man will war with those who brought the first flame of wisdom. Towers of smoke and fire will reach the sky. Then Pahana—the lost white brother bearing the missing piece of the sacred tablets—will return. With him will come the dawn of the Fifth World. The seeds of Pahana's wisdom will blossom in the hearts of those chosen to rebuild. Then will come the Emergence of the new world."

The voice died away with the breeze and the heavy desert

silence returned. Stargazer trembled violently as the experience left his body. He was the most renowned visionary in the entire Southwest and his mind was highly skilled at reading omens and signs. He understood that the sign of the scurrying animal juxtaposed with his remembrance of Adam had special significance. He realized that not only was the prophet under attack by persons as sneaky as the wildcat, but that his task had something to do with the prophecies of his people and the final breakdown of this age.

The warrior spirits of his people would finally be avenged when the civilization that crushed them was itself torn to shreds. Perhaps there was justice after all in this mighty universe. He was sure of one thing, however. There could be no justice for the prophet. Too many dark forces were surrounding him.

* * *

Renouveau was thriving on a constant flow of people. A dozen new buildings now covered the barren fields and gave shape to the desolate landscape. The community seemed to have a life of its own. The creativity released by exposure to the prophet's wisdom was generating an outpouring of variations on the theme of renewal. Some brought their gardening skills to create color and life in the monotonous environment. Trees were planted along the new roads winding through the budding town. A sculptor had donated a magnificent bronze statue of a mythic figure from antiquity who looked down upon the community with benevolence and encouragement.

The awakening of the spirit among the people who flocked to this place expressed itself in all the colors of humanity's cultures. African designs, Native American dream-catchers, giant Christian crosses surrounded with rose bushes, Arabic symbols—and most beautiful of all, children of all nationalities playing together.

Spring was in the air. The budding trees reflected the blossoming life of the community. As quickly as the new leaves came forth, so was this little oasis of renewed humanity arising with zeal and hope for a better future. People were now flocking to Renouveau no longer in search of a healer, but of a mighty teacher and prophet. Word was spreading that the spiritual healing power of the prophet was only a sign of a deeper power: his consciousness of spiritual reality and his ability to link it with the material world. Rumors were rushing about the globe through all forms of media and word of mouth that his mission was one of great magnitude and somehow related to the onset of apocalyptic events.

People around the world had left those fears behind after the birth of the twenty-first century which belied all the tales of doom that were said to come in its wake. They had settled into a precarious but acceptable existence. The fact that the planet continued to deteriorate psychically and physically did not seem to give them cause for worry. But here was a man who, once again, was stirring the primeval terror that an end was coming.

Among the guests at Renouveau were well-known writers and philosophers, and other spiritual leaders who felt the need to meet this special man.

On this spring day, the community was electrified by the appearance of a guru from India, known around the world for his genuine wisdom and beauty of soul. Swami Parasawna was in his nineties, but his lifetime of meditation had kept him extraordinarily young. Not a wrinkle creased his smooth bronze skin. His white beard, youthful face, and crystal-clear eyes were an amazing sight and proof that a spiritual world was carried within the walls of matter.

He appeared at Renouveau unannounced with an entourage of devotees. The first person to greet them was Jeremy, who happened to be mending fences at the entrance of the property. He immediately recognized the famous face and hurried over to the people getting out of the cars. At first, the entourage kept him away from the venerable old man, but upon telling them that he was Adam's close associate, they allowed him to greet their leader.

"Namaste," the swami whispered gently with a sweet smile as he brought his hands together and bowed his head before Jeremy.

Jeremy returned the greeting with great joy, hoping that perhaps Adam was going to bring together all the great enlightened beings of the planet and create a society whose allegiance would be only to the spiritual good. Such a new force in the world could change everything.

He led them to Adam's private conference room and went ahead of them to inform the prophet of his special guest. Adam stepped into the room to encounter the swami. Everyone disappeared from the awareness of the two men as they looked at each other with mystical recognition. This time the swami did not greet him in the traditional fashion, but took his hands and said, "My brother!"

Adam acknowledged the affection of the elderly wiseman. The two men stepped into another room to be alone. Jeremy sat with the swami's entourage for two hours, silently waiting for them to reappear. He tried to imagine the nature of their conversation and the incredible insights they were sharing for their ears only. He was disappointed at being left out of such an event, but he had the humility to recognize that on the spiritual summits of human consciousness, the air was rarified and not accessible to ordinary mortals.

Finally, the door opened and the two men emerged. Both were wrapped in a serene glow of peace and mutual understanding. The swami said to his entourage in a strong, clear voice:

"When I am gone, this is the man you must come to find. And when he is gone, there will be no Brahmins to turn to. So learn your lessons well, my children. Like Vishnu, this man is the herald of destruction as well as the bringer of new life."

He turned back to Adam.

"My heart overflows with joy. I did not hope to find one such as you in my old age. I can die happy now."

The dignified guru took his hands again and bowed to him. He swiftly turned away and moved toward the door. Jeremy was astounded that the man had crossed several oceans just for these two hours of communing with the prophet. If he needed any more proof that his friend Adam was so much more than he had ever imagined, this was it. The last doubts were chased away.

Shortly thereafter, the prophet was visited by another powerful individual. But this one was not a holy man like the swami. He was his very opposite, a bearer of darkness and evil. Stefan Zorn was a sorcerer and a ruler of the occult underground. He was also a giant physically—six foot five and built like a grizzly bear. He looked more like a wrestler than a metaphysician. His skulking features were intensified by thick, black eyebrows and his bulldog face was outlined with a finely cut beard.

Stefan Zorn was also a worldly man who enjoyed displaying his wealth. He wore four huge rings and several layers of necklaces around the tree trunk of his neck. Each ended in an ancient amulet thought to carry or attract certain powers.

When Adam was informed that Stefan Zorn was on the premises, he ordered that the man be escorted away immediately. He refused to see him, and seemed unusually disturbed.

"He drove all the way from the West coast just to have a word with you," Michelle insisted. "He simply wants to know if you're for real."

"No, he doesn't. He wants to compare his powers with mine," Adam replied. "Don't you realize who he is?"

"A strange man from the coast . . . " she replied hesitantly.

"No!" he said, uncharacteristically raising his voice. "This man is the Enemy. He serves those who seek to destroy everything good."

But it was too late. Stefan Zorn burst into the room, having found his way intuitively to the prophet's home.

"So you're the final one!" he cried out in a booming voice.

Adam stepped forward, his features turning to stone like a knight's visor slamming shut for protection.

"Why are you here?" he asked sternly.

"Surely, you expected me!"

"There is no reason for you to be here."

"That's for me to decide!"

"There is nothing you can do here," Adam stated almost as a threat as he approached him.

"Don't tell me what I can't do!" the large man roared.

Michelle hurried out the back door to get some help, realizing that the man was looking for trouble.

"I hoped that I wouldn't have to lay eyes on your kind," Adam said as he stared the man down.

"Sorry to disappoint you. But that's part of my job, isn't it?" Stefan Zorn blurted out with a sarcastic grin.

"Leave now. You'll have plenty to keep you satisfied when the time comes."

"Don't you know that nothing satisfies me? That's my curse and my power!"

"You have no power here."

"Really? Shall we find out?"

The two men faced each other in some unearthly showdown. Everything fell silent around them. Birds darted away, sensing an ominous event. Somewhere on the property, dogs began to howl.

"You dare to challenge me?" Adam asked in a calm, but somber voice.

"I'll challenge you until we achieve complete and permanent victory!" the man retorted as the thick veins in his forehead enlarged. His eyes were glazed with raw hatred.

"The time is not yet," the prophet said slowly. "But someday, we'll deal with each other decisively."

"This is that day!" the man growled as he took a step closer.

Adam raised his hand and his eyes flared with a powerful current of energy. The big man's face turned ghostly pale as he felt his very life-force seep out of him. His body sagged and his strength went out of him like air from a balloon. He lost control of his muscles and his mouth dropped open. He wet himself, unable to retain any control. He fell to his knees.

"Stop!" he cried out in a weak begging voice. "Stop and I'll leave!"

"Never come back here!" Adam ordered. He raised his hand higher.

Zorn began to sweat profusely. Drool fell from his mouth.

"Please, let me go!" he managed to mutter through his twitching features.

The sound of people running toward the building could be heard through the window. Adam lowered his hand.

"Get out now, if you don't want them to see you like this."

Stefan Zorn struggled to his feet. It took all his willpower to stand.

"Don't ever make the mistake of thinking you're more powerful than us!" Adam warned him. "Even when you have this world to yourself, it won't be for long."

A vengeful grimace turned the man's face into an ugly mask of hate.

"I know your time is short!" he mumbled.

Then he abruptly turned away and left the room as Jeremy and Andrew rushed in. They looked at the man curiously as he hurried away to his waiting car. They turned back to Adam who was still radiating the imperious power that he had used upon his wretched adversary.

The companions were stunned by his look.

"Who was that?" Andrew asked fearfully.

"You'll know soon enough."

He turned away and walked off before they could ask any more questions.

CHAPTER 22

It was five A.M. on a beautiful Monday morning. Michelle had, as usual, gotten up earlier than the others and gone to her car for her daily check-in with headquarters. She had parked some ways from the compound of buildings, in an area where she could make sure no one was witnessing her activities. She was surprised to find a message light on her computer. She pushed a few buttons and a recording of Jimmy's voice came out of the little speaker.

"Call me ASAP!"

It was dated three A.M. that same morning. Adrenaline shot through her and brought her out of her sleepy haze. She quickly pressed buttons on the tiny keyboard. Her friend's voice came on.

"Michelle! I'm so glad you got hold of me."

"What is it, Jimmy?"

"I intercepted a communiqué around midnight last night coming out of your area. It was from one of our agents but not directed to our department."

"What are you talking about? That's against the rules."

"That's why I wanted you to know about this."

"Is it one of the agents that I know of?"

"Yes, Jack Farris. But instead of sending it to Bracken, it's been sent to General MacDaniel."

"You've got to be kidding! Why would he do that?"

"All I can tell you is that he's done it, so here's the deal."

"How did you manage to intercept it?"

"My security clearance makes me privy to the codes, and I guess they figured I wouldn't be scanning that bandwidth. But I've got everything aimed at your area. So here's the message: the pigeon is in the cage. Being sent home at this time."

"Nobody uses that kind of language anymore. What the hell is that suppose to mean?"

"It's an old code. I had to look up some of the metaphors in an old manual that isn't even published anymore. Here's what I found: apparently there's been some undercover information gathered at your location that will create a significant change in the situation and is about to be transferred by hand to its destination."

"Why don't I know anything about this?" she asked angrily.

"Don't know. This is not ordered through Bracken, and I don't have the vaguest idea why the general's office is connected with it."

"It's gotta be Morgan's doing."

"Whatever it is, it's apparently serious business. You'll want to be careful. Who knows what avalanche might be started by it. I suggest you communicate with agent Farris and see if he'll tell you what's going on."

"What do you mean, if? Aren't we on the same team?"

"You tell me, Michelle. This is not according to standard procedure."

"Hey wait a minute! Doesn't 'pigeon' also refer to the work of an undercover insider whose more than an observer?"

"Yes it does."

"That means there is not only another agent on sight, but some other kind of infiltrator as well."

"Apparently so."

"This is terrible! I'm the lead agent and I don't I know anything about it? Somebody's got to have more control over this case!"

"Listen, Michelle, there's no telling what this is going to mean. They might even sweep you into the transfer if they need an extra pair of hands. Obviously they've got top priority since they're connected to MacDaniel."

"I'll look into it, Jimmy. Thanks for letting me know."

She turned off the computer and shook her head. This case was going off the tracks quickly. She also realized that she had mixed emotions about the Federation's role in this community. Her loyalties were becoming divided at an unconscious level in spite of herself. But for the time being, her professionalism caused her to focus on her task.

She pulled out a small communicator and entered a code. After a moment, a sleepy voice came on.

"This is 502. Who's this?"

"This is 375," Michelle responded.

"What's the problem?"

"I need to meet with you immediately."

"What time is it?"

"Doesn't matter. We're on duty twenty-four hours a day here! I'll meet you behind building five near the pond."

"Next to the willow tree they just planted?"

"Yes."

"Be there in ten. Over and out."

Michelle got out of her car and breathed in the fresh morning air. The skies were pink with the cool colors of dawn and promised the onset of a gorgeous day. But her emotions were overshadowed by a dark cloud. She realized that eventually something was bound to interfere with the beautiful experiment underway. She could only hope that it would be clean and swift. She hoped that it would also be an action that would minimize the damage to all involved.

Jack Farris showed up in jogging clothes just as Michelle sat down on the bench under the willow tree. He was the agent who had encountered Peggy several days before.

"Let's walk around the pond," he said. "Make it look natural."

They walked in silence for a moment, looking at a family of ducks slowly gliding through the still waters of the newly created lake.

"So you're Michelle Blair, eh? I've heard of your father's exploits. You were the first one on sight, weren't you?"

"Yes, I was. How long have you been here?"

"About a month."

"Pretty strange case, isn't it?"

"Oh, I've seen them all. So what can I do for you?"

"I've gotten word about the message sent to headquarters."

He looked at her strangely.

"What message would that be?"

"Oh, come on now, Jack, we're all in this together, aren't we?"

He did his best not to reveal his reaction.

"The Pigeon is in the cage," she whispered with irritation.

His poker face couldn't sustain itself. "How in the hell did you find out about that?"

"Never mind. You'd better tell me what's going on. This is against regulations. You're my backup. I have a right to know what you're doing."

They walked in silence for a moment, and she grew angrier with every step.

"Damn it, Jack, this is not right and you know it! Nothing like this ever happened in my father's day, sending messages to different departments and not communicating with other personnel on sight. This could endanger fellow agents."

"You're right," he finally said. "I don't like it much myself."

"Tell me, I'm on the same team."

"I know you are. I just followed instructions, that's all."

"We don't have much time. What's going on?"

"There's been a take-down. We've got pictures."

"A take-down?"

"You know what that means, don't you?"

"You've set somebody up?"

"We haven't, but it's been done."

"A sex thing?"

"Yep."

Her heart pounded in her chest. This was the messiest way to handle the situation.

"Who's the victim?"

"Bradshaw."

"Andrew?" she cried out.

He looked at her with concern. She said that name as though he was her friend.

"Andrew Bradshaw," she said again, without emotion.

"Right," he responded suspiciously.

"Somebody sent a whore up here to create a scandal?"

"You got it."

"Who's got the pictures now?"

"I do."

"Who's delivering them to their destination?"

"We are."

"Where to?"

"I'm waiting for instructions."

"You're sitting on this stuff and you don't know what to do with it? What kind of strategy is that?"

"They're not for us."

She abruptly stopped walking and took hold of his arm.

"What are you saying? This is not a Federation job?"

"That's correct."

"What the hell are we, the lackeys for somebody else's agenda?"

"What are you getting so excited for? It's all working out in our favor, regardless of who's making it happen. You're sure taking this awfully personal. That's not standard procedure either for level three agents."

"I just don't like it when we don't play by the rules."

"According to the rules, you should be the one to deliver the materials to our contact."

"What do you mean?" she said, trying to conceal her horror.

"You're the senior agent on this job and we're holding a priority one package. You should be the person taking responsibility for it."

She was about to insist on staying out of this sordid arrangement, but she noticed the intensity with which he was studying at her. Her gut feeling told her that he was testing her. She knew immediately that he would file a report directly to the top if he sensed that she was not fully committed to her task as a Federation security agent.

"All right, I'll do it. How do you want to make the transaction?" she said as businesslike as possible.

His facial muscles relaxed, confirming that she was right about the trap he had just set for her.

"We'll have the materials for you in one hour. Meet me here. They're the originals. That's why you should handle them. You're responsible for their safety."

"Who's the contact person?"

"I'm expecting a call on that matter in about fifteen minutes. That person will come to meet you halfway, in Ponca City. I'll have all the details for you. Now let's check our watches."

They set their watches to the same time and walked off in different directions. She moved rapidly down the road into the quiet countryside, trying to free herself from the turmoil within her. She was urgently attempting to locate the skilled agent she had been for over a decade, who was confident about her loyalties, and who could fulfill the requirements of this case. Never before had she had any question about the Federation's supremacy in her commitments. But she couldn't bare the thought of seeing this experiment in humanity's renewal completely destroyed by a cheap sex scandal.

Yet it all came down to her own job security and that, of course, was still her greatest loyalty of all.

She couldn't even imagine hitting the pavement looking for secretarial employment after the privileged position she had reached with such hard work. Nor did she want to shame her father by breaking the most fundamental rule of all: field agents were never to be confused by the circumstances in which they found themselves. Global security was at stake.

Michelle wandered off into a neighboring farmer's property. She realized that she had completely lost track of where she was and turned around to head back. She was shocked at the degree of inner confusion that caused her to be in such a daze. Where was the Michelle Blair that she was so proud to be—strong and utterly reliable, as good an agent as her father had been? In reaction to this anxiety, some part of her resented the prophet who had stirred old wounds and feelings that she had long forgotten about. She hated not having solid ground under her feet.

As she headed back to the building that was her temporary home, she realized that if she could hang on to that little piece of herself that was angry at Adam Hawthorn, she might be able to get her stability back and focus on the task at hand. She was ashamed at the vulnerability she had exposed in front of her colleague. For years they'd called her the "ice queen" because of her nerves of steel. Now she realized she'd behaved like an emotionally neurotic individual, one who couldn't even make it through the first course in security training. She swore to herself that she would not allow that to happen again, that she would make up for this momentary weakness. After all, she didn't give a damn what happened here.

She was senior investigator on a case and performing a professional task.

Michelle buried the feelings that she had allowed to grow in regard to the people here and their spiritual idealism. Even as she did so, she recognized that she'd gotten awfully good at burying other parts of herself. She knew it was a repulsive feature. But it worked, and that's all that counted now.

She returned to her room and washed her face in cold water, finding again the persona that functioned so well in the line of duty. She descended into the deserted kitchen and fixed herself a cup of coffee. As the caffeine worked its way into her system, she came in touch once again with that familiar accomplished individual that she took for herself.

An hour later, she was back under the willow tree, watching the baby ducks glide by in the pond. Jack appeared right on schedule and slipped a rectangular package into her hand.

"The ball's in your court now," he whispered.

"No problem," she responded.

He gave her a second look to make sure he could trust what he saw on her face. He was satisfied with the neutral and objective features of a Federation agent.

"All the information's inside. Let me know if you need anything," he said as he walked away.

She held the package tightly in her hand and looked around to make sure no one had seen the transaction. She stood up and headed toward her car. She got in and sat there for a moment, hesitating to open the package. She didn't want to see what was in it, but she knew that she had no choice. She turned to the package and abruptly opened the snaps. Inside was a stack of five by seven photographs that had been automatically printed by the state-of-the-art equipment provided for the entrapment.

Michelle turned over the top picture and immediately turned it back again. She couldn't bare the indignity of what she was involved in. No doubt about it, the images of nude bodies entangled together would do the trick and shout scandal loud and clear, making the whole community look hypocritical and untrustworthy. She didn't even want to imagine how Andrew was going to feel about them. It would destroy him. Most of all, it would damage the prophet's credibility, probably for good.

Michelle swallowed hard and shook her head at the dirty business she was suddenly thrown into. She picked up the paper that contained the instructions. The person who was to receive the package from her was a Reverend Harry Novak. The title Reverend seemed like a horrific blasphemy, even for someone who had no ties to religion. It made her shiver with disgust.

In the faxed note was a scanned-in, low resolution image of the man. He looked as pathetic and shifty eyed as she expected. She was to meet him in three hours at the Oasis Cafe, ironically the very spot where the prophet had first been spotted on his journey from Enid.

She put aside the information, closed up the package in a tight, neat bundle and locked it in a box between the seats. She leaned back and looked up at the trees above her. A soft breeze danced through the spring leaves, creating a sweet image of unspoiled nature, a sharp contrast from the grotesque deed in which she now was a participant. She could just imagine the creepy little clergyman and Robert Morgan pouring over the pictures, undoubtedly lusting over the nudity and giddy with the taste of victory over their enemy. They had gone for the kill and accomplished their aim.

She hadn't looked at the picture long enough to see who the woman was. Not that it mattered, but her curiosity suddenly revved up unexpectedly. She'd become part of the community and knew many faces there. She had to see who it was who had been the bait for the downfall of all the good that was occurring in this place.

In spite of her effort to resist, she unlocked the box and removed the package. She opened it again. This time, her fingers were trembling. She lifted up the stack of a dozen photographs and pulled one out from the bottom. It showed a clear profile of the woman in Andrew's arms. She didn't recognize the face, but saw instantly the look of disinterest that characterized her profession. The features burned into her mind and she put the pictures away quickly, as though they were vile things that the sun itself should not gaze upon. She locked the package up again and got out of the car. She didn't want to be in the same vicinity as the shameful material.

For the first time in years, she craved a cigarette, a sure sign that her nerves were on edge. The stern mask of professionalism that she had managed to recover in the previous hour was barely holding on.

She found herself walking again. As chance would have it, she came upon Lynn, Juanita and the baby just as she had three months before.

"Good morning, Michelle. Looks like we're in for a lovely day."

Michelle did her best to switch gears and act friendly, knowing that the last thing this day was going to be was lovely.

"You don't look like you slept too well," Lynn stated, noting her ragged look.

"No, I guess not."

"Is everything all right?"

"Sure, fine."

Lynn was not so easily fooled. "Why don't you join us for our little morning walk? We'll go around the pond a few times."

"I've got things I need to do, thank you."

"We'll see you at lunchtime, then."

"Adam's bringing a guest to lunch today. An Indian man," Juanita said. "You don't want to miss it."

"Oh?" Michelle said, trying to smile. "A guest?"

"Yes," Lynn responded. "His name is Stargazer. He's an elder among the Cherokee people—a friend of Adam's. He came in last night to see him because he's had visions that concern him."

"Visions?" Michelle asked as her throat tightened up.

"He's an extraordinary mystic. Apparently, he's seen something that does not bode well. I don't know if we'll get to hear about it or not."

Michelle tried not to flinch. "I hope it's not bad news."

"Hard to say. Stargazer hasn't been well and made quite an effort to get here. Must be something important."

"It's nice to know Adam has friends who care so much for him."

Michelle smiled and walked away, knowing she wouldn't be able to keep her mask on much longer.

* * *

Harry Novak waited nervously at the cafe, sipping black coffee and looking at his watch. He was sweating more than usual this day and taking deep drags on his cigarette. He didn't know who his contact would be, but he'd heard that the mission was a success. He was so excited over the anticipation of his enemy's demise that he could hardly sit still. He just couldn't wait to desecrate the man who made him look so bad.

A car pulled up in the dirt lot. Michelle got out with a package under her arm. Peering through the window, Harry knew what it must contain. She entered and looked around the room. A few farmers and old folks sat about finishing a late breakfast. She spotted the clergyman easily. There was no one else there whose very presence gave off the feeling of a treacherous snake.

The man revealed his yellow teeth in a big grin and looked her over, pleased to see that he'd be dealing with such a lovely young woman. She cringed as she sensed that he was undressing her with his eyes. She quickly sat down.

"Harry Novak?" she said coldly.

"That's me."

"You know what I'm here for, don't you?"

"Of course. And what's your name?"

"That's not important."

"Can I get you something to drink?" he asked as he waived the waitress over.

"No, I have to get back right away."

But it was too late as the waitress had already shown up.

"Coffee, tea?" Novak asked, trying to keep his eyes from heading back down to her chest.

"Coffee," she said, gritting her teeth.

"So it was a great success, I understand. Have you looked at the material?"

"Enough to know that it's what it needs to be."

"Let me see."

"You can't open that here!"

"Nobody will see."

"This is not the place to do this."

"What are you talking about? I paid for them, I wanna see what I got."

She had no choice. But she hesitated, knowing there would be no return from this decisive act.

"Come on!" he said impatiently. "I've been up all night waiting to see them."

The waitress placed the coffee in front of her. She then handed the package to him brusquely and looked out the window, trying to stay away from the feelings of shame and sorrow rising up within her. He put the package on his lap and opened it.

She sipped from her cup as he leafed through the pictures with the very look she had imagined. He was the most lecherous man she had ever seen.

"He's done for," he said triumphantly. "We got him now. Look at that. Talk about a compromising position. And the angle of his head is perfect for what we need."

"What do you mean?" she said, suddenly horrified by an intuition.

"We've got a couple photographs of Hawthorn from a few years ago, and one of them I know will fit perfectly in that position."

"What are you talking about?" she said in outrage, putting down her coffee cup.

"We're gonna put Hawthorn's face on the guy's body. That'll end his career right there."

She couldn't believe her ears.

"Your going to make it look like it's Adam Hawthorn in that picture?"

"Hell yes. We're not after Bradshaw. He's small fry. We want the big fish."

"You can't do that!" she said, raising her voice a little too loud.

"What do you mean we can't do that? We can do whatever the hell we want to do. There's only one purpose here, and that's to get rid of him. This picture here's gonna be in every news stand in the world, in every grocery store . . . they'll have to censor it a little bit, of course, but there'll be no mistaking what people are looking at."

She was so shocked that she couldn't speak for a moment.

"This isn't right, mister!" she finally blurted out. "It's bad enough that you entrapped this man, but if you retouch the photographs, you're breaking the law!"

"What law?" he said, confused by her rage. "Don't you work for the Federation?" he asked under his breath.

"Yes, but . . . "

"The Federation makes up its own rules, and you know it! Especially in cases like this. You guys are better at it than anybody."

"I've never known of a case where a picture was doctored to condemn an innocent man."

"Are you kidding me? Morgan tells me he knew a master of this art in your department. Frank Blair."

She lost control. "What the hell do you know about my father! Keep him out of your dirty business!"

"Take it easy, lady! What's your problem?"

"Don't you dare insult my father!"

"So he was your father, was he? I don't mean to insult him. But Morgan knew him and he says that he saw this kinda stuff firsthand. Your dad was one of the best."

"My father did not get innocent men convicted!"

"Innocence is a relative term, isn't it? I mean, Hawthorn is guilty, whether it's getting caught with a prostitute or filling people's heads with wrong ideas. It doesn't make a whole lot of difference. We've got to get rid of him, and that's all there is to it."

By now the people in the cafe were staring at them. Michelle knew she had to get hold of herself.

"For the sake of global security?" she said sarcastically.

"That's right. You've been out there for awhile. There are people from all over the world showing up. In fact, I was faxed a paper from one of our missionaries in Southeast Asia, and there was Hawthorn on the front page. If we don't stop him, the world's gonna think he's the Messiah come again. He's got folks on every continent excited about him, especially with that healing business. He's given false hope to millions with incurable diseases. If we don't put him out, he could become king of the world or something!"

"That's ridiculous!"

"In this day and age, with the right PR man, you can be heard and seen around the planet, even from this god-forsaken place."

The wheels of her mind started racing at full speed. She couldn't let them do this.

"When do you intent to start publishing this material?"

"Oh, I'd say it'll be about a week before we get all our ducks in a row. We've hired a media specialist to advise us on maximum exposure . . . so to speak."

He snickered.

"What happens if Mr. Hawthorn takes you to court?"

"He won't do that!"

"Why not?"

"Those who've been around him say that he doesn't have any interest in using the structures of our "decadent" society in any way. That's what he gets for not playing the game. Either you're in or you're out, and he's gonna be out for good. He shoulda known better than try to change everything. It just doesn't work that way."

Novak's eyes glazed with hatred. Michelle was repulsed by the bile that he was filled with. She'd seen the same look in Morgan's face.

"Why do you hate him so much?" she heard herself say.

"That's a stupid question," Novak responded defensively. "How can you ask such a question? You would hate him too if you knew him at all."

She couldn't help reacting to that ironic statement. She knew Adam Hawthorn just enough to recognize how extraordinary he was.

"He's the worst kind. Worse than a murderer or a rapist."

"What makes you say that?" she asked, trying not to show her outrage.

"He rapes the soul! He gets people to believe in things that can't ever be real for them, and when they fall off the pedestal of fantasy he's created for them, they're worse off than before."

"So what is it that you offer them as a minister?"

"I keep them well anchored in reality, that's what I do."

"And what is your reality?"

"It's not my reality," he said as his poisonous energy spewed forth again, "it's the same one we all live in! It's what we feel and touch and smell—it's what is!"

"Don't you have any sense of a spiritual dimension?"

"Don't talk to me about that crap! I studied it in seminary and read a truckload of books about it. Never did me any good."

"Did you ever try to access it somehow?"

"I've done a good deal of praying in my life, young lady, I'll tell you that. I never did hear God talking back to me."

She looked deeply into the man, in the way that she had witnessed Lynn doing. She saw a sordid darkness within him. She knew he'd never tried hard to climb out of the abyss in which he wallowed. He was too busy enjoying himself down there.

"You're taking the package to Reverend Morgan now?" she inquired as she readied to leave.

"That's the next step," he replied, still angry that she had asked him disturbing questions. But he was already back to looking at her like a man who'd spent his life around red light districts. She couldn't believe that he even pretended to be a clergyman.

"Tell me something," she asked as she stood up. "Are most of your colleagues like you?"

His eyes flared with rage.

"What the hell is that s'pose to mean?"

"Are most ministers as earthbound as you?"

She couldn't think of a more tactful way to put it.

"Sure they are! They're humans, just like you and me. What do you expect of us? To have wings under our suit coats?"

"No, I sure don't," she said, thinking of Adam and the light in his eyes. "See you around, Reverend," she said, heading for the door. She knew his eyes would be fixed on her buttocks all the way out of the cafe. She slammed the door behind her, hoping she'd never have to lay eyes on him again.

On the way back to Renouveau, her mind burned with a thousand thoughts. Whatever justification she tried to pin on what had happened, she simply could not stand for the horrific injustice that was about to take place. She could not conspire with men like Novak and Morgan for the purpose of destroying the goodness that she knew was alive in Adam Hawthorn and the people around him.

She remembered a quote she'd heard long ago about the sin against the Holy Spirit that couldn't be forgiven. She had never understood it, but it had scared her severely as a six year old girl. Over the years, she had sometimes found herself wondering about the nature of such a sin that was so cosmically unforgivable.

She now had her answer: hatred of good was the ultimate disgrace of the human spirit, for it left it hopelessly enslaved to evil. She knew that she would lose her job and her reputation before siding with such vile creatures. She had heard Adam say on many occasions in the last few months that the time had come to make a decisive choice. She'd never applied it to herself. But now her time had come as well.

There was still enough of the agent left in her to try to find some kind of compromise in this situation. Strangely, it was Novak who had planted a thought in her mind that kept coming back to her. It was as obvious as the light of day, although completely illogical. The fact was that one person could indeed speak to the world in this day and age and make his case if it was worthy of that kind of attention. And there was no man on earth whose case was more worthy than that of the final prophet.

Perhaps international attention would offset whatever was done with those pictures. She realized that there was hardly anything more difficult than to create such an event. She had no contacts with the media, other than a few reporters and some of her father's friends.

That's when it hit her. Her father had not only spent his life around the media empire, but he was also a close friend of some of the moguls of the industry. Maybe he could get her in the door.

The thought repelled her. She hadn't spoken with him in three years. They hadn't really gotten along since her teenage years. And though she knew he was proud of her accomplishments, they really had nothing in common as human beings. He was a staunch military man who had attempted to mold her to his way of thinking, repressing the creative and intuitive aspects of her nature. Though she had finally followed in his footsteps, it was only after a long detour that caused tremendous alienation between them. Now he lived alone, widowed for the past two years, somewhat of a recluse surrounded by hunting trophies and memorabilia of past glories.

She would have to get to him right away. The only way was with a Federation jet. She wasn't sure if he'd even want to see her after all this time. Even worse, he was not likely to be receptive to her situation. But there was no one else with contacts to such movers and shakers. If she could talk him into helping her, she might save Adam without destroying her own career. She would have to take some big risks and use all the pull she had to justify using the company plane and racking up the expenses this would require. But she was more afraid of what would happen if she did nothing than she was of the consequences of her foolhardy schemes.

She couldn't do it entirely alone, however. She'd have to have some assistance in covering her tracks. Instantly, her friend Jimmy came to mind. No one else would be willing to take such risks on her account, and she knew that he would do it just to please her. She realized it could cost him his job as well, but nothing measured up to the colossal disaster of destroying the prophet.

Her heart thundered in her chest as she considered all the pros and cons of the various strategies she'd have to employ. But what else could she do? She had just handed the ax to the executioner and that was intolerable to her. Perhaps she should have burned everything, but that was now useless hindsight. An hour ago, she was still trying to be a good agent. The thought hadn't even crossed her mind to commit such an infraction. Now she'd have to make up for such rigid thinking and that infraction would look like child's play compared to what she was about to do. She had made it very hard for herself, but she knew that her conscience would not give her a moment's rest if she didn't pursue this course of action.

She connected her car telephone and dialed a memorized number. It rang over and over with a loud, scratchy sound that wore on her frayed nerves.

"Come on! Answer the phone!" she muttered, wiping the sweat from her brow. She was taking a desperate leap off a cliff, with no idea how she would land.

"Hello?"

It was a deep, gravely voice. The familiar resonance brought back a flood of ancient memories.

"Dad! It's me!"

"Michelle?"

"Yeah. I'm calling from the field."

"Is there trouble?"

Frank Blair was an old pro to the bone. He knew that agents did not place family calls when on a case unless they were facing a potentially fatal situation. And even then, it was frowned upon, just in case some hacker was able to scan their signal.

"It's good to hear your voice," she said sincerely.

"Long time since we talked, daughter," the old man's voice responded in a cloud of static.

"I know . . . "

What could she say? Their relationship was not what she wanted it to be, but she had no idea how to fix it. He was one kind of person, she was another. Besides, there was a little girl within her who still resented the fact that he was never home for the first ten years of her life.

"I've missed you, honey," he said in a voice that was choking up.

Tears came to her eyes. She fought them angrily. This was not the time to start falling apart.

"I need your help, Dad."

"What can an old cripple do for you?"

She hated it when he referred to himself in such terms. All he had was a bad limp, but to him it was sign of being out of commission and useless. His whole adult life was based on maximizing his physical powers. Once they began to fade, he thought his purpose was over. That was only one example of their different view of things.

"This is serious, Dad. I need to come see you."

The phone speaker was silent. She knew he was shifting gears into his former super-agent focus.

"How soon can you be here?"

"Tonight?"

"On a charter?"

"Yes."

"Is it validated?"

"No."

She knew that he now understood how serious her problem was. It was outside the bounds of standard procedure and possibly illegal.

"Do you have to play it that way?"

"Sometimes the rules aren't the top priority, Dad."

"They were in my time."

"Do you want to help me or not?"

Another pause. She was ready to hang up on him.

"Yes, I want to help. Come see me."

Tears burned her eyes again. It was good to know that his fatherly love for her in this last chapter of his life allowed him to overcome his lifelong loyalty to codes and regulations.

She said good-bye and disconnected just as she pulled into the compound. The place was strangely deserted. She headed toward the main building. Her intention was to go to her room and pack a few thing, but as she walked by, Andrew stepped out of the newly constructed gathering hall.

"Michelle!"

She turned and nearly jumped out of her skin upon seeing the man whose life she had just handed over to his enemies.

"Where have you been? You're missing something truly incredible."

He came up to her, smiling and full of enthusiasm. She did her best to smile back.

"Where is everybody?" she asked.

"Didn't you hear? We've got a special guest here today. Come on in and listen to what he has to say."

"I really can't. I've got . . . "

He took her by the arm and led her into the building.

"You don't want to miss this."

A large crowd was gathered in the hall. People were seated at long tables and had finished their meals some time ago. At the far end of the room, on a platform, stood the old Indian elder, Stargazer. He was speaking with his eyes closed. Adam sat in a chair behind him.

"And so I have come to let you know that there are among you wolves in sheep's clothing as they are called. My people have other names for them, but I won't share them with you today. Utter destruction awaits you if you do not protect yourselves from such persons. They are here to kill the new world you are creating. They are more than weeds in a garden, for they not only seek to choke you, but to uproot and burn you!"

The crowd was intensely silent. Adam's features remained calm and unmoved, as though he was anticipating this warning.

The rugged bronze face squinted and turned hard. "If the Visitor is taken from you, there will be no more after him. The spirits tell me that you will vanish as surely as my people were destroyed. After his passing will come a darkness that will last even when the sun is at its zenith."

His hands drew an Indian sign in the air, emphasizing the ending of life. His features were now harsh and warrior-like.

"Without messengers, all the peoples of the earth will be enslaved by the devils that pollute the heart and spirit. The Visitor speaks the truth, and you must hear him before it is too late."

Stargazer opened his eyes. They fell instantly on Michelle who stood by Andrew against the back wall.

"The enemy is in this room now!"

Terror shot up Michelle's spine as she realized that he was speaking directly to her. Any second now, he would point and hundreds of angry faces would turn on her.

"Who is it?" several voices cried out.

Michelle felt her head spin and her life flashed before her. She looked around the room and spotted Jack Farris who was watching her and ready to spring to her rescue. He also recognized the danger of the moment.

"The Visitor is a man of peace. He will not raise his hand upon his enemy. But what will you do to protect him?"

"I'll kill anybody who tries to hurt him!" a man roared as he jumped to his feet.

Several others swore the same. The air filled with tension. Adam's features darkened as he saw violence in his followers' eyes. He was about to stand and speak to them when Stargazer aimed his finger in Michelle's direction.

"I see a destroyer of good, a servant of the dominators!"

Everyone turned around. Michelle froze like a deer caught in headlights.

"Grab her!" someone shouted.

She turned to Andrew and saw a look of rage on his face. He reached for her. Instinctively, she blocked his hand and pushed his arm aside. People were already jumping out of their seats and heading toward her. Jack Farris raced ahead of them.

"Run!" he shouted as he turned to the crowd in a valiant effort to protect her.

"See how they appear from under their rocks!" Stargazer said loudly, his voice booming through the speakers.

Adam leapt to his feet and took hold of the microphone.

"Stop!"

But his voice was lost in a deafening uproar of shouts and screams that exploded in the room. Jack struck the first few men who were rushing for Michelle. The blows acted like sparks on a lake of kerosene. A surge of outraged humanity fell upon him. Adam shouted for them to stop, but no one could hear him.

Farris fought with exceptional skill, displaying a mastery of martial arts that slowed his attackers. His fists struck out like lightning and his feet shot through the air with the power of coiled springs suddenly released. People fell to the floor all around him. No one there could match his power and skill. But the sight of blood only enraged the crowd and Farris was soon overwhelmed as dozens of men leaped at him and wrestled him to the ground.

Michelle ran to the door. A man jumped in front of her and blocked the exit. She kicked him in the stomach and struck him in the side of the head as he bent over in pain, slamming him against the wall. Insane with panic, she raced outside and dashed for her car. People burst out of the building after her.

Lynn and Jeremy pushed their way through the crowd and pulled people off of the agent who was already covered in his own blood. Adam jumped off the platform and also hurried through the crowd. People came to their senses when they saw him and backed away.

Adam kneeled by Jack Farris whose face was swelling up from the storm of fists and feet that had battered him. Jeremy held his head up to slow the bleeding.

"Save Michelle!" Adam said to Lynn. "They'll do the same to her."

He placed his hand over the agent's broken features and eased his pain. Jack Farris looked up at him in shock. His physical agony gave way to the soothing balm that radiated from the prophet's hand. He began to weep, not from pain, but from the unconditional love that poured down upon him, concerned for his welfare regardless of why he was among them.

Adam rose up and raised his hands. Silence fell over the room. Everyone stood still as he stared at them with a stern and outraged look. His outspread arms seemed to hold every person in their grip.

"Have you learned nothing?" he finally cried out. "Have my words made no impact on you? In one moment, you have gone from seekers of meaning to the vilest show of mob mentality. Don't you understand that if you do not eradicate violence from your being, it will overtake the world completely in every imaginable way? You have failed! Pray that others do not fall as quickly as you did or there will be no future for this planet! Help has been available to you, and you've rejected it again. I've been wasting my time and there is no more time to waste!"

Jeremy and Lynn had never seen such indignation in their friend's face. It was a frightening sight. His eyes were glazed with disgust and his face glistened with the intensity of his energy. He seemed to need all his mighty willpower to keep himself under control.

"In this one instant, you have revealed how little you have understood of all that I have said to you. You have witnessed miracles of the Spirit right before your very eyes. We have spent months together and yet you can in one moment throw it all away and give yourselves up to the most wretched of subhuman behavior! I am heartsick and unspeakably disappointed. What you did to that man you did to me!"

People wept openly. Some shook with uncontrollable emotion, sensing what was coming next.

"There will come a time very soon when you will be faced with terrible circumstances. How will you deal with them? Will you become savages again? There was only one reason for our being together. To prepare you for what is coming and to keep your humanity alive in spite of the approaching disasters. This experiment has failed. It is over!"

Great cries and moans filled the room. He raised his voice to be heard over the agonized sounds.

"Go home! Take with you whatever you manage to retain from

this experience and use it for the good of those around you. They will need all the courage and sacrifice your spirit is capable of."

Lynn, Jeremy and Andrew hurried to him and tried to change his mind, begging for mercy on these desperate people.

"I told you all along that this community was not the final aim of my work, nor that it was meant to be built to last."

The sound of weeping filled the room. Some people fell to their knees in remorse and shame. Jack Farris watched the scene in amazement. Adam stood before the crowd, statuesque and with eyes of fire.

"Don't you realize that the spirit world is closer to you than it's ever been! Angels walk this earth seeking to save you from your fate. Holy ones have poured their blood out for you. But you always choose the darkness! This cannot go on!"

"Please forgive us! Give us another chance!" someone cried out.

"I told you how serious your choice was and what was at stake. You must bare the responsibility. You'll never understand how much has been sacrificed to help you, and all to no avail. Mark my words—the day is coming when you will not have a choice to make. Maybe you don't deserve to be helped after all!"

The people cried out in agony at his words.

"There are no more chances!" he said in an imperative voice that exploded with finality.

Shouts and heart-wrenching cries for mercy shook the room. The prophet did not blink. Jeremy and Lynn turned to each other, horrified. They knew that he meant what he said.

Stargazer approached Adam and took his hand, whispering just above the moans of the brokenhearted crowd.

"Friend, I feel responsible for what has happened here. Don't punish them on my account."

Adam placed his hand on the man's shoulder.

"Each is responsible for his own action. You did what you felt you had to do, and what they chose to do was up to them."

"I too have the desire to protect you, friend," Stargazer said. "It's hard to see goodness come under attack."

"Everyone is under attack at all times. The battle is in each moment."

"You must not abandon them! They can't function without you."

"I won't abandon them. But they must function without me! That is the very reason for my being here."

"My people have known about visitors like yourself for five hundred years. In the last hundred, our spirit guides have given us many visions about what is to come. Your task is a difficult one. My visions tell me that you are the last of the visitors. Is this possible?"

"Your people should know better than any other the reality that all things come to an end."

"Will there be a spring after this terrible winter?"

Adam answered him only with a steady gaze. The old elder's lips trembled and sorrow darkened his features. The two mystics stared deeply into each other's eyes. They knew it was the last time they would ever see each other. Adam turned back to the wailing crowd.

"Why must it take so much to get through to you? You weren't meant to exist as violent, sub-animal creatures! You are spiritual children of the universe! Why will you not recognize your true nature?"

He turned his back on them and left the room. Lynn took hold of Jeremy's arm.

"We've got to convince him to change his mind! He can't throw these people out! It'll kill them."

"I can't change his mind. You know him."

"We can't end this community so abruptly. Please talk to him!"

"Lynn, he's told us that the human community as a whole is about to end this abruptly! We'd better be prepared for this kind of shock."

Lynn rushed out of the room and came up to Adam as he stepped outside.

"Adam, would you really abandon us?"

"It is not I who has abandoned them, it is they who have abandoned me! If they partake in violence, they not only abandon me, but they betray me. The price that is paid to lift them out of their miserable way of being is too high."

"Please don't abandon us! Not now, not when we're just learning how to live!"

He took her face in his hands and poured his gaze into her soul.

She saw that his compassion would never vanish, regardless of humanity's weakness and insanity.

Screeching tires made them look away. Michelle had jumped in her car and sped off in a cloud of dust. Several men leapt on her hood and grabbed onto door handles. But they all fell away as the car raced down the path and vanished in the distance.

CHAPTER 23

Michelle sat in her father's living room, weeping uncontrollably. Frank Blair was seated across from her, studying her sadly. He'd never seen her like this. At six foot four and some two hundred and fifty pounds, he was an ex-weight-lifter and judo champion. He still wore his hair in a military style, closely shaved on the sides.

He couldn't stand the sight of his brokenhearted daughter suffering so before him. He got up, sat on the couch next to her, and put his arm around her. She turned and put her head on his chest. In that moment, the bond of father and child surfaced with an intensity that hadn't manifested since her earliest childhood. Out of their unconscious memories came a love that had been unspoken for too long.

Her pain was contagious and he felt his throat tighten and his chest ache, absorbing her agony into his own heart.

"Now, now," he finally said. "We'll find a way out of this. We can do anything together!"

Those were the very words he had spoken to her many years ago when she had badly scraped her knee. He had run over to her, picked her up in his strong arms, and comforted her until the pain was eased. Somehow, the synchronicity of the words and the return of that distant memory brought a glow of hope back into her soul. The strength of their love and his fatherly affection combined to lift her out of her anguish.

He grabbed a box of Kleenex on a table behind the couch and handed them to her as she got control of herself. He dried her face as she looked at him through red eyes.

"I love you so much, Sweetheart," he said. "Forgive me for not telling you that for so many years."

"I love you too, Daddy," she responded. "I'm sorry for still being a rebellious teenager."

He laughed through his tears. They hugged.

"I'll tell you one thing, Darling. You can count on me this time. I'm on nobody's side but yours."

"You'll help me, even if it breaks the rules?"

"The hell with the rules. I've followed them long enough. My only rule now is to love you and support you like I should have done these last thirty years. You tell me what you need from me and you've got it."

"It could get real messy, Dad."

"Look, I'm just a few years away from my last breath. Things get a lot clearer when you face your own mortality. I just want to be your dad now. Not agent number 702."

"Will you make the call then?"

"You bet I will! I'll do more than that. I'll get in that plane and go see him myself. The only trouble is, I haven't put on a suit in five years. I don't know if I fit in any of them anymore."

"You look in pretty good shape to me."

"I've had trouble staying away from potato chips. But I still pump iron."

"You don't need a tie to see your old friend, do you?"

"Wait 'till you see his office. It's like walking into the Taj Mahal."

"So when will you be ready to go?"

"How 'bout within the hour?"

"That'll do."

He placed his large hand on her cheek. He hadn't touched her like that since grade school.

"I want you to know I'm doing this only for you. I don't understand anything about this religious man, but I trust your sense of right and wrong. Hopefully, I had something to do with instilling it in you. This time, you're the captain and I'll be the first mate."

She took his hand and kissed it gratefully.

* * *

Vince Kruger's office was indeed a palatial structure. He was the king of a media empire that circled the globe. He oversaw a personal fortune in the billions of dollars. Almost every major new development in the television industry in the past twenty years had come through his visionary teams. He owned half a dozen satellites orbiting the planet and had mastered the art of making entertainment an international monolith that incorporated the interests and needs of many different cultures.

At the turn of the century, he had recognized that the English language was not that of the majority of the world's population, and had invested in Chinese productions that were meant for the immense masses of Asia. These initial forays into previously untapped markets were made all the more profitable by turning them back toward the West as well. He had created international superstars out of actors from Malaysia and Pakistan who would have otherwise remained local celebrities only.

Kruger's companies branched out into music, motion pictures, books, computers and radio. There was no media in which he did not have some investment. Several other such moguls existed in the world, but they could be counted on the fingers of one hand. He was arguably the biggest one of them all. He had known Frank Blair for almost thirty-five years. They had been in the military together as young men and faced the horrors of war side by side. Blair had pulled him out of a fire fight after he'd been left for dead by his commanding officer. Those kinds of ties couldn't be broken with passing time or changing circumstances. They were forever the scared twenty year olds behind a rock whipped by enemy fire. In a great feat of heroism, Blair had dragged him across a mine field when no one else dared to come out of their shelters. The squeeze of Frank Blair's helping hand extended to him in his desperate time of need was still felt to this day.

The moment Vince Kruger heard that his old friend needed to see him urgently, he canceled everything on his packed schedule. Even stockholders would have to wait when Frank Blair called upon him.

Michelle and her father were shown into his office by several vice-presidents who had ushered them through the labyrinth of hallways in the building. The CEO's office was so large that he could hardly be seen at the far end of it. Giant windows looked out upon the sprawling metropolis, whose every house watched his programs. Thirty floors below was a battery of huge dishes communicating with satellites in orbit twenty thousand miles over the equator.

Vince Kruger looked like a king. He was short and stocky, exuding the power and confidence of a man three times his size. With multiple chins and a well-coifed mane of snow-white hair, he was wealth incarnate. His shiny herringbone suit looked like it cost as much as his employees' yearly salary.

He stood up from behind his gargantuan desk as they walked into the room and spread out his arms.

"Frank! How wonderful to see you!"

Blair hurried to him and the men hugged like dearest of friends, oblivious of any economic hierarchy separating them. That day beneath the bullets was still vividly present in this moment. Vince kissed him on both cheeks.

"What's it been? A decade or more?"

"Probably," Frank replied.

"I heard you retired some time ago."

"Yep. Isn't it time for you to do the same?"

"Not me! I'll be working 'til they carry me out with a tag around my toe. I heard about Grace. I'm sorry."

"Those things happen. She had a good life."

"You loved her well, Frank. And so this must be Michelle," he stated with a big smile creasing his face.

Michelle approached in awe. He looked at her through thick glasses bordered with golden rims that made his eyes twice as big as normal. She saw in them genuine pleasure at meeting her, as well as a temperament that could rain thunder down on his subordinates.

"Michelle! I last saw you when you were in pigtails. You've blossomed real nice."

"I've heard so much about you, sir."

"I understand that you followed in your daddy's footsteps. Those are big shoes to fill."

"They are indeed," she said humbly.

"I don't doubt that Frank's daughter can do the job. Sit down, please."

He called out to one of his submissive vice-presidents.

"Ed, you make sure nobody bothers us."

"Yes, sir."

The doors closed and they were left alone in the vast office.

"So what's this about, friends?"

"It's a difficult situation, Vince, and I wouldn't come to you if it wasn't terribly important," Blair stated solemnly.

"I know that, Frank. That's why I cleared my schedule. So what can I do for you?"

Blair turned to his daughter and motioned for her to speak. She swallowed hard.

"Sir, have you heard of a man by the name of Adam Hawthorn?"

The mogul's face wrinkled as he looked at her in surprise.

"Of course! There's been news reports about him on all my channels."

"I'm the agent investigating his case. I've been in his community for several months."

"Have you now?" he said with interest.

"I've come to know what he's about."

"You've seen him up close and personal, eh?"

"I have. And I've also been involved in a plot to discredit him through a trumped-up sex scandal."

"The Federation thought this up?"

"No sir, it's the work of clergymen."

"Clergymen?" he responded in amazement.

"That's right. Former colleagues of Mr. Hawthorn, who hate him with a passion, are terrified of his abilities and want to get rid of him."

"Let me get this straight," Kruger said as he leaned forward in his seat. "You're telling me that a bunch of religious men are conspiring with the Federation to destroy this man on false charges."

"That's what I'm saying."

"How can they have that kind of pull on the Federation to

involve its security agents?"

"One of the clergymen is president of the Ministerial Association and a friend of General MacDaniel."

Vince Kruger removed his glasses and stared at her intently.

"Are you talking about Bob Morgan?"

"Yes!" she said in astonishment. "Do you know him?"

"You bet I do! The son of a bitch has fought me for twenty years trying to get his religious tripe on the air. We went to court over it. I wasn't about to let him have a money-making operation on one of my channels. I'm not a spiritual man, mind you, but that guy makes my skin crawl."

"I know what you mean, sir."

"Don't you remember, Frank, he's the guy who gave the papers some dirt on me to try to undercut my merger with the networks. He and I are old enemies."

Michelle was suddenly filled with new hope that this crazy idea just might work.

"Within a week, Morgan and his cronies are going to distribute to the world pornographic images that have been doctored to look like Adam Hawthorn."

"Why is it that you're so concerned about this man?"

"He's the most extraordinary human being I've ever met. I've not only heard his words, I've seen him in action. This man is truly a sign of goodness and light in the world."

"You've come under his spell, have you?"

"No sir, I don't believe I have. I'm not a follower by any means. My dad will testify to that. I'm simply saying that I have witnessed his gifts of healing, and even more importantly, his depth of insight. What they're doing at Renouveau is nothing less than renewing humanity."

"Right," Kruger said with skepticism. "I've never been much of an idealist, but I will tell you what I am. Your daddy will back me up on this. I'm a fair man, I believe in justice the way some people believe in God. I can't stand liars and fakes. If you tell me this man is innocent, I'll believe you. But why come to me?"

"I believe that the only way to keep such a terrible injustice from taking place is to give this man the opportunity to speak to the world population and let it judge who he is and what he has to say, particularly since it is of ultimate concern to everyone."

Vince Kruger looked at her intensely, digesting what she had just said.

"You're saying that you want to get him on television?"

"On international television."

He thought for a moment.

"You know what would be an incredible media event?" he responded with enthusiasm. "If he spoke live around the world and everyone everywhere got to hear the same thing at the same time! That would be quite an event, wouldn't it?"

She was amazed at his idea. Frank Blair wondered what his old friend had up his sleeve.

"Frank, think of the marketing possibilities of such a deal! It could outgross a championship boxing match. Except that we'd make it free for everybody. The PR value to my companies would be worth their weight in gold. A charitable gift to humanity . . . "

"Won't it cost an absolute fortune?" Blair wondered.

"Sure, it would. Last time I did a live world link-up like that for some band whose name I can't remember, it took almost a hundred mill, inclusive of the pre-sell campaign."

"You have that kind of spare change?"

"Even I don't have that kind of money to throw around, but when I think of it as an opportunity for my companies' worldwide reputation, it's a different story. And I'd give a lot to get back at Morgan and his kind. That would be a blow he'd never get over!"

"I believe it might be, sir," Michelle stated excitedly. "He thinks he's won the battle already."

"Wouldn't it take months to set this up?" Frank Blair asked with concern.

"You don't know what kind of power I've got, Frank. I can get the word out on five hundred channels and in twenty-four hours so that three-quarters of the world's population will know about it. The next day, there won't be anybody anywhere who won't know about it except for a few hermits in the woods."

"You've got the world's ear, Vince?"

"Ears and eyes and more than those body parts, Frank! I figured out the game and I played it to win. I always told you that if you got control of where people live, you could sell them anything.

And where they live now is in front of their TV screens. For most people, that's all there is to live for: distraction. And I'm the king of distraction! It's the secular man's form of religious experience because it's an anesthetic to life. For many it's a lobotomy. That's how things are."

"So how would we go about creating such an event?" Michelle asked.

"I'll talk to my people today. You get us Adam Hawthorn and we'll do the rest. Can you deliver him?"

"I'm acquainted with his key people. I believe they'll recognize the importance of this opportunity once they know what they're faced with."

"I see. But I can't put anything in motion until I get something more concrete from you. We're dealing here with a major juggling of personnel, programs, and advertising. I can't make that move without knowing that we can get him for certain."

Blair looked at his daughter nervously. He'd heard the story of her departure from the community and was aware of how difficult it would be for her to return there.

"I'll work it out," she said as bravely as she could. "I'll get word to you as soon as I can."

"You do that."

He pulled out a card and scribbled on it with a golden pen.

"This is my personal business line. You let me know as soon as possible."

"You're doing the world a great favor, sir."

"Don't be naive, Michelle. I don't do things like this that aren't favorable to my enterprises. And you just promised to hand me on a silver platter the man who may possibly be the single most famous individual in the world. If not now, then very shortly. That makes for good television."

"You're not concerned with what he has to say?"

"Not a bit. I don't care if he wants to tell people that butterflies are angels in disguise. The fact is that he has become a celebrity and is therefore a marketable commodity. In my business, you put two and two together and you sometimes get an astronomical figure. This commodity obviously meets a need with the amount of interest he's generated. When you meet that need, the consumer will respond."

She was uncomfortable with his way of looking at the situation.

"Don't worry. I'm not just an old greedy bastard like many have said. I'm also a vengeful s.o.b., and if I can beat Morgan at his dirty tricks, then count me in!"

She was still distressed by his rather vulgar view of this critical event.

"What did you expect, Michelle?" Kruger said as he leaned toward her. "That I was going to become a true believer and put him on the air for some high and mighty spiritual purpose? What does it matter to you what my intentions are as long as they fit in with your aims?"

"That's true, Michelle," Blair added. "He's willing to do it, and that's all you need to know."

"Of course," she said, letting go of her unnecessary - requirements, like purity of motive. It was all a dirty game and she could only hope that something good would come out of it.

"I'll contact you in twenty-four hours, Mr. Kruger."

He stood up and shook her hand. "I hope this is helpful to you. I know it'll be helpful to me."

"You're doing a deed of great importance, sir."

Frank Blair approached his old friend and took his hand. "This means everything to my daughter, and therefore everything to me, Vince."

"That makes me happy, Frank. Next time you folks fly into town, stay around for awhile and we'll talk about old times."

"I'd love that."

Michelle and her father left the office and were escorted to the helicopter on top of the building that would take them to their jet. She realized that what had just taken place was the easiest part of her desperate efforts.

* * *

Jimmy was frantic. He couldn't locate Michelle's signal anywhere and hadn't gotten any messages in the last twelve hours. He had even contacted Bracken's office, but they had not received anything either. His gut feeling told him something was terribly wrong.

Hank Bracken didn't become upset until he learned that no reports were coming in from the backup agent either. Jack Farris had also fallen off the radar screen.

This was a code red situation: all communication was cut off. The entire investigative team was silent or silenced.

Bracken burst into the sub-basement room.

"Jimmy, you heard anything?"

"Nothing, sir."

"How can we lose two agents at once?"

Bracken looked over at the empty message screen. Suddenly, a red light came on followed by an agent's code.

"Jack, is that you?" Bracken called out.

"It is, Mr. Bracken," a voice responded amidst heavy static.

"Why the hell haven't you reported in?"

"There's been an incident."

That was the unofficial code word for a disastrous turn of events.

"Tell me!" Bracken said as he leaned toward the computer alongside Jimmy. "Don't wait for me to get an ulcer!"

"We've been uncovered. I haven't been able to communicate because I've been in the hospital."

"How bad are you hurt?"

"It was enough to keep me there for months, but instead it was only twenty-four hours. I was mauled pretty bad by a crowd."

"How about Michelle?"

"She took off. I don't know where she is now."

"Were they after her?"

"Yes, but I believe she's okay."

"What do you mean, you believe?"

"Well, I was informed that she left without being harmed."

"From a reliable source?"

"It was Adam Hawthorn himself, sir."

"He told you that?"

"Yes sir. He was pretty upset about all that's happened here. He didn't want his people to behave like that. In fact, he's so distressed about it that he's sending everybody home."

"What do you mean?"

"He called everybody to his study and decided who would stay and who had to leave."

"Is he closing the whole thing down?"

"No, but he said that if they hadn't learned anything by now, they never would. And he doesn't want to waste his time."

"So how are the people taking it?"

"You can hear them crying all day long around here. It's a tragedy. They're begging him to reconsider, to forgive them . . . I've had a hundred people come up to me and apologize. It's the weirdest thing I've ever been through."

"So where are you now?"

"I'm in my car and I'm on my way home."

"Excuse me?"

"It does no good to stay here, sir. My work is over. I've been exposed and, besides, I have no desire to spy on him anymore."

"Now is the time when we need you most in the area. To keep watch on the changing events."

"I'm not interested, sir. I'm off the case."

"You can't take yourself off the case! We don't do things that way around here. I'll tell you when you're off the case!"

"Sir, you can tell me I'm fired if you want. I saw the goodness in that man and I won't have anything to do with causing him trouble."

"What's gotten into you, Farris?"

"He put his hands on me when I was lying on that floor all broken up and I felt a love coming through his fingers that literally mended my bones. It was the most spiritual moment of my life and I'll treasure it as long as I live. The Federation can go to hell as far as I'm concern. I will not stay on this case. Over and out."

The screen went blank.

"Get him back up!" Bracken barked.

"He's shut off, sir. He won't be talking to us again."

"I've never known him to behave that way!"

"With all due respect, Mr. Bracken, if you'd seen all the news reports in the past six months, it would be clear to you that strange things happen to people out there."

"What do you mean?" he asked with irritation.

"Just like with agent Farris, people change around this man."

"How do they change?"

"I guess you could say the best part of them comes out."

"You don't really buy that stuff, do you, Jimmy? You've been sitting in the dark too long!"

"Sir, you heard it for yourself. As you know, Farris was one of the toughest security agents we had. Wasn't he some kind of championship boxer?"

"That's right. Jack was tough. I guess he's having some kind of nervous breakdown."

"I beg to differ with you, sir. He reacted just the same way that others have."

"What is he, a hypnotist or something?"

"I don't know."

"You don't think Michelle's gotten under his spell, do you?"

"Sounds like she had to run for her life. It doesn't suggest that she got caught up in all this. I think you should send someone out there to find out what is going on."

"Nobody's free now. We've got cases coming out of our ears."

"I'll go, sir," Jimmy said with all the courage he could muster.

"You?" Bracken cried out. "What's your qualification?"

"I don't look like an agent . . . "

"Well, that's true enough. How soon can you be ready?"

"My bags are already packed."

* * *

Within three hours, Jimmy was breathing in the fresh spring air as he stood on the edge of the property. He thought through the strategy that he had been instructed to follow in order to get information on Michelle. He was armed with a miniature message sender that was relayed via satellite back to headquarters.

On the way in, he had spotted news trucks several miles from Renouveau. They were permanently settled in as the news stories continually poured out from the community. A great media circus was underway, and he felt very uncomfortable landing in the middle of it. But he knew that Bracken was right. They could take no more chances with standard agents. Someone needed to be on sight to get information on Michelle.

Jimmy wandered about the place. Everything was quiet as construction had been interrupted because of the recent crisis. A decision had not yet been made to build again. He found himself near the front entrance of the property. In the distance, a low flying jet was landing vertically from the sky. He knew that it could only be a Federation plane. He looked about to make sure no one was in the area and pulled out his communicator. There were no messages for him. His curiosity kicked in. He had an intuition that Michelle was the passenger in the jet. Any moment now, he would spot a car heading his way. Sure enough, a dust cloud confirmed that a car was heading in his direction.

He didn't know what to do. He couldn't just stand there and wait for it to appear. But his lack of experience in this business left him without any way of dealing with the situation. Soon the car came off the main road and turned onto the dirt path leading to the compound. He sat on a bench and lit a cigarette.

The car bounced along the road and came to an abrupt halt alongside him. Michelle was at the wheel. He put out his cigarette and hurried to her.

"Is that you, Jimmy?" she asked in astonishment.

"Michelle! I can't tell you how glad I am to see you!"

"What in the world are you doing here?"

"Bracken sent me. We're worried to death about you."

"Is the whole department going to show up now?"

"We heard what happened to you. Jack Farris left. You have no more backup."

"Are you my backup now?"

"Bracken didn't want to take any chances on someone who might look like an agent."

"I see. Well, maybe you can be helpful to me. But it depends on whether you want to work with me or follow Bracken's instructions."

"We've been through that one already."

"Have you met the prophet?"

"No, not yet."

"Hop in. There's been a change of plans, Jimmy."

He hurried around the car and jumped in. He was thrilled to be near her once again.

CHAPTER 24

Just as Michelle suspected, Jimmy was more than willing to assist her in whatever she had to do. The first task was to find a way to speak with Lynn or Jeremy in order to get in touch with Adam. She knew she couldn't just walk through the doors, although Jimmy's report on the prophet's reaction to the violence of his people eased her concerns.

Jimmy's fresh, innocent face was ideal for her purposes. Soon he was wandering through the mission house, looking for someone who fit Lynn's description. He recognized the tall, lanky figure of Andrew Bradshaw that Michelle had depicted for him, as well as Jeremy and his curly red hair. But there was no sign of Lynn.

He walked over to her office where the administrative work took place. He came across Juanita and the baby with several others in a lounge area of the building.

"I need to see Lynn Wilkes," he said timidly.

One of the woman turned to him.

"She's very busy right now."

"This is urgent."

"You'll have to see someone else. Lynn handles administrative matters."

Juanita studied him carefully. Her sweet brown eyes had retained the maturity that had accompanied her back into this world after the prophet's healing. She picked up the baby and approached Jimmy.

"I'll take you to her. Follow me."

"You know Lynn is too busy," the woman protested.

"It's okay, Marla. Come with me."

Jimmy followed her through a hallway toward a closed door. Juanita walked ahead of him.

"It's about Michelle, isn't it?" she asked with her back to him.

A nervous shiver went through his body. He didn't respond.

"It's all right. You can tell me. I like Michelle."

His mind went numb. He couldn't understand what the girl had picked up on. She turned around, smiling.

"You don't have to be afraid. Nobody's going to hurt anybody here anymore. Not after what happened the other day."

She knocked at the door.

"Come in."

"Go on," she told Jimmy. "Don't worry."

Jimmy looked at her in amazement. He'd never seen a girl her age with such depth of character. He entered the small cluttered room where Lynn was busy at work on a computer.

She had been working for many hours. He hair was ruffled and her clothing wrinkled. There were mounds of paper everywhere. She turned her tired eyes upon him.

"Who are you?" she asked.

"My name's Jimmy. Michelle sent me."

She stopped her work and turned to face him completely.

"Is she all right?" she asked, genuinely concerned.

"She's here."

"She is? Does she want to make more trouble?"

"No, ma'am. Not at all. It's the opposite."

"Are you an agent also?"

Jimmy did his best not to react.

"Don't lie to me," she said, shaking her head. "Don't even try. What is it that she wants now?"

"Michelle wants to help."

"That's hard to believe."

"You've got to believe her! She's a good person. She never intended to cause any harm here."

"You're lying again," Lynn said calmly. "She was here under false pretenses. Had Stargazer not revealed her purposes, she would have done terrible harm to Adam."

"That's not right, ma'am. The harm is still about to be done and she's here to stop it."

"What do you mean?"

"Please come and see her. She knows that you'll listen to what she has to say."

"How do I know it's not some kind of trap?"

"Do I look like somebody who can trap you?"

Lynn smiled sadly.

"Take me to her."

Michelle sat in her car on the outskirts of the compound, doors locked just in case anyone recognized her. She had never prayed in her life, but an irresistible inner urge was calling out to whatever powers existed in the cosmos to help her save Adam from the evil that was about to befall him. Just as she opened her eyes, she saw the silhouettes of Jimmy and Lynn heading toward her. She knew it was an answered prayer.

Within an hour, Michelle was sitting across from Adam. Jeremy, Lynn and Andrew were in the room while Jimmy waited outside. Adam contemplated all that he had been told, seemingly unaffected by the information. Andrew stood in the corner, red-faced and humiliated to the core of his being by what Michelle had revealed. He could barely hold still and was sweating profusely. Jeremy was agitated and horrified by the information. Lynn held Michelle's hand, offering her the comfort of forgiveness and friendship.

Finally Adam spoke.

"This is the opportunity that was predestined. You've asked me in the past how people will hear this urgent call. Now you know. It will not be without sacrifice and you will need to be prepared for everything to change afterward."

"Maybe you should reconsider," Jeremy said.

Adam held up his hand to silence him. "This is not a decision for me to make. This is the path that has been traced. That's why, Andrew, though you must live through the penance of remorse, you must then let it go. Know that I forgive you and that you have played into the hands of destiny."

"What do you anticipate will happen next?" Lynn inquired, concerned by the seriousness of his tone.

"Once the word is spoken, everything will be unleashed. The cleansing process will begin as foretold by the visionaries of the past. Nature itself will be in turmoil and humanity will have to live with the consequences. We will enter the time of transition known as the Tribulation. You will each have to live by your spiritual sight. There is no guarantee of security."

"Are you predicting that a world catastrophe will take place in the near future?" Andrew asked in a trembling voice.

"I have known from the beginning that the work I am to perform will generate the onset of all that has been foretold. It will not only be human cruelty and ignorance that will bring on the disasters, but the earth itself will enter a period of agony and purification."

"What is the good of your message if we are doomed anyway?" Andrew cried out.

"It is when the storm rages that you most dearly need to have firm foundations beneath you. I am the last one to provide such an anchor before the storm."

"Have you seen the future then, Adam?" Lynn asked.

"Many have seen what is to come. I am both the last warning and the herald of its onset. After me comes the devastation. As it is written, the sun will no longer give its light and therefore you will have to find light within you in order to survive the dark night that will overshadow this planet."

"Are you then a prophet of doom?" Andrew asked in desperation.

"No, friend, we have not made this journey together for such a purpose. I offer the rope that allows those who can to climb out of the raging destruction that will soon wreck havoc across the world."

"Will your life be at risk if you do this thing?" Lynn asked, eyes sparkling with tears as though she already knew the answer.

"Life itself is a risk, Lynn. We are never secure here below. It is for this purpose that I have come and I cannot say what will happen once it is accomplished."

"Do you think the world will believe you?" Jeremy asked.

"That's not my concern. I did not come here to be believed but simply to state the facts."

Andrew suddenly threw himself at Adam's feet, weeping.

"I'll never forgive myself for what I've done!"

"You must!" the prophet said, putting his hand on the wretched man's head. "You were a pawn in destiny's unfolding. There is more work for you to accomplish, so you need to recover and make yourself useful again."

Andrew looked at him through his tears, gratitude dawning over his misery.

"Accept your humanity and get on with it."

"I'll do anything. My life is yours, Adam."

"Don't give it to me," he responded. "Give it to the purposes of goodness. Be a soldier of the Light."

"I'll never falter again!" he exclaimed.

"You are forgiven," the prophet said with a knowing look. Andrew's promise would be hard to keep.

"Tell us this, Adam, if you wish to ease our sorrow," Jeremy asked, "why does Stargazer call you the Visitor? Are you not one of us?"

"You're asking me if I am human? Yes, I'm made of flesh and blood, just like you."

"How did you acquire these gifts and this vision? How did you overcome human weakness?"

"I made a choice and did not turn back from it. As for the rest, that is between me and the Source of my arising. I will say this to you, however, any of you can be messengers of the most High if your motive is pure."

"Are you from another world?" Andrew asked, his anguish giving him foolhardy daring.

"What do you think, Andrew?"

"I think you're not one of us. I think you're from the distant future and have come back to warn us."

"Really?" He looked at the others. "And you, Jeremy, who do you think I am?"

"I think you're from another galaxy, here to save our species."

"What about you Lynn?"

"I think you're a lover of God whose love has set him free."

"And you Michelle?" Adam asked, turning his flaming eyes upon her.

"What does it matter what I think?"

"I'm asking you."

"I think . . . I think you're the Second Coming."

"People will say all these things of me after this event. Each will believe what he or she wants to. Be sure of one thing: the facts will not change. This earth is heading toward calamity and all must be prepared to contribute to the good or be swept away in tragic and meaningless deaths."

"Is there any hope that these catastrophes can be avoided?" Jeremy asked.

Adam looked at them solemnly. "There is only hope that you can withstand the trauma to come by anchoring yourselves in the spiritual dimension of your being. Survivors will have to be completely devoted to helping others even over their own needs, or renewal of life will not take place and it will mean the end of humanity."

"Do you think the world will believe you?" Michelle asked.

"As I've stated, it doesn't matter. Those who can hear will take action. Those who only want to play with ideas will suffer the consequences. And those who reject this last assistance will plunge into ultimate despair. This is a call for those who are willing to manifest that which they care most deeply about. It is in becoming that which they value most that they will make themselves useful. The days of the philosophers are over. Humanity can no longer afford the luxury of merely thinking about the good. They must become it."

Lynn turned to Michelle. "How do you think the Federation will respond to him?"

"They'll see him as a threat, destabilizing the population. The Federation's security blanket is in keeping people satisfied with the little comforts and pleasures that they can get out of life. If that's shaken, chaos and discontent are sure to follow. But they have no control over Adam's presence on international television. It will also depend on how the world population responds to him. If there is an overwhelmingly positive reaction, they'll be afraid to touch him."

"These things do not matter," Adam interrupted. "The World government is only a puppet show that will be blown away with the first cataclysm. They only think they have power, but they will not be able to control the fate of humanity. As for what happens to me, I have only one concern: to complete this last mission."

"How did you learn of your purpose?" Andrew asked, wiping the tears from his face, still sitting at his feet.

"The same way that you will learn of yours if you remain true to your commitment. The spiritual world does communicate to us. We simply don't listen. The subtleties of those messages are most often beyond our capacity to perceive, but that's the very purpose of the transformation of which I speak. If we are cleansed of the effects of the world, we become capable of interpreting the inner sensations and vibrations that come to us from beyond this three-dimensional realm. At the same time, the messages are becoming louder and clearer because of the urgency of the times."

"Why has patience run out for us?" Jeremy asked, eyes wide with fear.

"We have reached the point of no return, Jeremy. We have the intelligence to destroy ourselves in a matter of minutes and yet we have not developed the wisdom to make right use of our mind's inventions. The perversion of our abilities has poisoned the planet as well, and we have tested the greater powers that surround us to the extreme. We have simply run out of time.

"If you look back at the last century with its world wars, they represent the climax of a history of some fifteen thousand previous wars. This is the generation that is born to witness the cleansing of humanity's misdeeds. Perhaps some of you will be involved in a new start. But it will have to come out of the ashes of all the developments that have led us to this point.

"In a way, the global advances in communication were meant to make this moment possible. The world will not be able to say that it wasn't properly warned. Every nerve ending of electronic communication will be a channel for this final effort. Each human being will have the opportunity to know what he or she must do when the end takes place."

"What is the positive outcome of this communication?" Jeremy asked.

"Individuals could become conscious of their duty to the universe, and of their oneness with their fellow human beings. If the right shock is applied to their psyche, perhaps they can avoid being mere kindling for an apocalyptic future. Such a calamity is not merely an external event. It is linked with the general psychosis that has overtaken humanity. Each individual must aligned himself with his or her highest potential and thereby create a mass shift in the psychic atmosphere of this planet. Without that, there is no hope for avoiding utter annihilation."

"You believe that your speaking to the world will make possible such a sudden change?" Michelle asked skeptically.

"I don't know that it will create the change, but I do know that the option is there. Human beings need only have their consciousness raised, lifted out of the nightmarish sleep in which they wallow in order to redirect their lives and their relationship to the world around them."

"Will the religions allow their followers to accept the wisdom you present to them?"

"My task is simply to assist each person to encounter the source of wisdom within themselves, not to hand them a new set of rules and dogmas. The religions have become too rigid to delve into the deepest recesses of individual consciousness and break through to unitive consciousness. They can influence it, provide it with direction however limited, but they cannot keep a person from knowing what they know in their hearts."

"This could create revolutionary changes."

"That is precisely what is needed immediately. Without a liberation from the perversions of religious intolerance and separatism, the psyche of humanity cannot shift from the dark course that it has plunged itself into. This is the last chance for us to turn away from total destruction. The forces of light wish to make one final attempt to avert what is about to happen. It's a nearly hopeless situation, but it must be attempted."

"If you know yourself that it's almost hopeless," Andrew said, "aren't you asking for your own destruction by doing this?"

"Andrew," Adam responded, looking at him with deep compassion, "don't you understand yet that the only true path is that of self-sacrifice? It is in the dying of our egos that we are born, as the messengers of light have told humanity so many times. I'm not concerned with what happens to me personally. I'm concerned with fulfilling my charge."

"But if you are destroyed, what will happen to us?"

"If you keep focused on the path and remain aligned with your highest aims, then you will find the strength and the help to deal with what is ahead."

"We need your guidance!" Andrew insisted. "We can't be left like orphans!"

"What you must do is act on what you have learned, and become that which you most value. There is no time to linger. You must become your own teacher."

"I'm not ready for that!" Andrew cried out.

"No one is ever ready for the next step. It always requires a great effort, a great stretch of our capacities. That is precisely why it is the next step forward. This is true for all of us, both human and angelic beings. It is the way of spiritual evolution."

"Why does it have to be so hard?" Lynn asked.

"We make it hard," Adam answered gently. "Our selfishness, our blindness, our foolishness make it painful. If we could see things as they really are, if our hearts were cleansed of all the accumulation of misunderstanding and confusion, then it would be perfectly clear and straightforward. The only real fulfillment is in becoming a conscious participant in the grand designs of the universe. If we choose to live for ourselves, we become a cancerous cell of the cosmic organism. We do not exist for our own gratification, but for the benevolent purposes of the whole of which we are a part. To do otherwise is to fall away into confusion, isolation, and intolerable despair. The choice is ours."

"Can you tell us if anyone in this room will survive what is to come?" Jeremy asked.

"Survival is not the issue. Awakening is. If you awaken to your true nature and the purpose of your existence on this planet, then you will achieve the peace and fulfillment that your spirit seeks, regardless of external circumstances. Those who attempt to survive just to continue life as it is now will achieve nothing except a furtherance of misery."

"Why don't we build underground shelters?" Andrew asked.

"It is not my task to live on and renew humanity. That belongs to others. As to what you choose to do after this call has gone out to the world, that will be up to you. I will have no part in attempting to keep physical life alive when calamities overrun us."

"Isn't it a good thing to try to survive?" Andrew asked again.

"You'll have to decide that for yourself. I am not here to think for you. Once you have decided for the higher good, everything else will fall into place. You will know what you must do. But you will have to sacrifice your need to care only for your own life. If you choose to survive, it will have to be for others. Otherwise you will be useless."

Adam then called each one over to him one at a time. Andrew was the first. He took his hands and held them in the furnace of his palms.

"Andrew, release yourself from the grip of your intellect and open your heart. There you will find the truth you have been seeking for so long."

Andrew smiled through his tears and stepped away as the prophet motioned for Michelle to approach.

"Michelle, you must accept the part of yourself that is not strong and confident, but vulnerable and in need. That part of you will introduce you to your spirit and to your true strength."

"Please forgive me . . . " she whispered.

He placed a finger over her lips and gave her a look of unconditional love that ripped through her armor. She wept quietly as she returned to her seat.

Jeremy was next.

"My good friend, you will need to free yourself from the rational dogma of a religion that has lost its soul. In the same way, liberate yourself from your own closed view of reality. Learn that you know little."

Jeremy hugged him with great emotion. Adam patted him gently on the shoulder and turned to Lynn.

"Lynn, be willing to trust with your whole heart, even when uncertainty is the only certainty. Live in the faith that all things work for good for those who love. Be free of your childhood fears. This is your birthright."

She kissed him on the cheek and felt a new strength fill her inner being in the glow of his powerful eyes. She sensed that he was actually conveying this new strength to her, or at least giving her a taste of what it could be.

The group sat in silence around the prophet, each person turned deeply inward and face to face with the depths of his or her being. Together, they entered the holy of holies through their individual inner sanctuary. In their solitude, they found a bond that held them together in a profound intimacy.

* * *

Jimmy sat outside enjoying the warm sunshine on his pale skin that rarely communed with the star's heat. The peacefulness of the surroundings, along with the singing birds and chirping crickets, were foreign to him. For his entire life, he had known only the noise of traffic and the rush of people on busy streets. He had no idea that life was originally meant to be lived according to the rhythms of nature, rather than the frantic pace of the city.

He hadn't felt this peaceful for many years. The feeling brought back a vague memory of family vacations: a beach, and the company of relaxed adults—perhaps the rarest memory of all. He realized that he had grown up thinking that such inner peace and contentment was only meant for vacations, not as a daily way of life. Looking at the trees and open landscape around him, he understood that he had been terribly wrong. This was the way life was meant to be for human beings, and it was the one aspect of existence that the Federation could not regulate, package and deliver to the populace.

As he scanned the countryside, drinking in the renewing impressions of nature, he saw a pickup truck turn off the path to the compound. The thought came to him that it was rather odd for this vehicle not to be entering through the main gates. But he dismissed it, and turned his attention to a bed of flowers that was planted nearby. Within moments, he felt that something had entered into the deep peace of the atmosphere and disturbed it. Instinctively, he turned around and saw a stocky, unclean middle-aged farmer getting out of the truck and walking toward him. There was something wrong about this man's presence here. He was obviously not one of the prophet's followers. Jimmy stood up to encounter the man.

"Hello," he said awkwardly.

The man did not respond. His face was held in a vice of hate and violence which the shade of his old cowboy hat could not hide.

"Where's Hawthorn?"

"Do you have business with him?" Jimmy asked, surprised to find himself protective of the man he'd come to spy on.

"I sure do! My lands border his and I gotta talk to him about a broken windmill."

"You can talk to one of his assistants . . . "

"He's in that building, right?"

"Yes," Jimmy said with hesitation. "But he's in a meeting right now."

The man moved toward the door. Without thinking, Jimmy stepped in front of him.

"Just a minute, sir. I think you should wait until they're done."

"What's your problem? I got business with him, I tell ya!"

The silent scream of Jimmy's intuition shook through his being. He looked the man over. That's when he saw the bulge of a gun in his pocket. It was unmistakable.

"Is that a gun?" he asked, as adrenaline scorched his nerves.

The man's eyes glazed with anger. "I thought you worked for the Federation!"

"What?" Jimmy cried out, completely thrown off-balance by the unexpected statement.

"That's right, I've been hired by your people. So shut up and get outta my way!"

"You're no agent!" Jimmy whispered, his mind racing a hundred miles an hour, trying to figure out what all this meant.

"Look, son, that man in there took my daughter away from me. He won't let me see her. When the Federation called me, I was more than willing to be their delivery man."

Delivery man. That was a standard code word for a hired assassin. A shiver rushed through Jimmy's body.

"Who hired you?"

"Do I have to show my credentials?"

"The Federation doesn't work with people like you. They've got professionals."

"I was a sergeant in the Syrian war, boy. I know my way around killin' and maimin'! Got the bronze star and purple heart to prove it! I woulda done this job for nothin'. But who's going to say no to thirty thousand dollars?"

"Why would the Federation want you to do this?"

"Ask General MacDaniel."

"General MacDaniel contacted you?"

The question burst out of his throat which was shutting down on him.

"Yep! Called me up at my farm at four in the morning. I don't now how you guys found me or knew that I'd be happy to do this. Amazing organization. Now step out of my way, Jimmy."

"You know my name too?"

"That's right. They gave me the lay of the land. You shouldn't be so surprised. You outta know they've got their act together."

He stepped forward. Jimmy grabbed his arm.

"What the hell . . . !" the farmer growled.

"You can't go in there now! There's another agent with him."

"Blair, right? They told me about her. They said she can't be trusted. It seems you can't do the job you're paid for. So I'll do it for you."

"Wait!"

Jimmy insisted, squeezing his hand around the man's arm.

In a rage, the farmer tore himself free and struck Jimmy across the face with a hammer blow that cracked his jawbone. He fell on the deck like a broken rag doll. Blood gushed from his mouth.

"You stupid fool!" the man shouted angrily.

Just then the door opened. Andrew and Michelle hurried outside. They had heard Jimmy's cry.

"What are you doing here?" Andrew yelled out.

Adam appeared in the doorway and stepped in front of Andrew.

"You were told not to return!" the prophet said. "Why are you here?"

"You should know why, mister magic man!" the farmer said through gritted teeth.

He pulled out his gun and aimed it at Adam. Michelle shouted and leaped in front of the prophet before anyone else could react.

"I'll kill you, too! Good riddance!"

Suddenly Jimmy rose up from the deck and threw himself on the man. They fell down the stairs as Jimmy tried to grasp the hand that held the gun, but he was no match for the farmer's strength.

The man pulled himself away and fired the weapon into Jimmy's side.

He looked up to aim the gun at Adam and was met with the heel of Michelle's foot smashing into his nose with the full force of an expert fighter. He fell back as the gun went off, shattering a window. She struck him again with power punches that knocked his head sideways and backwards. He staggered, but remained on his feet. She grabbed the arm that held the gun, pulled it forward, twisted it inside out and brought down a knife-hand chop right over the elbow. The sound of bones cracking mixed with his yell of agony. He dropped the gun.

Andrew and Jeremy took hold of the man and wrestled him to the ground. Andrew picked up the gun and pressed it against the farmer's temple.

"Don't do it!" Adam said. "Remember who you are."

Michelle hurried to Jimmy who lay in a fetal position, groaning. A river of blood spread across the deck and cascaded down the steps.

"My God, Jimmy!" she cried out as she fell to her knees beside him, staining her clothes with his blood.

"Get a doctor!" she shouted to the others frantically.

"He won't make it!" Andrew responded. "The bullet must have severed an artery."

Michelle turned to Adam who stood behind her.

"Please help him! You can save him, I know you can!"

Lynn wrapped her arms around Michelle as she looked at the wound. The bullet had made a gapping hole as it exited the body, being especially made, to cause the greatest possible damage.

"There's no way, Michelle. You have to let him go."

"No!" she cried out in tears. "He can't die! He can't!"

She looked back at Adam. "He tried to save your life!"

Adam turned Jimmy over as his body went into convulsions. His insides were leaking out of the wound. Michelle wailed when she saw the horrific sight. She realized there was no chance of keeping him alive.

The prophet took Jimmy's head in his hands and leaned toward him. Jimmy opened his eyes. He was going into shock, but for a moment seemed to regain his senses.

"Jimmy, I'm taking you with me. You'll be safe on the other side. Your courage will be rewarded. Do you understand me?"

The dying youth became calm and his body stopped convulsing. He nodded as his breathing slowed.

"This is not the end for you. There is work awaiting you in another realm. Do you believe me?"

Jimmy nodded again as his life-force seeped out of him.

Michelle stopped crying as she saw a beautiful look of profound peace invade the features of her friend. He had never been so handsome and serene.

"Is the pain gone?" the prophet asked.

He nodded and smiled weakly. The others held their breath as they watched on. Adam raised his hand in the ancient blessing. Jimmy's eyes focused on the sign and his eyes lit up momentarily as though reflecting an unseen brightness radiating from the prophet's hand.

"Be at peace, Jimmy. Your life is only now beginning. You will be able to help your friend, Michelle, in ways that you never imagined. You will never feel lonely or humiliated again."

Jimmy smiled. Then his eyes rolled back and a hoarse expiration announced the passage of his soul out of his body. Adam blessed his spirit silently on its way into another sphere of existence.

CHAPTER 25

New York City—2020

The prophet looked directly into the camera lens. Despite the bright lights and large gathering of people in the shadows of the studio, he was alone with every soul that looked back at him on countless screens around the world.

"Religion has only one goal. To connect you with your true nature. When you find that, you find your Creator, your freedom and your purpose. In finding your authentic individuality, you find your relationship with your neighbor and with everything that lives. If you fail to seek out the best of yourself, you sink into the ignorance and depravity that has created the world we know too well.

"You are passing through space and time. You come from beyond and you will return there. How will you account for what you have done with this gift of life? It is brief, and if it is misused, it will turn against you. If life is used for a higher purpose, it will lead to another existence that is not dependent on the physical.

"Every messenger has said the same thing in essence. Every messenger has been betrayed by his or her followers. The message is not a set of rules or rituals. It is a map to your own sacred self."

Absolute silence filled the studio, the control room, and the offices where the prophet's unblinking eyes seemed to look through the television set. The entire ten story building was caught in the grip of his gaze and of his words. This same hypnotic intensity radiated out into space and was beamed down across the entire planet.

The prophet continued.

"Spiritual teachers have talked about their experience of the sacred self as cosmic consciousness, or the peace that surpasses all understanding, or the inner light, or becoming transparent to the divine. Whatever words are used to describe it, the result of encountering this inner depth is always the same: it allows us to enter a vast identity and wisdom which enables right action to be manifested in the world.

"We are each meant to live with peace, joy, and compassionate outreach to the world around us. We are meant to be masters of ourselves, capable of overcoming all the difficulties of life, even the most traumatic. This is our birthright. But in order to experience it, we must recognize how far we are from living in this manner, why this is so, and what efforts we must make to live in such a way.

"Perhaps you've had moments of experiencing such a liberation coming from these higher states of being. Moments of great joy, or gratitude for being alive. Moments when your awareness is lifted beyond the knots and tensions of your worries and concerns, and you are free to enjoy the experience of being here now and happy to be alive.

"You may have had such experiences as children when you were less weighed down by the things that now preoccupy you.

"We are meant to dwell permanently in this habitat of the soul where higher consciousness dwells.

"Our first obstacle is our wrong perspective on our lives. We take ourselves for granted. We think we know who we are, but we can't count on ourselves to be the same person from one moment to the next. We are made of many disconnected selves, all pulled to and fro by imagination and unintentional thoughts. Yet we think we are in full control of ourselves.

"We have developed masks to protect ourselves or to manipulate others. We have absorbed into our idea of ourselves the images that our cultures tells us are the acceptable ways of being a man or a woman. We have accumulated the imitations of our parents, of our peers and of our environment.

"We are our own greatest source of suffering as long as we live in this state of automatic and unconscious behavior.

"So what is your true self that religion and philosophy have tried to point out to you? It is the life-force beyond your mistaken notion of yourself that is seeking to come through you and accomplish its work of goodness in the world. It is that mysterious "presence" that can overcome solitude, meaninglessness, and despair. Not only is it always there—deep within—but it is seeking you more than you are seeking it!

"We are not merely separate, disconnected life forms as the senses suggest. We are all rooted in the deeper life that brought us into being. This habitat is our source of hope and sanity in a world of chaos. We are a part of the greater life from which all things come. With that awareness, we discover our real importance and our purpose in the world.

"Open yourself to this power at the center of your being, and you will be made whole and capable of truly caring for others. This is the only hope for the human species. The universe is watching and depends on you!"

Even the crusty cameramen, gaffers, and grips stood in awed silence. Though some did not understand the depth of his words, they all sensed the power emanating from the prophet. It was a phenomenon they had never witnessed before. Nor had they ever seen anyone in front of a camera with such magnetism, not even charismatic celebrities and professionals in the media. There was something utterly different about this man, and the cameras seemed to magnify an invisible element in his presence that communicated powerfully to the viewer.

In the control room, the director, Frank Ross, came out of his daze long enough to realize that the man had stopped talking and that they were confronted with dead air time on live international television. He was about to call for a cutaway to a graphics page to fill the space when the prophet spoke again.

Just then, the control room phone rang. An associate reached for the receiver.

"Don't answer that! We're in the middle of a live broadcast!"

"It's General MacDaniel from the Federation!" the young technician cried out, fear distorting his features.

"You're kidding!" the producer, Jeanne Fleming, responded as she stood behind the technician at the switch, looking over his shoulder.

"How did they pipe him into the control room?" Ross barked.

"The General can get into wherever he chooses. He wants to talk to you, Frank."

"To me? I can't do that! My cameras are being watched by the whole world right now!"

"You'd better talk to him," the associate insisted. "He's pretty wound up."

Ross turned to another associate. "Take over for me. Keep camera one on him and zoom in a little."

He took the receiver. "Ross here. It's an honor, General . . . "

Ross' face immediately turned ashen as a voice shouted through the phone. He answered "yes, sir" several times with uncharacteristic meekness.

"I understand, sir," he said, and hung up the phone.

He turned to his colleagues. Rex Conway, a vice-president of Kruger Media, and Jeanne Fleming looked at him intently.

"We've been ordered to black out the broadcast immediately or the military's going to blow up our uplink antenna!"

"They can't do that!" the arrogant executive responded.

"We got an angry four star general on our hands with the full might of the World Federation at his fingertips. I don't think he's bluffing," Ross stated anxiously.

"Why didn't he talk directly with Kruger?" Conway asked.

"He did, and Kruger told him to shove it. You know how he is. He's having a great time shaking everybody up with this broadcast."

"Isn't the Federation supposed to protect freedom of speech?" Jeanne wondered bitterly.

"This kind of freedom of speech," Ross said as he pointed to the studio, "is a little too free for them, I guess. The general says there are riots breaking out in cities from Calcutta to Lawrence, Kansas. Fundamentalists are taking to the streets, smashing TV sets . . . half a dozen countries have mobilized their armies to control the population. It's utter chaos. He's pouring fuel on fire across the planet!" Ross added as he looked at the solitary figure whose serene and intense gaze looked at them from a dozen monitors lined up over the editing bay.

"I can't imagine that's what this man wanted to accomplish," Jeanne whispered.

"If he really has prophetic powers, why didn't he know this was going to happen?" Rex Conway questioned sarcastically.

"Maybe he did," Ross muttered.

Jeanne Fleming crossed her arms and peered through the wall-length glass at the man under the lights.

"Maybe he's doing this for the few who can hear him beyond the noise of his detractors."

An associate burst into the room.

"Miss Fleming! There are hundreds of people gathering in front of the building, yelling and screaming. They want us to shut off the broadcast or they'll burn us down!"

"This is America, damn it!" she shouted back in outrage. "Since when do we have to cater to mobs dictating what we put on the air!"

Ross wiped the sweat from his brow. "If we're caught between angry mobs and the Federation, I don't know how much worse it can get. We gotta make a decision and fast!"

"Don't you think Kruger should be the one to make the decision?" Conway asked, always one to pass the buck. "It's his network!"

"I'm going to talk to him!" Jeanne said as she hurried out of the room and rushed into the narrow hallway.

She came to a nearby office that was perched above the studio. She knocked and entered.

Vince Kruger was sitting in the middle of the room, glued to a giant television screen. Several of his underlings sat next to him, dressed in expensive suits that couldn't hide their subservience to their powerful boss. The producer hurried to him.

"Mr. Kruger, we've got a critical situation on our hands!"

He waved her away. "Don't bother me now. This is great stuff."

"We've gotten a call from the Federation. They're going to shut off the program if we don't do it ourselves."

"What are they going to do? Blow up our antenna?" Kruger said mockingly as he stared at the features of the prophet on the large screen. "Don't they like good television? This is bound to make every self-righteous clergyman completely insane!"

"That's the point, sir. He is making people crazy, and not just clergymen. There's a mob outside our front doors. We're gambling with high stakes, Mr. Kruger."

The media mogul turned his haughty features upon her.

"This man is the most exciting personality I've ever put on the air. He's got the gall to sit there and tell a couple billion people that all their cherished beliefs are wrong, and that the whole world's going to fall apart if we don't change. With one blow, he's got everybody mad at him. You can't pay for that kind of publicity!"

His underlings dutifully agreed, although their faces betrayed gnawing worry and fear.

"We can't let the military make the decision for us, can we?" Jeanne pressed on.

"Nobody tells Vince Kruger what he puts on the air! Nobody! Not generals or clergymen or wild mobs! This is my treat to myself. I always enjoyed generating a little controversy, and now I've found myself the ultimate troublemaker!"

He looked back at the screen. "Listen to this man! I'm not sure he's going to make it out of the studio alive! And you know what? I don't think he cares."

He waved Jeanne out of the room. She left reluctantly, shaking her head.

In the bowels of the studio, the prophet's four companions— Jeremy, Lynn, Andrew and Michelle—were growing more and more nervous as they watched people running to and fro in agitated states. Lynn spotted Jeanne Fleming hurrying away from the main office back to the control room with a grimace of panic on her face.

"This is not going well," Lynn said in a voice weighed down by fear.

"I come not to bring peace to the world, but a sword," Jeremy whispered. The others looked at him, not understanding. Jeremy studied the prophet who sat tall and peaceful in front of the cameras.

"He didn't come here to make things better, but to initiate the final breakdown that will lead us to the next phase of our history."

"That's impossible!" Michelle said loudly. "He's a man of light, not a messenger of darkness!"

"Surely he anticipated the results of what he's doing here," Lynn said nervously.

"Maybe the only way for humanity to evolve is to go through a radical cleansing period and start again," Jeremy wondered.

"You mean he's a bringer of wrath instead of enlightenment?" Andrew cried out.

"Maybe both," Jeremy said, deep in thought.

Jeanne Fleming entered the control room

"Kruger won't shut us off. He's having too good a time watching the whole world squirm."

"There's a responsible attitude!" Ross mumbled.

"If we don't do something soon, there's going to be hell to pay," Jeanne insisted. "I say we wrap it."

"We might create a riot among those who want to hear what he's got to say," Rex Conway suggested. "There's no telling with this kind of thing."

"Well, he sure isn't doing himself any favors by telling the world that we've got nothing to look forward to," Ross stated grimly. "What good is that going to do?"

"You think we should keep them all numb to what's really happening?" Jeanne asked.

"You bet! It's the way of the Federation and they've held us afloat against all odds for a quarter of a century."

"Looks like the ship has sprung a leak," she responded cynically.

Outside the studio, several policemen tried to force the crowd to move back. The sound of shattering glass rose over the shouting mass of raging people. The policemen vanished beneath the flood of bodies rushing for the doors.

A helicopter hovered over the building. Through the craft's open door, a Federation agent watched the scene in horror and reported to headquarters, shouting into a communicator.

"That's right! I said they just trampled two policemen down there!"

A voice came through his headphones. "The General says let nature take its course."

"I don't understand! You gotta send backup! Those men are getting killed."

"I repeat: The General's orders are to stay away and simply observe. The crowd is playing into our hands. They may do our work for us. Is that clear?"

"Not at all!" the agent shouted angrily.

"You won't have to be the one to put a hole in the man's head when he steps out of the studio. Let them take care of it. Over and out."

Under the bright lights, the prophet continued his fateful words to a global audience.

"There was a time when the effort to evolve into your higher nature was less urgent. People took a lifetime to mature into their spiritual selves. This is no longer the case. What is called for at this moment is a complete and immediate reversal of your way of being. Literally overnight, you must jump off the ledge of your ego and sacrifice yourself absolutely to the higher purpose of your presence on this earth. If you fail to do so, you will be unable to deal with the impending catastrophes. They were seeded long ago and are now upon us. The time is up, the clock has run out on this cycle of human history.

"Famines, economic devastation, world war, unstoppable crime, and colossal transformations of the crust of this planet are around the next corner. There will soon come a time when crowds will war in the streets over bits of food. Money will be worth nothing. Coastal lands will be ravaged and large centers of commerce will vanish beneath the ocean. Those who live in the cities will flee, only to discover that agriculture is no longer possible. Droughts that will last for decades, catastrophic earthquakes, tidal waves, storms as the world has never seen . . . these are already underway.

"The earth's poles will shift and temperate climates will become ice-covered, as has happened in other ages.

"The continents themselves will be altered. Millions will die within moments. Others will die from radiation and killer plagues that are already reaching cataclysmic proportions.

"All these tribulations are about to take place. Not sometime in the future, but now, in this generation, among your families.

"Everything is about to change and those who have not aligned themselves with the inner light will be of no use to themselves or to others. It is time to turn away from your self-indulgence and your petty existence and commit yourself to the transcendent reason for your being. Only this awareness will remain solid and dependable when all else has disintegrated.

"You have been warned. When you are lost and in darkness, there will be no one to comfort or guide you unless it is someone who has heeded my words. Those who choose to remain under the illusion of living for material possessions and cheap gratifications will weep bitterly over their error, but it will be too late. I call upon you to turn away from all that keeps you from encountering your spiritual nature, whether it be infantile selfishness, violence, lust, or a religion of half-truths.

"The coming devastation is our own doing, not that of outer forces of darkness. They can only do their evil with our willing participation. Beware! These subtle forces work through our thoughts and imagination. But we are responsible for the choices we make and the actions we manifest. Only through you can they enter into the physical world.

"When the devastations come, you will need to turn to the power within. The only teacher will be yourself. Trust that your Creator has given you the capacity to be led inwardly without the need of priests and temples. They will all be destroyed. Make yourself the temple! And then perhaps the coming tragedies will lead to rebirth.

"I have spoken what was given me to say."

He stood up. The cameraman hurried to tilt his camera and keep him in the frame, but the prophet had already turned his back to the world and was heading off into the shadows.

Ross shouted in the microphone.

"Give me something to put up there! Hey, what's happened to our picture?"

Every monitor in the room was filled with static instead of the barren set. The phone rang and the associate answered. He leaped out of his seat.

"My God! This is the uplink engineer. He says the satellite's been blown out of the sky by a missile!"

Everyone cried out in shock. Another phone rang and Ross grabbed it as though his life depended on it.

"Yeah? I just heard . . . "

He hung up with a trembling hand. "Sure enough, our three hundred million dollar bird was blasted into a heap of scrap-iron. They don't know what country the missile came from."

The vice-president snickered in disdain at what had just happened.

"Kruger's really proven himself the eccentric with this madness. He'll have to bare the consequences."

"Are you kidding?" Jeanne Fleming said angrily. "Weren't you watching? What happened in that studio was incredible!"

"Oh yeah? Some spiritual wacko telling us that it's the end of the world? Give me a break! How many times do we have to hear that nonsense? Doesn't everybody know better?"

"You're a hopeless case," she answered. "But you can't say he didn't warn you."

"Did he make a true believer out of you, Jeanne? I didn't think you believed in anything."

"There's something about him that really shook me up inside," she admitted nervously.

Phones started ringing off the hook in the control room and in every office in the building. After the initial shock, the world was now reacting.

Ross changed channels on their main receiver. Commentators and leading politicians were on every channel, reacting to the prophet's words. One of the angry speakers was Reverend Robert Morgan, whose face was twisted in a nearly uncontrollable rage. He waved a Bible in one hand as he denounced the prophet and the media that let the world listen to him.

"I guess the world doesn't like being told of its demise," Jeanne Fleming stated with a knot in her throat. "Wait! Stop on that channel!" she cried out.

On an international station from the Middle East, the scanned features of Adam Hawthorn were displayed with a huge monetary figure beneath it.

"They've put a price on his head!" she raged.

Another switch of the channel revealed city streets jammed with vast crowds, chanting and screaming in instantaneous reaction to the prophet's warning. Many were weeping in terror and panic. The words had been received only as a message of doom rather than an opportunity for transformation.

"It looks like his own words detonated his prophecy! I haven't seen this volatile a situation since the last war!" Jeanne said to the others as tears filled her eyes.

Already, the images were turning into familiar nightmarish scenes: tanks running over frantic mobs, police and military beating anyone they could get their hands on, religious fanatics preaching holy war to large and wild-eyed crowds, reporters falling to the ground to avoid gunfire, a primal outrage etched in faces that had lost all hope.

These were the very images that the World Federation had struggled so carefully to avoid ever having to see.

"Do you know what this means?" Jeanne asked as she turned away from the monitor. "The world has given its answer. We've said no to his offer of change!"

She pointed at the violent images on the screen. "This is our choice!"

Vince Kruger hurried through the hallways, closely followed by his executives. His face was scarlet beneath his mane of white hair.

"What happened? What happened to our uplink?"

"It's been shot out of the sky!" Rex Conway shouted out as he joined the entourage of dark suits.

"The Federation wouldn't dare!" Kruger yelled back, looking like a man about to be struck down by a heart attack.

"We don't know who did it yet," Conway responded.

Vince Kruger turned to him and suddenly became calm.

"What does that mean?"

"Just what you think it means, sir. It's an act of war on the sovereignty of our nation!"

The billionaire was speechless, as though he'd been punched in the stomach. He never imagined that his method of getting global attention would turn into something so dangerous.

"One missile could start a world war!" he whispered in horror.

Jeremy and the others led the prophet through the back of the studio, trying to get to the parking lot as soon as possible. The previously silent crew members were now filled with a strange, frightening energy. The prophet's impact on them was causing many to fall into psychotic breakdowns. Several were weeping, one was rolling on the floor, others were filled with rage.

"We gotta get out of here right away!" Jeremy whispered.

Andrew waited for them at the elevators. He too had great concern etched on his face and was in a ready stance to protect the prophet.

"Come on, hurry up!" he said frantically.

Adam was completely oblivious to everything around him. As though in the eye of the hurricane, he walked silently through the growing storm. The elevator doors opened and they entered. Lynn looked back and saw several people running toward them, an insane look in their eyes.

"What has happened to them?" she cried out.

The doors closed just as the people grabbed at them.

"Why are they reacting like this?" Michelle asked in horror.

Adam said nothing.

"Some kind of nervous reaction," Jeremy stated. "Adam must have hit a chord deep within them."

It was clear that Adam did not wish to speak. They waited silently for the elevator to reach the bottom floor, with a growing fear of what awaited them outside if the people in the studio were any example of the mass reactions.

The doors opened and they stepped out into an underground parking lot.

"Listen!" Andrew said.

Outside, they could hear the rumble of angry voices in the streets—cars screeching to a halt, honking, police sirens going off.

"My God!" Lynn said with a shudder of terror. "This can't be in reaction to Adam, can it?"

Lynn looked up at the prophet. His face was utterly serene. They got in the car and Andrew nervously pulled out of the garage. He drove up the ramp. The man at the booth took his ticket. But when he looked in the car and saw Adam, he started shouting in a sudden wild rage. He hurried out of his booth. Andrew sped away as the man banged his fists on the trunk of the car.

They pulled out into the street. A giant crowd was gathering. People poured out of apartment buildings, offices, and cars, and blocked their way.

"We've got a problem here!" Andrew cried out. "What do I do? Start running over people?"

"Help us, Adam! How do we deal with this?" Jeremy begged, realizing that the angry faces had spotted them.

Adam put up his hand to calm him. He suddenly opened the car door and stepped out.

"Don't do that!" they all shouted.

A great roar rose out of the crowd.

"Adam! Get back in the car!" Jeremy shouted.

But the prophet had already walked to the front of the car. He was immediately recognized. A horde of people raced over to him in an insane rage. Andrew jumped out of the car, followed by the others. Adam put out his arms, ordering them to stay behind him.

The shouting was deafening. Words like "Antichrist," "fake," and "blasphemer" could be heard above the screams. Andrew was becoming a victim of the savage energy as it filled him with the violence of the crowd. Jeremy took him by the arm.

"Stay calm, Andrew," he said to his friend.

"I won't let them hurt him!" he shouted back.

Michelle frantically pulled out her communicator and called an emergency number for police protection. But it was too late. Stones flew threw the air and struck Adam in the head and chest. The others ducked, but he stood tall and silent. The mob rushed at them, swinging tire irons, fists, and bottles.

Andrew and Jeremy fought back the first wave of assailants. But they were quickly overwhelmed. The prophet was surrounded on all sides and pulled away from his friends. Lynn and Michelle tried to push people away from him but were thrown back. Adam was brutally beaten.

Soldiers in riot gear finally rushed in and pushed the crowd back. Adam lay in the street, arms outstretched and covered with blood. His companions raced over to him. They burst into tears and moans of anguish at the sight of their friend and teacher.

"Why have they done this to you?" Jeremy yelled in anguish.

Michelle jumped to her feet just as the angry mob broke through the barricade of soldiers. She knocked down the first two men with shuddering blows fueled by pain and outrage. Her companions rose up and were pushed away by policemen to avoid the rush of the screaming masses.

Andrew took hold of Michelle who was attempting to keep all of them away from the prophet. He pulled her away to safety. A dozen men surrounded Adam's body and beat him ferociously. They were lashing out at the inevitability of their fate, sensing instinctively that his prophecy was true and that they were the doomed generation who would suffer utter annihilation.

Panicked and searching for help, Lynn looked around for more policemen to come to their aid. She caught sight of something just ahead of them and cried out.

A luminous shape the size of a man was moving down the street toward them. As people saw it, they fell back and rushed away, terrified by the supernatural apparition. The being of light dispersed the crowd with every step forward.

"Look! Look!" people cried out.

Michelle shouted at the top of her lungs.

"What is that?"

More heads turned and cried out as well. In the gray sky above, lightning growled and crackled, releasing blasts of electricity. Windows shattered around them.

The crowd scattered in terror. Jeremy and his companions also jumped back. The street cleared as a thunderous explosion shook the air. Every window within a half mile of the sight shattered as terrified people ran for cover with their hands over their ears.

A strange smell filled the air as electricity crackled all around like golden sparks raining down upon them. Glass fell into the street and smoke rose from the cables and trees that had been charred by the strange atmospheric phenomena.

Those who were hovering over the prophet and beating him looked up as they heard the cries of terror. The shimmering silhouette stood before them, hand raised in a menacing poise.

He lowered his hand and a beam of light struck the men surrounding the prophet, throwing them with the force of ten thousand volts across the street. They crashed to the ground in convulsions. The light form stood over the prophet's body.

Jeremy took hold of Lynn's arm as he studied the figure from behind their car.

"My God! Look who that is!"

She squinted and stared at the blinding sight. Within the glowing light, the features of a man could be made out. Like a transparent and fluid image, the features within the layers of shifting light formed into the face of Anton Hogrogian. He looked thirty years younger than the man they had known and his eyes were brimming over with an unspeakable compassion.

Just as Adam had once done for him, so now the apparition raised his hand over him in a sign of blessing. He kneeled beside the broken body. Fingers of light took hold of the prophet's hand. The ghostly figure rose and gently pulled on the man's limb.

Light flowed from the ghostly figure's hand into the body of the prophet. Suddenly, Adam began to glow with light as well. He arose, blood flowing from his wounds, eyes fixed on the apparition. The luminous figure smiled at the bloodied face of his friend and put his hand on his cheek. The prophet's entire body began to radiate with light. The crowd watched in stunned silence.

Hogrogian blessed him again and turned away. Ecstatic tears streaming down their faces, Lynn and Jeremy hurried to Adam and took hold of him to keep him steady on his feet. Jeremy raised his hand as a farewell to his old friend and mentor. Hogrogrian's gleaming figure looked back and smiled at his former student.

Suddenly the luminous silhouette vanished from sight, as though evaporating into another dimension. The crowd screamed in terror.

They rushed Adam to the car and helped him into the back seat. His body was limp and he was barely conscious. Tires squealing, Jeremy drove off as the crowd snapped out of its trance and attacked the vehicle. On fire with emotion, he was ready to run over anyone in his way.

"We'll get you back to Renouveau!" Lynn said to him as she wiped the blood from his eyes.

"It's too late . . . " Adam whispered in great pain, "the military has overrun the community. We must get to the airport!"

"What do you mean, too late?" Lynn asked horrified.

"They've taken everyone. Even Juanita and the baby."

"They can't put a twelve year old in prison!" Andrew cried out.

"The Federation can do whatever it wants! Don't you know that? That's what our world has come to!" Michelle said angrily. "Believe me, I know!"

"We're being followed!" Jeremy cried out as he looked in the rearview mirror. Flashing lights and sirens raced after them, blocked by the crowd and debris. "What do they want with us?"

"They want to arrest us, that's what!" Andrew replied.

"No, they want to do more than that, Andrew," Michelle added nervously. "They want to liquidate us. What has happened here has lifted the illusory veil of security that the Federation had so carefully placed over the world. The game is up and they can't live with that."

"Did you know this was going to happen?" Lynn asked Adam, partly to help bring him back to consciousness.

"It had to be accomplished at all cost," Adam said in a raspy voice, eyes closed. "Maybe a few people will receive the message differently and understand what they must do."

"Apparently none of *these* people do!" Jeremy said as rocks bounced off the car and bodies flung themselves on the hood, spitting at them.

"Can't you go any faster?" Andrew said in near panic.

"We'll find a highway ramp around here any minute and leave these maniacs behind."

Suddenly, a military vehicle pulled in front of them, blocking the way. Jeremy slammed on the breaks and barely avoided crashing into the Jeep. Several soldiers jumped out, weapons in hand.

"Back up!" Andrew shouted.

Frantically, Jeremy peeled rubber from the tires as he backed away toward the crowd that was running after them. He took off in another direction, heading for an alley.

Lynn noticed that Michelle had drawn a small pistol and rolled down her window, ready to fire at the assailants.

"Put that away!" she whispered, nodding toward Adam, suggesting that he would harshly disapprove of her action. Michelle put the weapon away. Her respect for the prophet's wishes came before her safety.

Adam sat in the middle of the seat, head leaning backward, blood pouring from wounds all over his body. His eyes were closed and he breathed slowly and intentionally, as though seeking to keep his body alive by sheer will power.

Andrew tore off part of his shirt and gave it to Lynn to soak up the blood and stop its flow. The car careened through the small side streets. Though the crowd's yelling could no longer be heard, sirens screamed everywhere. The people who had been chasing them now stood in mute terror, heads to the sky, as they noticed the strange coloration of the atmosphere. The air had turned an - unnatural orange and the clouds were shades of green, like the war paint they wore in severe storms.

The stunned crowd wandered about aimlessly, mesmerized and disoriented by the bizarre changes occurring around them. The prophet's word had been spoken and the human species would now face the consequences of its history.

Police cars converged on them from all directions, as did military vehicles and Federation agents. The place had become a war zone as the prophet was hunted down.

"Go left!" Andrew shouted as he saw a Federation car tearing across a park to cut them off at the intersection. They raced down the city streets at a hundred miles an hour. Jeremy knew that if they were caught, none of them would make it out alive. They had violated the fundamental principles of global security. The punishment would be merciless.

"How's he doing?" Jeremy called out as he concentrated on the wild ride.

"We've got to get him to a doctor!" Lynn cried out.

"They'll arrest him right there on the gurney!" Michelle said.

A police car pulled in front of them, causing Jeremy to swerve onto the sidewalk and nearly crash into a wall. The police car wasn't so lucky and smashed into a lamp post, turning around in circles three times before coming to a crashing halt.

Helicopters hovered in the air. Andrew looked up and saw a man with a rifle hanging out of the craft.

"These people are insane! They're acting like we killed the President or something."

"You killed the illusion of safety," Michelle said grimly. "They won't let us get away with it."

Jeremy drove through back streets until he found himself utterly lost. He was desperately seeking a highway on-ramp that would lead them out of the city. An old woman came out onto the sidewalk as they approached and suddenly pointed commandingly to a little road off the square.

"What is she doing?" Jeremy asked in confusion.

"I think she's telling us how to get out of here!" Andrew replied, amazed by the sight.

"Maybe we have a few friends after all," Jeremy said with renewed hope.

He turned down the street. Soon they were in sight of the edge of the city.

"What do you expect will happen at the airport?" Andrew asked the blood-covered prophet. He looked over his shoulder and shuttered at the sight of his teacher.

"We'll head for the reservation . . . "

"The reservation?" they all cried out in unison.

"Remember our friend Stargazer? He has offered us a haven away from the forces of the Federation. There are sacred places in the desert where we won't be found."

"I didn't even bring a toothbrush!" Lynn said half-jokingly in a futile attempt to ease the tension.

Adam turned his wounded head toward Lynn and opened the eye that was less swollen. He smiled at her softly.

"It seems that every time we take off on a trip together, we bring fewer and fewer material possessions."

"The Federation won't let you get on a plane!" Michelle said forcefully. They'll have road blocks up before we even get there."

"Do you have any suggestions?" Andrew asked.

"It so happens that I have a Federation jet still at my disposal."

"They would let you have access to it after all this?" Jeremy asked.

"Until my security clearance is denied, I can commandeer it," she said as she pulled out a communicator and pressed a few buttons. A green light came on. "It seems that they haven't yet taken action to fire me. A minor oversight in all the chaos," she added as her voice became tinged with sadness. She had never consciously decided to ruin her promising career.

She pressed another button and a map appeared on the tiny screen. She entered a search and pinpointed their location. She pressed another button and a pilot came on the mini-speaker. She gave him her coordinates and a nearby field where they would rendezvous.

"Looks like we've got tickets to wherever we want to go," she announced.

"This is too easy, Michelle," Andrew suggested. "Surely they've got ways of knowing about this jet and can take control of it at any time."

"Maybe they want to assist in our departure so that they can be rid of us and not deal with the embarrassment of wrongful imprisonment," Jeremy offered.

"They wouldn't shoot us out of the sky, would they?" Lynn asked fearfully.

"I don't think so," Michelle responded. "Even the Federation must have a reason for that kind of action. Pull in over there, that's the location I gave him," she added as she pointed to a field on the outskirts of the city. "Just pull right off the road into the grass."

Just then a small aircraft came down through the clouds and landed vertically.

"Come on, let's go!" Jeremy said nervously as he got out of the car and scanned the horizon for their pursuers.

They boarded the plane. Michelle strapped herself in next to the pilot and gave him instructions. The jet lifted off just as sirens and unmarked vehicles came over the hill. Within moments the jet was above the clouds, high over the world that had gone into mass turmoil in reaction to the prophet's words. The utter tranquillity and stillness at this altitude was a stunning contrast to the madness and savagery they had barely escaped.

Jeremy put his arm around Lynn and kissed her gently on the forehead.

"We're going to be all right," he whispered.

"As long as we're together," she said, "I don't care what happens."

Jeremy turned to Adam. The prophet was in severe pain but had such control over himself that he seemed able to overlook his dire physical condition.

"What happens now, Adam?" he asked.

The prophet turned to him with his laser beam eyes.

"Now it begins."

He motioned for Jeremy to look out the window. The clouds had opened up and revealed the surface of the earth below them. In the distance, a strange orange glow filled the atmosphere. An eerie movement was occurring on the ground.

"What is that?" Jeremy asked, horrified.

Andrew studied the phenomenon. "It's an earthquake," he observed grimly.

"Look at the ocean!" Michelle called back to them from the cockpit, as the plane flew over the edge of the continent before turning inland.

The companions looked out to see colossal turbulence among the waves. A gigantic tidal wave was forming and heading for the city. Jeremy turned back to Adam.

"Already?" he asked in shock.

"This is the least of it," Adam stated weakly. "The real destruction will come from the hands of human beings."

"Will we find a place of peace anywhere?" Lynn asked the prophet with tears in her eyes.

"From this moment on, there will be no peace except in the souls of those who have discovered the place that cannot be assaulted by natural catastrophes and nuclear warheads."

The friends looked at each other in terror.

"Will you help us survive?" Andrew asked.

"Keep on the move," Adam said painfully. "Stay ahead of the evil ones."

"Who are the evil ones?"

"Don't you understand? The darkness seeks to conquer this realm forever. Its minions are here among us and you must fight to keep alive for the sake of the light."

"We're just weak human beings! We've got no powers!" Andrew said in terror.

"There's no one else. Start over again when you can. Build another Renouveau. Don't give up!" the prophet whispered hoarsely.

A loud voice came on the speaker in the cockpit.

"Return immediately! This is not an authorized flight. Repeat. Return to base immediately!"

The pilot grabbed the microphone.

"What do you mean, it's not authorized? I've got a security agent next to me!"

"There is a warrant out for the arrest of agent Blair. Repeat, return immediately, you are carrying unauthorized personnel who are wanted for questioning."

The pilot turned to Michelle, red with anger.

"Do you have an explanation for this?"

"I do," she answered. "Keep flying!" She pulled out her gun and aimed it at his forehead. "I suggest you disregard the orders of those who can't harm you and follow the instructions of those who can!"

"This is big trouble, lady!"

"Just do what I tell you! And remember that I can fly this plane without you."

The pilot looked back out at the cloud banks ahead.

"They'll get you no matter where you go."

"We'll have to take our chances," Michelle said with fierce determination. She had now paid the price of joining the prophet's friends—all or nothing. And she had given it all away. There was no going back.

Lynn leaned over Adam and studied him carefully. He was losing consciousness.

"We've got to get him to a hospital!"

"No hospital," Adam said weakly.

"We can't let you die, Adam! We need you."

"Bury me in the desert's sacred ground," he whispered.

"Don't talk like that!" Andrew cried out. "You'll get better."

"Why can't he heal himself?" Michelle called out as she saw him slipping away.

"I came to heal others, not myself . . . my work is done."

"How can you say that? The tribulations are here! Now is when we need you most!" Jeremy said in a trembling voice.

Adam motioned for Lynn to come closer as he grew faint. He whispered in her ear. A glow appeared beneath her tears.

She caressed his cheek. Only his eyes could be discerned beneath the blood; they were oceans of peace.

"Your work is just beginning," he said in a halting voice. "Keep the flame alive. After the devastation will come a new era . . . prepare yourself and others to be builders of that time . . . live what you know. Live as though you were already in that age to come . . . you must try to survive. Don't give way to despair. There will be help once again, greater than ever before . . . the Enemy will take advantage of the Tribulation. Don't give way, despite his power . . . "

The prophet's voice grew faint and raspy. His luminous eyes began to close.

Lynn leaned forward and kissed his forehead.

"The holy ones will return to this place . . . some of them are already born. Seek them out . . . but beware . . . others are also here. They will attempt to destroy you."

Lynn wept silently. Jeremy could hardly see through his tears. His head was swimming with emotion and awed terror at his words. Andrew dropped his head in his hands, while Michelle wiped the tears rolling down her cheeks and kept an eye on the pilot.

"He knows he can't make it to the desert! He knows he's not going to make it another hundred miles," Andrew whispered bitterly.

"The Federation won't let us get across state lines, not alive anyway. Am I right, Michelle?" Jeremy asked sadly.

"They'll blow us right out of the sky if they have to," she answered. "We might be safer on the ground."

"On foot?" Lynn cried out. She turned to Adam who was looking out the window at the sea of clouds, waiting peacefully for death to take him away. "Adam, what must we do?"

He remained turned toward the sun rays coming in through the small opening.

"Trust . . . trust that you will be used well if you allow it . . . trust that there's more involved here than sheer accident and human madness."

"How can we function without you?" Jeremy said tearfully. "You brought us together."

"My work is done. It was only to make clear humanity's choice. The mass response will decide the degree of purification required . . . I never expected to survive the ordeal."

"You mean you're some kind of sacrificial offering, served up to see what people's reactions would be?" Andrew asked in shock.

"That was my role this time."

"What do you mean, this time?" Andrew fired away again, his nerves badly frayed.

"You ask too many questions, Andrew," Adam said as he slowly turned and faced them. His features were ghostly pale, and his beautiful eyes seemed to be sinking back into their orifices in preparation for his soul's departure.

"Why can't you heal yourself?" Andrew asked again, despite the prophet's words.

"There comes a time when healing needs to be done without the body."

"I . . . " Andrew was going for another question. Jeremy put his arm around his shoulder to quiet him and soothe his grief.

"As I told you from the beginning, I came to ready some of you for the aftermath. I didn't come to comfort or ease your burdens. They are inevitable as the prophecies of past ages have warned all along. The transition is on its way at this moment. What you must do now is attempt to live as though you have already reached the dawning of the new age. In this way, you'll carry the seeds of a new evolutionary stage for humanity, even if they can't blossom during the harsh times ahead."

"How can we achieve this?" Jeremy asked, overwhelmed by his words. "How can we avoid being crushed by what is coming?"

Adam took a deep breath and seemed to regain some strength out of sheer force of will. He adjusted his dying body painfully so that he could look into the faces of his friends.

"When the Tribulation comes and you feel empty and abandoned, not just by people, but by the forces of light, know that these are symptoms of a condition called by centuries of spiritual teachers "the dark night of the soul." This "night" is a specific stage along the path of spiritual development. Not only are you not alone in this experience, but know that you are moving forward in the direction toward which your heart is yearning."

He paused, his mouth parched from the effort of speaking. Lynn helped him drink from a cup of water. He thanked her with his fading eyes.

"Don't talk," she said gently. "Save your strength."

"I must talk. I must tell you these things and complete my mission . . . the desolation of the human soul while the planet undergoes this transition is a purification from selfishness and superficial desires in order to clear the ground for the reception of greater wisdom. It will develop in you a new ability to perceive and understand. This will prepare you to participate in the creation of the new age to come."

He raised his bloody hands which trembled uncontrollably. Jeremy, Andrew and Lynn took hold of them.

"If you journey with perseverance through the seeming endlessness of the coming dark times, you'll be led to another shore. The very acceptance of these unacceptable times is part of the answer.

"Maturity of character and new depths of courage will eventually give birth to another Self. This is a Self that understands in ways that the mind cannot grasp, that has gone out of itself in order to find itself, and that sees what other eyes cannot see. This is the self that comes from the deep running river of Spirit, no longer from the sum total of your surface persona. This is the self that will build a new world."

Michelle looked at the pilot and noticed to her astonishment that he was listening intently. The words of the prophet were penetrating his heart and working their magic on his soul.

"You must face the fact that life is not meant to be a banquet of satisfactions for your particular interests," Adam continued in a weaker voice. "We are here for a much nobler purpose, one that integrates us with Creation as a whole. It's the feeling of being isolated entities that causes most of your dysfunction and sorrow."

He raised his head from the seat in a last burst of strength called forth from the depths of his being.

"Claim your true worth as children of the universe and recognize the self-sacrificial mission that has placed you here! We're not on this earth merely to gratify ourselves or to have every little passing wish come true. We are here as beings endowed with a higher consciousness and willpower for the very specific aim of being useful to the purposes of the Source of our creation!"

He fell back on the seat, exhausted and out of breath. Michelle knew that she no longer needed to aim her weapon at the pilot. He looked at her and nodded, allowing her to go to the prophet in his last moments among them. She hurried into the cabin. Andrew moved aside to let her be close to the man who had transformed her life.

Adam smiled weakly at her and placed his hand on her head as a blessing.

"Empty yourselves in order to be filled, like the mystics have always said. Your lives are about to be made empty in any case, whether you like it or not. And what can you be filled with eventually? The awareness of the sacredness of life. This knowledge will be essential in the aftermath of the devastation.

"Surrender yourselves into invisible arms that don't seem to be there, and you will become empowered with an awareness of a deeper reality that nothing can ever take away! Building underground shelters will not give you that security.

"Every human experience can be fuel for wisdom, even the most tragic and overwhelming. If there is any message that religions and metaphysics have taught us down through the centuries, it is that there is always cause for hope!

"Someday you will each be able to ask, 'Death, where is thy victory?,' even when death and destruction are all around you. Then you will be empowered to rebuild and start anew.

"The coming dark night of the human soul and of the planet itself will teach you to know through unknowing, to see in the darkness, to find meaning in meaninglessness, and communion in solitude. The mystery of mysteries, the deepest secret of all religions, will then be made known to you and the new age will begin."

The companions surrounded him with intense love and attention. Somehow they knew that their love for him was keeping him alive to share these final words.

"Accept your approaching pain, your mortality, say 'yes' to what must be, and you will enter into a transcendence that will free you from all the agony."

Adam turned to Jeremy and touched his cheek with great affection and gratitude.

"Dr. Hogrogian once told me that it was when he was most shattered by his war experiences in the last century that he truly encountered the reality of Spirit. Despite his despair and brokenness, he nevertheless felt himself mysteriously held up by a compassionate force. Having gone to the heart of hopelessness, he found there an inexpressible Presence that came to his aid and kept him going. The same will happen for you."

Adam's breathing was becoming more shallow and hoarse. He was in great pain, but smiled at his friends with unconditional affection and compassion.

"If you choose to be more than a slave to your every impulse and seek your true dignity as beings capable of witnessing the wonder of life and of participating in its caretaking, then you must be grounded in something other than your own desires and satisfactions. This is where the dark night of the coming Tribulation can be useful to you. It can create new foundations made out of patience, perseverance, and a faith in the ultimate goodness of the universe which nothing will be able to destroy!

"This will certainly mean sacrifice and acceptance of pain and insecurity. But that's what creates a spiritual being who can deal with the twists and turns of existence until it is time to enter into an even greater darkness—as I must do now—but this darkness is actually a wondrous light. Believe me! I am seeing it this very moment!"

Peace softened Adam's features as his spirit released itself from his mutilated body. His friends wept openly.

"Don't grieve for me . . . I know where I come from and where I am returning."

His eyelids slowly descended over the all-seeing eyes that had looked with compassion upon every being.

Jeremy whispered a prayer of blessing upon the soul that had briefly graced their lives. Then he prayed for them, for the strength and courage to endure what lay ahead.

The plane flew across the turbulent waters and shivering landscape, heading into a bleak and dangerous future.

As the sky darkened and the world fell silent in anticipation of oncoming storms, Lynn's fear turned to joy. She took the dead hand of the prophet and kissed it. Then she turned to her friends huddled together in the plane.

"We won't be left alone," she assured them. "We won't be left alone!"

BOOK 2

THE TRIBULATION

PROLOGUE

A Prophet had appeared in the early part of the twenty-first
century, the last in a long line of healers, visionaries and mystics
down through the ages. People around the world heard his message
of oncoming devastation and his warning that the only shelter that
would save them would be their own inner strength and nobility of
spirit. In response to his mission of compassion, the Prophet was
beaten to death by an angry mob. No one wanted to face reality,
not until it slammed into them in all its fury. A handful of the
Prophet's followers were left behind with instructions from their
beloved teacher to survive the cataclysms ahead as best they could
and start again.

Religions and technologies had failed humanity. Only these few
men and women inspired by the wisdom transmitted to them by the
final Prophet could offer desperate people a path to sanity and
renewal. But the odds were amassed against them. Not only was
the planet facing utter destruction from wild weather changes,
earthquakes, volcanoes, floods and a dreaded pole shift, but the
world government considered them their most deadly enemies.
These humble few were carriers of truth that defied all the illusions
which the iron-fisted Federation had instilled in the minds of the
masses. Such persons were as dangerous as the storms gathering
across the globe.

The time of reckoning was here. Everyone would have to face this
age of transition in one of two ways -- in utter horror and despair
or with the slim hope that renewal lay on the other side of
catastrophic earth changes. The second option would vanish

entirely if it was known what forces were at the heart of the destruction, forces that were darker and more savage than Nature's mightiest upheavals.

CHAPTER 1

The stench of cigarette smoke mixed with car fumes filled his nostrils and made him sick to his stomach. He'd only been in the city one day and he was desperate to get out of it. Life in the desert had given him a taste for an environment ruled by Nature and not by human beings.

Jeremy walked quickly along the city sidewalks. They were so thick with people that every step of the way someone's elbow poked him. He'd look back, but everybody was in a hurry or in some kind of trance-like state and hardly took notice.

Car horns echoed raucously against the steeples of power looming above the scurrying masses. Mounds of trash had taken the place of flower pots and trees that once attempted to beautify the concrete jungle which was the legacy of the twentieth century. The new millennium hadn't put a dent into the disintegration of urban life. Technology had continued to soar and conquer, yet it hadn't managed to clean up the garbage from the sidewalk nor out of the human soul.

Grey clouds were passing overhead, keeping the sun away from the filth and crime of the big city. A month in the barren purity of the desert had made Jeremy allergic to urban pollution. He found himself hoping that a thunderstorm would crash down upon them all and wash away the layers of scum that covered everything in sight.

An explosion nearly threw him out of his shoes. The synchronicity of his thought and its physical manifestation caused a tingle of vertigo to shoot through his nervous system. But he had too much to worry about to wrestle with the strange coincidence. Heavy raindrops struck the sidewalk, warning of more to come.

He barely made it to a doorway when the belly of the clouds opened up and a torrent of water blasted the city streets. Within moments, the sky turned nearly black as night. Lights came on even though it was only midday. Angry winds had swept in a strange storm indeed, just one in a series of bizarre occurrences that were plaguing the entire planet. This was no surprise to Jeremy. Adam Hawthorn had prophesied the oncoming devastation and Jeremy, as his first and most devoted disciple, had seen too much to have any doubts left, even for a rational, educated man. The mysteries of the cosmos so far outweighed human knowledge that it wasn't worth pretending anymore that he had any idea of what was at the heart of human existence.

In his late thirties, chiseled features framed by thick reddish hair and deeply inset eyes of emerald green on fire with vigilant awareness, Jeremy Taylor Wilkes stood out from the other passersby. There was a light on inside, just as clear as from a cabin's window in the deep of night. A light that was conscious of itself and generating itself as though creating its own world.

The strangely intense man looked older than his years. A deep wisdom emanated from his face, even though it was unsettled, interrupted with flashes of still unmastered emotions. His pale skin and sparsely freckled features added an aura of being 'different', even slightly unearthly. Anyone who could maintain any degree of inner calm and balance in these dangerous, tormented times was extremely rare. Self-mastery was a forgotten part of human development. Self-indulgence, instant gratification, disregard for any greater purpose in life had inundated human behavior and nearly conquered it.

Only infinitesimal pockets of individuals retained some link with deeper meaning, a link more life-giving than the ever more poisonous air that enveloped the globe. Deeper thought, ancient teachings, even some aspects of quantum physics had gone underground in the wake of quickly spreading global strife.

Just thirteen years into the millennium, under a highly sophisticated and intrusive but effective world government known as the Federation, the international political, religious, and economic scenes were boiling out of control. A lid had been kept over them during the first decade of the new unified government that held the world's military might at its disposal. Paranoia, invasion of privacy, arbitrary laws were leading the overcrowded and crime-ridden populations of the world into a gigantic police state more effective than any tyrant had hoped for in the previous fifteen thousand years of gore and mayhem which characterized much of human history.

Technological wizardry had betrayed the dreams of its original creators. Or had it? The immense speed at which globalization and interdependence evolved at the end of the second millennium had kept the race from perceiving the inevitable. Whoever controlled the information channels, controlled the minds of the great masses. Millions upon millions of all former nationalities could be compelled to emote, to rejoice, fear, rage, forget, buy with every flicker passing before their hypnotized senses.

Jeremy Taylor Wilkes, child of university professors, lifelong seeker of meaning, having briefly become an ordained minister in a desperate effort to live out in the world what he believed and felt in his inner world, was the unexpected principal leader of the most luminous of those pockets of outsiders whose beliefs were not molded by the Federation. He was the right hand man and trusted friend of the one known to the world as "the Final Prophet". The visionary messenger from above had come and gone like a whirlwind. The world had been warned, in every corner, all at once.

The Final Prophet's extraordinary live global broadcast had rung the last note. Then he was dead, torn to pieces for offering a last cosmic helping hand. His dying words to his friends would haunt them to the end of their days. More than haunting, they would compel them to fulfill the mission entrusted to them by the prophet—" Survive the oncoming world calamities, and rebuild a humanity of the future with the teachings I have imparted to you."

This was the fire in Jeremy's dark green piercing eyes. Everything was at stake at every moment.

Beneath the five inches of shelter that kept him from being soaked, he watched the scene around him turn into loud and messy chaos. Fender benders took place just feet away from him as the wet streets turned into ice-skating rinks and drivers just got mad instead of careful.

"What insanity!" he thought to himself. If people couldn't handle a rain shower without rage and havoc, what were they going to do when everything caved in?

"Die gruesome deaths!"

The words struck him like a two by four across the head. He turned to see who had answered his private thoughts. He found himself confronted by a wretched homeless man, as dirty as a human being could get and completely out of his mind.

"What did you say?" Jeremy asked as thunder shook the windows.

The wretched man laughed and skipped off into the rain like a child dancing in mud puddles.

"Wait a minute!" Jeremy called out. But his voice was lost beneath a curtain of rainfall that blocked out all other sounds.

Leaning back against the wall, he tried to digest what just happened. The man had clearly read his mind. But what difference did the gift of telepathy make in the ruins of this human being who couldn't even take care of himself anymore? On the heels of the previous synchronistic event—his thought of thunder right before the strike—he sensed some larger phenomenon taking place that his mind just couldn't bring into focus.

He shook off his inner confusion and looked out once again at the world around him. People raced to and fro and sirens wailed over the downpour. The stench of the city gave way to a cleansing scent of purifying rain. He couldn't tell if he was imagining the smell of wet grass or whether some drifting aroma of real nature was coming around the corner to reach him. It soothed his tormented soul and gave him a moment of peace. But his tranquility was quickly shattered again as his eyes fell upon a large silhouette standing directly across the street in another doorway, staring at him with vicious, glowing eyes.

Jeremy knew instantly who the man was. How could he forget, though he'd only caught sight of him for a split second once before. How could anyone forget the grizzly bear shape and evil aura of Stefan Zorn? The most famous warlock of the underworld had visited the Prophet's little community only three months before. He'd come to test the man of light and had lost. But now that the Prophet was dead, there was no one to stop him and the man of darkness was unrestricted. This was his world and he was master of it.

Jeremy shivered, not because of the cold dampness that came from the rain shower, but from icy terror that gripped him from his toes to the top of his head. He could feel the man's hate a hundred yards away. Jeremy suddenly understood that the strange mental events that had occurred just a moment before were linked with the presence of the evil man, as though he emanated a magnetic field of psychic phenomena.

Jeremy chose to follow his intuition rather than wait for his rational mind to catch up. He took off into the wall of rain and was immediately soaked to the bone, but felt nothing except raw fear snapping at him like a thousand piranhas assaulting a carcass in their waters.

Somehow he knew he was being followed, even though he couldn't bring himself to look back. He hurried through the crowd, pushing people aside with the skill of a lifelong city dweller. His hurried steps turned into a jog and finally into a fast run as he made his way through side streets. Before long, he found himself in back alleyways within the bowels of the city. He slowed his pace realizing that there was no one to be seen anywhere in this wasteland of condemned buildings and permanent garbage dumps.

The rain still fell hard, whipping at him as though telling him to hurry on. But he came to a stop, sensing a new fear in the eerie no man's land into which he had wandered. For the first time, he longed for the overpopulated sidewalks where at least there was some security, even among unfriendly strangers. Now he was alone and utterly vulnerable.

He turned around. The skeletons of abandoned houses rose up around him like the guardians of some infernal territory. He knew he had to get out of there fast before new dangers just as deadly as Stefan Zorn came after him. But it was too late. Four young men appeared from under the ruins of the city. Carrying chains, tire irons, and knives, they headed toward him with the aggressive glare of predatory animals hunting down their victim.

Jeremy turned to run in the other direction. Two other youths came out of a building. One of them pulled out a switchblade. The gang members approached and circled him, eyes sparkling with blood-lust in anticipation of what they were about to do to the unfortunate man who had entered their world.

At that moment, Jeremy could only think of one thing. His beloved Lynn, the one person he loved more than his own life. He was suddenly overwhelmed with the realization that he hadn't told her how deeply he loved her when he kissed her good-bye that morning on his way to the city.

The rattle of the chain brought him back with gruesome vividness to the situation at hand. He had never seen such brutal desire for violence in human faces before. These were creatures without a drop of conscience, like zombies fresh from the grave. Their only link with humanity was a superficial resemblance. But even that vanished behind the savagery in their features.

Every fiber in his body went into high alert. He knew he was going to have to fight for his life even if there was no chance of saving himself. Jeremy had trained to be a minister, a caretaker of human beings. He knew nothing about self-defense. Yet some primeval part of his nature came up from cellular memory and readied him to tear and break and claw like a wild man in order to survive.

He watched them like a trapped animal as they came closer and closer. He could now see the color of their eyes and the vile grins on their faces. He was outraged by the realization that they wanted to see him suffer. They had no idea who he was—one of the few who, if he ever had the opportunity to help any of them, would have gladly given them his last dollar. But they wanted to maim and destroy in some futile attempt to claim some power and control over their hopeless circumstances.

His eyes darted about looking for a weapon. He saw a three foot lead pipe lying on a pile of debris nearby. In a flash, the pipe was in his hands without his thinking consciously of picking it up. The young men stopped ten feet from him, surrounding him.

"Why don't you just put that down like a good boy and save yourself a lot of trouble!" one of them said. He looked to be no more than sixteen years old.

Jeremy tightened his grip around the pipe, prepared to crush the skull of the first one who moved. He could see the two others in his peripheral vision. He knew he would have to act at the slightest movement. Sweat poured from his body in streams. But he wasn't shivering anymore. Something had taken over in the recesses of his ancestry. The adrenaline flowing through his muscles was so intense that he couldn't even feel his fear. He was enraged that they wanted to take him away from Lynn merely for their entertainment.

"Put it down, man," one said. "We're gonna cut you either way."

Wild-eyed and silent, Jeremy waited for the first move. One of the young men behind him leaped forward. Jeremy swung with all his might. The youth ducked and jumped aside. Before Jeremy could regain his balance, he heard a whistle and was struck by heavy chains across the ribs. He found himself on his knees. The pipe was torn from his hands. He looked up. One of his attackers stood over him with the pipe raised high, about to bring it down over his head.

"Stop!"

The voice exploded through the alleyway, freezing the young man's arms in the air. They all looked into the shadows.

"Get outta here before you get hurt!" one of them shouted to the newcomer.

A silhouette moved forward.

"Did you hear what I said?" the youth yelled again as he stepped toward the stranger.

"Get rid of him!" one of his companions called out.

"The more the merrier!" another one added, shifting the knife in his hand.

The youth moved forward to confront the figure in the shadows. Suddenly, he let out a horrific, high-pitched scream. Jeremy turned his head as the other gang members shouted in shock. Their companion was on fire from head to foot. They raced over to help him as he threw himself on the ground, desperately trying to put the flames out. The silhouette stepped into the pale light. Jeremy recognized Stefan Zorn.

One of the youths let out a roar of animal rage and leaped at the large man. He caught himself, virtually in midair. It wasn't the six foot five, three hundred and fifty pounds size that terrified him, but the glare from the man's eyes. Framed in a finely cut black beard, shadowed by thick eyebrows, the man's bulldog features looked like the incarnation of Lucifer himself. It was the utter lack of fear and the intensity of power coming out of the man's small, gleaming eyes that frightened the youth.

Before the assailant could react, Zorn's big hand reached out and grabbed his throat. A crunching sound was heard and he threw the boy down like a broken rag doll. The three other punks jumped up and attacked him, letting out savage war cries.

With stunning agility, Zorn struck the first one in the eyes with his fingers and sent him to the ground screaming. The second assailant swung the chains at him. They wrapped around the big man's arm. Zorn let out a fearful laugh and tore the chains out of the youth's hand. He smashed him in the face with his forearm and swept his foot out from under him with a kick behind his ankle. The youth fell. Before he could get up, Zorn raised his foot and brought it down on his head with incredible power, crushing it like a spoiled egg.

The last youth stood in front of him, eyes wide with shock. Zorn looked at him and grinned with the very same blood-lust they had turned on Jeremy. Dressed in black, wearing gold necklaces covered with amulets and four rings on each hand, Zorn was a frightful sight. The young man turned to run, but Zorn pointed a finger at him and focused an unearthly energy on his back. The thug was frozen still and couldn't move, except for his eyes that turned back in sheer terror as Zorn approached him.

"You dare mess with me, Boy?" the man muttered in a guttural sound, full of hate and violence.

He teased his prey's terror, walking around him. The youth tried to move.

"You're gonna find out where you belong, son. It's not a pretty place."

He smashed his two open hands on either side of his head, bursting the youth's eardrums. Blood shot out of his ears and nose.

"This is nothing compared to what's waiting for you. It's just the appetizer. You're gonna be the main course for something much worse. And you asked for it."

He pressed his finger against the boy's forehead. His skin ripped across the length of his skull. By this time, Jeremy was standing.

"Don't do this!" he cried out.

The dark man looked over at him with an evil grin.

"You do-gooders are all alike. This slime was about to cut you to pieces. Now you want to be his friend?"

"Don't torture him!" Jeremy insisted. "You came for me, not for him."

"True enough!" Zorn muttered. "But you ought to be more grateful to me for getting these maggots off your back."

"Just leave him be."

"I can't do that," Zorn said as he looked back at his victim. The boy shivered in his frozen position, blood streaming down his face from the cut on his forehead.

"Don't you get any satisfaction from seeing your enemy suffer, Mr. Wilkes?" Stefan Zorn asked as he eyed his victim.

"No I don't," Jeremy answered. "Let him go."

"Oh, all right," the big man said sarcastically. He raised his hand. The young man's body suddenly flew across the alley and smashed against a wall like a ripe tomato. He slid down to the ground, lifeless.

Zorn turned his vicious features upon Jeremy.

"There, I let him go like you wanted," he said with a laugh that chilled Jeremy to the bone.

Stefan Zorn looked over at the bodies littering the ground. The one he had set on fire was now dead, burnt beyond recognition. The other one, whom he had struck in the eyes, was curled up in fetal position, moaning.

"Just for you, pastor," the big man said cynically, "I'll let that one live. He'll spend the rest of his days as a blind beggar. That'll teach him, don't you think?"

"Why did you protect me?" Jeremy asked grimly.

Zorn approached him until he stood inches from his face, looking down at him with disdain. Jeremy instinctively took a step back, unable to bear his oppressive presence.

"Don't think I did you any favors by keeping you alive. I've got my own use for you."

"What do you want from me?" Jeremy asked defiantly, outraged by this savage manifestation of evil.

"You were the Prophet's right hand man, weren't you? I want you to witness who has the ultimate power now and what foolishness it was to think that he spoke the truth."

"You'll never convince me otherwise."

"We'll see about that," Zorn said menacingly. "As long as you're alive, I have a link to the man who dared to defy me. I'll get my vengeance through you and those like you. If you survive what is to come, I'll make you my disciple instead of his."

"Never!"

Zorn raised his hand to strike him. His eyes were filled with a look of unbounded rage. But he managed to control himself and smiled mockingly.

"Either way, I'm gonna get you, Wilkes. And you'll see who the real master is. You will do my bidding some day."

"Go to hell!" Jeremy responded fearlessly.

Zorn let out a big laugh. "Look around you, fool! We're already there!"

He turned his back on him and walked off into the shadows. Jeremy watched him, overwhelmed with disgust. Zorn turned back one last time.

"Give my best to your lovely wife," he said with a snicker.

Jeremy wanted to run after him and strike him, but he remembered the teaching of the Prophet and realized that this was just another trick Zorn was playing on his psyche, proving how easy it was to make him his servant.

The man disappeared. Jeremy took a deep breath to calm himself. He looked up at the dark clouds above and noticed for the first time that the rain had stopped. He became aware of the whimpering youth whose eyes had been damaged. Instinctively, Jeremy went over to him and kneeled at his side.

He moved the youth's hands away from his face. His eyes were swollen and bloody.

"Help me!" he whimpered desperately.

Without thinking, Jeremy placed his hands upon the youth's eyes as he had seen the Prophet do many times. At first, he felt awkward, wondering why he was reaching out to this thug who had intended to brain him with the lead pipe, but the desire to heal brought back his memory of the Prophet with an intensity that overwhelmed everything else.

Jeremy had committed himself to the mission of the one who was the herald of the age of transition and the great Tribulation that was to strike all living things on this planet. He had told Jeremy many times that he had to make a decision from which there was no going back if he sought any kind of enlightenment and wanted to make himself useful to the forces of light.

It had taken Jeremy a long time to understand the full impact of that teaching, but it was becoming clear to him now. He had to choose again and again not to be a child of darkness despite all the horrors that surrounded him.

Now he held his hand on the youth's blinded eyes simply wishing to emulate the unconditional goodness he had seen manifested in the Prophet. Perhaps it was as much to honor his friend and teacher as it was for the sake of the wounded youth that he found himself kneeling there in the mud trying to help him. Whatever his reasons, in that moment of healing there were no thoughts, just the wish to be a channel of goodness.

He said a silent prayer for the lost soul moaning in agony. Then he felt his hand suddenly heat up and tingle. His desire for right action opened the floodgates of his heart and the vision of his beloved Lynn came into his mind. Now his chest warmed just like his hand. For an instant, he was no longer in a grim ghetto surrounded by dead bodies, but in an oasis of peace and joy that seemed to be the very apex of the purpose of life.

He basked in the inner sunlight of this spiritual tranquility and gave thanks to the mysterious forces that had kept him alive. He realized in that moment that he owed his gratitude not to the beast Stefan Zorn but to the higher powers that moved humans about like chess pieces on the table of destiny.

He became aware of his body again and realized that his face was wet, not with raindrops but with tears. He opened his eyes. He couldn't even feel his hand. It seemed to have turned into a wave of warmth like a sun-drenched beach where sun and sand become one. He looked down. His hand was swollen and reddish. It felt like a mass of hot vibration rather than flesh and bone.

Through his tears he noticed something and blinked several times to bring his sight into focus. He moved his hand away from the youth's face. The young man was staring at him, eyes wide with amazement and a new found serenity. It was as though he'd absorbed something of the state in which Jeremy had entered, and in that contact had become transformed from a vicious brute into the human being he was meant to be.

Jeremy couldn't believe it. Nothing like this had ever happened through him before. Not only was the swelling gone, but the youth's eyes were clear and bright. He radiated a new quality, as though he'd become aligned with the self he had lost long ago.

Jeremy stood up, unable to bear the mystery that had happened in the blood-soaked mud. The young man looked at him without a word, stunned by his act of goodness and the miracle that had accompanied it. Jeremy was just as amazed and shook his hand to bring it out of its numb condition as well as to release the pain that he had taken into himself from the wounds. He was struck with the realization that not only was the Prophet's teaching taking hold in his being but so was his power. Adam Hawthorn had sown seeds that contained miraculous possibilities. Jeremy's absorption of his words were not merely intellectual but transformational.

A ray of sunshine broke through the grey clouds and spotlit the desolate alleyway. Jeremy looked up, almost expecting to see the face of the Prophet gazing down upon him. A golden light shimmered above him. In this dreary place, it was the very image of the angelic realm.

He looked back at the young man who was still staring at him. Tears were rushing down his cheeks as well. The power of unconditional love was performing its magic in his heart. Jeremy heard himself say: "Don't hurt people anymore."

Somehow he knew that the youth would remember and abide by those words for the rest of his life. He turned away in a daze and stumbled out of the alley toward the noise and confusion of the city that made him feel safe. Beneath the blanket of activity and distraction, he could soothe his psyche from the world of mystery that had just revealed itself to him.

CHAPTER 2

The freak storm that had angrily blown over the city vanished as quickly as it had come. The oppressive clouds gave way to clear blue skies. Yet there remained a threatening electricity in the atmosphere. A tinge of green and orange blended with the familiar blue, warning of more to come.

A woman with thick locks of brown hair curled about her face by the hot wind stared out at the vast desert horizon. Her shimmering eyes drank in the view with an intensity that mirrored a powerful, deep soul rich with clairvoyant insight and warmed by a heart of gold. Lynn Wilkes sat at a picnic table behind the desert shack that was now her home. She wore her poverty with regal dignity and no one would have guessed the hardship that she and Jeremy endured.

Lynn had learned to find her way to a measureless peace within that gave her contentment which outer circumstances could not. The pain of life had taught her the hard way, perhaps the only way. She had given herself over to caring for whatever living being came her way, just as the Prophet had done.

This day she was less tranquil than usual. She disliked being separated from Jeremy. The greatest joy in the world for both of them was found in their togetherness and they were rarely apart. But this was one of those times when he had to be away from her side. The trip to the city was critical to them.

They had been living in the desert for nearly a month, hidden away in the rundown reservation under the protection of Stargazer, an Indian elder and friend of the Prophet. This excursion was their first resurfacing into society.

They had been assured safe passage by security agents of the Federation in return for meeting with General MacDaniel himself, the military's chief-of-staff and highest commanding officer in the

Federation. The world government was desperate to have them deny the prophecies in order to bring the world back to some semblance of peace. This was their only chance to save themselves from the Federation's wrath.

Lynn stood and walked along the dusty ridge that overlooked the barren plains stretching to all four horizons as far as the eye could see. A few rusty trailers and dilapidated farms dotted the barren landscape, but gave it little sense of life. This was the land of a proud people brought into submission under the yoke of extreme poverty.

In their desert hideaway, Lynn had come to know a number of Native Americans and admired their deep relationship with nature and their instinctive mystical intuition. Religious persons she had known in her past were far removed from the openness to the mysteries of life that she found among these barely educated people.

An old pickup truck bounced along a red trail leading to the isolated home where the friends of the Prophet were hiding. She recognized it as the elder's truck. Stargazer checked on them several times a week even though the journey through the rocky terrain was difficult for his aged body.

But there were no other choices. Lynn and her companions were on the Federation's most wanted list. The fact that one of them, Michelle Blair, was a former security agent enraged the Federation all the more and it was using the full power of its technology and limitless personnel to find and punish them.

Within hours of the Prophet's death, catastrophes had in fact begun to take place. But that didn't matter. The Federation had only one thing in mind. And that was to keep control over the massive hordes of panicked humanity. If cataclysmic earth changes were to occur, the Federation wanted the people of the world to die passively.

Lynn walked up to the ridge and waved at the oncoming truck. A hand appeared out of the window and waved back. Her heart warmed as a wave of gratitude washed through her in reaction to the kindness of the old Indian mystic. The truck pulled up in a cloud of dust. Stargazer painfully stepped out of the vehicle. A young man got out on the other side. He was the very opposite of the old elder, the incarnation of a vibrant Cherokee warrior.

They approached Lynn. "Good morning!" Stargazer said in a tired but resonant voice. "Meet a friend of mine. He's known to our people as Brave Eagle. But on his driver's license it says John Littlebear."

Lynn looked into the brown eyes of the newcomer and drank in the quality of his soul. She understood immediately why he was given that name as a result of his vision quest. A strong, honest presence radiated from him, one she sensed could be trusted.

"I brought him here to meet you and to take over for me. I won't be able to make this trip as often anymore."

Lynn turned to the old mystic, feeling that he was leaving something unsaid.

"You must have Indian blood in you," Stargazer stated with a gentle smile. "You don't need words to understand."

"How soon?" she asked, realizing that he had just informed her of his imminent departure from this life.

"Hard to say. The doctors tell me a few weeks, but their medicine is weak."

She knew that he was the kind of man who, once gone, could never be replaced. He held up his hand, as though putting an end to her sad thoughts.

"I'm at peace. I'm ready. I may be of more use to you in the spirit world than I am here."

She looked into his limpid brown eyes and saw the truth of his statement emanating from deep within.

"I'll be leaving you in good company. Brave Eagle is like my son. He's one of the few of his generation who's chosen to learn the ancient ways."

Lynn saw in the youth's serenity the kind of dignity of spirit and alertness of mind that was the characteristic of one awake and committed to the deeper mysteries of life.

"Where's Jeremy?" Stargazer asked.

"He's gone to the city," she said, knowing that the old man would not be happy at the news. He looked at her sadly. "There was no choice," she added. "We had to consider the Federation's offer."

Stargazer shook his head. "They can't be trusted. We'll need to move you to another place, further into the desert."

"I love these lands," Lynn responded. "But I don't know how much longer we can live out here, so dependent on your assistance. We need other means to take care of ourselves."

"I knew this day would come," Stargazer said somberly. "Maybe it's best in the long run. It's good that Brave Eagle can take over now."

"No one has been a better friend," Lynn said as she approached the medicine man and took hold of his wrinkled hands. He whispered a blessing for her in his native language.

"As the Prophet said," he spoke slowly, "you will have to live through hard times. Much harder than these."

"I'm ready," Lynn stated with certainty.

She hugged him, sensing that this was the last time she would see him. He patted her gently on the back.

"You must survive, dear Lynn, you must."

A dust-devil cloud suddenly swirled up at their feet and circled them, covering them with a mist of sand as they held onto each other for courage to face what lay ahead.

* * * * *

Michelle Blair sat in a dark restaurant, waiting impatiently for Jeremy's arrival. Her strong, graceful features were marred with anxiety and her forehead glistened with perspiration even though the day had become strangely cold after the storm.

She knew that she had ruined her career by committing the ultimate heresy and choosing the Prophet over the world government. She had brought disgrace upon her family name, but she had no regrets. Her conscience was clear. She had chosen Truth, even at the price of losing everything else.

However, she hadn't planned on returning into the belly of the beast to whom she had once given all her loyalty and talents. Her former colleagues considered her a traitor and the reputation she had reveled in was now one of infamy. Yet she knew she must face this dangerous turn of events if they wanted to save the Prophet's followers from certain death.

This fateful encounter was the last chance for her companions to make a deal with the Federation. Their stay in the desert had been severe and far too demanding for people use to the amenities of twenty-first century living. In this last months of the year 2016, it seemed absurd that they should live like primitive peasants scratching out a living in an unfriendly landscape. And yet something deep within her already knew that this harsh life-style was merely a foretaste of what was to come, not only for them but for the entire population of the planet.

A tall, lanky silhouette appeared in the doorway. Michelle sat up. It was Andrew Bradshaw. His eyes fell upon her immediately, as though attracted by a magnetic current. The instant their eyes locked together, electricity filled the air. These were two people on the verge of discovering that they were meant for each other.

Andrew made his way over to her and sat at the table. He gave her a warm smile.

"How are you holding out?" he asked.

"It's not easy," she answered with sincerity. She saw no point in hiding anything from him.

"I'm not going to let them hurt you," Andrew said, placing his hand on hers. The warmth of his affection was evident to the very marrow of his bones.

Michelle looked at him and received his proclamation of protection with gratitude and a tinge of hopelessness. She knew who they were dealing with. She had been one of them. And even the Prophet's devoted friends couldn't overcome the power of highly-trained, unscrupulous bureaucrats and military personnel.

"Jeremy's not here yet?" Andrew asked.

"He's late. That's not his way," Michelle said, worried.

"He'll be here," Andrew assured her. "It's been awhile since he's had to navigated through the city."

A waiter came up to them. Andrew ordered some coffee, though he hadn't eaten since the night before. He didn't have the money even to buy a side order. This felt very strange for him, having grown up in lavish wealth. He had never before experienced such severe shortage of the greasy green paper he despised so much. He sure could have used a warm sandwich, but he had nothing left except the shirt on his back. That was the price he paid for financing the Prophet's mission. The Federation had frozen all his assets.

"Have something to eat," Michelle said, reading the look in his face. She put a ten dollar bill on the table. "Come one, it's on me."

He looked at her in utter humiliation.

"Don't be silly. Take it. You have to be able to receive as well as to give, you know."

He nodded in agreement.

"Where are you getting money from?" he asked, still hesitant.

"Oh, I was able to gather some before I lost my job."

"Let's conserve it then."

"You're gonna need your energy for this, Andrew. That's more important." She had become intimate enough with him to know that he was hypoglycemic. He needed to be able to think quickly and sharply in their meeting with General MacDaniel and his cronies.

He looked at her with gratitude in his eyes, a feeling that went much further than the need for a sandwich. She was giving him new life at a time when he had lost everything.

Jeremy found his way to the restaurant and headed straight to the men's room to clean himself up from what he'd been through. He didn't want to frighten his friends with the ordeal.

He splashed cold water on his face, trying to wipe away the trauma of his psyche. He was in a strange condition, one mixed with horror and ecstacy, two opposite states that made for very uncertain emotional stability. He dried his hair with paper towels and combed it, breathing slowly and deeply to calm his jangled nerves. The event he and his companions were facing was dramatic enough by itself without the addition of this incident that had shaken his soul to its core.

He looked at himself in the mirror. He noticed for the first time the signs of wear and tear from the last few months. Dark circles under his clear, green eyes had permanently installed themselves, giving him a virtual mask over his fair and lightly freckled features. Several streaks of white spread through his red curly hair. He was never one to be concerned about the inevitability of aging, hoping that with it would come the kind of inner peace and fulfillment he'd searched and studied for these many years.

He noticed that the crow's feet had deepened and travelled nearly to his temples. Each wrinkle on his face was a scar from the white-hot intensity of the life he now led. As a minister, he had once enjoyed the rather bland and safe existence of a little community. Even hospital visits and funerals were easy compared to the colossal events that whirled around him like a deadly hurricane.

The Prophet had revealed what his generation was in for. Already, the news was screaming with stories of freakish weather and political unrest across the globe. It seemed that the entire planet was exploding with catastrophe, and the worst was yet to come. The fulfillment of the prophecies that had haunted humanity throughout the course of its history had now come to a climax in this age.

Jeremy was at the center of it all, aware of the cosmic struggle involved in this agonizing transition. There were no guarantees that humanity would survive this moment in history. After one last cleansing breath, he stepped out into the restaurant and spotted Michelle and Andrew awaiting at a table in the back corner.

They warmly greeted each other.

"Are you ready?" he asked them as he sat at the table.

"I don't know," Michelle said through gritted teeth, trying to keep the fear down. "I've got a bad feeling about this, Jeremy."

"What do you mean?"

"I know they can't be trusted and I know they want to put us away for good."

"Don't they need us for their propaganda more than they want to bury us?" Andrew asked.

"Sure," Michelle responded. "But if we don't give them what they want, then they don't need us anymore."

"Maybe we'll give them what they want," Jeremy stated flatly.

His friends looked at him in shock. "What's that suppose to mean?" Andrew cried out.

"I've been thinking about this a great deal in the last week, " Jeremy said with hesitation. "Whatever we say won't change the facts. If we satisfy the Federation's requirements, we'll be better able to survive what's about to happen."

"Wouldn't you feel kind of guilty about publicly denying the Prophet's words?" Andrew asked angrily.

"Eventually, they'll find us anyway," Jerry said in return.

"There's no guarantee we'll ever walk out of there. Not all of us."

"Do you think they'll try to keep you, Michelle?" Andrew asked as he put his arm around her. In these last months of common struggle, their nascent affection was coming into full bloom. Lynn and Jeremy had celebrated their developing attraction for each other. But now, in the face of such dangers, it was taking on a bittersweet quality.

"I'm a traitor as far as they're concerned," Michelle continued. "You know what they do with traitors."

"Can't your father influence them in some way?" Andrew asked as he kissed her cheek with a gentleness mixed with desperation.

"My father's retired and no longer has any power."

"They always liked a good deal. Can we bargain with them in some way?"

"That's the reason for this meeting," Jeremy interrupted. "Part of the results will be to free Michelle from their vengeance. Otherwise they'll just hunt us down."

"So how far are you willing to go in order to come to an agreement?" Andrew challenged.

"Like I said, I'll tell them what they want to hear. They can distribute it all over the world for all I care."

"I don't know if I can handle the shame," Andrew responded. "It'll blacken the Prophet's name and wreck his mission."

"He was never interested in his reputation. Whatever we say now won't stop what's taking place. But it might buy us a little time."

"Time to do what?" Andrew, always the pessimist, asked with renewed anger.

"You're not giving up before it starts, are you, friend?" Jeremy challenged.

"No, of course not! But we need to be building some kind of proper shelter for what's ahead."

"I thought the Prophet advised us not to depend on shelters," Michelle remembered with a trembling voice. Every time she thought about the man who had changed her life, deep emotion rose out of the wound in her soul.

"What he said," Jeremy responded, "was that our real security doesn't lie in underground shelters, but in our inner being and our effort to open ourselves to something higher than we are."

"That doesn't mean that we stand around and wait for our destruction," Michelle pointed out.

"Don't you think we should try to warn people so that they can take shelter as well?" Andrew asked, upset by the focus on their own safety when millions of lives were at stake.

"That's what the Prophet did," Jeremy answered. "He said it loud and clear. If people don't want to believe him, that's their problem. They had their opportunity."

"That's mighty cold of you, Jeremy," Michelle scolded.

"There's no more room for sentimentality. Everything's gonna crash and we must take care of ourselves so that we can eventually be useful to others."

"I can't imagine the Prophet saying such a thing," Andrew muttered.

"Damn it!" Jeremy slammed his hand on the table. His two friends were stunned by his violent reaction. But his nerves were still on edge from his earlier experience. "Let's not get caught up in arguing over what he would have wanted us to do or not do according to each one's interpretation. It's happened too many times before with other messengers. Let's not fall into that trap! We need to stay focused on the critical issue."

"And are you the one to tell us what that issue is?" Andrew asked with a scowl.

"Yes I am!" Jeremy replied with a commanding voice. "I paid the price from the beginning. I was his first assistant. And it's crystal clear to me that what the Prophet wants from us is to undergo these trials and carry the seeds for a future that will come after the Tribulation. That's the key."

"The odds are against us," Michelle observed nervously.

"That's right," Jeremy responded. "But some of us must try to make it, not for our own sakes, but because that's what he wants us to do. Remember, he said some day others would come along to help once again."

"Others?" Michelle asked. "What others?"

"Other Messiahs . . . " Jeremy said simply. "Messengers from a higher world."

The three companions sat in silence in the shadows, weighed down by the implications of what Jeremy had just stated.

The restaurant was bustling with activity. The growing fear across the world population was causing a resurgence of need for communal gatherings and the illusion of safety they seemed to provide. Public places were always packed now.

"Are we together on this?"

Michelle and Andrew looked at each other. That brief glimpse carried a lifetime of hopes and dreams. They wanted so much to be together and seek out the quiet joy of a life shared in love. But they were fated to exist in a time where peace would not be found in any corner of the world.

They nodded in unison. There was strength in the single-minded commitment that they shared. Jeremy looked at his watch.

"It's time. Remember, the Federation is not our greatest enemy."

The two lovers turned pale, understanding what he was referring to even though they didn't want to believe it.

"So beware not only of the outside dangers, but of the inner turmoil that will be created to throw us off-track. That's where the most deadly quicksands are to be found."

He stood and look at each of them in turn. "Remember," he whispered, "we carry the teachings of the Prophet that he passed on to us, the Light that must be saved from annihilation and forgetfulness. We have to keep it bright by living it. Then maybe we can share it with others in the future."

"If there is a future . . . " Andrew muttered cynically.

CHAPTER 3

Frenzy filled the air at the U.S. headquarters of the World Federation. Employees of the Science Division were running about, shouting to each other in hallways, and obsessed with the responses on their computer screens. News of yet another terrifying discovery had exploded among them like a neutron bomb. Their latest sonar cameras were sending back photos of an immense crack on the ocean floor. Careful analysis revealed that it had widened to twice its size in just the last few weeks.

The small earthquakes that had shaken the west coast of the continental shelf were warning signs that the mythic Big One was indeed about to occur. Yet the residents of the coastal states were taking the unstable earth in stride as they had for nearly two centuries. Under the influence of the Federation, the media was required to put the most positive and least alarmist spin on the information. News reports were softened to avoid mass panic.

Now at headquarters, across the continent, there were clear indications that it was not business as usual out in the Pacific.

"How in the hell can the earth crack open all of a sudden like that?" Brad Coglan, head of the Division, growled at three anxious scientists standing in front of him.

"I don't know sir. There's no natural explanation for it. But the facts are clear," the more courageous assistant stated, holding up the color printouts of radar images. "You can see for yourself."

He pointed to the jagged red line running across the image. "There it is, as clear as day."

Coglan grabbed the paper out of his hand and compared it with one that lay on his desk and was dated several months earlier.

"It's widened out all right. So what are your conclusions?"

"Sir, in my opinion, a killer quake is going to erupt any day now. There is no way the pressure isn't going to split that shelf in half and rip apart all the faults like never before."

"What magnitude are we talking about? Seven, eight?"

"Off the charts, sir. California will float out to sea."

"Get outta here!" Coglan called out.

"And there's another thing," the third scientist pipped up. "A lot more serious than that."

His boss looked at him incredulously.

"What could be more serious than losing a piece of the country and millions of people dropping into the ocean?"

"Well, sir, I believe we've got definite proof that the earth's axis is undergoing a shift."

"A what?" Coglan may have been head of the Federation's Science Division, but he was no scientist. He'd been in the core of engineers, but when it came to things of a cosmic nature, he was utterly ignorant. They had placed him in management for his leadership skills, not for his intellectual abilities.

"A complete lithospheric reorientation of the earth's crust."

Coglan didn't want to reveal his ignorance in front of his underlings. He didn't have to. They already knew his limitations.

"We're talking about a pole shift, sir. It's also known as an earth crust displacement. If you imagine removing the peel of an orange and then reattaching it, you can see how the peel could easily move over the inner layers. We can expect a tilting of the earth's axis, changing the centrifugal balance of the crust and generating massive surfaces changes."

"So what would that result in?" Coglan asked, already knowing the answer.

"Some continents could sink and others rise from the depths. The oceans will back up in their basins at an average velocity of two to three hundred miles an hour. We can expect gigantic tidal waves some three thousand feet high inundating the continental shores."

"Has this ever happened before?" Coglan barely managed to ask as his throat nearly shut down with anxiety.

"Our geological and geomagnetic records suggest that this cataclysm occured nearly fifteen thousand years ago."

"That's why we've found skeletons of sea animals in the Himalayas and tropical coral reefs in the Polar Circle," another man in a white coat offered. "Coal deposits in Antarctica tell us that there was a great forest up there once."

"When you consider the results of the greenhouse effect," another scientist continued, "and the buildup of ice at the South Pole, it makes the globe all the more unstable."

"Are you telling me the climates are going to change?"

"Dramatically!" the scientist responded with enthusiasm. He was fascinated by the geological phenomenon and seemed to have overlooked the damage to the planet's population. "Some of the warmer countries will become ice-covered. And ice-covered lands will thaw."

"That's too strange!" Coglan cried out. "How can you be sure about this?"

"Well, it's happened before. That's one of the theories about the demise of the continent of Atlantis, you know. Some believe it's hidden under miles of ice in the arctic."

"Don't be talking to me about Atlantis, damn it! Let's stay focused on reality, shall we?"

The scientist held up a six inch thick folder.

"Got the data right here, sir. Six months of research."

"That could explain the fast increase of the fault lines on the ocean floor. The entire globe is under incredible pressure now."

Brad Coglan stepped away from his colleagues and looked out the window, staring at the doomed city beneath them.

"Maybe that man they call the Final Prophet was right after all . . ."

* * * * *

A black limousine, shaped in the latest aerodynamic style, swept around the corner and glided to a halt in front of a dilapidated church. Two men got out, obviously highly-trained bodyguards, and scanned the area for any trouble. They nodded to each other and opened the passenger door. The glistening dome of a bald head appeared from the car. A man of medium build stepped out, covered in a large raincoat. Beneath the flaps of the coat appeared shiny medals.

Under thick black eyebrows, steely eyes darted about searching the environs for potential enemies. General MacDaniel was the hero of the turn of the century Syrian war and feared nothing, expect perhaps renegade holy men. At his side, he wore the latest heat-seeking, laser driven pistol. Despite his years, he moved about with catlike grace and vitality.

He checked his watch and motioned for the men to open the old church door. This abandoned sanctuary in a forgotten corner of the city was a perfect rendezvous. Close to the waterfront, surrounded by discarded factories of another era, it was a no man's land. Not even the homeless and dope dealers ventured into this landscape.

The men muscled their way through the door into the dark room. They were greeted by giant cobwebs and an overwhelming wave of musty aroma. The old orthodox church had once been home to a thousand worshipers. Now it was more like a rotting cadaver than a place of reverence. Left to disintegrate soon after the beginning of the third millennium, no one had ever come to revive it. The angelic hymns and mystical chants that had once resonated in its walls had given way to a deep silence that in some ways was even more mysterious and compelling. Its very desolation spoke volumes about the times.

Educated people no longer thought about getting on their knees, unless it was to work with the latest technological wizardry. This gutted church was a symbol of a death at the heart of civilization which, like a black hole, sucked in all the dislocated pieces of societies into its barren vortex.

The general stepped into the cool shadows of the old sanctuary. He coughed as the dust choked him. For a man who hadn't had a spiritual thought in forty years, this place was very irritating. Irritation, in fact, was his antidote. He buried any intuitive feelings that might have opened his eyes to another dimension of reality deep in the morass of negative energy which stirred within him where they were sure to be swallowed up and forgotten. At least for now.

He smiled at the paradox of being a man of darkness in this "hallowed" ground. The blasphemy tickled his atheism.

It took him a few moments to adjust to the darkness of the Gothic setting. The heavy aroma of mildew filled his nostrils, further confirming the fact that religion had been defeated long ago by men like him. Impatience burned through his veins as he sought out the man he had come to see. "Where the hell are you?" he finally called out, after bumping into several columns of cold stone. The electricity was out. An orange, flickering glow came from a few newly lit candles beneath a disintegrating statue of the "Mother of God."

"Turn on a flashlight," he ordered angrily. One of his men lit a high-powered lantern and aimed it around the room. A beam of light shot through the darkness, illuminating icons, candles, crosses and broken pews.

"What the hell do they want to meet here for?" the general muttered as he looked upon the religious objects with disdain. "I guess they can't let go of the old fantasies of the race. They haven't entered the modern world yet. That's their whole problem."

The general took off his raincoat and tossed it to one of his men. He wore a carefully tailored military uniform. Tight riding pants, shiny boots, a sharply creased shirt with insignias of his four-star rank. An expert horseman, he liked to wear the clothes that came with the sport even though the animals were as anachronistic as this ancient church in an age where nothing mattered but high speed and efficient control. He wandered about the large space, looking at the ruins of another time.

"This all died out with the last millennium," he said arrogantly, looking up at an icon of a mother and child whose gaze were warmer than his. "We've entered more enlightened times. Do you know how many wars were fought over these myths?" he asked his men without expecting any answers. "At least our wars have a rational purpose."

The purpose was straightforward indeed: the destruction of maverick rulers and political terrorists, and the domination of the world population. For a planet on the brink of collapse, the strategy made a lot of sense. Especially to a man whose only insight on human beings was to crush them into submission.

The general stumbled over an object and kicked it away from him, cursing. It was a porcelain angel wing. It shattered against the wall.

"It's all junk!" he said angrily. "I don't know why anyone ever fell for it. It sure didn't do him any good," he added as he paused below a crucifix.

But he quickly turned away, disturbed by the sensation he felt gazing upon the face of one who was called the savior of the world. He moved off abruptly.

"I can't believe I'm wasting my time with these fools."

He looked at his watch again. "I have to be in Paris in a few hours."

"Sir, I think I see them coming," one of his men called out as he looked through the crack in the door.

"You two disappear. We agreed to a one on one. Needless to say, shoot anything that looks suspicious. And I mean shoot to kill!"

The men vanished in the shadows as they pulled out their weapons. The general leaned back against an old wooden table that had once been a holy altar where the sacraments were distributed to the faithful. The door opened, sending a ray of light into the room which immediately filled with a myriad dancing dust particles. The silhouette of Jeremy Wilkes appeared in the doorway. He stepped into the sanctuary.

At first he didn't notice the presence of the man he was to meet. Jeremy was struck by a memory with the force of a bolt of lightning. His early spiritual encounters as a child in an old church swept through him like a tidal wave crashing on the shores of his consciousness, rekindling all the feelings that had changed his life and put him on this path. In the next instant, it was lost again. He was back in the dangerous present.

His eyes first saw the shiny leather boots, so terribly out of place in the old sanctuary.

"General MacDaniel?" he asked in a voice strengthened by the remembrance of his commitment.

The general said nothing, still leaning on the altar as though it were a bar.

"You'd be Jeremy Wilkes."

"That's right. Are we alone?"

The general stood up straight and stepped forward. "I'm here. Isn't that enough for you?"

"I've got two friends waiting outside who are prepared to speak with you as well."

"The deal was one on one."

Both men knew that his friends were there to witness any possible betrayal.

"I take it one of them would be Michelle Blair," the general muttered hatefully.

This time it was Jeremy who didn't answer.

"I'd like to see her again," he added with an evil grin.

He approached Jeremy swaggering with the confidence of an all-powerful, merciless leader.

"I'd like to look into her eyes and ask her if she's happy with the decision she made."

He was now just a few feet from Jeremy. They could see each other's features well. Jeremy was disgusted by what he witnessed in the cold eyes, and he stared back defiantly at the bravado of the arrogant military man.

"So you're the Prophet's right hand man, eh?" he asked almost mockingly.

Jeremy let the insulting tone slip by and studied the angular features of his adversary. This man had seen more dead bodies than Dante had described in his gruesome vision of the inferno. He was in the highest echelons of a world government that controlled the planet more effectively than any empire before it. And yet it was teetering on the brink of utter collapse despite the increasing military control.

Jeremy smiled to himself at the irony. This man so full of pride had to lower himself to meet an ordinary person. That alone was an admission of the underlying weakness and fear within the Federation.

"Let's get straight to it, shall we!" the bald warrior said impatiently. "You've heard the terms of the deal. You declare the prophecies untrue and we let you live in peace."

"How can you guarantee us safe passage?"

The general's little eyes caught fire with rage. "You're talkin' to a four-star general, son, the commander of the western military branch of the World Federation! My orders are sacred. When I give a command, it's obeyed without question."

"Are you a man of honor?" Jeremy dared to ask.

The general's jaws clenched tight. He did his best to maintain his composure, unwilling to let himself be thrown off balance by this nobody.

"Are you?" he shot back.

"That's why I'm here, general," Jeremy said fearlessly. "So what exactly would you have me do?"

"We want to call a news conference and have you make a statement to the world press. We want you to say that the Prophet was wrong."

"And what do you think that will accomplish?"

"It will keep the world population from utter panic."

"What if his words aren't wrong?"

The two men glared at each other through the shadows of the silent sanctuary.

"Then it will keep them content," he said with a subtle smile. The man might as well have told him that the Federation was the wizard of Oz. More illusion than power.

"But he is wrong!" the general continued. "I don't see the earth caving in under our feet."

"Not yet . . . But I know you've seen other reports from across the globe. There's no denying that geological and political unrest are coming to a climax."

"We've handled difficult situations before."

"I'm sure you have. But this one is even beyond your powers, general. There's going to be a clean sweep and men like you will have no authority."

The general winced as though he'd been hit in the face.

"How dare you?" he responded. "I could splatter you against the wall right now with my bare hands."

For a moment, it seemed as though he was going to follow through with his threat. But Jeremy was no longer worried. He understood that his work was to step into the lion's den and say what he must.

"So what's your proposition?" Jeremy asked coldly.

The general paced back and forth, moving away from Jeremy, trying to control his desire to kill him.

"I'll set up a news conference tomorrow morning. It will be the largest ever assembled. I want you there with whomever else will stand at your side. I want you to state that the prophecies are—at best—disturbed imaginations and not to be taken seriously."

He glanced over at Jeremy, knowing how much he was demanding. "You can qualify that however you wish. Tell the world that your friend was under stress, ill, or whatever. Just give people something else to think about besides total destruction."

"And what will you do for us?" Jeremy asked, biting his lip, forcing himself to continue forward with this bargain.

"As soon as the news conference is over, if you have achieved what we require, my soldiers will escort you to the edge of the city. No one will harm you. All you have to do is never show yourself in public again."

"This would include all those who are with me?"

"That's right."

"Even Michelle Blair?"

The general flashed a hate-filled glare at him. "Even Michelle Blair," he said through gritted teeth.

"I thought the Federation never forgave its rogue agents. Isn't that official policy?"

The general's dome glistened with sweat as his emotions roared within him again. He walked up to Jeremy and tried to stare him down.

"We'll make an exception for this case. There's too much at stake to waste our time with one traitor."

Jeremy peered into the fierce light coming from his eyes, seeking to detect what he was really thinking. The general relaxed his facial muscles, as though backing off from a frontal assault.

"Look, Wilkes," he said in a calmer voice, "we're trying to keep the world from annihilation, don't you understand? For all our military strength and surveillance capacities, we're at the mercy of madmen and terrorists, some of whom have uranium in their possession. One spark could ignite a war that would kill us all. Your Prophet has just raised the odds that we're not going to make it. So now it's up to you," he said, sticking his finger against Jeremy's chest, "you're the one who can make the difference. If it wasn't so, I wouldn't be wasting my time with you. I deal with world leaders, not bohemians and religious fruitcakes."

Jeremy had to repress his instinctive reaction to the man's poking finger. He had learned the hard way not to let himself be victimized by his every response. This effort was at the heart of the Prophet's teaching.

The man was so close to him that he could smell his cigar-laden breath and could sense his inner violence.

"It's up to you, Jeremy Wilkes, to keep us from a disaster from which we cannot recover. You don't even have to condemn your friend, just give people another option besides the total devastation which the Prophet predicted."

"I repeat, general. What if there is no stopping what he said was on its way? I can't blind them to what's before their eyes."

"Young man, I've been in the business of world government for twenty years. I've learned that reality is not the issue—perception is. If some kind of end of the world is coming, I want to avoid the hundred revolutions that will explode before its onset. At least we can limit the bloodbath."

"Since when were you concerned with human life?" Jeremy asked in a challenging voice.

General MacDaniel studied him from beneath his thick eyebrows. His angular face tightened again into a knot of disdain. "Son, I deal with the things of this world. You may be interested in another, but my feet are planted solidly on the ground here below. If I have to take lives to save other lives, then that's how it's gotta be."

"Aren't you just repeating what has always been the curse of human history?"

This time the general lost control. He grabbed hold of Jeremy's collar and choked him.

"You bastard! How dare you judge me? What have you ever done for your country? I stood in front of enemy fire. Where have you shown your courage? Don't you dare judge me! What have you done for your fellow human beings?"

"I've never tried to choke them!"

The general released his grip and walked away from him.

"Are we agreed?" he asked in a loud, angry voice.

"What if I don't agree?"

The general turned around and pulled out his pistol.

"Then I'll waste you right here, son. You're of no use to me."

Jeremy didn't flinch. This would be the easy way out to end it all right here in this old sanctuary.

"You've now given me the experience of facing enemy fire," he said serenely.

"How does it feel?" the man asked, arming his weapon. A red light came on and projected against Jeremy's heart.

"You have no power over me, general. Go ahead, shoot!"

"Is that really how you feel about it?"

The general held his weapon with both hands and aimed at him.

"Do you want your wife Lynn to come here and mop you off the floor?"

Jeremy was stunned at hearing his beloved's name come from the vicious man's lips.

"Don't you think we know all about you, Wilkes? Who do you think you're dealing with? We know what time you go to bed at night. We know you're hiding in the desert somewhere and we're going to smoke you out like rats. Every one of you. So think of your friends before you play the hero."

Jeremy's mind went into hyperspeed. The faces of his companions appeared before him beginning with his soul mate, Lynn, and followed by Stargazer and his people who had protected them. And beyond the welfare of his friends, the mission that the Prophet had bequeathed upon them—to stay alive and survive the Tribulation in order to help the race begin again.

"It's a deal, general," Jeremy said, his heart sinking, knowing there was no other way.

CHAPTER 4

The phone rang in the Indian elder's shack. It was one of those old touch tone phones from the previous century, predating the era of satellite transmitted calls, even before the use of fiber optics. Very few such phones were still in operation, except in rural areas and among the marginalized.

Stargazer sat in a gutted sofa with a cup of water in his hand. He looked over at Lynn who was sitting on a tattered couch across from him. The old man studied her, eyes sparkling with concern. He nodded for her to pick up the phone. She did so with a trembling hand.

"Hello?"

"Lynn?"

Jeremy's voice reassured her.

"Are you safe?" she asked breathlessly.

"I am."

She detected a grim tone to his voice. "Tell me," she said, not sure she wanted to hear.

"We've made a deal. But it's going to be costly."

"What do you mean?"

"They're going to leave us be, all of us."

"That's great! What do we have to do in return?"

There was silence at the end of the line.

"Jeremy?"

"They want us to publicly reject the Prophet's words."

Lynn's face turned ghostly pale.

"We can't do that!"

"Not all his teachings, just his statements concerning the predictions of global disaster."

"What predictions? They're already here!" Lynn cried out.

"They don't want to know that. They believe there's security in ignorance."

"We can't deny his words!"

"Do you remember what his first requirement was from us?"

"Of course I do."

"That's what this is about—survival."

"Not at the cost of rejecting him publicly. I can't do that. I didn't think you could either."

"Damn it, I feel bad enough as it is, Lynn! Don't make it any harder! This is the only way out. Otherwise, they'll slaughter every last one of us and bury us in some mass grave in the desert."

Lynn turned and looked at little Angel, the six months old infant who had been saved from death by the Prophet's mysterious powers. Her mother, barely fourteen years old, had also found new life through him.

Lynn turned to Stargazer. The old man was staring out the window, but listening intently. He too was suffering from the desperation of their situation.

"Lynn, we've got to do it. It's the only card we can play."

"What makes you think we can trust them?" she asked, trying to find a way out of the unthinkable.

"I spoke directly with MacDaniel. You can't get higher than that. The Federation is ready to do anything to calm the world population."

"Don't they realize that people can see for themselves what's taking place? You can't very well overlook earthquakes and giant storms!"

"They've been manipulating people's minds for so long, they believe they can keep them from seeing what's in front of their faces. In any case, it's only temporary. They're buying time just to keep control."

"Jeremy, I can't believe you would do this."

"What the hell do you want from me, Lynn?" he shouted through the phone line. It was the first time he had spoken such angry words to his beloved wife. She was shocked, speechless.

"I'm doing this to save our lives!" he said more calmly.

"I don't want my life saved at that price."

"All right then," he responded with irritation. "Don't think about your life, think about the mission we've been given. We've got to make it through this for the sake of the future."

"I don't want to carry that kind of responsibility on my shoulders, Jeremy. I just want to be true to what I believe in."

"It's too late to back out now, Lynn! You were right there when we made our promise to him. If we give up now, he will have died for nothing."

His last words struck her in the chest like a sledge hammer. Nothing could get her to betray the Prophet, except his own legacy. She knew her husband spoke the truth. If they were destroyed, nothing would be left of what the Prophet had brought to humanity. His mysterious mission, which was still so unclear to them, could vanish like dew at sunrise and be lost for all time.

"Lynn, darling," Jeremy said gently, "people are becoming more insane than ever. They have no idea of the madness taking over their own souls. They're easy victims of deception. The Federation knows this all too well."

"So we'll participate in the deception?"

"No," he answered, no longer angry, but feeling her pain. "We'll create an oasis of sanity for those who can find us."

"When must this happen?" Lynn asked in a weary voice, resigned to what had to be.

"Tomorrow morning."

"Tomorrow?"

"The sooner the better."

"Don't you realize what tomorrow is?"

"No."

"It's the anniversary of our first encounter with Adam Hawthorn."

Another silence came over the phone line.

"I'll be back by the weekend," Jeremy finally stated.

* * * * *

A gigantic bank of fog had fallen upon the city during the night. It drifted through the streets like some lost ghostly monster. By daybreak, nothing could be seen more than ten feet away. The world appeared captured by a thick mist that wandered over it unhindered. Clouds of fog seemed to rise from the ground like puffs of smoke exhaled by some unseen creature.

An eerie silence hung over the vast jungle of buildings as though all life were crushed by the mammoth clouds dragging their bellies across concrete pavement.

A black car, headlights beaming bright, made its way through the empty streets. It came to a halt in front of a television studio. Three security agents jumped out and scanned the area for safety. A limousine swept around the corner and pulled up in front of the building. Four bodyguards exited the car, followed by General MacDaniel who was dressed in a colorful, fully decorated uniform. He adjusted his cap on the shiny dome of his head and approached the entrance.

Suddenly, a light tremor shook the ground beneath his feet. He caught himself on the stair railing as the building shuttered. The men looked at each other, trying to conceal their fear generated by this interference of nature's instability. This was especially difficult for the general. He was heading to a news conference that would assure the world population that there were no imminent catastrophes ahead.

The tremors stopped after a few seconds. Everyone stood still. No one breathed. Each man remembered the dire warnings of the Prophet, despite their denial of them. The general was the first to break out of the fearful trance that held them all in its grip.

"Let's take care of business, shall we!" he said gruffly. They headed into the building.

One of the bodyguards looked back before closing the door behind him. The streets were quiet as the strange fog wound its way between the buildings. There was something threatening in the air, something ominous. The man could sense it like a jungle animal knowing that it was being watched but unable to detect the presence of its adversaries.

Jeremy, Andrew and Michelle were already waiting in the conference room, along with a crowd of reporters summoned there by the Federation.

The trio sat at a table covered with microphones. Their faces were grim, but determined. The tremor had made them even more uneasy about what they were doing, and yet Jeremy was certain of the necessity for pushing onward. They could barely hide their nervousness, however, as military men—some with weapons strapped to their sides—filled the back of the room.

General MacDaniel entered and gestured to an assistant. Immediately, everything went into motion. Lights came on, reporters opened their notepads, cameras rolled.

An army officer pointed to a reporter, ordering him to ask the first question.

"Reverend Wilkes, you were a key associate to Adam Hawthorn, better known around the world as the 'Final Prophet.' You were with him from the beginning."

"That's right," Jeremy replied solemnly.

"Why have you called this news conference today?"

"We're here as friends of the Prophet to dispel misunderstandings concerning his announcement to the world prior to his death."

Jeremy paused. The room was utterly silent. Andrew looked over at him, tense and worried.

"The Prophet was here for more reasons than forecasting oncoming calamities. He taught us in very specific ways how to live with meaning and purpose."

General MacDaniel leaned against the wall in the back of the room, grimacing impatiently at Jeremy's delay in getting to the point.

The reporter, coached by the Federation, pressed on.

"What are you trying to tell us?"

"The reason for this news conference," Jeremy continued grimly, "is to let people know that the prophecies they heard broadcast around the world which have caused such panic are not the central purpose of the Prophet's mission."

General MacDaniel barely managed to keep himself from smacking the wall with his fist. The military men in the room looked at their superior with concern. The man hated double talk.

"What are you saying about the prophecies then?" another reporter asked.

"We are here to tell you that they should be disregarded because, whether they are true or not, they are not the point of his teaching."

"Are you telling us that you do not believe in the prophecies?"

Jeremy swallowed hard. He felt as though his heart was being pulled out of him. He glanced over at the general who eyed him fiercely.

"I'm saying that they are metaphors rather than statements of fact."

"What do you mean by metaphors?" the reporter insisted.

"The Prophet did not merely warn us of oncoming natural catastrophes. He saw them only as reflections of the spiritual devastation of humanity. We should be more concerned about the death of conscience among us than about dramatic weather changes.

"He told us of the invasion of the walking dead among us, people so alienated from their spiritual identity that they are devoid of all feeling and reason. Such legions of pathological individuals are capable of every kind of atrocity. This is the real disaster. Not whether the earth shifts on its axis.

"The Prophet spoke of demonic predators seeking to destroy the very dignity of being human. His emphasis was placed on each individual's personal effort to avoid sinking into the endless night of human degeneration.

"What I'm saying is that people have focused on the wrong issues. It doesn't matter whether or not we're destroyed by wars and natural cataclysms if our souls are lost to greed, selfishness, and perversion."

Jeremy leaned forward toward the microphone.

"The real tribulation that is coming stems more from the cataclysms within the human soul than from wars and weather conditions. The most dangerous battles will not be conducted with bombs and bullets but with unseen forces pitted against each other whose battleground is at the center of every human being."

"What kind of mumbo jumbo is that?" someone cried out.

Jeremy didn't blink. A new serenity had suddenly taken over where uncertainty and confusion previously ran rampant.

"Everything is connected. We know that by now. Our physicists have told us that each of us is at the center of the expansion of the universe. Each of us is also the center of the destruction of the universe. And everyone of us must become aware of the real struggle before we can do anything to protect ourselves and change what is coming. Our own inner demons are the cause of what we see around us. Either we exorcise them through new awareness and effort or we're all going down in flames."

"How are your statements different from the Prophet's message?" a reporter asked, taking the words right out of General MacDaniel's mind.

"Don't look without, look within," Jeremy said simply. A strange silence fell over the room, as though his words had jolted his listeners into that very experience..

"People around the world are making the mistake of seeking shelter from external danger because of the Prophet's words," Jeremy continued. "But his true message has to do with the dangers within us."

"So you're saying that the world population is not in such imminent danger. It's more of a spiritual thing, eh?" a reporter asked with a mocking grin.

Jeremy did not answer, letting people draw their own conclusions. In the back of the room, General MacDaniel shook his head in anger and disgust. He was entirely unsatisfied with the direction of the news conference.

"Do you take any responsibility for what the Prophet has unleashed across the globe? The panic, the suicides, the general mayhem that is upon us? Could the world have been saved from this if his words had not been broadcast on television?" another journalist asked.

Jeremy leaned into the microphone again. "I'm sorry that people have suffered unnecessarily by making wrong decisions based on their misunderstanding of the call that he sent out. But I'm not surprised that his message was reduced to such limited interpretation."

"You people ought to be thrown in jail!" someone called out. "Somebody's gotta be held responsible for the anarchy that's so rampant now!"

"It would be absurd to blame the messenger for the message," Andrew responded angrily. "The natural cataclysms that we witness everywhere around us are certainly not of his doing!"

"But you did kill the messenger, didn't you!" Michelle suddenly blurted out.

Jeremy looked at his companion whose emotions were bubbling to the surface. Andrew took her hand, worried. But she couldn't contain herself.

"You beat him to death! Now you suffer the consequences. This man could have changed everything! Now we're left with the results of your rejection!"

The general leapt like a tiger from his position at the far end of the room and shouted an order as he personally tore the microphone's cable out of the wall.

"You're under arrest!" he cried out.

"What are you doing?" Andrew exclaimed, his face turning scarlet with anger.

"This news conference is over!" the general shouted, motioning for his men to rush the cameras and shut them down. He called for two soldiers nearby to draw their weapons.

"Arrest her! Your irresponsible accusations are treachery!"

"You promised us free passage!" Andrew yelled as he jumped between Michelle and the approaching soldiers.

"False accusations are tantamount to betrayal!" the old warrior thundered.

Jeremy jumped up and came face to face with the general.

"This is not going to look good at all for the Federation to be seen as untrustworthy. Not in these times!"

His words stopped the general cold.

"It was a live feed," Jeremy continued, "just like we agreed. The whole idea was to show your magnanimity, wasn't it? And quiet the fears that are threatening the entire civilized world. Arresting her won't help meet those goals."

The general held up his hand, stopping the soldiers.

"Get outta here now," he whispered between his teeth. "Don't ever let me see your face again, or I'll shoot you myself!"

Jeremy looked into the steely grey eyes and sensed that he meant exactly what he said.

"Good luck," Jeremy whispered back sincerely. He knew the man was going to need it to keep civilization afloat against all odds.

CHAPTER 5

The companions hurried out of the building. A black van was double parked next to their car, surrounded by a dozen heavily-armed soldiers. The friends looked at each other as a feeling of terror shot through them.

"They've betrayed their promise!" Michelle whispered hoarsely. "Just like I knew they would."

"We've got to make a run for it!" Andrew said as every muscle in his body tightened in fear.

"Don't panic!" Jeremy ordered. He slowly moved down the steps ahead of them. "I think they're going to let us go."

Excitement made his heart beat wildly as a feeling of certainty filled him with new hope. Andrew and Michelle followed, suddenly struck with the same sensation.

They came to the bottom of the stairs and stopped in front of the van and the ring of soldiers. Jeremy unlocked the doors to his car with his remote control and motioned for his friends to get in.

"Now what?" Andrew muttered under his breath once inside the vehicle.

Jeremy looked back at the building in expectation. The doors opened and General MacDaniel appeared at the top of the steps. His face was distorted with a fierce anger as he motioned to the soldiers to follow their orders.

Several men opened the back of the van, revealing a group of men carrying submachine guns.

"I don't believe it!" Michelle whispered in horror. "Hurry!" she suddenly cried out.

Jeremy looked up in time to see the general command his soldiers to fire.

"Get us out of here!" Andrew shouted.

Jeremy threw all his weight onto the accelerator. The car hurled forward, slamming into the soldiers who had appeared from the van and were preparing to shoot. Jeremy managed to maintain control of the vehicle as it flew around a corner under a hail of gunfire.

The car raced toward the outskirts of the city. Just as they reached the highway, an old trailer truck appeared on the road directly ahead of them.

"We're done for!" Andrew shouted.

The truck stopped in the middle of the road. Someone jumped out of the passenger seat and waved them down. It was Lynn.

"Is that who I think it is?" Michelle cried out.

Jeremy slammed on the breaks, barely avoiding a collision with the huge vehicle. At the wheel of the truck was young Brave Eagle, motioning for them to get into the trailer.

Jeremy pulled the car off the road and came to a screeching halt behind a clump of trees that would provide camouflage from their pursuers.

"Come on, let's go!" Jeremy said nervously as he jumped out of the car and hurried toward Lynn. He took her in his arms.

"What a woman you are! You'll never cease to amaze me!"

"I hope not!" she responded with a big smile.

They jumped into the truck and headed into the countryside.

Jeremy put his arm around Lynn and kissed her gently on the forehead. They sat on thick layers of Indian blankets that padded the inside of the vehicle.

"How did you know where to find us?" Jeremy asked as he caught his breath.

"We've been following the news conference on the radio. Stargazer told us to be ready to meet you by the highway. He had another one of his visions. This time, I knew better than to question it."

Jeremy pressed his lips against her warm forehead.

"We're going to be all right," he whispered.

"As long as we're together," she said, "I don't care what happens."

* * * * *

That night, colossal storm clouds thundered all around the

world. Gigantic lightning crackled across the skies, terrifying animals and humans alike. Fires broke out everywhere. Transformer plants exploded beneath the electrical bolts. The stratosphere seemed to be retching violently upon the blue planet and its inhabitants that had so polluted their own nest.

Power outages created immense blackouts that shut down entire states across the North American continent. Computers crashed by the millions, television screens went blank, cars crashed into each other on every highway. The lightning looked like monstrous arms slamming down upon the earth as cosmic sledge hammers savagely assaulting their helpless victims. Armies were mobilized to prevent the population from massive looting. The World Federation declared a global state of emergency as communication systems failed all across the planet.

In the national office for Scientific Research, Brad Coglan stared in stunned silence at the reports coming through their emergency backup system. The high tech computers they had taken so for granted were as useless as empty beer cans. Hundreds of power transformers had been put out of commission.

"Has anybody ever seen anything like this?" he shouted out with uncharacteristic frenzy.

Several colleagues gathered around him, hair and clothing askew from the frantic work they had been doing for the last few hours.

"Never! Not in forty years on the job," one of the scientists said.

Another associate took off his glasses and cleaned them pensively on his disheveled shirt.

"There's never been such a thing in the annals of weather history. I don't even know what to call this phenomenon. It's as though the entire magnetic field of the planet has been disrupted."

"Maybe it's that axis shift you were talking about," Coglan suggested in spite of his disbelief.

"It may well be," James Fuller, the oldest scientist on staff responded as he joined the group.

"What can we expect next if that's the case?" Coglan asked, uncertain that he wanted an answer.

"That's a hard one," the old man stated, scratching the grey nubs on his chin. "It's never happened before. But if I were to guess . . .

"

"Go ahead, guess!" Coglan said with irritation.

"Well, I suppose the plates would shift."

"You mean the continental shelves?" Coglan asked with a new rush of fear.

"That's right," Fuller said sadly.

"We're talking earthquakes all around the globe on top of this?"

"Probably."

"Under these conditions, no one can be rescued!"

"That would be a correct deduction," Fuller said in a low, somber tone.

"Thousands, millions maybe, are gonna die!" Coglan cried out as he wiped the sweat from his brow.

"Yep."

"What can we do?" Coglan asked in a voice that was now trembling.

James Fuller looked at him with mournful eyes. He was tormented by the fact that his vast knowledge and experience were useless.

"Pray . . . " the old man said in spite of himself.

* * * * *

Thunder echoed across the vast Southwestern desert and slammed into parched earth that hadn't seen a drop of water in months. But still the skies were barren. No rain fell despite the storm.

Young Brave Eagle stood by his mentor Stargazer at the entrance of a deep cave and watched the dangerous lightning crash all around them. The elder shook his head as he studied the strange sight with great intensity.

"This is a sign . . . I've never seen such manifestations before."

"What is it saying to us?" the young man asked in frightened awe at the freak cosmic event displayed before him.

Stargazer listened to the crackle and explosions shattering the great silence of the desert, as though seeking to hear what the spirits had to tell him.

"He said this would happen . . . " the old man whispered.

"Who did?" Brave Eagle asked.

"The one they call the Prophet. He spoke of oncoming devastation, the end of the age."

"Our seers have also spoken of this, haven't they?"

"Yes, but what they did not say was that these events would come about because of the darkened souls of human beings."

"But this is nature's doing!" the young Cherokee warrior said to him.

Jeremy came up behind them from the back of the cave, leaving the shelter where his friends were huddled.

"He said that poison emitted by wrong action and the spiritual death of people everywhere would alter the magnetic field of the planet," Jeremy stated. He looked out at the purple sky furiously hurling thunder to the earth. "This has been building up for centuries and has reached critical mass in this age."

"What you call critical mass," Stargazer said sadly, "my people call the victory of the evil ones."

"It seems that we are the evil ones," Jeremy replied softly.

"All the dark deeds that humanity has committed are preserved in the spheres of the Great Spirit, like dust caught in the folds of a giant cloak."

"So the massacre of our people is part of this downpour of rage?" Brave Eagle asked in a whispered voice.

"That's right," Stargazer responded. "The Spirit World is releasing its fury over the cries of the innocent."

Just then, an explosion of lightning ripped across the horizon and shook the rocks around them. The men were unable to restrain a startled reaction at the great roar that followed upon the mystic Indian's words.

"It has always been said that evil deeds would be remembered. We thought it was our elders who would be the rememberers, through the stories they passed on to us. But maybe it's the cosmos itself that remembers."

"That's what the Prophet told us, Stargazer," Jeremy said. "In the East they call it Karma and it seems that the effects of countless terrible causes are now being played out."

"Must the innocent suffer as well?" the young man asked, lips trembling with the implications of his question.

"We must all suffer now," Jeremy answered. "Guilty or

innocent, we're all in the same boat."

* * * * *

From his office in the headquarters of the World Federation Military Sector, General MacDaniel ordered a state of emergency across the entire North American continent. The unprecedented weather conditions gave him the excuse he'd been waiting for to increase his power over the population. Military control had been hidden just under the surface for years, but now it would come out into the open with full force.

Reports were arriving over secret military satellite systems from every major city describing massive looting and violent anarchy. Vast urban areas were blacked out from the storms. The festering brutality and anger barely under control for the past half century was erupting with vehemence. People who had been reduced to cogs in the great machine of the social structure were now rebelling with insane fervor as they saw the system begin to fall apart. The youth of the day, whose family unit had been broken down since the last century, were without parents or conscience and were eager to destroy the civilization that had given them their miserable lives.

The active black market of weapons and drugs which formed a toxic mix that nothing could contain were now surfacing, adding deadly fuel to the firestorm. The Prophet had warned his friends that the cities would be the most dangerous place to be when the time came.

"Have you found them yet?" General MacDaniel barked as he studied the half dozen monitors on the back wall of his huge office.

"No sir, but we're on their trail," a military officer answered nervously.

"What the hell does that mean?"

"We know they're in the southwest and most likely on an Indian reservation."

"Then what are you waiting for? Bring them all in! Anybody who shelters them is an enemy of the Federation."

"Well, sir, we've been through every shack in that stinking hole. They must be out in the desert somewhere."

General MacDaniel stood up and stared fiercely at his officer.

"I don't care if you have to bulldoze the entire southwest! You find those rebels and you bring them to me dead or alive! This is the wrong time to have people like that on the loose!"

"I thought the Prophet spoke against violence."

"Well, he's not here anymore, is he?" the general shouted. "All his people ever wanted was to cause anarchy and destroy our system of government."

He pointed to the monitors on which news reports from around the world were being piped in, every one of them a picture of devastation from the freak storms across the globe.

"If ever there was an opportunity to take advantage of the situation, this is it!"

"Sir, we've got two regiments out there looking for them. Are you sure we should be using that kind of manpower? They're needed elsewhere."

"You questioning my orders, captain?" he asked as he stepped up to him. The soldier wasn't sure whether his superior officer was going to smash his knuckles into his face. He stood at attention and looked away, hoping for the best.

"Continue to follow my instructions to the letter, is that clear? I'll let you know when I'm ready to release the men for other purposes. That'll be all!"

The captain saluted stiffly and hurried out of the office, his jaws clenched.

He stepped into the antechamber and took a deep breath to control his anger. He looked around at the secretaries and people waiting for audience with the powerful general. He shook his head, realizing MacDaniel was more of a dictator than a military officer. He'd known for years that the puppet civilian government would eventually disintegrate and give way to the real power which always belonged to the men with the weapons.

The captain felt a strange heat in the right side of his face. Instinctively, he turned and saw in a corner of the room a large silhouette with gleaming eyes boring holes into the side of his head as though reading his mind. The soldier flinched. He'd never felt such a sinister sensation.

"What in the world is this man doing in here?" he wondered to himself as he looked away from the dark, massive figure.

"You'll find out soon enough!" came an answer in his head. The captain's eyes widened in shock. The man had read his mind and responded. He hurried out of the room, unable to deal with the strange phenomenon.

Stefan Zorn smiled slyly as he watched the captain walk away. One of the secretaries approached him.

"The General will see you now, sir."

He stood and adjusted his heavy black coat. He was dressed in a dark suit and tie and had removed the rings from his hand so as to look more like a business man than the occult magician that he was. He entered the general's office.

MacDaniel lit a cigar and watched Zorn approach with steely, suspicious eyes.

"I've heard a lot about you, Mr. Zorn."

"I'm sure you have," the big man said with an evil grin.

"Do you know why I called you here?" the general asked as he sat himself in the manner of an emperor on his throne.

"Of course. You need my skills."

The general did not respond and puffed on his cigar, unwilling to acknowledge his statement.

"Have a seat," the general said coldly as he pointed to one of the comfortable furnishings decorating the room.

"I'd be interested in learning how you came to find me, general."

"Now Mr. Zorn, you should know that the Federation's security forces can find anyone."

"You have a file on me, do you?"

"Certainly."

"What am I identified as?"

"I beg your pardon?"

"Am I under 'W' for warlock?" he asked sarcastically. "I didn't think the Federation had any interest in the supernatural."

"Officially we take no interest in these matters, because they have no reality for us. But the Federation can't be foolish enough to disregard anything completely."

Zorn let out a deep, booming laugh that startled the general.

"I'll bet you've got some department buried in a sub-basement somewhere conducting experiments with the unmentionable."

"You're partially right, Mr. Zorn. We've looked into telepathy, hypnosis and other such things. They can be powerful weapons."

"Indeed!" Zorn responded, sending a glare toward the general that reduced his own to shame. "So what conclusions have your bureaucrats come to?"

"No conclusions," MacDaniel said coldly, barely hiding the dislike he was developing for his visitor. "But we want to fight fire with fire."

"Aaah . . . fire. I know about that."

"You know that the world government's stability is threatened as never before, particularly because of the unfortunate spectacle that was made by the man they call the Final Prophet. I assume you saw that."

Stefan Zorn shifted in his chair. He was never comfortable talking about his nemesis.

"Did you know him?" the general asked.

"Who?"

"The Prophet."

"I met him once," Zorn replied with a distant look in his eyes, clearly uninterested in pursuing this line of conversation.

"Ever since he appeared on world television warning of dire things to come, we've had a rash of religious fanatics come out from under their rocks."

The men sat in silence. Zorn waited for him to continue. The general studied him carefully.

"How does this concern me?" he finally asked impatiently.

"We need someone who can identify their degree of "power" and then terminate them," MacDaniel said bluntly.

"You've got an army of hired assassins on your bank rolls. You don't need me for that kind of work."

"No, but we don't have a single person at any level of the government who would know how to deal with people with strange powers. We thought that perhaps you could identify these persons. We'll do the rest."

"Let me get this straight. You want me to be like a hunting dog."

"You can call it that if you want. We can't afford to have any more dangerous mystics appear on the world scene. It's worth a lot to us."

"A million dollars a head."

"They told me you had expensive tastes," the general said without flinching.

"Indeed I do. So do you by the look of things," he added as he waved at the decorations that filled the large office.

The general ignored his comment. "For a million dollars, you'd have to convince us that the individual in question was truly a person with dangerous powers."

"That's right."

"Is our information correct? You can detect such things?"

"I can detect them all right. And I'll be happy to tell you all about it for a million dollars. Add another half million and I'll kill them for you."

"We don't use that word around here."

"Ah yes, terminate. Tell me, how do you know you can trust that I'm not the very kind of person you're seeking to "terminate"?"

The general sat back in his chair and let out a circle of smoke.

"My people tell me that you don't care for those religious types anymore than we do."

"This is true."

"They also tell me that you're exclusively devoted to the dark side, as they call it."

Zorn did not respond, but held the general's gaze defiantly.

"You don't believe in such mythology, do you general?"

"No, I don't. The only power I'm interested in is at the end of my laser gun. The rest is irrelevant. But I know what loyalty is. If you're loyal to the enemies of the Prophet, then you're on my side."

Stefan Zorn revealed his big teeth in an evil grin. "If you're looking for the Prophet's archenemy, you've found him all right."

The general looked at him with satisfaction. He knew he had made the right decision by making a pact with the malefic man. One way or the other, he would come out the winner. Whatever it took.

CHAPTER 6

Jeremy returned deep into the heart of the cave where the storm sounded only like distant canons and the howling of ghosts from ancient wars. He made his way down a narrow corridor that descended into the bowels of the earth. Primitive lanterns hung on the sides of the walls, barely lighting the steep natural stairway created by waters that had once carved their way through the stone.

He descended further and further underground, sometimes having to slide between the wet walls through spaces hardly wide enough for an adult body. After awhile there were fewer lanterns to light his way and he had to grope in the dark. The sound of the freak storms could no longer be heard and a heavy silence, akin to the one heard only in the depths of the ocean or in the infinite vistas of outer space, filled Jeremy's senses. Somewhere in the belly of the earth, the slow drip of underground water echoed loudly, intensifying the eerie impression of intense isolation from the rest of life, a feeling that was comforting under the circumstances.

Flickering light appeared far below at the end of the steep corridor, a vision that would have terrified Medieval painters of a literal Hell. Jeremy came out into a vast chamber whose ceiling was higher than any cathedral ever built by human hands. It was lit up by torchlight on all four sides. The shivering light illumined giant Indian paintings created in primordial times. An overpowering sense of sacredness was given off by the symbols and images that climbed to the very top of the huge chamber. The place had once been a secret ceremonial temple for peoples who had disappeared long ago. Stargazer was the last of the elders to know of its existence. The secret would have died with him had he not chosen to make it a refuge for the friends of the Prophet. Nothing less than the end of civilization would have caused the old mystic to let outsiders into this holy place.

Colorful blankets covered the stone floor throughout the chamber, except in the center where a large fire crackled and warmed the humid walls. A slit in the ceiling served as a chimney, releasing the smoke into the upper rooms of the colossal cave.

In the far corner stood three large tepees, looking strangely out of place. They served as private rooms for the unlikely guests. Jeremy headed for the nearest one. He lifted the flap and peeked in. Blankets and furs made the space cozy and warm. In the midst of them, his beloved slept peacefully. Jeremy smiled at the sight of the woman he loved more than anything in the world.

Lynn moved slightly and opened here eyes as though she'd sensed his presence. She smiled a radiant smile and raised her hands for him to come into her arms. He entered the makeshift home and laid next to her. They hugged warmly, both keenly aware that their embrace was the only peace and joy to be found for them in this doomed world. They kissed passionately.

"Has the storm abated?" Lynn asked as she looked lovingly into Jeremy's bright green eyes and moved his wave of red hair dangling on his forehead back into place.

"Not at all. I've never seen anything like it."

Lynn's cheerful expression darkened. "Then it has begun!"

Jeremy shook his head. No words were necessary.

"My God! He was right!" Lynn whispered in shock.

"You knew he was right all along, Lynn, before any of us really understood what he was saying and how much he knew."

"But it's not the same when it actually happens." She tightened her embrace around Jeremy's strong shoulders. "I'm scared."

"There's reason to be, sweetheart. There's plenty of reason to be scared. Any sane person should be."

"Do they know what's going on out there?" Lynn asked in a trembling voice.

"You mean the Federation and the general public?"

"Does anybody understand what's taking place?"

"I don't think so. Not yet. You know how people are. It's gonna take recurring cataclysmic devastations to get their attention. By then, of course, it will be too late."

"Do you think we can make it through this?" she asked, pressing her warm, soft cheek against his.

"We have to, Lynn. Just like the Prophet wanted us to."

"How can we ever have a family under these conditions?"

He looked deep into her glistening eyes. The light blue of her pupils made him think of a cloudless spring sky in more peaceful times.

"You have to hold onto hope, hold on real tight. That's all we've got."

"Hope for what?" she asked breathlessly.

"For our happiness."

"I can be happy right now with you here in this place."

She kissed him gently on the lips. He felt a thrill rush through his body at the contact of her wet, quivering touch. They'd been married five years and madly in love every day, yet he'd never felt so loved as in this moment.

"Yes, we can be happy now," he whispered. "Like you said so many times, as long as we've got each other."

"Don't ever leave me, Jeremy. I couldn't handle this without you."

"I won't."

"I mean, never. No more trips away from me. Whatever we do, we do together now. And if we must die, it's gotta be together."

"Don't talk like that, darling. We're gonna make it. We've got to."

"What about the others?"

"You mean Andrew and Michelle?"

"No, all the other students of the Prophet who were dispersed when the security forces overran our community?"

"They'll learn to take care of themselves. You know that some of them have regrouped and are creating little communities all over the world. Think of Max and his people in the Bay area. They're thriving again. More and more people are joining them in response to the Prophet's words. They're better off than we are."

"I wonder why the Federation doesn't go after them?"

"They don't have time for the small fry. They want the ones closest to the source of power. The ones who can influence public opinion most."

"I sure don't feel close to the power right now . . . " Lynn whispered sadly.

Jeremy kissed her passionately and held her tightly in his arms.

"Why did he leave us with this responsibility?" she asked after a moment. "Who are we to carry Light into the future?"

"I guess we just happened to be in the right place at the right time."

"No, it doesn't work that way." She leaned back into the furs and looked up at the sides of the tepee where torchlight moved in a bizarre dance of color and shadow. "It had to take long preparation for us to end up here."

"What do you mean?"

"I don't know . . . Maybe people live many lives. I just feel that this couldn't be sheer accident that we're the ones to be given this awesome task. I can hardly bring myself to think about it."

"Then don't! Live for right now, in the moment like he always told us."

"But we're not him. We don't have any of his powers, and barely a drop of his wisdom. How can we live the way he did?"

"He gave us knowledge. He gave us strength by his example. And, who knows, maybe he'll sustain us even though he's not here."

Tears streamed down Lynn's cheeks. It was like this any time reference was made to the Prophet's death. It was an open wound in her heart that would never heal. Adam Hawthorn had given her a unique vision of unconditional goodness and self-sacrifice.

"Don't cry, Lynn," Jeremy said softly. "He wouldn't want you to keep suffering like this."

"I can't help myself. It hurts too much."

Jeremy had to stop himself from trying to convince her not to feel her pain. He'd learned by now that the intellect was useless as a tool for healing emotions, so he gently caressed her face with his hand and kissed her on the forehead and cheeks. He shielded her with his love. He knew that was the only way to ease her agony.

After a while, the tears slowed and she regained her composure. A muffled groan came from the tent next to theirs which housed Andrew and Michelle. Jeremy and Lynn looked at each other and tried to hold back their reaction. They smiled and broke out in soft laughter.

"Are they at it again?" Jeremy managed to say.

She nodded merrily. "They're as bad as we are." He kissed her full, sensual lips. He'd always loved those lips. They were like the fruit of Paradise—luscious, vibrant, overflowing with love. He knew he would never tire of tasting those lips as long as he lived.

"Privacy is going to be a problem from now on," he said after a moment. "We're gonna have to get used to a lot of new things."

He leaned over her and pressed his cheek against her soft, brown curls. He ran his fingers through them and breathed in her sweet scent. It immediately brought back the memories of the first time he had been that close to her.

They had found each other under strange circumstances, the kind that were suspiciously more than mere accident. At that time, Jeremy was in his mid-twenties, trying to make sense of the insanity around him. He was one of those intense loners who searched high and low for something more than the oppressive, materialistic society that dictated its version of reality to all its citizens.

He had landed in some sprawling urban setting after having traveled the continents like a bohemian wan-derer searching for meaning. Coming out of a subway one day on his way to some menial job he had managed to acquire, he noticed a poster advertising a lecture on the mystical origins of Christianity. Upon closer inspection, he saw that it was to be given by a Dr. Hogrogian, professor at some seminary in the Southwest. Jeremy didn't have much use for academics and their vain mind games, but something seemed familiar about this man's name. Perhaps he'd read an article in some obscure esoteric journal and retained the memory of the author's eastern European name.

That night, Jeremy entered a shabby public hall where the lecture was to be held. Fancy, high-tech meeting rooms were not available to people interested in these matters. Few persons were attracted to such ideas, partly because the world government had so thoroughly purged them from public consciousness. Only the outsiders and outcasts, those with no money or power, supported these events.

Jeremy looked around the room. Two dozen people sat in old metal fold-up chairs from the past century. He was curious about the individuals who would gather for such a lecture and studied their faces as best he could—loners, artists, rejects from the corporate world, all keeping to themselves. They were the laughing stock of the comfortable elite of the world. Most were dressed in wretched clothing, although some of them wore their simple garb with a dignity that transcended their poverty. Nobility of character shone in many of the faces. He observed a few potential sociopaths, the inevitable by-product of any group called together around the word "mystical." But most seemed stable, intelligent people.

No one seemed interested in socializing. They were here for one purpose, to seek knowledge and food for their starving souls.

Jeremy's eyes fell upon thick brown curls hanging over a black cloak which a young woman held around her tightly. Her clothing suggested that she wasn't a street urchin like the others, but came out of a more cultivated and successful world. His curiosity got the best of him and he walked down the aisle until he could catch a glimpse of her profile. He was immediately struck by the graceful lines of her face, the fullness of her lips, and most especially, the brilliance in her eyes. They emanated a gleam of intelligence and awareness that he had rarely seen before.

Then she turned and looked at him. He knew immediately that she had sensed his gaze and that she was a person with psychic powers. Their eyes locked and he stood mesmerized by the directness and sincerity in those sky blue eyes. He knew in that moment that he'd found his soul mate. Concerned that he was going to lose his balance, he decided to step forward.

"Is this seat taken?" he asked, pointing to an entire row of empty chairs.

A soft smile came across Lynn's features and she shook her head. That was the beginning.

The old professor entered and they were both completely absorbed by his words. He was a man of extraordinary wisdom, and a mysterious capacity to see into the soul of each person he looked upon. Jeremy knew that he would be his student some day, although he had no idea how close they would become.

Afterwards, he and Lynn spent the entire night at a local cafe discussing the radical ideas expounded by Dr. Hogrogian. Higher consciousness, autonomy of spirit, psychological liberation, detachment, awakening, all potent concepts on the evolution of humanity that thrilled their hearts and minds.

From that moment on, they were inseparable. Neither of them could stand being away from the other for very long. As their knowledge of each other grew, it became crystal clear to them that they were destined to be together. Each in their own way understood that they had found their other half, someone who shared mutual understanding, all-consuming affection, and a wondrous harmony in the balancing of each other's nature. They had no other desire but to merge their lives together.

Jeremy and Lynn joined forces in their common search for the deeper meaning of their existence and were ecstatic that they were no longer alone in their solitary journeys. They were lovers, companions, friends, co-workers in the effort to find meaning and purpose in their allotted time on earth. It wasn't long before Jeremy felt the need to enter seminary in his desire to study the illumined souls of the past. Lynn dropped everything to accompany him on this new path, even though she had grave doubts about the viability of religious institutions that were Federation approved. Nothing was sacred or safe anymore. Every aspect of society was reduced to the purpose of efficiently assisting the world government's effort to keep chaos at bay.

It was in seminary, under the tutelage of Dr. Hogrogian, that they encountered Adam Hawthorn, the man they would come to know as the Final Prophet.

Now they were at a new stage of their journey. And this underground home made it clear how dramatically different life would become for them. The Prophet had made them promise to make every effort to survive the oncoming devastations so that they might carry the seeds of the wisdom he had brought forth in them for that day when a new beginning was possible. But such a time was far off. First they would have to endure the unimaginable. Along with the danger of planetary catastrophes and the Federation Security forces, Jeremy knew that Stefan Zorn would be seeking them out. He chose not to tell Lynn of his encounter in the city, knowing that it would only cause her more distress at a time when he wanted so desperately to find some sort of peace despite the circumstances.

He also knew that it wouldn't be long before she detected his state of mind and uncovered the horrific experience he'd had in the ghetto. But with it would also come the revelation of his strange new ability to heal. He still needed to keep this event to himself until he could confirm that it was not a one time freak occurrence. The opportunity to find out was not far off.

* * * * *

"General MacDaniel, sir, this is Brad Coglan calling." The scientist wiped the sweat from his brow and did his best to keep his voice from shaking.

"What is it, Coglan?" the general asked in his usual bad mood.

"I've got some data that you need to know about."

"Can't you send it through the normal channels?"

"No sir, this is something you need to see before word gets out."

"Talk to me."

The scientist swallowed hard and struggled to find the right words to begin.

"Hurry up, I've got a conference in ten minutes."

"Well, sir, it's like this. We have reason to believe that the planet is going to experience a shift in its axis that will have terrible repercussions for the world population."

"What do you mean a shift?"

"It's happened before in the planet's history, and it seems that it's in process as we speak."

"Tell me in plain English what this means."

"Well, the weather patterns are going to change drastically. We can expect major earthquakes, volcanoes, and tidal waves, some of which may cross over entire continents."

General MacDaniel was speechless, perhaps for the first time in his life. For a moment, he couldn't think. This was an enemy that he didn't know how to combat.

"Keep me informed on a priority one basis." He hung up the phone and looked over at Stefan Zorn who was still sitting in his office, smoking one of the general's expensive cigars.

"Do you know anything about this?"

"Of course I do, general. It's been predicted for centuries by every warlock and visionary I know of."

"You're kidding!"

"I don't do that, general. You should have been reading those books you banned."

"I never had time for that supernatural crap."

"Well, now you'll have to deal with the consequences."

"There's not anything you can do about this problem, is there?"

"I'm afraid not. I can conjure up a few things for you, but I can't keep a cosmic event from taking place. You'd better get the Federation's leadership in underground shelters and plan on total anarchy spreading across the globe."

He smiled with evil glee. The general was disgusted.

"But you've got a great opportunity now, general. You can clamp down with your military might like never before. Get rid of a lot of people you don't want opening their mouths. Declare martial law in every country."

"This is unbelievable! How can the earth change so drastically and so quickly?"

"It's not just the earth that's changing."

"What do you mean?" the general asked, placing a hand on the back of his chair to steady himself for more bad news.

"Not only is the planet mutating, but so are the creatures who live on it."

"Go on . . . "

"The electromagnetic transformations that are occurring as the magnetic poles shift and reverse are having an impact on the subatomic levels of our physical being. We are nothing other than organic energy transformers. The increased energy in the atmosphere will cause our molecular structure to vibrate at higher frequencies. Our cells will be infused with new electromagnetic impulses. There is information encoded in our DNA that is now being activated. We can expect an acceleration of the nervous system which will also trigger a temporary weakening of the immune system."

"What does all this mean?"

"For one thing, you can count on a greater level of aggressive agitation. People are going to be overloaded with such energy that they won't know how to channel it. These greater frequencies will diminish the boundaries of the physical self. There will be more out-of-body experiences, and greater contact with beings from other realms."

"That's insane!" General MacDaniel cried out. He couldn't take anymore of this kind of talk. Or perhaps he couldn't bare to hear anything that didn't fit into the rationally constructed world that he helped to govern.

"The electromagnetic fields in the solar system are shifting and we little organic creatures are going to be profoundly affected by those forces," Zorn said slowly in a voice heavy with warning.

The general sat down and took a reflective puff on his cigar. "What are you telling me, Mister Zorn?"

"Our species is undergoing a transformation at the cellular level."

MacDaniel coughed on his cigar and poured himself a shot of cognac.

"Our DNA will evolve from two helixes to twelve or even fourteen strands which correspond to energy centers, what the ancient East called chakras. I'm sure you know that our cells are light-encoded filaments, threads of energy that carry information. These threads are detaching so that energy flows through us more - easily."

"What would that result in?"

"People will experience physical vibrations that are odd and uncomfortable to them. Our endocrine systems may speed up or slow down, impacting our hormonal balance. This will create everything from strong feelings to intensified memory to new psychic abilities. It will depend in part on a person's capacity to consciously receive these new energies."

Zorn inhaled on his cigar and studied the general's reaction. The military man remained poker faced.

"People are going to lose control," he continued with arrogant certainty. "You'll see many cases of what was once called possession. Some will be able to communicate with entities from other dimensions."

"Enough of this nonsense!"

The general slammed his fist on the table. Zorn stared him down with an eerie calm.

"I don't have any more time for this babble!" MacDaniel grumbled. "Our security forces will call on your services when needed. Good day, Mister Zorn."

Zorn did not move from his seat.

The general raised his voice angrily. "I said good day!"

Zorn slowly put out the cigar in the ashtray and stood without taking his eyes from the powerful military man.

"You're making a big mistake, General MacDaniel. People in your position can't afford to make these kinds of errors in judgment."

"I want you out of my office right now!"

"You're going to regret not paying more attention to what I'm telling you, sir. Even your blind scientists who think the world is only what their senses can perceive will be reporting on these matters. They won't have any choice. You'll be hearing from hospitals and psychiatric wards. You'll see it in the streets, in every city and town across the globe."

"I told you to get out!" the general roared.

"And then you'll come looking for me, sir, but it'll be too late. Because by then you'll realize that I'll be the one with the power!"

He turned abruptly and headed toward the door.

"Is that a threat, Zorn?" the general cried out.

He turned back as he opened the door. A sinister grin twisted his features. He said nothing and turned away.

"I asked you a question!"

The door slammed behind the dark man.

* * * * *

The storms finally abated and the sun broke through the clouds only to reveal massive floods on every continent. Engorged rivers everywhere spilled out across the land. The Hopi tribes had prophesied the cleansing of the earth in this age, but as the natural disasters increased, the earth began to rumble deep in its core and corruption surfaced as never before, not only on the mineral level but among the peoples of the planet.

Beneath the thin veneer of civilization held up by the world government, the wretched disintegration of the human spirit had continued its free fall that had accelerated in the last century and was now on an unalterable course. The vilest pornography was now available everywhere, anytime to everyone. The vast ocean of television viewers had gone from fantasy gore at the movies to the viewing of real deaths on their living room screens watched with a perverse lust that was sub-animal.

The market in child prostitution was one of the largest industries in the East, second only to opium and heroin. The illegal drugs that gave people an escape from the meaninglessness of their lives made up only a fraction of the drug market. The rest was generated by the international medical community that had no answers to the physical and mental troubles of the great hordes of humanity knocking on their doors. The majority of people were on some kind of tranquilizer or antidepressant. The men and women in white coats were doing their best to keep their patients as numb as possible.

Tension between the races was at an all time high as people searched for excuses to release their rage and frustration at a life that had lost its natural foundations. The work place was a giant oppressive force where everyone was terrified of being thrown out into the outer darkness of unemployment and hopeless misery. The streets were teeming with abandoned children who were quickly turned into super-predators by their ugly life of survival. There were miles and miles of concrete jungle, cemeteries of prosperous days gone by where no one ventured, not even the well-armed police forces. Savagery lurked around every corner.

It was a world that only the likes of Stefan Zorn found appealing. Evil was emperor. Only a very few still held onto some kind of faith in the goodness at the heart of the universe. But they were so marginalized that no one ever heard a word from them. History had come full circle. The Dark Ages had returned, even in the midst of extraordinary technological developments. Now that the foundations of human decency had been utterly eroded, those of nature itself were collapsing. Chaos and terror were creeping across the planet like the great shadow of a meteorite about to slam into the earth.

As the military branch of the World Federation expected, it took no time at all for guerilla leaders and warlords to emerge and take advantage of the destabilized societies. Like rats scurrying in the darkness, they felt safe under the cloak of catastrophes and mass confusion. Many of these new leaders had no intention of making the world a better place. Like most everyone, they'd given up hope on that a long time ago. They were from a generation that wanted to urge forward the degeneration of their societies. They wanted to insure the destruction of the world, not save it from its terrible fate. Like vultures circling a body near death, most of these troublemakers were lovers of death and corruption. What they did, they did with an insane zeal for self-annihilation. And they had no trouble finding followers. People were so emptied of meaning and purpose that any cause would do to wring out some kind of momentary satisfaction.

Hordes of youths who had never known a family hearth were eager to throw themselves into the furnace of self-destruction as long as they could take somebody with them. The world religions had reached their ultimate failure and left the species without any sense of direction.

Religious leaders began to appear with the speed of poisonous mushrooms after a spring shower, spouting the wildest brands of teachings ever brought forth by the human imagination. It had been so long since the world population had any exposure to the deeper truths of religion that anything was acceptable and worth considering. People wanted to be told what to do and become submissive to someone else's fantasy of deliverance from a world sterilized by greed and materialism. Underground cults that had been hidden for decades from public view now began to surface, revealing that a vast undercurrent of subcultures and separate societies had grown in the shadows of the dominant civilization. Some of them had stockpiled weapons for half a century. Among these obscure figures claiming some sort of divine knowledge was one man in particular who embodied both revolutionary furor and religious zeal. He lived in both worlds—the hidden realm of believers in metaphysics and in the very earthy world of assassins and paramilitary organizations. This unholy alliance gave him a power that few of the other self-proclaimed leaders could summon up. Stefan Zorn thrived on the wretchedness of the times.

CHAPTER 7

"What's wrong with this thing?"

Oliver Lance studied the homemade satellite receiver with an expert's eye. In his mid-thirties, he was at the height of his physical and mental powers. Rugged good looks, wild and thick hair flying in all directions, somehow never clean-shaven, Lance was the very incarnation of a maverick guerilla fighter. Hard bodied, weather-beaten skin, and intense dark eyes got him attention wherever he went. With the animal magnetism of a leopard and the single-minded devotion of a crusader, no one questioned who was in charge when he entered a room.

Lance braided several strands of wire and turned the system on again. This time, an image came through the static on the ten inch screen.

"We got him!" Loretta cried out as she adjusted her headphones. She shot a twinkling smile at Lance and turned up the volume on the sound board. Hardly into her twenties, Loretta looked nothing like an electronics engineer. She could have been a model, with her sunshine curls and harmonious features. But her devotion to the cause sent her off-course into the underworld of dangerous revolutionaries like the man standing at her side.

Loretta would have been accepted into the best of the international corporations who preyed on multi-talented, highly-trained graduates with relentless tenacity. Now she sat in a dingy, poorly lit room somewhere in the desert of New Mexico, following Oliver Lance on his one way path.

"Talk to him," she said enthusiastically.

Lance grabbed the microphone. "This is Omega One. Come in Master Zorn. Come in."

A faraway voice echoed out of the homemade loud speakers.

"This is Stefan Zorn. I read you."

Lance leaned toward the monitor and examined the unfocused figure. Despite the dim light source, there was no mistaking the hulking, powerful frame of the warlock. His coal-black hair and haughty features gave him a demonic look.

"Is it him?" he asked softly.

"He's too close to the camera," Loretta whispered.

"Looks like the photo they faxed us."

"You can't trust those things. Not with the new scanners. His face could be made out of four different people."

"You'd better talk to him before the connection breaks down again," Loretta insisted.

"I'll just have to risk it," Lance mumbled to himself.

Loretta smiled. How many times had he said that line before? Risk was what they did on a daily basis. It wasn't simply that they were so recklessly daring, or so devoted to their cause. There simply was no other way. Either they stepped out into the insanity of international social upheaval or they stayed home and watched reruns.

"Commander, we have completed our task. The time and place are set."

The little image in the monitor stared blankly at the camera as though digesting the meaning of those words crossing over the continent.

"Very well. Let us proceed to stage two."

They glanced at each other as a surge of adrenaline sent their hearts pounding in unison.

"Do you copy?" the voice came crackling through the speakers.

"We copy," Lance responded. "I will set things in motion immediately."

"Good. Until next time . . . "

The image vanished into a tiny dot of metallic light and the screen went dark.

"Next time? He's optimistic," Lance observed with a strange smile.

Loretta tried to mask her nervousness. But her companion knew the signs only too well. He took her in his arms and kissed her aggressively. Danger was a powerful aphrodisiac for this mercenary. She pulled away, disturbed by the violence of his passion.

"It'll all work out fine. What could go wrong?" he said as he studied the fear on her lovely features.

"You're kidding!" she cried out, finding it hard to control her growing uncertainty over both the mission and the man she worked for.

"Look at it this way. The worst that could happen is that we get killed."

"And you don't have a problem with that?"

Lance sat next to her and gazed into her large brown eyes.

"What's the alternative? To go on living in this madness? Without freedom or privacy? Civilization is only an excuse for powers-that-be to control us all the way to the grave. So why not take out as many as we can when it's our time to get outta here?"

"Is that what this is about? Some kind of cynical death-wish?"

Lance pulled out a crumpled pack of cigarettes from his shirt pocket. He fished out a bent cigarette and placed it between his lips.

"If we don't make something happen, everything will just stay the same. And this "sameness" is not static. It's heading downhill fast."

"I know that," Loretta said with a twinge of guilt for her hesitation.

"So we help shake things up a bit. At least we'll show we care."

"By killing dozens of people?"

Lance took her face in his hands. "This is not the time to get the jitters, baby doll. You've been with us, what, three years now? You knew this was planned all along."

His gaze darkened as he studied her closely. "I can still count on you, can't I?"

She tried to keep herself from shaking. Whether it was the look in his eyes or the upcoming event, she wasn't sure.

"Of course you can. I'm sorry."

"That's better," he said with strained warmth as he stood up. "Are you clear about your next step?"

He could see her mind racing, probably imagining the gory devastation that would soon be on all the newscasts around the world. He grabbed her by the shoulders to snap her out of it.

"Think of the result. We're lighting the spark that will bring on the shift in power. The Master will take over and the Federation itself will become his puppet. We just have to clear the way by liquidating the only people who could stand in the way."

"I've never been responsible for the death of innocent people before."

"You haven't?"

She looked up at him, horrified by his implication.

"What the hell do you think we've been doing all along? You don't think those diplomats were innocent?"

"They were part of a repressive coalition . . . "

"They were sacrificial victims on the altar of destabilization."

Loretta's breath caught in her throat and her face turned a scarlet red. Oliver leaned over and touched her cheek with unusual tenderness.

"Am I not the one who pulled you out of your meaningless little life and gave you the kind of excitement that made it all worthwhile? Hasn't it been really good?"

She nodded hesitantly, unable to speak.

"Who else would you want to have by your side when everything crashes? Who's the best protector you could ever hope for?"

She raised a finger and pointed at him.

"Then trust me. Trust Master Zorn. We'll take you places you've never dreamt of, not in the wildest throws of ecstacy."

Her fear vanished beneath a growing smile as she recalled all that they had shared together. He took her in his arms again, knowing that this would be the quickest way for her to conquer her fears. And after he'd satisfied himself, he had a bullet with her name on it when the time came. He wasn't taking any chances. No one, not even a pretty face, would interfere with the job he'd been hired to do.

* * * * *

A death-like silence weighed heavily over the dark seacoast. Across the bay, the famous silhouette of the San Francisco skyline sparkled like jewels in the moonlight. But on the other side of the waters, a strange motionlessness held the landscape in its grip. Something cataclysmic was about to happen.

In the midst of this nowhere land, where only seagulls and a few seals wandered by, a car suddenly appeared on the dirt road. Its headlights were out but the dim moonlight glimmered on silver designs revealing a Rolls Royce.

The elegant car pulled off into the grass. It sat there strangely out of place, engine running, waiting. Within moments, another car crawled quietly over the gravel. The Mercedes Benz also moved in the dark, lights out. It came up behind the Rolls and waited.

Then a line of cars appeared from the shadows—three, four, five, all without lights. They gathered around the Rolls. A tinted back window slid down into the innards of the door. A gloved hand appeared and pointed upward toward the top of a cliff. An old manor overlooked the ocean. A porch light illumined the nineteenth century home like a fragile candle soon to be snuffed out. The gloved hand abruptly gestured forward with regal authority.

The cars moved off toward the solitary home. A face looked out from the Rolls. The vicious eyes of Stefan Zorn sparkled with eager anticipation in the pale haze of moonlight. His face radiated power, strength, and most of all, hatred.

A silhouette detached itself from the tree line at the bottom of the cliff. Dressed in black, Oliver Lance was ready for battle.

* * * * *

It was in all the headlines: "Bizarre Bloodbath" . . . "Grotesque Massacre." Reporters bested each other on adjectives to describe the indescribable. Something had happened that had never been seen before. Those who had the misfortune to go to the scene were in shock. Forty-five bodies lay in and around the old mansion on the remote slopes of the mountain, each one more unrecognizable than the other.

Doctors argued among themselves as to what exactly had taken place. Bodies were exploded, not like victims of war struck by bombs but from within. Corpses were splattered on walls, dripping down staircases, split to pieces. Something, a power never seen before had destroyed an entire community. The fact that the dead were followers of the man who was called the Final Prophet only intensified the imaginings of the local inhabitants. Police felt incapable of dealing with such an abnormal atrocity and the Federation's security forces were called in immediately. But the best of them could not come up with any theory. What had happened was unearthly, unholy and unknown. The only question that could be dealt with was: would this happen again?

Detective Ernest Sloane was first at the scene, having gotten a call on his radio on his way home from work. By the time his colleagues joined him, he was knee deep in blood and knew he wouldn't be eating for a week. Nor would he ever order a rare steak again. Detective Sloane was a twenty-five year veteran, at the top of his game. A large, muscular man who had played pro football before a lineman ripped the cartilage out of his knee, Sloane lacked manners but made up for it with an unusual dose of common sense.

"What do you make of this, detective?"

Sloane turned from the grisly sight and studied his questioner. A young man, thirty-something, stood before him.

"Looks like a tornado passed through here."

"The lab boys are looking for explosives. We're also checking the wiring," Sloane mumbled with a mix of fatigue and disgust.

"You think it could be a short circuit, eh?" the young man said, a smirk on his face.

"What's so funny?" the detective responded with irritation.

"How 'bout a gas leak?" the young man suggested sarcastically.

"Who are you?" the detective asked suspiciously as he stood and looked down upon the man whose humor seemed so out of place..

"Name's Tom Wells."

"Who are you with?"

"Uuh, the Times . . . "

"Let me see your press card."

Tom pulled out a card, swallowing nervously. Sloane studied it closely and gave it back to him.

"How did you get in here? This is a crime scene. Official police business."

"You haven't put up the demarcations yet, so I thought . . . "

"We will any minute. Get out before I throw you out."

"I might be able to help you, detective."

"I don't think so," the detective said as he turned his back on him.

"Have you seen this?"

Sloane turned around and looked at the object Tom was holding up. It was a medallion.

"Where'd you get that?"

"Right by those steps over there."

"You mean you picked up evidence? You wanna go to jail?"

"Nobody'd found it."

Sloane tore it out of his hand. "You might have covered up finger prints!"

"Sir, I believe I can help you. I can assist in identifying the symbolism of this medallion."

"What are you, some kind of expert?"

"As a matter of fact I am. I have been studying occult sciences for fifteen years."

"Anybody can look into an encyclopedia."

"Sir, there are no encyclopedias with this kind of information in them. That's a three thousand year old symbol that comes out of ancient Egypt. I'd date it around the Nineteenth Dynasty, in the reign of Amenhotep. "

"You're not expert enough to know not to pick up evidence at a crime scene. Get outta here!"

"You don't think this is the work of your neighborhood syndicate, do you?"

"Maybe, maybe not. A little analysis will tell."

"Analysis?" Tom responded, amazed at the man's blindness. "I think you're going to be in for a surprise, inspector."

"How's that?"

"There are no bullet holes or knife slashes on the corpses. You just might have to look in another direction."

"What other direction?"

"The realm of dark forces," Tom whispered with a gloomy look in his eyes.

The big detective studied him for a moment with a look of disdain.

"Get outta here!"

"You're not dealing with your average maniacs here, inspector. There is something . . . demonic about these killings."

"Don't bother me anymore!" the man growled as he turned back to the grisly mess around them.

"When was the last time you saw a body smashed against a wall like a ripe tomato? What do you plan to do? Look for fingerprints?"

"That's right! And take pictures and measurements, and those things I've done for twenty-five years to put these puzzles together. And I've been highly successful at it, thank you very much. Now get outta here and don't waste my time!"

Tom didn't move. He watched the detective search through the gore.

"With all due respect, sir, your narrow mind is going to get a lot more people killed. And you're going to keep walking through these massacres with your head up . . ."

The detective turned around and grabbed Tom by the collar.

"You push me any farther, bigmouth, and I'm gonna have you arrested!"

"I'm not the enemy, inspector," Tom said as calmly as he could.

Sloane let him go and walked away. Tom shook his head at the man's stubbornness. The stench of death was beginning to make him sick to his stomach. But his curiosity would not let him turn away from the gruesome sights. He walked over to his rusty Oldsmobile and leaned against it. From this distance he could survey the activities of the investigators. Personnel from the coroner's office were invading the premises with loads of body bags.

Tom knew that the media would be here soon with their cameras and remote trucks. In no time there would be a wall of people and equipment between him and the old mansion. Television sets and newspapers across the world would package the story and fit it into a framework that might be understandable: Victims and villains, weird religions and violence . . . Nothing new, really. There were more bodies at Jonestown.

But Tom was certain that there was something radically new about the horrid event. It wasn't only the inexplicable manner of death and the vicious slaughter of everyone in the house without exception, but the fact that such carnage was signed with a symbol lost to humanity for eight hundred years. Tom felt goosebumps raise the skin from this bones. Something very big was surfacing, something that did not belong to this plane of reality.

Tom had been a writer for over a decade but had only published two books. The material he researched was too esoteric for the marketplace. Few wanted to hear about secret orders and ancient teachings when, for the same price, they could acquire pornography and brutality as food for their imaginations. The young man knew that his path would keep him in poverty, but he was committed to that direction. Whether out of choice or because of the hypnotic attraction he had for mysteries that transcended human reasoning, he did not know. He studied sages, mystic knights, and obscure communities separated from the bulk of humanity because of their experience of transcendent realms. He knew more about these things than most professors. Unfortunately, it kept him eating pasta and soup. But he was adapting to his fate, unwilling to waste his time on more trivial things like satisfying the public taste. Now that his isolated love affair with arcane matters was blending with front page news, he felt that perhaps he was living a relevant life after all.

His dark auburn hair and bright eyes wrapped in a face that could have been in the movies made him a potential catch for the opposite sex. But he hadn't been very successful in that area either. In fact, his relations with all humans, male or female, was reduced to small talk with the waiter in the coffee shop where he did his writing and with the owner of a used bookstore. He didn't have time for anything else. There was so much to learn from the buried wisdom of humanity that he scarcely noticed the world of the twenty-first century. And it returned the compliment.

So his treatment at the hands of detective Sloane was no surprise to him. He smiled sadly at the trouble his sight gave him in the land of the blind. He pictured the symbol to himself: the sun with rays extending all around and ending in human hands. He knew that its origin came from the time of Amenhotep, also known as Ikhnaton. The pharaoh had so shaken up his times, that at his death, the stones of his monuments were buried beneath new constructions so that the world might forget him altogether.

There was one thing that Tom knew for certain: The people who had been massacred in this ungodly display of mysterious forces were clearly connected to a group with great knowledge. He'd given up years ago finding people with such interests. It wasn't until he saw the Prophet on that infamous international broadcast that he dared to hope that others were drawn to the deeper mysteries of life as he was, instead of being chained to the wretched treadmill of this age. He had searched in vain for the Prophet's followers. When he learned of his death, he gave up in despair and returned to his melancholic reflections.

But the medallion had stirred his hopes again. Perhaps what had happened here was related to the Prophet's mission. He remembered that while he sat mesmerized in front of the TV set listening to the Prophet's searing words, something he said made him think of the ancient pharaoh. He had been one of those few people in human history who had attempted to unite religious teachings in a deeper synthesis that lifted the veil from the uncreated One behind all forms. Now in the twenty-first century, another man had raised his voice for that cause and been killed for it as others had before him. The Prophet had warned of dramatic - changes that would shift world history off of its tracks, just as Ikhnaton had done in his day. He had torn down all the idols of his people that had reigned over them for three thousand years. For one brief shining moment, he offered them a greater understanding that might enlighten their short journey through time and space. He worshiped a formless being, the energetic form that acted through the sun, the divinity immanent in all things, Aton the intangible essence of all creation.

Another man grasped his vision and carried it to another people—the former Egyptian prince known as Moses. Tom's studies had clearly shown him that there was a link between the mystic pharaoh and the man who took the Hebrews to the Promised Land and opened the way for the tradition of the universal Messiah.

It made perfect sense to the lonely writer that in the Final Prophet's lightning streak through history, there should reappear signs of past visionaries, reminding the world of the roots of his message. Tom had heard about the followers of the one called

Adam Hawthorn. He had eagerly sought them out and would have been thrilled to speak with the least of them. Anyone who was privileged enough to be around such a man must have worked hard for it. It would be among such people that these treasures of humanity's lost wisdom would be found.

The amateur sleuth wandered around the parameters of the crime scene, looking at every detail with intense attention. He felt in his gut that there was something for him to find. The sense that this atrocity was related to the man called the Final Prophet kept growing within him with irrational zeal. Suddenly, he became aware of the gravel beneath his feet on the far edge of the property. He looked down and found that he was standing in front of tire marks. Discreetly, he followed the tracks which were visible for just a few feet before they vanished onto the paved road. The Federation security forces were too busy walking through the slaughter in the mansion to have examined this area. His heart - began to beat to the cadence of a tribal drum. He knew he was going to find something. His eyes scanned the ground with an eagle's beam. That's when he saw it.

The dim sunlight partially hidden behind incoming fog from the bay created a sparkle that revealed an object in the gravel. Tom look around to make sure no one was paying attention to him. He quickly kneeled down and grabbed a handful of gravel that surrounded the shiny object. He stood, walked off toward the trees lining the road and stepped into the shadows. He closed his eyes, took a deep breath and then opened his hand. In the middle of his palm was a tiny diamond pin, an ornament for expensive glasses. It had apparently fallen from the rim unnoticed by its owner.

Tom brought it to eye level. The hair thin golden pin was topped by a small diamond-encrusted shape. There was no doubt as to what the symbol was. Fifteen years of study had trained Tom's eye to recognize it instantly. It was an upside down cross, the sign of the beast, the Antichrist as history had once called him in days when people believed in deeper mysteries than the senses revealed.

Sweat broke out over his entire body and a wave of nausea sparked by unspeakable terror shot through him. For the first time in his life, he realized that the mythology that had fascinated him all these years was no fantasy.

The sound of a car screeching to a halt nearby pulled him out of his state of shock.

Tom looked up, instinctively wrapping his fist around the pin and slipping it in his pocket. A shiny Mercedes Benz with dark tinted windows was stopped next to him. He couldn't see any of the passengers but he immediately sensed the presence of evil. Though he was more of an intellectual than a mystic, there was no denying what his intuition was telling him.

With a slight electronic buzz, the window slowly rolled down and the face of a striking older woman stared out at him. She had strong aristocratic features and her piercing green eyes were set wide apart and shaped at an angle, giving her an unsettling feline look. She stared at him like a tiger studying its prey.

"May I help you?" Tom heard himself say.

The woman peered into his eyes as though trying to read his mind. Tom froze, seeking to keep any thought from revealing itself to her. He felt his hand tremble in his pocket.

"Did you find something?" she asked in a husky voice deepened by years of cigarette smoking.

"What do you mean?"

The woman's strange eyes narrowed as she studied him carefully, as though she were trying to detect a lie.

"A friend has lost something precious. Have you seen it?" she asked again.

"I don't know what you're talking about," Tom said, giving the best performance of his life.

The woman did not respond and suddenly rolled the window up. The car took off and quickly vanished around the steep corner. Tom stood there for a few moments, uncertain as to whether he was going to collapse from fear. He had just looked into the face of unspeakable darkness. And it had stared back at him with fierce hatred. He had seen a practitioner of the occult who had most likely been part of the horror that had taken place in the mansion. He would have been less mortified had he stared down a hungry lion on the prowl.

Somehow he knew that this was not the end of the affair. He sensed that she recognized his lie. He hurried away toward his dilapidated car and headed back to the city, wishing this had just been a bad dream.

CHAPTER 8

Jeremy walked along the ridge of a dusty cliff just as the golden orb of the sun rose above the razor-sharp edge of the desert horizon. His loyal friend Andrew Bradshaw walked alongside him, a tall melancholic silhouette contrasting sharply with the intensity of his companion

"We can't stay here," Jeremy whispered as he looked at the glorious sunrise spread out before him.

"What do you mean? This is a perfect hideout."

"They'll kill everybody on the reservation to locate us. We can't do this to Stargazer's people."

"There's no place for us to go. As soon as the authorities spot us, they'll put us away for good."

"It's not just the Federation that is looking for us," Jeremy said almost unwillingly.

"What do you mean?" Andrew responded, stopping dead in his tracks. Jeremy turned around and looked at him sadly.

"Don't you get it, Andrew? We've taken sides."

"Sides?"

"By choosing to go the way of the Prophet, we've made some terrible enemies, some of whom are much more dangerous than the Federation. Even with all its surveillance gadgets and deadly weapons."

"Are you talking about some kind of force of evil?"

Jeremy shook his head. He couldn't bring himself to acknowledge it out loud.

"Don't you remember Adam telling us about it?"

"Only in the vaguest terms!" Andrew said angrily. "I thought it was more philosophical than literal."

"It's literal all right. I've looked in its eyes."

"What are you talking about? Demons?"

"They're human beings who have devoted themselves to very different powers than those of light and evolution. They're now the servants of destruction and degeneration."

"I thought that kind of thinking went out with the last millennium."

"That doesn't take away the reality of the matter. There's so much that we don't know that what we do know is either irrelevant or so fragmentary that it has to be wrong! But you can be sure of this. By choosing to support the Prophet's mission, we have made enemies in high places. They won't waste any time coming after us. And there won't be any deals like we had with General MacDaniel. What they want is our death, physical and spiritual."

"I wish we'd been warned about this early on."

"Why? Would you have backed out? To do what? Wander around in chaos and confusion like you had before? Don't be ridiculous, Andrew. There was only one way for us. We're the lucky ones. We've found some kind of meaning in this madness. Whenever our lives end on this plane, we'll have found some kind of purpose."

Andrew turned red, embarrassed by his reaction. He looked across the desert wasteland toward the mountains to the north.

"What can we expect?"

"I don't have the answers. But we'll have to be watching our backs every moment. Not only that, we'll have to be attentive inwardly, because they may come at us in more ways than one."

"How's that possible?"

"They'll attack us in our thoughts, our imagination, our feelings. They'll confuse us, stir us up emotionally."

"How are we suppose to cope with this?" Andrew asked in terror.

"We'll definitely need all the help we can get from the higher regions. And I think we can expect to receive it. The Prophet has not left us alone."

"It sure feels like it!"

Andrew kicked at the sand, still feeling betrayed and abandoned.

"Jeremy!"

Lynn's voice echoed across the ridge. He looked up, immediately concerned. He raced back toward the entrance of the cave and found Lynn standing there, arms wrapped around herself to keep from shivering.

"What happened?" he cried out.

"A horrible premonition . . ."

She was as pale as a ghost. Her lower lip trembled like a child about to weep. Jeremy took her in his arms.

"Tell me. Was it a dream?"

"I was stirring the fire. I thought I saw something in the coals. A vision came to me."

"What did you see?"

"Our friends . . . Max and the others . . ."

"What about them?" he asked as he tried to comfort her.

"I think they've been killed!"

Jeremy pulled back and studied her. He knew better than to reject her intuition. He'd learned over the years that, when she intuited something in this way, it was no fantasy.

"What did you see?" he asked again.

"Something terrible . . . Something not of this world. Everybody's dead. The coals glowed like devil eyes. The hiss of the wood was like evil laughter. The eyes were full of hate and violence. Then they seemed to turn on me!"

She looked at her beloved, eyes glistening with tears.

"They're coming after us, Jeremy! They killed our friends, but it's us they want! They seek to wipe out all traces of the Prophet's presence among us."

Jeremy flinched. The synchronicity of his conversation with Andrew and Lynn's vision only intensified his feeling that she was right. A thought came to him.

"We should tell this to Stargazer. Maybe he knows a way to shield us from this kind of evil."

"We've got to warn all the others before it's too late! If they could find the teaching house in San Francisco, they'll locate all our other friends!"

"They're scattered about everywhere."

"We can't just let them all die like sheep sent to the slaughterhouse!"

"Andrew can reach a few of them on the WorldNet, but that'll expose us to the Federation's scanning devices."

"Our people would be better off in prison than left vulnerable to these creatures!"

The sky suddenly rumbled with a powerful roar of thunder. Jeremy looked across the horizon to see a pitch black mountain of violent clouds headed their way. It struck him that these dark forces were rising out of the earth's agony, as though the instability of the planet opened the way to the entrance of infernal powers.

* * * * *

Oliver Lance came out of the basement where he'd been hiding out and stepped into the light of day for the first time in two months. He took a deep breath and felt immediately invigorated. The subtle scent of sea breeze coming in off the bay gave him a thrill he didn't expect. Oliver wasn't a sentimental type. He'd had his emotions crushed years ago by a disinterested mother, a broken family, and a dreary career in the corpse of some mega-corporation. When he finally rebelled against a society that had never given him any value or attention, he sold his soul to a wretched cause that turned him from a disenchanted citizen into a cold-blooded mass murderer.

The joy of nature's sweetness was a rare experience for him. But even to one as dead as he was toward the beauty of life, two months in a windowless concrete basement was enough to entice his need for contact with the world around him. The sun had not yet burned through the fog that covered the area since morning. He liked it that way—grey and overcast. He had no use for sunshine and blue skies that reflected a happiness and lightheartedness which would never be his.

Oliver Lance walked down the sidewalk heading toward famed Union Street where he could mingle through the crowd undetected. He felt exhilarated by the success of the operation for which he'd been a key point person. He was the one who had located the Prophet's followers and he could take a good share of the credit for the destruction that had occured at dawn. In his twisted mind and frozen conscience, this was a good thing. He was a success in the eyes of people he admired. People like this Master Zorn, the most mysterious figure he'd ever encountered. And also the most powerful. Oliver was proud to be a trusted member of his elite secret organization.

He didn't even know what his leader's objectives were or who it was that he worked for. He just knew that this was a man of action who could make big things happen. That was good enough for him. It seemed that his boss's agenda was primarily death and devastation, something he had lusted for since his teens. It was the only thing that could get him up in the morning. Life had no purpose, so he'd chosen to find it in death.

He still enjoyed the taste of good food and the company of women. But even those sensations couldn't justify a life that had no direction. Now he had a cause, even if it was in opposition to everything good.

Oliver wandered by the shops and studied the crowd. He glanced at the passing faces. Some of these people could be his future victims. That thought gave him a power he'd never felt before. He entered a shop for no particular reason and found himself in a bookstore. Oliver hadn't picked up a book in ten years. But he was drawn by the obscurity of the atmosphere and the smell of coffee that came from a small reading area.

He ordered a strong coffee, grabbed a newspaper, and sat at a small table in the shadows of the room. Several intellectual types sat at the other tables. He looked at them with disdain. He had no use for people who used only their minds. He was a man who lived by his muscles and instincts. Oliver's athletic prowess had always been his greatest asset. In his teen years, he was the best of his generation across the entire state. No one was as strong, as quick, as graceful in the use of his limbs as he was. He didn't know why his body was so good at throwing footballs or combination punches. He'd never met his father so he couldn't trace it back to ancestral genes. But it was the only gift that came with the package. His mind was ordinary, his imagination mediocre. But his hands and feet were amazingly coordinated.

Unfortunately, he was too small to make a career out of these skills. He had hoped to enter the elite world of the Federation's security forces, but he failed too many tests. The world government had no place for powerful bodies with limited intelligence. Their agents had to combine top engineering education with physical ability. The days of dull-witted tough guys had vanished with the previous century. Degrees in computer science had to go with sharp shooting skills.

So Oliver was left at loose ends with no prospects but the most menial manual labor. His ego had been far too aroused by cheering crowds in high school to accept such a fate. It was at his lowest point that he came across an underground figure who introduced him to the world of terrorism. Oliver realized that behind the name of Stefan Zorn was more than a military renegade or political anarchist. He knew there was something else motivating him, something supernatural. But like virtually everyone else in this age, he had no capacity to grasp what that could mean, so he dismissed it from his mind.

His eyes wandered across the shelves of books surrounding him. The very thought of reading fatigued him. As far as he was concerned, the Nazis of the last century had the right idea when they made bonfires of all that intellectual babble. It had too much influence on gullible minds. He looked at the readers sitting around him, sipping their expensive coffees. He stared at them with disgust. It made no sense to him that the human body should sit motionless absorbing something that didn't strengthen tendons or exercise circulation. He was a true product of a society focused on the surface of life. People were judged and measured according to the flesh and bones that were visible. The depths of their mind, heart and soul—that invisible realm where the vaster part of life resided—was utterly closed to the general consensus on what constituted reality. Oliver had swallowed the government approved version of truth hook, line and sinker, even though he rebelled against the oppression of the Federation's tentacles.

His eyes fell on a young man who was furiously writing in a notebook. Oliver realized that he was looking at a producer of books. He imagined pulling out his hidden weapon and blowing off the top of that overworked head. That would make clear which one of them was the superior man. Raw power was the only yardstick he had for proving his worth.

Suddenly Tom Wells looked up and their eyes locked. Oliver was caught in the glare of Tom's vision with his disgust and hatred revealed in their primal ugliness. Tom was stunned and then angered by what he saw in the man's face. What right did that unshaven, ragged-looking character have to despise him like that? Hatred and anger mingled together like toxic energies and before they knew it both men were on their feet.

"What is your problem?" the young writer asked between clenched teeth.

"Why don't you step outside and I'll show you!" Oliver responded, losing all control of whatever reason he had.

Tom realized that he was dealing with a completely irrational creature, as dangerous as a wild dog who had torn himself free from his chain.

"What did I do to you?" Tom asked more calmly.

"I don't like your kind!"

"What kind would that be?"

"Are you man enough to come out on the sidewalk?"

By this time, the other customers in the bookstore were watching the scene, horrified.

"I don't want to fight you," Tom said quietly, trying to ease the tension.

"I knew it. You're all talk and no action. It's up to my kind to make things happen."

Tom said nothing. He glanced over at the employee who served coffee and noticed that he was already on the phone to the police.

"You don't like me because I write? Is that it?"

"That's right!" Oliver spit out. His hatred of all life shot through him like acid. He looked at the other faces staring at him.

"I don't like any of you! You're all a waste of space on this planet! You'd be better off as fertilizer!"

Oliver suddenly grabbed Tom's collar. Tom's adrenaline burst through his veins and he pulled himself free, jumping back and landed in a karate stance.

Oliver snickered. "You've had some training, have you?"

Tom didn't answer, waiting for his adversary's next move. A police siren reverberated down the street. Oliver froze and came to himself. The last thing he wanted was trouble with the authorities. Not on this day. Stefan Zorn would never forgive him. He unclenched his fists and looked around for a quick exit.

His eyes fell on the newspaper headlines that screamed in giant bold letters of the predawn massacre. Tom watched his adversary's face change colors. Oliver looked up quickly. Their eyes met. In that split second, Tom saw that Oliver was connected to those terrible headlines. The glare in Oliver's dark eyes revealed that he also perceived Tom's recognition. He was about to reach for his gun when a police squad car screeched to a halt in front of the store.

Oliver suddenly dashed toward the back door and was gone before the officers entered. A shiver shot up Tom's spine. He knew that he had made a deadly enemy. The man would kill him if they ever encountered each other again. Yet his fear was tempered by the excitement that roared through his veins. He had unwittingly been given a clue to the occult murders that had taken place only hours ago.

Before his mind had a chance to stop him, Tom ran out of the store on Oliver's heels. He'd never followed anyone before, although he had written many pages carefully describing the experience. Now he had to live his fantasy into action.

He caught sight of Oliver racing toward the end of the alley and turning onto Gough Street. His eardrums pounding with the frantic thump of his heart, Tom hurried through the shadows keeping his eyes on Oliver's vanishing silhouette.

Sliding against the wall, he tripped over a garbage can and fell in a heap on the ground. He turned rigid with fear, expecting the dark-eyed man to come around the corner with a pistol aimed at his head. But no one came. Beyond his shuddering heartbeat, he could hear the man's hurried footsteps moving off in the distance.

Tom scrambled to his feet and carefully looked out onto the steeply inclined street. He saw Oliver turn toward a house at the top of the hill and descend a set of stairs leading to a lower level entrance. Tom fell back against the wall and slid to the ground.

"I must be totally nuts!" he muttered to himself. He wasn't in the habit of talking out loud when no one was around, except when he was in the heat of inspiration for one of those novels that he couldn't get published. But he was beside himself with a schizophrenic combination of bloodcurdling fear and ecstatic excitement.

The last thing he wanted to do was to tangle with the likes of Oliver Wells. Until a few moments before, he had only met that kind of individual in his darker fantasies as they spilled out onto paper. Never before had he been threatened like that. But the very intensity of the threat convinced him that he had stumbled onto the trail of an extraordinary story, the like of which he had never dreamt up, not even in his overactive imagination. Moreover, he sensed that the immensity of evil he had encountered across the bay hinted at the other side of the equation. Such dark forces could only be out to crush a manifestation from the higher realms. And who else but the one called the Final Prophet could fit that bill in this day and age?

Twenty years of studying metaphysical texts made this conclusion as clear and solid as crystal.

It was rumored in the underground of spiritual outsiders that the Federation was hunting down all the Prophet's followers. They had dispersed almost immediately after his murder, scattering in all directions. It made sense that one of those directions would be the west coast. A number of the Prophet's disciples had come from Asia and the Pacific rim was a perfect stopover for those who needed to vanish into obscurity at a moment's notice. Besides, the Bay Area was still the last refuge of maverick thinkers despite the long years of intellectual drought inflicted on society by the world government.

Tom now had the opportunity to not only resolve the mystery of the massacre at the old mansion, but to also be brought into contact with those who had been close to the Prophet. They would surely reflect something of his influence. A man with that kind of power and enlightenment hadn't appeared on earth for nearly a century. Tom didn't expect to be around for the next "visit" from the celestial realm, so he considered this chance his one shot at coming face to face with a wisdom not of this world.

He stood up and dusted himself off. He knew he couldn't just walk into the house that Oliver had entered. It would mean certain death. First he would have to find some of the Prophet's students, not only to warn them but also to call for reinforcements. This was not a conflict he wanted to tackle alone.

* * * * *

Andrew tapped away on his keyboard, sending urgent messages

out over the WorldNet. He sat in Stargazer's shack, his laptop plugged into the only outlet within five miles. Michelle stood by the window, keeping a vigilant eye on the horizon. Any sign of approaching vehicles and they would rush back to their more secure hideout. In the back of the room, Lynn and Jeremy were engaged in whispered conversation with the old Indian mystic. Tension filled the small, cluttered space. They all knew that change was in the air. After three months buried in the soothing silence of the desert, they were being compelled to step out into the madness of a world in chaos and before the all-seeing eye of the Federation's security forces.

But they had no choice. Within moments of logging on, Andrew had found the gruesome news flash of the killings on the west coast. There was no time to mourn the dead. As the leaders of the Prophet's former community, they had to assist those in immediate danger regardless of the risk to their own safety.

After sending a general word of alarm across the globe to whomever might receive it and relay it onto friends of the Prophet, the first order of business was to contact those who were left in the Bay Area. Andrew's genius with computer communication would not be enough to fly under the radar of the Federation's constant scan of the WorldNet. Nothing was private anymore in cyberspace, but the sheer volume of global business and babble might give them a few precious moments to make vital contact.

They could only hope that someone out there happened to be online at the time. E-mail would be detected by Federation agents before it was ever retrieved from in-boxes. Technology had become as much an oppressive force as it was a producer of ease and efficiency. The pioneers of the last century would be turning over in their graves or wandering the halls of their nursing homes in misery and despair. What had been unleashed on humanity was not a gateway to new opportunities but an enslavement to the powers of international dictatorship. There was no room for individuality on a planet that was ablaze with anarchy and terror.

"Marla's on!" Andrew cried out.

The others turned to see little yellow letters forming on the blue screen.

"All dead . . . Except for Juanita, the baby, and Maxim

Ivanovitch. They were staying with us overnight because the baby was sick. Can you get us out?"

Andrew looked up at Jeremy, despair in his eyes. Juanita was a thirteen year old whose life and that of her baby Angel had been saved by the Prophet. Marla and Ivanovitch were loyal members of their former community who had joined the Prophet in the early days.

"Answer yes!" Jeremy stated with determination. "Tell her we're on our way."

CHAPTER 9

Jeremy looked into the rearview mirror as the car roared down the highway. A white car travelled at a certain distance behind them. His stomach suddenly tightened as he realized that he had seen this same vehicle just to his left for the last half hour. It seemed obstinately stuck behind him at a constant hundred yards away. A wave of hot adrenaline shot through him from head to foot, pouring out of some primeval instinct telling him that he was being hunted. Once, the white car had come close enough for him to catch a glimpse of the driver's features. He saw a bulky, powerful silhouette with a crewcut that suggested military training.

If his suspicions were right, the man was good at his job, seeming distracted and completely uninterested in giving his attention to the car ahead of him. Jeremy tried to convince himself that he was being paranoid, that the car was merely traveling in the same direction. The vehicle looked at least ten years old, although it clearly had an aerodynamic structure that could move at great speeds.

By now he'd lost tract of the conversation his friends were having. He suddenly realized that he was hearing Lynn's raised voice calling out to him.

"What's going on, Jeremy?" she asked, worried.

"What do you mean?"

"I called you twice. You didn't respond."

"Sorry, I guess I'm a little tired. I was daydreaming," Jeremy said, swallowing hard. He knew he couldn't lie to Lynn for a moment. But he had to try anyway. At least for a little while, until he was sure that they were being tracked by a Federation agent, and probably many more who were not within view.

Jeremy drove on for some time along the isolated stretches of the desert highway. Few cars were on the road, except for that white vehicle, tracking him relentlessly. His mind started racing. Should he pull off the road, confirming whether the car was indeed following him? Should he try to lose him somehow? Or should he continue to pretend that he was unaware of the threat that hung over him? The more he studied the car behind him, the more he realized that the Federation was too skilled to have such an obvious plant. The security forces were not merely following them, but closing in on them.

"Do you want me to drive for awhile?" Andrew asked, jolting Jeremy out of his intense watch of the enemy.

"No!" he responded louder than necessary. "I'm fine, thank you."

The highway curved up ahead and forked off into an exit toward some community nearby. Jeremy watched the white car pull off toward the right lane and head off the ramp. His momentary sense of relief was interrupted by another car appearing in the far distance and rapidly approaching. The high-powered vehicle slipped into place with professional ease.

Jeremy understood then that things were worse than he had imagined. Undoubtedly a helicopter lurked somewhere in the distance, and perhaps a jet's surveillance equipment was focused on them high in the stratosphere. The Federation spared no expense against those it considered a danger. Jeremy and his friends were listed as public enemy number one on the world government's list. The Prophet's dark predictions of the future had so shaken the world population that no more influence from his followers could be tolerated. Every word was sedition and betrayal. Even the simplest wisdom teaching was a political matter. How could it be different when the Federation's only real power was in the distraction and sedation of the great hordes of humanity, keeping mass attention focused on its priorities and view of the world?

This time the car followed them even closer, more brazen than the previous one. He could clearly see the figures in the front seat, both large, stocky men with close cropped hair and features that reflected a violent past. Still he didn't want to tell the others yet. Nothing could be done, except to try not to be overwhelmed by fear. He knew they'd angered one of the most powerful men in the organization and there would be no mercy, and certainly no safe passage for them now.

"Have you noticed the sky?" Lynn asked.

Jeremy switched his gaze from the little car behind them and leaned forward to look at the heavens. The familiar soothing light blue had turned a strange translucent orange.

"What is that?" Michelle wondered as she stared out the window. "I've never seen anything like it!"

"It's too early for sunset, isn't it?" Andrew asked.

"We're hours away from that," Jeremy responded, conscious now not only of time but of each passing second.

"Some bizarre weather phenomenon, I guess," Michelle whispered.

"Maybe it's going to storm again," Jeremy suggested.

"But there hasn't been a cloud on the horizon," Michelle observed.

Jeremy looked back at the car following them, only ten feet away now. He could see that one of the men had a cell phone against his ear and was relaying information. The tension of the moment seemed to fire an inspired idea into his mind. Though it wasn't in Jeremy's nature to think like a survivalist, he knew it was their only chance.

"Start looking for paths coming off the highway!" he ordered.

His friends looked at him, instantly cognizant that danger was imminent.

"Don't look back but we're being followed, and they're about to close in on us. If there's a strong downpour and visibility goes down, we might be able to lose them in the canyons."

Just them a rumble of thunder echoed across the vast desert sky, promising a hard rain.

"It's going to come down hard!" Andrew announced, familiar with the southwestern weather's temperament.

Michelle, being the highest trained among them for these conditions, quickly calculated their situation.

"They also know the rain will make things more difficult, which means they're going to move quicker. We need to outsmart them. Our only chance is surprise. They undoubtedly have reinforcements up ahead along with air surveillance. Don't take a road that ends in someone's homestead. We need to get into the wilds where there'll be lots of dust and mud."

"They've got small, thick wheels, front drive probably . . . "Jeremy muttered. "Their vehicle is at least twice as powerful as ours."

"How close are they?"

"I can see the whites of their eyes."

"Then we must act in the next thirty seconds or it'll be too late. We're about to run into a road block."

Without any warning, light vanished from the sky and the strange translucent glow turned a violent purple. A massive explosion ripped open the sudden darkness. Jeremy switched on the car's lights, disoriented by the appearance of night in the middle of the day. A curtain of rain crashed onto the ground, drilling holes into the cracked dirt. The precipitation looked like steel rods connecting heaven and earth.

"There!" Michelle yelled, pointing to a path leading off the highway. Jeremy turned the wheel with brute force. The car swerved off the road, nearly falling on its side. But it worked. The vehicle behind them was unable to slow down in order to follow them. It took their pursuers several hundred feet to come a halt, turn around and head off in hot pursuit.

Dust on the surrounding rocks rose like steam as the rain slammed upon them. A foggy veil overtook the landscape and within moments visibility was nearly gone.

"Keep moving!" Andrew cried out as Jeremy checked his rearview mirror while trying to keep the vehicle on the dirt path. "Can you see them?"

"No, but that doesn't mean anything. I can hardly see anything at all back there. Look for another path heading off this road. If we can get up into those hills before they find us, we'll lose them for sure."

The friends held on tight as the car bounced and swerved along the increasingly slippery path.

"Do you see anything up ahead?" Lynn asked as she peered through the blinding shower.

"There's a farm on the right slope on the other side of the ridge," Michelle noted. "I think this road will lead us right by it."

Lynn saw Michelle retrieve a small pistol from her coat pocket.

"Put that away!" she said angrily. "We can't shoot at security agents!"

"Why not?" Michelle retorted. "They're going to shoot us if they catch us."

Lynn looked into Michelle's eyes which glared with an energy that was ready for battle.

"We don't want to be like them," Lynn said softly, "otherwise, what's the point to all this?"

"The point is to stay alive!" Andrew interrupted. "Whatever it takes. Isn't that what the Prophet said?"

"Not at the cost of compromising everything that we believe in!" Lynn insisted.

"Stay focused!" Jeremy yelled. "Keep an eye out for another path. If we don't get off of this road they'll be on our tail any second."

"Too late!" Michelle cried out as the little car appeared out of the mist at high speed. It nearly crashed into the back of their car. Michelle could see a laser guided weapon in the hands of the passenger. She knew what would come next.

"Damn it, they're not taking me alive!" she roared, cocking her pistol. "I know what they do in the sub-basement of the Federation headquarters!"

She leaned out the window and fired, striking the passenger right between the eyes.

"My God, you killed him!" Lynn shouted in horror.

"Yep, and I'm gonna kill the other one too!" Michelle responded with eerie calm as she carefully aimed her pistol.

The driver veered off the path trying to avoid her skilled aim. But he was going to fast. The vehicle smashed into the rocky hillside rising up at the edge of the road. The car was thrown across the road, crashing into the other wall of granite. It burst into flames. The twisted metal kept barreling down upon its prey.

"Faster!" Andrew shouted. "It's gonna hit us and we'll all blow up!"

Lynn held her face in her hands, more horrified by Michelle's act than by the danger that was bearing down on them. Jeremy slammed the accelerator into the floor. The car jumped forward just as the out of control vehicle swung past them and exploded into the hillside. A jet of twisted metal struck the car and cracked the two side windows.

Jeremy took his foot off the accelerator and held on tight to the wheel as the car slowed to a more controllable speed.

"We're in for it now," he said grimly. "They'll come after us with everything they've got."

"That's already what they're doing," Michelle said. "This won't make any difference."

"Of course it will!" Lynn cried out, her outrage boiling to the surface. "How could you do that?"

"This is war, Lynn. We have no other choices. It was us or them."

Jeremy pulled off the road onto another path heading deep into the desolate landscape. They all stared in silence at the violent skies shedding tears upon the ground, echoing the feelings within them. Lynn began to weep. Jeremy took her hand as he drove along.

"The Prophet's mission was to bring life, not take it!" she said, choking on her agony.

"I know," Jeremy whispered. "But everything's gone helter-skelter. If those men had stopped us, that would be the end of the Prophet's legacy."

Michelle leaned forward and put her hand on Lynn's shoulder. Lynn pulled away, disgusted. A look of great sadness came over Michelle.

"Please Lynn, don't hate me for this."

"I won't have anything to do with violence and death. I'd rather be dead myself."

Michelle looked over at Andrew, silently asking for help. He leaned forward in turn.

"You have to accept the situation we're in, Lynn. Be realistic. The last thing the Prophet told us was to stay alive. We've got work to do."

"Not that kind of work," she said.

Michelle sat back, heartsick. Lynn was the best friend she'd ever known. She couldn't stand the rejection. A feeling of guilt began to creep into her soul, even though she'd acted for the welfare of her friends. In her days as a security agent for the Federation, she had seen death up close and had shot government enemies in self-defense. But now she was experiencing the killing in all its ugliness, apart from any justification. It was as though Lynn's feelings had invaded her being. She bitterly understood the horror that her friend was experiencing—the horror of extinguishing a human life. There was something cosmically blasphemous about it.

Andrew took her in his arms, seeing her emotional faltering.

"It's okay," he whispered in her ear. "You did what you had to do."

Michelle wept quietly. She was no longer the person she once was. The military mindset she'd grown up in was evaporating rapidly. The memory of the Prophet's serene presence was the strongest source of this transformation.

"Where are we headed?" Andrew asked, trying to break the tension.

"I'm not sure. I think we're going north again," Jeremy replied. "We'd better find some other entryway onto that highway so we can get ourselves on the right direction. If the Federation's reinforcements track us down out here, we're done for. They'll have a tougher time in the cities."

Andrew opened a map and tried to get his bearings. One way or the other they would reach the coast and locate their friends.

* * * * *

A fourteen year old girl of Mexican descent walked up the steep sidewalk of an old San Francisco street, pushing her six month old baby in a carriage. There was something about her carriage and her luminous dark eyes that made her immensely more mature than children her age. She was the miracle child whom the Prophet had brought back from death, saving both her and her baby. They named the infant Angel, even though she was the product of incestuous rape. The mystery of her birth had transcended the conditions of her conception. Juanita loved her with her whole heart and never failed to remember the features of the man who had saved them both and brought a new spirit of joy and hope into her life.

Though he was dead now, his spirit remained with her,

surrounding her with a glow of protection. She was as confidant in the reality of this invisible protection as she was sure of the existence of the buildings alongside the sidewalk. With the fear of the great earthquake looming in everyone's mind, the structures were more unstable than the reality she believed in but could not see.

She looked down at her child and smiled at her lovingly. The Prophet's friends, especially Lynn, had assisted Juanita in her first steps as a new mother. She had been a quick learner and developed the skills of a woman twice her age. She was privately tutored by other members of the Prophet's community and took classes every day with her mentor Ivanovitch with whom she and several other disciples lived. Ivanovitch was a Russian immigrant in his mid seventies who had been trained as an educator and a philosopher. He had been fired from several universities for his old fashioned mystical ideas which were unacceptable to the world government in its obsessive effort to control the population. When word of the Prophet's appearance reached him, he dropped everything, sold all he had, and came to join him in the Southwestern desert. The Prophet had charged him with Juanita and Angel's care and Ivanovitch took this responsibility with the utmost seriousness. The charge which the holy man had left him helped him stay in touch with the mystical presence that had graced his life.

After the Prophet's death, the community had been raided by the Federation's soldiers. Ivanovitch returned to his home near his old alma mater, Berkeley. He gave shelter to several other students. There were three such homes in the Bay Area where the Prophet's disciples had found refuge from the Federation and lived in quiet seclusion. Unfortunately, none of them paid much attention to the news broadcast across the media. They studied together, read the notes they had kept from the Prophet's teachings and tried to apply them to their daily lives. They had no time for the interference of a world gone mad. They knew nothing of the massacre and went about their lives in the usual manner—serene, peaceful, attentive to the things of the spirit. The earth changes were no surprise to them. The Prophet had said they were oncoming and they expected colossal destruction to sweep civilization away. They accepted their fate with courage and dignity, their greatest hope being that of living out the Prophet's message of spiritual transformation in the midst of chaos.

Ivanovitch poured a can of soup into a bowl and stirred it. At seventy-five, he was the senior student of the Prophet's community. Half of his life had been spent in the twentieth century, at a time when searching for meaning was still a viable option for human beings. Already past his prime by the time of the Mideastern wars in the early part of the third millennium, he watched society's total transformation at the hands of the world government. The very nature of reality had been redesigned by the centralized powers of the media.

He had seen a gradual snuffing out of interest in the intangible things that were not in the order of consumer goods or fiscal improvement. Much like the Bolchevic strategy in the Russia of the previous century, the leadership managed to block the masses from their own perceptions and intuitions of reality. People's minds were shaped by the dominant forces of world culture. The razzle-dazzle of celebrities and of stimulating entertainment was all they needed to keep the reins tight.

Ivanovitch had seen the complete demise of individual freedom for the sake of the collective security. Surveillance was everywhere, privacy was inundated through every channel, and the dreams of unity had yielded to a world military state. He had seen the tragic end of his generation's fantasies for a better world. Despite radical efforts to get control of the global situation, things couldn't be worse. Not only had the earth and its resources been throttled, but the human spirit itself seem to hang lifeless on the gallows of materialism and secularism. There was nothing anyone could do about it. Not until the appearance of the Prophet.

Ivanovitch had lost hope long ago of coming across such a luminous human being. He had given up on the possibility of gaining a wisdom that would save him from despair. Not even nature was around anymore to provide some transcendent pleasure and bear witness to a world that was not dominated by human ignorance. There were very few parks left in the cities. Whatever bit of nature was to be found in the hinterlands was private or government property.

Ivanovitch was an unhappy man. Most of his life had been spent

depressed over the lost dreams of the former century. He was one
of the very last from that other time when the hopes of humanity
had been renewed with the transition to a new millennium. Then
everything happened very quickly. The complete disintegration of
the so-called "New Age" philosophies, world economic collapse,
global instability dragged the human psyche back to its most basic
survival mode. All things of a higher order were put aside in a
frantic attempt to stay alive.

Ivanovitch was among the few to hold on at all cost to the ideas
and teachings that had given his life meaning. But all around him
everything else fell into ruin. The tidal wave of spiritual hunger
that had swept across the second half of the twentieth century
crashed on the shores of a harsh realism that could see nothing but
the bleak law of eat or be eaten.

By the time the World Federation was set in place, there was
nothing left of the idealism of former times. Once again, humanity
was lost in the dull work of day to day living without any reference
to a higher purpose. For people like Ivanovitch this was unlivable.
He had longed to die years ago. Somehow some primeval will to
live kept him plodding along until the day when the Prophet
appeared.

He had almost not survived the Prophet's death. But the
teaching had empowered him with a new sense of purpose and
responsibility. Now the attention that he gave to those placed in his
care by the Teacher himself was enough to satisfy his need to
contribute to the universe. He knew that in the wake of the Final
Prophet's mission, he was now aligned with an event of great
significance. Ordinary tasks were no longer ordinary. He was
especially honored by the gift of caring for Juanita and Angel. It
was clear to everyone that they were very special to the Prophet,
the first signs of his powers. Ivanovitch was devoted to them as
though they were his own grandchildren, and he lived to protect
and nurture them along with the other students who had come
West with him.

Despite their age differences, Ivanovitch had accepted Jeremy
Wilkes' leadership, recognizing in him an utterly devoted soul, the
first one picked by the Prophet. That was enough to qualify him as
far as Ivanovitch was concerned. When word reached him that

Jeremy, Lynn and the others were on their way to his home, he was filled with a joy and lightness of being that he had not felt for most of his adult life. It kept him rushing about like a man half his age. He was particularly fond of Lynn, whose sensitive spirit reflected the very mysticism that he had witnessed in the Prophet's eyes.

He pensively stirred the meal boiling on the stove, then checked his loaf of bread in the oven. The man still made his own bread even though it had gone out of style more than half a century ago. Electronic gadgetry now made everything, but he hung on stubbornly to a former way of life that kept human beings closer to nature. He loved the sight of earth's bounty transformed into nutrition for the organism that housed the human spirit.

The large loaf was golden brown, just about perfect. He thought he'd give it another few seconds so that his special guests could enjoy it all the more. His busyness kept him from considering the feeling that disturbed him somewhere in the recesses of his being. He felt that something was wrong, terribly wrong, for the most wanted members of the Prophet's community to come out into the open. Perhaps they needed to flee to Asia as some had already done. Of greatest concern to Ivanovitch was the fact that the sudden announcement of their trip came on the heels of the horrific massacre that had taken place the day before. He did his best to keep himself from thinking about it. If such forces were after them, then all was lost.

It was one thing to hide from Federation agents and their tinker toys of surveillance, but there was no hiding from occult powers bent on total destruction. Ivanovitch had been around metaphysical circles long enough to know better than to imagine that there was no such thing as evil. It was more than merely human ignorance and selfishness. It was more than bad habits and tempers, and perverse behavior. There was something ancient, relentless and all-consuming about it. Humans were mere puppets in its hands, though each one was capable of choosing to become a willing slave of its demonic desires. Even before the Prophet, he had learned to keep a close watch on his impulses and thoughts. He guided the ship of his psyche with the sure hand of a captain committed to making it to his destination without wrecking on unseen rocks.

It was one of the few works he had accomplished in his life—control over himself and devotion to a higher purpose than satisfying his every desires. Now the payoff was upon him. He had developed a gift of discernment and he could tell when some external force was seeking entrance into his heart and soul, attempting to pollute his efforts toward a purer life and throw him off the path of awakening to his true purpose.

When he first came across the news of the horrific murders of his friends across the Bay, he sensed immediately that his household was in grave danger. But he chose not to tell anyone for fear of causing a panic that would make things worse for them. So he kept a close eye on his companions. But the contact with Andrew in cyberspace had suddenly confirmed his fears.

Ivanovitch moved to the window and looked past the little enclosed garden toward the steep streets over which the home was perched. His aged eyes encased in layers of wrinkles sparkled when he spotted the graceful teenager wandering along the sidewalk, pushing a baby carriage ahead of her. With the back of his hand, he brushed a wave of snow-white hair that had fallen from the striking mane that he wore long but carefully controlled. The natural regal dignity that accompanied him at all times was his last refuge from inevitable disintegration. He would be taking nothing with him except his stalwart and honest spirit.

Too many of his old friends had died in utter despair, damning a world that had purged all mystery and wonder from its essence.

Ivanovitch's square jaw, aquiline nose, and high forehead added to the impression that he was some mysterious count who had lost his estate. But it was the quiet serenity of his energy that was most captivating about his presence. Long practiced in the art of continual awareness and the bodily harmony of Tai-Chi, he was a silent witness to the peaceful centeredness that was possible for everyone—if they would only reject the crush of their frantic life-styles.

But few people were given the privilege of his company. Only the Prophet's disciples shared his time and attention. Most of his days were spent indoors, reading long-forgotten books or doing domestic work for the sake of his friends. His forays into the outside world were limited to the garden, that little piece of planet

Earth not covered by concrete. He often sat in the shade of an oak tree engaged in deep conversation with a student or offering advice to Juanita.

Ivanovitch removed the bread from the oven. The mouth-watering aroma filled the kitchen and drifted out the open window. A passerby looked up, shocked by the smell of homemade bread. Tom Wells stopped in front of the house and noticed Ivanovitch's silhouette in the midday light.

His amateur sleuth's imagination had led him to this neighborhood. It was one of the last strongholds of artists and independent thinkers. They were left undisturbed by the Federation despite its phobia of free spirits. No rebel leader could come out of this caricature of the past and lead an uprising against government-approved reality. No one would take seriously individuals stamped with the stigma of west coast foolishness. Three generations of media-fed children had been trained to mock any new trend coming out of California. Too many "original thinkers" had been - revealed as frauds and neurotic megalomaniacs. The overburdened world had lost patience with the descendants of the flower children.

In his urgent search for remnants of the Prophet's following, Tom had learned of a group of people characterized by a strange peacefulness completely out of step with the fear and anguish that burned through the city like wildfire. For Tom, this was a sure clue that these people were in touch with a living wisdom teaching. Self-transcendence and inner peace at a time of global catastrophe were no accident. These people were applying specialized information that had transforming power on their daily behavior. There wasn't a guru on the coast who could generate such knowledge. Not anymore.

The golden age of "New Age" philosophies had gone down the drain with the ideals of world peace and environmental rehabilitation. A cynicism had settled in that melded comfortably with the atheism of the dominators. The wretched ghosts of Mao, Lenin, and Stalin were giddy with victory. The world had fallen into step behind their march to nowhere without even trying. No more speeches, propaganda, or secret death squads were necessary to turn people's minds toward the cattle barn of serving the state.

A grocery clerk had further informed Tom of an aristocratic old man who never spoke and bought supplies for a large family. Tom noticed that the elderly gentleman who at the window had taken notice of him and slipped discreetly out of sight. That was all the mystery writer needed to convince him that he had found what he was looking for.

His mind went into overdrive. How could he communicate with these reclusive people? How could he tell them that he was a friend at a time when the whole world was their enemy?

"Hi there."

Tom nearly jumped out of his skin. He turned around to find a sweet face with wide dark eyes staring at him. Juanita was returning from her stroll with Angel.

"Hello," Tom replied as best he could. He felt like he'd been caught doing something wrong. He sensed the flush of embarrassment turn his face red.

"I need to get by," Juanita said softly. Tom realized that he was standing between her and the gate of the house where he'd seen the mysterious old man.

"You live here?" he asked as casually as he could.

She nodded. Her bright, happy features suddenly became overcast with worry. She had been taught to distrust snoopy individuals. Tome felt certain that he stood in the presence of someone who had known the Final Prophet.

"I'm a friend," he whispered. "Don't be afraid."

Her face turned sunny again.

"I need to talk to your leader," he stated more boldly. "I've got important information . . . "

"How can I help you?"

The voice was a rich baritone booming just behind Tom's head. He turned to find Ivanovitch standing over him with the wrath of God in his eyes. If ever there was a lion protecting his pride, this was it. Tom tried to gather his wits as quickly as he could.

"I'm a friend," he said nervously.

"I heard you say that already. What does it mean?"

"We shouldn't be standing in the street," Tom suggested. "Can we talk indoors?"

"Only as far as the garden," Ivanovitch ordered. He motioned for Juanita to enter the property ahead of them, all the while keeping his eagle glare on the young man. "Don't try any funny business. I may be aged, but I know how to use this."

He held up a thick oak cane sculpted in intricate designs. "And I don't use it just for walking."

"I understand," Tom said, swallowing hard. He knew the old gentleman had the power to brain him before he could turn to run.

"I'll let you in the garden," Ivanovitch said sternly, "because it is clear to me that you are not a security agent."

He motioned for Tom to step into the garden.

"How can you tell?" Tom asked as he walked past him through the gate, hoping to ease the tension.

"You obviously don't know what you're doing."

Tom's face turned a deep red. "This is true," he admitted as Ivanovitch locked the heavy brass doors behind them, sealing them off from the outside world.

Ivanovitch pointed to a chair and sat in his favorite one beneath the tree. He proceeded to study Tom from head to foot. The young man felt stripped of all masks. At the same time, a state of euphoria began to rise within him as he realized that he was in the presence of an advanced student of spiritual matters. His knowing eyes, gazing out from beneath white eyebrows, were the ultimate proof that this man had learned from the Prophet himself.

"I'm looking for the friends of the Prophet."

The old man did not so much as blink. His noble features betrayed nothing of his mind's activity.

"Why look here?" he finally questioned.

"It's a matter of life and death. I had to take a wild guess."

"Sheer accident brings you here?" the old man asked suspiciously.

"I like to think of it as intuitive deduction."

"Where did you develop such skills?"

"I've been a student of the paranormal for years."

"What do you do for a living?"

"I write works of fiction."

"Books? No one reads books anymore. They went out when I was your age."

"So I'm a writer with no money. I also create interactive cd-rom stories for education and entertainment companies."

"How do your studies fit into those products?"

"They don't. Strictly bread and butter. Although my interest in history and literature help me out."

Ivanovitch stared at him as though weighing his soul in the palm of his hand. Tom twitched with discomfort.

"So what makes you think that you've come to the right place?"

Tom smiled. "I can see that you are different."

"Different than what?"

"Different than the assembly line produced masses so effectively developed by the Federation."

"That's dangerous talk."

"Maybe."

"You're playing with fire, son," Ivanovitch stated in a strong voice full of warning.

"Sir, I've been playing with fire all my adult life. Now I want to burn."

The trace of a smile came and went across the old man's face. He knew about burning. Burning for the need to find something all-consuming which alone could feed the soul. But he was still on his guard.

"How do I know you're not a spy working for the Federation.

Tom's eyes widened, as though exposing his soul to Ivanovitch's seeing eyes.

"See me . . . Know me. That will be your answer."

A tense silence ensued as the old man pierced into the heart of the youthful visitor. He peered deep into the core of his being. A breeze fluttered through the burgeoning branches overhead, the only sound in the garden. For a moment, the intensity of their encounter silenced even the traffic in the distance.

"Son, if you walk across this bridge, there's no going back."

A shiver shot through Tom's body and caused his features to twitch. "I've got nothing to lose."

"You've got everything to lose."

"I've got nothing holding me back."

"Really?"

"The world doesn't buy my writing anyway. I'm ready."

"For what?"

"To take the plunge."

"There are no guarantees."

"I know that."

"Everything must all be paid for up front."

Tom knew that the man was not speaking about cash, but about hopes, dreams, fantasies, ambitions. If he was to step into the inner circle of the Prophet's followers, he would have to step out of society's version of comfortable living.

"Can you use me?" Tom asked with deep sincerity.

Ivanovitch smiled. "We can always use an honest, devoted seeker of truth."

"You have found one."

"Apparently, you've found us."

Tom beamed at the admission that his intuition was indeed correct. He was looking into the face of one who had been close to the Final Prophet. The old man stood with unusual grace and dignity and approached him. Tom rose from the chair in time to grasp the extended hand.

"You are welcome among us. I hope you don't regret the decision you've made today."

"No sir, I . . . "

Ivanovitch raised his hand to silence him.

"Don't be so certain. None of us are unified enough to be so certain. There will be days when parts of you will feel very differently."

Tom realized that he was looking at a man who had climbed the treacherous mountain of self-mastery and paid a heavy price for it. He understood that there was no getting around the long, hard labor involved. He couldn't expect to conquer himself overnight, no matter how committed he was, no matter how much he longed for the deeper truth of his being.

Ivanovitch escorted him into the house. Soon Tom was surrounded by half a dozen men and women listening with full attention to his concerns. He told them what he had found at the sight of the massacre, of his encounter with Oliver, and of his intuitions that this was an intentional attack on the Prophet's followers. When he finished talking, there was a long silence as everyone digested the implications and realized the danger they were in. Finally, Ivanovitch spoke.

"Friends, I'm not surprised at this news. I believe that is why Jeremy and the others are on their way. They should be here by tomorrow evening. We'll figure out then what to do next. In the meantime, everyone needs to stay in the house. I don't want anyone to answer the door."

"A locked door is not going to keep these creatures of darkness away," a man said in a trembling voice.

"No, that's for sure," the old man responded. "But until we talk to the others, we're stuck."

"You mean, we're sitting ducks, deer caught in the headlights," another said.

"Not quite," Tom stated firmly. "There's another option. We can be proactive. If some of you will help me, we can check out this man who threatened me in the restaurant. I can tell you this. He may be dangerous but he's an ordinary mortal."

"What would this accomplish, besides exposing us to danger?" Ivanovitch asked.

"We might get a headstart on the adversaries. Find out more about who they are. Get a clue on their activities," Tom suggested.

"I'll go," a tall man with a powerful frame and bright, intelligent eyes said.

"Me too!" another man standing next to him said. Allan was the very opposite of his friend John. Shabbily dressed and unshaven, his hair hadn't seen a comb in several days, his eyes lit by some erratic energy that never seemed to calm down, he was one of those outsiders who had wandered in the more bizarre realms of the occult searching for something to give purpose to his life. Allan was a man who had seen it all—drugs, cults, perversion. He had made some terrible mistakes until the day he came across the Prophet's community.

Ivanovitch raised his hand before anyone else could talk.

"Friends, you are considering something completely irrational and possibly fatal. As Tom describes this man who assaulted him, it seems that we're dealing with some sort of mercenary. Those men shoot before they ask questions, you may be sure of that. They've made a craft out of killing other people."

"What choices do we have, Ivanovitch?" Allan pressed on. "I

don't want to sit here and passively be slaughtered like happened to William and the others in Marin County."

"If we were to run," John added, "they will simply chase us and overtake us. If they take my life in this effort to help my friends, I will consider it well spent."

"Let's wait until Jeremy and Lynn get here," Ivanovitch insisted. "They may have another perspective on the matter."

"We cannot wait, sir," Tom stated boldly. "If you value your lives at all, we've got to counter attack right away. The scientists tell us that we're about to get hit by the Big One any day with the polar shift taking place. I'm sure these people will take advantage of the chaos and finish their work."

"Friends, remember this man is a writer of fantasy," the old man said sternly.

"He may also be saving our lives," Juanita spoke out in a calm, serene voice.

"He's a Godsend," another woman agreed.

"I think the Prophet sent him," Juanita added. "From the place where he protects us."

They all turned and looked at the young woman who had been brought back from the dead by their Teacher. The certainty in her innocent face left no room for argument. There was something so ethereal about the look in her eyes that they took her words as a message from the higher realms. Ivanovitch finally lowered his head.

"You have my blessing to pursue this course of action. But please be very careful. You can only help us if you stay alive."

* * * * *

Tom drove his two companions past the house and slowed down as they approached. The sun had set and the moon was hidden behind a bank of growling clouds. The streets were barren. In the darkness, the ghetto was more fierce and grim than in the light of day. Ruined buildings, boarded up homes that weren't fit for human habitation, rose out of the concrete for miles on end. The emptiness of the streets added to the feeling of the death of civilization. Every once and awhile, a few silhouettes moved furtively in and out of the shadows, obviously up to no good.

A stray dog wandered through the rumble, searching for some place to spend the night. The feeling of desolation and gloom was overwhelming. Tom had never been so deep into the heart of disintegrated society. He felt his mouth turn dry and his muscles tighten with nervousness. The threatening figures were hardly more disturbing than the remains of buildings from another century rising as disfigured monuments to the failure of the past. The acrid tinge of danger raced through his nerves. He took a deep breath in a useless attempt to relax. This was a place where no one should venture, especially after the midnight hour.

Every square foot of this ugly landscape screamed pain and misery. Tom found himself longing for the comfortable neighborhoods that had been his world until now. This third world country was just down the road from the other sights and sounds he had known. It was terribly unsettling to him. How could such a gruesome world be in such proximity to the seeming security that he took for solid ground. It struck him that a whole lot more of the planet looked like this dark, mean ghetto than like the suburbs of his middle class acquaintances.

A shiver rushed through him as he considered the possibility that further economic decay could turn every place on earth into this sunken underworld. The brokenness of the ghetto could become a way of life for everyone. He saw a man walking down an empty street and was astonished that he seemed so uncaring of the dangers lurking in every shadow. Within moments, he could be lying in a pool of his own blood, split open for pocket change. Apparently, human beings could get used to anything and overlook the reality of their situation.

They drove around in circles, studying the house in every detail. They drove down streets that looked more like a nightmare than arteries of a twenty-first century city. A strange terror began to eat at Tom's insides. He suddenly felt caught in the web of some monstrous spider seeking to suck the life force out of him. Every street was worse than the next.

Soon Tom and his two colleagues were in the shadows across the street from the house that Oliver had entered. They had worked out a daring plan with the help of Ivanovitch and the others. Allan would keep watch across the street while John and Tom attempted to enter the house. It was decided that the only way to deal with this situation was directly, that John should knock at the door and draw Oliver out. Tom would then enter and see what he could find.

"Allan, you'll wait here. Be sure you stay against the wall so you can't be seen. Are you ready?" Tom asked.

The men nodded.

"Not too nervous?"

"I gave my life up when I joined the Prophet and his mission," John stated calmly. "There's nothing for me to lose. I've found what I needed."

Tom smiled sadly as he looked into the determined eyes of his new friend. The man had encountered something that was still out of his grasp. He was ready to die and he would be at peace with himself. Tom envied him.

John crossed the street and approached the house. It was agreed that he would first try the front door and claim to be looking for someone else.

A half hour later, John had not yet reappeared. Tom decided that they couldn't wait any longer.

"If I'm not back in ten minutes, return without me," he told Allan solemnly.

"I can't do that!" Allan responded, horrified.

"Don't argue with me. We can't risk any more lives!"

Tom crossed the street, leaving Allan trembling in the shadows. He knocked at the door aggressively, pumped up with adrenaline.

A young woman dressed in a strange combination of Hindu attire and homemade designs answered the door.

"What do you want?"

"I'm here to see a friend . . . "

She tried to close the door in his face, but he blocked it and pushed his way in. She flattened herself against the wall, terrified. Tom spotted a stairway leading to a large door and headed in that direction.

"You can't go up there!" she cried out. "This is a temple!"

"Why don't you call the police!" he shouted back

"Amir!" the young man shrieked. "Amir! Help!"

As Tom reached the top of the stairs, the door opened and a man appeared, blocking his way. His dress was also mid-eastern, but more authentic than the woman's clothing. His skin was olive colored and his eyes flashed with dark intensity.

"You cannot enter, sir!" he said angrily.

"I don't want any trouble. I just want to find my brother who was here a little while ago."

"There is no one that you would know here."

"Who are you people?"

"We are the children of Anavirn, followers of his Holiness Shri Halameh."

"What religion is that?" Tom asked, trying to look over the man's shoulder suspiciously.

"It is the unifying Path to ultimate Truth, gathering the heart of all other teachings brought down by the true masters," Amir responded with artificial serenity.

"And my brother believes in this?"

"If he is, he's no longer your brother. We are his true brothers in the spirit."

"So you won't let me see him?"

"This is sacred ground. You cannot enter without being purified."

Suddenly, Tom pushed him out of the way and dashed into the room. Persian blankets covered the large room and incense burners filled the air with smoke. Candles illuminated the exotic decor. Long curtains hung down from the ceiling, covering the walls. Tom frantically searched for a door behind the heavy colorful cloth.

Within moments, he'd found a small entrance. He entered quickly and found himself in an obscure chamber. An old man with a long white beard and dressed in eastern garb, sat in lotus position at the far end, surrounded by mesmerized students. No one reacted to Tom's sudden entrance. Tom was momentarily taken aback by the immobile forms sitting in the shadows. Amir entered behind him and threw him back into the main room, closing the door tightly.

Tom scrambled to his feet as Amir approached him, his whole body tense with rage. He flung off one of his long shawls and took a karate stance. Tom backed away just as Amir kicked him in the side of the head with lightning speed. Tom quickly regained his balance and dashed for the door. The young woman blocked his way, holding a switchblade in her hand.

Tom grabbed an incense burner and threw it at her. She evaded it, but Tom took hold of her arm and sent her flying into Amir as he charged him. Tom raced through the front door, down the stairs and out of the house. He ran toward the back of the building and found himself in the garden of the cult house. Breathing frantically, he searched the area and found an iron bar near the garbage cans. He broke a basement window and entered.

He found himself in a dark room filled with crates. The eerie sound of chanting echoed from the floor above. Tom searched for a door and entered into a narrow hallway. He heard footsteps up ahead and hurried to another door. He entered quickly and leaned against it, trying to catch his breath. The footsteps passed him by and faded away down the hall. Tom moved forward and stumbled over a large object which he caught just as it went crashing to the floor. He set the expensive vase back on its pedestal just as a dim lightbulb came on, illuminating the room.

In the corner of the room, an emaciated man in his late twenties, head shaved and clothes tattered, stared at Tom with eyes of doom. A drug overdose kept him in a near comatose state.

"Who are you?" he mumbled.

Tom did not answer, terrified that the man would reveal his presence.

"Are you a student? Did you also find out?"

Tom approached him cautiously.

"Find out what?"

"God, I came here to find answers . . . and I found more lies!" the broken youth cried out.

Then he snickered tragically. "Maybe that's the answer. It's all lies. What do you think?"

Tom realized the man's mind was nearly gone. He studied the room to find a way out.

"I thought if I put on a robe and listened to a guy with a big white beard that I'd be enlightened . . . I'm not even sure his beard is real now!"

The man started flaying his hands about, unable to move his legs. Tom noticed that he'd been severely beaten.

"I came out here looking for a true teacher . . . Let me tell ya, nobody gives nothin' for free. Especially Truth. Hell, I'd go to India tomorrow if I thought I could find God there. But you know what? He isn't. He isn't in the pockets of some wrinkled old guru or priest or inside some shrine . . . "

Tom had stopped listening. In one of the crates, he had found large plastic bags. He sniffed them and was stunned to discover that they contained hashish and heroin. The man continued to talk to himself, tears welling up in his eyes.

"This is the fourth group I've joined to find God . . . And it's another caravan to nowhere. I'm through looking on the outside, man."

He grabbed Tom's leg as he stepped near him. Tom pulled away and continued his search of the room.

"You know, I've spent a year and a half working two jobs seven days a week to pay for the privilege of receiving crumbs of knowledge from these people. There's about twenty-five other poor fools doing the same thing in this house alone. And they've got centers in five other cities . . . They've got a lot of competition in the secret initiation business. It's open season year round for desperate seekers . . . "

The door suddenly burst open. Amir entered with five other students.

"Get him!" he barked angrily.

The men leaped on Tom and beat him savagely. Horrified, the young man in the corner managed to stand up in spite of his condition.

"What the hell are you doing?" he cried out.

"He's a danger to our family," Amir said angrily.

"But surely his Holiness didn't order this treatment!"

"He asked me to question him, in whatever manner necessary," the fanatic follower replied coldly.

"Question him about what?"

Amir turned a glare full of fire upon the sickly youth. "This is not your affair, brother. Remember your vows. You have renounced the maya of this world!"

"Is that maya I'm looking at?" he raged, full of a righteous indignation. "Is this cowardly beating an illusion?"

"Don't be swept away by negative energies, brother Massu. Try to remain objective. This is a test for you. Use it to your spiritual advantage."

"But this isn't right!"

Amir took hold of his arm and pulled him out into the hallway as the others continued to beat Tom mercilessly.

"You've chosen to follow the path of enlightenment as given to us by our teacher. Things are not what they seem for those of us who follow him. Each experience is for the growth of your understanding, regardless of its seeming appearance of wrong. You must absorb the energy of this scene and separate yourself from your subjective attitude. This will strengthen your internal work."

Amir shut the door so that the ugly sounds were less overwhelming to the young student.

But brother Massu shook uncontrollably.

"I've been here eight months, Amir. I was really hoping to learn from you people. So I've done what I was told, and I never questioned your knowledge. But this . . . this is not acceptable."

"It's a great test for you," Amir said with exaggerated theatrics.

"Why don't you just let him go?"

"He can't go home. He's desecrated our temple. Besides, our master wishes him to stay."

"What for?"

"He could be injurious to our family. That's what master says."

"How?"

"Don't question his holiness!" Amir shouted with fury.

"But he's not a threat . . . "

"How dare you resist the will of our teacher?"

"If you kill this man, I'll go to the authorities!"

Amir suddenly slapped him hard across the face. Brother Massu turned back, eyes gleaming with a new determination.

"Is this an example of your spiritual awareness, brother Amir?"

"You're still attached to the outer world. Can't you see that? You must learn to lift yourself above those illusory ties."

"Check out this illusion, you freak!" Massu shouted as he lunged at him. They fell back against the wall and the frenzied young man pounded his fists into the man who had dominated him for so long.

The young woman who had let Tom into the house appeared in the hallway. Her graceful facial features turned grotesque as a villainous expression came over them. Out of her cloth belt she pulled a razor-sharp knife curved in the Arabic fashion. She hurried to the battling men and took hold of the long hair of the one they called brother Massu. Without blinking, she slit his throat in one quick and deadly motion. Amir jumped away as the blood shot out and sprayed the wall with red designs.

CHAPTER 10

It was almost three in the morning when Jeremy and his friends pulled up in front of the house. They checked the address and confirmed that they had reached their destination. Lynn was the first one out of the car. She looked up at a lit window on the second floor of the old mansion. The curtain moved slightly and Ivanovitch's silhouette appeared in the frame. He held up his hand in a loving sign of greeting to the woman he admired so much.

Lynn smiled with great joy. She hadn't felt such a rush of happiness in a long time. The thought of seeing people she loved and cared for during their communal experience under the Prophet's leadership was an unhoped-for gift. Her heart beat faster at the thought of embracing Juanita and Angel, the children first put under her wing. Every time she saw them, she perceived the presence of her beloved Teacher. Within moments, Ivanovitch was unlocking the gates. Other lights appeared in windows as the house awoke and word of their arrival spread.

Lynn was the first to stand before the old man.

"Lynn . . . " he whispered in a voice weighty with unspoken affection.

"I didn't think I'd see you again, Ivanovitch," she said as her eyes sparkled with tears.

Their hands clasped warmly. He kissed her forehead with a serenity and unconditional love worthy of a sage.

"Are you surviving?" he asked with paternal concern.

"We're managing so far," Lynn responded. "We've been well-cared for by Stargazer and his people."

"I'm sure," he said, recalling the wise Indian elder who had come to visit the community and shared his confirmation of the Prophet's mission.

Jeremy came up behind Lynn.

"Are you well?" he asked his elderly friend. Ivanovitch moved his gaze from Lynn's radiant features to the strong, thoughtful eyes of her husband, the Prophet's right-hand man.

They looked at each other without speaking. A nonverbal contact, more powerful than any words they could express, filled the space between them. They peered into each other's souls and communed in brotherly affection.

Both men had developed a level of awareness that could see deeper than most people. They also shared unshakable commitment to the higher realm that had sent them a messenger who pointed out the way the rest of their lives should be lived.

Lynn observed the silent communion between her two favorite people. The sheer power of their presence to each other allowed them to empathize in a telepathic manner. Ivanovitch saw in the features of the dynamic young man before him a pioneer of future times. He sensed the weight of the world on his shoulders and the awesome responsibility with which the Prophet had charged him. His curly red hair, lightly freckled face and intense green eyes presented the unmistakable image of the peaceful warrior. He had given himself heart and soul to a higher cause and lived a life of unconquerable integrity. In the shadowy light, the old man who stood at the summit of his own existence perceived a clairvoyant vision of this strong, vital face in the distant future. The same eyes would be there, perhaps a bit more at peace, but all the more penetrating, and framed in white hair and a beard worthy of the hermits of old.

His heart leapt. He realized that he was the sudden recipient of a gift from the angelic realm where such timeless vision was commonplace. He sensed that the momentary glimpse was a message for him. What he had finally found at the end of his life would blossom and seed the future in a way that was of ultimate importance to the human race. In knowing that, Ivanovitch was given the gift of seeing the value of his contribution to this sacred cause. For the first time in nearly eight decades, he felt a profound sense of fulfillment. He had achieved the goal of his lifelong search. His presence among these special people had brought him the wisdom, enlightenment and purpose that had eluded him for many tormented years.

Lynn looked up at the profile of the dignified old man and saw in the light of his eyes the timeless inner vision that overwhelmed him. She turned to Jeremy and witnessed the same light in his face. A new quality of depth and knowing scintillated in those intense emerald eyes that she had looked into so often.

Behind those eyes, Jeremy was also seeing a flash of insight. He perceived that the old man who was so close to the grave would not become dust in the wind. The soul that Jeremy could see coming at him through those aged eyes would be part of his life in the future after the body that encased it was left behind. At the same time, he realized that an entire ocean of conscious souls was present in this moment, surrounding them like the darkness of space, shimmering with awareness like the stars above and the sparkle in the pupils looking at each other. They were not two men standing in the night air, but centers of awareness linked to the continuum of the vaster awareness that lived in a nonmaterial dimension and somehow interpenetrated the reality of the five senses.

In the old man's face, soon to leave this world, Jeremy witnessed the immortality of the spirit, especially of a spirit awakened during the life of the body. Jeremy realized that if he could sense the continued presence of this man after his death, then the infinitely vaster soul of the Prophet was also with him somehow, linked to him in the invisible world and aware of his hopes and fears.

The old man in turn saw in Jeremy's vital features the undying hope for the victory of light over the darkness of human ignorance. As long as someone carried the torch and passed it on, the Prophet's living teaching—itself a summation of all the enlightened teachings of the past—would continue to feed human beings of the future. It was not a lost cause despite the hardships of the presence, and neither the Federation nor the evil ones could extinguish it altogether. He could die in peace, saved from the despair of hopeless.

Soon, they were in the comfort of the old house, being offered tea and lemonade. Ivanovitch quickly brought them up to date. He told the newcomers of Tom's appearance among them and of their effort to gather information on the group that had massacred their friends.

"We've got to get all of you out of here immediately!" Jeremy said. "It's far too dangerous to stay in the area. How soon can you pack up?"

The dozen friends responded as one. "By sunrise."

"You can only take what's necessary. Do you have enough vehicles to accommodate everyone?"

"We've got two vans and several cars," Ivanovitch responded.

"That should do it," Andrew stated. "Why don't you start packing now since everybody's awake."

"What about the three who are out in the city?" Michelle asked with concern. "How do we get them back here safely?"

"They're due to call in at six a.m.," Ivanovitch said. "If we haven't heard from them by then, we'll have to go look for them."

"I wish they hadn't done that," Jeremy muttered. "It complicates matters greatly."

"What happens if they don't show up by the time we're ready to leave?" Lynn asked.

"We'll have to go without them."

"No!" Juanita cried out. "We can't leave without John and Allan."

"We've got to consider everyone's safety," Lynn said gently as she caressed her cheek. "Time is critical."

"We've got to get you out of here without delay," Michelle stated in the commanding voice of one who had been in dangerous circumstances before. "Anything could happen at any moment. There's no time to lose."

"We can't abandon them!" the frightened girl insisted.

"We won't!" Ivanovitch replied. "I'll go find them myself. I allowed them to go in the first place."

Jeremy looked at the old man with worried eyes. "We'll need to send someone else."

"You mean a younger person? I'm perfectly capable of driving around the North Beach area."

"What about the danger?"

"No matter what we do, that's going to be unavoidable as you know so well. Please don't argue this point with me. It's my responsibility. I want to handle it."

"Andrew," Jeremy said as he turned to his friend. "How about if you go with Ivanovitch?"

"No, I insist," the old man responded. "You need him with you. You'll need all the help you can get. Don't disperse your forces. Let me handle this alone."

Jeremy looked at the frightened faces around him. He had known all these people in a better time, when the Prophet was among them, and the possibility of peaceful living seemed at hand.

"Where will we go?" one of the students asked.

"We'll have to head north," Michelle suggested. "Find some isolated community where we can discreetly hide out. We'll need to stay away from earthquake and volcanic activity as best we can. It'll have to be away from the west coast."

"One of those barren places like Wyoming or Montana?"

"Someplace like that where we are less likely to come under surveillance."

"What about Stargazer's cave?" Lynn asked.

"Not for awhile," Jeremy answered. "The place will be crawling with agents, especially after our little encounter on the way here."

"We can't possibly stay unnoticed by the Federation," an older woman with a European accent stated. "There is no place isolated enough."

"Besides, the earth changes will affect everything everywhere," an Asian man spoke out.

"Friends," Jeremy said calmly, "there is no safe haven. But if we're together, at least we can use our minds to stay a step ahead of the next catastrophe."

Some of the people began to weep, faced with the harsh facts of the uncertainty of their lives now.

"We knew this was coming," Jeremy added. "The Prophet told us loud and clear. He also told us to weather the storm. We do this not for ourselves but for whatever purpose we might serve in the future."

* * * * *

Ivanovitch drove into the neighborhood where his friends had gone. He drove past the house several times and noticed that all the lights were out. No sign of anyone. On the third time around, he spotted a silhouette coming out of the basement door and furtively moving into the shadows. He turned off his headlights and pulled the car against the sidewalk where he couldn't be seen.

The moonlight illuminated the features of a muscular man. For Ivanovitch there was no doubt that this was the individual who had assaulted Tom in the bookstore. Everything about him revealed a soldier of fortune—the arrogant swagger, the careful scanning of his surroundings. Ivanovitch took his car out of neutral and followed at a distance. As they approached the center of town, he saw the man duck into a bar whose crude neon lights blended with the shimmering colors of the city.

Ivanovitch drove past the bar and noticed that it was some sort of strip joint. He had never been into one of those places and he sure didn't want to start now. But he had no choice. Too much was at stake. He pulled into the overcrowded parking lot and stepped out of his car.

It was dark and noisy inside. Low-lifes of all kinds littered the place, drowning whatever was left of their souls in poison that was sure to finish the job. It was the kind of place that generated violence and criminal activity like some unholy nest of vipers.

The old man immediately spotted Oliver at the main bar, ordering himself a drink. It was clear that he had no idea he'd been followed, especially by an old gentleman who sat himself several tables away from him. A buxom woman with too much makeup appeared before him, her body hanging out of her clothes as part of the titillation that made their clients pour their money out faster than the liquor was flowing.

Ivanovitch was sick to his stomach. He hadn't seen the low end of humanity up close for a long time. He couldn't believe how degenerate it had become since the turn of the century when he was last exposed to it. Both men and women were brazen about their animal instincts, grabbing each other publicly, exposing their lust without any conscience or natural dignity. A pigsty had more formality over the mating ritual than this place.

He looked over toward the far corner of the room and immediately turned away. On a small stage, a woman was gyrating with hardly an ounce of clothing on. The last thing he wanted to see was a human being humiliating herself with masochistic verve.

Unlike all the other men in the room, he didn't see breasts and thighs, but rather a lost soul—someone's daughter, someone's - mother, someone's sister—destroying herself in order to pay the rent.

He turned his back on the ugly scene and took a sip of the soda he'd ordered. He glanced up at Oliver. He could now see his unshaven profile. There was no question this was the man who had confronted Tom. His face looked like war itself—aggressive, merciless, violent. The old man felt terribly out of place among these people. He wished he hadn't made the decision to follow him here. But what else could he do? There was no more time. Either he found his friends, or they would be left to survive on their own. He could stand that idea even less than putting up with the grotesque atmosphere of this human destitution.

On a giant TV screen at both sides of the bar, a bloody boxing match was under way, fitting in just right with the ugliness of the place.

"You here for some action, grandpa?" a female voice said right behind him. He turned his serene features upon the young woman who leaning toward him, seeking to display her merchandise. She reacted as though she'd been struck by a baseball bat between the eyes. The calm, penetrating eyes of the old man completely threw her off her professional persona. She felt as though her own father was peering into her soul.

For an instant, she was utterly ashamed. In the next second, she regained control and turned her shock into rage.

"What the hell's the matter with you, old man? Lost interest in women, have you?"

The insult didn't even make him blink. She wanted to yell and scream at him for revealing to her who she was and what she was doing, but his silence was too overwhelming. She turned away and hurried into the crowd. Ivanovitch watched her go with deep sorrow bubbling up from his soul. How humanity had disintegrated! He thought the previous century had hit rock bottom, but it was clear to him that the twenty-first century was even worse. For all the wizardry that humans had created, there was nothing left of deeper values. A great black hole was at the center of the human soul, sucking out all that was valuable about being human. Self-gratification and greed were the order of the day, especially now that things had become so uncertain.

He scanned the room with his sharp eyes and remembered the ancient Persian saying: "Eat, drink, and be merry for tomorrow . . . " What a tragic way to use one's days on this wretched planet, he thought to himself. It struck him that all of the great wisdom teachings the world over had fallen on deaf ears. People were as barbaric as ever. It didn't matter that prophets, philosophers, poets and martyrs of all stripes had sought to kindle an awakening to humanity's true potential. It had all gone down the drain and now he sat in the spiritual sewage of his fellow man, each one more lost and pathetic than the other.

He turned back to look upon the reason for his being in this cesspool. Oliver was on his second drink, and beginning to loosen up. Ivanovitch knew this was not a good thing. It was all important that he have no sense of being watched. For once, being old and physically weakened would be useful to him. He checked his watch. Jeremy and the others would be leaving within two hours. He couldn't just sit here and watch time evaporate. Three lives were at stake. He would gladly give his to save theirs. Living had become exceedingly tiresome to him. He had learned from the Prophet what he needed to know and he could die happy now.

A large, burly man entered the bar. His fierce energy drew Ivanovitch's attention immediately. Without question this was a merciless warrior hidden in civilian clothes. Tattoos crawled up and down his arms and his bone mass was the heaviest he'd ever seen. The man must have been a professional sportsman prior to - developing the skills for hunting humans. The man spotted Oliver and walked straight over to him, paying no attention to anyone else. He stood next to him until Oliver became aware of the mass of muscle behind him. Ivanovitch was close enough to hear them talk to each other.

"What the hell are you doing here?" Oliver asked, doing his best to hide the fact that the man's appearance disturbed him.

"What are you doing here?" the big man responded. "You were told not to do this anymore."

"I do whatever the hell I want to!" Oliver replied, partly inebriated.

"No you can't, not anymore! Come with me."

"I just got here."

The burly man's features spread into a vicious smile. "Am I going to have to convince you?"

The words fell on Oliver's arrogant ego, instead of on his common sense.

"Don't you dare threaten me!"

"You've got an obligation to your boss now," the man stated, every muscle preparing for combat. "Either you cooperate, or you don't. Those are your choices."

"I'll show you my choices!" Oliver said in a louder voice than he should have. He suddenly tossed the rest of his drink into the man's face.

Ivanovitch felt his adrenaline rush through him. He knew what was coming next. The big man took hold of Oliver by the neck and tore him off the bar stool. People immediately scattered in all directions. Oliver responded by swinging his elbow into the man's temple with professional skill. The blow loosened his grip and Oliver pulled away, turning around to face his adversary.

"You're a damn fool!" the man said.

"You're the fool!"

Oliver's foot shot out and struck the man in the abdomen. He fell back against the bar, sending glass flying across the room. Cursing and roaring with fury, he leaped at Oliver whose blows bounced off of him as though they didn't phase him at all. Despite Oliver's training, he was no match for the brute force of his adversary. Within moments, the man had twisted an arm behind his victim and wrapped his own powerful arm around the man's neck.

"You just made a big mistake!" he whispered in his ear as he pushed through the crowd toward the exit. No one dared say a word. The fierce glare in the man's eyes was enough to keep everyone at bay.

Ivanovitch followed them out of the bar, leaving behind the startled crowd that had stopped all activity. People knew when greater forces—such as the Federation's security agents—were involved in mayhem. They were more frightened by the obvious military training of the two men than by their brawn. The ordinary citizen was used to stepping aside when these powers manifested in their lives. Everyone wanted to remain safe, or at least out of the spotlight of the Federation and its legions of cronies.

Ivanovitch stepped outside into the shadows. He scanned the alley where he expected to see the two men pounding on each other, but there was no one there. An emergency bell went off in his mind, bypassing his logical reasoning and telling him loud and clear that something was terribly wrong. How could the men have suddenly vanished?

He looked the other way and felt his heart shoot up into his throat. The two men were standing next to him, staring at him. They shared in common an evil glare that could kill. Without taking his eyes off of him, the big man said to Oliver:

"I told you you had a tail!"

"We flushed him out all right," Oliver muttered between gritted teeth.

Before Ivanovitch could react, powerful hands grabbed each of his arms and forced him into the back of a van waiting nearby. The old man fell to the floor of the vehicle. He immediately tried to sit up, but a fist struck him in the side of the temple and knocked him across the seat where he lost consciousness. His age made no difference to these thugs. The van took off with squealing tires.

* * * * *

Juanita strapped the baby in the car seat as Jeremy placed the last bag in the trunk. Three cars, a van, and a pickup truck formed a caravan. The drivers stood around Jeremy and an open map, studying the road that would be taken. They were to head northeast to the heartland, as far from civilization as possible. Lynn watched on nervously, her whole being resonating with a dark intuition. She sensed that some great calamity was looming over them, like a tidal wave rising to its peek and about to crash down upon them.

She had already urged Jeremy to hurry and get the caravan moving. It had been delayed several hours, awaiting the return of Ivanovitch and the others. There could be no more delays now. Jeremy felt her gaze and looked over at her. The tense, glassy look in her eyes worried him. He knew she didn't get that way very - often, that something momentous must be on its way for her to feel it so strongly. He folded up the map, gave final instructions. Just as the drivers stepped into their vehicles, the earth began to shake.

It wasn't like any quake they had ever felt before. It started as a shiver along the surface, causing loose objects to clang like ominous drum beats. Then all of a sudden, a powerful sensation jerked the ground back and forth. It felt like a gigantic whiplash. People screamed in terror.

"Let's go!" Jeremy shouted over the rising noise of shattering glass and tumbling debris.

"We can't drive under these conditions!" Andrew cried out.

"We've got to!" Lynn said urgently. "We've got to get out of here before it gets any worse."

"Worse?" Michelle asked in horror as she watched the old mansion shake like a palm tree in a strong wind. "We can't get on the highways. Take the back roads!"

"Follow me!" Jeremy ordered.

He started the car and headed past the gates. The others followed, terrified, as the entire city shivered in the grip of a monster quake.

"It's got to be a seven or an eight!" one of the passengers who'd lived a lifetime on the coast said. "This is not just a tremor!"

"What are you saying?" Michelle cried out as she held on to the dash board.

"This is the big one!"

"No!"

"Look over there!"

Through the shaking houses, they could see the Golden Gate bridge sway back and forth, sending cars flying off the edge to the waters below.

"Oh my God!" Michelle shouted out.

All around them, buildings began to collapse with frightful noise. The vehicles raced down the side streets inland, away from the turbulent waters of the bay.

"Make sure everyone's behind us!" Jeremy called out as he held on tight to the wheel.

The car danced over the unstable pavement as debris flew through the air. The shaking became more intense. Sidewalks buckled and cracked around them.

"We can't drive through this!" Michelle insisted again. Even her warrior spirit was terrified by this sudden cataclysm.

"We've got to! We've got to get away from the epicenter!" Jeremy insisted.

Sirens wailed as smoke rose all around them. Fires broke out, gas lines cracked, people ran into the streets in utter panic. Shards of glass, metal, and brick flew through the air. Structures collapsed everywhere.

The little caravan rushed away from the city, heading for the countryside where the danger was less intense. After a moment, the shaking stopped. Jeremy gunned his engine.

"It's just the beginning," Melissa said somberly.

"How do you know?"

"Believe me, I know. I've lived here too long not to know. This is just the appetizer."

They dodged debris in the street and the cars that had crashed into each other when the shaking started. They drove by crowds wandering about in a daze. Thick black smoke drifted over the city.

"Stay off the highways!" another woman stated emphatically as she pointed to a shattered overpass where cars had fallen into an abyss of death, crashing on top of each other three layers thick.

"Can we get out of here without the highways?" Jeremy cried out.

"Take a left here."

"Better slow down. The others won't be able to keep up," Michelle suggested as perspiration rolled down her face.

"Watch out!" one of the passengers yelled as an old telephone poll fell ahead of them.

Jeremy swerved and barely missed it, flying up onto the broken sidewalk, scrapping the side of the car against the ruins of a building that had fallen forward. He pulled the car back out onto the road and came to a halt. He turned to make sure the other cars were avoiding the obstacle and joining them. He looked at the terrified faces of his friends crowded in the vehicle.

"We'll make it! We'll make it. We didn't come this far to fail."

He put the car back into drive. "Failure is not an option!"

He took off at high speed as the second shock began to rumble across the doomed city.

* * * * *

At the Scientific Headquarters, panic had set in. Brad Coglan and his colleagues stared at the information coming over the computers. There was no question that a catastrophic earthquake was ripping open the San Andreas fault like never before.

"It's the tension of the axis shift, I'm telling you!" an assistant whispered in a trembling voice. "It's gonna cause the Big One."

"What are you talking about!" Coglan said, hardly able to bear any more bad news.

"It's gonna crack the Bay Area right off the continent."

"Let's not get carried away!"

"Look at this! Shocks are coming in one after the other, and getting worse in intensity."

"Get hold of the military!" Coglan ordered. "I'll call the general."

"Look at this!" the assistant exclaimed, staring intently at his computer screen.

The group of scientists hurried to his cubicle in time to see a graph appear full screen.

"My God, it's an eight point five!" one of them said. "We've gotta airlift people out of there!"

"There are eight million people in that area alone. There's no way!"

"We can't watch them all get crushed to death!"

Coglan picked up the phone. The ghostly pale face of a scientist on the west coast came on the screen.

"Help us! Everything's coming down! Get us outta here!"

Coglan hurried to the terminal and picked up a microphone.

"Give me a report, Jim."

The man was in tears. "Entire neighborhoods are sliding down the hills! Fires everywhere! Lakes of fire in the streets from broken gas mains. A third of the downtown buildings are down! We're not going to make it, we're trapped! Get us out!"

"I'll see what I can do," Coglan said grimly.

"Do better than that, Brad! You know damn well what the emergency plan is! Federation people get top priority!"

"I can't control the military in a situation like this!"

"What do you mean?" the man yelled, eyes wide in horror. "This was always the plan!"

"You really think they're going to save the scientists before the politicians and the CEOs?"

"I thought level three personnel were top security and priority one!"

"Just on paper, Jim."

"What the hell are you telling me, Brad?"

"I don't know what's going to happen. We never really expected anything like this. You're on your own for now."

"On our own? There's suppose to be a helicopter here within ten minutes of such an emergency, according to our contract!"

"I'll remind General MacDaniel."

The picture started fading in and out.

"Oh God, there goes our backup system!" the scientist shouted. "You know we're perched on top of a hill. The whole laboratory's gonna head for the ocean! Help me, Brad! You know my family!"

"I'll do what I can, Jim," he said as his throat tightened with guilt.

Suddenly, a terrible sound came through the speakers.

"Oh my God!" the scientist screamed.

Then the screen went black. Coglan stared at the empty screen in shock. An assistant approached him.

"Mr. Coglan, what is it?"

"It wasn't suppose to happen like this."

He dropped the microphone. "Our technology was suppose to withstand this kind of thing."

"No one planned on the impact of an axis shift, Mr. Coglan."

"All this stuff is useless!" he said as he waved his hand across the vast array of technological wizardry surrounding them. "It's all useless!"

He dropped into a chair, thunderstruck with despair.

CHAPTER 11

An old secluded house stood alone on a cliff overlooking a desolate seashore. A dozen people wandered around the unkempt grounds. With their grim expressions, cold eyes and absolute silence, they looked like the walking dead.

The sound of a violin echoed from one of the many barren rooms in the crumbling home, strangely out of place in this abandoned setting.

Tom wandered through the dark hallways, lost and confused. He was still in a haze from some narcotic with which he had been injected after the beating. He vaguely remembered having been driven through the night to this new location. He'd been deposited in an empty room of this isolated mansion, unguarded and seemingly left to himself.

A silhouette appeared before him. He blinked, uncertain as to whether he was hallucinating or seeing a living being. A young woman of rare beauty and of rarer intensity, studied him curiously. She was dressed in a simple, full length dress that had gone out of fashion two centuries ago.

"Would you come with me, please," she told him in a commanding tone.

He followed her in a virtually hypnotized daze. They walked through chambers decorated by old works of art that looked like orphaned children hidden away in these barren rooms.

Tom stopped in front of a huge Medieval tapestry depicting a unicorn hunted down by knights.

"Beautiful, isn't it?" she stated simply.

"That it is," he whispered, awestruck.

"A true work of art. Have you noticed the expressions on those faces? They're full of vitality and emotion, unlike most medieval works."

"Yes indeed . . . " Tom said, surprised by her obvious education.

"The earliest historical accounts of the unicorn are handed down to us by the Greek philosopher Ctseias who visited India in the fourth century B.C. Have you seen the others in the series?"

"No, I haven't," he said, mesmerized by his mysterious hostess.

"The unicorn was one of the strongest metaphysical analogies of the Middle Ages. He had to be sacrificed, or killed, in order to be tamed. It was said that the unicorn could only be caught by a maiden upon whose lap he would rest his head and thereby be easily taken by hunters."

"You haven't told me your name," Tom whispered breathlessly.

The young woman turned her striking violet eyes upon him. For an instant, he thought he detected a glimmer of warmth. But it vanished beneath a glare of suspicion.

"Oriana," she said coquettishly after deciding that the information was safe to share. She swiftly turned back to the tapestry in order to avoid his admiring smile.

"It captures the spirit of the times, doesn't it? Truly an image of darkness. With an ominous feel . . . Notice the castle in the distance. A man stands on the ramparts. He looks like some sort of mystic, calling down doom upon the merciless hunters."

"What makes you say that?"

"Look at his clothing. Mideastern, I'd say. Despite the Dark Ages, rays of light seeped through to individuals and secret sects who were forced to remain invisible—or in this case, at a distance—for fear of being burned at the stake."

"That's very perceptive," Tom said, genuinely impressed.

"See the knight in the foreground?" she continued, as though swept up in the power of the ancient work of art. "You see the scars of many battles on his face and arms. He exudes a strong, physical sense of life. He likes to fight and gallop and hunt . . . but all the while there is this sword at his side with the symbol of the crucifix—the vertical or spiritual dimension of life—at his side."

"A mighty paradox . . . " Tom observed, enthralled by her sensitive reading of the symbols.

"His zest for the sensual life drives him away from a spiritual quest, yet carries with it the sign of what he is escaping."

She stepped back and examined the painting from another

perspective, eyes glowing with a mysterious fascination.

"The very instrument of destruction which directs his way of life—and which is about to kill the unicorn—denotes the path of regeneration that directs the journey of his soul. Instead of raising the blade, he raises the hilt. He's turning his life around, confronted by the purity of the unicorn."

Tom was no longer looking at the artwork. His eyes were focused on the young woman before him whose beauty was more than skin deep. She felt his gaze and turned her back to him.

"Come with me."

They made their way to a patio overlooking a rocky precipice that fell straight into a turbulent ocean. They approached a table, carefully set with plates and food. The young woman motioned for him to sit down.

"Eat. It's not poisoned."

"Would you mind telling me where I am?" Tom asked as he seated himself and proceeded to satisfy his ravenous hunger.

"No."

"Who are you people?" he asked again with a full mouth. "What do you want from me?"

"You're the bait."

Tom stopped eating.

"The what?"

"The bait," the woman said with a coy smile. "We're going to catch our fish with your help."

"What is that suppose to mean?"

She approached the edge of the patio and looked out at the sea.

"See the ocean out there? It comes and goes and comes back again . . . We're like the ocean. We come and we go. And sometimes, we leave unfinished work behind. Or we leave certain "valuables" that we have to find again."

She looked back at Tom who was suddenly no longer hungry.

"That's what we're doing. We're looking for something."

"What's that got to do with me?"

"You'd have an answer to that question if you knew what you were."

"Do you know what I am?" he asked sarcastically.

She nodded. "You're what is called . . . a finder."

"A finder?"

"You will lead us to the people we need to find in order to accomplish our mission."

"Are you suggesting that I'm not here by accident?"

"Of course you're not. We've been waiting for you."

"That's ridiculous."

"You may think so, but the masters don't."

"Who?"

"You wouldn't know them. They don't show themselves, except to those who know what to look for."

"Are you talking about spiritual beings or what?"

"The masters are a form of energy that can manifest through various channels, generating new degrees of consciousness in certain receptive witnesses. The masters are a bridge between human beings and a higher metaphysical intelligence. Most people are only capable of receiving certain kinds of impressions that are beyond the visibility range of our senses. The masters can only be perceived by more conscious receptors. Sometimes they send a shock through otherwise ordinary experiences, stimulating new insight on the part of the one who can detect their presence."

"I don't understand . . . "

"They are comparable to a powerful voltage of electricity running through ordinary life, giving to whatever they touch a new quality and purpose. They can add an otherwise imperceptible energy to circumstances that someone with the right knowledged will perceive. Then one senses that a higher intelligence is present."

"What is their purpose?"

"What they might be trying to express is sometimes very obvious, especially when their appearance, so to speak, takes place in synchronicity with moments of enlightened perception. Sometimes they 'speak' through others."

"Are they good or evil?"

"I . . . It depends on your definition of those words," Oriana hesitated. Tom noticed tht she trembled slightly.

"They seem pretty black and white to me."

"We don't look at reality that way. We know there is a larger picture than our senses deliver to us."

"Who's we?"

"The Fellowship."

"The Fellowship?" he asked with his writer's curiosity suddenly peaking.

"Enough!" a voice cried out from the house.

They turned to find a fierce older woman standing in the doorway. Tom instantly recognized her as the woman he had seen in the mercedes the morning of the massacre.

"Who gave you permission to speak with him?"

"I thought . . . "

"Don't think! Just do what you're told! Keep your mouth shut and make sure he doesn't try to leave before we're done with him."

She turned around and walked away quickly. The young woman's feature turned red with humiliation.

"Eat," she ordered with the same anger expressed by the older woman.

"I'm a writer, Oriana. I've spent years observing people, sensing their energies, their emotional states. I notice things. And you're a neon sign, Oriana."

"Don't analyze me!" the young woman responded angrily. "You think you can slap quick labels on human beings and have them all figured out in one blink of your all-seeing eyes? Who do you think you are?"

"You're laboring under terrible tension," Tom continued calmly as though he hadn't even heard her criticism. "You're one of the most tormented individuals I've ever met. You intrigue me."

"I'm not a character for one of your books! I'm not a plaything to titillate your scrutiny! I'm not interested in your theories of what I am!"

"This volatile energy only supports what I sense about you."

"Stop this!"

"I want to be your friend, Oriana. I want to help you. You're surrounded by some mysterious tragedy and you're drowning in it. Let me throw you a lifeline."

"You're in no position to help anyone!"

Oriana stood up and hurried onto the patio. Tom followed her.

"What is so terrifying to you?" Tom asked softly.

She stopped at the edge of the patio and stared out at the vast expanse of barren countryside.

"Do you believe in Fate, Tom?"

He was surprised by her sudden question. "Why certainly. It drives us forward, just like it makes the planets rotate. In fact, I think that's a perfect analogy. I believe Fate creates circles. We return to the same points, in different periods of time."

"How can you feel so certain about these things? It all sounds theoretical to me."

"I can only trust the deepest whispers of my soul. Where else are we going to find confirmation?"

He stood at her side and looked out at the quiet scenery. Almost unconsciously, he put his arm around her. She received his comforting touch as though it were a familiar, natural feeling that they had shared forever.

"We humans are such tiny creatures in this universe," he said in a dreamy voice. "Not much at all really. We're born, we love and struggle and feed ourselves. Then we die. We can't possibly conceive of the larger side of life, that infinite ocean of space and consciousness. But we can look out of our eyes and marvel . . . "

"Marvel at what?" she asked in a shy tone.

"This aspect of reality. The birds, the sky, your smile . . . "

She turned to him as her lips spread into the first happy expression he had seen on her features. He held her closer. The heat of their bodies intensified and merged.

"You know, I decided not to be conquered by the tragedies of this earthly existence. I refuse to forfeit my birthright to find contentment, if not out-and-out happiness."

He took her face in his hands and looked deep into her eyes.

"Live your life fully, Oriana. Don't smother it with melancholy and fear."

Their lips met and they kissed.

"What the hell do you think you're doing?"

The voice rang out across the patio like thunder. Oriana and Tom instantly separated and turned to the newcomer. A shock wave nearly knocked Tom off his feet. In the doorway stood Oliver, the man who had confronted him at the bookstore.

The same shock registered on the violent man's face.

"You!" he cried out. His mind seemed to shut down as his

instincts took over. He lunged toward Tom. Oriana stepped between the two men.

"Stop this!" she shouted as she blocked Oliver's way. "He's here because the master wishes it."

"Does he wish you to kiss him also?" he asked venomously.

Tom immediately understood that his adversary was completely under the spell of Oriana's dark beauty.

"That's my business!" she answered angrily.

"Get out of my way!" Oliver muttered through his teeth, unable to contain the rage that boiled in his limbs. "I'm gonna teach him a lesson!"

"You're not going to touch him!" Oriana ordered angrily.

"Oh yeah? Does everybody think they can boss me around?"

"You'd better control yourself, Oliver. You've been warned before."

"I've told you what my feelings were for you, Oriana."

"You have no feelings, Oliver! You're not that kind of a man."

"I'll show you feelings!"

He suddenly pushed her aside and faced Tom. It was now the writer's turn to burn with fury. Seeing Oriana tossed aside like a rag doll was more than he could bear.

"You son of a bitch!" he yelled as he took a swing at Oliver.

The man blocked it with expert force, nearly breaking Tom's wrist, then slammed a vertical push directly into Tom's chin. Tom fell back against the balcony, almost toppling over it into the ocean. Oliver grabbed him and held him up.

"I'm not done with you yet."

Wild-eyed, the brutal man struck Tom with hammer fists that would break a board.

"Stop it!" Oriana cried.

Tom valiantly tried to fight back. He landed several punches even though he was blinded by his broken nose. Oliver didn't even blink at receiving the blows. Oriana grabbed hold of his arm just as he held it up to send a mighty blow against Tom's temple. Insane with anger, Oliver turned around and slapped Oriana across the face. She fell in a heap on the patio. Just then, a bone-thin, cadaver-like creature dressed in a suit that had gone out of style two hundred years ago, stepped through the doorway.

Oliver froze upon seeing the hideous looking man. Dr. Tagore stared with imperious outrage at Oliver for a moment that seemed like forever.

Tom fell to his knees, blood flowing from his face.

"You're through," the strange man grumbled as he raised his hand and pointed a crooked finger at the mercenary.

Oliver's hand shot to his side, grabbing a hidden pistol. But it was too late. A current of energy from Dr. Tagore's finger snapped between them like a lightning bolt, lifting up Oliver's body with extraordinary force and hurling it over the balcony. The man's scream could be heard all the way down the steep cliff until his body smashed against the rocks below.

Dr. Tagore helped Oriana to her feet.

"Are you all right, my child?"

She nodded, placing her hand against her red cheek. He turned to Tom.

"Is he responsible for this?" he asked as he pointed a finger at the writer. Oriana grabbed his hand and moved it away.

"It's not his fault."

"Are you sure?" the gruesome man asked, turning his shark-like eyes upon her.

"I'm sure. The master wants him alive."

Tagore looked back at Tom who was holding his bloody nose. He grimaced with disdain.

"Don't make any more mistakes, Oriana," he whispered hoarsely. "There is no more time for delays."

He promptly walked back into the house. Oriana hurried to Tom's side. She helped him raise his head back to stop the flow of blood.

"I'm so sorry," she said.

"It's okay," Tom whispered. "It'll make good descriptive material for my next book," he added with a painful snicker.

She grabbed a napkin from the table and cleaned his face.

"How bad is it?" he asked, still barely able to see.

"The bone is cracked. You'll probably never have the same profile. But it will heal by itself."

"I didn't care much for its previous position," he said, trying to be cavalier. "Was that the man I saw playing the violin?"

"Yes, that was Dr. Tagore."

"What did he do to Oliver?"

"It's a skill that certain people develop. Very efficient."

"I guess. It's also what killed the Prophet's disciples."

Oriana looked at him coldly and said nothing.

"What's a beautiful girl doing in the company of people like that?"

"You ask too many questions."

"That's what a writer does. Why would you want to destroy followers of the Prophet?"

"It's been ordained for a long time. You wouldn't understand."

"Try me," he said as he leaned his head back to stop the bleeding.

"There's nothing more I can tell you."

"Answer me this, Oriana. Are you human?"

She looked at him strangely.

"Of course, Tom. What else would I be?"

"I don't know, but what just happened here on this patio wasn't human."

"Paranormal powers, that's all."

"Do you have such powers?"

"No, I do not . . . But a number of people do possess them. This is a turning point in human history. There are great forces at work."

He touched her cheek and felt her soft flesh.

"Oriana, are you evil?"

"Why do you ask me this?"

"The people around you are servants of darkness."

"They work for other purposes," she corrected him.

"How can someone like you be among them?"

"You don't know anything about me."

"I know that your lips are soft and warm. So must be your heart."

"You talk too much."

"Why would you seek to destroy good?"

"Some of us don't have choices, Tom."

"We all have choices."

"Some of us are not like others."

"So you're not human?"

"I couldn't have kissed you if I wasn't."

He took her in his arms again, despite the pain, and kissed her passionately. Her warm response convinced him that she was indeed human.

"I don't want to see you get hurt, Tom. The Fellowship is merciless with those who interfere with the mission."

Oriana lifted a necklace she wore and revealed the ornament on its end that was hidden by her clothing. Tom's eyes widened as he recognized the upside down cross he had found near the mansion.

"Do you know what this is?"

"I've seen it in books . . ."

He wanted to grill her with more questions, but understood from the dark look on her features that he could get no more information from her.

* * * * *

The sun dipped behind the ocean's horizon, taking with it the last golden shades of the day. Tom witnessed the cosmic phenomenon, eagerly awaiting the oncoming darkness. He knew he had to escape this night. It was his last chance.

He hurried to the door that he had taped open, listened for any sound on the other side, and stepped into the hallway. He hurried through the large house, searching for a way out. The deep silence disoriented him. Everyone seemed to have vanished.

Then he heard a low hum rising from the floor below. He stopped to listen and recognized the sound as some kind of chanting. His curiosity took control of him. He had to see what was going on before leaving this strange place. He followed the sound. It led him to the basement.

Tom quietly made his way down the stairs. The further he descended, the more the surroundings changed from a shabby, disintegrating mansion into an underground cathedral.

He made his way toward a large, dark room from which the morbid sound emanated. He peered through a crack in the wall. The whole group was gathered there, dressed in dark ceremonial robes. They hummed a chant unlike any Tom had ever heard before. It carried a Mideastern tonality, but seemed more ancient than the melodies that came from the land of Islam.

In the center of the room, the large figure of Stefan Zorn stood like a great dolman, hovering over his disciples, controlling them with magnetic power.

"The time is here . . . " he proclaimed dramatically in his deep, gravely voice. The stars are aligned to open the way. The stage is set. The actors are in place. We who have dedicated our lives to the destruction of the enemy are now worthy of completing our mission. Remember the ancient saying of our forebears: "When Oros will have returned from His long journey round the throne of Osiris, then shall the days of desolation dawn again with the souls of men, and the child of Baphomet will be born from the flames of wickedness!"

Tom listened intently. Under the spell of the mysterious scene, he lost all sense of personal safety. The name Baphomet stirred a faint memory from his vast studies of the occult. But he was too fascinated with the scene before him to reflect upon it. What he saw in the dim light was part Gothic theater and part nightmare, much like a recurring dream that had plagued him all his life. The familiarity of the sight hypnotized and terrorized him at the same time

Stefan Zorn looked at the strange assortment of faces staring at him with total devotion and fanatic zeal. They were young and old, of all races, and their eyes gleamed with a common intensity.

"You know that for centuries the Fellowship has been preparing for this event. The Grand Masters have guided us to this moment and we are the generation that will carry out the Mission. The forces that have brought us together have made it abundantly clear that the long awaited moment is here. Everywhere across the world, we are making entryways into the halls of power. It won't be long before the World Federation itself will be fully infiltrated.

"You know the signs by which we recognize each other. Some day they will become the code of all who are in positions of power. In the meantime, let us maintain absolute secrecy. Above all, we must not fail. The Prophet nearly derailed our work and we will not let it happen again. Victory is within our reach."

"What will be the sign of the time to act?" someone asked.

"When the planet's upheavals have reached their apex."

"What can we anticipate in the days ahead?" another follower asked.

"We are entering the era of a new cosmic process, one of disease, corruption, and crime," Zorn responded. "In this process, form breaks loose from its natural subservience, and reduces the whole to dead matter. What is taking place on a planetary scale can be seen in the same way as disease in the human body.

The comparable condition on the planet would be for one segment of nature to step out of its role and destroy the general balance. Humankind has been doing this throughout its history and that is why we find ourselves at this moment of cosmic revenge.

"This process represents the rebellion of the part against the whole or, more simply put, crime, cosmic crime. Hence our presence here as . . . jailors if you will."

"Could this have been prevented, master, or was it ordained from the beginning?"

Zorn moved pensively to a large throne-like chair and sat.

"As I said, it is a natural process, the result of many causes. Could it have been prevented? Yes, if another process had been initiated, which is what the so-called Final Prophet was here to accomplish. The process of healing and renewal. It represents the rediscovery of spirit by matter, through the mediation of our enemies, those who come from the places of light."

"You are referring to the intervention of solar forces," Dr. Tagore muttered hoarsely.

"That's right," Zorn responded. "This is the counter-activity to disease and crime that has plagued our Fellowship throughout the centuries. By creating an order similar to that created by a higher power, people can acquire in little the nature of that power. Saints and great teachers, emulate the solar source of light and themselves achieve it.

"But as most of you know, any process of regeneration of natural or human forms must consist in unlocking more and more of the matter of the body from mineral first into molecular and then into electronic state. In such a condition, a being could, as with light, exist in all parts of the Solar System simultaneously. And this is entirely unacceptable to the Forces that we serve."

"Tell us why, Master Zorn," a follower called out, eager for the dark knowledge.

"It's very simple. such unlocking of energy runs counter to all natural growth, to the whole process of creation, which consists in the locking up of solar energy into complex forms. The process of regeneration is against nature and against creation!"

Zorn turned to Dr. Tagore, his first lieutenant, and motioned for him to step forward.

"Tagore, you're our metaphysical expert. Explain this to them once and for all."

Tagore stepped into the middle of the room and looked about with a stern expression. Then he closed his eyes and began to speak like a professor to his class.

"What is the Sun in relation to humans? As we descend the scale of worlds, on each level the number of possibilities contained in matter diminishes. When we come to this level of earthly elements, the possibilities are already clearly defined and limited. Atoms of carbon, oxygen, nitrogen and hydrogen contain the possibilities of all living matter. But they do not contain the possibility of becoming each other.

"At a still lower level, the world of the moon, nothing can change into anything else and is condemned to remain eternally what it is. This is the antithesis of the absolute, the end of creation. And it is as it should be. In a sense, we are the guardians of the right order of created existence. Those who seek to rise to higher levels are seeking to destroy our ways and the very laws of our world.

"At the level of the sun, however, one element can change into another. A carbon-atom one moment is a nitrogen-atom the next. One element contains in itself the possibility of another element. A hydrogen atom contains within itself the possibility of all other elements."

A man stepped forward from the crowd of onlookers.

"I'm not interested in physics! I gave my life over to this Fellowship for in the name of the Dark Ones!"

Tagore smiled coldly at him and continued calmly.

"In splitting the atom, humans succeeded in chipping one electron off to release an energy never seen before. They introduced to this realm of creation a phenomenon which does not belong here, but rather is from the world of the Sun. The hydrogen bomb involved the actual creation on earth of a miniature sun. In other words, humans compromised solar force to produce death."

Tagore turned a dark glare upon the man who had stepped forward.

"What do you think they will do if they achieve such transformation at a spiritual level?"

The man turned pale beneath the fire of his gaze and moved back among his colleagues.

"Our Grand Masters have taught us that the universe is divided into several major planes of matter or consciousness," Tagore said in a haughty voice. "Humans are endowed with subtle bodies that interpenetrate each of these planes of matter. And even though spiritual writings and teachings that have emerged from every culture contain this concept, the vast majority of people have failed to discover these entryways into other dimensions. We must keep it that way!"

"Is this the violation of dark matter that our teachers have spoken of?" a woman asked.

"Dark matter is associated with mystical matter from other planes, the matter that also constitutes the subtle bodies of humankind. Our teachers have revealed to us that this dark matter was present before—and thus responsible for the Big Bang which created visible matter. It therefore has consciousness, primeval consciousness."

Tagore noticed the puzzled look on several faces.

"The explanation of "dark matter" is not so mysterious. It is matter which is not composed of electrically charged particles. This simple property makes this matter invisible to our normal vision, and also would give "dark matter" the ability to pass right through visible matter . . . ," he added with a sinister twinkle.

Zorn leaped impatiently from his great chair.

"Enough! There is no more time for lessons. Now is the time for action! If you haven't understood the big picture, then just obey orders and leave the rest to your leaders!"

Zorn motioned for someone to begin the chant again and the group resumed its mind-numbing activity.

Tom listened in a trance of fascination. Until a hand fell on his shoulder. He nearly jumped out of his skin and turned around to find Oriana staring at him sternly. She motioned for him to follow her upstairs.

He followed her sheepishly, feeling like a little boy who'd been caught with his hand in the cooky jar. It irritated him that she would have such an effect on him. But he couldn't help it.

As they walked down the hallway, they heard the group coming out of the basement. In a near panic, Oriana grabbed his arm and they slipped behind a curtain decorating the otherwise dark and dreary home. Dr. Tagore and Madame de Belmar walked past her.

"What do we do with this Tom Wells when he's fulfilled his purpose?" the odious doctor asked in his gravely voice.

"We hand him over to you, doctor."

Oriana peeked out from the shadows in time to see an evil grin spread across the man's gruesome features. She turned to Tom and whispered in his ear. The sensation of her breath on his earlobe startled him.

"You've got to get out of here immediately."

"What?"

"I can't let them turn you over to Dr. Tagore! Come with me."

She pushed him forward into a nearby empty room and hurried to the windows. She unlocked the steel shutters and opened them wide.

"What's going to happen to you?" Tom asked nervously.

"Don't worry about me. This is the first decent thing I've done with my life. Let's go!"

They slipped out the window and hurried through the darkness.

Oriana took his hand and they ran to a tall fence on the edge of the property. The faint sound of Dr. Tagore's melancholic violin floated toward them on a cold breeze. Tom thought he heard the music become menacing, as though the freakish man knew what they were doing.

They managed to climb the fence and jumped to the other side. Dashing across the rocky cliff, they ran toward the ruins of a deserted seaside resort.

Tom stopped her just before entering the ruins. "Stay here. I'm going to take a look around."

She hid in the shadows as Tom investigated the area. He spotted a fisherman making his way up the beach toward a car parked near the road. Tom hurried back to Oriana. As he came around the disintegrating walls, the figure of Dr. Tagore appeared before him, a savage look in his eyes. The fiendish man aimed his finger at him and hurled him through the wall.

Oriana jumped up from her hiding place at the sound of the crash and raced toward them. She came between the two men.

"Run, Tom, run!" she cried out.

"I can't leave you," he responded as he rose from the debris.

"For the future!" she shouted as she sent a beam of light straight into her adversary's face.

Tom raced wildly for the beach as several silhouettes hurried toward them from the mansion, led by Madame de Belmar.

Dr. Tagore wiped the burning flesh from his features and laughed at the brave young woman. He swung his arm and an entire side of the resort came crashing down on her in a great cloud of dust. Oriana barely escaped the tumbling debris and fell to her knees in terror and despair. Tagore gave her a disdainful look and headed off into the darkness in search of Tom.

The desperate young man made his way to the road and saw the fisherman gathering his gear from the trunk of his car.

"Please help me! Help me!"

The man turned around, frightened by the terrified pleas. Tom came up to him, drenched in sweat.

"Take me into town."

"Do what?"

"I have to get to the police!"

"Hey, I don't want no trouble."

"Then give me your keys!" Tom shouted as he approached him.

"Hold on now!"

Dr. Tagore appeared on the road and walked calmly toward them. Tom grabbed the keys from the trunk lock and hurried to the driver's side.

"What's the big idea?" the fisherman cried out.

As Tom started the car, he suddenly realized that it was already moving. The vehicle began to pick up speed as it weaved down the road, pushed on by Dr. Tagore's mysterious powers. Tom jumped out just as the car was lifted into the air and hurled down the hillside.

He tried to run but stumbled in pain from a twisted ankle. He fell and helplessly watched the evil man approach. The fisherman hurried to Dr. Tagore.

"What the hell is going on here?"

The vicious man slowly turned and looked at the fisherman. Horror filled his victim's eyes as he saw clearly the evil nature of the creature he was confronting. Dr. Tagore waved his hand and the man exploded into bloody pieces. He turned to Tom, snickering. But the young man was nowhere in sight.

CHAPTER 12

Within twenty-four hours, the cult on Gough Street in San Francisco had vacated the house and stripped it bare of any signs of their activities. Everyone was moved to the property further north where Tom had been taken.

It was here that they brought their new prisoner.

A dozen students were sitting at a long table for lunch while others served them. They all looked up at the old man limping alongside Amir who watched him closely. Ivanovitch was stunned by their expressions. They each had vacant eyes and quietly went about their chores like hypnotized people. The entrance of the stranger seemed to disturb their routine, temporarily jolting them out of their odd state of somnambulance.

"Return to your chores!" Amir ordered. He turned to the old man and looked at him haughtily. "One of our teachers will see you now."

"Who?" the old man asked, disoriented.

"Our teacher. You should be grateful that he respects your age."

The student escorted him up the stairs. Ivanovitch followed passively, knowing that they were seeking to manipulate his mind and throw him into confusion.

Ivanovitch was brought into the hidden inner temple. The "teacher" sat on a small ornate sofa. He stared at the newcomer intently. Amir motioned for the old man to sit in a chair across from the sofa.

"I welcome you to our home," the teacher said slowly.

"Thank you," Ivanovitch responded with suspicion.

"You have questions for me?"

"I do," the old man said, playing along. "I suppose everyone does. What do you teach your students about God?"

"God . . . " the theatrical teacher whispered. "The power of the universe. The power within you."

"The power of the universe is in me?" Ivanovitch questioned, trying to draw out the man's opinions.

"We are all the center of the universe."

"Is this power love?"

"Love? This power is power. It is objective."

"Isn't there objective love as well that is both impersonal and unconditional?"

"Love as we know it is merely a sentiment. And sentiment is frailty and illusion."

"But humans are frail. "

"We seek release from frailty."

"I see . . . " Ivanovitch responded, studying the man closely.

"My teacher and his teacher's teacher bring to humanity a message that is concrete, practical. A message that makes sense: Discover your latent powers and develop them with all the discipline and consciousness available to you."

"Why develop them?" Ivanovitch asked suspiciously.

"In order to reach your ultimate destiny."

"Is our destiny to end in God?"

Our destiny is to find our higher selves, and thus immortality."

"Are our higher selves the same as God?"

"There are many theologies," the man answered evasively.

"What do you believe?"

"I believe nothing. In time you will know."

"That's an evasive answer if I ever heard one. So I'll ask you another question: When do your students get to think for themselves?"

"When they have a self."

"Is there any room for compassion in your teachings?" Ivanovitch wondered sadly.

"There is room for knowledge."

"You don't concern yourself with the human needs of your followers?"

"We concern ourselves with that which is more than human."

"But isn't the divine spirit everywhere, even in the most ordinary, the most human? Isn't the spirit present in that which is most human?"

"I don't know what the divine spirit concerns itself with. I know what I concern myself with."

"And what would that be?"

"The achievement of powers that are not available to the ordinary person."

"They call you the teacher. Are you the master here?" Ivanovitch asked, suddenly suspicious. He studied the man carefully. He was of Indian decent and had the ideal look for an exotic guru, along with the right words and voice intonation for the part. The very perfection of the presentation struck Ivanovitch with a feeling that came deep from his belly and shot up into his brain with the thundering power of insight.

"You're not the master here, are you!"

The soft-spoken, bronze-colored man was taken aback by the statement. His serenity lost its balance. For a split second, Ivanovitch saw in his eyes a look of absolute terror. The mysterious brown pupils soon regain their outer calm, revealing the powerful control the man had over himself. But it was too late. The Final Prophet's disciple had seen enough.

"You are a front for something else, aren't you?"

The guru was back in his seat of stability and was able to play his part to perfection again.

"I don't understand what you mean."

"Sure you do," the old man said, sick and tired of the abuse he had undergone and distressed that he'd missed his chance to leave with Jeremy and his friends. The fact that his life was in danger made no difference to him at all.

"Someone else is in charge. You're not the teacher. You're just a smoke and mirror trick."

"I don't understand why you are insulting me, sir," the man said, keeping control as best he could over his heart rate.

"You may be a knowledgeable man," Ivanovitch continued, his eyes burning into those of the guru, "but you're no teacher of higher wisdom. I've met a true Teacher. I've seen a great soul. You're just a servant of something . . . evil."

This time he'd gotten through. The guru was losing his cool.

"I am Swami Saravida! I abhor evil!"

"You may hate it, but it pays your bills!"

"That's absurd!"

"Either you're completely disconnected with reality or you have powerful buffers in place, Mister Swami. You're looking at a nearly eighty year old man who was roughed up by two brutes, driven face down in the back seat of a car for hours and brought here by men who just as soon cut my heart out as look at me. How dare you lie to my face when evil is all around you!"

The dark brown eyes twitched. They turned wet. The man tried so hard to stay in control that he couldn't speak.

"How did they get you to sell out? Surely not the cheap gimmicks of indulging your weaknesses," Ivanovitch whispered as he looked around.

A look of profound sadness shifted the musculature in the man's features. His posture slumped slightly. The guru looked away.

"I won't divulge your secret," Ivanovitch said softly. "I'm a dead man. They won't let me out of here alive."

The Indian swami looked back at him, eyes filled to the brim with tears.

"I too am a dead man . . . "

"Then we are brothers!" Ivanovitch said with an ironic smirk. "Why not speak the truth to each other?"

"They captured my soul," the man said in a whisper. "Not with money, not with the flesh . . . They gave me passive students, and a position of authority that I always wanted. Back in my village, I admired the great swamis of the previous century that had gone to America and were surrounded by adoring students for sharing the simplest crumbs of our teachings. You Westerners were so starved that anything from the East was gold, even the weeds. I would have made a good teacher. But I was a farmer's son, stuck where I was born. They came and lifted me from my outcast position and answered my prayers."

"Who is they?" Ivanovitch asked.

"Don't you know?"

"Enemies of the Prophet, that I know!"

The swami uncrossed his legs and his body curved downward, overwhelmed with the weight of his inner misery. "I thought they were merely rich Europeans who would take care of me and let me teach what I had learned from my culture. I never meant to hurt anyone."

Ivanovitch's anger receded as he observed the broken man before him whose mask of detachment and wisdom had cracked open.

"So who are they?"

The Hindu looked up, a wild look in his eyes.

"The Dark Ones!"

Ivanovitch was struck by the answer as by a spear. His mind didn't know what to do with it. The guru who had fallen into line with the wrong masters began to weep like a child. Ivanovitch knew better than to ask him anymore questions. Besides, he had the information he needed. He had already sensed the forces of evil in this house and knew that they were more than human, even though incarnated in transient form.

A door suddenly opened, tearing through the moment with a sinister creak. Ivanovitch looked up in time to see the very manifestation of what he had just been sensing. The hideous figure of Dr. Tagore stood in the shadows, eyes gleaming like a savage wolf. The guru immediately brought himself back into his facade of serene disinterest. Ivanovitch felt his muscles tense with anger and disgust, knowing that he was in the presence of all that was hateful.

"So we have another of the prophet's devotees, do we?" Tagore said in a sadistic tone.

Ivanovitch stood up. "Who else have you brought here?"

Tagore stepped forward and eyed the old man intensely.

"You're in way over your head, old man. You should be watching television in a nursing home, waiting to die comfortably instead of how you're going to die now."

"What have you done to my friends?"

"I'll be frank with you out of respect for the fact that you're not going to live much longer. One of them is splattered in a back alley off of Gough Street. The other has just gotten away from us, temporarily."

Ivanovitch's throat tightened in agony. "Which one?"

"I didn't check his identification papers. I believe Oriana called him Tom."

Ivanovitch did his best not to smile. If anyone could get away from these monsters, it would be the daring young writer who had appeared in their lives from out of nowhere. He felt certain that Tom would somehow reunite with the others. His heart ached for John and Allan, but he also knew that his friends' troubles were over, unlike his own.

"What are you going to do with me?"

"That depends on what you're going to do for us," Tagore said with an evil grin revealing his rotting teeth.

"I can answer that for you right now," Ivanovitch responded defiantly. "I'm not going to do anything for you." He would die a thousand deaths before serving the wishes of his murderous captors. He felt a new energy rush through him, a youthful vigor that hadn't run through his veins for decades.

A strange sensation came to him. Like a strong wind in his solar plexus, he suddenly felt the presence of the Prophet and his heart was filled with courage and strength. The experience covered his body with goose bumps. Despite looking into the eyes of death, he rejoiced in the feeling that the spirit of the man who had so changed his life was in this room.

"I wouldn't speak so quickly, old man," Dr. Tagore said menacingly. "You don't know who you're dealing with."

"Oh yes I do!" Ivanovitch stated as he stared him in the eyes. "I've fought you all my life!"

Tagore was taken aback by his answer.

"You knew the man they call the Final Prophet, did you not?" Tagore asked between gritted teeth.

"I did."

"And you know his leading disciples?"

"I do."

"And you know where they're headed at this moment."

Ivanovitch nodded, almost daring the man to tear the information out of him. A grin spread over Tagore's gruesome features. He knew that no torture would get it out of the loyal elder.

"We flushed them out, you know."

"How do you mean?" Ivanovitch asked with sudden fear from his companions.

"We killed your friends by the bay knowing that it would bring the leaders to your aid. The plan worked."

Ivanovitch did his best to repress his outrage.

"Shall I describe to you how your friends died?" Tagore asked, taunting him. "Those still living will suffer the same fate."

"No they won't!"

"You seem awfully sure of yourself, old man, for one who is about to die."

"I know that evil will not be victorious in the end."

Dr. Tagore burst out in a high-pitched laugh that sent shivers through Ivanovitch.

"A true believer, eh? What a fantasy! Look around you, old man. I'm sure you felt the earth shaking on your way up here. Tidal waves are headed this way as we speak. The city by the bay will be under water within a few days. This is the end. We've already won."

"You haven't won anything!"

Tagore slapped him across the cheek with incredible power, virtually shattering his jawbone.

"You fool! You have no idea what you're saying. The human race is done for. It's a failed experiment. Whatever is left of it will be under our power. It is written!"

"Not in the books I read it isn't!"

"Not only will we conquer your world, but we'll have the full assistance of your fellow human beings. Don't you understand?"

Tagore leaned toward him, exhaling a vile breath in his face. "Humanity has wished this fate upon itself! Humanity is the vessel of evil."

"This specimen is not!"

With the force of a volcano about to erupt, a boiling rage filled the old man's soul. He'd never been this furious in his life. It was taking over his mind and body like a hurricane tearing everything down in its path. He felt his hands turn into fists. Just as he realized he was losing control of himself, the face of the Prophet appeared to his inner eye, as sharp and clear as though he were standing in front of him.

"Remember who you are!"

The words echoed in his mind like thunder blasting across mountain peaks. He was flooded with the Prophet's teachings, as though remembering them all at once. Every idea was summed up in those four words: Remember who you are.

In that instant, Ivanovitch understood that if he gave way to his murderous outrage, he would descend into the outer darkness where Dr. Tagore and his legions awaited him. With a supreme act of will power, the old man held back his rage and unclenched his fists. The very act of making that choice had an alchemical effect on the energy shooting through him. The violence and hate of an instant ago was now neutralized into pure consciousness. All of that power was channeled by his memories of the Prophet and now reinforced his highest potential, keeping him from falling into the gutter with his enemies.

Everything around him became more clear and bright. He was aware that he could hear better. Aromas were more intense. And the horrific figure of the beast before him faded from the center of his focus, becoming just a dot in the reality around him. He could hear the birds outside and the choppy, disturbed waters of the ocean crashing against the rocks below.

He sensed a cool breeze coming through the window, and with that feeling he knew that he had been blessed by the Prophet and saved from madness.

Ivanovitch was taken to the basement, into an empty room made of concrete walls where bloodstains were the only decoration. Dr. Tagore promised him a dreadful end if he did not cooperate. Ivanovitch accepted his fate. Nothing could shake the transcendent experience he'd just undergone and the undeniable encounter with the presence of the Prophet.

As he sat on the cold floor in a corner of the room, his only regret was that he could not tell his friends about what he had discovered. Though the Final Prophet's body was no longer with them, he was alive in spirit!

A rumble shook the ground beneath him. Ivanovitch was aware that something cataclysmic was taking place. He had felt the car bounce across the road hours before on his way to the cult mansion. But this time the vibrations of the earthquake made it clear to him that some unprecedented catastrophe was in the works. The old mansion rattled and cracked beneath the strain. Dust clouds entered beneath the locked door. As one who'd lived his life on the west coast, Ivanovitch understood that the structure would not remain standing. Perhaps it was a blessing that he would die crushed rather than tortured. Either way, he had accepted the end of his life and was content to leave.

* * * * *

Tom ran along the side of the road as it quivered like a living thing convulsing in the death grip of continental shelves slamming into each other. He fell several times but got back up and kept on his frantic race away from the horrid place. He had no idea where he was or where he was going. The world around him seemed to be crashing in, a perfect expression of his own inner world. He was completely thrown off-balance by what he had encountered over the last few days.

Despite dodging rocks sliding down the hillside toward the road and pavement cracking under his feet, he couldn't get Oriana's features out of his mind. At thirty two years of age, he hadn't really been in love yet, and this strange woman mesmerized him utterly. He couldn't believe he would never see her again. At the same time he realized that there were terrible things in her life that were leading her down a path of no return. He wanted to save her, and bring her into his own life, guiding her into light instead of darkness. How she had gotten herself involved with such evil was a mystery that burned him with intense curiosity. No story he had ever dreamed up could hold a candle to this one.

He stopped running, completely out of breath. He'd quit jogging ten years ago and couldn't sustain the physical effort, even with death at his heels. He looked around. A hundred feet from the road, the ocean waves were rising to heights he'd never seen before, crashing beyond the beaches onto land that had never tasted sea water. The sight was virtually psychedelic. The waters seemed like furies rising up in outrage, seeking to break out of their confines and attack the people of earth. The ground vibrated as though in the grip of some cosmic python squeezing the life out of it. The sky turned a bizarre color—purple and green.

No drug he'd taken in his younger years had ever given him such a vision. He looked back toward the mansion on the distant hill and cried out involuntarily.

"No!"

The roof had already caved in. The walls shuddered as though about to explode. Tom's mind went blank. He lost all contact with his reason. He could only think of the young woman who had stolen her way into his heart. Before he knew it, he was running back toward the mansion. It didn't matter if the beasts inside could kill him in a heartbeat. He didn't care that he had no weapon and no means of defending himself. He knew that if he didn't try to save Oriana, he would never be able to live with himself. He'd rather die at the hands of the evil doctor.

By the time he reached the property, the old mansion was collapsing in on itself. People ran out in panic, hurrying away from the cliff that was on the verge of plunging into the hungry waters. Tom hid behind a clump of trees and kept a close eye on all the people exiting the house. He recognized Madame de Belmar and Dr. Tagore who headed with a few students to their Mercedes and dashed off without looking back. Everyone seemed to be on his own. No surprise for such dead souls, Tom thought to himself.

As the house emptied of its inhabitants, he rushed forward, staying low behind bushes and shrubs. He reached the side of the mansion. The old walls cracked and whined with the terrible stress ripping through the structure. The ground shook like a tight drum skin relentlessly pounded on by a mad drummer. The door frame had slipped off the foundation and the door hung open like a dead limb. Tom ran in without any concern for his safety. He was certain that they had abandoned Oriana to her fate. He ran through large rooms and hallways that were filled with dust, sacrificial victims about to be consumed by the devastation.

He hurried toward the main stairway and came face to face with the guru who was slowly descending the stairs, oblivious of the danger. Tom was taken aback by the desolate, empty look in his eyes.

"Where's Oriana?"

"Have they abandoned her as well?" the man asked in a somber voice.

"Where is she?" Tom yelled.

"I saw her head toward the basement . . . "

"Why isn't she getting out of the house?" Tom cried out,

looking up at the huge beams shaking back and forth above his head, rattling like old bones.

"There's an old man down there. She probably wants to save his life."

"Which way to the basement?"

"Over there," the guru said as he pointed. "But you won't make it out alive if you do this, young man."

Tom hurried away and called back. "Don't worry about me. You'd better get out of here yourself!"

"I'm not going anywhere."

Tom looked back, shocked at the answer. The look of despair in the Indian man's eyes said it all. He was anxious to escape the wrong that he had done and to find peace and forgiveness in another dimension. Tom hurried to the stairs just as the first beam came crashing down on the very spot where the guru stood, burying the man beneath its mammoth weight.

Tom made his way with great difficulty down the stairway that shook back and forth brutally, slamming him against the wall several times.

"Oriana!" he shouted. "Oriana, where are you?"

An ear-shattering rumble overwhelmed his senses as he stumbled about in the dark labyrinth of the vast basement. He couldn't tell whether it came from the crashing down of the house or from beneath the earth as the continental shift created havoc along the coastline. He knew it was useless to call her name now. Nothing could be heard above the roar of nature's agony.

He pushed his way through several doors leading into empty chambers, his heartbeat pounding in his head. Any moment now, the entire structure would cave in and bury them alive. At the same time, a new energy filled him with the ecstacy of learning that the woman with whom he'd fallen in love had a good spirit after all and was sacrificing herself for the sake of someone else. Nothing could better express the goodness at the heart of the spiritual teachings that he loved so much.

Dust blinded him as both the floor and the ceiling shook wildly. He could barely hold himself up anymore. He turned down a dark hallway and headed toward one last door. It was locked down by the twisted frame. He would have to break his shoulder on it to open it, perhaps for nothing. This was his last shot. He knew there was no more time to search.

He stepped back and rushed at the door like a mad bull, releasing a war cry as he crashed through it. He landed in a barren room. He didn't notice the pain in his damaged shoulder as his eyes fell upon the most amazing sight he'd ever seen. In the far corner, lit by a single ray of light coming through the window, stood a serene Ivanovitch face to face with Oriana. They held hands and spoke to each other silently, no longer aware of the devastation around them. Tom instantly recognized that the old man was, out of gratitude, feeding her spirit with his wisdom in a manner that was telepathic.

Tom's entrance caused them to break away from their hypnotized attention.

"Tom!" they both cried out at the same time.

"Mister Ivanovitch! What are you doing here?" he said as he scrambled to his feet and hurried to them.

"I was looking for you," the old man said with a half-smile.

"Well, I guess you found me," Tom responded as he took hold of both them. "Let's get out of here!"

"It's too late!" Ivanovitch insisted.

"No, it isn't! It's never too late to try."

He helped them through the broken doorway and led them down the hallway.

"This young woman came to save me, Tom. She doesn't even know me. She just knew I'd been left here to die."

Tom looked back at Oriana's strangely quiet features and smiled at her.

"I knew you were one of us."

The ceiling cracked overhead and tumbled down behind them, burying the chamber in a mound of debris. Tom took hold of Oriana's hand and pulled her to his side, intending to push her up the stairway.

"Wait for him!" she said as she reached the first step.

Tom turned back. What he saw cut him short. Only Ivanovitch's head and shoulders could be seen beneath a pile of heavy concrete. The old man looked up at him. The peace in his eyes was a mind-bending contrast to his circumstances.

"Go!" he whispered. "Find Jeremy! Fulfill the Prophet's mission!"

Tom stopped dead in his tracks in spite of the shattered debris flying all around him.

"I can't let you die here!" Tom shouted.

"My time is up! Find the Prophet!"

"What do you mean? He's gone!"

Ivanovitch made a supreme effort to force his crushed body to speak.

"Help him find you!"

"Come on!" Oriana shouted, seeing a glimmer of hope for survival. Above the stairway, a dim flicker of greenish light called to them. There was still a chance to get out this deathtrap. But Tom was in the grip of the old man's dying words.

"What are you saying?" he shouted through the dust and the falling cement blocks.

"Fulfill the Prophet's mission!"

Just then another chunk of concrete crashed down on the old man, ending his time on this earth. Tom turned back to Oriana, hoping she hadn't seen the gruesome sight. But she had and she screamed hysterically. Tom picked her up in his arms and rushed up the shaking stairway. One of the steps cracked under his footing, and his leg fell through, pulling every muscle in his thigh. He shouted in pain and rage, calling forth a force in him that lifted him back up on one leg, still holding Oriana tightly in his arms.

He limped into the hallway. The place was unrecognizable. The floor stood up almost vertically, cracked open by the force of the quake. Tom had no idea where to find an exit.

"Help us!" he cried out in spite of himself, uncertain as to whom he was calling to. His mind harkened back to the old man and his last words—*fulfill the Prophet's mission*.

"I can't do it without your help!" Tom cried out again, watching the rest of the mansion crash around them. "Help us so that we may help you!"

He'd never done this in his life, but it was clear to him that this cry from the depths of the heart was true prayer. They crawled through the shattered remnants of the home, squeezing past huge chunks of flooring and devastated walls. The contents of the second story had buried the first.

"Where's the exit?" Tom shouted through his vertigo. The old man's last words rang through his being like an urgent siren. He knew beyond reason that Ivanovitch had given him a legacy to pass on to the world he was leaving behind.

The debris had shut off all light now. They wandered about blindly, quickly losing hope. They fell hard against shards of material, as though on a ship tossed about in the grip of a mighty storm. Tom suddenly saw a thin golden light pierce through the rubble, revealing a path to the outside.

"Look!" he cried out in a state of wild wonderment. "That way!"

"What is that?" Oriana shouted. She could tell that this was not ordinary light.

Tom tightened his grip on her hand and pushed his way through the ruins, eyes transfixed on the point of light. Like a magnet, it urged him onward as though some gravitational force gave him strength to tear through toward its mysterious source.

Bloodied and covered with dust, they made their way to a small opening, the remnants of a doorway that was nearly buried by broken masonry. The golden light vanished, giving way to the greenish hue of the outdoors.

"We'll have to squeeze through this!" Tom said. "You go first."

He helped Oriana into the narrow passageway. A piece of glass cut through her shirt and tore a red line across her back. She hardly felt it as she scrambled out. The remains of the house moaned like a dying man as the tension shot through its foundations and lifted it up off the ground. The hillside itself was in convulsions.

Tom noticed that the exit space was diminishing rapidly. The odds were high that he would be crushed trying to slip through it. He took a deep breath and forced himself into the passageway. He had just gotten his leg and arm through when the entire structure shifted and the wall above them came down on him, trapping him like steel jaws. His head and arm were still inside the house. He could hear Oriana shrieking and trying to pull on his limbs that had made it out. He let out a yell of agony.

"Help me, Prophet! Help me reach the future with your message!"

Tom didn't even know where those words came from. Suddenly,

out of the ruins a figure appeared. Tom let out a shout of utter terror as he recognized Ivanovitch moving toward him over the mounds of debris. He was bloody from head to foot and broken bones stuck out of his flesh. The corpse approaching him was dead even though something living looked through his eyes. Tom's terror gave way to a state of utter shock that made him virtually catatonic as the dead man came closer to him. A strangely serene look emanated from the shattered features. A light vibrated around the cadaver, providing the supernatural force that moved it forward.

The broken body approached him and placed its bloody hands on the frame that had trapped Tom. In one astonishing motion, the corpse lifted the mammoth weight, causing the walls to quiver and groan above the roar of the earthquake. Tom slipped through, eyes fixed on the gruesome yet radiant sight before him. As he fell to the ground, he saw the old man's corpse lay itself against a chunk of flooring. The light surrounding it evaporated like mist at dawn.

Tom shivered in the wet grass and started losing consciousness. Oriana shook him.

"Tom! We've got to get away!"

He opened his glazed eyes, completely traumatized by the experience he had just undergone. His very soul was in shock from the unnatural phenomenon that had saved his life.

He knew that it was a direct response to his prayer and he knew that he would never be the same. The experience had initiated into a dimension of reality that recreated him at the very roots of his being.

Oriana's striking features came into focus and brought him back to the moment. He found himself admiring a black curl of hair that had fallen on her dust-covered forehead. In spite of the fear in her eyes, he could only see the graceful image of the mysterious woman who had set his heart on fire.

"We've got to get away before the rest of the house falls!"

She helped him to his feet. They limped away over the shaking landscape as the rest of the mansion fell in a great crash, crushing everything within it. They collapsed on the edge of the woods and held each other tightly as they looked out at the quivering countryside. They were alone now. All the members of the cult had vanished, leaving them to their fate, assuming that they were buried in the tomb that had once graced the hillside.

For awhile there were no words, just the sensation of their bodies held tight against each other. Their mutual warmth eased the trauma they had undergone and slowed their racing heartbeats. They examined each other's wounds. Tom had severe gashes on his arms and hands, but he couldn't feel any pain. His experience of being saved by a corpse brought back to life and freed from the rubble for that purpose had sent him into a state that kept him barely attached to the physical world. Oriana's warmth alone kept him linked to the realm of the senses. He felt as though his consciousness was on top of a great mountain summit and that his body was far down in the valley below. He soared in the undiscovered country of his spiritual nature, rocketed there by the astonishing events that had kept him alive for a purpose that transcended his own desires.

CHAPTER 13

The small caravan of the Prophet's disciples made its way inland through the agonizing countryside. Everyone was utterly silent in the six vehicles, stunned to have survived the destruction of the city that had literally fallen to its knees all around them just as they headed out into the relative safety of the surrounding golden hills.

The grim faces reflected what each person was thinking. The suffering and death behind them was monumental. Hundreds of thousands, perhaps millions, of bodies would be found some day beneath the rubble. It just so happened that they were packed and ready to leave as the devastation began. Everyone else was caught unprepared. They thought about the friends they had left behind, certain now that they would never see them again. Despite the warnings of the man who had transformed their lives, it was impossible to conceive the scale of the destruction that was at hand. They also knew from the prophecies that this was only the beginning, the first in a terrifying list of cataclysms.

Their destination was unknown. They had to escape the more populated areas, far from skyscrapers and glass buildings that were turning into guillotines for the people below. All the signs of human self-importance and achievement were crashing down upon their builders and vanishing in the wind like the grandiose statues of the Pharaohs of old. Once again, human arrogance would turn to dust, but this time the likelihood of starting over again was uncertain at best.

Jeremy and his passengers remembered the words of their Teacher. Now that the cosmic trauma had begun, they knew that a domino effect would take place and that one disaster would lead to another. It wouldn't simply be the results of the axis shift that would devastate the earth. Terrorists, tyrants and fanatics would take advantage of the chaos and intensify the horror. The glee of demonic forces was already palpable as the earth shook and violent storms gathered overhead. A monster lightning bolt ripped through the sky with an explosion that nearly shattered the car windows. Everyone jumped in terror.

"My God! What was that?"

"Creation itself is mourning in travail, as the writings say," Jeremy uttered grimly.

* * * * *

The shaking finally stopped. Thick smoke filled the sky as a strange silence settled briefly over the catastrophic destruction. Nothing moved, as though Nature itself was in a catatonic state.

Then, all of a sudden, sirens and screams exploded through the momentary peace. Every city along the coast—from Seattle to San Diego—had become a death trap to its citizens. Eighty percent of the structures were in some stage of devastation. The ocean roared like a crazed creature stirred from its lair and taking its rage out on the ragged edges of the continent.

It would be weeks before an approximate body count could be collected and months beyond that before basic necessities were restored. The gold coast had finally reached its inevitable encounter with its geological destiny. It was gold no more. Despair and crime would wander through the rubble for years to come. Not even the World Federation could handle such epic devastation. In a few hours, California had returned to its lawless condition out of which it was born. The wild west was back, this time with neither lawmen nor code of honor. Out of the wreckage of civilization would arise sadistic beings who would put their infamous ancestors to shame. Only the most violent would survive—though not for long.

Those who could band together and reach the desert were more likely to stay alive than those stuck in the ruins of the cities. Instantly, barbarians were in power. Decent people were unfortunate prey sure to be attacked by some roving gang.

A lieutenant colonel hurried into the War Department of the World Federation Headquarters. The vast windowless room was filled with anxious generals and other high ranking officers standing over large computer screens displaying constantly shifting maps of the world.

"Where's General MacDaniel?" the frantic lieutenant-colonel cried out.

"He's on the phone with the President. We're expecting him any moment," an older general answered grimly.

"Have you seen this?" the newly arrived officer asked as he opened a file he was carrying.

The general looked at the colored fax that was handed to him.

"What am I looking at?"

"There's been a catastrophic calamity in Asia. It's bound to send shock waves to the west coast that it will not be able to sustain. I think we're going to lose a chunk of California."

"That's crazy!"

"Sir, as we speak there is an 8.5 earthquake going on out there."

"I know . . . "

"You add to that the Tsinamu on its way and the pressure that will create on the plates, and we're in for something we've never seen in our lifetime."

"Are you guessing here?"

"I'm pretty sure, sir."

"Pretty sure won't do it, soldier. We've got a worldwide catastrophe on our heads. Every continent is in utter chaos. We've sent war planes to the Middle East to survey the danger zones. We expect anarchists to take advantage of these disasters."

Another officer came running up to the two men.

"Sir, we've been tracking a giant storm over West Africa. Our satellites have picked a picture you've got to see."

"Another storm?"

The man handed him a large photograph depicting the coast of Africa.

"Look at the size of those lightning strikes. You can see them on the photograph for God's sakes! It's wiping out entire cities and shows no signs of abating. It's crossing the whole continent."

"Is this the same storm we spotted last week?"

"That's right, sir. It's only gotten more powerful."

"What kind of a storm is that?" the man cried out, horrified at the huge red spots on the satellite images.

"Nobody's ever seen anything like it. Every city it comes

through is completely blacked out. There's massive looting and total disorder in its wake. Even Federation posts are under attack."

"Why don't they shoot the bastards?"

"Sir, they've been overrun. There are thousands of panicked people in the streets. There's nothing we can do."

"What do you mean, there's nothing we can do?" General MacDaniel shouted, red-faced as he approached them. His fellow officers turned to him, sad and silent.

"Send the Air Force out there!"

"They don't have the heavy equipment to dig their way through the mess."

"Then order the Navy's largest ships into every harbor."

"It's not safe. There'll be aftershocks, and that means tidal waves."

"We can't leave millions of our citizens without food and water, or medical attention, or protection!"

"People are gonna be on their own for awhile, sir. There's no way around it," one of the older generals said sternly. "We'd better concentrate on the situations we can do something about."

"Explain yourself!" MacDaniel ordered.

"The storms in the Midwest have created blackouts in at least a dozen cities."

"There's massive looting going on," another officer pointed. "We've got to get the army in there and restore order! There's no telling how long the electrical systems will be done. There are so many transformers blown, the blackouts could last for weeks."

MacDaniel ran his hand across his bald head, removing the beads of sweat that had gathered there. A thought came into his mind. For some reason, the image of the dark man who had visited him recently formed on the screen of his inner eye. Why exactly he would think of Stefan Zorn in this moment was unclear to him. But the thought stuck there, obstinately, refusing to give way to more practical matters in this moment of crisis.

"What are your orders, general?"

MacDaniel turned his back on his officers, trying to rid himself of the image of the big, evil-eyed man that was interfering with his rational mind. He'd never had such a problem before. Then it dawned on him. The occult leader might be in possession of mysterious knowledge regarding the global cataclysms taking place. Perhaps he had some inexplicable way to counteract these overwhelming events.

A surge of anger rushed through the general's nervous system. That was the most ludicrous thought he'd ever had. But it remained nevertheless, unwilling to evaporate and give way to logical reasoning. A cold shiver shot through him as another thought came to his mind. Had the evil man done something hypnotic to him, locking down his capacity to function and forcing him to think in a certain way?

That was too much for him to deal with. He let out a bear-like growl and turned around.

"I want military units dispatched to every city that the storm has passed through. I want you to reestablish contact with all authorities that are still functioning on the west coast. And make arrangements to drop supplies from the air to citizens that can't be reached otherwise. Let's do it now, gentlemen!"

The officers immediately dispersed to their various phone centers. An assistant approached the general with a handful of faxes. MacDaniel waved him away and walked over to a corner near the giant world maps etched on glass that surrounded the room. He took a deep breath and concentrated his mind. His iron will had been his strongest gift throughout his life. Zorn's sinister dark eyes remained stuck in his mind like some ghostly freeze frame that couldn't be removed. He had to confront him and deal with this phenomenon before it interfered with any other executive decisions. He hurried back to his office.

He made no eye contact with anyone along the way. He opened his address book in his computer and found the man's cellular phone number. He clicked on it. Within moments, the intense features of Stefan Zorn appeared on his computer screen. He was driving his car on a road leading toward the headquarters.

"Hello, general," Zorn said with a knowing smirk.

"How did you know it was me?" MacDaniel asked, more confused then ever.

"I'm already on my way."

"You knew I wanted to see you?"

"Yes I did."

"Don't come to my office. Let's meet in a secure location."

"I have several. I know you do as well."

"There's no safer place than the Corridor."

"The what?"

"Corridor 600. It's long been our most secure military location for high level gatherings. I wouldn't want to take any risks. Not now."

"Very good, general. By the way, don't bring anyone else with you. I wouldn't want to get nervous and do something . . . unnecessary."

"You're not threatening me, are you , Zorn?" the general asked, his face turning beet red with outrage.

"No sir, I just wouldn't want to find out that you're planning on arresting me."

"Can't you foretell that?" the officer asked sarcastically.

"As a matter of fact, I can. But I just wanted you to know that I would know if you made that decision. It wouldn't be the smart thing to do."

"Who the hell do you think you are?" MacDaniel yelled, unable to control himself. "Don't you realize who you're talking to?"

"Yes sir, I do. The man who thinks he's got all the power, but who needs to talk to me because he now knows that he doesn't."

MacDaniel's insides felt like they were melting with shame. It was the worse defeat of his career. He couldn't argue with the beastly man. He had to resolve this situation before it interfered any further with his self-mastery.

"Don't be late!" MacDaniel said menacingly.

Zorn smiled slyly. "I'm almost there already, general."

MacDaniel shut down his computer. He looked around his office to make sure that no one could have heard that conversation. This was a secret that he couldn't afford to let leak under any circumstances.

Suddenly the room filled with a loud mechanical screech as a dozen seismographs shook back and forth. They were receiving signals that were off the charts, shattering the equipment. The officers jumped in fear as sparks and smoke flew out of the machines as the needles ripped through the paper charts running through them.

"What the hell is that?" MacDaniel yelled over the noise.

"We've got seismic activity that's never been recorded before, sir! It's so intense that it's destroying our measuring equipment."

"Where is it coming from?"

"Everywhere!"

That one word said it all. A strange terror filled the room as the building itself began to shake, confirming the fact that every continental plate on the globe was rattling under the strain of incredible pressure.

"What does this mean?" MacDaniel asked as he held on to a table and watched chairs skip across the floor.

"It's gotta be the axis shift, sir" an officer shouted back over the chaos.

"Is the whole planet gonna explode or what?"

"Nobody knows, sir. This has never happened before," the science officer said as he held on for dear life. Everyone knew that if this uniquely designed building was shaking, structures in every other city were tumbling to the ground.

After a moment that seemed like eternity, the shaking stopped. A grim silence fell over the room. Only one of the seismographs still functioned. The others hung loosely from their boards, shattered beyond repair, witnesses to the mammoth destruction that had just taken place.

The officers gathered around the broken equipment.

"Has anyone every read about anything like this?" MacDaniel asked somberly.

"No sir. This has not happened before in recorded history."

"For all the plates to be affected at once, it can't be anything less than the planet shifting its axis. Nothing else could account for that kind of unilateral stress on the earth's surface," another officer stated.

"I hate to see what it's like outside," a general muttered.

"We've got to get control as best we can," MacDaniel responded the only way he knew how. Tight control and overcoming the enemy were the only solutions he knew how to employ. But this time the enemy was larger than anything he'd ever faced.

* * * * *

Stefan Zorn's black luxury car swerved past huge piles of debris and large cracks in the pavement. Smoke covered the city like a thick mourning veil. Sirens and flashing lights were the only signs of life in this traumatized landscape of twisted metal and broken concrete.

The bulletproof vehicle screeched to a stop in front of a side entrance to the Federation's headquarters. Several officers stood in the doorway awaiting him. They scanned the area to make sure there was no one in sight. The large, evil-looking man got out and surveyed the surrealistic environment. The glow of gas fires could be seen in the distance, but here in this desolate section of the city the atmosphere felt like a cemetery.

He looked up at the huge fortress of concrete, somewhat surprised that it was still standing. The steps leading up to the side doors that were camouflaged as a maintenance entrance were cracked from top to bottom. Zorn could not hide a smile. He was thrilled that he was finally entering the ultimate halls of worldly power. This was the holy of holies for political leaders and military commanders who thought they controlled the world's destiny.

It took him a few moments to adjust to the darkness of the labyrinth of secret hallways and large iron doors. After fifteen minutes of following a silent officer up and down lengthy stairways, irritation started to burned through his veins. Zorn was finally led into a long, darkly lit hallway deep below ground level. The officer opened one of the heavy doors and gestured for him to enter.

Zorn wandered in the shadows of the vast, barren room. After a few moments, General MacDaniel entered. His visitor seemed to have vanished in the darkness.

"Where the hell are you?" the general finally called out, after bumping into several columns of cold stone. The backup electrical system was dim and weak. He heard a noise to his left and turned toward it. The massive frame of Stefan Zorn appeared just a few feet away from him, causing the general's instinctive combat readiness to go for his gun.

"Easy, general. This is not a Syrian battle ground."

The general approached him and stared angrily into his dark eyes. Zorn waited patiently for him to speak, full of arrogance and the certainty of his greater power.

"What have you done to me?" the general whispered hoarsely.

"Whatever do you mean?" Zorn replied with a smirk of disdain.

"You know damn well what I mean, Zorn! You've done some hypnotic trick to my mind."

"Do you think so?" the man asked with a mysterious glint in his eyes.

The general looked away, realizing that if he was right, the man could manipulate him even now without his knowing it.

"I want you to undo what you did so that I can perform my duty unhindered!"

"But I didn't do anything, general."

MacDaniel turned purple with rage and pulled out his weapon with great speed, pressing it against Zorn's thick cheek.

"I'll blow your face off right here and now if you play games with me! Tell me what you've done! Now!"

"Please remove your weapon from my face," Zorn said coldly.

The general cocked his gun and prepared to pull the trigger.

"If you kill me, general, no one will be able to help you."

"So you did do something, you son of a bitch!"

"Nothing serious, general."

"Then undo it immediately!"

"I'd be happy to, but you'll have to remove your gun."

The general pushed it deeper into his flesh. "No tricks Zorn, or I swear I'll drop you right here and leave you for the rats to gnaw on."

"I believe you, general. But I can't help you under these conditions."

MacDaniel reluctantly removed the gun just far enough for Zorn to turn his head toward him.

"How dare you mess with my mind!"

"Believe me, general, it kinda happens automatically with me. Nothing personal. It sort of comes with the territory."

"What the hell are you talking about?"

"Most people I come across are affected in that way, sir. I don't even have to try."

"This has never happened to me before. Undo it."

Zorn focused his intense glare upon the harsh features of the general. His arrogant smirk turned to ice as he shot of beam of energy into the man's soul. The general did his best to hide a tremble that shook his body. There was none braver in a war zone, but this was too foreign for him. He didn't know how to deal with it. He never had any use for occult matters, but he distinctly felt an uncomfortable energy exchange that left him with a feeling of vertigo. His body went limp and he felt his will power diminish. He tightened his grip on his weapon.

"You're a dead man, Zorn, if you're fooling with me."

"Take it easy, general. I did as you requested," Zorn said with a mysterious smile as he stepped back and the glazed intensity left his pupils.

"How do I know you didn't do something else with your magic tricks?"

"I'm not a fool. I've no desire to have your wrath turned upon me. I wish to be an ally, not an enemy. We can be helpful to each other in these difficult times."

"Why did you mess with my mind in the first place?"

"As I said sir, it was unintentional. Just magnetic effects rather than the hypnotism you're imagining."

"I know I didn't imagine what was happening to me. If it happens again, I'll . . . "

"You've already made that clear, general."

"How did you fix the problem?" he asked as he replaced the gun back in its holster.

"Difficult to explain, general. Sort of a release if you will. I'm sure if you become aware of yourself, sir, you'll find that you're particularly clear-minded and sharply focused."

The general turned his awareness on himself and sensed the truth of his words. He felt rested and was more aware of his surroundings, as though his peripheral vision had expanded. He shook his head in dismay at the strangeness of it all.

"You people are too weird for me," he said in disgust. "But I did learn one thing from this. I do realize that you know things that I do not, Zorn. So I'll ask you again. Is there anything that can be done to alleviate the crisis that is taking place around the globe?"

"As a matter of fact there is, general."

"Tell me, then."

"This will require more than deployment of military personnel."

"I'm ready to try anything."

Zorn did his best to keep a look of victory from spreading across his features. The general waited eagerly for a response.

"You have to understand, general, that the source of these cataclysms is not in the physical world but in the psychic realm."

"Go on."

"The magnetic fields of the earth have been contaminated. I'm referring to a dimension that your scientists know nothing about this even with advanced theories of quantum physics. I'm talking about the electromagnetic influence of the cosmic forces that surround us like the ocean surrounds a fish."

"Tell me more," the general muttered reluctantly.

"You see, general, we humans aren't what we think we are. We are receivers, transformers you might say, of planetary energies."

"What are you talking about?" the general asked disdainfully.

"We're part of the thin slice of organic life that covers this rock and which absorbs the influences which come to us from space. You see, general, we humans are only a coating on the surface of this planet, which is merely an organ buried in the far reaches of the cosmic body which is the universe. We blend with the electrons emitted by the sun, the magnetic waves from the orbiting planets, and the raw minerals of earth. This organic life that we're a part of is nearly seventy percent water so we are obviously under the gravitational power of the moon. And beyond that we are subjected to the different subtle energies from distant star configurations as the earth rotates throughout the year. What we call our history or fate is the result of our cosmic interactions that we know nothing about. Influences from celestial bodies are received by our nerve antennae and stimulate our endocrine glands. These secretions create the overall psychological conditions we find in the people around us."

"How is this possible?" MacDaniel growled impatiently.

"These electromagnetic impulses reach us through our nerve plexuses, which then stimulate our endocrine system. In fact, each planet of the solar system corresponds with our endocrine glands."

"Don't waste my time!" MacDaniel said angrily, confused and disturbed by the strange information.

"Each gland passes its accumulated energy from planetary influences into the bloodstream and therefore into our psychology," Zorn continued, oblivious to the man's dismissal. "The sun itself produces cycles of varying influences on us poor humans. The fluctuation of the amperage, if you will, of the planets' magnetic fields affect our nerve systems and our glandular secretions, thereby impacting our behavior. The glorious history of humanity is a manifestation of these cycles of influence."

A mocking smile wrinkled Zorn's features, as though the man before him was the incarnation of this puppet behavior so arrogantly called history.

"Are you saying that everything we think and do is related to rotating rocks in space?" the general challenged.

"The sun affects the thymus, which stimulates the process of regeneration. The moon influences the pancreas, which directs the process of refinement."

"What do you mean by refinement?"

"This is one of six cosmic processes that form the dynamics of what we call reality. The process known to metaphysicians as refinement is characterized by developments in the quality of human culture. The gradual evolution of technology could be considered refinement, if it hadn't led to this state of affairs. From the first uses of the wheel to travel on the surface of other planets, we can see a process of development that has positive influences on human life. You could also include developments in politics, in the entertainment field, the expansion of our cities. As you can see, we have come to the end of that process."

The general moved away from him, pacing the floor with nervousness and a gnawing uncertainty. This was all too bizarre for his rational mind.

"The thyroid," Zorn stated as though he were tutoring a freshmen, "has an affinity with the planet mercury which stimulates crime. The parathyroid is linked to the planet Venus which stimulates growth. The adrenals stimulate fight or flight and are affected by mars, of course. The posterior lobe of the pituitary has an affinity with Jupiter which, like the sun, stimulates the process of regeneration. The anterior pituitary is affected by Saturn and calls forth the process of invention."

The general stared at him, speechless before this outpour of knowledge.

"What is the bottom line, general? Simply this: the combined electromagnetic irradiation of the planets as they orbit our world directs the general movement of human affairs. Each of these celestial influences carry with them cosmic laws under which we place ourselves according to our degree of consciousness. We are currently under a great density of hydrogen and live in the darkest state of psychological captivity. We've been this way for a long time. That is why we have reached this crisis point, general."

The two men stood in the dark cathedral in somber silence as the general absorbed the information he'd been given.

"How can we influence the situation?" he finally asked in words that he could barely make himself speak. This was a reality he hated to recognize.

"There are methods, general, that have been known for a long time. Rituals, manipulations of energies can alter the atmosphere from which the disturbance is coming. But this requires massive control of the population. We need to harness a critical mass to generate the necessary tone of energy."

"How do we do that?"

"First, you'll have to remove those who might distract people from participating in the mass mind. At the top of the list are the so-called Final Prophet's disciples. They'll throw a monkey wrench in this thing, believe me. As long as they're around, people will consider alternatives and we'll have a lack of unity in the population's focus."

"What will it take to get the population's attention harnessed?"

"Very simple, general. Something you're good at and that will make perfect use of your skills."

"What are you talking about?"

"We need a war, general, a world war in which millions will die. The slaughter and all that goes with the events of war will generate the psychic substance that will balance out the magnetic fields."

"That's the craziest thing I ever heard!" the general grumbled, while at the same time a surge of excitement filled his whole being. He had trained all his life for just this sort of thing. War was something he could understand and accomplish to perfection. He felt back on familiar ground. The relief was palpable. The rest of the mumbo jumbo was irrelevant.

Zorn could read his mind like an open book. He knew he had his man where he wanted him.

"So this release of substance is like a purging of some sort?"

"You might say that. Human beings are simply organic transformers of energy. We serve a purpose like plants, but in a more complex way. Every once in awhile the planetary systems need what we might call mass psychosis for purposes that have nothing to do with the politics that seem to generate it. The universe itself is a series of processes and transformations. The small cells that we represent in the body of the solar system have a function that is far different than we imagine it to be. Death and destruction may not be pleasant to those who undergo it but they have their own value beyond their impact on human beings. We're kind of a compost heap for celestial gardeners."

"Enough of that! You're giving me a headache. Any suggestions on how we go about this?"

"That's your department, general. I'm sure you can find a way."

General MacDaniel looked at his watch.

"We'll stay in touch. Let's be sure to keep this relationship entirely confidential. I'm not interested in your cosmology or metaphysics, but if you can help me get things under control, then I'll take your counsel on these matters."

"You can count on me to assist you in every possible way."

MacDaniel headed for the great door, then turned around. He studied the big man standing silently in the dim light. A wave of suspicion crashed upon his feelings.

"What's your purpose for helping us?"

"I live on this planet too, general. I have no desire to see it wrecked beyond repair. I'm a man of responsibility."

"What's in it for you, Stefan Zorn?" the general asked again, unconvinced.

The dark man stared back at him, an inscrutable look in his eyes. The general took a step back, eager to get away from his overbearing presence.

"You're not wanting to take over the world, or something like that, are you?"

Zorn let out a loud laugh that echoed across the concrete walls surrounding them.

"I leave that kind of power to men like you. I don't need it. I'm not a conqueror of territories. My interests are elswhere."

"That's what I'm asking you, Zorn. Where are your interests?"

"What does it matter to you?"

"If we're going to be allies, I have to have some kind of trust in you. To be honest about it, it's hard to come up with."

"I don't blame you, general. You're a man of war. Everyone's a potential enemy."

"It's not that, Zorn," MacDaniel said impatiently. "You think I'm an idiot. You're not a lamb, you're a wolf. Don't try to pass yourself off as some kind of innocent, patriotic citizen."

"You'd be surprised, general," Zorn responded with a certain melancholy in his voice. "I've been sidelined from mainstream society all of my life because of my interests. But I'm not what people think I am. Everyone has their specialties. Does that mean they can't be good citizens?"

The general stepped forward angrily, sick of his playacting.

"My spies tell me that you're involved with evil things. They say you drink the blood of the innocent!"

"It's a myth," Zorn stated, looking back at him unblinking. "I'm surprised you fell for that superstition from the Dark Ages. I'm a . . . philosopher."

"Who do you really work for, Zorn?" the general asked, his face contorted with distrust.

"I don't work for anybody. Maybe that's my greatest interest. Personal autonomy."

"Why don't I believe you?"

"I don't know. You're beginning to hurt my feelings, general. I've offered my talents to you in a sincere wish to help an agonizing world. We've desired to help for a long time."

"You've known about this all along?"

"We have information from ancient sources that a crustal slippage of global proportions occured around fourteen thousand and some odd years ago. It's part of a cycle. This may have happened several times in remote antiquity."

"What does this mean for us today?"

"We can expect a complete lithospheric reorientation of the earth's crust. Hudson's Bay could end up where the North Pole is currently located. The Antarctic continent may rotate away from the South Pole Axis as much as forty-five degrees south latitude. If this happens, we can expect the oceans to back up in their basins at an average speed of two to four hundred miles an hour, creating gigantic tidal waves. In a period of eight to twelve hours, Chicago could end up at the North Pole and a three thousand foot wall of water will come down on the empty ocean basins at a velocity of a hundred miles an hour."

The men stood in silence, stunned by the gravity of the future hurdling down upon them.

"It is also said," he continued, "that a huge magma bubble is pushing up beneath the United States."

"A what?" the general cried out, distressed by a new tale of horror.

"A magma bubble. They're caused by ice buildup at the poles. This in turn causes an instability in the earth's rotation, and that creates instability in the earth's magma and core."

"What will be the result?"

"Land fractures. Expect great migrations of people out of California, Oregon, Washington into the deserts of Arizona, Utah, New Mexico, Nevada and Colorado."

"What will happen to the land west of the fractures?"

"They'll break up further, become inundated, and some will turn into islands. There'll be a seaport in Nebraska. Denver will become a seaside resort," he added sarcastically.

"What about the east coast?"

"Half of Manhattan will go under water. Most of Rhode Island and a third of Maine will be submerged as well. Forget about Long Island. We'll lose a good chunk of Florida. There'll be other phenomena as well that you might not expect . . . New land will rise up out of the shifting oceans."

"New lands?"

"Well, not so new. We hope to see part of Atlantis resurface."

"Don't give me that babble!" the general cried out, red-faced.

"You might get to walk among the ruins of its great cities and see for yourself, general. They'll rise out of the water between

Florida and the Bahamas. We'll see ruins come up out of the Sargasso Sea and the Gulf of Mexico."

"What about the Midwest?" MacDaniel asked, trying to change the subject.

"The Mississippi will expand into a huge seaway. The Great Lakes will turn into an inland sea due to melting polar ice caps. Changes will also come because of those endless storms and floods we're seeing now."

The general brought his hand to his forehead. The fingers trembled ever so slightly. This was an enemy he had never faced before. Zorn snickered at the man's primal fear. It was the sensation he most enjoyed stimulating in others. It was in fact the source of his power.

The general looked at him, stupefied. He had left himself wide open for Zorn's hypnotic influence to seep deep into his soul. Zorn continued like a boxer smelling the kill.

"We humans are part of a much larger organism which has little interest in our survival. We're created primarily to serve the purpose of digesting energies that cannot be absorbed by the earth and moon. Without us, sunlight simply becomes heat when it penetrates the atmosphere. It's the same with the magnetic rays from other planets. The bare minerals of the moon can't do anything with them without a mechanism that will transform these energies. That's us. The masses are here to produce greenhouse gases that conserve the sun's heat. Most humans are obedient cells, or rather a digestive secretion. Nothing more."

"You're talking nonsense!" MacDaniel shouted, feeling his very essence drained out of him.

"Consider this. Before food can become nourishment, it must be refined. In the earth's early history, the sun fell on swampy forests; as the ferns died they formed thick layers of rotting organic material. The climates changed, the continents moved, the swamps became seas, mountains, deserts. These sedimentary materials that were once sun and water became buried under immense pressure and transformed or digested by the earth. Ages later, they are extracted as coal and oil and turned into gases. In other words, the sun's heat, buried countless centuries ago, is released, just like the storing and burning of fat in hibernating animals. Humans simply serve a purpose. The question is—whom will you serve? The sewage of a growing planet or ethereal forces that belong to another plane of existence?"

The general's face was glistening with sweat. Along with his hands, his lips now trembled. He was entirely at the mercy of the man of darkness. He turned his back on Zorn, unable to bear the unearthly tension.

"I don't want to see you again face to face, unless it's absolutely necessary," MacDaniel said coldly as he walked away. "You know how to reach me. Let's keep our communications to a minimum. When I need your input, I'll contact you. Don't call me first."

He moved into the shadows, his army boots resonating on the cold stone floor. An officer entered and escorted Zorn out of the room and down the secret corridor. His big features broadened in a victorious smile as they walked in silence through the underbelly of the military headquarters. He knew he'd won an important battle for his cause, which was most certainly not that of humanity's well-being.

CHAPTER14

The mega earthquake unleashed tsunamis that wiped out most of the Hawaiian Islands. One thousand miles further east, the first new land mass appeared from under the waves. The ancient continent of Lemuria, covered with incalculable treasures from a primordial history, emerged from the deep for the future and the past to meet, if anything was left after the cataclysms.

Japan's fate was the most dire as it faced being utterly swallowed up by the shifting ocean. The catastrophe was so colossal that the world population could only watch in horror, although most people were too concerned for their own safety to worry about the annihilation of another country. Adding to the rising misery and destabilization was the an odd phenomenon soon detected by the Federation's scientists. A hum, just below the capacity of human hearing, caused by tectonic plates sliding against each other, began to create erratic behavior in animals and a variety of symptoms among the human population. Cases of chest pains, nausea, heart failure increased overnight as millions reacted to the inaudible sound.

Large solar flares announced the certain return of super-mega quakes and the further breakup of the continents. Weather changes were turning dry places into wetlands and wet areas into deserts. Monstrous storms thundered across the face of the earth, increasing the relentless devastation. Ironically water was becoming a rare and valuable commodity as salt water contaminated inland reservoirs. Volcanic activity in the Pacific was sending a giant black cloud across the globe, threatening to turn day into night for months on end.

Food shortages and massive rioting kept the ruined cities in a frenzied state of panic. Plagues appeared out of the destruction, like some toxic poison arising to chase after the survivors. It wasn't long before jammed hospitals detected a new strain of the AIDS virus, one that was transmitted through the air. Electromagnetic disturbances generated great disruptions of the technological world on which civilization relied completely.

Throughout Europe, elevations below three hundred feet were inundated by the seas. All the land from the Mediterranean north to the Baltic Sea was in danger of collapsing. Upheavals in the Arctic and Antarctic created volcanoes and were generating the dreaded pole shift that would utterly transform the planet.

Dense clouds were spreading out over large portions of the globe, the result of increased volcanic activity. In their wake, they carried a sense of gloom as rain fell continuously. The ferocious winds brought forth the tales of ancient peoples. The Mayans spoke of a terrible wind destroying entire forests and leading toward the end of the world. Its name was Hurakan. The Hindu Vedas and the Persian Avesta, as well as the primordial Epic of Gilgamesh told of a cosmic hurricane that would sweep the land, devastating humanity. This same mighty wind was known to the Polynesians as Taafanua, to the Arabs as Tyfoon, and to the Chinese as Ty-fong. The Maoris tribes of New Zealand foretold of a wind that was to descend upon creation and turn ocean waves into high mountains. The Buddhist text Visuddhi-Magga described a world cycle that would destroy the inhabitants of earth by wind.

The sacred book of the Mayans, Popol-Vuh, and the Annals of Cuauhtitlan further detailed an age when the sun of fire-rain fell upon the people. The Voguls of Siberia also knew of the time when a sea of fire would fall upon the earth, along with aboriginal tribes from the East Indies who told of the "water of fire".

At the same time, a bright blue comet appeared in the night sky. At least, observers thought it was a comet for awhile. It wouldn't be long before it was discovered to be a star—a new sun. Ten times brighter than the planets and other stars, this new cosmic presence stirred distant memories of a Hopi legend about a blue star they named Kachina. Other mystics had foretold of its appearance and perceived it as the domain of great spiritual forces. In the daytime, it was visible in the sky as a small white light, similar to the moon. At night, it lit up the skies as one of the brightest lights in the galaxy.

This new and inexplicable phenomenon only added to the chaos and panic. In the first week of the onset of global disasters, the Federation set up relocation centers for the millions made homeless. The roads heading inland were jammed with bumper to bumper traffic. Terrified refugees mingled aimlessly toward some place of security that did not exist. Rich and poor travelled side by side, victims of a colossal catastrophe that had suddenly made everyone truly equal. Money was quickly becoming useless as businesses shut down and the economy grounded to a shuddering halt. People were suddenly on their own to stay alive. The promised security of the world Federation had vanished with the first onslaught of devastation.

* * * * *

Tom and Oriana wandered along the road that led inland from the ocean. They'd been in a daze for hours. The world was no longer the one they had known the day before. The pavement was split in half. Trees were uprooted, laying on their sides like petrified corpses, as though they'd been plucked out like weeds by some colossal giant. The few homes located in this sparsely inhabited area were completely demolished. The people inside were most surely crushed beneath the flattened structures. Thick black smoke covered the horizon, coming from the towns and cities further inland that had been devastated by the terrible quake. Behind them, the ocean swirled angrily, sending twenty-foot waves over the coastline, with the promise of more to come. Seafaring eyes would know that this turbulence was the front edge of a killer Tsunami coming in from the open waters, created by the movement of the continental shelves.

The skies were odd shifting colors of purplish green. Cloud formations carried with them that frightful look of the birthing of tornadoes. Everything was in a state of trauma.

Tom and Oriana were desperately thirsty and couldn't make it much farther on their own. His wounds were still bleeding although Oriana had bound and cleaned them with expert care. They were too tired to talk even though they'd walked side by side for hours. They felt like companions in some terrible nightmare that wouldn't fade away with daylight. Even Tom's insatiable curiosity couldn't stir him to find out more about this strange woman and the stranger circumstances in which he had encountered her. He had only one thing in mind, and that was to survive this ordeal.

They came over the top of a hill and were struck by the panoramic view of a small town below them. Not a building remained standing. Vehicles were scattered everywhere, now worthless heaps of scrap iron. There was no sign of life anywhere. It looked like a ghost town in which some angry poltergeist had vented his wrath for past wrongs.

"There's gotta be somebody alive around here," Tom whispered hoarsely.

"Can you make it down the hill?" Oriana asked, looking at his battered condition.

"I'm not sure, but we've got to get food and water . . . or find a phone."

She took his arm and helped him down the hill. They both knew that one fall and their chances of staying alive were over. It didn't matter that they were such different people. Perhaps they would discover that they could never be together, that their romantic feelings couldn't last, but for now they were stripped down to their essential humanity and nothing else mattered than to take care of each other.

As they came closer to the shattered town, a pack of dogs suddenly appeared ahead of them, barking fiercely. They were an odd assortment of different breeds, formerly domesticated and now suddenly reverted back to their primeval ways. The animals were as disoriented as the humans. The dogs raced toward them, baring their teeth. Tom frantically looked about for some kind of weapon.

"Sit down!" Oriana ordered.

"What? They're gonna rip us to shreds!" he cried out.

"Please do as I ask. I know about these things."

In spite of the energy coursing through his system and his desperate urge to run, Tom followed her instructions. They both sat in the grass as the dogs raced toward them.

"Be very still," she said in a strange calm that contrasted dramatically with the dangerous moment. "Don't let them smell your fear."

He looked into her eyes and was astonished by her courage and self-control. He was ashamed of the terror pounding through his nerves. Her serenity was contagious and he felt himself able to find shelter in her peace even though he could already imagine the fangs tearing into his flesh.

He heard the dogs approach and instinctively turned toward them.

"Don't look at them!" she said in a peaceful voice. "Just look at me."

He turned his gaze on her again and was transported out of the terrifying situation.

The dogs charged at them and stopped suddenly a few feet away. They sniffed about. Some of them barked loudly at them, but none attacked. Tom felt a cold nose against his arm. It took all the self-mastery he could muster not to jump up. Oriana's quiet gaze kept him still.

Soon the dogs turned away and headed off into the woods, searching for other prey.

Tom released his tension by taking Oriana in his arms and hugging her with a gratitude and affection he'd never felt before.

"How did you know to do that?" he asked.

"Just a trick from the old country my grandparents told me about."

"You're one brave lady," he said as he touched her soft cheek. "You never cease to amaze me, whoever you are."

She looked at him oddly, realizing that there was indeed much about her that he did not know and that he might feel quite different about her once he found out. He sensed the turmoil in her heart and struggled to get up in order to escape the implications. With new vigor, generated by the adrenaline rush they had just been through, they descended into the town below.

The rubble was spread all across the street, shattered into piles of wreckage. Here and there an arm stuck out from under the mounts.

"These folks never had a chance," Tom said. "They were too close to the epicenter. The San Andreas fault must have split wide open," he added as he surveyed the disaster.

They hadn't walked far before they saw a restaurant front spread out halfway across the street. A side of the building was still standing. The old luncheonette's floor was covered with smashed dishes. A refrigerator lay on its side.

"Let's try this," Tom suggested. They walked carefully through the twisted chaos, trying to avoid sharp objects and hoping they weren't stepping on bodies.

Tom made his way to the back of the restaurant and looked in a cupboard that stood at a forty-five degree angle. It was filled with loaves of bread and hamburger buns.

"Open sesame!" he cried out. The simple food looked like a lost treasure to him.

Oriana pulled out a couple of plastic bottles from the broken refrigerator.

"Well, we're going to live another day," he said as they stumbled out of the destroyed restaurant.

They made their way to the middle of the street and sat on large blocks of concrete that had once graced the town's courtroom.

"Bon appetit!" he said as he raised his bottle.

They ate ravenously, in a near state of starvation, completely oblivious to the bizarre scene—a picnic in the midst of desolation. Tom noted in his writer's mind how amazing it was that people could adjust to virtually anything. The world had fallen apart, but it was still lunchtime and life had to go on, with or without civilization. That thought caused a feeling of fear to interrupt his meal. He realized that it wouldn't be long before the criminal element ruled over the chaos.

He looked around and was relieved by the absolute stillness of the surroundings. Death weighed heavily over the countryside. Nature itself had to catch its breath after what it had been through. There were no bird whistles coming from the groves around them. That in itself intensified the eerie atmosphere. The silence was unnatural.

Then he heard a distant pounding.

"What's that?" he asked as he stopped chewing.

Oriana listened carefully. "I don't hear anything."

"It's kind of a rhythmic beat."

She put down her food and listened again. "I do hear something."

Before she could say another word, the sound was overhead. They looked up and saw a small military helicopter appear above the tree line. Tom's first instinct was terror. But he thought better of it.

"Maybe they're surveying the destruction."

"I don't think so," Oriana responded in a tone filled with dark premonition.

A voice came over a loud speaker on the helicopter.

"Do not move! We have you in our sights. Repeat, do not move or you will be shot!"

"What the hell..!" Tom whispered with a sudden case of indigestion.

Ropes shot out of the craft and several soldiers swung down, landing in the middle of the street just a few feet away from them. As soon as they hit the ground, they aimed their weapons at them.

"Freeze!"

"What's the matter with these guys?" Tom said angrily, sick of the relentless trauma that kept coming his way. "Is there a problem?" he called out.

"Shut up and raise your hands!" an approaching soldier ordered.

"We haven't done anything!" Tom protested.

A gunshot exploded through the air, whizzing right above his head.

"I said keep quiet!" the soldier said as the four men rushed toward them.

"Better do as he says," Oriana whispered.

Tom quickly pulled out a piece of paper from his pocket which Ivanovitch had given him. On the crumbled paper was scribbled Andrew's email address, the only link left with the Prophet's disciples. He placed it in Oriana's hand, closing her fingers around it.

"If you want to help me, try to contact this person."

His action made no sense to him since he knew they were both being arrested. But somehow he sensed that she would have a greater chance of being set free.

The soldiers violently took hold of them, turning both of them around and handcuffing them. Tom turned to Oriana to see a soldier push her forward brutally.

"What are you doing?" he said angrily.

A rifle butt cracked him in the back of the head. He fell forward unconscious.

CHAPTER 15

The caravan pulled into a little town in the foothills of the Sierra Nevada mountains. Marysville was lost in the woods of northern California, a refuge for loners who still believed in the American myth of rugged individualism.

The cars and vans stopped at a gas station to refill their tanks before heading further into the hinterlands away from the faults that were destroying the geography of the continent. Jeremy got out of the lead car and stretched his legs. The earthquake had been felt that far north. Pavement was cracked and several structures were partly shattered, but it was a far cry from what they had left behind.

Lynn escorted Juanita and the baby to the restrooms while Andrew and Michelle came up to confer with Jeremy. They opened a map.

"We can make it to the Oregon state line by nightfall," Andrew said as he studied the mileage.

"We're in luck," Michelle added. "The Federation has its hands full for now. They won't be looking for us until we're in the Montana wilderness. We just might make it."

"Let's find a restaurant and feed everybody before we cross the state line," Jeremy said.

"Do you think there'll be something open after what's happened?" Michelle asked.

"The damage isn't too bad," Andrew observed as he studied the surroundings. "We'll find something. People have to keep making a living no matter what."

They were interrupted by a light beeping sound coming from Andrew's car.

"What's that?" Jeremy asked, surprised.

Andrew was stunned. "It's my computer calling me!"

A frown darkened Jeremy's features.

"Who would know how to reach you?"

"Not many, that's for sure. I changed my address after the community was disbanded. Mr. Ivanovitch would be the only one to know . . ."

"You'd better answer it, then," Jeremy stated. "Just be sure the Federation can't track the location, otherwise we're sunk."

Michelle took Andrew's arm. "Get the identity of the person before you respond. They can track you down in seconds. You can be sure agents are lurking everywhere in cyberspace. It's one of their chief means of surveillance."

Andrew listened to her carefully, knowing that her years of experience as a Federation agent gave her inside information into the wicked oppression that ruled the earth in the name of security. He hurried to the car and pulled out a small laptop from his satchel. A red light was blinking on and off. He pressed a button and his email appeared immediately on the screen.

"Tom. Who's Tom? I don't know any Toms."

"Yes you do," Michelle said as she looked over his shoulder, a worried look on her face.

"I do?"

"That new guy that Ivanovitch told us about. The one who was with Allan. The one we waited for this morning."

"That's right. If Ivanovitch gave him my address, he must really trust him."

"I don't understand that. How could he trust him so much after only a few hours of knowing him? That's awfully quick," Michelle wondered.

Jeremy walked up to them. "Well, I count on Mr. Ivanovitch's perceptions. If he thought it was safe, then open the message."

Andrew moved the tiny arrow to the envelop icon and pressed the key. A few lines of print appeared full screen: *Tom arrested. Charged with looting and aggravated assault on an officer—both outrageous lies. Will be arraigned in court on Thursday. Please help. They intend to put him away and throw away the key. Somehow they know of his connection with you. Oriana.*

"Who the hell's Oriana?" Andrew cried out, adrenaline turning his face red.

"Scroll down, there's a P.S.," Michelle said.

He did so and another line appeared on the screen. *I am a friend of Tom's. We survived the quake together. He saved my life. Gave me your address just before the arrest. You can reach me at the community address below in San Anselmo.*

"What is she doing in Marin County? It's gotta be a total ruin."

"I thought it had fallen into the ocean already," Michelle added.

"The aftershocks will surely take it out," Lynn said as she joined the group around the computer.

"What can we do for him?" Michelle asked.

"We've gotta keep going," Jeremy stated emphatically. "We can't stop for this. We can't do anything about it."

"What do you mean?" Lynn asked, horrified. "We can't let them destroy this person!"

"We don't even know the guy!" Jeremy said irritably. "What we do know is that we can't walk into a Federation courtroom and pull him out."

"What about this Oriana?" Lynn asked again. "She must be in terrible circumstances as well."

"Everybody's in terrible circumstances, Lynn," Michelle stated somberly. "We've got to get our friends to safer ground."

"We cannot let these people be swallowed up by the Federation! Tom was trying to help us. And who knows where Mr. Ivanovitch is? At the very least, he deserves our careful consideration of this matter!" Lynn insisted.

"I don't know what there is to consider!" Jeremy turned to her and looked deeply into her eyes, trying to find something more rational within her. "What is there to consider, Lynn? We can't sacrifice ourselves for one person. Surely you know that. What we have to do is too important. You know what the Prophet expects of us."

"Yes, I do. And what he expects is that we be compassionate human beings first and foremost. Otherwise we're of no use to the future anyway."

"This is true. But it doesn't mean we should be unreasonable."

"If we let this person be destroyed without trying everything we can to help him, we will be guilty of the sin of omission and we will lose our right to represent the Prophet."

"What do you think we can do?"

"Think about this way, Jeremy. What would the Prophet do?"

Jeremy smiled sadly, remembering their mysterious friend and teacher who was so unlike anyone else. "He would probably go sacrifice himself to help him."

"Can we do any less?" Lynn challenged.

"What about the lives of the people in our charge? What about Juanita and the baby? Do you want to sacrifice them to?"

Lynn was stung by the remark. It was very rare that they had bad feelings toward each other. A hurt expression glistened in her eyes, but she controlled the anger that arose from the pain he had caused her. Talk of the Prophet made it difficult to fall into the standard stimulus-response routine that ruled most lives.

Jeremy witnessed the transmutation of energy in her soul. Her resistance to her own response in spite of his impatient irritation filled him with gratitude for her unselfish efforts to reach for her higher potential and not give way to old habits.

"I'm sorry," he whispered. "Let's think this through carefully."

He took her in his arms and hugged her. It took her a few moments to release the tension in her body, but his touch was magic to her, second only to that of the Prophet himself. Their closeness quickly healed the alienation that had risen between them.

"What do you think we should do?" he asked her in a calm, even voice.

"One of us will have to return and find out what they're charging him with and how his relationship to us is involved in all this."

"What if it's a trap?"

"Then we do what we have to do. If they're destroying this person because of his brief contact with us, maybe they'd be willing to trade."

It was Michelle's turn to be irritated now.

"So which one of us do you suggest ought to give himself up as a burnt offering?"

"I'll do it," Lynn answered softly.

"No you won't!" Jeremy stated in a voice that would not tolerate any disagreement. "You've got other work you must do."

"I'll go," Andrew said solemnly.

"What are you talking about?" Michelle cried out.

"I owe it to the Prophet," he said grimly.

"He told you to stop feeling guilty over what you did in the past. Let it go."

"I'm the right person to go," Andrew insisted.

"What about us?" Michelle asked, her anger now mixed with grief. "Can you just walk away from me like that?"

"It's not about us, Michelle. It's about him," Andrew said gently.

"Who, this Tom person, someone nobody knows? We're worth more than that, aren't we?"

"It's about the Prophet. If we run off like cowards and let other people pay the price for us, then we are not worthy of representing him to the future."

Michelle turned away and walked off to hide her feelings. She knew there was nothing she could say to that and the pain was too intense. Lynn hurried after her and took her by the arm. Michelle pulled away angrily.

"Leave me alone! I blame you for this!"

"That's right, it's my fault."

Lynn took hold of Michelle's arm again and forced her to turn around. The former security agent instinctively took a defense stance, ready to strike. Lynn didn't blink.

"I simply reminded us of our mission. Our lives are worth nothing if we can't be what the Prophet has called us to be."

"If Andrew goes to his death, I'll never forgive you!" Michelle hissed, eyes narrowing with hate.

"I thought you were totally committed to the Prophet's cause," Lynn said calmly.

"I am! Don't you dare question it. You know what I've sacrificed already. It's got nothing to do with this. We're wasting a good man for nothing!"

"Justice and truth are not nothing . . . They're everything."

"Don't get high and mighty with me, Lynn. I knew him also. You weren't the only one who was close to him."

"I'm just trying to remind you of not only what we have to do, but what we have to *be*."

"We can't *be*," Michelle said sarcastically, "if we're dead, now can we? Sending Andrew back into the jaws of the Federation in this moment of crisis is asking him to immolate himself on your lofty principles. Don't you think he'd be much more useful to us in our attempt to survive for the long haul in the wilderness? That's where we need him! Not in some Federation prison cell!"

"That's right, we need him. But it's not worth surviving at all if we can't live rightly."

"So saving this stranger who didn't even know the Prophet is the way to live rightly?"

"You're looking at this so negatively, Michelle. Maybe this can be dealt with quietly without too much trouble. We're just talking about investigating the situation."

"Investigating in the middle of the worst earthquake to hit the coast in recorded history? Don't you know how insane the government is right now? They'll shoot people in the streets for no reason at all. This is the opportunity the Federation's been looking for to turn into a completely fascist organization. General MacDaniel will issue shoot to kill orders for the slightest offence."

"So we let this person die for having gotten in touch with us?"

"He made his choices, just like we all did."

"It seems that Andrew has made his choice as well."

Michelle grit her teeth together, grinding them into her jaws. She had the urge to strike the woman who was taking her lover away from her.

"If he dies, I'll hold you responsible."

"You'd better be responsible for your own behavior, Michelle," Lynn said coldly. "I thought you'd learned to better control the violence of your nature. You know what the Prophet had to say about that. It's all a waste of time if you're just going to wallow in the ghetto of your nature."

"Wallow?" Michelle cried out. "How dare you?"

"Look at yourself. You're ready to draw blood from me. Isn't there another way? Isn't what this is all about?"

"Don't preach to me, Lynn! You're taking away from me the only thing I've got left. How do you expect me to feel?"

"I expect you to remember what's at stake and what the Prophet died for."

Michelle turned away from her.

"Don't you realize Michelle that behaving this way turns you into one of them?" Lynn continued. "The whole point of the Prophet's mission was to create a remnant that doesn't respond with violence and hate. They're not even considered an option. If we can't do that, there is no chance of renewal after the Tribulation."

"You really think we're going to survive these catastrophes?" Michelle asked as a cynical grimace distorted her features.

"Of course! We must! If we don't, the Prophet's work is wasted!"

"You think a lot of yourself, don't you, Lynn?"

"Why do you say that?"

"We're just ordinary people. Why should we be the ones to somehow renew humanity. That's pretty grandiose thinking!"

"What's happening to you, Michelle? You didn't think that way when the Prophet was among us."

"That's right. He cast a spell over me. Made me think I could be somebody I'm not."

Lynn was horrified by her friend's words. "What's come over you? There's nothing else in life worth doing than to seek your highest potential. Otherwise you're useless to the universe."

"Right now I'm useless to myself and to Andrew. I don't give a damn about the universe or the human race for that matter!"

Lynn took hold of her shoulders and shook her. "What demon has possessed you? Snap out of this!"

Michelle pulled away and pushed Lynn back with a sharp strike of her palms against her chest. Lynn fell back against a tree. Watching from a distance, Jeremy stepped forward but Andrew took hold of him.

"Let them work this out or it will never be resolved."

"She'd better not hit her!" Jeremy said. The words caught in his throat as he realized that the poison polluting Michelle's mind and heart was contagious, taking hold of him as well.

"Let them work it out, Jeremy," Andrew said calmly. "You know it's how it's gotta be."

Jeremy turned away, disgusted at himself and at the alienation that was taking place among close friends.

Lynn stared at Michelle sadly, realizing that she was eagerly awaiting for an excuse to attack. The deep sadness in Lynn's eyes acted as a mirror and Michelle became aware of herself. She looked down at her closed fist.

"What the hell am I doing?" she cried out.

She stepped out of her warrior stance and relaxed her muscles, letting go of the savage energy.

"What am I doing?" she whispered again, on the edge of tears.

"Don't you see that's how the enemy conquers us. It begins inside each one of us. One moment of inattention and we can be bulldozed by these dark forces. We lose our will, our ideals, our knowledge. We become slaves!"

Michelle looked away, shaken to the core of her being. It no longer mattered what the initial stimulus was that had sent her into this abyss of violence.

Andrew came up behind her and put his hand on Lynn's shoulder.

"I'll take care of this, Lynn."

He hurried after Michelle and took her in his arms. She broke down in bitter sobs. Lynn returned to the car where Jeremy awaited her.

"This is too hard," she whispered. "I don't know how he imagined that we could live up to his expectations."

"The Prophet only asked us to stick to our choices. That's what you're doing, Lynn. Let Michelle make her own."

She looked up at her beloved husband. "Do you think I'm making a mistake?" she asked, no longer sure of herself. He shook his head, smiled lovingly at her, and leaned forward to kiss her full, warm lips.

Andrew walked away from Michelle who hurried off further away from the group to hide her pain and shame. He spoke somberly with Jeremy. It was agreed that they would stay in electronic contact and that he would meet them in two weeks outside of the Indian reservation where the secret caves would keep them safe. The men hugged warmly, knowing it could be for the last time. Andrew turned to Lynn and hugged her as well. In so doing, he let her know that he did not hold her responsible for his decision. The burden of his future would not be on her shoulders.

* * * * *

The city of San Francisco was in a condition of utter disaster. Electricity had been out for days and bodies still lay rotting in the rubble. Emergency teams could not put a dent in the gigantic catastrophe. The army had been called in and swarmed down upon the city like an invading force. Platoons moved through the debris, shooting looters on sight. Though the government claimed to still be functioning and some attempt was made at returning to normal procedures as though civilization could limp forward through this cataclysm, details like individual rights were forgotten about. Any kind of semblance of law and order could only be maintained at the point of a gun.

Andrew drove carefully over the shattered roadways winding their way toward the city. The closer he got to the Bay Area, the more catastrophic was the damage he encountered. He felt like he was in some kind of bad dream taking place in a surrealistic set that wasn't even trying to look like the reality he once knew. Cars were turned upside down and abandoned like the carcasses of giant metallic bugs littering the countryside. Houses had slid down cliffs and formed bizarre sculptures of death at the bottom. Even the ocean had changed color into a freakish yellowish tint that was profoundly unsettling. Something was wrong at the very heart of Nature itself.

He had contacted Oriana over the WorldNet and was to meet her in a park on the outskirts of the once luxurious haven in Marin County. From miles away he could hear sirens rising with the smoke that darkened three quarters of the sky, announcing the degree of devastation.

The day was heavily overcast by a mixture of thick smoke and grey clouds weighing heavily over the damaged landscape. A harsh wind whistled ferociously and raced about in all directions, carrying with it the stench of decay and toxic fumes. Some turbulent disturbance in the atmosphere was also traumatizing the air currents.

The Bay Area was still in shock from the catastrophe. Emergency crews continued their nonstop efforts to save broken bodies from under the rubble. But now people were so tired that they worked mechanically as though going about some ordinary business. Sirens weren't as blaring anymore or were so taken for granted that they no longer pierced through the air as they once did.

The gas fires were pretty much under control. Thousands upon thousands of homeless were gathering in shelters, haggard and disoriented. It was the first day of relative sanity since the monster quake.

Dressed in jeans and a sweatshirt, Oriana waited patiently near a collapsed concession stand in the park. Her features were marred by fatigue and a strange, distant look in her eyes. This young woman whose mysterious past had entangled her with the freakish cult now found herself with one foot in each camp. The extremity of the situation rendered her as displaced as the sea of homeless refugees who surrounded her for miles around.

She raised her melancholic brown eyes upon hearing a car pull up. Andrew appeared in her field of vision—tall, slender, intense. She watched this man, one of the Prophet's key disciples, approach her. This would be the first time she encountered someone from the inner circle of the man who had announced this terrible drama. She stood to let him know that she was the one he had come to find, although there was no one else in the area.

He came within a few feet of her and stopped.

"Oriana?" he asked coolly.

She shook her head and studied his angular features. The former intellectual had been remolded by the shattering experiences of the recent past. There was a quality of sensitive perception shimmering in his eyes, born out of his close encounter with the Final Prophet and the traumatic events that had followed in his wake.

"What do we do now?" he asked.

"Let's talk," she answered, eyes glazed over with an emotionless expression.

Andrew looked around to make sure the area was safe. There was not a soul anywhere. The place was abandoned as people went about the business of meeting their immediate survival needs. Andrew sat down at the concrete picnic table that had survived the upheaval. He studied her carefully as she removed a wave of dark hair wrapped around her face by the angry wind.

"Who are you?" he inquired in a suspicious tone.

"All you need to know is that I'm a friend of Tom."

"I don't know that person."

A surprise look came over her. "Then why are you here?"

"If we can help him, we will, just as he tried to help us. How did you meet him?"

"That's not important," she replied.

"Do you know where he is now?"

"They've got him locked up in the county jail down the road."

"It survived the quake?"

"It did. Frank Lloyd Wright designed it, you know. I guess he knew what he was doing."

"How are you managing to survive?"

"I'm all right. This is not about me."

"Do you have any suggestions as to what we can do for this Tom?"

She removed another strand of hair from her eyes. "You're one of the Prophet's disciples, right?"

Andrew hesitated before responding. His gut told him that it was dangerous to answer that question. But his mind still ruled over him. He hadn't learned yet to give priority to those fleeting intuitions.

"I am."

"And you were traveling with the others before coming here?"

"That's right," he answered, suddenly concerned by her questions. "Why do you ask?"

"I don't understand why you risked coming back," she said sadly. "Where were you headed?"

"With all due respect, that's none of your business."

"I'm sorry ... I was just curious as to why you came back. Would you like to see Tom?"

"Do you think that's possible?"

"Certainly. You can pose as his lawyer or something."

"You mean the government is still doing business as usual in the midst of all this?"

"That's all they know how to do."

"How can we get him out of there?"

"They've got no charges against him. He's done nothing wrong.

I'm sure all they want is to locate your friends."

"Well, that's not gonna happen."

"Maybe we can use the system itself to get him out."

"Not if they've declared martial law. All the rules are suspended."

"We might convince them that a swap is possible?"

"How do you mean?"

"Maybe you can make a deal with them and give them false information for his release."

"Surely they're not that easily fooled."

"You'd be surprised. Especially now that everything's in such chaos."

"I'm prepared to do whatever I can. That's why I'm here."

"Thank you."

Oriana leaned forward and placed her hand on his wrist. He was surprised by her action and unsettled by her soft skin on his. Suddenly her hand squeezed tightly around his wrist and turned into an iron grip.

"What are you doing?" he cried out as he tried to pull his arm away. But he couldn't escape her grip. Before he could make another move, she rose and twisted his arm inside out, a savage look in her eyes. The motion slammed his head against the concrete table. Adrenaline surged through his body on a wave of rage. He tried to jump to his feet. At that moment, the palm of her hand crashed with full force against his extended elbow. He let out a shout of agony as he felt his cartilage tear.

He attempted to stand again in a wild effort to strike back at this sudden attack on his person. But another pair of hands took hold of his head and pulled him back with brute force. He fell off the bench, slamming to the ground on his back. An army boot came down on his throat, cutting off his ability to breathe. He gasped and looked up to find himself staring at a Federation soldier aiming a machine gun in his face. Completely disoriented by the pain and surprise assault, he turned to see Oriana standing a few feet away. At her side stood several soldiers and the most bizarre looking man he'd ever seen. A sadistic grin creased Dr. Tagore's gruesome features. Then everything turned black as he passed out from lack of oxygen.

* * * * *

Andrew was led into a large room lit by dim, sickly green light. The room's atmosphere had a quality of desolation and hopelessness. Several policemen stood in the far end of the room with sullen expressions on their faces that never changed, almost like androids fulfilling their duty.

Raised high over the chairs and tables was the judge's bench. A stern old woman in black robes lorded it over the fellow humans brought before her. Most of the people there were the scum of the earth, uneducated and poor people whose future had died out long ago. There in the center of this wretched crowd and cold authority stood Andrew. He couldn't feel more out of place. Handcuffed criminals were brought in, men who had committed violent acts for a lifetime. They sat in a chair that he soon would sit in beneath the all-powerful robed representative of the Federation.

Prosecutors and lawyers spoke to each other in a language all their own. The lives of the human beings involved seemed irrelevant. It was all a chess game. In the last few decades, no one had outmaneuvered the rule of law. Prosecutors adhered more and more rigidly to the letter of the law instead of its spirit. People were tossed into tiny cells for endless years, regardless of the severity of their crime. The only way to keep order in these chaotic times was to be merciless. No one seemed to notice that it didn't work. Desperation was such that crime continued to soar, people continued their free-fall into psychotic behavior, and jails were packed beyond capacity.

Andrew realized for the first time that once he entered the cave of this monster, he wouldn't come out the same. They wouldn't let him. All the power belonged to the authorities and their primary interest was to crush any deviance from their requirements. The law had long ago forgotten the philosophy that one was innocent until proven guilty. In this day and age, everyone who walked into these dimly lit warehouses ironically called halls of justice was considered guilty. The old statues of blindfolded justice now had new meaning. Justice was indeed blind, but not as it was once understood. The balance that the goddess held in her hand didn't stand for fairness but for control.

Andrew could smell the stale odor of cigarettes and uncleanliness all around him. He wondered if the judge was raised above this mass of miserable humanity to avoid having to take in its stench. Case after case was processed ahead of him. People were sent off to lives of confinement without expectation of rehabilitation. Punishment was the name of the game.

He watched as desperate criminals were presented to the judge and led through a door in the back of the room toward a fate that made his hair stand on end. How did he get to this point? He thought of the insane series of events that had brought him to this unimaginable moment where he was being handed over to the lions who would devour him for certain. The machine of the law would destroy him more effectively than the punks in the street who lusted for blood.

Files were passed back and forth between the judge and her assistants. People were moved through the system at amazing speed. The woman behaved with a strange condescending attitude toward all who came in her presence, acting the part of a benevolent and impartial observer when in fact she had the power to decide human destinies at the blink of an eye. Andrew knew that behind the mask of smooth control and politeness was a Federation-trained puppet whose only purpose was to protect the state or in this case the world government against people like him who refused to step into line with the rest of the sheep. He knew that the moment she opened his file and saw the charges, she would treat him more vehemently than she had the common criminals who filed past her day after day. He was a choice grist for the mill that crushed those who could not be controlled.

He found himself shaking with fear. He had never felt so completely helpless. Already he could imagine the sensation of cold handcuffs squeezing his wrists and the horrifying walk through that back door to a world where there was neither freedom nor sunlight. He thought of the betrayal that had taken place. How could Oriana have done this to him? The woman had no remorse at all. He could almost accept the fact that the lovely young lady was part of some dark conspiracy with the dominators to destroy whatever good was left in the world. What he couldn't accept was that no help from beyond was pulling him out of the grips of this merciless system. He would be rendered useless to the Prophet's cause and his efforts to do right in this wretched world would come to nothing.

The hope that the Prophet's spirit would be present with some of his follower now stirred intense rage. Why was he left out? Wasn't he the one who had given all his material goods to the Prophet's community and risked his life to help his friends? Now when it was his turn to be in need, he was not only betrayed but abandoned by all and left to a fate that no one deserved, least of all those who sought to be helpers of the human cause.

He looked up at the dull panel walls bathed in green, depressing light and listened to the droning on of the judge's voice and the case numbers called out by the bailiff one after the other. There was no room for human feelings here, only efficient destruction of lives. No one who came through this room would be the same afterward and most would wish they'd never been born. Andrew felt that way now, heartsick that he was being thrown into the abyss for having tried to help his fellow humans. He would have been better off becoming one of the dominators like his father before him, a rich contributor to the status quo and guaranteed a life of comfort and luxury. All he had to do was not care what happened to those who were less fortunate. Even with the world devastation, the super wealthy could find ways to protect themselves and satisfy their bodily needs while others died in the cold.

Andrew dropped his head in his hands, trying to clear his mind. He felt nausea rising from the depths of his soul. It was all so unfair. He had given up on human justice long ago, but he held out hope that some cosmic check and balance was in operation. He remembered the moment this set of circumstances had fallen into alignment. Like dominoes, one thing led to another, each furthering his descent into this place of despair.

CHAPTER 16

Andrew was taken into an empty, dimly-lit concrete room in the lower levels of the police station. A wooden table and several chairs were the only furnishings.

"Sit down!" a policeman ordered as he pushed him toward one of the chairs.

Andrew looked back at the brute and shook his head. The man turned red with anger and smacked him in the temple.

"What the hell you looking at? Do what I tell ya!"

He kicked Andrew in the back of the knee, causing him to lose his balance and shoved him into a chair.

"When I tell you to sit, you sit! Is that clear?"

The man abruptly left the room, leaving Andrew in the grim silence of the underground chamber. The contrast to the noise of the courtroom made him dizzy. He was so stunned by the sudden turn of events that he couldn't think straight. He had barely stabilized himself long enough to become aware of his own breathing when footsteps echoed outside the door. A quick pattern of beeps announced the unlocking of the entrance. Two men entered. He was too worn out and distressed to look up.

They sat at the table on either side of him.

"So how are you feeling today, Mister Bradshaw?" a gravely voice asked, full of sarcasm.

Andrew looked up and found himself face to face with the freakish Dr. Tagore. Strands of white hair hung from his skull. The skeletal thinness of his face and grizzled skin from illness or burns gave off an aura of evil. But it was the eyes that especially revealed the reality of his nature. They sparkled with sadistic glee. Andrew had never looked into such perverse energy before. Except perhaps for the fleeting glimpse he'd had of Stefan Zorn when he'd come to their community. He felt certain that the association he had made in his mind between this man and the occult leader was no accident. He sensed that they were linked together, both servants of darkness.

In that moment, he remembered the Prophet's words that they be prepared to face a powerful enemy. It was not until now that Andrew understood what he had meant. His words were more than symbolic. They referred to the very incarnation of evil.

"Do you know what we want?" the strange cadaver-like man asked, eyes sizzling with lust for violence.

Andrew looked over at the other man and saw that he was a high ranking officer in the military. They made a very odd pair. Andrew's mind went into high gear. Obviously, the man of darkness was somehow allied with leaders of the Federation.

"No idea," Andrew said calmly.

Dr. Tagore let out a hoarse chuckle. "Nice try." He turned to the officer.

"Colonel, tell this poor man what he's in for if he doesn't cooperate."

"We've been ordered to apply all available means in order to get the information we need from you," the military man said as though he wished he didn't have to. It was clear that he was under orders and not happy about dealing with the likes of the evil man across the table from him. Strings were being pulled from high up the chain of command.

Andrew looked at the officer. He seemed like a decent sort and he was obviously not looking forward to being turned into a torturer. In that instant, Andrew felt sorry for him.

"Who is this man?" Andrew asked the Colonel, as though he were asking a fellow human about some alien being.

"You don't ask the questions. We do!" Tagore responded.

"Is he part of the government?" Andrew continued, staring directly at the officer, seeking out some kind of humanity in him.

"You're really asking for it, Bradshaw!" Tagore said again, eyes widening as his pockmarked skin turning purple with rage.

"Don't I have a right to know who I'm talking with?" Andrew pressed on, staring at the Colonel. "I'm still a citizen of this country."

"You've got nothing left!" Tagore spouted out venomously.

"Enough!" the Colonel barked, unable to withstand the strange civilian's flaunting of authority. There was only so far he would allow him to invade his territory.

"You're here because you are an enemy of this government and you've confessed it already."

"What do you mean?" Andrew asked, confused.

The Colonel pulled out a small digital tape recorder from his pocket and pressed the play button. Andrew's conversation with Oriana instantly came out loud and clear. It was cued to his words about tricking the government in order to help Tom.

Andrew shook his head. He couldn't believe the immensity of the trap he'd fallen into. His situation was hopeless.

"You have a choice," the Colonel said. Either you give us the information we need and we will provide you with immunity, or you talk to us because you'll want to very badly."

"What are you going to do to me?" Andrew asked defiantly.

"It's gonna hurt real bad," Tagore said, revealing his large brown teeth. He looked more like a demented mummy on the loose than a living human being.

The Colonel looked at him with growing irritation. "We'll fill you with enough truth serum to tell us whatever we want. Surely you know that we have the technology necessary for such purposes."

"I know my rights! I won't say another word until I have a lawyer!"

Dr. Tagore let out a high-pitched cackle. "Everything's changed, Mr. Bradshaw. Nothing is like it used to be. You should know that."

"What do you want with my friends, anyway? We're not going to hurt anybody."

"That's for us to decide," Tagore said, eyes narrowing into slits.

"Who's we?" Andrew asked defiantly.

"Just won't stop asking questions, will he?" Tagore said to the officer. "What are we going to do about this, Colonel?"

"You'd better answer us, mister," the officer muttered coldly, "or we're going to take you downstairs. You don't want to go into the subbasement, believe me."

"This is the United States of America, damn it!"

"This is the world Federation at a time of dangerous chaos," Tagore corrected, "and you and your friends have only added to the instability."

"And *your* friends aren't?" Andrew challenged. He turned to the Colonel. "I'll bet you don't know who this guy is either, do you? Well, I've got a pretty good guess. He works for the forces of destruction. He's your enemy, not me!"

"Be silent!" Tagore shouted. "You have no power here. Your situation is hopeless. Don't make it worse for yourself. Just take him downstairs, Colonel. This is a waste of my time."

Andrew looked sharply at the military officer. "Are you going to obey this goon from Hell? Is that why you rose up the ranks? To be a slave to evil?"

Tagore jumped up and swung his ivory cane at Andrew's head. With surprising speed, the Colonel leaped up and blocked it with his forearm.

"You don't do that!" the Colonel shouted, his face scarlet red. "Law and order still prevail, regardless of whose strings you're pulling."

Tagore turned an unsettled look upon him. He couldn't afford to lose the man's cooperation. He had to swallow back his hatred of Andrew who had outmaneuvered him, even from his position of weakness. The savage man couldn't tolerate not having absolute power. It was his one and only aphrodisiac. But he was too smart to let whatever emotions he had rule over him.

"Sorry about your arm, Colonel," he said apologetically.

"You'll be a lot sorrier if this happens again! This man is in my custody, and we'll follow the rules of war laid down by the Federation."

"Yes sir," Tagore responded, a sarcastic smile distorting his gruesome features. Andrew thought he was going to salute him in mockery. But the man knew better and sat down, straightening his old-fashioned smock.

"Mr. Bradshaw, I'll give you one more chance to save yourself. We're going to find your friends anyway, so why don't you just make it easier on us and on you. They've got no place to go. There's nowhere they can hide. Not from the world Federation."

A strange thought came to Andrew's numbed mind. It had the

flash of sudden inspiration, so he acted on it.

"I'll make a deal with you. You release Tom and let him go free, and I'll do what I can to cooperate."

Tagore looked at him suspiciously.

"Why would you want to do that?"

"That's why I'm here. To let this innocent man go free and take his place."

Tagore focused his gaze deep into Andrew's soul, searching for the strategy he knew had to be there. Andrew stared back at him with a blank look on his face, knowing the man was trying to read his mind. He did his best not to think any thoughts.

"My orders were to free this man. So that's what I'm going to do."

"If you're trying to trick me," Tagore hissed, "I'll have you skinned alive! You have my word on that!"

"You'll do no such thing!" the Colonel responded, outraged. "We'll proceed by the book!" He was getting tired of the freakish man's savage violence.

This time Tagore ignored him and kept staring at Andrew, letting him know silently that his promise would be fulfilled. Unspeakable horror awaited him if he dared to betray him.

"Do you want your information or not?" Andrew said bitterly, wishing he could get his fingers around the evil man's thin throat.

The violent urge struck him like an electric shock. He heard a voice in his head.

"Violence is contagious."

A chill ran through him and beads of sweat appeared on his forehead. The voice was that of the Prophet himself. It echoed in his head more vividly than any memory he'd ever recalled. It was as though his beloved teacher had leaned over and whispered in his ear. The message also came through loud and clear. He realized that the desire to kill had been stimulated by the bestial brutality emanating from the wretched creature across the table from him. The toxic energy had penetrated unconsciously into his psyche. He found himself behaving at the level of this creature from the Netherworld.

Dr. Tagore watched him intensely, seeing the disturbance flash in his eyes. He tried to detect what was going on within him.

"Seal yourself!" the voice said again imperatively.

Andrew focused all his attention on the benevolent order he had just received. An invisible wall rose up between him and Tagore, cutting off the influence the man was having upon him and shielding his vulnerable soul from the dark energies to which he was exposed. His heart raced within him and a hot flash made him nearly faint. This time he knew that those words were not memory but immediate communication from the man whom he had watched die not long ago. The sense of his presence was so powerful that he felt certain the Prophet's spirit was in the room with him, standing behind him and helping him become hermetically sealed to the evil that confronted him.

It was as though the degree of Dr. Tagore's darkness had beckoned forth a light from beyond where the Prophet now lived.

"Are you all right?" the Colonel asked, noticing the change in skin color as Andrew turned ghostly pale.

Andrew managed to control himself enough to nod his head affirmatively.

"I've been fighting off the flue," he responded.

The Colonel accepted the answer, but Tagore knew better. A fierce glint in his eye revealed the heat of violent hate that burned forever in his black soul. He knew that something mysterious was taking place and that worried him greatly.

* * * * *

Oriana sat in the dark room which was hardly larger than a closet and served as her bedroom. She needed silence and obscurity to cover her shame. On the other side of the wall, she could hear the whispered conversations of the other members of her group, the only family she had ever known.

Now every time she saw them, she was filled with repulsion. They had asked too much of her and her lifelong training in the occult arts was not enough to obliterate the feelings rising out of her heart. She was still a human being, despite all the careful efforts of her teachers and companions who had relentlessly attempted to mold her into the perfect servant of their aims, which were now revealing themselves as darkness and destruction.

From earliest childhood, she remembered participating in

mysterious activities and going into trances. Early on, she had become fascinated by the strange tales and rituals that were as much part of her daily life as the making of peanut butter cookies was for other children of her age. Her world was Gothic, grim, and shrouded in secrecy. Madame de Belmar was her aunt, but had been a more of a mother to her since her birth mother had died in a tragic fire that had also taken the life of her father. Dr. Tagore had come in and out of her life at every stage of her development. She had become habituated to his gruesome features long ago, but in the recesses of her soul she was still as frightened of him as when she was child. The evil emanating from him was tangible.

In spite of their bizarre ways and the myths they discussed as though they were headline news, these people nevertheless lived the life of a tightly knit community. They provided her with the basics for survival. She was never in need for food or money. They had taken her to Europe several times where she was treated like a princess by foreign members of the sect. She had adapted well to their secretive life-style and learned all the esoteric texts and teachings that were so important to them. But she had never played with anyone her age or gone to school with her peers. She lived alone like a rare and precious jewel carefully tended and monitored by the dozens of people who made up her family.

Oriana had always been a serious, reflective person. Her inherited clairvoyant gifts were legendary among her companions. Her parents had been key members of the organization, as had their parents before them. They were masters of the more psychic elements of the teachings. Their death had been a terrible loss, even though the details were left unspoken. Among the many ways in which she had been manipulated into becoming a perfect member was the painful fact that they had intentionally distorted her development. Her childhood had been barren of play; her youth was devoid of romance; and now her adult years were entirely focused on the requirements of the group.

Despite their best efforts, tender feelings still bubbled to the surface and the increasingly difficult tasks they gave her only intensified the awakening of that repressed part of her nature. Tom had been the first man to break through the ice of her carefully sculpted facade. The destruction of the Prophet's disciple had served to break in the door completely. Andrew's last tragic look at her before passing out haunted her relentlessly. She couldn't get the image out of her mind. It was stuck there on the screen of her inner eye like some broken monitor that couldn't be turned off.

No book, no tale of ancient fellowships and beings from other realms could overcome the breakthrough of her conscience. All of her training, from advanced self-defense to the study of lost languages, collapsed before that look of agony that pierced her soul. She had never been taught about good and evil, but only about power and weakness. Her companions had fed her subconscious with a sense of duty toward her departed parents. She had to carry on their legacy with this lofty and ancient secret society whose roots reached back into antiquity and whose destiny was finally to be fulfilled in this age.

Never before had she experienced such an encounter with this burning, gut-wrenching sensation of guilt. She'd had nothing to be guilty for prior to these events. Now at the very dawn of her maturing into a full-fledged member of the group, her whole world was collapsing before her. No one had ever told her about right and wrong. All the teachings she had absorbed were couched in the context of warring cosmic forces that titillated the mind but never engaged the heart. There was no avoiding those eyes that had looked upon her and reached into the very depths of her being with one all-consuming question—*why?* Andrew's question was now hers.

Her companions would have given her a quick answer. He was the enemy, interfering with their centuries-old plan, and he had to be destroyed. But that wasn't good enough for her anymore.

She stood up and paced back and forth in the darkness. The makeshift home they had found after the quake was not large enough to provide everyone with private space. This was not the first time that she found herself camping out with the cult members. Life had always been a bohemian journey on the outskirts of society and she had enjoyed the variety that it brought into her life. Until today. Everything had lost its savor. What was once an adventure now felt like a gloomy repetition full of sound and fury signifying nothing. Nothing except the destruction of other people.

If she could question one aspect of their mission, then everything was up for grabs. The look in Andrew's eyes was inescapable. Something was terribly wrong and no brainwashing in the world could keep her from seeing the tortured eyes of the man she had trapped and captured to satisfy the secret goals of the mysterious group. Somehow, the Egyptian symbolism and ritualistic formulas, talismans and antique ornaments now sounded empty and looked old and withered, even absurd.

Pacing in the tiny room, she became aware that the narrow confines surrounding her represented perfectly the condition of her entire life. She had never been let out of the closet. She had lived an inbred existence, fed only what the group wanted her to think and feel. They had never let her out in the light of day where she might form some opinions of her own. Despite her brilliant intelligence and encyclopedic knowledge, she suddenly realized that she had never had a thought of her own. She was a machine full of recordings she had stored away in the libraries of her mind. She could teach postgraduate classes all they'd ever want to know about the sources of Freemasonry and the secrets of the high priests of early Egyptian Dynasties. She could write a whole series of books on occult symbolism and its travels through time, but she couldn't tell simple right from wrong.

Oriana was horrified at the creature she had grown into. She felt like vomiting every time the sensation came back to her of twisting Andrew's arm and cracking his elbow. She was a black belt in Goshu Shorei karate and had long gotten use to physical contact as though it was merely mathematics of the body or some intensified dance. It never penetrated her heart that it was savage and brutal. Even physical abuse was justified by the principles and mission of the arrogant group. When she was younger, she couldn't dare question the wisdom of her ancestors and the awesome figures that were quoted to her on a daily basis—Madame Blavatsky, Jacques De Molay, Pharaoh Sequenenre II, Aldous Huxley and all the rest. They were mythic figures, heroes of her past. She had come to know them in a way that other children enjoyed the heroes sold to them on television. She'd been told that the man known as the Final Prophet was the arch enemy, the one who would interfere with the ultimate purpose of this ancient lineage, a purpose which was nothing less than the domination of humanity.

She'd been given a thousand reasons why higher intelligences needed this work accomplished and what the consequences would be if humans were not brought to their knees in the worship of forces who were said to rule this part of the universe. Gnostics myths and archetypal psychology had taken her so far from simple reality and common sense that she had lost sight of her humanity.

She brought her hands to her face and was surprised to find that her cheeks were soaking wet with salty tears. She couldn't remember the last time she had wept. That again was a clue as to how far she had drifted from her essential self on the current of illusion generated by her leaders. Now Madame de Belmar, Dr. Tagore and the rest of them seemed so ugly, evil, and dark. How was it that she had never seen that before? She remembered how the beady, glimmering eyes of the repulsive doctor had lit up with a perverse joy at Andrew's capture and literally turned her stomach. Madame de Belmar had taken the place of her mother long ago, but behind her dignified, aristocratic features she was as cold as ice. The high curvature of her eyebrows now revealed the haughtiness of her nature rather than the stamp of nobility Oriana had always attributed to her. In one horrifying shift of scenery, these people were now revealed in all their sordid nakedness— grisly, heartless creatures who served ignoble purposes.

Oriana had never really been told what the great mission was, but she was assured that she would be initiated into the secret when she got older. She had accepted that, patiently and with reverence. Now two men faced possible death because of her naivete and her lack of discernment that had allowed her to betray both of them for some fantasy she no longer even understood.

The door to her room swung open. The tall silhouette of Madame de Belmar stood in the light.

"What's the matter?" she asked in a husky voice.

The woman peered at her with the eyes of a cat on the hunt, searching out the mind of the young woman who wept in the dark.

No words came to Oriana's mind. She spoke four languages, had memorized an entire Thesaurus, but not a single word—not an adverb—came to her mind. This woman whom she had admired all her life, though she'd been distant and unaffectionate, now seemed like a predatory fiend. Her changes in perception were happening so fast that Oriana thought she was losing her mind.

"I asked you a question," the woman stated coldly.

"I'm confused," Oriana finally said.

Lying was foreign to her. She didn't know how to do it, although she had learned to repress her more vulnerable feelings over the years.

"Don't let that man poison your mind."

"What man?"

"The man from the park."

"He's not . . . "

"Yes he is!" Madame de Belmar interrupted. "You're upset with what you had to do, aren't you?"

Oriana nodded, although it was only half the truth. But it was close enough. She realized that lying wasn't that hard after all. It could be very safe.

"His poison is contagious. Beware."

"Why did we have to do this?"

"We've discussed these matters thoroughly! We thought you were mature enough to deal with this. Don't disappoint me, Oriana."

"I don't want to do that," Oriana said, lying again.

"We thought you had the inner strength and skill to be useful to us."

"I did too," Oriana mumbled, finally speaking the truth.

"It certainly doesn't look like it. Why can't you just see it as crushing a nasty bug to protect your garden?"

"He's not a bug, he's a human being."

"He is a bug!" the woman growled. With that sound, all of her feminine beauty vanished, revealing eyes full of hate and violence, a terrain where no beauty could grow.

"This man would enjoy seeing us all shot! Why do you feel sorry for him?"

"I no longer understand why he's our enemy . . . He seemed like a good person."

"Don't be so naive, Oriana!" the woman responded angrily, her features tightening with disdain. "I've told you before. It's a problem you've got to deal with head on. You know nothing about the world and you're easily fooled. Besides," she said pulling out a thin cigar from a gold case which she lit with the expertise of long habit, "being a 'good' person is not something to be admired. It's weakness and foolishness as the masters have said. Instead of whimpering in the dark, you should be proud of what you've done."

She leaned against the doorway and inhaled the acrid smoke, letting it return into the air through her tight, thin nostrils. "You overcame an adversary with physical force. That was an initiation for you and you succeeded. This behavior you're exhibiting now is very disappointing to me."

She turned her glare upon the young person she had brought up as her own.

"I thought you had reached a new level of strength."

For her entire life, Oriana had submissively accepted the reprimands of this harsh woman. But this time, something struck her as unbearably wrong. She couldn't be passive anymore. She stepped into the dim light in the doorway.

"What is so brave and noble about luring someone into a trap and breaking his arm while having a friendly conversation?"

A slight smile crossed Madame de Belmar's heavily made-up lips. They clashed with her blonde-died hair. Despite her deep beliefs in esoteric philosophies, she was as intent upon delaying the ravages of age as any woman who lived on the surface of her nature where vanity ruled.

"Think of the big picture. Think of our mission and the culmination of generations who are a part of you. You're fulfilling their dream. You're a player in a mighty drama and you took center stage for a moment. We all depended on you and you came through. This whining makes me sick!"

She inhaled the sweet smelling smoke and released it with a long sigh. "Get hold of yourself. I don't want the doctor to find you like this."

She had always referred to Dr. Tagore as "the doctor." After all these years, Oriana still didn't know what kind of doctor he was— medical or academic. Maybe he wasn't a doctor of anything. She had only recently begun to wonder what the history of this strange couple might be. They had been together her whole life, an odd platonic twosome united around common goals. She was a stunning aristocratic beauty while he was a man whose ugliness was unparalleled, except perhaps in burn wards. Now Oriana was being told to shape up in order not to disappoint him also.

"I did what you wanted me to do. Isn't that enough?" she blurted out.

"No, it isn't!" the woman said, looking into her eyes. "We need to count on you still. We can't afford to have any doubts. It's all just beginning. There is a long way to go."

"You expect me to brake someone else's arm?"

Madame de Belmar placed the thin cigar between her teeth and gritted the stem with anger. "I expect you to do whatever we require of you and have no opinion on the matter! Just like everyone else here."

She stepped forward, within inches of Oriana. "Maybe I've spoiled you too much. You think you're different from the rest of us. But you're not. You'll give your all to our mission—your life if you have to—and you won't complain or question ever again!"

The women studied each other defiantly. Oriana knew that their relationship would never be the same. It was the first break with the woman's hold on her soul. Madame de Belmar saw it all in her eyes.

"And if you don't show your total loyalty at all times, I'll turn you over to the doctor."

Her eyes narrowed with a hatred that made Oriana's blood run cold. They had never been close, but she had never seen such venom in the woman's behavior. Nor had she any idea of what the implications were in the threat. But she could sense that much was left unsaid as though the woman was somehow jealous of her. - Apparently, she had been standing between Dr. Tagore and Oriana's safety for many years.

"And if that doesn't take care of things, I'll go to the master himself."

The master . . . Oriana had only seen him a few times in her life. But it was all she needed to know about real power and danger. Stefan Zorn had only glanced at her and she'd had nightmares for years afterward.

CHAPTER 17

The jail door slide open with a strange iron hiss and Andrew was pushed into a dark, smelly cell. The force of the policeman's thrust landed him against the humid wall. He heard the heavy door slide back and an electronic lock shut him in like the lid of a coffin.

For a moment, he remained in that position, his cheek pressed against the cold concrete block. He had a sudden urge to weep, to let go and release his emotions in a torrent of angry tears. Instead, he took a deep breath and fought to regain control of himself. He couldn't afford to crack, not now, not after experiencing that extraordinary contact with the Prophet.

With great effort, he turned himself around and faced his situation. It took a moment for his eyes to adjust to the darkness. The small room was lost in shadow, except for the shape of a bed which detached itself from the darkness. He looked for a light source and noticed that there were no lamps anywhere. The cell was intended to remain in darkness. That alone was cruel and unusual punishment. But Andrew was not surprised. He knew in whose hands he was in now. Anything was possible.

The fact that the Federation was somehow in league with the servants of darkness was enough to know that his fate was sealed, as well as that of the planet's inhabitants. If the earth changes didn't destroy everyone, a corrupt world government would. He'd always sensed that there was something rotten at the Federation's core. All its efforts for effective control of the global population were not motivated from care but from the need to dominate. Why should he be surprised to find that they were in league with demonic powers. Wasn't that the fuel of every other world power throughout history, from the Third Reich to the Roman Empire? If such allegiance did not directly involve them with the sons of darkness, as the Essenes named these forces, at least the key leaders were manipulated by these forces. How else could one explain the atrocities inflicted on humankind?

An onslaught of gory visions filled Andrew's mind—thousands of crosses lining the road to Jerusalem, on which victims cried out in a chorus of unbearable moans. Then he saw, in a flash of fire and smoke, countless stakes raised through the centuries to burn people accused of thinking for themselves.

Andrew shook his head, horrified at the sudden appearance of these awful images in his mind. He didn't know where they were coming from. He had the odd feeling that these terrible sights lingered in the wake of Dr. Tagore's aura. The man's very proximity made Andrew frantic with the need to wash himself. He had never been so close to pure evil. It took another breath for him to find stability. He remembered that the Prophet had warned them in no uncertain terms as to the nature of their enemy.

Someone coughed.

Andrew turned with a jolt toward the bed. A form detached itself from the darkness. It was sitting on the bed, staring at him. An intuition struck Andrew again. Ever since the Voice had rung in his ears, he'd been flooded with intuitions passing through his mind like shooting stars.

"You wouldn't be Tom by any chance, would you?"

The silhouette reacted strongly to hearing his name.

"How would you know that? Who are you?"

"I'm the guy who came to help you out!" Andrew said with a twinge of irony in his voice.

Tom approached him. A greyish light leaking in through the door's tiny square window illuminated the two men's features as they faced each other. Deep circles were carved in Tom's features beneath his eyes and he hadn't shaved for days. He was as pale as a ghost, although no paler than Andrew. Both men were traumatized by having fallen into the Federation's grip.

"Who are you?" Tom asked.

"That's the question I have for you," Andrew said, trying to see his features in the shadows.

"You must be one of the Prophet's people," Tom responded in a sudden burst of hope.

Andrew shook his head sadly. "I am, but as you see I've failed in my efforts to assist you."

Tom grabbed his shoulders, filled with enthusiasm. "I'm so glad to see you! I had a feeling that I wouldn't be left alone."

"Take it easy, Tom. I'm not gonna do you any good."

But his words had no impact on Tom's joy. "I knew someone would come!" he said again.

"Why would you think that?" Andrew asked, suddenly haunted by another intuition.

"Because the Prophet came to my rescue!"

Now it was Andrew's turn to be filled with energy. "What are you talking about?"

"I heard his voice as clear as I can hear yours!"

Andrew heard his heart pounding in his ears. But he was still suspicious.

"How did you know it was his voice? You never knew the man."

"I knew it was him ... He brought one of his disciples back from the dead to save me when the quake struck!"

"What are you saying?" Andrew cried out, his face turning a scarlet red.

"This old man, a Mister Ivanovitch ... "

"What about him?" Andrew asked urgently.

"He was crushed by a huge cement block. I saw him appear out of the wreckage when I was unable to get out of the house. There was no way that he was still alive. A supernatural power held him up ... as an answer to my prayer."

"How do you know it was the Prophet's power?"

"Because he spoke to me, and I just knew it was him."

Andrew couldn't question him any longer. Having heard the voice himself, he knew that it was more than familiarity and memory that identified it as that of the Prophet. Something about its very presence carried with it the identity of the being who voiced it.

The two men looked at each other for a moment, not knowing what to say. The fact that Andrew had just experienced the same phenomenon made it more difficult for him to reject Tom's statement. He was still in shock himself from his encounter.

"So you came to help me ... That's a beautiful thing," Tom

said, tears glistening in his eyes.

"Doesn't look like I'm going to do you much good," Andrew responded grimly.

"But you found me and have come to my side. That gives me incredible hope . . . "

"Hope for what?"

"Hope that anything might happen."

"Those are pretty thick doors locking us in. And the Federation has a special interest in our case. They won't let us fly away."

"Still, they've put us together. Why would that be, do you think?"

Andrew's mind suddenly came into full focus, as though he'd been kicked awake. There could only be one answer to that question. One that he hadn't caught onto right away. They were being electronically monitored. Every word was carefully recorded. To his horror, Andrew realized that they had already let out the mystery of the Prophet's contact with them. He looked into Tom's eyes and the hardness of his glare quieted the young man. He strained to understand what was being said to him in silence.

After a brief moment, he got the message and he also realized that it was not for his convenience that the two had been put together. Tom swiftly turned around and went to sit on the bed.

"Can you tell me about him?" Tom finally said, unable to restrain his need to know.

Andrew stood in the shadows, listening to his heartbeat pounding in his ears, knowing that someone was listening to his every breath. But he also knew that to describe the kind of man the Prophet was could not possibly hurt anyone. It could only be a comfort to them and of no value to the Federation.

"His eyes were incredible," he said slowly, drifting back into golden memories of his time with the one they called the Final Prophet. "He could see right through you, to the depths of your being. Sometimes I felt like the little boy I'd once been when he looked at me, as though he could see my whole life at once and conjure it forth out of my subconscious. I also felt he could see the future, my future and who I would be. The first time he ever looked at me, he knew me better than I know myself."

Tom smiled. He'd been waiting his whole life to hear about

someone like this. He had tried to invent him in his little paperback fictions, but he'd never come close to the real thing.

"When he spoke, his words came out of the deep silence where he lived. They were serene, and brilliant with wisdom. He never spoke too much or too little, just the right words at the right time."

Andrew's throat tightened as he remembered the man who had become more than a teacher, but a friend as well. He slid down to the floor and crossed his legs in half lotus position, resting his body comfortably for the first time in days.

"His calm was palpable. Yet his aura was so intense that it was like feeling an ocean breeze in your face every time you came near him. His peace, stability and goodness were contagious."

They sat in silence, letting the words soak in.

"There was also power, electric, radiant, supernatural power all around him. He was like walking thunder. But it was always kept under control, never used in negative ways although there was the sense that he could fry you alive merely by focusing his attention . . . Maybe that was the most amazing thing of all—his awareness. Every time he came in a room, everybody's consciousness heightened because of his. He was aware of everything all around him. Before such a presence, it was impossible to be in a slumbering, automatic state in which things happened just out of habit and momentum. Every gesture, every instant of time was filled to the brim with this electrifying awareness that absorbed everything and yet was affected by none of it. He was his own universe, though intimately linked with the external one."

A shiver went up Tom's spine and he felt goose pumps cover his body. He'd never thought he would cross paths with such a person in this day and age, even in such an indirect manner.

"He could be full of humor and simple joy, like a child," Andrew continued. "You could tell that he loved colors, flowers, the ordinary things of life. He appreciated them more than anyone I've ever seen. He never missed the aroma of cut grass or of oncoming rain. His senses were more acute than anyone else's. And yet there was always the awareness that there was something there besides his senses, which enjoyed what they received but was also master of them. He told us once that our consciousness was not tied to the body, that even if our brain was dead there could be the presence of consciousness. It is not the result of organic activity, but a magnetic field that surrounds the body and is independent of it.

"He taught us to tap into that field and live there rather than merely in the sense-based world."

"Have you achieve such a state?" Tom asked timidly.

"Just in moments . . . Then I'm dragged back down by anxiety or fear or simple daydreaming. But when I'm in those moments of awareness and remembrance of my higher nature, I enter a peace that passes all understanding. These are the moments that make life worthwhile."

Tom realized that this experience was what he had always sought for. He had intuitively sensed that someday he would find it. Little did he imagine that it would be in a Federation cell, facing his mortality like never before.

"You've spent all your time in fantasy land, Tom," Andrew said firmly, as though reading the young man's mind. "You are now given an opportunity to come face to face with the real thing."

"You mean, this situation?"

"I mean the fact that your life's at stake. The Prophet says that it's only when you're intensely aware of your mortality that your perceptions become cleansed and your priorities clear. No more time to waste. Every moment counts."

"So where does all this work on oneself lead?"

"To the capacity to be useful to the human race and to cosmic plans that we know nothing about."

"That's a rather grandiose assertion."

Andrew peered at him harshly through the shadows.

"At a time like this, when everything's up for grabs, we have to think big, no matter how pathetic we are as individuals. Everyone is needed."

"How do individuals combat the Federation or natural cataclysms?"

"Precisely by living more consciously within themselves. Instead of being terrified creatures seeking only to survive, we can maintain some link with meaning and right action. The Prophet says that's when we become useful."

"Does that mean that I could be useful?" Tom asked in a hushed voice.

"You bet!"

The two men looked at each other in the darkness. Tom sensed a new energy rush through his body. Despite his precarious situation, Andrew's words were a call to arms, a call to join the ranks of the warriors of light where he'd always wanted to be.

"How can we be helpful under these conditions?" Tom wondered, pointing at the walls that stood between them and their freedom.

"We are meant to be instruments of higher forces. They will help us get out of here!" Andrew stated with a faith he had never thought himself capable of. In these dangerous moments, a new confidence arose from a place he'd never encountered within himself and that he didn't know existed.

"We both heard this voice," he continued. "We both have proof that we're not alone!"

"A voice can't break walls down!"

"I wouldn't be so sure about that. I've heard of a primitive Indian tribe who would gather around a tree and shout at it until it fell to the ground. The same thing can happen from the psychic realm."

Andrew suddenly put his hand in front of his mouth. "We're doing it again!" he whispered, waving his arm in the air, motioning to an invisible surveillance system that tracked every word they spoke.

For now, they would have to wait in silence.

* * * * *

Stefan Zorn's garden was a bizarre, Gothic design thick with exotic vegetation and gargoyles. Statues from Greek mythology appeared beneath heavy foliage that was carefully landscaped to look wild and threatening. A small waterfall added the odd impression that nature's sanctuary had been caged in with these dark statues, reflecting the presence of the underworld. The earthquake and storms had shattered a third of the statures, but even in their cracked and dismembered state, the stones fit right in with the ghoulish landscape.

This garden was Zorn's private space where he did much of his nefarious thinking. The home itself was designed according to the finest technological standards and could withstand the earth's most violent shaking. Some shingles and windows were shattered, but the high-tech structure had survived.

Sefan Zorn walked through the greenery, followed by his two faithful servants, Dr. Tagore and Madame de Belmar. He was impeccably dressed in a black satin shirt and tuxedo pants, as though he were preparing for an entrance to some formal engagement. His charcoal locks were greased back away from his massive face and tied into a small pony tail at the top of his thick neck.

He might have been considered a handsome figure by some if it weren't for the hateful glare knotting his heavy eyebrows together and making his eyes black and fierce. He turned around and aimed his toxic gaze at the strange couple.

"Why didn't you tell me this earlier?" he bellowed.

The two aristocratic leaders had lost all their arrogance in the presence of their master. They looked rather like terrified school children, fearing punishment and ashamed of their ignorance.

"We thought you would know," Madame de Belmar ventured, her lower lip trembling in sheer terror.

Stefan Zorn growled, sounding more bearlike than human. "Your job is to inform me of every development, especially when it comes to the cursed Prophet's followers."

"We sent word as soon as he was arrested, sir," Dr. Tagore said in a high-pitched whisper.

"When did it become clear to you that he was being communicate with?"

"I myself did not hear anything. I saw a change in his demeanor and a feeling in the atmosphere."

"What are you talking about?" Zorn asked impatiently.

"Something electric was in the room that had not been there a moment before. I sensed a presence."

"And you waited twenty-four hours to let me know?"

Zorn moved toward him with unleashed fury. Tagore turned more ghostlike than his usual freakish appearance.

"I'm sorry, master."

"That's not good enough!" he shouted, blowing strands of the doctor's hair away from his forehead. He poured his dark glare into Tagore's fearful eyes. "There will not be a next time!"

"No, master."

Zorn turned his violent hate toward the beautiful, aristocratic woman who now looked like a wilted plant. "When did he inform you?"

"Last evening . . . "

"And you waited twelve hours to get the information to me? Wanted to get your beauty rest, was that it?" Zorn asked with a sneer.

Dr. Tagore cleared his throat to keep his voice from trembling. "Master, we did not realize that this matter required your immediate attention. There is no way to tell if this was imagined or not."

"Since when did you confuse imagination with the spirit realm? I thought you were a more advanced initiate!"

Tagore couldn't answer. He looked down at his feet, humiliated. Zorn stalked away and looked at a pile of debris that had once been an expensive antique statue. Though he was often consumed with rage, he had developed his will power to such a degree that he knew how to stay focused on the priorities at hand. He would deal with his followers' incompetence at a later time. Now he had to confront this unexpected occurrence before it interfered with his plans.

"Here's what I want you to do," the dark man said without turning around. "Bring me this Andrew and we will get the information we need from him, I'll guarantee it!"

CHAPTER 18

Lynn awoke with a frightened cry and bolted upright. Her face was gleaming with sweat and her body convulsed in shivers. As her eyes focused, she looked around in the darkness, completely disoriented. She didn't know where she was. After a moment, she recognized the dreary motel room that they had rented for the night. Its alien shadows and grim surroundings did not comfort her in the least.

Jeremy was pulled out of a deep sleep from her anguished sound and sat up beside her. He placed his arms around her.

"Sweetheart, what is it? Another nightmare?"

She couldn't speak and just shivered in his arms. He tried to soothe her.

"Another nightmare . . . " he said as he pressed his lips on her moist forehead. "Tell me . . . "

"This was more than a nightmare," she finally managed to verbalize.

"Another vision?" he asked, suddenly alarmed. His wife's nocturnal experiences were often brimming with clairvoyant insight. "What was it?" he asked again, hoping that her talking about it would exorcise it from her psyche.

"Andrew . . . " she whispered in horror.

"What about him?" Jeremy asked, a knot tightening in his stomach.

"He's surrounded by evil."

"Tell me more!"

Adrenaline flooded Jeremy's mind and body, awakening him completely. "The Federation?"

"No, worse, much worse."

"What could be worse than that?"

"Evil itself."

It was Jeremy's turn to feel a shiver of terror rush up his spine. The shadows of the room turned menacing for him as well.

"What else?"

"They want something from him. They'll torture him for it. We've got to save him!"

"How?"

"I saw the girl . . . "

"What girl?"

"Oriana, Tom's friend. She'll help us . . . even though she's one of them. My God, we sent him right into a trap!"

An intense shiver shook Lynn's body, this time not from the nightmare but from the guilt she felt. "She can help us!"

"Why would she do that if she's one of them?"

"She didn't want this. I can feel it. She's not like the others. There's some humanity left in her soul."

"How do you know?"

"In the dream, I looked into her eyes and I saw it. More than that, she was calling to us."

"What if this is just fantasy?" Jeremy had to ask.

"I just know," Lynn said firmly. Jeremy understood that when his beloved knew in such a way, it came from a place that couldn't be questioned. He had confirmed this too many times in their life together.

"How will we find this person?"

"She'll find us if we make ourselves available."

"Can we risk endangering all of us?"

"No, just me."

"No way!" Jeremy cried out.

"She's got the gift. We'll find each other. No one else can interfere."

"You're not going anywhere by yourself, that's just not going to happen. Not when the world's crashing in on itself. If you feel you must go back, then I'll go with you. Michelle can take the others to safety."

"She'll insist on joining us. We won't be able to keep her from doing so. And it wouldn't be right to stop her from helping Andrew now."

"She's the only other one who knows the way to the caves."

"Contact Brave Eagle. We're not that far. Have him lead them the rest of the way."

"It's going to take my finder's ability to get to him."

Jeremy shook his head. He hadn't heard her use that word in ages. But he certainly knew what it meant. The gift had manifested several times at crucial moments. Lynn was indeed a finder. Her clairvoyance and intuitions made it possible for her to perceive the path to a certain goal, to find the right person, to be at the right place, to discern the right moment. She was like a magnet, pulled toward what was destined to occur. He knew better than to question that skill. It was the very one that had linked him with the Prophet and their ultimate destiny.

"Just look out there," Lynn said, pointing toward the road winding below the motel and drawing his attention to the bumper to bumper traffic that shut the highway down to a crawl for hundreds of miles. "It'll take us a week to get to the next state."

Desperate people were fleeing the epicenter of the quake, not realizing that the earth changes were occurring everywhere. There was no place to hide.

"Look at the lanes going the other way," she observed. They're completely free of traffic. No one is heading back to the devastated cities along the coast. "It would be easier for all of us to go back and do what we need to do. By the time we get back to this spot, we won't be far behind where we'd be if we went forward now."

"How do we keep the others out of danger? We can't expose Juanita and the baby to any of this."

"We'll have them stay outside the city limits while we go in."

"Why not let them stay here? We've got enough money to pay for several weeks of rent."

Money was the least of their problems. Andrew's generosity had seen to that. Despite the out of control inflation that was doubling on a daily basis, they had enough to keep themselves going for months.

"You've got to convince me how you're going to find this person before we make the decision."

"She's a seer. I will contact her telepathically."

"That's not much of a guarantee."

"Jeremy, if you'd seen what I saw in my dream, you wouldn't

wait another five minutes. Andrew's fallen into the hands of sheer evil. They will destroy his soul as well as his body. We've got to get him out at all cost."

"Just a few days ago you were arguing the other side, saying it was better to sacrifice one for the good of all."

"Not this kind of sacrifice! It would overshadow anything we did in the future."

Jeremy stood up and went to the window. He waited in silence for the decision to make itself known. Strangely, his mind was vacant of all thought. He found himself intensely present to the moment, breathing in the cool night hear seeping through the window. This was a terrible decision to make and it made him feel ten years older. If he were to catch his reflection in a mirror, he wouldn't be surprised to find streaks of white hair on his head. He took a deep breath and listened to the peacefulness. In the distance, countless refugees headed toward a promised land that would not be there.

"All right, we'll go back. I'll leave Robert in charge and we'll stay in touch with our radios as long as our batteries last."

Lynn closed her eyes and said a silent prayer, not for themselves but for Andrew who was caught in the jaws of hell because she had sent him there. She felt better already knowing she might be joining him in that abyss. Fear was less intolerable than remorse.

* * * * *

The giant earthquake seemed to have broken the ice. A domino effect expanded across the globe. Fierce winds whipped over the continents. Volcanoes erupted like never before. The entire country of Japan was swallowed up. Within a week, the world's economy had collapsed. International commerce was interrupted by the cataclysms. Societies crumbled overnight under the weight of the calamities. Hospitals that were still functional were crammed with the wounded and the dying, always packed and serving as temporary morgues.

The Federation's world army turned on its people and tried to save some vestige of control over the absolute chaos that inevitably came with mass destruction. Cities in every country were in ruins and destitute of order. Electricity was cut indefinitely to millions upon millions who had depended on it in every way. The complex technology on which twenty-first century civilization was built revealed itself as a fragile giant with no footing. Once the plug was pulled, two centuries of advancement fell into a black hole, taking humanity back to a dark age, this time without the wherewithal to survive. Nature was now a constant threat, humankind's greatest enemy. Once the cosmic mother of the species, providing for all her children's needs, she now turned against them. Her fury was unquenchable. She had been raped for too long and the time had come for retribution.

As lights went out on world civilization, Nature herself was plunged into a new age of dramatic upheaval. The shifting poles disfigured lands everywhere. Weather turned insane—shattering rains no one had ever seen before, winds whose velocity could snap the necks of people caught in their grip, and thunder that fell on mutilated ground with the ferocity of bombardments from above, as from enemy war planes.

Two thirds of the population were without proper shelter. Nature seemed to take advantage of their exposure to ensure their destruction. If falling debris didn't crush them, then the elements would. People banded together in desperate groups, instantly becoming animal-like in their efforts to stay alive. Along with the shutting down of the computer age, the light in the human soul seemed to go out as well. Humanity had been preparing for a century to enter this age of horror where basic goodness and decency no longer even made sense. Generations of unloved children and even more generations devoid of wisdom regarding their purpose for being, set the stage for the species' self-destruction. The specter of a global death wish had shown itself vividly in the international media that fed the masses like a mother's milk. People who loved to see barbaric acts and violence could now live them out in the shadows of devastated societies. Murder, rape, pillage were a daily occurrence and as ordinary as rush hour traffic had been just a week before.

The gruesome jungle law of the survival of the fittest was all that was left of the wisdom of humanity.

General MacDaniel relished his new role as ruthless dictator. This was the part that he had readied for all his life. There were no boundaries now. Men of war could run rampant over civilians with orders to shoot to kill. They no longer needed to face a specific - enemy. Everyone was the enemy. People were shot in the streets for the smallest infraction. Encouraged by Stefan Zorn's suggestions, the general turned the world's nightmare into his private playhouse. The military's emergency communications system was all that was left of the WorldNet. Once people's batteries had died out, there would be no way to communicate except through the secret systems of the Federation. The world was theirs to dominate and plunder. But even this was an illusion. They could never shoot enough people to bring order back. The mayhem was out of control and descending at warp speed into a savagery that would eventually consume the Federation itself. Brutality and madness was contagious and spreading through the military ranks as well as the civilian population.

Corridor 600 became the busiest hallway in the military complex as secret meetings took place. Around the clock, the fate of nations was decided in these back rooms where a dozen high ranking officers and financiers made choices with the stroke of a pen or a phone call. Satellite cameras pumped in live video from the most explosive regions where infantry could not penetrate and where rebel leaders were threatening to engulf other populations. The secret audience simply picked and chose who would be carpet bombed and permanently "stabilized".

General MacDaniel was at the center of it all, and the most influential voice whispering in his ear was Stefan Zorn whose powers had completely locked onto the military man's mind and soul like tentacles from a deadly octopus. Zorn had made himself his most trusted advisor, even satisfying his more private desires with his accomplished devotees, sending the man's soul reeling down into an abyss of perversion that made him the perfect instrument. The arrogant officer went about his gory business certain that he was the only one in charge with the world's power at his fingertips. Yet every day he became more of a puppet to the true beast who was holding the reins of humanity's future.

Zorn not only discovered the general's fetiches and dark fantasies, but instilled, intensified and aroused them to deepen his hold on the man's will. The more the general thought that he was master of himself, the more he became entwined in the web of the dark master.

"Use it, use the bomb . . . " were words that kept recurring in the general's head as he wandered down the super secret corridor of power on his way to another decisive meeting. Zorn had made sure those words were repeated in different ways, under different circumstances until they were burned in the man's mind and would come forth at the right time. Once the first nuclear bomb had been dropped, the second one would be easier, further disintegrating the last shreds of civilization. Zorn knew the key to the complete annihilation of humanity's soul. The more perverse and violent the act, the more its evil would spread and repeat itself through the darkened unconscious of a species gone mad. It was such a simple affair—pull the rug of comfort and security out from under human beings and they became capable of the most horrific behavior. In this theater of blood and destruction, he had found the way to pull the rug out from under every individual on the planet.

* * * * *

The long, narrow hallway bathed in dark shadows looked just like a secret corridor of power would be expected to appear. Lights were dim but sufficient. The silence was tense. Doors of magnificent polished oak were closed to the world. The corridor was guarded twenty-four hours a day by heavily armed soldiers and the best in surveillance equipment

The gigantic figure of Stefan Zorn appeared at the far end of the hall. Zorn's eyes shimmered in the darkness like black pearls, strangely illumined from within. He wore his usual excessively expensive tailored suit which looked out of place in this Spartan, serene atmosphere known only to grim-faced men in dreary uniform.

But Zorn was not here on usual business. This was the day he would do more than consult and advise the men who held access to the world's weaponry. This was the day when he would apply the final coup de grace in his total dominance of their psyches.

He came to one of the unmarked doors and knocked. It opened and he stepped into a large room that looked like a five star hotel suite. It served as a lounge for the elite in power, but this day it was redesigned as a playroom. The lights were low, giving off the sense of a dungeon rather than a modern conference room. Zorn had arranged the redecorating himself. He was providing a special birthday present for the man whom he had bound in invisible strings. This gift would wrap the most valuable string of all around General MacDaniel who still imagined himself one of the most powerful men in the world.

The general stood in the shadows, oddly out of uniform in a silk robe, and hiding his features out of a last sliver of shame. Other top brass with similar tastes stood in the room, awaiting the ringleader who would expose them to forbidden pleasures they had never dared seek out before.

Zorn was a consummate actor and played his part to perfection.

"Are you gentlemen ready for the time of your life?" he asked slyly.

Whispered responses confirmed that they were now in the palm of his hand. This orchestrated perversion would chain them to him forever. Zorn turned his back on them for a moment to conceal a grin of satisfaction.

He stepped back into the hallway and motioned for the guards at the end of the hall to open the door. Six women and young men entered the corridor, dressed in long black coats meant to hide what they were not wearing. They carried bags stocked with toys that would provide pleasure and pain.

They filed past Zorn with strange, deadpan faces, looking like zombies covered in lavish makeup. They were ready for the job for which they were highly trained but had lost all passion for the freak show they put on. These creatures were skilled technicians and had turned human deviance into an art form.

Zorn watched his employees with cold, calculating eyes. They had long ago ceased to please him. His only aphrodisiac was his dark mission which was now finally manifesting in colossal proportions. His former indulgences had melted down into one all-consuming interest.

He stopped the last woman as she entered the room. Decorated with tattoos and pierced with jewelry, she turned savage, feline eyes upon her master.

"Make sure they take their time," he whispered. "Double the

doses if you have to. I don't want any of them standing when it's all over."

She nodded with no expression.

"If they want to go beyond fantasy, and take somebody out, you let them have their fun. Understand?"

Her icy trance-like look sparkled for a moment.

"You mean . . . all the way?"

He shot a ferocious glare at her.

"That's right. If death turns them on, then give it to them. Sacrifice somebody. It's for a glorious cause."

A wicked grin turned her face evil as she headed into the room.

Zorn watched as the women unpacked their wares and removed their coats.

"Happy birthday," he said in a voice filled with irony.

He closed the door behind him and walked off into the darkness, past secret rooms where the affairs of the world were being determined. But he knew where the real decisions were being made and what would truly generate the future.

* * * * *

Oriana raised her head from her pillow and listened intently. The crumbling mansion was silent except for a whistling breeze shooting through the cracks in the walls and broken windows. She quietly pulled the covers back and got out of bed, stepped carefully onto the wooden floor, and slowly applied her weight to the creaking planks. She tiptoed to the closet and removed her gown. She quickly changed clothes with jeans and sweater that were waiting for her. She hung up her gown and closed the closet door.

Oriana returned to the bed and placed her pillows under the cover to make it look like a form was asleep there. She moved to the door and held her breath as she slowly opened it. She peered out into the hallway. A cemetery silence filled the dark shadows. She knew that someone had to be awake. There was always a watch. She moved passed the closed bedroom doors toward the stairway. Peaceful snoring sounds came from the rooms. Someone groaned in their sleep, stirred by some dark dreams. Her heart leapt.

She made her way down the stairs. At the bottom, she saw a

light seeping below the closed door of the library. She walked passed it and heard a sound from behind the door. She bent down and looked through the keyhole. Dr. Tagore was sitting on the couch in his silk robe, drinking from a large liqueur glass and staring vacantly into the darkness.

Oriana moved on quickly. She knew it was now or never. She made her way to the front door and slipped out into the night. She didn't know where she was going, but she knew she would find what she needed to find. Several hours before, she'd been struck with a strong intuition that the people she needed to discover were nearby. As she had learned to do since childhood, she quieted her mind and followed her intuition. She sensed that the people she was to encounter also had the gift and would find their way to her. This was a first. She'd never met her equal in telepathic insight. But she understood that in this colossal metaphysical crisis, - everything was possible.

She found herself walking in the street, alone and without the protection of street lamps. A great instinctive fear swept over her. She'd never been left to herself in this way, had never walked down a city block all alone. The cult had protected her as though she were royalty. She knew now that whatever purpose they had for her could only bring sorrow, and however much she had come to care for some of them, there was no going back now. She had no doubt that if Stefan Zorn, Dr. Tagore, or her stepmother learned of her treachery, she would be dealt with mercilessly. All those years of upbringing and nurturing would mean nothing. Not for the followers of Stefan Zorn.

She wandered into the night like a lost waif, trusting that each passing breeze would lead her to the shelter she had never found. The only thing that balanced her terror was the sense that the people she would encounter might bring something into her life that she had never known—simple kindness which she longed for now more than life itself. She had gone far into occult esoterica and found it all shallow and worthless without the goal of goodness at its heart.

She wandered through the cracked asphalt that rose in frozen waves all around her, creating an unreal stage for her escape. She had no idea where she was headed, but she knew she was not to stay with the cult a moment longer.

She turned a corner and found that she was heading toward the park. Suddenly, out of the shadows, three men in rags appeared before her.

"Where are you going on this dark night, darlin'?"

The man addressing her was at the far end of human destitution. She knew that she had the ability to deal with his frail stature. He stepped toward her. She could smell his breath and decided that he'd come close enough. With lightning speed, she turned her hips and shot out a side kick, striking the man right at the point where his diaphragm met his solar plexus. He let out a groan and fell backwards into the mound of trash he'd come out of.

The second man stepped forward, this one much bigger and stronger. Neither drunk nor weak, he was one of the many brutish predators who were taking over the city as quickly as the rats that had begun to crawl out from the destruction. For an instant, she thought she'd run back to the house, but then realized what would await her there if she drew such attention to the cult. She would be better off dead.

"You're a pretty one," he said with a wicked smile. The other one grunted, already enjoying the rape he expected to commit.

She stepped back to create a fighting space between them. She threw a kick but the bigger man grabbed hold of her ankle. She was suddenly completely helpless, unable to move her legs and position herself.

"You're mine now, girl!" the other man said as he grabbed her arm and twisted it behind her back. He was already unbuckling his belt.

Frozen in terror, she became incapable of thinking. Any training she had received was washed away in a tidal wave of fear. The young naive woman that she was stood helpless before these sadistic criminals. Then she heard it. A voice different from any she'd ever heard before.

"I am with you. Will you be with me?"

It was as loud and clear as the snarling sounds coming from her attackers. The voice was filled with a strange tranquility that inexplicably gave her new hope.

"Yes!" she cried out. "Yes, I am with you!"

The men looked at her strangely.

"What did you say?"

She was hardly aware of them as a blinding light spread out before her inner sight. Her entire body was set aflame with the thrill of beauty and goodness that entered her consciousness.

"Who are you?" she cried out.

One of the men thought she was talking to him. "You want to know my name?" he asked stupidly. "So you can tell the cops? They're too busy to take care of your problems, that's for sure."

She looked around as though expecting to see a materialization of the voice. The light was nearly blinding her sight.

"*I am with you,*" the voice said again.

Her heart pounded no longer from fear but from the joy of this supernatural encounter, liberating her from everything that had ever hurt her or caused her sorrow. She felt as though cool waters were cleansing her soul from a lifetime of unhappiness and confusion. She blinked her eyes and realized that her sight was crystal clear, despite the darkness, as though the inner experience was intensifying her senses.

"I am with you!" she cried out.

"I know you're with me!" the assailant said as he grabbed her waist.

A car suddenly pulled up alongside them from out of nowhere. Jeremy jumped out.

"Is there a problem here?" he asked angrily as he approached the men.

"You'd better scram boy, or you're gonna get yourself hurt!" the bigger one of the two growled.

"Do you think I'm gonna let you hurt my friend?" Jeremy warned as he looked at the amazed young woman.

"You know her?" the smaller man asked in a hesitating voice.

"That's right! And you'll have to walk over my dead body to touch her! Are you ready to do that?"

The man backed away, but his partner stepped forward.

"If that's what it takes!"

Jeremy stared hard into his adversary's bleary eyes.

"You should be ashamed of yourself, Jim Doyle!" he heard himself say, not knowing how the words came out of his mouth.

The man's eyes widened in shock. "How do you know my name?"

Jeremy had no idea. It had just flashed into his mind.

"You've made your mother suffer over your wrongdoings enough, haven't you?"

Once again, some foreign power had taken control of his vocal cords. The man raised his arm to strike him. Jeremy did not react to protect himself. He heard himself speak again.

"You've done enough damage in your life, Jim Doyle. It's time to stop."

Jeremy's serene voice struck the man in a place deep in his soul, as though his own buried conscience were talking to him. He turned pale and lowered his arm, backing away from Jeremy. Something was tearing him up inside, bringing forth some primordial remembrance of who he once was. Tears sparkled in his eyes, along with immense, incomprehensible fear. He turned away and ran as fast as he could, followed by his companion.

Jeremy was in shock as well. He had only witnessed this sort of thing once before, when the Prophet had spoken to a darkened soul in such a way. Jeremy was certain that it was his teacher and friend who had spoken through him. His whole body resonated with a sense of his mighty presence. A feeling of exhilaration swept through him.

Lynn hurried from the car and took his hand. Her eyes glittered with tears.

"It was him! He's with us!" she whispered in ecstasy. She turned to Oriana who stared at them wide-eyed.

"You're Oriana, are you not?" Lynn asked, knowing the answer already.

The young woman shook her heard, unable to speak.

"My name is Lynn. I've been looking for you. Or maybe it is you who is looking for us. Come." She took her hand and led her like a child toward the car. Jeremy stood on the sidewalk in a trance. Lynn smiled and grabbed his arm. "You'd better get used to these things. The miracles are just beginning."

They got into the car and drove off into the dark night.

CHAPTER 19

"You can't just take off with our prisoners!" the general said angrily as he paced his office. Dr. Tagore stood in the shadows like a scarecrow from another time.

"I was told that you would cooperate with us," he said calmly.

"We have some laws and regulations left in spite of the chaos!"

"Mr. Zorn assured me that you would make an exception for this case."

The general reacted oddly to the sound of the name his visitor had mentioned. But he caught himself and turned with anger.

"He can't have everything he wants! No one can."

The doctor smiled slyly, knowing better.

"This is not a request, general, this is an urgent necessity and we will do whatever we must to procure this man."

"What the hell does that mean?" the general asked, sensing a threat.

"General, I don't want to go into embarrassing details . . . "

"What are you talking about?"

"We have tapes from Corridor 600 that you would not want to see broadcast on world television."

The general rushed at him and grabbed him by the collar, ready to tear his throat out.

"Who do you think you are? You can't blackmail me! I'll crush you like a bug, freak! How dare you threaten me?"

Tagore looked at him fearlessly. Though he'd trembled before his master Stefan Zorn, he had absolutely no fear of ordinary human beings, not even those with control of the world's armies.

"General, I mean no disrespect. If you permit me to show you where we stand, perhaps that will make everything clear."

"What?" the general asked suspiciously.

"Mr. Zorn would like you to take a look at our position."

The general winced at the name and released his grip. He uncharacteristically backed away from his adversary and became passive, though his jaws were still clenched. The name of Zorn had hypnotic properties that affected him in spite of his soldier's will power.

"Go on!"

Tagore put his hand in his coat pocket. The general instinctively went for his pistol. Tagore smiled and slowly pulled out a videocassette. MacDaniel let go of his weapon but was no less concerned.

"May I?" Tagore asked as he pointed to the television set in the corner of the room. The general noted reluctantly.

Tagore walked over toward the large set, trying not to snicker. He slipped the tape into the video player and pushed the play button, knowing that by that little motion of his finger he would gain control of the powerful general. On the screen instantly appeared an orgiastic scene from the dark room in Corridor 600. The general was in the foreground, partially undressed and on his knees before two of the women who had been brought to him as a birthday gift from Zorn.

MacDaniel's face turned dark red. His eyes bulged out of his head. There he was with his perverse sexual predilections exposed for the world to see, and in as humiliating a position as could be imagined.

"Turn it off!" the general cried out.

Before Tagore had pressed the stop button, the general rushed to the video player. He ejected the tape and crushed it under his foot. He looked up at Tagore, ready to kill.

"It's only a copy of course," Tagore said calmly.

"How did you turn my own surveillance system on me?"

"Perhaps you don't understand, sir, that you are not the only man in power."

The general pulled out his weapon with the speed of a gunslinger and pressed it against Tagore's forehead.

"I'll splatter you all over this room! We'll see who's got the power!"

Tagore didn't even blink.

"It would only make things worse for you, general. Don't you think this has all been carefully thought out?"

"Zorn betrayed me!" the general shouted, cocking the weapon and eager to spread blood on the floor.

"I wouldn't say that, general. He provided you with entertainment to your liking and thought perhaps you'd enjoy reliving the moment. The tape was a gift."

"Cut the crap!" the general screamed. "You're trying to blackmail me! What kind of a fool do you think I am?"

Dr. Tagore's silence gave him the answer he didn't want to hear. In spite of a lifetime in the military, he had stepped into a trap that a schoolboy could have recognized.

"What would you do with this?"

"Distribute it by the thousands and put it on international television, or what's left of it."

"You don't have the power to do that!"

"You'd be surprised. You don't seem to realize who we are."

"Who exactly are you?" the general grumbled, keeping his gun pressed against Tagore's head.

"The future."

"What the hell does that mean?"

"We will bring order to this planet . . . with your help. A future of unimaginable wealth awaits you if you cooperate."

"You think you're going to take over the world government?"

"There is no world government now, general."

"How dare you say? I've got millions of soldiers at my command!"

"You must come out of denial, general. The current devastations are only going to get worse and destroy all means of communication. Every society will disintegrate in a very short period of time. Humanity will be reduced to barbarism. No army will keep this from happening."

"So how do your people propose to control things?"

"We have other means."

"What kind of means?"

"From the realm of the occult."

The general holstered his gun and stepped away. "I don't want to hear that nonsense."

Tagore smiled knowingly. "Of course not. But the facts are what they are, regardless of whether you can understand them. As Mr. Zorn has made clear to you, we can work together to our mutual satisfaction."

"How do I get you to destroy the tapes?"

"Cooperate with us. Begin by giving us the prisoner we want."

"Why is he so important to you?"

"No questions."

"Damn it, I'm in charge!"

"Whatever you say, general," Tagore stated, knowing better. "I can tell you this. The prisoner is a follower of the one they call the Final Prophet who was a personal enemy of ours. We have reason to believe that they seek to harm us, which would not be good for you or the ordained future of humanity."

"How do I know you'll destroy the tapes and not use them against me?"

"We will hand you the master copy for your use only. You have our word of honor."

"That's the last thing I'll count on!"

"Mr. Zorn has no desire to create conflict between us. He would not stoop to blackmailing. My job was merely to give you the tape, not to threaten you with it. We wish to work with you, not against you."

"Do you have the master copy on you?"

"We will deliver it to you this very day, as soon as I leave here."

"You do that and tell Zorn not to pull anymore tricks on me."

"As long as we understand each other. Besides, the tapes only show that you are a lucky man. I never had a birthday party such as that. Next time you should invite me."

The general looked at him in surprise. Tagore gave him a lustful snicker as he left the room.

* * * * *

Andrew and Tom were let out of the jail cell, taken down to a lower level toward an underground garage. They walked in grim silence, knowing that nothing good awaited them. The guards were silent and somber as though they too sensed something of the gruesome fate that awaited these men. Both prisoners looked down at the ground, their eyes seeing nothing, their consciousness buried deeply within, seeking to connect with something from another dimension that would comfort them in their trials ahead. They especially didn't want to be present to the realm of the senses that was soon to be horribly violated.

They came out into the garage area. Great fissures cut through the thick cement walls and ceiling. The earthquake had not managed to tear through the high tech fortress of one of the Federation's most secure prisons. Nevertheless, Andrew came out of the recesses of his being long enough to feel a new terror wash over him. This concrete tomb was the wrong place to be at a time of colossal continental shifts. He suddenly felt an unbearable urge to get out of the garage. He looked at Tom who was lost in his own melancholy. Tom felt his gaze and turned to him. He immediately recognized the worry on Andrew's features. In that instant he was struck with the same intuitive urgency to get out immediately. The two men turned to each other and realized at the same that they were receiving a simultaneous communication. This was not imagination or anxiety, but a message from beyond telling them to get out—now!

Andrew searched for an exit as the guards led them toward the armored van and turned their attention to unlocking its doors. It took both of them to slide back the grill inside the vehicle that caged the prisoners. Andrew spotted a light seeping in from an open maintenance door. He looked at Tom and motioned with his head. Without thinking, they both dashed for the door.

"Hey!" a guard yelled. "Don't be stupid!"

The prisoners ran as fast as they could toward the open exit.

"It only leads to the jail courtyard, fools! You can't get away!"

The guard let out a laugh. "That's going to cost you!" he said, pulling out his club. His motion was arrested by the sudden sound of a low vibration that seemed like a growl from below the earth.

"What the hell is that?" he cried out.

Then the ground jerked fiercely below his feet, throwing him against the van. The other guard went sprawling on his back. He shouted as another jolt shot through the ground with such violence that a slab of concrete cracked open and shot upward toward the ceiling, sending cars flying about like insects.

"Get out!" the guard yelled in terror.

A rumble deafened them as the wall and ceiling began to gyrate wildly in the grip of some savage force field. The guards tried to get to their feet but couldn't maintain their balance. The entire surface of the garage was moving up and down as though it was made of liquid, ripping the structure apart. Vehicles slammed together with such force that they were crushed like beer cans. The prison van flew up to the ceiling and came crashing down on the chest of one of the guards. Dust filled the underground chamber, cutting off all visibility. The noise was such that it seemed a giant train was crashing through the walls at full speed.

The ceiling and upper stories slammed down on the shivering garage floor, instantly flattening everything. Tom and Andrew rolled across the courtyard, bounced like rubber balls by the convulsing earth. All around them, everything loose was flying through the air. A soldier on the watchtower crashed through his window and was thrown to the ground, followed by a third of the wall on which his post was perched. The two men looked up at the building behind them steadily sinking in on itself, one cell block after another flattening into the ground, shooting out fragments of metal, glass, and concrete with the force of a machine gun.

"This way!" Tom shouted over the noise. He managed to get on his feet and staggered like a drunkard toward the large breach in the crumbling wall that revealed the countryside. The prison fortress was on the outskirts of the city.

Andrew followed him. They looked like two sailors on the deck of a ship tossed mercilessly by the ocean waves. They leaped through the ruins of the wall as other sections crashed all around them. They fell in the grass on the other side and rolled down a steep hill that shook like a creature gasping for breath. Behind them, the great structure collapsed with a loud roar as tons of concrete shattered over hundreds of people trapped inside.

At the bottom of the hill, Tom and Andrew continued to bounce on the flat surface. It shook back and forth as some nearly supernatural force uprooted trees and ripped roads in half. Despite being unable to stand, the men were grateful that no structure was nearby to crash over them, unlike the millions in the city on the horizon where giant clouds of smoke rose ominously. Though it was only midday, the sky had turned dark purple as the weather responded with spasms of violent reactions to the earth's agony.

Tom felt wet earth beneath him and realized that the ground was cracking open all around them, plowing up the topsoil. Nature had become as terrifying as being in the hands of their torturers.

"Is it ever going to stop?" Andrew shouted as he tried to get control of his body. He felt he was riding a wild bronco whose only aim was to throw him off.

"Watch out for crevices!" Tom shouted back over the roar.

Andrew didn't quite understand at first until he felt his hand enter a hole that hadn't been there a second before.

"My God!" He shouted. "This is no earthquake!"

The smell of fresh mud filled their nostrils as fractures appeared in the grass. An intense gust of wind suddenly swirled around them, sending an icy breeze whipping across their faces. Debris flew by, wrapped in dust devils. The vicious wind shot down from the west with all the force of El Nino. It was as though the continents had moved several degrees and were entering a new latitude ruled by the winds of the open sea which were sweeping across land.

By now boulders from the destroyed prison were flying down the hill, bouncing about like giant soccer balls.

"We've gotta get outta here!" Andrew shouted.

The shaking shifted direction. The men managed to get to their feet and dashed away from the hill, stumbling further out into a field. That very moment, the heavens turned bright with immense thunderclaps.

"Great!" Andrew shouted as they fell into the dirt.

A heavy downpour burst over them, instantly turning their surroundings into thick mud. The men crawled on all fours into the field, creating more distance between them and the deadly fragments of the once mighty stronghold.

A thought came into Andrew's mind, relieving his terror. At least the Federation would be too busy to hunt them down, for awhile anyway. That is, if anyone survived this freakish cataclysm.

* * * * *

The entire west coast was in the thralls of a shattering force that shook the continental shelf. The dreaded polar shift was under way. For the next eight hours, the crust of the earth shifted from its former position as the magnetic fields pushed the planet's core in the other direction. The cosmic tension was so extreme that ocean basins were emptied of their contents. Formerly dry land became the bottom of a new sea. Lands in the north were shifting toward the Equator. No place would be what it once was. No human being would experience life in the same way again.

Giant waves shot across the lowlands, destroying everything in their path. Millions upon millions drowned. Death and destruction were everywhere. Whatever was left standing would be unsafe, all the rest was rubble. Great dams broke, inundating the population below them. It would take generations for the order and symmetry of humanity's architecture to return, if future generations were to rise again.

By the end of the day, as the sunset—made glorious as it sent streaks of light through mammoth clouds of dust and flames that turned global destruction into a thing of beauty—the shift had come to an end. The ground was stable again, but the weather systems were out of control. The magnetic turbulence had whipped up colossal storms and killer winds that would rage for weeks. Any hope now for the maintenance of order and the continuance of civilized life was lost for the foreseeable future. People would have to group together in small communities to sustain themselves with whatever was left of the ruins of technology. Orbiting satellites could still send images from the Federations world headquarters down to receivers, but a third of the viewing audience was dead and the rest scrambling for shelter and food.

Such devastation had not been seen since the atom bombs over Hiroshima and Nagasaki in the previous century. Worst of all were the oceans, raging wildly as though rebelling against the forced transformation of their home. All coastal areas were inundated. Great walls of water tore through everything in their way. Fires were everywhere, from broken gas pipes and downed electrical wires. Explosions would flare up every few moments all over the globe, causing more trauma and tragedy in a situation that was already impossible and unbearable. The Tribulation, foretold by Prophets of all cultures, was upon humanity in full force.

Only the super-wealthy who had prepared for such a catastrophe were in a position to survive it. None was as ready as Stefan Zorn. Before the first shivers had been felt, he had boarded a private supersonic plane that flew him into the quiet space of the stratosphere. There he watched the world crashed in upon itself. Everything was going according to plan. He sat in a large study in the center of the plane, smoking a cigar and listening to television and radio reports from around the world coming out of a bank of monitors and speakers. His wildest fantasies had come true. The world was crumbling at his feet and he would become its master. Then he would turn it into the kind of place desired by the dark forces—a gruesome work colony serving their purposes.

Zorn was one of the few people to know that pain and suffering were energies which fed certain dimensions of the cosmos. It was his mission to harness vast amounts of this substance and he was eager to do so. He turned to another bank of static monitors near the windows of the plane whose shades were drawn. He pressed a few buttons. After a moment, a middle eastern face appeared on the screen.

"I am here, master," the man said in a thick accent. He had the look of an Islamic imam, with beard and turban. But obviously his god was not that of Mohammed nor of the other revealed religions. He was a priest in the teachings of darkness coming out of antiquity before Moses had taken his sandals off on Mount Sinai. His dark eyes made clear what he worshiped.

"Is everything prepared?" Zorn asked.

"All is as planned."

"How many can we count on?"

"Five thousand strong, grandmaster."

"I was hoping for more, Sa'id."

"Some of our people were either killed or made refugees by the cataclysm."

"Weren't they prepared for it?"

"Most of us were. But some were foolish enough to go about their business as usual."

"What about our friends further east?"

"I've just spoken with Ying Chang. They were more careful. We can count on another ten thousand."

"Very good. Stand by."

"Certainly," the man said, bowing his head in submission.

Zorn pressed a few more buttons. Another monitor lit up. A European aristocrat appeared on the screen.

"Lord Havisham, how are you on this fateful day?" Zorn asked with a sneer. "How do we stand with your people?"

"Our brothers and sisters are at your service, and have been in shelters for over a week. Your predictions were most accurate. There are three thousand of us in the U.K., and another six thousand on the continent"

"Very well. Keep them organized and focused on their mission," Zorn ordered.

"Count on us, sir," the Englishman said respectfully.

A few more buttons were pushed and another image formed on a third monitor. A Russian woman appeared, with the features of a bulldog and eyes of fire.

"Madam Oskya, good to see you again."

"It has been a long time, master," she responded with reverence.

"Is everyone safe over there?"

"Da, we knew what to expect."

"I want to speak to all of you at once so that you know that everything is under control. We have access to the power needed to accomplish our goals. There is, however, one detail you need to know. There seems to be some trouble brewing with the followers of the so-called Final Prophet."

"How do you mean, sir?" the aristocrat asked with concern.

"It appears that they have received some communication."

"What sort of communication?" the mid-eastern man questioned.

"From the spirit realm!" Madame Oskya grumbled.

"Precisely," Zorn answered. "There seems to be some contact being established, perhaps by the Prophet himself."

"This is not good," the mid-eastern man stated angrily. "I thought we had taken steps to avoid this."

"There are some things that cannot be fully controlled," Zorn stated coldly.

"Then we must wipe out the followers as soon as possible," the Englishman suggested forcefully.

"That has been one of our goals all along, and we are beginning to accomplish that. There are only a very few left. However, you need to locate those persons who may be in your countries. Only you can identify them. Search them out and destroy them immediately. Even those who are not susceptible to this kind of contact. Anyone of them can become a vehicle for the Enemy. When you take over the communications systems, I want you to send undercover people in nests of resistance that may be forming and burn the rats out as soon as possible. We don't want any interference when we begin the next phase."

"What kind of powers do you think might be conveyed to the followers?" the Russian woman asked.

"None that we cannot overcome, I'm sure of that. But it will motivate them to continue the struggle and that could be contagious. We need people to give up all hope. Then they will be ours. Place your key leaders in positions that we've outlined. Make sure that we have control of police forces, local magistrates, and that we can proceed quickly. You know how to reach my people for funds and directions."

All three nodded.

"Be sure to stay in contact with people in your regions and inspire them to intensify their efforts for the Cause."

He abruptly shut off the monitors and leaned back against his large padded chair. He took a puff from his cigar, deep in thought. He knew that the only people who could stand up to him now were those influenced by the spirit of the Prophet. That was the only antidote left to the influence he would spread across the globe. He had to stamp it out before they created a stronghold against him.

"Damn you!" he whispered to himself, remembering the man who had stood up to him and defeated him once before. Even in death, he was a threat that wouldn't go away. But for now, Zorn was the one in control, and he knew how to wield power for his purposes.

He looked out the other windows at the quiet zenith around him.

"It won't be long now," he whispered to himself with great satisfaction.

CHAPTER 20

Mammoth clouds of dust filled the skies all around the globe, veiling the sun's light. Cities around the world smoldered in ruins. Smoke would continue to rise for days on end, like a slow death. Some places were completely devastated.

Destruction was everywhere. Although some buildings had managed to resist the cataclysmic shaking, highways were broken like twigs and the oceans contorted in wild convulsions. Some basins had been completely emptied of water, sending tidal waves across the land, turning green pastures into sea floors. The winds mirrored the frenzied waters and tore across the world mercilessly as weather patterns readjusted to the transformation. Places that had been warm were now cold, and the polar regions were becoming temperate, melting the ice rapidly, which assured new catastrophes.

Oriana, Jeremy, and Lynn had camped out in the safety of the park during the hours of the violent shift, keeping away from crashing buildings. When peace settled upon the land again, they ventured out to the edge of the park. They stared in shock at the devastated landscape. Nuclear bombs could hardly have created worse destruction. They knew that life would never be the same. The last shreds of order and civilization were gone. Everyone was left on their own to survive. The future of the species was uncertain. It would be years before societies would be able to rebuild and recreate a semblance of a familiar way of life.

"We knew this would happen generations ago," Oriana whispered. "The ancient foretold it. I've seen this very image in dreams. This very scene."

Lynn put her arm around her. In the dark moments of the shift, they had become friends holding on to each other as the earth convulsed.

"Who is we?" Lynn asked.

The pale young woman turned her large dark eyes on her new friends. They glistened with tears.

"Those who worship the darkness."

"Were your people looking forward to this?" Jeremy asked, disgusted.

"Oh yes. The masters understood years ago that the crippling of civilization would be their opportunity to gain control."

"For what purpose?" Jeremy wondered, sensing the answer already.

"To be masters of humankind and manipulate their behavior to satisfy certain needs."

"What needs?" Lynn asked, not understanding.

"The creation of death and violence and evil on a mass scale release certain kinds of energies into the magnetic fields that feed other realms of the universe."

"Spiritual realms you mean?" Lynn asked again.

"Something like that," Oriana whispered. "You know the power struggle has always been there between those various forces in the unseen world."

"How is it that you chose the dark forces?" Jeremy wondered cautiously.

"I never had a choice. I was born into it. I was taught the mysterious, grandiose side of the teachings that hid its uglier aspects. It seemed to be more about the development of personal power than about the worship of evil. They had me fooled, me and many others who are still fooled. It actually seemed like the right path to take, entering the arcane mysteries and experiencing new psychic capacities. It took me a long time to realize what the ultimate goals were."

"What are those goals?"

"What seemed like personal empowerment is really servitude to masters like Stefan Zorn."

Jeremy and Lynn both reacted in shock.

"I take it you know the name," Oriana said observing the look on their faces.

"He came to our community once to see the Prophet."

"So you've met him?"

"Just very briefly. Do you know him?" Lynn wondered.

"Oh yes. He has come in and out of my life from my earliest memories. He always terrified me. But for years I thought it was because of his great skills. Now I understand that it was because of his black heart. He is very happy right now at what has taken place. This is the moment he has been waiting for and he will undoubtedly accomplish his aims."

"Not as long as I'm alive," Jeremy said.

Oriana looked at him with a certain pity. "You can't fight a man like him. He's got connections in high places."

"So do I!" Jeremy said with new confidence. "And I'm certain of one thing. Even though humanity is helpless right now, and may play into his hands, there are other realms that will not be passive at his takeover."

"Can you call down legions of angels?" Oriana asked sarcastically.

"No, but I'll be a thorn in his side and will create the opposite of what he's trying to do. That's what the Prophet prepared us for."

"I'll help you however I can," Oriana said, her face radiating with sacrificial courage.

"That means a great deal to us, Oriana," Lynn said. "The first thing we need to do is find Andrew."

"In the midst of this chaos, it will take a miracle," the young woman said sadly.

"We count on miracles," Lynn responded. "We live for them. Be sure of one thing. Stefan Zorn and his minions don't have all the power. There is another source. It's power is even greater!"

* * * * *

Before the giant dust clouds had begun to settle over the land or drifted off into the upper layers of the atmosphere, a convocation of the most powerful individuals in the world was called to order in the bowels of Corridor 600, the only safe place left on the planet.

General MacDaniel stood at the head of a vast oval table around which sat the richest and most influential people across the globe. Each one had been flown in on private jets under military protection. In this one room was gathered the very axis that kept the world's economy in operation—CEOs of international corporations, government dictators, arms dealers, billionaires. Two dozen men and women kept the world population at work, fed it, and fueled the system called civilization, a system that made them richer than kings.

In the midst of this powerful group sat the impassive but magnetic figure of Stefan Zorn. No one but the general knew his identity, yet somehow he fit right in with this group of ultimate dominators. Oddly enough, in the midst of utter global chaos, the reins of power were being pulled tighter than ever.

"I call this emergency meeting to order!" the general said, standing before the group in his dress uniform sparkling with rows of medals across his chest. "I need not tell you why you are here. Whatever country you call home has experienced a devastation unlike any other seen before in recorded history. Had we actually faced each other in another world war, the results could not have been worse."

Several men around the table chuckled at the idea, having attempted for years to create that very war.

"The world's communication systems, agricultural activity, and economies are at a standstill. Millions have died, millions more will soon die, and so it is. It is up to us to start the engine again and save our world from slipping back into a dark age from which it may never recover. We have among us the most powerful leaders in the world gathered together for the first time, thanks to the Federation's military communications system which has not been entirely destroyed. You were all personally chosen to be in this meeting by the executive council of the Federation. You are considered to be in positions to actively participate in keeping our civilization from sinking into annihilation altogether. Each of you is highly respected in his or her field. At this table, ladies and gentlemen, is the power of the world. It is we who will control its destiny."

The general paused for dramatic effect. Stefan Zorn looked around the room, keeping a poker face before these people who knew nothing of him. He had a strong desire to release a mocking smirk. These people only imagined they had power. As he humbly sat there among them, without any of the resources or fame the others held, he knew nevertheless that he would some day control them all. With the patience of a master craftsman, he watched his plan unfold before his very eyes. He knew when his time would come to take over.

"Our first duty is to sustain the food distribution as best we can," the general continued. "We will have to make some hard decisions. There are some parts of the world that we will have to let starve so that others may survive. Our decisions cannot be made politically. That is why you are here, being practical, levelheaded business men and women. What is needed here is the common sense that will keep the majority alive. There can be no room for misplaced compassion that would seek to care for everyone's needs. It is simply impossible and I know without taking a vote that you all agree with me.

"The second order of priority is to gain control of the weapon stocks and nuclear armaments that are so vulnerable right now. Have no doubt that rebel leaders will surface like rats rushing out of the sewers. We must crush such individuals mercilessly before they have a chance to set up power bases that will be counter to our plans. I'm sure you'll agree that the Federation has done a fine job in this past decade unifying the military power of the world. Now we must do more than that. It is necessary to make use of that unification by stamping out all of our detractors."

The general glanced at Stefan Zorn who had masterminded the plan for global martial law and delivered it freely to MacDaniel with his blessing to take credit for it. Zorn watched him steadily, enjoying the precision of his manipulations. The general made a slight motion with his hand and half a dozen officers appeared from the shadows. They placed bound manuscripts before each of the people at the table.

"You will find here a methodology to accomplish our common goals, a systematic breakdown of the ways in which we can ensure control of the population, even under these extreme conditions. Your role is carefully defined in these documents and I believe you will be pleased to see how we have made the best use of your skills."

He watched the people open the manuscripts and scan through the material with great interest.

"Rest assured that your comfort and enjoyment of the life-style to which you are accustomed will be well guarded and increased."

"This is the work of a genius," an Asian man stated enthusiastically, having quickly perceived the thread of the ideas on the pages.

The general acknowledged the compliment with false humility and made sure to keep his eyes averted from Zorn.

"But do you have the will to make these plans a reality?" the man asked in a challenging tone.

MacDaniel hesitated. He wasn't sure what that mysterious Chinese mind was seeking out.

"It will take a great deal of . . . clamping down," a woman with a European accent asked.

"A lot of blood in streets," a large Turkish businessman pointed out bluntly.

"This is a new approach for Federation forces," the Asian man continued. "Can you achieve your desired results?"

The general's face turned hard and cold. He let the assemblage witness the appearance of the killer within him.

"Let there be no mistake! We will wipe out all resistance even if it takes a scorched-earth policy to do so!"

"Your soldiers will be willing to shoot civilians on sight?" an Indian woman wondered suspiciously.

"We will place the officers who fought in the Syrian conflict of the last decade in command of our urban squadrons. They'll be happy to follow these orders, believe me. I've seen them in action. And many of them know how I deal with insubordination."

"The armies of the world turned on their own people . . . "an African leader muttered. "That's not a new idea. However, it could backfire and cause greater conflict."

Some agreed with him and turned to the general for his response.

"When you read the material more closely, you will note that we are preparing a vast program that includes the establishment of detention camps the size of our largest stadiums, the training of special death squads whose sole purpose will be the hunting down and termination of dangerous individuals, the creation of interrogation centers that will rival the fear struck in the hearts of the population in the last century by the Gestapo. Our surveillance networks are still operational for tracking dissident groups. And we will invest all of our armed forces with the power to destroy on sight anyone who poses or seems to pose a threat to them. A zero tolerance policy will be in place. We will quickly show by example that we mean what we say. The people will fall in line or they will end up in ditches by the roadside."

The assemblage sat in silence, satisfied by the general's words. They were unified in the knowledge that only the iron fist of total control could maintain them in power and positions of privilege in a world that had lost all semblance of order.

Stefan Zorn sat back in his chair, content with the direction things were taking. His steady climb to the pinnacle of domination was well underway.

* * * * *

Tom and Andrew wandered through the colossal ruins on the outskirts of the city. The horizon was black with dust and the acrid smoke of thousands of fires. Day was turning to night as the sun was buried from view behind the global clouds of destruction. The Earth vomited its misery into the skies as though sending desperate signals to other worlds. But the belching of smoke and toxic vapors would only serve to further the planet's distress. Stirred up by great winds and shrieking storms, the mountains of dust and debris fell over the wounded landscape like a veil of sorrow.

Muddy, black rain fell on the dead and dying from Bangkok to New York City. Rivers of blood, gasoline, and sewage rushed through the streets of every city, from Istanbul to Paris.

The story of human accomplishment would have to start again from scratch.

Andrew and his new companion were mute with shock. Only the fierce, howling wind broke the stillness, punctuated by explosions in the distance.

The city skyline, already splintered by the recent quake, was a horrific mangle of twisted silhouettes smoldering and groaning like a great beast in a death grip. Andrew wanted to turn away and run back to the countryside where at least they were less likely to find mounds of corpses at every corner. Tom suddenly grabbed his arm and shocked him back into the realization that he had to face and endure the very thing that his beloved Prophet had told him would be coming.

At the far end of the road they traveled on, a group of soldiers were pushing people up against the wall of a building. The two men watched in horror as the soldiers struck the civilians with the butt of their rifles, brutalizing them as they searched through their clothing. Then the soldiers stepped back, one of them shouted, and a burst of machine gun fire tore through the helpless people who convulsed and fell to the ground.

"God in heaven!" Tom shouted, unable to control himself.

"Quiet!" Andrew whispered. But it was too late. One of the soldiers turned and spotted them. He pointed in their direction and shouted at his companions. The soldiers rushed toward them. Tom and Andrew raced into the jungle of ruins. Shots echoed around them and bullets exploded in the concrete, splattering dust on them.

A strange thought went through Andrew's mind as he stumbled over the debris. Maybe it would be simpler to turn around and let them shoot him. Why should he keep living this nightmare which only seemed to get worse by the hour? He started to turn around and meet his death.

"*What are you doing?*"

He turned to Tom who was scampering over the slabs of shattered buildings. He realized that Tom was too busy saving himself to have spoken to him. Andrew suddenly understood that the voice in his head was *the* voice that had saved him before. It was the voice of the Final Prophet.

"*What are you doing?*" the voice said again.

Andrew felt terribly ashamed and suddenly redoubled his efforts to escape, this time not for himself but for the cause for which he had been chosen.

They ran through back alleys and a labyrinth of destruction that protected them from their pursuers even though every step was treacherous.

Out of breath and faces streaked with sweat and dirt, Tom and Andrew finally made their way to a quiet square that seemed like a clearing in the forest of rubble. The space they came upon was strangely peaceful in the midst of all the destruction, a kind of sanctuary at the heart of the devastation. They made their way through a narrow corridor in the debris and stopped to catch their breath in the old-fashioned square, complete with fountain and storefronts. The fountain was cracked and the water burst out of broken pipes like a wild geyser. Shattered glass covered the streets and all the doors were torn off their hinges, hanging sideways like dead men tied to an execution post.

They leaned against the fountain, splashed water on their faces, and drank deeply. The soldiers had long given up their pursuit in the catacombs of destruction that the city had become.

"Any idea where we are?" Tom asked when his voice returned to him.

"None," Andrew answered, still struggling to catch his breath. "This place is my hometown and I can't recognize a square inch of it. This must be the Forest Hills district, or what's left of it. I don't see any point in wandering any further into the city. What do you propose we do now?"

"We've got to find a way to contact our friends . . . if they're still alive."

"How do we do that? I'll bet there's not a working phone for fifty miles."

"Cell phones are still operational, at least for awhile. I have the strange feeling that Jeremy and Lynn are looking for us."

"You said they were somewhere north of Marysville."

"That's right. I just feel them close by somehow. It makes no sense. But nothing does anymore."

"At least we're alive," Tom pointed out.

"I'm not sure that's doing us any good," Andrew responded, still unable to find any peace with being alive. It would have been easier if the garage ceiling had crushed him like a bug.

"I heard the voice again," he blurted out.

Tom turned to him eagerly.

"When?"

"Just a little bit ago. The soldiers were right behind us. The voice has saved my life twice in less then twenty-four hours."

"It saved my life as well. What do you make of it?"

"Obviously, there's a new breakthrough between us and the spirit realm. I've never in my life encountered phenomena like this.

It could be that the terror of the situation is creating new possibilities."

"It should give us hope anyway."

"Don't forget I saw how the Prophet ended up. I'm not sure what there is to hope for. If he didn't escape a gruesome fate, why should we?"

"Because they need us."

"Who?"

"The higher forces. They can't operate on this plane without human agents, no matter how imperfect we are."

"You've been living too long in a world of fantasy," Andrew retorted sarcastically.

"How strange for you to say that, as one who witnessed the Prophet's miracles up close."

Andrew's face turned red with guilt. Tom had struck him where he was most vulnerable. There was no denying what he had witnessed with the Prophet. He couldn't return to a cynical, secular mind set anymore. He knew too much.

"Sometimes I wish I'd never met him," he heard himself say in spite of his wounded conscience.

"You don't mean that!" Tom barked at him. "It's the greatest privilege you could have hoped for."

"To endure unspeakable hardship and accept it serenely?"

"Don't you realize, Andrew, that you and your friends are perhaps the only people in the world who have any purpose and meaning to cling to now? Everybody else is in state of total despair and wretchedness. You've been prepared. You've got a mission."

Andrew looked at the crushed city around them and held up his arms.

"How can we possibly start again?"

"We're not suppose to rebuild a city. We're suppose to rebuild the human soul."

Andrew turned to Tom with irritation. "Awfully arrogant from someone who wasn't even there to hear the man speak!"

Tom shrugged his shoulders. "I'm just telling you what I feel in my heart of hearts."

Andrew suddenly remembered the words of the Prophet about receiving messages from the humblest sources. Everything could speak to one who had ears to hear and eyes to see. Even a down on his luck writer with no future could be a channel of wisdom. Andrew put his hand on Tom's shoulder.

"I'm sorry. I'm not thinking straight right now."

"I don't blame you," Tom answered. "It's been a rather rocky day."

They laughed sadly at the understatement.

A loud speaker suddenly crackled to life and a booming, authoritarian voice burst through the air.

"Attention! Attention! This is the voice of the Federation. Everyone who is able must report to the nearest relocation center where food and blankets will be provided. Repeat: if you are able to walk, you must report to one of our relocation centers immediately! Anyone found in the streets within an hour of this announcement will be arrested. All able persons must report to the relocation center nearest them. The wounded will be cared for by our medical teams."

The voice died away in a haze of static crackle and the message was heard starting again in the far distance.

"Relocation centers?" Tom cried out. "That doesn't sound right."

"It's not just the earth that's undergone changes, Tom. Our government has changed dramatically as well. Its mask of benevolence has been dropped."

"You don't think what we saw back there with those soldiers was an isolated incident?"

"No, I think it's the order of the day. We'll be next if they find us. We've got to get out of the city. It's one giant prison now."

Andrew closed his eyes and seemed to listen to some inner prompting. Tom looked at his new friend whose haggard features were now radiant with a strange tranquility. He waited patiently even though his survival instincts screamed at him to get going.

After a moment, Andrew opened his eyes.

"They're here!" he said in a whisper with a soft smile.

A shiver went through his companion. He wasn't sure whether that was good or bad news. What he did know was that his friend was manifesting clairvoyant gifts which Tom knew had not been his the day before. Transformation was occurring before his very eyes.

"Who?" Tom finally asked.

"Jeremy and Lynn are nearby. Follow me."

Andrew hurried off to the end of the square that led toward a small wooded park.

"The city limits are that way!" Tom called out, pointing in the other direction. "We've got to get out of here!"

"We need to go this way first!"

"Don't tell me you know what you're doing or where you're going!" Tom cried out.

Andrew looked back at him. "I don't! But I know I'm being guided. That's even better."

CHAPTER 21

Triage was taking place in the streets. Damaged cities throughout the world were turning into vast tent dwellings as survivors tried to protect themselves from the fierce elements and adapt to a life without any twenty-first century comforts. Hospitals especially were overwhelmed. Many of them were destroyed and there were such great numbers of wounded and dying that only the worst cases could be treated. Everyone else was bandaged up and left to be cared for by relatives, if they had any left. The streets were a permanent jumble of broken glass, twisted metal and junks of concrete. Only military vehicles could get through, crushing everything in their way.

The world had turned into a war zone, and the enemy did not come from another nation, but was the planet itself as it convulsed in the grips of its cosmic trauma.

Highways everywhere were broken up like the partial skeleton of great dinosaurs still hovering over the land they once dominated. Sirens were always screaming somewhere as new fires broke out or a building tumbled over. The countryside seemed to be the only sane place to be after centuries of vacating it. But even there nothing was the same. Bridges that remained standing were unstable, rivers were overflowing their banks and washing into people's living rooms. Those who lived in remote areas were entirely on their own in ways they had never wanted to be.

Gun shots echoed constantly through the urban areas. Battalions armed to the teeth hurried through the rubble, attempting to restore order against all hope. The population was in a frenzy, and crime was rampant everywhere. It seemed to be the only way to stay alive, at least for now. Certain elements took advantage of the situation, looted whatever they could get their hands on and murdered with abandon, finally freed from society's boundaries. It wasn't long before people gathered in groups to organize themselves as the realization sunk in that the government could do little to help them. Secret subcultures had been waiting for this time for decades if not centuries. They were in their element now, with underground shelters, hoarding their precious food and weapons for themselves, and considering all who were not part of their privileged group to simply be out of luck. Compassion was the first victim of the destruction.

No one had time for another person. Children were left to expire under the rubble while adults desperately tried to find a morsel of food or a way to stay warm. Humanity's arrogance and certainty that it could control its destiny and the forces of the planet had received a death blow. It would be a long time before the species could fool itself again.

People huddled around battery-operated television sets and radios, listening to Federation information and commands, feeding on the illusion that if someone was in charge, things would be put back in order some day, even though the terrible reality of this catastrophe was all around them. The death wish of three generations had finally been granted. Around the world, mass suicides were occurring hourly as people gave up all hope. Death rose into the atmosphere with the toxic fumes and surrounded the earth with a gruesome melancholy that hovered in the dark clouds.

Occult leaders, revolutionaries, brigand rulers appeared overnight like mushrooms sprouting in the dark. This was the world that the Prophet had depicted, only to be hated for it. No one wanted to believe, not until it was too late, until they had to live it out in utter misery. This was also the world that Stefan Zorn could harness for his purposes.

The occult societies that paid allegiance to Stefan Zorn and worshiped the same forces of darkness were the most prepared to meet the new conditions on the planet. They quickly began to infiltrate the makeshift centers of power that attempted to create structure out of chaos one community at a time. Along with fulfilling a centuries-old mission, there was another top priority on the agenda. Across the world, word was out to search out and destroy all of the remaining followers of the Final Prophet.

No group was better organized than Zorn's minions to maneuver in the chaos. This was their element and human suffering created a perverse pleasurable atmosphere for them. Around the world, super-secret occult societies were stepping out of the shadows to take charge. They had the greatest resources at their disposal, the most sophisticated underground survival systems, and most of all, a carefully rehearsed plan. Entire regions would soon fall under their well-orchestrated manipulations. Relocation centers, food banks, even police stations would soon be run by members of Stefan Zorn's groups. The lights had gone out on gigantic portions of the globe and virtually all that was good about human civilization. No computer technology could provide a quick fix.

* * * * *

As soon as Tom and Andrew stepped out of the rubble onto a wide street, they spotted a car coming out of the park and heading slowly toward them. At that moment, a ray of sunlight pierced through the thick, unnatural darkness, shot through space, and landed directly on the vehicle.

Andrew's attention turned to the car that seemed to glow in the momentary appearance of the star's light.

"That's them!" he said as his heart pounded like never before. "That's Jeremy and Lynn!"

"It can't be!" Tom cried out.

The car came to a stop a short distance from them. Jeremy jumped out.

"Is that you, Andrew?" he cried out.

"Jeremy!" Andrew shouted in a burst of gratitude, relief, and joy. "Yes, it's me, Andrew!"

The passenger door flew open and Lynn stepped out and raced toward them. Andrew met her halfway. They hugged intensely.

"Thank God! Thank God!" she whispered, "thank God we found you!"

She looked up at him and held his face in her hands. "Are you all right?"

He nodded, tears streaming down his face. She kissed his cheeks fervently.

"Forgive me for putting you through all this!"

"It was meant to be," Andrew responded. "We're just

instruments."

Jeremy approached Andrew. They hugged silently with deep emotion. When he was able to speak again, Andrew turned to his companion.

"This would be Tom," Jeremy said as he extended his hand. "Welcome among us!"

"You must be Jeremy," Tom said in a wavering voice. "The Prophet's first disciple."

"We've been looking for you," Jeremy said. "Lynn insisted that we come to your rescue."

"It didn't have to be so dramatic," Tom responded, gesturing to the devastation around them.

Their laughter was interrupted by the appearance of Oriana who stepped out of the car and stood at its side, shivering with remorse.

"What the hell!" Andrew shouted with sudden rage and totally confused. "What is she doing here?"

Tom's eyes nearly popped out of his head. "Oriana! What a day of wonders!"

Andrew grabbed hold of his arm. "She's the one who entrapped me and got me arrested!"

"That's impossible!" Tom said.

"Believe me, there's no mistake. She assaulted me."

Oriana wept silently. Jeremy stepped between Andrew and the young woman.

"Everything's changing, Andrew. She's with us now."

"How can you possibly trust her after what she's done?"

"I'll explain it to you in the car. But know this. Incredible things are happening, not only in the outside world, but in the spirit realm. She's been touched by the Prophet."

Andrew wanted to argue, but realized that it was all too mysterious for him to understand. It was not up to him to judge what miracles might be granted to people around him, since they were happening within him as well. They got into the car.

"What do we do now, Jeremy?" Andrew asked as he wiped tears from his eyes.

"Don't you realize this is what the Prophet prepared us for, this very moment. We know what we have to salvage and keep alive in spite of everything."

"How do we stay away from those who seek our destruction?"

"Oriana will help us keep one step ahead of them."

"How can she do that?" Andrew asked suspiciously.

"She knows their ultimate plan. That will help us anticipate their next move."

"How will we communicate with the outside world and pull people out of the vortex?"

Lynn took Andrew's hand with the greatest gentleness. "Some will find us. We need only build a place that they can come to and start again."

"Do you think anybody cares anymore about the deeper things of the spirit?" he asked as his voice caught in his throat.

"Now more than ever, Andrew," she said, eyes sparkling with intense certainty. "Everything else they've held onto has crumbled. Some will realize that the only solid ground is not made out of matter. Those who are truly seeking for something other than sheer survival will find their way to us."

Tom and Oriana held each other tightly in the back seat of the car, overwhelmed with the joy of being together again against all odds. Andrew leaned over the front seat and whispered to Jeremy and Lynn.

"I've heard a Voice . . . "

A radiant smile softened the tense features of the two soul mates.

"So have we," Lynn said.

Jeremy turned to his friend. "In ancient times, the Essenes told of the battle between the sons of Light and the sons of Darkness. It was taken as symbol and myth, full of esoteric meaning. Today, it's literally true. We have chosen sides."

"Maybe we've *been* chosen," Lynn said softly.

"That could be. In either case," Jeremy added, his jaw clenching with determination, "now it begins!" He turned to his beloved and kissed her waiting lips to give himself courage and to promise her that his love would never die, whatever might happen to him in this life.

"What's that noise?" Tom said suddenly, turning his attention to the window.

Everyone listened as a growing whirling sound filled the air.

The eerie, rhythmic noise sounded like the heavy breathing of some monstrous creature or a huge bird flapping its wings.

As it became louder and louder, Andrew finally cried out:

"A helicopter!"

They looked up to the dark skies just as a huge military helicopter burst out of the clouds right above them. They could see the murderous eyes of the soldiers in the cabin.

"Do not move! Stay where you are! Repeat, do not move!" a voice from a loudspeaker shouted, shaking the car windows. "This is a Federation order. You are wanted for questioning. Step out of the car slowly! You will be shot if you do not cooperate!"

The companions turned to each other, terrified.

"What do we do?" Lynn whispered with dread.

"We have no choice," Andrew responded. "We're sitting ducks!"

Jeremy turned back to the wheel and threw the car in gear. The voice echoed again as the helicopter descended to barely fifteen feet above the vehicle.

"Step out of the car now!"

"Hold on tight!" Jeremy yelled as he floored the accelerator.

The car tore off in a cloud of dust and squealing rubber. It swerved frantically over the cracked pavement littered with rubble, heading toward a ray of light that shot through the black clouds and fell over the distant countryside. The helicopter followed swiftly after them, descending to within five feet of the hood of the car. On the horizon, a dark line suddenly appeared and headed at dizzying speeds toward the scene of the chase. A dozen helicopters separated out of the line and formed a circle that would soon surround the vehicle.

* * * * *

Pale beams of dying sunlight shot through colossal grey clouds, illuminating the shadows hovering over the ruins of the city. A great silence crept through the empty streets, resisted only by the angry howling of the wind. All life seemed to have vanished. A terrifying tranquility announced the onset of more dangerous storms.

A fierce crash of lightning split through the embers of sunset, echoing across the twisted skyline of the ruined city. Within moments, the bellies of great clouds, pregnant with rain, would spill onto the earth.

An old man, of unusual height, overgrown with wild strands of long snow-white hair and a huge unkempt beard, slowly moved through the barren, sinister landscape of devastated buildings. The clothing beneath his heavy, mud-stained trenchcoat from the previous century was tattered and of coarse material. A silver amulet hung from his neck, fashioned in an emblem of strange geometric design. The old man's eyes shimmered with striking intensity. Deep in their dark caverns, they sparkled like rare stones and pierced the object of their attention with the power of a killer hawk's gaze. Though of great strength for his age, the solitary figure supported himself with an antique cane which gave him the appearance of a desert prophet. Yet to most passersby and to the military police that constantly combed the streets, he seemed like a typical homeless vagabond with not much time left to live.

He stopped in front of a cheap motel and observed the flickering neon lights of a broken sign that partially spelled the words "no vacancy". For an instant, the fiery eyes closed and a whisper escaped from the solemn lips.

"Finally . . . " he whispered with a mixture of relief and exhaustion as he knocked on door number forty-four.

The sound of several locks being opened shot back from the other side.

Michelle peered suspiciously through the cracked door. The old sage stood patiently in the dim light.

"Are you the one I've been waiting for?" she asked with a trace of awe in her voice.

Michelle studied the old man, as though searching his soul for some miraculous answer to her secret hopes. A gentle light appeared in the eyes of the sage.

"I have come . . . "

"At whose request?"

"Yours."

The old man smiled gently beneath his forest of beard. Michelle opened the door wider.

"Do I know you?"

They stared into each other's eyes as a deep silence filled the room. For a moment, the outside world utterly vanished beneath the intensity of their gaze. Soul opened to soul, penetrating the solitary regions of that invisible landscape where their true natures dwelt.

"Why are you so familiar to me, old man?"

"We have met in your dreams."

The night visions which had haunted Michelle's sleep for years suddenly flashed before her inner eye. Each was weighed down by an overpowering presence which seemed to watch and guide them. It was that presence which had a familiar quality to it. It was that presence which she recognized in the old sage.

"How can this be?" she let out in a terrified whisper.

The old man stepped forward.

"There is nothing to fear, Michelle."

"This is sorcery!"

"No!" the strange man cried out in outrage.

The old man's voice was at once filled with implacable power. His imperative reply silenced all her thoughts. Her fear disappeared like morning mist in the heat of the rising sun.

"This is your destiny," the sage announced solemnly.

Michelle opened the door wider and let the strange man into the motel room. As his aged eyes adjusted to the dark shadows, he noticed other people huddling in the corners. Among them was Juanita and her baby who smiled merrily at the newcomer. The others weren't so trusting.

"Don't be afraid," he said softly to the glistening eyes full of terror. "I'm a friend."

"We have no friends," Michelle responded, "unless you are a follower of the Prophet."

The old man turned to her and his face became radiant. His eyes vanished behind wrinkles and sparkling tears as his features lit up with warmth and a strange smile.

"Yes, I'm his follower . . . But he followed me once . . . I'm his grandfather."

Robert leapt to his feet, angered by the man's statement. "He had no family! Everybody knows that!"

The old wiseman turned a patient, melancholic look upon the aggressive youth.

"Didn't he teach you to rid yourself of violence? What you say is true . . . The Prophet had no family. I became his adopted grandfather, many years ago."

Juanita approached him in awe. "You knew him when he was a boy?"

The man shook his head affirmatively, pleased to find acceptance in the girl's wide, innocent eyes. He leaned forward and gently touched her cheek.

"I gave him food, shelter, and books. But what he learned and who he became was not my doing. That was entirely his work and that of greater powers."

"He saved me from death, me and my baby," Juanita said in a whisper of ecstatic joy and gratitude.

"I was told of this miracle. I knew long ago that he would do wonders in this world."

He straightened up painfully and turned to the others. "I also knew that he would meet a tragic end. All of you who love him are also in great danger. I was sent to help you."

"Who sent you?" Michelle asked, still uncertain of his motives.

The white-haired man pointed upward. "They did . . . In a dream. I have such dreams more and more often as I approach my departure from this plane."

"Your dream revealed to you where you would find us?" another student questioned in disbelief.

"Oh yes. It even showed me what bus to ride in order to reach this place. They are closer than ever, you know."

"Who?" Michelle asked, confused.

"Why, the messengers of course. Including the one you call the Final Prophet."

"How do you mean, closer?"

"The drama all around us has called them forth. Without them, we will be utterly destroyed. They have a stake in our survival. There are other forces who seek the opposite and the more they attempt to fulfill their wishes, the more the forces of light seek to counter them."

"How can you help us at a time like this?" another person

questioned, studying his frail condition.

"I know of a safe haven . . . Besides, I'm all you've got."

"We're awaiting the return of our friends," Michelle said with determination. "We don't go anywhere until they come back to us."

"Your friends are not coming back," the old man said sadly. "I saw that in the dream as well."

"I don't believe it!" Michelle cried out. "I don't care what your dream told you! They will return to us safely and I will die waiting for them rather than leave without them!"

"Me too!" Juanita said courageously.

The sage studied the intent faces around him, realizing that they all felt the same.

"Your friends are in grave danger. They've fallen into the hands of the evil one."

Michelle let out a gasp as others burst into tears and moans.

"But they are not alone . . . That I know with more certainty than the fact that I stand here before you! They will not be abandoned in their hour of need. Not now."

"How can you know this?" Robert inquired in a trembling voice and wiping tears from his face.

"Because the forces of light need them as much as your friends need their supernatural assistance. Without your little group, there is no hope for the accomplishment of the Prophet's mission. And that mission has ultimate importance, not only to the human race, but to the galaxy."

"How is that possible?" Michelle asked, trying desperately to find hope in his words.

"Don't you realize what you're involved with? Do you think the Prophet appeared merely to offer you a few bits of wisdom? Your awakening is necessary to the existence of the sun, and of the living being we know as the Milky Way. If we all fall under the influence of darkness, there will be no one to generate the finer energies that keep the solar system from . . . "

He felt that he was saying too much to people who were unprepared to hear his revelations.

"From what?" Robert asked eagerly.

"From being sucked into the black hole that is forming at the center of the galaxy!"

A heavy silence filled the room and his words seem to hang in the air like an ominous cloud. No one moved as the implications of his strange statement slowly sunk in.

"I've come five hundred miles to find you . . . and you know what the conditions are like out there. So I'm here to stay. I'll wait for your friends with you."

"Then let's make some tea for you," Michelle ordered as she pointed him to a chair. "What is your name?"

"Tobias Hungerman."

"Mr. Hungerman, we welcome you . . . "

"Call me Tobias," he said as he gratefully sat at the table and rested his weary limbs. The companions joined him around the table. Juanita sat next to him, holding her baby lovingly in her arms.

"Tell us about the Prophet when he was young."

"Let the man rest," someone said.

"I'd be glad to tell you about him, young lady. That story was the most beautiful period of my life. I was much younger then of course, and handsomer too. It was just before the turn of the century. Things seemed normal then, although we knew that something immense lay out with the new millennium. I had moved to a small town not very far from here, at the edge of the Sierra Nevada mountains. I'd been a lifelong student of philosophy and metaphysics. My beloved teacher had just died and I wanted to get away from the centers of culture."

"Don't you like people?" Juanita asked innocently.

"Most of them were so immersed in the foolishness that passed for culture. Even then I knew it was all headed for what the Federation's made of it—a senseless, hypnotic trick meant to deaden the human soul."

One of the students brought out a cup of steaming tea and placed it before him.

"Thank you," Tobias said gratefully. He sipped it as they all watched him. "Haven't had such good tea in decades!"

"Linda's from England," Juanita said merrily. "She really knows her teas."

"I can tell . . . Anyway, my closest neighbor in those days was a strange old lady. Everyone thought she was plain crazy. I wasn't so sure. We didn't talk much but she knew that my hobby and addiction was truth seeking. And I guess she appreciated that. One day, she showed up at my door. She looked terribly distressed so I invited her in. She told me she'd be dying soon and that she needed my help. I tried to convince her that she looked healthy to me, but she was certain of it. She told me that she did not live alone as we all thought. She had a young child with her that nobody had ever seen. It was an abandoned baby boy that she had found three years before, left to die in a wooded area in the foothills of the Sierra Nevada mountains."

"Someone just left a baby in the middle of nowhere?" Juanita asked in horror.

"She told me she always suspected that the child was a changeling . . . "

"What's that?" Juanita asked.

"There's an ancient Celtic myth that changelings are children born from the tuatha de daanan peoples, the fairy folk, and left for people to find and raise as their own. In other words, he'd come from another dimension. The woman almost had me convinced that she was indeed insane until I realized that she had loved and cared for that child at the cost of great sacrifice. She kept him hidden away because she was afraid the community would take him away from her. And she knew there was something very special about him. Even as a small infant, there was a unique healing heat in his hands. She told me he had the eyes of an old wiseman. He didn't behave at all like other children. He was thoughtful and reflective even at that early age. He seemed to understand her without words, as though he could read her mind."

The friends listened in awe as the old man told them of the early life of their beloved Prophet, the man who had changed their lives forever. The little motel room was filled with a reverence and silence worthy of a great sanctuary as the old man quietly whispered about the wondrous presence of the one called the Final Prophet.

"Was he from this world or not?" Robert asked impatiently, always the sceptic.

"I lived with him for ten years. He seemed human enough, in

spite of the old soul that lived inside him. One day he looked at me and said: it's time for me to go. I nodded, knowing this time would come. Then he was out the door and I never saw him again. But I - always knew he was here for a special purpose."

"You didn't answer my question," Robert said firmly.

"I think the Prophet came from the stars, that's what I think. But I'm just an old man . . . "

A stunned silence fell over the group, as though a veil was being lifted on some cosmic truth that was too vast to be grasped by the human mind. The dark motel room seemed to morph into an ancient chapel.

"But it's his teachings that matter," Tobias said in a whisper after awhile. "That's why he appeared among us. Be sure that sustained desire to make his ideas come alive within you is never lost, even in the face of such utter catastrophe."

"I feel like the external trauma around us has entered into my very soul," Michelle stated sadly, unable to hide the guilt in her tone of voice. Tobias turned luminous, compassionate eyes upon her.

"He taught you to know yourself, did he not? Surely, you remember his observation about our nature and how to begin the process of transformation. Life is indeed a constant interference with those aims. In a more natural world, people should be able to have time to be quiet, to think or reflect, to move at a slower pace. We have been aborted from a natural life and the necessary suffering resulting from this is hard to take for everyone. And yet . . . The Prophet said over and over again that life's in-your-face distractions end up being our best teachers.

"That's still a problem for me. Especially now that life is nothing but destruction," Michelle whispered.

The old man reached out and placed a warm hand on her shoulder.

"I know that you were one of his closest students. Remember his fundamental revelation to us—using negative energy for transformation means neutralizing the negative momentum that generated it and rechanneling this available energy for conscious work. If you pull the irritation out of your irritated reaction, what you have is new energy circulating within you. The effort of not going with the current, which is now drowning people by the millions, creates a sort of alchemical effect which refines that energy and may give you an intense moment of self-awareness and intensified presence to the instant of your life.

"Don't forget that the Prophet's teaching deals with awareness of and intentional uses of energy, harnessed for the aims of awakening. The "enemy" is not in the external world, not even with the Federation after you, but up close and personal—within you. It is that which becomes irritated which is your troubles, not the apparent cause of that irritation. Use it to remind you of what you are really trying to accomplish."

"Sometimes the observer within that he taught us to become forgets and sometimes the observer separates and remembers the teaching," Michelle stated as her throat tightened.

The old man took a sip of tea and looked around at the faces staring at him breathlessly. Tobias understood from a place deep within that it was his duty to feed these distraught disciples who were so lost and without direction. Though he hardly felt worthy of the task, he realized that there was no one else available to remind them of all that the Prophet had taught them at the cost of his life.

"It is more complicated and more subtle than this, although it is true that ultimately the presence of your authentic self is already behind or within your current state of consciousness. But vanity creates pictures and assumptions that provide us with other identities that are so far removed from the "One" you are that there is real fragmentation. If you truly follow the Prophet's teaching, you will become another person, and yet be more truly yourself than you have ever been. You will not be subject to the knee-jerk reactions, requirements, expectations, and concepts of reality that you are now.

"Most of you experience yourselves as your opinions, feelings, etc. But you are something else, something inescapably spiritual. Don't ever forget what the Prophet told us—we must travel the path of self-becoming in order to encounter lasting meaning and purpose.

"There is a critical part of you that is missing. It will not appear until you have conquered your weaknesses, old habits and illusions.

"We have to develop new psychological 'muscles'", a student stated with emphatic certainty.

"This is not correct," the old man said bluntly as his shimmering eyes turned upon the man who thought he understood. "This a partial truth. We begin with new muscles of attention and awareness. But that is just the tip of the iceberg. This "iceberg" leads to the source of your being to which you must become transparent.

"The fact is that we are all shattered into many contradictory - pieces and the outcome of our personal spiritual battle is still uncertain. To "know thyself" is to come face to face with the tragic and dangerous reality of this condition. Once that happens, the real journey and struggle begins."

Everyone silently absorbed what the old man with the strange glowing eyes had said. They each shared the same inner excitement, as though their beloved Prophet had returned in the shape of this ragged tramp and once again offered them life-giving wisdom.

"The ticket," Tobias continued, " to enter into this is nothing less than sacrificing everything to what is best in us. There is much old snake skin to be removed so that conscience, heart, spirit, can be unburied and bring forth the light of new understanding."

"I feel that my life runs it course and ultimately is of little significance, value or meaning. I want to know what is on the other side of the curtain," someone in the back of the room said in a faltering voice.

"This is true and not true," the old man responded. "You are seeing only partially and "through a glass darkly." This is a stage. You will move beyond this. Many seekers have stayed there and died in those feelings of emptiness and meaninglessness. You do not need to do that. You have already been given material to start peeking behind the curtain. There is more than the world of senses and even of mind. There is mystery, wonder, help, power, love, light available to you. A wiseman from the last century, whom the Prophet loved to quote, said one day to his students: 'Open the door and let yourself be found. That is the whole thing.'

"Most of our inner efforts are aimed at removing obstacles that inhibit the experience of deeper things which will answer many of your questions and transform your understanding. Having encountered the Prophet and his disciples, you are on the right track, you have been given pieces of the most important puzzle there is. Trust that you will be helped to put it together. Just remember that if you get close to the fire, it burns. But the burn can be more than pain. It can be transformation."

"The difficulty for me sometimes is the inability to find meaning or value in anything," Michelle admitted from the depths of her soul. "The feeling that our death and the uncertainty of what occurs thereafter permeates everything around me with a 'unreality'."

Tobias suddenly took hold of her chin and raised her face. Tears streamed down her cheeks as he stared fire into her eyes, sending a new force into her crushed spirit. When the tears had stopped, evaporating in the heat pulsating from the old man's aura, he spoke to her with a distant, serene calmness.

"It is urgent to your life that you begin to integrate that awareness with the "other reality" that is before you. This is a cornerstone development. The mystics speak of immanence and transcendence simultaneously, or eternity in time. Some of them were called "witnesses to eternity." At the same time, they were fully engaged in life.

"Your deepest longings are directly linked to your mundane everyday life. The Prophet wants you to translate that lofty knowledge into "being" which incorporates common sense, strength, devotion, sacrifice, self-transcendence, acceptance, forgiveness, and sometimes righteous indignation at darkness and intentional evil."

He patted her cheek with infinite gentleness, then turned to the others.

"Listen to me, all of you. Don't let the destruction of everything you've known fool you. There are ultimate, eternal realities that cannot be torn down. Believe this until you know it with every fiber of your being. An ancient saint said that you must believe before you can understand. You must open the door to the possibility of such reality before you can encounter it. Part of your soul knows there is something more. Find that part of yourself and remember it always.

"The Prophet wished with extraordinary compassion and

empathy to awaken you to a reality that can change everything for you and make you who you are truly fated to be. But know that you are wandering into holy territory, dealing with sacred things. You must eventually develop a new sensitivity toward the reality of the "higher," the divine, the transcendent, the immortal. The Prophet came to remind us of our obligation to existence itself.

"What I am here to say to you is this: Be careful not to forget all that has been given to you. The Prophet's teachings have power you know not of. You can receive help from beyond the reality you know. And in fact you already are. So be humble and focused and committed to your heart's deepest longings."

The old man raised his hands, sending an energy of blessing over the group.

"Be at peace. Even now, in the midst of the Tribulation. Trust the mystery that caused your path to cross with that of the Final Prophet."

CHAPTER 22

Jeremy, Lynn and their companions were forced into a steel room beneath the Federation's military headquarters. Several soldiers stood in front of the bolted door, machine guns in hand. They were still in shock from the abrupt end to the chase as helicopters had landed ahead of them and the tires were shot out from under the car.

"We're lucky to be alive . . . "Jeremy mumbled. He knew it wasn't true, now that they were all caught in the enemy's net.

"How did they manage to find us?" he asked to break the terrible silence.

Andrew shook his head trying to hold tears back. "They must have planted some kind of tracking device on us when we were in the jail. That's the only way I can figure it. We brought them straight to you. I'm so sorry!"

"Don't be," Lynn said softly. "This is all part of the play."

"What do you mean?" Andrew asked, eyes brimming with tears.

"Do you remember what the Prophet said about accepting what is and in doing so finding the traces of purpose and meaning behind the events? Even now, there's no reason to give up hope. We may be exactly where we're suppose to be."

"That doesn't make any sense!" Jeremy said. "What are the others going to do if we get executed? The Prophet's mission is over."

"The Prophet's mission is not dependent on just us. It's much bigger than that," Lynn insisted. "If we don't succeed, someone else will step forward."

"You think so?" Jeremy challenged. "I don't agree. I think we're it, we're the remnant. The others who were with the Prophet are scattered."

"Maybe we shouldn't talk about this anymore," Andrew

suggested. "You know they're listening."

"It's all nonsense to them," Jeremy continued. "Military officers don't have mystical inclinations."

"I'm not so sure we're just dealing with the military, Jeremy."

"What do you mean?"

"Ask her!" Andrew replied, pointing to Oriana. She looked at them, pale as a ghost.

"What's he talking about?" Jeremy asked.

"He may be right," Oriana said in a trembling voice. "The cult has ties to the highest levels of the Federation."

At that moment, the heavy door unbolted loudly and swung open. The large silhouette of Stefan Zorn suddenly appeared in the corridor. He entered the room like a cold gust of wind, accompanied by two savage-looking bodyguards. The door slammed and bolted behind him.

He silently studied the group, walking around them as they stood in the middle of the room. He stopped in front of Jeremy and glared at him for a moment.

"So you're the Prophet's right hand man?"

"I was his friend," Jeremy said softly, showing no fear of the vicious man.

"He's dead and gone. Why are you still making a fuss about it?"

"His words came true."

"I could have told you what was going to happen just as easily!" Zorn said, his eyes sparkling with anger.

"You couldn't have told us how to endure it," Andrew called out.

Jeremy turned a look upon his friend that told him he shouldn't have made that comment.

"Told you how to endure it?" Zorn asked with a curiosity he couldn't hide. "You've got a secret anecdote to disaster? How are you going to fix the global devastation?" he asked, inches away from Andrew's face. "Tell me what you meant!" Zorn ordered.

"Just that he told us we would have to develop the moral courage to deal with these conditions."

Zorn peered into his soul silently, searching out a deeper answer. Andrew tried to still his mind so that the occult master would not steal anything from it.

"He taught you how to be in touch with another type of consciousness, didn't he?" the man growled.

Andrew turned pale but did not respond. Zorn looked at Lynn who stared back at him defiantly.

"He taught you how to resist external stimulus . . . so as to build an independent state of being. Am I right?"

He stepped in front of Lynn who didn't blink at the nearness of his repulsive presence.

"Am I right, young lady?"

"What does it matter to you? Do you need to control everyone, is that your ambition?" she responded.

"Pretty much," he retorted with a sly smile. "I don't appreciate independent souls. They aggravate me and interfere with my plans. You can understand that, can't you?"

He stepped back and looked at the group.

"We can't have people thinking for themselves when we need cohesion and obedience at a time like this."

"Do you expect to brainwash the entire population?" Tom blurted out angrily.

"Yes, I do! Starting with you."

"Go ahead and try!" Tom said with foolhardy courage.

"I take it you're not one of the Prophet's followers," Zorn observed as he approached him.

"I didn't know him," Tom answered with a new uneasiness, surprised that the man knew this.

"You didn't learn from him like the others did. You're just blowing your horn out of sheer arrogance, aren't you? You don't know what you're talking about or who you're dealing with."

Zorn's features darkened while a strange light seemed to emanate from his eyes. Tom let out a shout and fell to his knees as though a bolt of electricity had gone through him. He trembled in near convulsions.

"Don't fool with things you know nothing about, boy. Next time, I'll fry your brains."

He turned to Jeremy. "You need to teach him some manners. If the rest of your group are as stupid as he is, this is going to be a piece of cake."

"Why are we such a threat to you?" Lynn asked, hoping to save

Tom from any further torment.

"What if I told you I just disliked your kind?" Zorn replied disdainfully.

"It wouldn't be worth this much trouble," Lynn continued. "I'll tell you why we're a threat to you."

"You will?" Zorn retorted merrily, enjoying her courageous nature.

"You can't control us, no matter what you do! You can't have power over us."

"You might be surprised, young lady," Zorn grumbled.

"You think pain is a form of control? You can break someone, but you'll never win their souls over."

"I don't give a damn about your soul!" Zorn suddenly shouted in a rage.

"Maybe you don't want people to know about your plans," Jeremy stated, calling the wild man's attention on him.

"You don't have any idea what my plan is, even with the traitor among you," Zorn said as he pointed at Oriana. She turned away from him in revulsion and fear. He turned back to Lynn and looked deeply into her eyes.

"Do you want to live?"

"Of course," she answered simply.

"You love this man," he said pointing to Jeremy, "and you want to have a long life with him in spite of the hardship out there."

She nodded and looked over at her beloved who sent her his love silently.

"And you also know that I have the power to end it all for you right here and now. One click of my fingers and these soldiers will fill your body with holes, toss you into a mass grave, and that'll be the end of that."

He let the words sink in for a moment and walked among them, looking down at them disdainfully.

"General MacDaniel once gave you a choice," he continued, "to ease the people's fears instilled by your pesky prophet. That didn't work out so well. I'm willing to give you another chance."

He peered into each one's eyes, except for Oriana who kept her head turned away from him.

"Come work for me. Help the people understand that their only chance is to fall into line with the new world order which will take us out of this free fall."

"You must be insane!" Lynn said coldly.

Zorn raised his bushy eyebrows in mock surprise. "That's not very nice. I'm offering you your life."

"You want us to support you?" Jeremy cried out. "We are devoted to the other side!"

"What makes you so sure that I'm evil?"

"The Prophet told us," Jeremy said defiantly.

"Aah, and he knows all . . . But the fact is that you don't know anything about me. Maybe I'm devoted to the cause of the human race and my aim is to get us through this cataclysmic time."

Oriana could take no more. She turned around to speak up and reveal what she knew about this man. At the same moment, Zorn turned his glimmering eyes upon her and deadened her voice. Her vocal chords became paralyzed beneath his fiery gaze. With all her might she tried to speak, but nothing came out.

Zorn turned back to the others. It had happened so fast that they noticed nothing. Zorn had merely turned away for an instant.

"I can use people who want to sacrifice themselves for the betterment of their fellow humans. I know your motives are pure. I can give you the opportunity to help humanity."

Jeremy stepped forward, wanting to get the man away from his loved one. "How can you do that?"

"I am interested in power, this is true," Zorn said more gently. "But it's not merely personal power. It's for the sake of the big picture—the welfare of this planet and its inhabitants. It should be clear to you that under these conditions there must be a new kind of control or we will disintegrate completely into dark ages and never rise again. Ultimately, my plans are benevolent even though they may not look that way."

"What are you asking of us, then?" Jeremy demanded.

Lynn took his hand. "Don't bargain with him, Jeremy!"

"You shouldn't listen to the little lady all the time, Mr. Wilkes. You should make your own decisions. I'm giving you the chance to find fulfillment in caring for the needs of desperate people on a large scale. I'll put you in charge of our food distribution and medical services. Think about it. In the blink of an eye, you would go from penniless vagabonds to people with the ability to touch millions of lives."

"We don't have the same goals," Jeremy protested.

"It doesn't matter what our differences are!" Zorn insisted. "We have to journey on the same road for awhile. I'm telling you that I need people who mean well to do the kind of work I need done. I'll put others who do a different kind of work in other positions."

"You mean like the death squads out in the streets?" Andrew stated bitterly.

"We call them cleanup crews. How would you handle it? You got some better ideas?"

"It seems to me that murdering people on street corners doesn't qualify as an idea at all!"

"Well, I'm a common sense sort of fellow. We have to do what we have to do. I'm also a very busy man so I will end this conversation and leave you with this opportunity. Think about it. I'm handing you charitable work on a silver platter. Take it or leave it. Makes no difference to me. Either way, I will win. You'd better accept that."

He turned around dramatically and looked at Oriana.

"You, however, are another matter! You're gonna have to come with me."

"No!" Tom cried out.

"You haven't learn your lesson yet, son?" Zorn said angrily. He waved his hand and Tom's body was thrown back against the wall with full force. The crack of his bones echoed through the room. "Doesn't pay to be so hardheaded."

He turned to the soldiers. "Take her!"

The soldiers grabbed her as she screamed. "Please help me!" she managed to cry out as they dragged her across the room.

Lynn jumped between Oriana and the soldiers.

"Wait!"

One of the soldiers raised the butt of his rifle to strike her. Zorn held up his hand.

"Just a moment! Do you have something you want to say to me?" he asked, careful to hide a victorious smile.

"Don't take her," Lynn begged. "I'll convince the others to consider your offer seriously."

"What is she to you?" Zorn wondered, looking with disgust at Oriana.

"A treasured human life."

"Are you telling me that you'll change your position completely for her safety?"

Lynn nodded with difficulty.

"Then you can keep her for now. Your cooperation is more important to me than her punishment."

With that he turned and walked out the door swiftly.

Oriana hurried over to Lynn and hugged her.

"You can't do this. He'll only use you."

"We're not going to let him take you away to some dreadful fate."

"What am I to you?" Oriana asked in tears. "We haven't known each other twenty-four hours. My life was doomed from the beginning. I was born to this."

"No one's life is doomed like that! In this short time with us, you've heard the Voice. You know that there is another force in the world."

"I do! But for the moment, it's the dark one that's winning. I know he will eventually destroy me. I have too much information. And he hates disloyalty more than he does goodness of heart."

"What about those things he said about charitable work?" Jeremy asked.

"Believe me, Stefan Zorn is evil to the core. He has no interest in humanity's welfare. His kind have been preparing all these centuries for the manifestation of forces that use humanity for their own dark purposes. These purposes have nothing to do with our welfare. He's not about to change. I may have seen a new light, but he never will. He's offended against it too often."

"So what is his mission?" Andrew questioned impatiently.

"He's right that it's a secret I was never privy too. But I can tell you this. There's an intent to use human beings as organic transmuters of energies to feed certain needs of the cosmos. The wars that have been fought were not really for conquest or defense, but for the generation of certain emanations that are nutrition for another world, the one that Stefan Zorn works for. That world thrives on human suffering and death."

"Maybe we can do some good in spite of him . . . play along with him for awhile," Tom suggested, rubbing his bruised shoulder.

"Once he's accomplished his aims, you'll be done for. He'll never forgive the Prophet for humiliating him," Oriana stated sadly.

"Our first priority is to safeguard the lives of the people around us," Lynn said with determination. "If we can't do that, we're of no use to anyone."

"I don't understand," Oriana retorted. "You told me you were charged with a mission to reawaken the human spirit."

"That's right and in order to do that we must exemplify that in our own lives, which begins with the things and people closest to us. There were plenty of helpers of humanity who worked for the larger good and disregarded those nearest to them. That's not what the Prophet taught us. If we're devoid of that kind of authentic care and love, we can't do anybody any good."

"I'm not worth all this!"

Lynn took Oriana by the arms. "Even if you did sacrifice yourself, we'd be stuck in this situation. We must make the best of where we are now. And if we're butchered at the hands of Stefan Zorn, then so be it. We will not sell our souls to him for our own safety. Besides, there are too many clues that we are receiving help. Andrew and Tom were pulled out from their clutches once before. It could happen again."

"I think you're fooling yourself!" Andrew said angrily. "How can we possibly do anything useful when the evil ones have all the power. Now that we know that Zorn is in tight with the highest echelons of the Federation, it means that he'll control everything. The rebuilding process is already a lost cause."

A loud noise announced the unbolting of the door. They all turned to see the gruesome figure of Dr. Tagore appear in the dim light. They reacted in revulsion to the spectral figure. He looked at them haughtily. But his eyes didn't carry the glint of fierce hate that was his typical expression. A deep melancholy darkened his features. His usually erect posture was slightly stooped beneath its weight.

"Are you looking for me again?" Andrew said, hoping that the demon would focus his evil intent on him rather than on his friends.

"Where's Oriana?" the man said in a hoarse whisper.

"I'm here," she responded, stepping into the pale stream of light coming through the doorway.

"Oriana . . . How did you get yourself into this?" he asked with deep sadness.

"I had to leave. I didn't belong with you anymore."

"I've loved you since you were a little girl," the man stated, his voice quivering with rare emotion. "How could you leave me?"

"You loved me? I never saw it."

"Since the death of your parents, I've been like a father to you. Don't you remember? We use to go for walks in the park together. You liked holding my hand."

"I don't remember."

"It wasn't that long ago!"

"Why did you come here?"

"I can't let him have you. I know what he'll do to you."

"You would disobey your Master's orders?" she asked, stunned.

"I told you, you're the only being I've ever loved. The sweetness of the little girl you once were was the only joy I've known. I promised your parents I would care for you. I didn't know what it would do to me."

"So you've come to say good-bye?"

He shook his head. "I've come to take you with me."

Her mouth dropped open. "He'll roast you alive!"

"I know some safe houses."

She looked fearfully at the half dozen soldiers surrounding him and armed to the teeth.

"What about them?" she asked in terror.

"They're paid mercenaries. They do my bidding."

"He'll find you!"

"Even he doesn't know all the secret places we've established. That was my department."

"I won't leave without them."

"What?"

"You'll have to take my friends with us."

"I can't do that, Oriana."

"Then I stay!

"I came for the little girl who once called me 'papa'."

Oriana knew this was her only chance to save her friends. She swallowed hard and placed her hand on his scarred cheek.

"She's still in here, papa. I do remember your goodness to me. You were the only one who was concerned for my welfare. I'll always be grateful for that. I'll go with you, but we must bring them along. We can drop them off outside the city."

"Zorn will have my hide for sure."

"What difference does it make since you've already crossed the line?"

"You'll stay with me?"

"I will."

"It will be like it use to be, when I bought you lollipops at the fair?"

She had always known that he was disturbed. Now it was clear to her that he was completely insane.

"I'll hold your hand like before."

"No time to waste, then!" Dr. Tagore growled as he motioned for the companions to join them.

Stunned by the turn of events, the friends hurried behind the soldiers as they rushed down the hall to the docks below. A dark van awaited them. The friends were ordered into the back and told to hide under blankets and behind boxes that littered the vehicle. The soldiers piled in and the van headed toward a heavily-guarded post.

A soldier peered into the vehicle. Dr. Tagore held up an official pass. The officer saluted him and waved them on.

The van hurried through the smoldering city. Crowds wandered the streets in a daze. Sirens and loudspeakers filled the air with confused sounds that intensified the chaos. Inside the van, an eerie silence contrasted with the outside noise. Everyone was mute, except for an occasional order from Dr. Tagore to the driver. Oriana sat next to the grim occult leader who held onto her hand like a drowning man. She did her best to hide her disgust and thought of her friends hidden behind her. Their breathing kept her sane as he caressed the back of her hand. She turned to him and looked into his freakish features. Buried behind the scars and decades of encrusted dark energy was the faded light of a fatherly love. She was his only link to his human side. She sensed that he would be good to her . . . until his mind went completely over the deep end.

Soon they reached the boundaries of the ruined city. Trees and grass appeared as a reminder that life could start again, even after the worst catastrophes. The van turned onto a dirt road and came to halt in the middle of nowhere.

"Get out!" Dr. Tagore roared at the companions.

Lynn took Oriana's hand. "Come with us," she whispered.

Oriana turned a look of terror upon her. She was too frozen to respond.

"Get out before I change my mind!" Tagore shouted in a frenzy.

Jeremy pulled Lynn out of the van as the others followed.

"We can't leave her with him!" she murmured in horror.

"We've got no choice," Jeremy said, trying to comfort her.

Lynn leaned back in the van to say good-bye to her new friend. Dr. Tagore turned to slam the door in her face. In doing so, his coat opened, revealing the butt of a revolver protruding from his belt. Without thinking, Oriana grabbed for it and tore it free. Tagore turned around to find the gun cocked and aimed at his forehead. His wild eyes turned dark with anger.

"How dare you turn on me? I took care of you . . . "

One of the soldiers moved abruptly, trying to raise his weapon. Oriana fired the gun at him and the man slammed against the van, hit in the shoulder. She turned back and aimed the smoking pistol directly between Tagore's eyes.

"You're next . . . "

"Oriana," the man begged, "why don't you love me?"

"Because you're a beast, not a human being."

"I'm human! If you shoot me, I will bleed."

"Shall we find out?"

"I put my life in danger to save you . . . I don't understand."

"Tell your soldiers to put down their weapons and step out of the van."

"Have you no gratitude?" he asked cynically, his face turning hard and losing all warmth toward her.

"For what? For being tutored in your dark ways and

brainwashed into thinking that what you did was right?"

"I took you to the fair . . . . " he muttered between his teeth.

"You're the one who molested me!" she blurted out suddenly.

Tagore's face turned red. "What are you talking about?"

"I've had nightmares for years and a vague memory . . . The silhouette of a man . . . colored lights behind him!"

She prepared to shoot.

"Wait!" Lynn cried out. "Don't kill him. It won't help us."

She motioned for the others to disarm the soldiers as Oriana held the gun in a tight grip. Andrew and Tom pushed the soldiers out and checked them for additional weapons. Jeremy took hold of Dr. Tagore and helped him out of the vehicle. Oriana followed, the weapon still ready to fire.

"You'll regret this!" the freakish man warned. "I swear you'll regret this!"

The companions got into the van as Tagore and his men watched helplessly.

"Maybe she ought to shoot him," Tom suggested. "That'll keep him from coming after us."

"What are you saying?" Lynn retorted angrily. She placed her hand gently on Oriana's shoulder. "You don't want to be like them, remember?"

Oriana looked into Lynn's eyes and became aware of the violence and hatred polluting her heart. She handed the weapon to her and turned away, ashamed. Lynn quickly closed the van's door.

"Let's get out of here!" she called out to Jeremy who put the vehicle in gear and tore off in a cloud of smoke which covered the grim men left behind with dust and humiliation. Tagore's eyes beamed with evil intent as he watched the van disappear.

"I'll find you!" he muttered hatefully. "I'll find you wherever you go."

* * * * *

The Federation's armies amassed over the most devastated areas of the world, where populations were decimated by the catastrophes. In one terrible day, a thousand planes roared back and forth across the wreckage, bombing it into oblivion. There was no way to help the wounded and the world's resources would be toppled over trying to salvage what the typhoons and earthquakes had left alive.

In the Middle East, squadrons filled the skies over territories where revolution was anticipated. Religious fundamentalists were sure to make the most of the devastation. They were already organized to force the starving, confused and desperate hordes to do their bidding. Their agenda was power, not care for the masses they controlled. On the same day as the bombs fell over the last shreds of southeast Asia, so did they rain upon Iran and Iraq until the populated lands were as inanimate as the surrounding deserts.

The Federation forces then turned upon Africa. Smart bombs hit refugee camps where survivors were gathered by the hundreds of thousands. In a few hours there would be no one left to carry contagious diseases across the borders. Nor was there anyone to interfere with the military raids. No one was organized enough to shoot back or to create a renegade army. This was indeed the moment to strike, just as Stefan Zorn had advised. Hundreds of special forces lived in the skies, refueling in midair, flying from place to place according to the high command's urgent orders. Wherever surveillance or espionage had warned of rebellious action, the planes would break the sound barrier overhead and drop their deadly cargo upon the suspects. The plan was simple—to keep the world population on its knees until it was completely at the mercy of the dominating forces.

Military installations and nuclear plants were guarded by carpet bombing their surroundings so that nothing within a hundred miles could come near them. Only the Federation's jets could descend out of the skies into the precious locations. It was a novel plan, to destroy the enemy before he even appeared on the horizon. At the same time, satellites sent messages twenty-four hours a day to huddled masses living in the ruins. The messages were designed to bring some measure of hope for normalcy's return. The makeshift studios in the Federation's various headquarters uplinked images of stability and strength to a world where no such thing existed, except on the flickering screens of the remaining television sets.

Staged presentations of food shelters created in cavernous warehouses were beamed across the world, making it seem that the benevolent dictators were solving the famine problem. People were fed with pictures of other people being fed and given the illusion that they were next. Every so often, wanted posters would appear on the screens, faces of individuals who were on the short list for execution. The Federation's expectation was that desperate people would turn them in for the reward and just as important would stay away from these hunted persons who were doomed to be caught eventually.

Certain politicians, major criminals, serial killers who were out of control even for these times, were shown several times of day. Every few hours, the photos of Jeremy, Lynn, Andrew, Michelle, Tom and Oriana would appear in the ghostly light of some TV screen in all parts of the globe with a resonant base voice warning all to beware of these persons and promising large stores of food and money for those who would provide information leading to their arrest.

The world was on fire. Nothing was left of decency, kindness, compassion. All power was in the hands of dominators who knew how to keep the people in absolute need and terror. The human spirit had reached its darkest hour. Only those who had learned to stay alive inwardly despite their circumstances according to the great teachers of wisdom could hang onto their sanity.

Ideas that had taken centuries to develop—freedom of the individual, democratic government, religious liberty—had vanished like dust in the fierce winds that howled across the planet. As the ancient prophecy had warned, the sun no longer gave its light, neither the cosmic sun shrouded in clouds that would linger for years, nor the sun of the human spirit. As in the days of the holocaust in the previous millennium, all sense of a benevolent force in the universe had crumbled beneath the trauma of the moment. Humans were reduced to the most basic survival instincts and like sheep led to the slaughter accepted the Federation's stranglehold over their lives.

Reconstructing the structures of the world would take immense labor but rebuilding the human soul seemed like an impossible task. New generations brought up in this devastation, parented by people long devoid of depth and meaning, would become little more than two legged animals without conscience, without learning, living from sensation to sensation. Their lives would be brief and focused on finding the next meal. If the inherent nobility of the human race was to be salvaged, it would have to be with help from beyond. As never before in history, the time was at hand for the return of the messengers of light . . . before it was too late.

THE END

Made in the USA
Lexington, KY
23 May 2017